Praise

Rogues & Rebels

'The English Civil War is brought vividly to life in Jo Field's first novel. Her characters are swept into a breathless adventure of heroism, intrigue and romance. It is a cracking good read. Her readers will be captivated.'

Historical novelist, HELEN HOLLICK

ROGUES

&

REBELS

Jo Field

DA

This first edition published in Great Britain in 2008 by
DA Diamonds – a Discovered Authors' imprint

A CIP catalogue record for this book is available
from the British Library

ISBN13 978–1–906146–69–6

Available from Discovered Authors Online –
All major online retailers and available to order through all UK bookshops

Or contact:

Books
Discovered Authors
Roslin Road, London
W3 8DH

0844 800 5214
books@discoveredauthors.co.uk
www.discoveredauthors.co.uk

Printed in the UK by BookForce International

BookForce International's policy is to use papers that are natural, renewable
and recyclable products and made from wood grown in sustainable
forests wherever possible

BookForce UK Ltd.
Roslin Road, London
W3 8DH
www.bookforce.co.uk

FOR MUM

*My sternest critic and greatest friend who never
failed me and who will now never know how it ends
– or perhaps she does. I hope so.
Love you my Mum.*

ACKNOWLEDGEMENTS

I would like to extend my gratitude to Ken Dykes, for his encouraging comments; to Phil Hinton, for ploughing through my draft and sharing his knowledge of boats; to Liz Pile – still waiting for the ending! – and to CuChullaine O'Reilly of the Long Riders' Guild, who so kindly put me right on matters of seventeenth century equestrian travel. A big thank you to my publishers, Discovered Authors, principally Graham and Michaela. My thanks also to Chris Collingwood for his invaluable help and advice and to Jag Lall for his skill and patience in creating the cover I wanted. I should also mention Caliver Books for keeping me supplied with source books on the English Civil War; Google – which rarely failed me; the Old Map Company for allowing me to reproduce a copy of their Speede map of Devonshire and Exeter (www.oldmap.co.uk); and finally, 'Torrington 1646', who so kindly offered their advice on firing a musket and wearing a petticoat!

Thank you to my lovely sister Wendy, my brothers, Nick and Bose, my dearest friend Maggie, and my sons, Simon and Julian, for their unfailing support and encouragement. Also to my friend and mentor, historical novelist Helen Hollick, for her unstinting help and advice and for convincing me I have the makings of 'a writer'! And to the late, lamented genius Dorothy Dunnett, who was always my inspiration.

Finally, to Capt. Jesamiah Acorne, whose cheerful profanities have kept Alexander going on more than one occasion – yo ho mate!

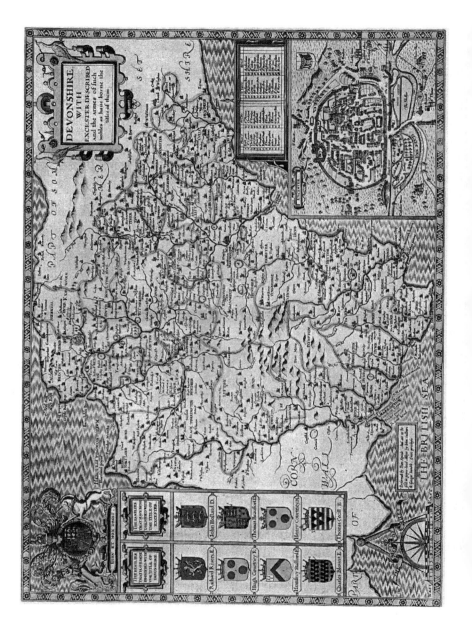

John Speede map of Devonshire circa 1610

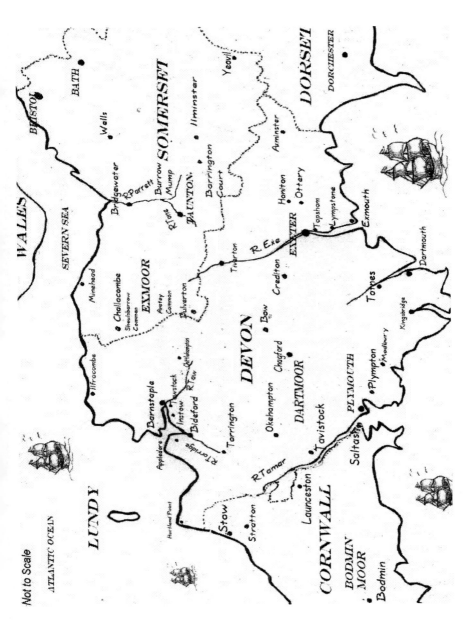

Alexander's Travels in the South West

*'Rogues; rebels; are not they content to be rebels, themselves,
but would have me in their number?'*

(Charles, Prince of Wales, 1645)

1

Saturday 24th September, 1642

He was trussed like a Michaelmas goose, the bonds at his wrists pulled tight around his ankles, arching his body backwards on the stone floor of the cellar where they had thrown him. Grunting, he mumbled obscenities to himself and belched, emitting a sour gust of wine from between the blackened stumps of his teeth. He squinted up at the face looming over him. Pock-marked and shiny with sweat in the candlelight, it filled his limited vision. A vein pulsed on the flushed forehead and flecks of spittle glistened on the stained, grizzled whiskers. Beneath the pitted, fleshy nose, a tongue protruded wetly from full dark lips. He giggled, hiccupped and with studied insolence, belched again.

The sound exploded from his throat as a heavy boot thudded into the soft corpulence of his belly. In a blur of movement a fist descended. 'What's your name? Why are you here? Who sent you?' A vicious blow punctuated each question. 'I will have your answer.'

Lights cascaded in his head. Tears of pain spilled from his eyes and tracked the livid weals on his cheeks. Gasping hoarsely he whispered, 'Domnhall. My name is Domnhall O' Néill.'

'Hah! Found your voice for you, have I? And what kind of a name is that?' His tormentor bent over him and grinned, fist poised for another blow.

Flinching, the prisoner cried out, his voice subsiding to a

whine as he tried to turn his face away. 'Don't hit me no more, Sir. I am named for *Domnhall Ua Néill* of *Magh dá chonn* and descended from the *Déisi Kings* of the *Uí Cheinnshealaigh*.' He spoke with the slow concentration of the very drunk. 'Sure and it's the name my mother gave me.'

The trooper gave a shout of laughter. 'And I'll wager she don't know who fathered you, eh? Hear that, Captain?' He looked over his shoulder at his comrade who lounged against the cellar wall idly picking at his fingernails. 'We've gone and got ourselves a king,' he snorted. 'A king! As if the one we've got weren't bad enough we've got ourselves another.' He grinned. 'What are you? A misbegotten Irish bastard hatched in hell, that's what you are.' He worked his mouth and spat.

The spittle landed on the prisoner's cheek and slid down to his chin. 'I didn't say I was a king,' he slurred petulantly. Behind his back, fists clenched, his fingernails gouged blood.

'So, Dunghill O'Neill,' the trooper sneered. 'Who sent you?'

'Nobody sent me.'

'No? Then why are you here?'

'I'm a pedlar. I travel about... I sell gloves... ribbons, lawn and lace,' he said with difficulty, his gaze resting on the trooper's hand. 'And tabby, sarsnet... very fine... and pots and pans and trinkets, pretty trinkets for pretty maids.' And altogether too many eshes he thought, and hiccupped.

'Eh? A pedlar? What kind of a fool do you think I am? God's Bones! I'll give you peddling.' The man struck him again, splitting his lips like a ripe plum.

'It's the truth,' the prisoner sobbed, bubbling blood. 'Soldiers' doxies, bless their generous hearts, they've pennies aplenty to shpend on pretty ribbons... and well earned you'd say, well earned.' He leered up at the trooper, wincing as blood spurted from his lips, streamed over the dark stubble on his chin and dripped into the folds of his grime-encrusted shirt.

'Pah!' The trooper grasped his chin and forced his head back. 'And what about this? How did you come by this, eh?'

The prisoner screwed up his eyes in an effort to focus on the package the trooper was waving under his nose. 'Found it on the road I did.'

'What road?

'Don't know what road. Don't know thish country.'

Releasing his captive's chin the trooper cuffed his head from side to side. 'What else did you find, you piece of filth?'

'Naught but a dead man,' the prisoner gasped, added, 'he was in the ditch. Still warm he was. Still warm...'

'Pah! What manner of a man?'

'A poor man; no boots on his feet, no coat on his back, no lace on his collar, no rings on his fingers. Hish horsh was dead too,' the prisoner mumbled sadly.

'You filthy, lying, snotty-nosed, toad-faced, long-haired, stinking Irish beggar, what else did you find?' Again the trooper raised his fist.

Whimpering, his victim shrank back. 'Nothing else... nothing... he'd been robbed,' he cried out as the fist descended.

'You're lying. There was no man was there!'

'To be sure there was. His head was all stove in.' The prisoner's voice sank to a whisper. '*Saoth liom an ceann an bhir laim...*'

'What's that you say? Speak English, you scum.'

'Nothing... it's the truth.' He let out a guttural cry as the trooper's boot thudded into his ribs.

'So – you found a man, but he was alive when you found him, wasn't he? You killed him, didn't you, then robbed him blind. You fat, snivelling Papist – you wouldn't know the truth if it hit you between the eyes. You're a thieving, murdering, godless, lying incendiary and hanging's too good for you.' The trooper aimed a vicious kick at his victim's groin and smiled as he screamed, vomited, voided the contents of his bladder and lost consciousness.

'Leave it, Hooper, you'll kill him.' The captain spoke curtly. Moving forward from the shadows he held up the sconce and looked with contempt on the inert body at their feet.

'So? The vermin's better dead, Cap'n Dewett, Sir. I'd be doing 'im a favour,' Hooper muttered defensively.

'Here, give me that.' Dewett held out his hand for the package still clutched in Hooper's fist. 'Where did you say you picked him up?'

'Ilminster – we had reports of a stranger in the tavern. By the time my patrol got there this sot was out in the road capering about with a fiddle and demanding they open the gates for him. We thought he was naught but a vagrant – he seemed harmless enough. We'd have left him for the Watch, excepting we found this down his shirt, so we brought him back for questioning.'

'You did well, Sergeant.' Fingering the slim package with distaste, the captain gingerly unwrapped the oiled cloth and drew out a sheet of folded paper. 'You found nothing else? What about a body? Was there a dead man like he says?'

'No.'

'How far did you look?'

'About a mile in both directions,' Hooper lied. 'All we found were a couple of packhorses straying up the road loaded with fripperies, and poor beasts they were too. We let the Watch have 'em.'

'So he could be telling the truth. We don't know where he came from. He could have found it like he says.'

'Nah. The miserable puggard is lying. More likely stole the beasts, murdered their owner and took it off him thinking it might be worth something.' Hooper paused, scratching at his beard. 'Mind you, it could be he's a deserter; they've been fleeing like hares before bratchets since the Earl of Bedford moved against them, cowardly Royalist bastards.' He spat roundly at the floor. 'And we know they've been filling their ranks with Irish, devil take their murdering Papist souls. I'd wager he's bin soldiering – see here, his face is scarred under all that filth. An old sword cut looks like.'

'That means nothing – and when did you last see a fat

soldier, Hooper, eh? No, he's more likely a thieving gypsy, but it's still possible he's carrying messages for the enemy.'

Hooper frowned. 'Surely even they would not use this pigswill as a messenger?'

'You think not? Beggars can't be choosers. Lord Bedford has them pinned down at Sherborne and they're heavily outnumbered. By now they'll know we've taken Portsmouth. Even if they were to break out there's nowhere left for them to run. Nobody round here will lift a finger to aid them.' He brought the paper up under the light to examine the seal. 'I'd wager this is a plea for reinforcements. It would be useful to know where he was taking it.'

Hooper's fingers strayed to a lump on his chin. 'He didn't want us to have it that's for sure, he felled three of us before we got it off him.'

'Three of you?' The captain snorted with derision. 'A fat, unarmed fiddler and drunk into the bargain?'

'He's right handy with his fists for all that, and he broke a few heads with that damned fiddle.'

Dewett grunted. Carefully breaking the seal, he unfolded the paper to peer at the closely written page. 'One thing's for sure, we'll not find out if you kill him now, and we'll get no sense till he's sober.'

'What does it say?'

'How the devil should I know – I'm a soldier not a cleric. No matter, Colonel Strode will make sense of it.' Dewett refolded the paper and tucked it into his coat. Wrinkling his nose he bent over the motionless body, stirring it with his foot. Loud bubbling snores emanated from the open mouth. 'S'death, I wouldn't want his head when he wakes. He's an ugly brute, isn't he? Certainly has the look of a gypsy.' He eyed the fat mound of the prisoner's belly, the despicable clothing, the black hair matted with ordure and plastered like rats' tails round the dark, puffy face. 'Ugh! Plague take the man, he stinks. What did you do with his boots?'

'He weren't wearing any.'

'No? Can't have travelled far without boots.' With his mind already straying to other, more pleasurable things, the captain held up the sconce and glanced cursorily around the room. His shadow loomed on the steps that led out of the cellar and slid over a pile of casks stacked against the back wall. On the opposite wall was a rack of dusty bottles and tipped up beside them a long trestle table-board. Nothing more. Reaching for his knife, Dewett grasped the rope at the prisoner's back. The candles flared and guttered adding thick fumes of smoking tallow to the acrid stench of sour wine, vomit and urine.

Hooper put out a hand to stay him. 'Pardon me, Cap'n Dewett, Sir, but I'd leave his bonds secure. He's a deal more dangerous than he looks.'

Shrugging Hooper's hand off his arm Dewett sliced through the rope and pushed the prisoner face down on the floor. 'I don't want him choking to death when he spews, Sergeant. Don't fret; his wrists and ankles are still bound and he's more than three parts dead already,' Dewett said, striding towards the steps. 'Come on, there's nothing more we can do here tonight.'

Reluctantly Hooper followed, shaking his head. 'No offence, Cap'n, but I think you're too soft.'

Dewett looked down his nose. 'Has it not occurred to you that the Colonel will want to question the prisoner? He'll not be best pleased if he's dead, will he?' He grinned. 'Besides, there's more ways to kill a cat than by skinning it. He'll have such a thirst on him come morning he'll sell his soul for a drink. You mark my words. If there's anything more to tell he'll tell it then. Kill him after if you must. Now stop blathering and come on, I've better things to be doing with my time.' He winked, exaggeratedly cupping his groin. 'Too soft, you say?'

Hooper laughed grudgingly. 'Whoremaster! Which one is it this time?'

Dewett leered. 'That's for me to know and you to guess.' Chuckling, he took the steps two at a time, pulled open the heavy door and waited, tapping his foot. 'I'll report this to the Colonel when I've done with her. You're in charge meantime.'

'Hell's teeth. It's alright for some.' Hooper grumbled under his breath as he shuffled up the steps.

The prisoner feigned unconsciousness until he heard the bolts slide home, then cautiously opened his eyes. A glimmer of moonlight filtered into the cellar through two small gratings high in the wall. Dimly he could see the barrels, grey humps stacked against the opposite wall. Apart from the steps there appeared to be no other way out. Grinding his teeth, he forced himself to think. He had a hazy recollection of being dragged through a kitchen and along a passageway before they threw him down the steps. He looked again at the barrels. Was he under the brewhouse? If so, surely there was a trapdoor? From where he lay, he could not see one. Gingerly he tried to move and swore softly. Flexing his long fingers, he curled them around the knots at his wrists. Ignoring the pain that fired in his veins as his bonds slowly loosened, he worked at them until his hands were free. '*Saoth liom an ceann an bhir laim…*,' he murmured again, the half remembered Gaelic phrases of his childhood coming unbidden to his lips. '*Ni doilge leam ceann eile … ceann Domnhall ī Néill bhūige.*'

He gently probed the deep cut above his left ear, repeating the ancient words in English to take his mind off the pain: 'Grievous to me the head in your hand. *No sadder to me the other head, the head of Donal, grandson of Neill* – Godamme!'

He let out a cry; his ribs hurt, his head throbbed and judging by the blood on his breeches, his thigh wound had re-opened. But nothing broken, please God, nothing broken.

With a muttered curse he inched gingerly onto his side and reached for the knots at his ankles. With shaking fingers he loosened them, gasping with pain as the rope finally fell away. Gorge rose in his throat, he retched, and dragging himself on to all fours like a dog, spewed up a gutful of wine. For a moment he slumped back to the floor, his face pressed into the foulness, pinpricks of light spiralling behind his eyes.. Lifting his head he eyed the barrels speculatively and started to crawl, his progress hampered by the size of his girth. As he dragged himself slowly towards them he was acutely aware of the minutes ticking by. He would be naught but roast meat for worms once Colonel Strode learned of his capture. The foul thought spurred him on. 'Pray God Captain Dewett's lust will not be quickly slaked,' he muttered.

Fighting waves of nausea he reached the bottom row of barrels and rested on his elbows, his eyes wistfully level with a tap. The smell of malt sweetly filled his nostrils. He ran his gaze over the stack – mostly ale, but a few smaller casks – probably sack. His mouth watered. No, it was not a good idea. To distract himself, he started to count. Twenty-three hogsheads? He eased himself on to his knees, muttered, 'Fifty-four gallons in each, that's twelve hundred gallons.' Still calculating, he manoeuvred himself into a crouch, his murmuring barely audible between his gasps for breath. 'Assuming a generous allowance of, say, two quarts of ale per man per day, with a small garrison of around twenty men, that's nearly eight months' supply, give or take.' Grunting with effort, he clung to a barrel for purchase, slowly pulled himself to his feet and stood swaying. Waiting for the dizziness to subside he looked up, running his gaze along the great oak timbers above. Yes, he'd been right: a little to one side of the topmost barrels, hard to make out in the gloom and partially concealed by a joist, was a trapdoor. Was it bolted from above? There was only one way to find out. He started to climb, cursing as splinters embedded in his raw, slippery hands. At the top he paused for breath, listening, but all he could hear was the blood pounding in his ears.

Balancing on the uppermost cask he reached out to grasp the joist and stretching sideways pushed against the trapdoor. 'If it's bolted, I'll drink this cellar dry,' he promised himself.

But creaking, it gave against his hand. 'Careless, Captain Dewett,' he murmured. 'Very careless.' Beneath his toes the cask wobbled, threatening to dislodge from the stack and bring the whole lot tumbling down. He steadied himself, repositioned his feet and summoning all his strength shoved upwards. For a breath the trapdoor teetered at its apex, then crashed backwards sending a shower of dust and cobwebs into his hair. Somewhere in the house a slumbering hound barked half-heartedly. He held his breath, waited for the shouts and curses, the sound of running feet. The bark subsided. With a shuddering gulp of air he started to breathe again. A rope dangled from pulleys above. At full stretch he grasped it and hauled himself up and out of the cellar.

The room above reeked of hops and malt. Grey light from a meshed window revealed the mashing tubs and brewing copper, a shovel leaned against it, beneath it, a scattering of coal. A salt-encrusted tub glistened under a window and beside it was a chest filmed with ash and cluttered with utensils. By that was an outside door. Edging across the room towards it, he found with a sob of relief that the bolts slid back easily. He grasped the latch and cautiously pulled open the heavy door. The hinges were well greased, their protest muted. Letting himself out, he stood with his back against the wall, listening.

Something scuttled squeaking in the shadows. A rattle of dead leaves hurled at his feet. Somewhere a loose shutter was banging rhythmically. He shivered. Between racing clouds the moon fitfully revealed a cobbled yard surrounded by a range of outbuildings. He could see the entrance, a gated archway with a lodge on either side. From one a light flickered. Straining to hear, he caught the faint rumble of voices and spasmodic, muffled laughter. A smattering of rain started to fall. Keeping to the shadows he limped towards the gate, supporting himself against the buildings as he passed them: still house, bake house, buttery and dairy, coach house, cart shed and stables. He could hear the dull thud of restless hooves. The gatehouse door was not barred.

He pushed his way through, almost tripping over four bodies variously slumped in a comatose heap, muskets and flagons scattered around them. The guards! His luck was holding. Avoiding them he stumbled on, creeping past the adjacent cattle yards. The garrison was almost certainly housed in there. A little bit further and he was over the carriageway and out into the meadow beyond. He paused to get his bearings. Barrington Court was behind him. Looming on his left were the dark shapes of the Black Down Hills. Beyond them was Taunton, strong for Parliament, as was Yeovil to his right. Bridgwater and the Severn Sea lay ahead, but before then, spread out between the Quantock and Polden hills, were the marshes and safety. He had some eight miles to cover – he was not sure how. Would it be pushing his luck to steal a horse? He half-turned, hesitated, changed his mind and cursed. He felt as ungainly as a pregnant sow. The wads of linen wrapped around his belly and thighs had seemed like a good idea; they made him look fat and to an extent had protected him from that godammed trooper's fists, but by God, he could not wait to be shot of them. What had the bastard called him? Dunghill? In other circumstances it would be almost funny. But at least they had not got his real name out of him. Had they known he was Sir Ralph Hopton's scout, they would have smelled a rat and all his efforts would have been for nothing.

His capture had been no accident. Since midsummer he had been with the King's Western Army – a grand name for barely four hundred ill-equipped men – under the command of William Seymour, the Marquis of Hertford. For weeks they had been defending Sherborne castle, blockaded there by the rebel Earl of Bedford and several thousand foot soldiers mustered by Parliament from all over Devon and Somerset. The Marquis had been so sure reinforcements would come to his aid. Alexander snorted; it had been wishful thinking. But they had not known it then and had made lightening attacks to keep the road clear, charging out of the castle to sting the enemy when he least expected it. It was during one of those skirmishes that his thigh had stopped a musket ball. He had been barely aware of it at the time, but was acutely conscious of it now as he dragged his abused body away from Barrington Court. Those sallies had been costly in men's lives, but they had bought rewards. The rebels had begun to desert, and the Earl of Bedford, lacking the heavy artillery he needed to break down Sherborne's walls and fearing all his greenhorn recruits would melt away, had moved back a couple of miles to Yeovil while he waited for the siege guns to arrive from Portsmouth, only recently surrendered to Parliament.

As soon as Bedford was out of sight, the Marquis of Hertford had abandoned Sherborne. Under cover of darkness he had led his army to Minehead, certain he would find boats in the harbour to carry them to Wales and safety. That too had been wishful thinking. Oh, there were boats aplenty, but only two of them were seaworthy, Tom Luttrell had scuppered the rest, the Puritan dog! Him and his feisty wife, who had fired down on them from Dunster Castle and wounded two dragoons. Mind you, it was a miracle they had got as far as they had unscathed. They had been clubbed and stoned by screaming hoards of locals in every village twixt Sherborne and Minehead.

The two boats were big enough to take the Marquis and his infantry, but not the horses – almost two hundred of them – so Hertford had ordered Hopton to ride on round the coast to Ilfracombe and find more boats. But Sir Ralph was not a man to give up so easily; he was damned if he was going to hightail it to Wales and leave the South West to that scoundrel Bedford. The Cornish were loyal; if he could only get to Stow and unite with Sir Bevill Grenville they might yet raise an army for the King. Hopton had been eloquent and the Marquis in no mood to argue. He advanced Sir Ralph to act in his stead as the King's General of Horse in the West, wished him Godspeed, loaded up his foot soldiers and with barely a backward glance embarked for Wales.

Hopton's plan was a bold one; the shortest route to Stow was across mist-hung, bog-ridden Exmoor, the road little more than a meandering sheep's trail. Men and horses were bordering on exhaustion and the Earl of Bedford's army was only four miles behind and closing. It was then that Hopton's eye had lighted on his trusted scout, Alexander Dynam. Hastily appending erroneous information to a letter he had started to his wife and not had time to finish, Hopton had given it to Alexander with instructions to see it found its way into enemy hands. God willing, it would serve as a decoy.

That had been last night. Now, struggling to stay conscious and alert for sounds that the alarm had been raised, Alexander stopped for a moment to get his breath back. So far, so good. On the far side of the meadow a dark belt of woodland offered cover. He limped towards it, his breath rasping painfully in his throat, his bare feet catching in the soft, tussocky grass. Reaching shelter beneath the tossing branches, he had time only to register relief before the ground came up to meet him.

'Alexander!' Someone was anxiously saying his name. 'It's me, Lyddon, can you sit up? Here, drink this.'

He felt a hand under his head, liquid fire running into his mouth, trickling down his throat. He tried to swallow and choked. Still spluttering he squinted up at the figure hunkered beside him. Hugh Lyddon, one of his men whom he had last seen in Minehead yesterday. Lyddon wore a woollen cap pulled well down over his ears, his narrow, bearded face was in shadow and his short, wiry frame was concealed beneath a baggy smock, but the voice, unexpectedly deep and rich in a man so slight, was unmistakable.

Alexander frowned. 'Hugh? What the devil...?' Grunting, he eased himself onto his elbow, reached for the leather bottle held out to him and took a long pull. The aqua vitae caught in his throat making him cough. 'For God's sake get your poking fingers off me,' he muttered hoarsely with no trace of Irish brogue, pushing Lyddon's hand away. 'I don't need a nursemaid.'

'No?' Bringing the shielded lanthorn nearer, and holding it high in one hand, Lyddon continued probing with the other. 'From what I can see you look as if you have been mauled by a bear and you stink like a rotting carcass. Anything broken?'

'Maybe a rib or two, I had to put up a convincing amount of resistance and they seemed disinclined to be gentle.' Gingerly Alexander put a hand to his head and winced. 'I suppose I may have said a few unkind things about their parentage. I don't quite remember.' He handed back the bottle and frowned up at Lyddon. 'And anyway, what the devil are you doing here? As I distinctly recall, my orders were for you to return to St Michael's as soon as the Lord Marquis had sailed and make no attempt to follow me.'

'Yes, well, the situation changed,' Lyddon said defensively. In a feeble attempt to justify his actions, added, 'we had not expected the rebels to withdraw and I wasn't sure how it would affect your plans.'

Alexander grunted. 'Just as well for you I'm damned pleased to see you. I take it Hertford got away – and Sir Ralph?'

'Aye. His lordship will be safe in Wales by now. I can't say about Sir Ralph; he and his men took the coast road to fool Bedford's scouts. They were going to double back inland by Dunkery. We've sent to Tawstock for a guide to meet them at Chittlehampton.'

Lyddon peered towards Barrington Court. The house was in darkness; there was nothing to hear but the wind gusting through the trees. Satisfied, he sat back on his heels and contemplated his captain's swollen face. In the small hours of this morning, when Alexander had ridden away from Minehead, none of his men had expected to see him alive again. Soon afterwards they had been caught in a stiff exchange of musket fire, which turned out not to be the Earl of Bedford's vanguard as they had supposed, but Tom Luttrell's garrison which had followed them from Dunster. Bundling the Marquis of Hertford into a quayside inn, they had beaten off the attack just as scouts brought welcome news that the Earl of Bedford, apparently believing he had successfully driven them to Wales, had turned tail and was withdrawing his army into Dorset.

Acutely aware that here was not a healthy place to linger, Alexander contained his patience as Lyddon briefly related this sequence of events, ending, 'And then, when I learned Bedford was headed for Dorchester, I was afraid you were risking your life for naught, so I hightailed it back to St Michael's, got some help, filled a cart with casks of sack and set out to find you. By chance, we picked up your trail to Ilminster and learned you'd been brought here.' He grinned sympathetically as Alexander crawled painfully to his knees. 'We were about to stage a rescue when you appeared.'

Alexander feigned a disgruntled expression. 'By rights I should have your hide for disobeying my orders – and so I would had I the energy to thrash you. Please tell me it wasn't our best sack you used on those damned greenhorn guards?' He held his hand out. 'Don't just stand there like a moonfaced clodpoll. Help me up, dammit!'

Relieved to be getting off so lightly, Lyddon pulled Alexander to his feet where he stood for a moment holding on to a tree. A gust of wind caught the overhanging branches cascading water onto his head. Covered with wet leaves, hair plastered around his soot-streaked face, his padded stomach thrust before him, he looked more like a woodland sprite than the captain of hardbitten mercenaries.

Lyddon cracked out laughing. 'Sorry, but with that girth and all those leaves, you look like Shakespeare's Bottom! Wherever did you find such a guise?'

'Scratch my head, Peas-blossom – where's Monsieur Cobweb? No – I don't think so – my ears aren't long enough! By happy chance I met with Cobb. He was on his way to find us.' Sticking his finger in his mouth, Alexander hooked out the beeswax and wadding packed in his cheeks, grimaced, worked his mouth and spat. 'Like chrysalides we changed our shapes. He got to be the butterfly and I got his britches, which, as you can see, are a good deal too big for me.' In fact the gypsy had been extremely useful, but there was no time to go into detail now. Grimacing, Alexander shrugged out of his jerkin and began to strip off his shirt to remove the padding, but changed his mind. Given how painful it was to breathe, there was a distinct possibility that some of his ribs were indeed broken. Wincing, he pulled the jerkin back on.

Lyddon grinned. 'So Cobb has surfaced again?' Added, 'How did you get away – those psalm-singing bastards surely didn't let you go?'

'They were careless and I was lucky. They weren't sure if they'd caught themselves a fat Irish deserter, an itinerant gypsy, an enemy spy – or all three. Their exact words were a little more colourful,' Alexander added dryly. 'So, how many men are with you?'

'Three; over yonder with the cart and there's a mount for you.' Lyddon gestured into the trees. 'I've brought you a cloak and a sword. Why the devil did you go into Ilminster? And what happened to your boots? I didn't think to bring any spare.'

'Sweet Hugh, you'll make someone a lovely wife.'

Alexander started limping towards where Lyddon had pointed, anxious now to be on his way. 'It was easier than trailing Bedford's army to Dorchester. I knew the Barrington patrol would pick me up.' He paused, chuckled, 'I truly do not remember what happened to my boots.' He threaded his arm around Lyddon's shoulders for support. 'Enough – I'll fill you in later. We've been lucky so far. Best not push it. Where's this horse you've got me? I must ride after Sir Ralph.' Stepping on a sharp branch he suppressed a yelp, eyed Lyddon's boots, said with dark humour, 'And seeing as how you need to be reminded about obeying orders, I'll have those off you. And there's another thing: there's an exceedingly well-stocked cellar in yonder house, and since you've made the entire garrison drunk on my sack, you can damned well replenish supplies.'

Moments later he was hauling himself precariously into the saddle. Swaying he looked down at Lyddon's anxious face and attempted a smile. With fresh blood trickling from his lips the result was grotesque. He raised his hand, turned his horse and rode into the darkness, saying over his shoulder, 'St Michael's is on my way – I'll send you back some help – and your boots!'

Standing in his stockinged feet, Lyddon watched him go, breaking into a grudging chuckle as his captain's melodious voice floated back to him: '*There was a jovial tinker which was a good ale drinker, he never was a shrinker believe me this is true…*' The man was insufferable! More than two parts dead and singing, for God's sake. Lyddon stood listening until the sound was lost on the wind.

Tired beyond reason, Alexander made his way towards the village of Fivehead. Where were Sir Ralph and his men by now? Had they come to grief in a bog? It was likely. The moor could be treacherous if you did not know the ways. What if they failed? It did not bear thinking about. The King could kiss goodbye to any chance of victory in the South West, that was for sure. But Hopton was nothing if not resourceful, Alexander liked and respected him for that. There were no airs and graces about the man, what he lacked in flair he made up for in determination. He smiled to himself. God's Truth, the man was ill-favoured with his high forehead, close-set eyes and very long nose. Nor was he a man to cross, but he was plain speaking and sincere, which was something of a rarity in these troubled times, when everyone was afraid to speak his mind.

Riding with a loose rein, Alexander tried to concentrate on the parts of his body that did not ache: they were few. He screwed up his eyes; the megrim was getting a grip, a cast iron band tightening about his temples. Had Lyddon said something about Adam being back? Alexander hoped so. Adam Hartley was his second-in-command, and also a damned fine physician. It would be good to see him again after these interim months. When had they parted company? August, was it, just after the skirmish at Marshall Elm? That had been the start of it. First blood. Even then nobody had wanted to believe the quarrel between the King and Parliament had escalated to civil war.

Alexander's reverie came to an abrupt halt as his horse stumbled, almost throwing him from the saddle. He cursed explicitly. The wind had dropped and the rain thinned to a fine drizzle; he was already soaked through. Ineffectually wiping his face with a corner of his cloak, he climbed the ridge to Swell Woods.

It was dark under the dripping trees and ominously quiet. Apprehensively, his hand going automatically to his sword hilt, Alexander slowed the bay gelding to a walk. Guiding the horse with his knees, back prickling, every aching muscle tensed, he crested the ridge and slithered the animal on its hocks down the steep descent on the other side, attempting to look more menacing than he felt and trusting the horse to negotiate the fallen branches.

With a sudden screech, an owl stooped directly in their path. The horse squealed in fright and leapt sideways. Riding the shy, Alexander let out a yelp of pain and bit off a string of crude curses – he could not afford to be unseated out here! He steadied the startled creature, smoothing his hand down its lathered neck and murmuring soft words of comfort. He noted wryly that he was quivering almost as much as his mount and they were both drenched with nervous sweat.

Emerging from the trees, he passed between great banks of withies and picked up one of the many droves that criss-crossed the weeping land to Sedgemoor, disturbing chuckling coots as he squelched by. He hunched painfully in the saddle, his thoughts turning to the news Cobb had brought him. It had led him to change his plans, but he trusted the gypsy implicitly. He'd known him for long enough, God knows.

Must be all of ten years since they first met. It was when they were soldiering in the Netherlands. Alexander smiled ruefully at the memory. He had been naught but a greenhorn boy just turned fourteen and it was his first battle. Cobb had found him puking up his guts in a trench, picked him up and taught him how to stay alive, and for that he would always be grateful. Months later, he had repaid the kindness, almost lost an eye saving the gypsy from being skewered on a pirate's blade. Since then Cobb had attached himself like a doting hound – more like a bear than a hound, Alexander thought, chuckling at the analogy – as big anyway, and bald as a coot, bellied like a toad and cunning as a fox into the bargain – a walking menagerie! Alexander liked the old rogue, but even had he not it was a useful alliance. Cobb was a king among his people, a nefarious bunch of tinkers, pedlars, strolling players and animal keepers, their innocuous trade gaining them entry into all manner of unlikely places. They had been keeping close to the Earl of Bedford's army for some weeks and Cobb had been passing back information.

The gypsy and his pack train had emerged from the trees into Alexander's path this morning. On the strength of what Cobb told him, he had delved into the packs for a likely disguise, borrowed a couple of beasts, left his horse and a complex set of instructions with Cobb, and gone looking for Goody Redhead. He had tracked her down at the Queen's Head in Ilminster: a whore with a heart of gold, she had laughed so much at the sight of him she had almost given the game away and he had been forced to play the clown to cover her mirth. The subsequent revelry had not been part of the plan, but as it turned out had perhaps been of useful service. He had known Goody's considerable charms would prove an irresistible distraction to Dewett, bless her. Even so, Alexander was aware he had been lucky to escape before the lustful captain reported to his commanding officer. Colonel Strode would have seen through the disguise in no time. Thinking about it now, he could only hope that after all this effort Hopton's fake letter got to the Earl of Bedford in time. Sir Ralph was far too dangerous an adversary to ignore. As soon as Bedford's scouts reported Hopton had not sailed with Hertford, he would go after him – in the wrong direction if the ruse worked, pray God.

The harsh crake of roosting herons broke into Alexander's thoughts. The drizzle had stopped and the sky was clearing. Sedgemoor was behind him. Ahead, grey in the cloud-dulled moonlight, lay the flat expanse of Stan Moor bordered on two sides by the rivers Parrett and Tone. Mist rose eerily from ditches that threaded the moor with silver. The Levels would soon be impassable on foot.

He picked his way along a drove to the first bridge and crossed the Tone above the point where the two rivers converged. The roar of the water masked all other sound; new earth had been thrown up along the banks and sandbags piled at vulnerable points in readiness for the flood. For the few people who lived here it would, as usual, be a losing battle. On the other side of the river, floating on the mist like a witch's hat was the conical tor of Burrow Mump.

According to legend, the great King Alfred had built a fort here. Alexander could quite believe it. The Mump was an island in the marshes, a superbly defensive position that commanded extensive views across the flat reaches of the Levels, south as far as Glastonbury Tor and north beyond the Quantock hills to Bridgwater and the sea.

Speaking softly to his horse he slid from its back and holding on to its neck made his way to the second bridge just below the surging waters of the confluence. He crossed over and limped into Burrow Bridge. From there it was but a few steps to the Mump and the steep track to the church on the summit.

2

Although the ancient church of St Michael was still used for worship by the few inhabitants of Burrow Bridge, in recent years it had begun to fall into disrepair. Weeds sprouted from its walls and chunks of masonry from crumbling buttresses lay strewn, moss-covered, beneath them. Perhaps that was why it had so far been overlooked by marauding Puritans: the altar rails and crucifix remained intact, though the churchwarden had circumspectly removed the alabaster Virgin Mary from her niche and hidden her away. The place had an eerie, derelict feel, Alexander reflected as leading his horse, he climbed laboriously through the mist, slipping and sliding on wet scree and wishing Lyddon had bigger feet.

On such a night as this it was easy to imagine restless spirits wandered here, still marshalling their ghostly forces to repel invading Danes. Lost in thought, Alexander caught a blur of movement ahead. Indistinct in the mist a white shape floated into his path. He gasped, stopped short, the hairs rising on the nape of his neck. Behind him his horse baulked, snorting.

'Easy boy, steady now,' Alexander murmured, reaching up to still the tossing head. 'What fools we are,' he chuckled. Tugging at the reins he continued on his way as the startled sheep jumped back into the shadows.

For centuries St Michael's had served as a refuge, for although the monks had begun in King John's time to drain the land hereabouts, and spasmodic attempts had been made ever since to keep the waters at bay, the Levels still flooded for half the year or more. Each autumn the villagers dusted off their stilts and rafts, carried their meagre valuables to the church and herded their livestock onto the Mump to wait for the waters to recede. Theirs was an island mentality. News travelled slowly in the Somerset wetlands. Life went on as it always had and arguments between the King and Parliament were of another world. Perhaps that was why, along with the many kindnesses that had come their way since Alexander had found his way here, the recent comings and goings of mounted men and the growing stack of weapons in the church remained – as yet – a closely guarded secret.

Last April, when Alexander had returned home from captivity in London, Adam Hartley and Hugh Lyddon had soon found a path to his door. Was there going to be a war? Was he going to fight for the King and if so, could they join him? There were others of like mind, all good men; would he consent to lead them? At first he had refused, shunning the responsibility. He preferred to operate alone. For almost a year he had been confined in the Tower for his alleged involvement in the Army Plot: a treasonous conspiracy to free the Earl of Strafford and subdue Parliament with a show of force. Kicking his heels in the dank confines of a prison cell, Alexander had ample time to consider both sides of the argument that raged outside it. He had no liking for zealous, uncompromising Puritans: men like John Pym, who had stirred up resentment against the King, shouting that his taxes and monopolies were against the law. Trumpeting the atrocities perpetrated by Catholic rebels in Ireland to inflame people's fear of Papism until mobs rioted in the streets, desecrated churches and assaulted anyone suspected of being a Catholic sympathiser. And yet, despite himself, Alexander had understood why Pym and his supporters cried out so vehemently for reform. Cocooned in the extravagance of his court, the King seemed oblivious to the poverty and suffering his taxes were causing – especially the hated Ship Money. He refused to listen to his people's fears, failed to understand that they could see no difference between Papism and his High Anglican reforms. Misery and frustration swelled like pus in a boil and Pym – 'that round-headed man', as the Queen had dubbed him – stood poised with a scalpel.

While the world turned upside down outside the walls of his cell, Alexander had taken pains to befriend his guards, gleaning tidbits of news over protracted games of cards that he endeavoured to lose. He had even begun to question his own loyalty, yet to go against his King was unthinkable. There was a gentleness about this tiny, elegant monarch for all his faults; a sweetness of temper that bound one to him in love and protectiveness as to a wayward child. And yet he was also autocratic and distant, emotionally insecure and politically naïve. Was it wise to allow such a man to govern unchecked? But what was the alternative? Anarchy? A puppet King manipulated by religious zealots and power-hungry men? Was that any better for the people? With his thoughts going round in circles, Alexander had grown increasingly bad tempered as the weeks dragged by. Then, in March, when no proof of treason could be found against him, his guardian had paid the heavy fine for his release. Still undecided what to do, Alexander had gone home to watch and wait, but as war became inevitable his friends had at last persuaded him to follow his natural inclination to side with the King.

He had sought out Cobb and set in motion a means of gathering and exchanging information; sent a message to Sir Ralph Hopton, under whose command he had engaged in clandestine activities during the last Scots War, declared his allegiance and offered his services. He had delved into his dwindling resources to house, feed, equip and train a small company of thirty men. He paid them well and in return demanded exacting standards, meting out stern discipline and pointing out when they grumbled that they were not obliged to stay. So far not one had left. He expected – and usually got – unquestioning obedience, employing them only on those terms. They may not always like him, but he knew he had their respect.

As he neared the summit, Alexander paused to catch his breath; the Mump had never seemed so steep, his feet were damned sore, the padding round his belly hampered his movements and despite the cold, he was running with sweat.

'Feeling sorry for yourself won't get the job done, my boy,' he muttered, echoing a phrase of Cobb's. Softly cursing, he hugged his ribs, leaned against the bay's muscled shoulder and looked up at the dark bulk of the church tower silhouetted against the sky. He had expected to be challenged before now, could not believe the men had not posted a watch on the Mump. Careless bastards! He would have something to say about that.

Once he had firmly made up his mind to commit himself to the King's cause, with Adam's help he had spent some weeks knocking the company into shape: had shown the men how to fight as a team, charging down the enemy like a battering ram and holding their fire until the last possible moment. He had taught them to ride like acrobats and provided them with flintlock pistols with sharply curved butts that could be tucked underarm and fired single-handed – they were from Arabia and had cost him a small fortune. The men had spent hours on horseback each day, turning in the saddle to shoot at moving targets, dodging and slicing at straw men with turnip faces, competing in races, engaging each other in combat and honing their swordsmanship until each one was an expert and had the scars to show for it. It was new, it was exciting, it was exhausting: they thought he was mad and they loved him for it. When at last they were fashioned into a close-knit team, he had sent eighteen of them with Adam to help train Prince Rupert's new cavalry. Two more had gone as spies to join Parliament's armies, masquerading as Roundheads and using Cobb's web of messengers to pass back intelligence. Four had been with him in Sherborne, the remainder were based here at St Michael's – the name they had taken for their company.

Wearily hitching his whickering horse by the linhay near the church, Alexander limped to the porch, discarded his sopping cloak, felt his way around the saddlebags, sheepskins and food sacks piled there and let himself in. A single wax candle burned in the chancel, its light glowing dimly into the nave. He bowed his head and stood for a moment, leaning against a pillar and absorbing the peaceful stillness of the little church. He could hear the murmur of voices and see light shining from under the door of the tower room, which they had repaired and now used as a communal living space. He walked down the shadowed aisle towards it, his hand caressing the pew ends as he passed them. Gently he eased open the door.

Under a sweet pall of tobacco smoke, six of his men were seated companionably at a table, the remains of a meal pushed to one side. There was another, a stranger sitting with his back to the door. They stopped talking abruptly as they saw Alexander. Benches clattering backwards, they reached hurriedly for their swords, clay pipes scattering and shattering on the floor.

'Easy, gentlemen,' Alexander drawled, raising a sardonic eyebrow. 'Good to know you're staying alert.' He looked at their sheepish faces and was glad to see Adam was there. Beside him was Will Mohun, a fiery redhead who enjoyed taking mechanical things apart to see how they worked and if he could improve on them – he usually could. James Chichester was grinning as usual, a jovial bear of a man, more skilled with horses than anyone Alexander knew. Jonathon Southcott, his notary, whose penchant for devising and breaking ciphers was so useful, looked nonplussed. Francis Sydenham stood beside him, tall and thin, a lawyer with a brain as sharp as his blade. Finally, Rob Pollard, his quartermaster, who no matter what he wanted would somehow find it for him. They were all the friends of his boyhood – those halcyon days when he had led them into one mischievous exploit after another and driven their long-suffering parents to despair. Most of them came from landed families, younger sons whose income was as limited as their choices: marry money or live by their wits. Like Alexander, they had so far chosen the latter.

As Alexander limped into the light of the tower room, Rob Pollard shouted with delight. 'It's Tawford, by God! We weren't expecting you so soon.'

'Clearly!' He grinned bloodily. 'Nor anyone else apparently.'

For a heartbeat they stared at him, then all started laughing at once – except the fair-headed stranger, a handsome, exquisitely dressed youth whose features were vaguely familiar and who looked Alexander up and down with thinly veiled contempt. Raising a quizzical eyebrow, Alexander looked back at him.

'It appears we have a ganymede in our midst,' he murmured. 'You have me at a disadvantage, Sir.'

Before the youth could reply, James Chichester broke in with mock formality. 'Tawford, allow me to present my cousin, Richard Chichester of Hall, lately come from Ireland. Young Dickon here wants to join the world of men,' he teased, 'and since he's recently sprouted a little fluff on his chin, I suggested he join us – if that meets with your approval?'

'Or even if it doesn't, it seems,' Alexander said mildly. 'I assume you have him sworn to secrecy and have warned him I will slit his throat and feed him to the crows if he betrays us?' He spoke softly, but none doubted the underlying menace of his words.

'I will vouch for him, you need have no fear as to his loyalty and if you don't mind my saying so, you do smell as though you could use a body servant.' Grinning, Chichester held his nose. Amidst the laughter he turned back to his cousin. 'Dickon, this is our lord and master whom you so wished to meet: Alexander Dynam of Tawford, ward of Lord Robert Dynam, Viscount Westley.'

'Delighted.' Alexander gave a polite smile and attempted to make a leg, bending over his corpulence in a courtly bow so incongruous it started another gale of laughter.

Embarrassed, the youth responded with a curt nod at the fat, slovenly fellow posturing before him who looked as if he had come off worst in some vulgar tavern brawl. Dickon, annoyed with James, had no intention of demeaning himself to be this or any other person's body servant. He had come to offer his sword in the King's cause and was keenly disappointed. If this disreputable clown was the fabled Tawford, he would take his sword elsewhere.

'Thank you, but I think not,' Alexander murmured, admiring the youth's shining lovelocks falling to his elaborate lace collar, the black velvet doublet, sleeves fashionably slashed to display a fine embroidered shirt. Suddenly he placed the youth's features. 'And how is your illustrious cousin? You bear a marked resemblance to his Lordship.'

'If you mean Viscount Carrickfergus, he is well thank you,' the boy's eyes were chips of ice. He looked superciliously down his nose, added, 'Though I find it hard to imagine you are that well acquainted.'

Alexander's eyebrow shot up. The sudden quiet was palpable. 'Enough of these pleasantries,' Adam Hartley interjected hastily. 'You look dreadful, man, come and sit down.' Dickon was no match for Tawford's biting sarcasm, few were, and the boy clearly had no idea he was being duped.

The moment passed. A barrage of questions met Alexander as he was manhandled to the table and pushed onto a hastily up-righted bench. A mug of beer appeared at his elbow and a trencher of cold mutton was placed before him. His stomach heaving, he pushed it away and stood up.

'Forgive me, gentlemen.' He looked around apologetically at their expectant faces. 'I have to leave again shortly. I'll answer your questions before I go, but first, Master Chichester?' He directed a cool gaze at Dickon, 'Perhaps you would see to my horse and then pick out four fresh mounts. Bridle them all, but saddle only two – use the lightweight saddles with sheepskins under. You'll find them in the linhay. I want the rest of you, except Hartley and Sydenham, to make ready to ride to Lyddon's aid. Also, from now on I want a guard posted on the bridge. See to it,' he snapped. He abruptly left the room, calling over his shoulder as he went, 'Hartley, I need you, come.'

Stunned into silence, the men stared after him. 'He was ever a high-handed fellow,' Will Mohun murmured.

'So you should be used to it by now,' Southcott responded dryly. 'I wonder what's going on.'

Chichester shrugged. 'He'll tell us in his own time. Come on, best do as he says, you know what he's like and the last thing I need right now is a tongue-lashing.' He gave his young cousin a shove. 'Go to it, my boy. What's the matter? Too grand to take orders now, are we? Or is it that doublet you're worried about? I thought you wanted to serve our infamous captain. Not what you'd imagined, eh? I'll allow he's on the portly side and his personal cleanliness is a little wanting – but you should see him with a fiddle.' He clapped Dickon on the shoulder as his colleagues howled with mirth. The youth, his ears bright red, went reluctantly to do his bidding.

Adam, who had been watching Alexander closely, moved hurriedly from the table, grabbed a lantern and followed, found him in the shadows of the nave, bent double, silently retching.

'Oh dear,' Adam murmured. 'You are in a bad way. Come on, old chap.' He helped his captain into the small side chapel, which had been cleared of fallen masonry and made watertight for Alexander's personal use. It was sparsely furnished with a trunk for his clothes, a table spread with books and maps, a stool and a truckle bed, which the villagers had produced and lugged up the hill for him when he had first found his way here. The churchwarden's wife, a motherly woman, had soon taken Alexander to her ample bosom and ensured he did not want for fresh food and clean linen.

Alexander eyed the bed longingly for a moment then proceeded to strip off his filthy jerkin, retrieving a tiny, silver brooch pinned to the underside. It was fashioned in the shape of a gillyflower, the centre set with an amethyst. He had meant it for Goody, in all the commotion had forgotten. It was a pretty trinket, Ellen might like it; luckily Sergeant Hooper had missed it. 'It's good to see you Adam – Hugh said you were back – you have news of the King? How does our noble monarch?'

'Much as you would expect in the circumstances, he misses the Queen more, I think, than he will allow. But his courage and resolve remain firm, largely thanks to Prince Rupert. The King sends an urgent plea for arms and bids me tell you he knows who his true and loyal friends are and when he is restored to London, they will receive his gratitude in full measure.'

Alexander snorted. 'Whatever that may mean now the Queen has pawned the crown jewels!' He fumbled with his points, tugging at the ribbon cord, stepped out of Cobb's voluminous breeches and tossed them on the bed. 'What we need now is troops and weapons, not promises.'

Adam put the lantern on the table and watched as Alexander began unwinding the yards of linen encasing his belly, grimacing as he saw the welts and bruises being revealed.

'Here, let me help you. As to that, there's news: the King has asked Lord Ormonde to start peace talks with the Catholic Confederates in Kilkenny. He means to free up supplies and troops from Ireland.'

'Godamme!' Alexander gave a low whistle. 'That'll set the cat among the pigeons. Pym will have a field day.'

'For sure.' Pursing his lips, Adam dropped an armful of linen on the bed. 'Wherever did you get all this stuff – and why, for God's sake?'

'It's complicated. You were saying?'

'Ormonde will send what troops he can spare now – a few hundred – but if there's a truce in Ireland he will have tens of thousands for us, and with Bristol, Plymouth and now Portsmouth in Parliament's hands, they will have to be landed at Falmouth. Pendennis must accommodate them until they are mustered.'

Alexander grunted with pain as Adam eased away the last of the padding stuck bloodily to his thigh. 'I take it Nick Slanning knows his role as Governor of Pendennis is about to get a deal more taxing?'

'No – the King dare not trust this information to the usual channels. He would lose a lot of support if folk knew he was preparing to negotiate with Irish rebels. He asks that you convey it for him personally – "as you have done so ably in the past", he said.'

'Did he indeed! As well I go to Cornwall then,' Alexander swayed.

Adam shot out a hand and grasped his elbow. 'Sit down before you fall down and scrape that wax off your teeth. I need more light in here. I'll be back shortly.' Alexander obediently did as he was told. Adam Hartley was a man who inspired trust; clean-shaven, he wore his mousy brown hair to his shoulders, had a square, honest face and kindly eyes. Softly spoken, of average height and build he went unnoticed in a crowd, yet there was about him an air of quiet professionalism that commanded instant respect among the men. Aside from Cobb, he was Alexander's closest friend and had been the natural choice for his second-in-command.

Moments later Adam reappeared with another lantern, a bowl of water, soap, cloths, towels, bandages, an assortment of medicaments and a chunk of raw meat, which he slapped onto Alexander's eye. 'Hold it there for a moment.' Carefully setting down the lantern and bowl, he released the rest of his load onto the bed.

Setting to work on his captain's abused body, Adam listened to Alexander's cultured tones recounting events since they had parted company after Marshall Elm. When his voice tailed away, Adam sat back on his heels for a moment. 'Do you think Sir Ralph will get through to Cornwall?'

Alexander shrugged. 'Who knows? If he manages to find his way over the moor he then has to get to the border without attracting attention, which means crossing the Taw under Barnstaple's nose, and the town is strongly garrisoned – five hundred or more last I heard – Sir Ralph can't outface them, he has fewer than two hundred mounted soldiers with him. Then there's Torrington, though they've yet to show their colours and will most likely look the other way rather than risk a confrontation.' He gritted his teeth as Hartley examined his thigh.

'Where did you get this? Whoever stitched it for you did a good job.'

'Outside Yeovil – a skirmish on Galleon Hill – don't ask! A horse surgeon tended me and judging by the size of the needle he thought I was a horse.'

Hartley chuckled. 'What does Sir Ralph mean to do?'

'Join up with Sir Bevill Grenville; they will raise an army between them. Bevill will – ouch!' He winced as Adam's competent fingers probed his head in an attempt to clean the blacking out of his matted hair.

'Sorry. You were saying?'

'Only that Bevill has a lot of friends – everyone loves the dear man – with Sir Ralph's help he will soon rally the Cornish. Hartley, desist – that will do – really,' he protested as the physician continued tugging.

'Be still. You have a nasty cut on your head and I need to cleanse it.' Lapsing into silence, Adam finished tending Alexander's hurts then stood back to admire his handiwork.

'There. If you insist on leaving now, that is all I can do for you. You've cracked a couple of ribs, but the binding should help. Your thigh has partially reopened, but it's clean. Thank God the ball missed the bone. You really ought to get some rest. Can I not persuade you? Just for an hour or two at least?'

Alexander shook his head. 'No time; what if Sir Ralph loses his way? He is our only hope. I must ride after him.'

Adam shrugged, resigned. Had it been anyone else he would have insisted, but he knew it was pointless to try: no man drove himself harder or with more restless energy than Alexander. 'Be it on your own head then.' Adam held out a cup of dark, noxious smelling liquid. 'Here, drink this, it will help keep the megrim at bay, at least for a while.'

'You know me too well, Adam.' Alexander grinned weakly.

'I thought I was managing to hide it.' He took the cup and drained the contents. 'Ugh!' He screwed up his face. 'That's foul, whatever's in it?'

'Endive, camomile and horse-mint, with a touch of cinnamon and ginger in white wine to settle your stomach, tincture of willow bark for the pain and powdered hyssop to keep you awake.'

'I should have known better than to ask!'

Hartley's mouth twitched. 'You really ought to eat something to go with it.'

'I will, at the first opportunity,' Alexander promised. Washed and salved, his chest bound and his thigh dressed and tightly bandaged, he climbed into fresh clothes.

'Will you call in at Tawford Barton to see Ellen?'

Alexander's face softened at the mention of Ellen, Lord Westley's sister, who lived with Alexander and kept his household together for him while he was away – which seemed to be most of the time these days. 'It rather depends on what transpires. I will if I can.'

'What about Lord Westley? Won't you see him?'

'No. I will not.'

'You should make the effort. He is not a well man and he is desperate to talk to you.' Adam spoke without thinking. He both liked and respected the man everyone thought was Alexander's father, though Westley had never publicly acknowledged that fact.

Alexander's eyes narrowed. 'I have nothing to say to him,' he said shortly.

'Dammit, man,' Adam protested, ignoring the warning signs. 'He's done his best. It's not his fault...' He clamped his lips together, but it was too late to recall the words.

With an obscene curse, Alexander grasped the empty cup and threw it violently against the wall where it shattered, sending shards of pottery flying across the room. 'No? Then who else's? Keep your mollycoddling nose out of my business, Hartley. When I want your opinion, I'll bloody well ask for it!'

Stung, Adam bent to pick up the pieces, mentally kicking himself. Alexander's customary self-control and the silver-tongued mockery with which he wielded authority made it easy to forget how young he was – and how vulnerable, particularly where Lord Westley was concerned. An intensely private person, Alexander kept his emotions carefully in check. Few were permitted to see the man beneath the habitual mask of devil-may-care. That it had slipped now was a measure of his exhaustion, which Adam knew with a stab of compassion, his captain was trying hard to conceal. He clowned an expression of abject apology, 'Forgive me for speaking out of turn. As you say, I should mind my own business. God's Wounds!' He had caught his fingers on a sharp piece of pottery. He shook his hand spraying blood all over his shirt, swore again and sucked at the wound.

'Serves you right, you sanctimonious bastard!' Despite himself, Alexander's lips twitched. 'I've arranged for the arms to be shipped out at the end of the week. The men can spend the next few days gathering up whatever the rebels have not yet seized: muskets, powder, bullets, match – anything still useable. I know Lord Poulett has been stockpiling weapons at Hinton St George and there are others of like mind. I want you to see to it. Take them by barge to Bridgwater and ask at the Anchor for Billy Baines, he is Master of the *Gabriel*. To all outward appearances she's being re-fitted and has only a skeleton crew, so nobody's paid her any attention as yet. She is due to sail to Dublin on Friday and is putting in at Swansea to pick up more crew. Baines will offload the weapons for us there. You'll have to send someone with her to see to them at the other end.'

Adam nodded. 'How will she get through the blockade?'

'Most of Parliament's ships are concentrating their efforts on Bristol, they may not spot her if she slips out on the evening tide, but she's a fast lugger, built to outrun the Dunkirkers: plenty of sail, very manoeuvrable and six cannon to fight her way out of trouble. She'll be damned unlucky not to get through.'

'And afterwards – do we join you in Cornwall?'

'Not sure till I've spoken with Hopton; I'll send word, give me ten days – if you hear nothing by then take the men to Prince Rupert. In any event, we must move out of St Michael's. The Levels are flooding, the villagers will soon be needing the space.'

'What about young Chichester, shall we keep him with us?'

'No; too much of a liability – does James think we're a company of bloody nursemaids, for pity's sake?'

Adam's brows shot up. Alexander had been much the same age when he'd gone off to the Netherlands to fight for the Prince of Orange, but he held his tongue.

Fully clothed, Alexander was grunting with the effort of pulling on his boots. 'I'll take him with me and drop him off near his home. We'll just have to hope he keeps his mouth shut. The last thing I need right now is to be harried by irate parents. It'll be a hard ride, I hope he's up to it.'

Adam frowned. 'More so than you are just now I suspect,' he murmured.

As if on cue Dickon hesitantly entered the chapel. He looked searchingly round the room, his gaze taking in the discarded clothes and swathes of bloodstained linen on the bed. 'But you're not...' He stopped in confusion as Adam snorted.

'I assure you that I am.' Alexander's tone was coldly polite.

Dickon stared, jaw dropped, at the slim, elegant figure standing before him. Only the bruises remained of the man to whom he thought he had been introduced. Alexander's short, tousled hair, still streaked with lampblack, was the colour of bleached straw. Between livid bruises his skin, now free of filth, was deeply tanned. A thin slanting scar pulled at his right eyelid giving him an indolent expression curiously at odds with the restive energy he exuded. His teeth were even and white and his lips, though crusted with blood, were full and perfectly shaped. The eye that returned Dickon's stare – for

45

the other was still swollen shut – was green and fringed with ridiculously long, fair lashes, but the strong, dimpled chin, stubbled with two days' growth of beard, belied any hint of effeminacy. Dressed for the road, Alexander wore a russet doublet under a sleeveless buff leather jerkin. A plain, but freshly starched white collar adorned his clean linen shirt and his muscular legs were encased in warm, worsted breeches and thigh-length boots. A pistol in a calfskin holster was attached to the belt at his waist, also a leather pocket to carry powder cartridges, shot, a small knife and money. From right shoulder to left hip he wore a sword belt and had slung on an oiled cloak. In one gloved hand he held a wide-brimmed black hat, which he now placed gingerly on his head.

Alexander tolerated Dickon's scrutiny with a glint of amusement. 'Well? Do I pass muster?'

Flushing, Dickon looked away. 'I'm sorry, Sir – I thought…' He faltered, grinning. 'They let me think you were… the rats. God, what an idiot.'

'I know what you thought. Appearances can be deceptive – you might reflect on that, young man. Are the horses ready?'

'Yes, Sir.'

'Right, get mounted, you're coming with me. We'll lead one each and travel as lightly as possible. We need to ride fast and you might like to wear something a little more suitable? I would prefer we are not taken for Cavaliers should we be observed, proud as we are to be called so!' Alexander buckled on his sword. 'Of course, if you'd rather stay…?'

Dickon's eyes lit up. 'Yes, Sir, that is… no, Sir. Do you mind telling me where we are bound?'

'Later.' Seeing Dickon's crestfallen expression, Alexander relented, briefly outlined the events of the past few hours and the purpose of their journey, smiling slightly as the boy's eyes widened in unabashed admiration.

'I'll be ready directly, Sir.' Dickon turned away, tripping over his feet in his eagerness.

'Dickon,' Alexander called him back.

'Sir?'

'For pity's sake, drop the Sir! Tawford will do. We tend to stick to second names at St Michael's, but if you don't mind I'll continue to call you Dickon – having two Chichesters in our little band will be all too confusing.'

'I would be honoured, S..., that is..., I mean, T-Tawford.' The boy flushed, tongue-tied.

'Go on then, jump to it,' Alexander said kindly.

Adam feigned a sigh as Dickon scrambled away. 'Oh Lord – now he thinks you're Alexander the Great reincarnate.'

'Hardly – his father thinks I'm a murdering traitorous bastard and would hang me from the tallest tree. I daresay the boy will soon have cause to agree.'

Adam doubted it, but held his tongue. As always, Alexander was blithely unaware of his power to bind men to him, particularly youngsters like Dickon who lived for the chance to prove their courage.

Moving to the door, Alexander hesitated and turning clasped his friend's shoulder. 'As always, you have wrought miracles. Thank you. May the Lord keep you safe, Adam, for in truth, though it may not always seem like it, I do not know what I would do without you.'

Smiling gently, Adam met Alexander's gaze. 'God go with you too, my friend.'

Companionably they left the church; men were milling around outside, retrieving their horses from the linhay, tightening girths and adjusting straps, disturbing the pigeons that fluttered and grumbled in the loft above. Handing over Lyddon's boots, Alexander rattled off orders as Dickon, plainly attired in ill-fitting, borrowed clothes, scrambled breathlessly out of the porch. Alexander gave him an approving look.

'Better!' Turning, he slithered down the Mump with Dickon and four horses in tow.

Once over the bridge, they mounted up and each leading a spare horse, set off at a fast pace towards Wiveliscombe. Dickon's chief anxiety, as he followed Alexander's flying figure through the night, was keeping his seat. It was not easy when his horses were jibbing and snorting at shadows. The thought of disgracing himself was not to be borne.

Varying the pace they stopped from time to time to change over mounts and let the horses blow. Then off again, the way silvered by the moon riding high in the sky. Above Dulverton they stopped to water the horses before wading the River Barle, fast flowing, but shallow. From there they skirted the southern fringes of Exmoor along deep, winding lanes that led sometimes up onto open moorland, their progress slowed by drifts of tall rushes and tussocks of sedge, or down into wooded combes, splashing through streams and sinking in cushions of moss, their faces scratched by overhanging branches of beech, blackthorn and alder.

As the sky was beginning to lighten and Dickon knew neither he nor his horses could go much further, Alexander reined in, looked at the youngster's set face appraisingly. 'Not much further now, lad. We're on Courtenay land – this is Anstey Common. We're about two hours from where I believe Sir Ralph and his men will cross the Taw, if indeed they have not already done so. But we have asked more of these poor beasts than anyone should, so I propose we make a short detour.' He gestured into the mist-hung landscape. 'There's a place yonder where we should be able to get fresh mounts, but keep your wits about you. The Courtenays are divided, we may not be welcome.'

Dickon, too exhausted to care one way or the other, nodded assent and followed, sucking and squelching along a boggy ridge and down into a rocky gorge. At the bottom, Alexander dismounted. Dickon followed suit, staggering a little, thighs stiff and aching, backside on fire.

Leading the foundering horses, they turned up a deeply rutted track to a farmstead. It was tucked away in the lee of the hill, a group of low stone and thatch buildings clustered round a yard. On the windward side stood a belt of stunted trees, their skeletal branches bent almost horizontal. Half a dozen milk cows waited patiently outside a byre, steam rising from their backs, hens scratching beneath their feet. A pair of curs rushed up noisily heralding their arrival, tails wagging.

'Ho there, Jester, down, Poll, good dogs, where's your master?' Alexander stooped to fondle them. It was an unnecessary question as from between the cows and squawking hens an old man had emerged carrying a pitchfork threateningly before him.

'Josh, hold up, it's me.' Alexander walked forward to greet him, the dogs fussing around his legs.

The old man peered at him with short-sighted eyes. 'Maister Alexander, be it yourzel?' Under his floppy hat, his wizened face creased into a toothless grin.

'It is indeed. How are you, Josh? It's been a long time.'

Josh Randall lowered the pitchfork. 'Awiz achin an crakin I be, but like the wive do zay to I, thee can't have two vorenoons in one day, Josh.'

'And you still in your prime,' Alexander teased.

'Gid on, thee bist a vule as ever was.' The old man's smile widened with pleasure. 'Ow be yerzel? Bain wraxling I zee an ad a woppit roun the yurole, you'm zor brit bouta vace. An what be doing yr vaur day when honest volk be abaid an who be ur behind ee spuddlin 'bout? Ur looks wisht like ur's gwain to vall awver.' He stared at Dickon. 'Ur be a Chichester or I baint Josh Randall.'

Grinning wearily, Dickon gave up trying to follow the old man's broad Devon speech.

'I see you're as keen-eyed as ever, old man.' Alexander nodded. 'Yes. This is Master Richard Chichester of Hall. We've had a hard ride and our horses have foundered. We have to make haste. Have you a couple of mounts you can spare and could you see to these for me?'

Taken with a fit of coughing, Josh leaned on his pitchfork and spat down at his feet. 'Might've. How long vor?' He wheezed, wiping his mouth with the back of his dung-encrusted sleeve.

'That's a nasty cough you've got there Josh. Not long – a

few days at most.'

Randall's eyes gleamed. 'Ow much?'

'Two shillings.'

'Dray.'

Alexander laughed. 'Very well, you old rogue, three shillings it is, if you'll spare us some milk into the bargain.'

The old man grinned. 'I can do that right nuff an more azides. Wude ee come een back an zee the wive? Er'll be zore upzot if thee disn't. Er's bin bakin vor an ower gone,' he added persuasively.

Alexander hesitated, took a quick look at Dickon's white face and nodded. 'Just ten minutes then, thank you, we'd be pleased to.'

'Proper job,' Josh wheezed.

They followed him into the house where a delicious smell of freshly baked bread assailed their nostrils as Mistress Randall, hands outstretched, came bustling and beaming towards them.

At that precise moment, in Barrington Court, Captain Dewett was tentatively raising his hand to tap on the door of Colonel Strode's upstairs parlour.

3

Sunday 25ᵗʰ September, 1642

Colonel Strode, his two favourite hounds lying in a greying, somnolent heap at his feet, was just partaking of a light meal, as he customarily did after gathering his household together at dawn to lead them in prayer. Today was the Sabbath and later he would take them to church to listen to Amos Turner's – doubtless – lengthy sermon, but for the moment he had some respite from his pastoral duties.

It was a pretty room this, in the west wing of the house, the mullioned windows overlooking the garden that his wife, Joan, so enjoyed and where she grew roses and lavender, leaving sweetly smelling baskets of them strewn about the house to dry – but not lately. He pondered anxiously on her condition. It was her fourteenth pregnancy and she had been complaining of a backache all week. The midwife was already installed in readiness and Joan had taken to her bed. She was not a young woman – they had been wed twenty-two years, had not expected to be blessed again, but one did not question providence. The Lord had been good to them; five sons had survived to manhood and the future of his family, pray God, was assured. He hoped this one would be a daughter to comfort them in their old age, and if Joan survived this one more time, he would not go to her bed again, but would mortify his lustful flesh until his hungers subsided. Sighing, he whispered: 'Forgive me Lord, I am but a weak and sinful man—' A rap on the half-open door interrupted his prayer.

William Strode was a devout man, a Presbyterian who strongly resisted the Papist practices that had steadily increased under Archbishop Laud and which he believed to be the workings of the Devil. He was also an astute businessman, had made his mark as a clothier, learned everything about the trade from the bottom up and soon gained a reputation for integrity and honesty. He had made a great deal of money from shrewd investments and his subsequent purchase of Barrington Court, a Tudor manor house nestling in the Somerset heartland, had fulfilled his aspirations for social advancement. Member of Parliament for Ilchester, Strode took his duties in the Commons most seriously, siding energetically with John Pym in the desperate struggle that was now taking place to rescue the King from his corrupt advisers – those evil men who subverted the law and threatened to destroy the true Protestant religion.

In July, when half his mind had been occupied with the gravity of this situation and the other had been on the forthcoming harvest and whether his rams were being properly conditioned for tup, William Strode had hired and armed a garrison to protect his family, his property and that of the local community. Just as well, he now reflected, for in early August, the Marquis of Hertford had arrived in nearby Shepton Mallet to publish the Commission of Array for the King. This Strode viewed as blatantly illegal; the law had been changed and it was now Parliament's prerogative to control the militia. Saddened and outraged, he had ridden into town with a few men at arms, told the townsfolk to ignore any attempt to muster them and demanded that Hertford and his soldiers depart the town immediately. In the ensuing scuffle Strode had been struck from his horse and arrested at sword point by a minion of Sir Ralph Hopton's. Gratifyingly – and a little surprisingly, for Strode was a modest man – a large crowd had come to his aid, forcibly obtaining his release from the terrified constable into whose charge Hopton's agent had entrusted him. Since then, Strode had been assisting the Earl of Bedford at Sherborne, but expecting the blockade to persist for some weeks had taken a short break from his military duties, pleading leave to attend his wife.

Hearing Dewett's tentative voice behind the door, Strode sighed, pushing his plate away. He was not entirely happy with the captain of his garrison, for although the man had come well recommended and seemed a capable soldier, he was too familiar with the men under his charge, lax in his manner and prone to the sins of the flesh. Again Strode sighed. He should perhaps have listened to his wife, whose initial reaction had been to say, 'Twas a pity the new captain was somewhat lacking between the ears'. But beyond this tart observation, Joan, far too loyal to openly criticise her husband's choice, had thought him out of earshot when she had added to herself, 'Too handsome by half and knows it – nothing but trouble will come of it, you mark my words.'

She had been right, Strode reflected gloomily. By anyone's standards, James Dewett was good to look upon. He was tall, lithe and athletic, his regular features unmarked by pox, with full lips, white teeth, and eyes of startling blue. His thin moustache and short, pointed beard were always carefully groomed, as was his hair, which fell to his muscular shoulders like polished jet. Aside from his misshapen fingernails, bitten to the quick, he appeared to be physically flawless and as Joan had predicted, his presence had an unsettling effect on the women of the household, each one vying for the captain's attention and neglecting her duties whenever he came in sight. It was not Dewett's fault, perhaps, that he was so sought after by the ladies, but he lacked the moral fibre to resist their sweet temptations. Strode was himself a lusty man, but feeling most strongly that such urges should be confined to the sanctity of marriage and the procreation of children, he took a very dim view of lecherous behaviour and Dewett, who should be a role model for his men, was the worst offender. Determining to speak to him on the matter, Strode dabbed at his grey whiskers and called upon the captain to enter.

Dewett, blissfully unaware of what was occupying his commanding officer's mind, tore his thoughts away from Goody Redhead's milky-white thighs and attempted to focus on the matter in hand. He walked a little unsteadily to the table, stood to attention and held out the captured document.

'Sir, we arrested a vagrant in Ilminster last night and found this on his person. The man was of no account, but I thought I should bring it to your notice.'

'Stand easy, man.' Strode reached for the grubby package held out to him, inspected the torn seal, drew a sharp breath and rapidly scanned the page. He directed a tense gaze at Dewett. 'At what time did this occur?'

'At about nine o' clock, Colonel.'

The colonel let out an exasperated grunt. 'Then why, in heaven's name, have you waited until now before bringing it to my attention?'

Embarrassed, Dewett struggled to find a convincing reason. 'I didn't like to disturb you, Sir, what with your good lady being... that is to say...'

'Very well, very well.' Strode frowned. 'Where is the prisoner now?'

'Confined in the cellar, Sir. He was reported as a stranger by the town watch. We questioned him, but could get little sense out of him – he was drunk, barely conscious when we brought him in. He says he is a pedlar and found this letter in a ditch.'

'And you believed him?' Strode's bushy eyebrows shot up and he stared at Dewett. 'Well? What does he look like? Did you get his name?'

'O'Neill, Sir – Irish,' Dewett grimaced. 'He's the look of a gypsy, dark and swarthy, has a belly on him like a pregnant sow.' Fingering his thin moustache, Dewett searched his memory, 'And a scar on his face, puckering his eyelid, Colonel.'

'What!' Violently, Strode pushed his chair back from the table and tried to stand. His feet came up against the sleeping hounds, arms flailing he overbalanced and fell spreadeagled to the floor. Tails thumping, the hounds covered his face in wet kisses, scratched, yawned and settled back to sleep again while Strode, flushed and breathless, pulled himself up by the table leg, felt for his discarded napkin and mopped his damp cheeks. 'Take me to him,' he spluttered.

With an effort, Dewett kept his face straight. 'Yes, Sir.'

'At once!' Strode snapped, recovering his dignity. He followed Dewett down the back stairs and through the house to the kitchens, drumming his fingers while the captain, smirking at the fluttering maids, selected a freshly lit sconce and led the way through the scullery and along the corridor to the cellar. Sliding back the bolts, Dewett flung open the door and descended the steps, holding up the sconce to light the way. On the bottom step he stopped suddenly. Colonel Strode cannoned into him with a grunt and gave Dewett an irritable push. 'What is it, man? Move on.'

Dewett, his mouth dry, stepped into the cellar and paced around it looking wildly about him, the sconce flaring in his hand. Catching his thigh on the corner of the trestle table, he suppressed an obscene curse as burning wick jolted onto his fingers. Not only had the prisoner gone, but aside from the table and an upturned empty wine rack, the cellar was completely empty. At a loss for words, Dewett swung round blankly to face the colonel.

Wrinkling his nose at the foetid air, Strode tapped his foot on the floor. 'Well, Captain?' He waited as Dewett struggled to compose himself.

'The prisoner would appear to have escaped, Sir, but I don't know how, for we left him tightly bound and the door securely bolted. I can only assume that one of your servants...' Dewett faltered, silenced by Strode's thunderous expression.

The colonel looked in horror at the empty space where his carefully garnered stocks of wine and ale had stood, turned his gaze to Dewett, whose mouth was opening and closing like a landed perch, said bitingly, 'My servants had nothing to do with it.' He craned his neck to peer at the ceiling. 'Did you by chance fail to check the trap door to the brewing house?'

Dewett flushed to the roots of his hair. Devil take it! He had been in too much of a hurry to think about it. Not for the first time he regretted his accursed lust. Uncomfortably, he gestured at the empty space where the barrels had rested. 'The man must have had an accomplice, even so, Colonel.'

'I am fully aware of that,' Strode hissed. 'And what do you suppose the guards were doing while this was going on?'

'I don't know, Colonel, I was not at my post, I left Sergeant Hooper in charge for the evening.' Dewett faltered, his face ashen. 'The guards must have been overcome, Sir.'

'Do you think it likely that an armed guard of thirty men could possibly have been overcome, as you put it, without a single shot being fired?' The colonel's voice rose to a shriek. 'Or is it that you think the entire household is stone deaf?'

'No, Sir.' Dewett bit his lip.

'Do you take me for a fool, Captain? Oh yes, the ungodly varmints were most certainly overcome.' Strode's face was puce. 'Overcome with drunkenness, with gluttony and avarice. Overcome by the Devil's work, that's what, Captain!'

Dewett flinched. Like Strode, he could guess what the garrison had been up to in his absence. Somehow they must have got hold of a fair quantity of strong liquor, but from where? His jaw clenched as realisation dawned.

'How could you let this happen?' Strode was shouting. 'What was it that was so urgent it took you away from your post?'

Dewett looked at the floor, his attention caught by a spider scuttling towards his boot. He raised his foot to stamp on it, thought better of it, shuffled uncomfortably.

'Well? I repeat, why were you not at your post?'

'I had a prior engagement, Colonel. It was quiet and Hooper is an experienced man. I saw no reason not to keep it.' Dewett knew he was blustering.

'Engagement?' Knowing perfectly well from Dewett's demeanour the nature of this "engagement", Strode let out a harsh cry, beside himself with rage. 'I should have you strung up and flogged for your negligence.' Seething, he paced to the far wall, looked up at the trapdoor, turned back to Dewett, his lips drawing back in a humourless smile. 'You have been duped, Captain.'

'No! I mean... that is not possible, Colonel.'

'Is it not?' Strode's voice cut across Dewett like a whiplash. 'Then explain to me, if you will, how an unconscious prisoner managed not only to release himself and escape from a trapdoor in the ceiling, but also spirit away three and twenty hogsheads – my entire winter's supply – eh?'

Dewett shrugged helplessly and remained silent, his gaze on the darkly stained floor, his mind going over what he could remember of the wretch they had interrogated.

'I'll tell you, since you seem incapable of working it out for yourself.' Strode's voice dripped acid. 'This man was no more an Irish gypsy than you or I, Captain.'

Dewett's head jerked up. 'He's Irish, Colonel, I'd stake my life on it.'

Strode grunted, took a deep breath. 'Whatever you may want to believe, Captain, it was a masquerade and you have been taken for a fool. You have let an important enemy agent slip through your fingers, you... you...' Unable to find a sufficiently derogatory expletive without blaspheming, Strode, quivering with frustration, spittle spraying from his lips, screamed at Dewett, 'You incompetent nincompoop!'

Dewett's handsome face blanched a shade whiter. 'No, Sir – that could not be. When Hooper apprehended him, the man was capering about with a fiddle and falling down drunk. If he was an enemy agent, he would not have brought attention to himself in that way, surely....' He was silenced by the look on his Colonel's face.

Strode, not normally a violent man, did not trust himself to speak. Clenching his fists, he brushed past Dewett and rapidly ascended the steps out of the cellar.

Chewing at his fingernails, Dewett reluctantly followed,

imagining exactly what he would do to the Irish bastard when he caught up with him, and more immediately, what he was about to do to his men – by God, he would have their hides! He remembered thinking it was unusually quiet when he had returned, barely an hour ago from Goody's bed – damn the slut for her lusty ways.

Colonel Strode hurried along to the brewhouse and stood looking down at the trapdoor. It had been carefully bolted back into position, the many fresh footprints evidence that several men had been here. Turning, he looked around the room, his gaze resting on the chest by the half-open door. He strode towards it and exclaimed in rage. There, crudely drawn on the dusty surface, was a smiling face.

Taut with spleen, clasping his hands behind his back to keep them from Dewett's throat, Strode swung to face him.

'For your information, Captain, the document you considered so trivial it could wait on your pleasure was a letter written by Sir Ralph Hopton to his wife at their home in Witham Friary, and since it is not far from here, Hopton's men made a detour on their way to deliver it, plainly intent on robbing me – quite possibly at Hopton's bidding. Because of your negligence, Captain Dewett, they have succeeded.' Strode's mouth twisted in repugnance. 'It was a ploy, you damned fool; this so-called "Irish gypsy" placed himself deliberately in the way of your patrol in order to gain access to my house.'

As Dewett, shaking his head in denial, opened his mouth to protest, Strode raised an imperious hand. 'Be silent! I have good cause to remember that scarred face, Captain. It belongs to Ralph Hopton's agent, the very man who held me at sword point in Shepton Mallet!'

Dewett gasped, a worried frown creasing his brow as he took in the implications of what Strode was saying. Again he opened his mouth to speak, changed his mind.

Strode gave an exasperated shake of his head. 'Never mind that I was robbed, it is the least of it. Hopton's letter contains vital information. The Royalists have escaped from

Sherborne. The Marquis of Hertford and half his army have sailed from Minehead to Wales, but the other half, led by Hopton, are still in the locality and on their way to Ilfracombe to find more boats.' Strode paused, cleared his throat. When Dewett made no response, continued. 'Clearly you are incapable of comprehending the gravity of the situation.' With a contemptuous sigh, he regarded Dewett's ashen face. 'Let me explain it to you. Had you reported this to me last night, we might have been in time to prevent Hopton's escape. Thanks to you, Captain, he too may by now be on his way across the Bristol Channel and the opportunity slipped through our fingers. Strode paused, drew breath, continued, each word succinct. 'You will take this captured document to the Earl of Bedford immediately. You will tell him what has transpired and you will put yourself at his disposal. You can only pray he will treat with you more kindly than I am disposed to do.'

Dewett snapped to attention. 'Sir.'

'Before you leave, I will write a letter for you to take to his Lordship. Go and pack your belongings. I do not wish to see your face here again. Not ever. Do I make myself clear? Now get out of my sight!'

Dewett thought to protest, changed his mind, turned on his heel and left Colonel Strode staring bleakly down at the face smiling up at him from the dust.

Dickon was feeling satisfyingly replete and a good deal better, though very sleepy as they took their leave, their pockets stuffed with oatcakes and apples by Mistress Randall. Somehow ten minutes had stretched to twenty and by the time they emerged, the sun was a dull red globe on the skyline and the mist just beginning to disperse. Dickon snorted with derision when he saw the fresh mounts waiting patiently outside the byre. Small, moorland beasts with dark, tufted coats and broad, dished faces, their protuberant eyes peeping out from forelocks reaching almost to their mealy muzzles, long tails brushing the ground. Alexander mounted without comment.

They picked their way back down the track accompanied by the dogs who stopped at the end, tails waving, to watch them go. Alexander set off at a trot along the narrow, deeply banked lane towards a patch of woodland. Dickon, unused to the short stride and his feet so close to the ground, joggled uncomfortably behind. 'I thought you said the Courtenays were great landowners and Josh one of their most valued tenants,' he said, probing his teeth for crumbs. 'Call this a horse? More like a donkey!' He was still grumbling as they rode into the wood in a shower of falling leaves, their way softly carpeted in drifts of red and gold.

Turning, Alexander directed a lazy smile at the youth. 'Don't be fooled, these little moorland beasts are sturdy and big-hearted. They'll take you anywhere you want to go, live for twenty years or more and survive winters so harsh as to blacken your toes. More to the point they are extremely docile and can be relied upon to keep their heads in a disturbance,' he paused, added conversationally, 'such as the one coming up on your left.' Before the youth could react, Alexander had leapt from the saddle, his sword appearing as by magic in his hand.

Four swarthy men jumped out of the trees into their path, fists bristling with cudgels. At the sight of Alexander's long blade they hesitated. It was enough; as they rushed him he leapt among them, ducking and diving like an acrobat, his sword flickering and wounding. 'Some help would be appreciated, if you can spare the time, Dickon,' he called.

The boy fumbled with his pistol spilling the powder in his haste. With trembling fingers he rammed home the ball, aimed at the nearest back and squeezed the trigger. The gun misfired. With an oath, he flung the weapon away, leapt from his baulking horse and drawing his sword charged into the mêlée as Alexander, gasping with helpless laughter disappeared under the weight of grunting bodies.

The footpads turned to face Dickon, but seeing his flailing steel thought better of it and fled raggedly into the trees. Whooping with glee he made to follow, but Alexander, struggling to rise, stayed him.

'There but for the grace of God – and anyway, we've already tarried too long.' He wiped a smear of blood from his chin.

Disappointed, Dickon helped him up, exclaiming as he saw his captain's thigh. 'You're bleeding.'

Alexander looked down. 'So I am – but you should see the other fellow.' He laughed, 'It's naught but a scratch.'

Reassured, Dickon bent to pick up Alexander's hat, dusting it against his knee as he found his pistol and retrieved the horses, which had wandered off and were unconcernedly nibbling at brambles under the trees. Completely unaware that his captain had barely the strength to lift his sword, never mind do serious damage with it, Dickon handed him hat and reins. 'You could easily have killed them, why did you not?'

'You think so? It felt remarkably like the other way round.' Alexander mounted up and trotted forward. 'Besides, I knew you'd see them off.' With a laugh, he kicked his horse into a gallop and surged ahead. Grinning, Dickon puffed up his chest and followed – he was getting the hang of this little beast now.

Scattering rabbits in their path they rode cautiously through North Molton, descended the Mole valley, skirted South Molton to cross the River Mole and came at last to Chittlehampton, just as the bell ringers were unknotting their ropes. The sun was well up now and the town basking in unaccustomed warmth – a rare respite in the dismal string of wet, windy days of past weeks. Of Sir Ralph Hopton and his men there was no sign. Ignoring sideways glances from the worshippers hurrying to obey the summons of the discordant clangour from the church tower, they clattered through the square. Seeing a young boy leading a heavily laden donkey, Alexander drew rein.

'Not going to morning service, lad? Shame on you – I trust your master can afford the fine?' He looked severely down his nose.

The boy stopped in his tracks, his beast shedding some of the logs perched precariously on its back. 'What's it to you, stranger?'

'Keep a civil tongue in your head, boy,' Alexander frowned. 'Has a body of mounted men passed this way?'

Observing the poor, moorland beasts and their riders' sober, mud splattered garments, the boy decided he was on safe ground. 'Aye, they came in the night.' He thumbed his nose, gestured down the road and spat. 'They rode out not two hours gone.'

Alexander produced an apple from his pocket. 'Who were they, do you know?'

The boy licked his lips, his gaze fixed on the apple revolving slowly in Alexander's fingers. 'No, but I know one of their names.' He held out his hand.

'Which is?' Alexander waited patiently, holding the fruit just short of the boy's reach.

The boy stared at him for a moment, then shrugged. 'It were a Mister Bold.'

Alexander raised an eyebrow. 'And how would you be knowing that?'

The boy gave a cocky grin and pointed towards the inn. 'He lodged over there and my master's the tapster.'

'Ah,' Alexander placed the apple in the grubby, outstretched palm, smiling slightly as the boy inspected it, polished it on his sleeve, tugged at the donkey and went on his way, deftly catching the coin Alexander tossed after him.

'Cheeky young sod,' Dickon grinned. 'Was it Sir Ralph and his men? Who is Mister Bold? Do you know him?'

'Yes – Peter Bold – he is the Earl of Bath's man, which means Lyddon's warning got through to Tawstock. Bold will guide them by the back ways into Cornwall. So long as they have crossed the Taw without alerting Barnstaple's garrison they will be safe. Come on, Dickon, look lively, the crossing is but a mile or two down the road and if there's any trouble that's where we'll find it.'

Leading the way at a fast trot through the main street, Alexander drew his sword and kicked his beast into a gallop as soon as they were out of sight of the town.

4

As Captain Dewett spurred out of Barrington Court towards Dorchester, one overriding thought was occupying his mind: to recapture the accursed Irishman, be he a gypsy or a spy; nobody made a fool of James Dewett and got away with it. His lips curling back from his magnificent teeth, he bunched his fists, thoughtlessly jerking his horse's head. Fingering the crackling pages of Colonel Stride's damning letter, sealed and tucked with the captured document in the leather pocket at his belt, Dewett pondered on how he would present his case to Lord Bedford and what he could do to redeem the situation. The further he travelled, the greater his temptation to turn off the road and seek employment elsewhere. He could find another garrison a long way from here – in the current climate of uncertainty and upheaval, who would question it? But a belated sense of duty carried him onward. A little further along the road and another thought struck him: why hand over Strode's letter at all? If he volunteered to lead a troop in pursuit of Hopton, he could cover himself in glory before his deception was discovered; his transgressions would soon be forgotten and, what was more, if Strode was right and the Irish scum really was Hopton's agent, there would be an opportunity for vengeance at the same time. Heartened, Dewett quickened his pace.

Dorchester was packed and bustling. Soldiers spilled out of billets swelling the crowd gathered in the marketplace to listen to the preacher. The cleric stood precariously atop a mounting block like a demented crow, his black gown flapping in the breeze. Dewett could see he was clutching an open prayer book, his mouth opening and closing, but his words were lost as the crowd, roaring its approval, burst into song: *'While my enemies are driven back they shall fall and perish at thy presence...'* Above the commotion, as though on invisible wires, a flock of pigeons swooped and fell. Humming the psalm under his breath, Dewett forced a way through the press, stopping to ask directions from a trooper who obligingly attempted to clear a path. It was some while before he located the quarters he sought.

William Russell, Earl of Bedford, Member of Parliament for Tavistock and Lord Lieutenant of Exeter and Devon, had requisitioned the finest house in the High Street: the Earl enjoyed his creature comforts. It was built of local stone and richly furnished, though a little on the dark side, most of the windows facing north and the walls hung with gloomy, smoke-blackened tapestries. But it served his purposes admirably for the short duration of his stay.

A mild-mannered man, Bedford's loyalty to Parliament was considered by some to be, if not questionable, then sadly lacking in enthusiasm. Even so, he had been appointed Lord General of Horse in the West, with orders to strengthen and co-ordinate the militia in Devon and Somerset, apprehend the Marquis of Hertford and his deputy, Sir Ralph Hopton, and assist in bringing the South West to heel. An astute man with an eye to the various possible outcomes of this unhappy conflict, Bedford intended to follow his orders insofar as he could, while avoiding bloodshed if at all possible.

Thus far it had been a tiresome campaign alleviated only a little by the lavish entertainment heaped on him by numerous obsequious local dignitaries, one of whose houses he presently occupied. Bedford, alarmed to discover the enemy had broken out of Sherborne, had reluctantly given chase. He had been more than a little relieved when Tom Luttrell's messenger brought news: the Royalists had passed by Dunster and were apparently intent on embarking for Wales. Luttrell would attempt to pin them down in Minehead until the Earl caught up. For Bedford it had solved a ticklish problem: Hertford was an old friend and colleague and he had no wish to see him dead. The Royalists' departure to Wales spelled the end of resistance in Devon and Somerset, thus achieving Parliament's objective. With a clear conscience, Bedford had ordered Luttrell to let them go and had turned back to Dorchester. Now all that remained to do was to organise the local militia to pick up any stragglers, he could then focus his attention on advancing at a leisurely pace to address the next problem: Cornwall.

At this precise moment Bedford's attention was focused on his long awaited breakfast. Sat at the table in the downstairs parlour, his mouth watering in anticipation, he had just tucked a napkin under his many chins when he was told there were three messengers without, all claiming extreme urgency. The Earl was not best pleased. Regretfully pushing aside the fresh coddled eggs that had by some miracle been found for him, he saw first the messenger from the Commander in Chief of Parliament's armies, the Lord General the Earl of Essex.

'My Lord!' The mud-splattered dragoon all but fell into the room, 'There has been a skirmish outside Worcester, at Powick Bridge. Our cavalry were cut to pieces.'

Throwing aside his napkin in consternation, Bedford rose from his seat. 'When was this?'

'Two days since, My Lord, they came upon us by surprise, cut down our flanks like corn. They are demons, General, and Prince Rupert the Devil incarnate – him and that great white dog of his – we could not stand against them.' The soldier tried to swallow. 'I have a message for you, My Lord,' he said hoarsely, his Adam's apple bobbing painfully in his throat.

'Take your time, trooper,' the Earl said kindly, motioning his aide to give the man a drink.

The trooper took the tankard gratefully, spilling it in his eagerness. After a moment he squared his shoulders, took a deep breath, looked up at the ceiling and proceeded to recite his message by rote.

'The Lord General the Earl of Essex is approaching Worcester. He humbly requests you bring your army North to meet him with all possible haste leaving only as small a force as you reasonably can to maintain the blockade at Sherborne. The King's army is in Shrewsbury. His Majesty is preparing to march South and means to seize London and turn his guns on Parliament. It is imperative he be stopped or the war is lost.' Visibly drooping, the trooper ended his recital and wiped his mouth on his sleeve.

Bedford very much doubted if Robin Devereux, Earl of Essex ever did anything humbly and this was no 'request', but he could see the urgency. He smiled encouragingly, 'Thank you, Corporal...?'

'Fletcher, My Lord, with Colonel Fiennes' troop of Horse – the London Blues, your Lordship.'

'You are a credit to them, Corporal Fletcher. Go now and find yourself some food. When you have rested, obtain a fresh mount and return to My Lord of Essex. Give him my compliments and tell him we have taken Sherborne and driven the Royalist army out of the South West. I am confident that here at least, the war is won for Parliament. Tell him also that quantities of ordinance from Portsmouth are already on their way to him and assure him that I will make all speed North.' As Fletcher bowed and stumbled away, Bedford called for his Captain of Horse and snapped out a string of orders. Cornwall would have to wait.

Sitting back at the table, he beckoned in the next messenger, another from Dunster, listened with increasing dismay and uncharacteristically let out a string of blasphemous curses, to the discomfort of the man cringing in the doorway: he was only the messenger, it wasn't his fault Tom Luttrell had ordered the Minehead boats scuppered. Fearfully he kept his head down as the great Earl of Bedford vented his spleen.

The Earl's confidence deflated like a pricked pig's bladder: Hopton still at large in Devon was the last thing he wanted to hear. His face flushed, spittle clinging to his whiskers, he waved the messenger away. Tom Luttrell, damn his efficient hide, doubtless expected gratitude! 'Find a scout familiar with the North Devon coast,' he barked at his aide, just as Captain Dewett was ushered into his presence.

The Earl listened sourly as Dewett, with a certain amount of bravado – Strode's letter safely concealed in his saddlebag until he had a chance to dispose of it – launched into his version of events at Barrington Court. Neglecting to mention the circumstances in which the prisoner had escaped or Strode's suspicions as to the man's identity, Dewett delved into his coat and with a flourish, handed over his much-thumbed prize.

'You are to be congratulated, Captain.' The Earl quickly scanned the contents. 'This corroborates the intelligence I have just received from Dunster. It appears Sir Ralph Hopton is still at large in Devon and from this, that he is on his way to Ilfracombe....' The aide, returning with a bleary-eyed trooper still struggling with buttons, a musket clamped under his arm, interrupted the Earl's flow.

'And you are?' Bedford eyed the trooper's dishevelled appearance with distaste.

'Sergeant Cary, My Lord.'

'Mmm.' Bedford grunted, but let it pass. 'You know the road from Minehead to Ilfracombe? How long would it take a flying column to traverse?'

The scout thought for a moment, scratched his nose. 'It be mighty steep, My Lord, narrow too, and sheer to the sea over to Countisbury, and what with all the rain we've bin having, well the Lyn will be in spate I daresay and fearsome to cross, but assuming the weather were kind and the horses good...'

Bedford banged his fist on the table, barked, 'Dammit, man! How long?'

'About four hours, mebee five, My Lord, but like I do say...'

Bedford cut across him 'Very well. Take a couple of good men and find out if a body of enemy horse has arrived in Ilfracombe and if so, where they are now. Send a man back with news, but stay on the enemy's tail until you are sure where he is headed. Is that clear?' Bedford swivelled in his chair. 'Yes, Captain?' He drummed his fingers, turning impatiently to Dewett who, in a state of agitated subservience, was trying desperately to attract his attention.

'Please, your Lordship, I had hoped you would allow me to pursue the enemy. If you could spare me a troop of horse it might yet be possible to apprehend Hopton. I would like to try, My Lord.'

Bedford looked down his nose at Dewett. 'A moment, will you?' Turning back to Cary still hesitating in the doorway, the Earl waved him away. 'Go. I want confirmation of the enemy's movements as soon as possible. Now, man!'

As the scout scuttled away, Bedford looked at Dewett, eyes narrowing thoughtfully. 'Your arrival is propitious, Captain. As it happens, I have another task for you.'

'My Lord?'

'I have received a warrant to arrest the Earl of Bath for his hostile activities in North Devon and his refusal to obey summons to attend Parliament. The Committee for Safety has declared him delinquent and ordered the sequestration of his property. The Earl is to be taken forcibly to London to answer for his malignancy to our cause.'

Guessing what was coming, Dewett's heart sank. Confound it! He was going to be lumbered with escorting some puffed-up Royalist Earl all the way to London while someone else took the glory for apprehending Hopton. Worse, he would miss the opportunity to get his hands on that Irish scum and squeeze the bastard's throat until all the breath ran out of him. Dewett, his fists clenching involuntarily, ground his teeth.

Glancing at the disappointment etched on the captain's face, Bedford smiled. 'I am giving you a small troop of horse. You will proceed with all haste to expedite this warrant. I suspect you will see as much action as you can handle, Captain.'

'I hardly think so, My Lord.' Dewett bridled.

'Mm,' the Earl grunted. 'Then consider this. I am not sure

about this letter you bring me.' He gestured to the crumpled document, pursing his lips in annoyance as he saw that he had unwittingly dropped it onto his coddled eggs – cold by now – he sighed. 'I think it may be a ruse. Hopton would hardly send military information to his wife, least of all by means of a drunken Irish gypsy, wouldn't you agree?'

'But he wasn't...' Dewett bit his tongue.

'Wasn't what, Captain?'

'Wasn't necessarily all he seemed,' Dewett responded lamely.

'My point exactly.' Bedford clicked his fingers at the hovering aide, pointed to the portable writing slope he had left on the floor by the fireplace, waited as the aide hastily retrieved it and placed it carefully on the table.

Dewett shuffled uncomfortably and looked at the wall behind the Earl's head, his gaze drawn to the tapestry: a once-white hart pierced by an arrow, the blood from its wound trickling onto the naked breasts of a nymph lying sorrowfully at its feet. Reminded suddenly of Goody Redhead, Dewett suppressed an answering twitch in his groin. He could hear men marching in the street outside, horses trotting, gun carriages rumbling, became aware the Earl was addressing him.

'I think you do not quite understand, Captain. I know Sir Ralph Hopton of old. He cut his teeth on the Dutch wars and is not a man to give up easily. He is an able soldier, popular with his men, one of the few men loyal to the King who might yet raise the South West against us.' Bedford lifted the lid of his writing slope, pulled out a bottle of ink, quill and paper. 'Which, were I in his misguided shoes, is exactly what I would do, not scuttle to Ilfracombe to find a cattle boat and slink to Wales,' he wrinkled his nose, closed the slope and looked up to meet Dewett's gaze. 'I believe Hopton will attempt to unite with his friends in Cornwall and is even now on his way to Tawstock to present his services to the Earl of Bath, who will doubtless assist him. We know Bath has been stockpiling weapons and has a large force of armed men hiding at his house. These malignant traitors must be stopped, Captain. The task I give you is of far greater importance than you seem to believe.'

Dewett's stomach lurched as he considered what Bedford was saying. Was it possible? His heart beginning to lift, he watched as the Earl scribbled a note, the quill spraying droplets of ink on the page.

As he wrote, the Earl rapped out orders. 'You are to ride with all haste to Barnstaple. I can spare you only twenty dragoons. If you learn Hopton and his men are indeed at Tawstock, you will not attempt to engage them without assistance.' Waving the sheet of paper to dry, Bedford held it out to Dewett. 'You will take this to George Peard. It confirms you are acting under my orders. Peard is Member of Parliament for Barnstaple and patron of its garrison. He will see you have enough men to engage the enemy with some chance of success. I warn you, Captain, if Hopton has already gone over the border, under no account attempt to pursue him. Barnstaple's men would desert and you would not last five minutes, which would be about as useful to me as a musket without balls. Do I make myself clear?'

'Yes, My Lord.' Dewett caught the aide's amused glance and grinned.

Bedford grunted. 'Of course, it may be my instincts are wrong and Hopton is already at the bottom of a bog or on his way to Wales, eh Captain?' He beamed up at Dewett. 'So much to the good! Either way, you are to arrest the Earl of Bath. I want him, his officers and his weapons to be taken under guard to London.' The Earl paused, his expression sombre. 'And, Dewett.'

'My Lord?'

'I do not want Lord Bath harmed. If he resists arrest, use only what force is necessary to subdue him. I mean it. Under no circumstances is he to be hurt.' Bedford scrutinised Dewett's eager face and was satisfied by what he saw. 'When you arrive in London, take the prisoners to the Gatehouse and report to the Earl of Pembroke. There is an opportunity for advancement for you here, Captain.'

Dewett made a leg, sweeping his hat to his knees. 'Thank you, My Lord, I will not fail you.'

'Mmm,' Bedford held Dewett's gaze for a moment. 'Very well. My aide will direct you to my Captain of Horse who will see you have everything you need. God be with you, Captain.'

Dewett swept another low bow, but the Earl, preoccupied, had turned away and was gazing out of the window. The Earl of Bath was his cousin, his mother's favourite nephew in fact, she would never forgive him for this, nor indeed would Bath's formidable Countess. Bedford sighed. Why could the King and Parliament not reach an accommodation? Whole families were divided by this sorry business and he was caught in the middle of it. Dammit! Irritably pushing the congealed mess of his breakfast away, he called for his manservant.

Dewitt found the Captain of Horse directing proceedings in the midst of chaos as the army prepared to march. He was most helpful, cutting out twenty dragoons and calling over a trooper loitering nearby. As it happened, the man, whose name was Fane, knew the roads into North Devon and using the butt end of his musket drew a map in the mud at Dewett's feet, comprehensively describing the shortest route to Barnstaple. Within the hour Dewett headed West out of Dorchester, leading his troop at a fast trot through the marketplace past the ranks of shouting men, shrieking horses and rumbling wagons that were assembling in the opposite direction. Grinning in anticipation as he mulled over his orders, he had soon left the cacophony behind. He failed to see a lone pigeon pacing the column above him, nor was there any reason to notice when it wheeled away to the northwest.

It was quiet at St Michael's. Most of Alexander's men had gone off in different directions to requisition firearms, only Adam Hartley and Francis Sydenham remained. They were loading barrels of muskets and gunpowder onto sleds when the pigeon circled above the church and landed on the tower.

Dropping an armful of muskets, Adam fetched a handful of corn from a sack in the porch and scattered it in front of the linhay. The bird hopped from one foot to the other, its leg was daubed with yellow dye.

'One of Fane's,' Adam shouted.

The pigeon put its head on one side, peered down at the corn, black eyes winking. After an agonising moment it fluttered to the bait. Slowly Adam edged towards it, grasped it firmly about the wings with both hands and tucked it under his arm.

'Clever little bird,' he soothed, stroking the ruffled feathers. Carefully detaching the tiny capsule from the pigeon's leg, he retrieved and unrolled the scrap of paper within. The message was written in cipher.

'What's it say?' Sydenham strolled over.

'Bad news, I fear. Bedford hasn't fallen for the ruse. He suspects Hopton's gone into North Devon and has sent a troop of twenty dragoons to Tawstock with a Captain Dewett – 'Sblood! I wonder if that's the same Dewett who interrogated Tawford at Barrington Court – they are to apprehend Hopton and arrest the Earl of Bath.' Adam looked up, grimaced. 'Let's hope Sir Ralph is over the border by the time they get there.'

Frowning, Sydenham peered over Adam's shoulder. 'Bastards! Tawford got himself beaten up for nothing then.'

'That's odd...,' Adam paused. 'There's a postscript. What the...?' He grinned at Sydenham. 'Fane says he's given Dewett directions to Tiverton via Axminster as instructed.' Thumping Sydenham on the shoulder, Adam laughed delightedly. 'Tawford must've found out about Lord Bath's arrest from Cobb. I'll wager he's hatched a surprise for the Roundheads and asked Fane to send them by the right road.'

'The wrong one more likely!' Sydenham guffawed. 'Tawford might have mentioned it, arrogant bastard. It all sounds a bit chancy to me.'

'You know what he's like – ever the gambler. Besides, he probably meant to tell us and forgot – hardly surprising after the beating he took. Could you catch me up a bird? I imagine Tawford's alerted Lord Bath, but there's many a slip… best to play safe. I'll send this on to Ellen in case his plans go awry.'

Sydenham was already on his way up the ladder. He crawled into the reeking pigeon loft, sneezing and spluttering as the startled birds sent a cloud of dust and feathers onto his head. He selected a bird with red dye on its leg and took it to Adam, who initialled and replaced the note in the capsule, attached it to the pigeon's leg and threw the bird into the air. Within moments, it was heading westward, a black speck in the cloudless sky.

5

The track dropping steeply from Chittlehampton to the river was churned with hoof prints and hock deep in mud. Clarts of it flew up into Dickon's face, half blinding him as he struggled to keep up with Alexander, his stomach churning, palms sweating, ears straining for the sound of gunfire. Behind the hedge a flock of sheep were startled into a bleating run, streaming away over the shoulder of the hill like a slick of flotsam on the outgoing tide.

The two men rounded a bend and came at last in sight of the Taw, disturbing crows from the trees clustered on the riverbank. In a flurry of raucous alarm the birds flew up and flapped away downstream. The crossing was deserted; no bodies in the mud, nothing to see but moving water. Dickon, suddenly aware he was holding his breath, exhaled and gasped a lungful of air as they galloped the remaining few hundred yards to the river.

Alexander reined in his blowing horse and dismounted, bending to examine a pile of fresh dung. He picked up a handful and crushed it in his palm, looking up at Dickon as the boy skidded breathlessly to a halt behind him. 'Stone cold! Saints be praised, Barnstaple's been caught napping. Sir Ralph and his men are long gone.' Limping to the waters' edge, he hunkered down to cleanse his hand, wiping it dry on his breeches. 'So, young Dickon, it seems we have endured a gruelling ride to no purpose. I'm sorry, lad.'

Busily replacing his sword in its sheath to hide his trembling fingers, Dickon forced a nonchalant shrug. 'You could not have foreseen that. Besides, I enjoyed it.' Actually, he thought, surprised, that was true. His nausea forgotten, he fished out an apple and bit into it with gusto.

With an approving look at his young companion, Alexander led his horse onto the wooden bridge. It had been erected beside the ford to carry packhorse trains in winter and was so narrow the rails were buffed smooth and shiny by overhanging panniers. The river was level here and relatively shallow. In summer the bridge was hardly used, but now the Taw was in spate, a torrent of water frothing over shining jags of rock, swirling under the bridge and splashing up through gaps in the timbers beneath Alexander's feet. Stopping halfway across he leaned out over the side and looked thoughtfully at the struts beneath.

'Anything wrong?' Dickon had to shout above the noise of the water.

'No, just looking.' Alexander pulled himself back onto his horse and trotted ahead, drawing rein on the bank to wait. Upriver a wisp of smoke rose from the Bassetts' house, the erstwhile home of Kit Bassett who had been at Barrington with Lyddon last night. Unable to suppress a painful grin he gazed at it, wondering how things had gone and whether Strode yet knew he had been robbed.

'Do we ride after Sir Ralph?' Clattering across the bridge, Dickon finished his apple and flung the core into the river. 'What about Torrington? Will they give him a fight?'

Alexander quirked an eyebrow, murmured, 'I doubt it, but if they do I think it safe to assume he will manage to beat them off without our help.'

The sarcasm was lost on Dickon who looked disappointed. 'So what now? Do we return to St Michael's?'

'Eventually, but first I have messages to take to Cornwall. And before then, I've a mind to go home and get some rest. So, my kinchen, this is the parting of our ways. I thank you for your company, but now you must return to your Papa lest he add kidnap to my crimes. Can you find your way home from here?' He pointed upstream. 'Hall is about five miles that way.'

Biting back an angry retort, Dickon flushed; he resented being called a child and did not want to go home. His father would be hopping mad, give him a severe beating and confine him to the house for weeks. As for his mother, having only recently got him back from Ireland she would be weeping, wringing her hands, calling him her 'dear baby boy.' It was not to be borne, but he had a feeling it was best not to confess this to Tawford, who was looking at him quizzically, one eyebrow mockingly raised.

'I know perfectly well which way it is,' Dickon said stiffly, 'and I am not your kinchen.' He looked down at his hands, fiddled with tangles in his horse's mane, mumbled. 'I am not a child, Tawford, and I am not expected home.' Inwardly hating himself for the note of pleading that crept into his voice, he looked up to meet Alexander's gaze. 'I would lief ride with you. I know I can be of service if you'll let me.'

Alexander gave the boy a considering look. It was not difficult to guess what had chased shadows across Dickon's expressive face. His father, a staunch Parliamentarian, would be filled with murderous rage when he discovered what company his son was keeping. Alexander did not relish the prospect of crossing swords with the senior Richard Chichester just now. It might be best to keep the boy at his side for a while longer, at least until this day's work was done. 'Very well, but at the first opportunity you will write a note to your father explaining you have placed yourself in my service willingly. I will ask the Lady Ellen to pay him a visit and deliver it for you, but I must warn you, I cannot allow you to stay with me if he objects. Is that clear?'

Tawford's expression brooked no argument and Dickon's heart sank; not only would Papa object, he would be in a blind, bloody rage, which a visit from Lady Ellen Seymour would do nothing to alleviate, though Mama would be impressed. He had often heard her talk of Viscount Westley's sister in glowing terms: 'That woman is a saint,' she was wont to remark. 'I don't know how she puts up with the dreadful goings-on in that family. For all young Alexander is her bastard nephew, why she stays and mothers him is quite beyond me. They say he was the death of his own half-brother and it wouldn't surprise me if it were true and now Lord Westley's a widower, his poor lady wife gone to the Lord before her time, poor soul, and he's like to stay that way by all accounts, his sister could be mistress of Marley Court if she'd a mind instead of keeping house for that young devil with all his wild, murdering ways...'

His Mama rarely drew breath once she warmed to her theme, but Dickon voiced none of these thoughts, saying with a taut smile, 'Perfectly clear. My mother will be reassured – she thinks your aunt is a saint!'

'Most people do.' Alexander nodded affably. 'Keep your eyes open. If we are stopped let me do the talking and leave your blade in its sheath – and Dickon,' he sighed, 'could you at least try to look a little more humble like a Puritan?' With a mocking smile, he turned his horse and set off at a brisk trot downstream.

Dickon followed, his momentary relief tempered with guilt about his parents. Three nights ago he had run away from home. Had not dared tell anyone he was going with James – his cousin was the black sheep of the family since he had taken up with Tawford – instead he had left a note to say he was following his conscience and taking his sword to the King. That was bad enough. He knew what Papa's reaction would be: 'Young whippersnapper, what can he possibly know of conscience. By God I will whip some sense into him when he comes home with his tail between his legs at first sight of blood.' As if he were some greenhorn boy who had never been in Ireland and seen the things he had seen; things that turned your guts to water and made grown men puke and weep. Papa didn't know the half of it.

Dickon sighed. It wasn't that his father was disloyal to the King, far from it; it was a deal more complicated than that. Over the last few weeks, since he and his brother Edmund had come home from Ulster, there had been nothing but arguments in the

Chichester household: Papa wagging his finger at Edmund, Edmund shouting back. 'The King is not above the law, boy. He has violated the privileges of Parliament and should be held accountable. He has forgotten his duty to protect our ancient rights as free Englishmen and we needs must protect them for ourselves, for without them, my son, we are but slaves ruled at the whim of a tyrant. Surely you can understand that?'

'But Papa, the King's Grace is sacrosanct, he cannot break the law – he *is* the law. He rules us by Divine Right. It is our bounden duty as free Englishmen to protect him from his enemies. That is the way it has always been and that is how it should be, otherwise we are condemning our country to anarchy – and what use our ancient rights then?'

Listening to them, Dickon had tried to understand why they argued when it seemed to him there was little difference between their points of view. Both were committed to the true Protestant religion, wanted to preserve and uphold the law and protect the Church of England, but Edmund believed in the King's unassailable right to control the army, while Papa emphatically did not. 'It is Parliament's prerogative now, lad. The law was changed for a very good reason. King or no, he is not to be trusted; he is too easily influenced by the evil men who surround him. How can we know he will not abuse us – the very people he is sworn to protect? Remember Buckingham? And what about Strafford and Laud? And as for that Papist Queen of his, eh? She leads him by the nose, turning him away from Parliament. And what if she should persuade him to use our own army against us, eh? Dammit! She has already tried it once, with the help of Tawford and others of his ilk. Treason! They should have hanged the devil while they had the chance, not let the traitor go. Lord Westley must have been out of his mind to pay the fine. I'd have left the thrice-damned murderer in the Tower to fester even if he were my own bastard son!'

Edmund had protested. 'No, Papa, that's not true, Tawford was vindicated of treason and it is only gossip that brands him a murderer. His brother's death was an accident, I am certain of it.'

'Don't contradict me boy, you were not here,' Papa had roared. 'Oh yes, Edmund, you're right about one thing, we should protect the King from his enemies – get him away from them, that's what! Bring him back to Parliament and urge him to listen to us. If we fail, we will lose our freedom and our Church, of that you can be sure. Look what happened in Ireland, eh?' He had grunted triumphantly. 'You of all people should know what is at stake here, Edmund. Do you want us to be murdered in our beds, our privy members cut off and stuffed into our mouths, made to watch our women raped before they're slit from breast to belly, their babes' brains dashed out before their eyes? Is that what you want for us, son? Eh? Because that's what will happen, you mark my words.'

As always, Papa had silenced Edmund with talk of Ireland.

It was an emotive area for both Dickon and his brother, but more so for Edmund, who had been caught up in the sickening retribution that had followed the Papist rebellion.

Remembering he was supposed to be staying alert, Dickon pushed these thoughts away and looked around him. The road meandered by the Taw winding through a belt of trees, their gnarled trunks green with lichen and moss, leaves twirling from branches to settle in wind-piled drifts of gold. The river had broken its banks and turned the low-lying fields into a lake. Dickon caught glimpses of sun-spangled water dotted with seabirds, watched a heron fly up, stretching its great wings to soar downstream towards the estuary, was so engrossed he almost missed seeing Alexander turn up a steep, narrow track at the edge of the wood. Dickon eyed his captain's back with concern. Tawford was riding loosely, his head lolling forward as if he had fallen asleep in the saddle. The boy made to call out, hesitated, knew instinctively that his captain would resent the intrusion. He moved closer, ready to put out a steadying hand if needed, grinning as a thrill of excitement coursed through him: his captain! Even yet he could hardly believe it. Not since that first heart-stopping moment at St Michael's when he had feared he had made a dreadful mistake, had he doubted Tawford was a man to follow – and that is what he meant to do, dammit, follow him – with or without Papa's consent! He squared his jaw; he simply could not go home. It was out of the question. He would have to think of something.

Unaware of the thoughts occupying his young companion, Alexander concentrated on staying in the saddle and thought about Tawford Barton, the home he had not seen for several months. His guardian Robert Dynam, the Fourth Viscount Westley, had gifted it to him on his fifteenth birthday. It was a poor enough gift at the time having stood empty and neglected for many years, the river constantly flooding the low-lying pastures and the farmhouse in ruins. Even so it had set tongues wagging and confirmed – for any who had doubted it – that he was indeed Lord Westley's by-blow.

The first Viscount had built the Barton as a summer house overlooking the estuary, so his beloved wife could sit in comfort to watch the great merchant ships from which his wealth derived, coming and going over the bar. It lay along the seaward edge of the Westleys' Marley estate, the land sloping steeply from the high moor to the flat marshes of the Taw. The second Viscount had reclaimed much of the marshland, improved the pasture and extended the summerhouse into a sprawling farmhouse for his own son, Cleve Dynam, Robert's father. Cleve had disliked 'that windswept, drab little place on the marshes' and on his rare visits home from Cork had chosen to live in Marley Court. As, in turn, had Robert, and over the years the Barton and its land had fallen into disrepair. When Alexander returned from soldiering in the Netherlands, resisting advice to finish his education at the Inns of Court, he had set about it with a will; constructed a dyke, mended ditches, repaired and extended the house and built half a dozen tithe cottages. Before long his husbandry had begun to reap rewards, the rich, fluvial pasture and sun-drenched slopes bringing him a reasonable income, even without his other activities.

Riding at a leisurely pace, Alexander followed the path bordering the Earl of Bath's great Tawstock estate, up and out of the Taw valley onto open grassland, enjoying the soporific warmth on his back and the gentle breeze, sweetly laden with meadowsweet. It was enough to make a man nod off, he thought sleepily, plucking blackberries as he rode and looking around at the green and ochre landscape: deep wooded valleys tinted russet and gold, cornfields dotted with neglected greying stooks and lines of bent gleaners salvaging what they could of the ruined harvest before teams of oxen ploughed it under, so late this year, the rye, which by now should be showing a fuzz of green, had yet to be sown. Trying to forget his aches and pains and enjoy this unexpected morning, Alexander anticipated the moment when the full grandeur of the Taw and Torridge estuary was laid out before him. As he crested the ridge he drew rein, kicking his feet out of the stirrups and letting the little horse nose at the sward.

On such a day as this the view was incomparable: the water a flat expanse of milky-blue shimmering like shot silk beneath an opaline sky. Out to sea, beyond the white foaming crease of the bar, the water was dotted with vessels waiting for the tide to lift them into the estuary. Alexander searched the horizon for Lundy Island and found it, a mauve smudge on the skyline. Sometimes it was so clear he felt he could reach out and touch it, at others it vanished in the mist like the mythical Isle of Avalon. Looking westward at the distant hills hugging Bideford bay, he could just make out Hartland Point, the jagged teeth that had claimed so many lives were today lost in a haze of blue. Alexander's gaze followed the sweep of the River Torridge upstream, past the ship building yards to Bideford, where the great ships unloaded their cargoes: tobacco and exotic plants from the Americas, cod from the cold, treacherous waters of Newfoundland, gold, spices and precious stones from Africa and the Indies. The thought of it sent shivers up his spine. Were it not for Tawford Barton he might have made a living from the sea. He never felt so free as when his feet straddled the deck, salt wind singing in the rigging, the intricacies of navigation occupying his mind. He sighed, turned to look eastward up the Taw towards Barnstaple. Here the quay would be no less busy: wharves piled high with bales of cloth and crates of pottery; pens of thin, travel-weary cattle awaiting slaughter; mounds of sea coal carefully guarded by thickset mariners; merchants strutting in their fur-lined coats, clerks trailing anxiously behind clutching bills of sale; tax collectors totting up their tally sticks with eager, sweaty fingers.

Gathering his horse, Alexander rode down from the ridge, his gaze skimming over the distant, brooding slopes of Exmoor and the vast wedge of sand hills beyond the Taw, to the foreshore of Instow, alive with curlews and oystercatchers searching for grubs and shellfish among the weed. He caught sight of the ferry bobbing across to Appledore, a flurry of gulls squabbling in its wake, and was reminded suddenly of his boyhood, the day when he, Hartley and Lyddon had patched up an abandoned ketch and named it *'Revenge'*! They had sailed and bailed that damned boat up and down the river all summer long until it had disintegrated beneath them. Happy days! Alexander sighed, closing his eyes to shut out the view, a wave of nausea rising in his throat as the megrim began to disturb his vision. He became aware that Dickon had ridden up beside him and was softly quoting poetry. *'How can such joy as this want words to speak? And yet what words can speak such joy as this?'*

Alexander turned to the boy in surprise. *'Far from the world that might their quiet break, here the glad souls the face of beauty kiss...'* he capped. 'You're an admirer of Giles Fletcher?'

Blushing, Dickon nodded, speaking in a rush to cover his

embarrassment. 'I've not been up here before. It's a splendid sight, is it not?' He pointed below. 'Is that your home?'

Lying a few hundred yards back from the bank of the Taw, a long, ramshackle farmhouse, built of stone with central porch, casement windows and thatched, gabled dormers. It formed one side of a yard. A barn and various farm buildings joined by an arched stone gateway formed the other three. Behind was a walled garden and beyond that an orchard, a track leading through it to a row of cottages partially concealed by a stand of windswept trees: willow, birch, and alder.

Alexander nodded. 'It is indeed and there, my friend, we will find good cheer, soft beds and some precious hours of oblivion. Come.' Avoiding the potholes, he led the way down the track to Tawford Barton.

In the walled garden, Lady Ellen Seymour, though still in her Sunday best, was on her knees taking advantage of this unexpectedly fine day. Some years before, returning widowed to Devon, she had gone against the wishes of her brother and chosen to live at Tawford Barton with Alexander rather than at Marley Court. The first thing she had done was to make a garden, carefully picking a site behind the house, but still the salt-laden winds had reduced most of her efforts to spindly brown stumps of rotting vegetation. Giving in to her pleas – for he could deny her little – Alexander had deployed some labour to surround her plot with a high wall. He had also hired a man and a boy to help her: Francis Lewin, came highly recommended from the Countess of Bath – herself a keen gardener – and his young son, Todd, was both willing and strong.

Along the west-facing wall, which now dripped with fruit, Ellen had trained apples, figs, and pears. She also grew cherries and hops, and had cultivated a physic garden of medicinal roots and herbs bordered by low hedges of rosemary and lavender. She had purchased the new edition of Gerard's Herbal, the old one having fallen to pieces with use, and this she had studied at length along with a much-thumbed volume entitled: '*Profitable Instructions for the Manuring, Sowing and Planting of Kitchen Gardens*', which Alexander had found on a bookstall in Shrewsbury one time. Undeterred by the popular view that vegetables were a mere bagatelle to meat, Ellen interspersed a wide variety among drifts of flowers, and in one corner of the garden was experimenting with forcing cucumbers out of season, growing them on hotbeds of fresh horse manure protected on the top by woven mats of straw. Alexander teased her mercilessly, but her salads had become quite a talking point in the neighbourhood and she was always swapping recipes with like-minded housewives. So green were Ellen's fingers that her garden now yielded far more than they could eat and Todd made regular trips to Instow, his handcart loaded with produce for the almshouses. Her latest idea was to install some hives, feeling that the garden would be a haven for bees, but this summer had been so dreadful that so far she had not had much success.

Most of the flowers had gone over now and Ellen, returning from morning service, had not been able to resist stopping to cut them back, carefully saving the spent seed heads. And as always in the garden, one thing led to another and time flew by. It was warm in the sunshine and wasps gorged drunkenly on fallen fruit. Discarding her cloak, Ellen made a mental note to ask Lewin to harvest the last of the pears, when she heard the horses. She was not expecting visitors. With a spasm of fear she pushed herself up from her knees, seeds spilling from her basket as she plonked it down with her trowel, picked up her skirts and hurried round to the front.

Alexander saw her starting up the track towards him and cheerily waved. A tall, slim woman in her early thirties, Ellen had married well, but cruelly lost her husband and baby daughter to the great pox. Now a widow of some worth with a good many suitors wooing her hand – more likely her fortune, she said tartly – she had chosen not to remarry and Lord Westley had at length ceased urging her to do so. Considered by many to be plain, even a little manly, she had strong brows, high cheekbones, an aquiline nose and an unfashionably wide, generous mouth. But as she ran to greet Alexander, wiping her muddy fingers uncaring on her now bedraggled skirt, he saw only the sweetness of her expression, her beaming smile, the smear of dirt on her nose, lace cap perched askew on tousled ringlets the colour of burnished copper.

'Alexander, is it really you?' She stopped half way up the path, concerned as she caught sight of his black eye and bruised, swollen face. 'Ugh! Don't tell me – you've met your just desserts at last. Was she worth it?' Ellen lifted a sardonic eyebrow so much like his own.

'Almost.' He grinned down at her. 'You hoyden, how can I introduce you to my fine literary friend here?' He turned to Dickon. 'This is the Lady Ellen Seymour, but you'd be forgiven for thinking she's one of her less successful scarecrows, much pecked about by contemptuous crows.'

Reaching into her pocket, Ellen pulled out a pear and threw it at him. He ducked and it whizzed harmlessly past his ear. 'Never trust a redhead, Dickon!' Then, dismounting, he was in her arms and laughing.

Smiling at their banter, Dickon scrambled off his horse, hat in hand and waited. If gossip were to be believed this was Tawford's aunt. There was a faint resemblance, he supposed. They were of a height – she was tall for a woman – but their likeness was more in their mannerisms than their features. That they were easy with one another was plain, and thinking about the reserved dealings he had with his own aunts, Dickon was both surprised and intrigued.

Disentangling herself, Ellen gave Alexander a long look and murmured something. He responded, shaking his head. He seemed to be reassuring her and they stood talking softly. Then, flushing, Ellen turned and walked up to Dickon, held out her hand. 'Please forgive our ill manners, you must think we don't know how to behave.'

Dickon responded with a slight bow, taking her grubby

fingers to his lips. 'Please don't apologise, there is nothing to forgive. I am Richard Chichester – I expect you know my cousin, Edward?'

'Viscount Carrickfergus? Yes, of course. You are very like him. But you must be tired of people telling you so. May I call you Dickon, too?' Ellen smiled, gold lights winking in her hazel eyes.

Warmed by her smile, his heart already won, Dickon felt immediately at ease. 'Yes, my Lady, please do, all my friends call me so.'

'Then we are already friends and you shall dispense with "my Lady" and call me Ellen. Come, you must be tired and hungry after your journey.' She threaded her arm companionably through his and drew him down the path to the house. 'How long were you in Ireland? It must be so good to be home. I expect your mother is overjoyed, and how is your brother, Edmund?'

Alexander watched Ellen weaving her magic; like everyone else, Dickon would in very short order be her slave. Meanwhile, Ned, the groom, had appeared on his way home from church and was retrieving the horses that were straying purposefully towards Ellen's roses.

'How's it going, Ned?' Alexander called.

'Brave, Maister.' The little man removed his hat. 'Those are Josh Randall's beasts.'

'Be they?' Leading the animals, Ned walked towards him, boots squeaking. He was a man of few words and Alexander had long ago given up trying to draw him into conversation, but his horsemanship more than compensated for his taciturnity.

'Turn them into the orchard for now, Ned. Perhaps you would have Todd return them to Josh in a day or two and fetch my horses back here? Tell him to go armed, there are footpads in the woods above North Molton.'

'Aye, Master.'

Alexander looked over to the paddock. 'Where's Tweed?'

'Er be indoors.'

'Not a problem, is there?' Alexander was particularly fond of Tweed, a promising roan filly he had acquired while on a mission for the King in Berwick. He had sent her back for Ned to bring on and earlier in the year she had been covered by one of James Chichester's stallions.

Ned creased up his weathered face, looked skywards and scratched his head. 'Ers voled, 'bout three days gone. A mite early, but tiz no bad thing vor a maiden.'

'All's well with her then? And the foal?'

The groom's eyes twinkled. 'Aye. You'll be wanting to know what er's dropped?'

'In your own time, Ned!' His head hammering, Alexander frowned, struggling to hang on, both to his patience and to Mistress Randall's fresh bread that he had so unwisely eaten.

The groom gave a slow smile. 'A filly, bit winnicky mind, but very fine, and er'll soon graw.'

'You'll own I'm a good judge of horseflesh then?' Alexander raised a mocking eyebrow.

Ned's smile widened to a rare grin. 'Aye, mebee. You'll be wanting to see they?'

'I certainly will, but later, Ned.'

The groom nodded, crammed his hat on his head and trudged away, mouth pursed in the soundless whistle of one whose days are spent enveloped in horse dust, Josh's amiable little beasts following along behind.

Swaying a little, Alexander turned and limped to the house, cursing under his breath and pulling his cloak forward to hide the fresh blood on his thigh.

The house was always quiet on Sundays. It smelled of lavender mingled with beeswax and roasting meat. He missed Blue's uproarious welcome as he entered the corridor. Ellen's old greyhound had died earlier in the year. The place felt appallingly empty without him; he would have to find another for her.

Dickon was seated on a bench in the front kitchen supping a mug of spiced ale. He looked up sleepily content as Alexander came in. 'I am promised fresh beef – the first of the season – and whortleberry pie with cream to follow, can I only keep my eyes open to eat it!'

'Don't worry, the noise your belly is making will keep you awake.' Alexander passed through to the back kitchen where Ellen was busily getting dinner. She insisted the servants had the day off on Sundays to visit their families after church, but Mistress Wilmot, the cook, ably assisted by Rose, the kitchen maid, had as usual left little for her to do.

'You must be hungry, it won't be long.' Ellen looked up with a smile. 'Oh, my dear!' Her ladle clattered to the floor as she leapt towards him, calling for Dickon.

Alexander, smiling apologetically, had slid gently to the floor.

Between them they carried him up the stairs to his chamber and laid him on the bed. 'We were set upon by thieves, he told me it was only a scratch.' Dickon gasped at the blood spreading through his captain's breeches. 'I had no idea he was this badly hurt.'

Ellen, efficiently discarding Alexander's cloak and pulling off his boots, smiled tersely at the boy. 'Don't worry, he didn't want you to know, it's not your fault. Can you give me a hand – quickly, before he comes round, get him undressed and into this while I fetch something to staunch the bleeding.' She rummaged in a chest and pulling out a clean nightgown, threw it at Dickon.

By the time she returned, Alexander was naked and Dickon was manfully attempting to pull the nightgown over his captain's head, being lacerated for his pains by a steady stream of vituperative invective.

'Leave the boy alone, he's only trying to help,' Ellen said smartly, wincing as she saw the welts and bruises that spread below the binding on Alexander's ribs. 'Dickon, hold this.' She handed him a bowl of warm water and proceeded to unravel the blood-soaked bandages from her nephew's thigh. 'How did you get this?'

Alexander attempted to rise. 'Stop fussing, woman. What happened to modesty? Go away and leave me alone. All I need is some sleep. *Sleep is reconciling. A rest that peace begets, doth not the sun rise smiling....*' His words slurring, he continued reciting poetry under his breath, pushing feebly at her hands and attempting to cover his manhood as she gently washed and cleansed his wound.

Ellen captured his long fingers in her own and stayed him.

'Be still, foolish child and let me make you comfortable. There's nothing here I haven't seen before and it's nothing to write home about!'

Standing awkwardly by the bed, Dickon suppressed a grin as Alexander gave her a baleful stare. How many folk could say that to Tawford and get away with it? The gossips were right; Ellen had to be his aunt! He shot his captain a look of sympathy, seeing him in a new light.

Ellen gazed at Alexander, but he had lapsed into silence and closed his eyes in an expression of pained resignation.

'It's a shot wound, isn't it? When did it happen?' She turned to Dickon. 'Do you know?'

Dickon straightened his face, perplexed. 'No, the footpads were armed only with cudgels and knives.' Into his mind came the image of the chapel and a pile of bloody linen. 'But Adam Hartley treated him before we left St Michael's. I'm sorry, I had forgotten – we left in rather a hurry. Tawford let himself be captured by the rebels yesterday to pass them false information about Sir Ralph Hopton – did he tell you? Obviously they beat him severely. Perhaps it happened when he escaped. I'm sorry, I don't know any more than that and he said nothing about it.'

'No, he wouldn't.' Ellen set her lips and frowned. 'But it did not happen yesterday. It is not a fresh wound, look, see here where the ball entered – thank God it missed the bone. Someone extracted it and stitched him up afterwards. You say Adam Hartley saw this?'

Dickon nodded. 'I think he must have done, yes.'

'Well I'm surprised at Adam, he should never have let Alexander ride. But what am I saying? As if anyone can stop Alexander doing anything unless he wants to be stopped. He is his own worst enemy.' Ellen sighed. 'I need to re-stitch this wound, Dickon. Can you place your hand here, so.' She demonstrated. 'I'll be back shortly. If he wakes, ignore him – don't worry, he's too weak to hit you.' She hurried from the room, leaving Dickon nervously pressing his hand as instructed to the lint on his captain's thigh. Moments later she was back, this time with needle, thread and fresh lint spread with a sticky red ungent. Catching Dickon's questioning glance she explained. 'It's Ointment of Egypt, it will cleanse the wound and stop it from festering. Be prepared to hold him down.' White-faced, the boy nodded.

Alexander tried to swim through the water, striving to get to the shore, but his arms and legs were trapped and he could not get free. He was cold, so cold. He could see the woman on the sand. As always, she was yearning towards him, her arms outstretched, her huge green eyes spilling with tears, her hair like yellow silk billowing around her. He wanted desperately to reach her, struggled, but the reeds were clasping his leg pulling him down and he had no strength to resist. Gently he let go, drifting into darkness as the water closed over his head.

Dickon, hanging grimly onto his captain's flailing arms, fidgeted anxiously as Ellen stood back to admire her handiwork before tightly binding Alexander's thigh. 'Is he going to be alright?'

'Yes, of course he is. He fainted from blood loss and exhaustion, he has at least two cracked ribs and he almost certainly has a megrim, but the wound has not festered – probably thanks to Adam – and will heal if he will only let it. You go and have something to eat, Dickon. I will stay and watch him for a while. You will find everything you need in the back kitchen, just help yourself to whatever you want.'

After Dickon had gone, Ellen stroked the hair back from Alexander's face, dabbing at the sweat on his brow with a damp cloth, all the while scolding him softly, as she had done so often when they were children and he had come home the worse for wear from one escapade or another. But this was a good deal more serious than a grazed knee! He murmured something unintelligible, his head threshing on the pillow, his hair clinging to his head, dark with sweat, his eyes moving rapidly under bruised, swollen lids. His face was a mess. Ellen tried to imagine the resolve that had enabled him to endure riding through the night after so bad a beating and in the grip of a megrim. That he had courage was never in doubt, but always he drove himself too hard. She sighed, was he even yet punishing himself for Henry's death? It was an accident. Would he never come to terms with it? Lost in thought, she became aware that his breathing had changed. One eye flickered open, registered her presence. Flecked like moss agate, it stared into her own.

'Oh Lord! You're still here.' He tried to sit up and grimaced. 'And you have me swaddled like a babe. Can a man get no peace around here?'

'Hush, you ungrateful brat. I have cleansed and stitched your wound. Is it my fault you take no care of yourself? And when did you last eat?' A tear slid unchecked down her cheek.

'Sweet girl, stop scolding. I am stuffed to the gunwales with Mistress Randall's wonderful bread. There is nothing wrong with me a few hours' rest won't cure.'

'So you have wind colic to contend with as well as everything else?'

He smiled weakly. 'It was very fresh bread.'

'Drink this.' From the embroidered pocket dangling at her waist she fished a small, dark bottle and held it to his lips. 'It will take the pain away. When you wake, you shall tell me all about it, but now you need to sleep. Just for once, Alexander, please do as you are told!'

He eyed her for a moment, hesitated, then obediently he swallowed, the pungent taste of poppy filling his mouth as he lay, drifting, watching her move around the room gathering up his clothes, smoothing the sheets and drawing the heavy curtains across the window to shut out the sun.

Ellen stayed, anxiously watching over him until she was sure he was asleep then went in search of Dickon. She found the boy fast asleep at the kitchen table, his head resting on his arms, a platter of uneaten beef at his elbow. Her face softened, he was so young, far too young to be involved in this wretched war.

Gently she woke him, brushed aside his stumbling apologies, reassured him that all was well and led him upstairs and along the corridor to the guest chamber in the quiet end of the house, promising to wake him if Alexander should need him. She went back downstairs to the kitchen and reaching for a plate, found she had lost her appetite. Feeling at a loose end, she cleared away the food and Dickon's uneaten meal, wandered aimlessly through to the parlour. It was always the same on Sundays. So quiet and still, even the distant shushing of the sea seemed muted. It was a shame to waste this lovely day, but she had lost the urge for gardening. She sat on the window seat and picked up her sewing, needing to keep her fingers as busy as her mind.

Alexander had escaped this time, but what of the next? Ellen bit her lip. He was always so careless of his own safety – he and others like him, the men of St Michael's who had so eagerly taken up the King's cause, their heads filled with derring-do as though it were some big adventure. Men! An exasperated sigh escaped her lips. They were all alike, so stubborn, so puffed up with pride, like so many fighting cocks – as if the only way to win an argument was with sword and pistol.

The King was no better! Why could he not have compromised, listened to his people's fears and beliefs? And why did Puritans have to be so stiff-necked and dour, as if being dull and miserable were the only way to attain God's infinite love and mercy?

If only women had a say in politics things would never have come to this pass, Ellen thought angrily, then smiled wryly at the thought: the very idea! But surely there was a middle path they could have walked, these men, to avoid a war. She had no doubt that many would die before this damnable quarrel was resolved. And it was women who would be left to pick up the pieces when they were done with killing each other. It always was.

'Why, oh why does it have to be like this?' she murmured sadly, her hand reaching out automatically for Blue, who was no longer there to comfort her.

6

James Dewett was not a happy man: the road from Dorchester was so indescribably awful he had to travel at a snail's pace or risk the horses going lame. Some had, even so, and finding replacements was proving difficult, so many had been taken for the army. Dewett, seething with frustration, wished he had ignored Trooper Fane's advice: this may well be the shortest route to Barnstaple, but it was surely not the quickest. It was too late to turn back now.

In a village just short of Axminster some sort of a fair was in full swing. Dewett, at a loss to understand how this had been permitted on the Sabbath, made enquiries: it seemed the Minister had been called away to a dying relative in the next village and had not yet returned. Similarly, the constable had gone off before dawn to investigate reports of sheep stealing on outlying farms. In the absence of anyone in authority and blithely ignoring the Puritans among them who shook their heads in appalled sanctimony, the villagers had welcomed the gypsies and their wares with open arms.

Deciding it was no business of his and would in any event take too long to disperse, Dewett shrugged and signalled his men forward. They rode past booths laid out with all manner of temptations: trinkets dangled, ribbons fluttered; stalls were heaped with beads, buttons, bows and bangles. There were silks and satins, pots and pans, mouth-watering pastries, honey cakes and sweetmeats. Children were apple bobbing, jumping with excitement and getting under everyone's feet. Tumblers, jugglers, fortune-tellers, barking dogs, fighting cocks and a weary, battle-scarred bear added to the general hubbub.

Passing with difficulty along the crowded street, Dewett became aware that his men were falling behind beguiled by the appetising smells wafting from the roadside. He had just managed to whip them all back into line, when someone released a pen of greased piglets. The terrified creatures scuttled squealing under a booth and emerged all of a clatter, trailing a string of pots and pans. A stream of lads whooped after them, followed by several fleabitten curs, their gleeful baying contributing to the general uproar. Upturning a barrel of apples in their path, the piglings made unerringly for the column of troopers, scattering between the legs of their plunging horses and into the crowd. As the riders struggled to regain control, guffaws of ribald laughter turned suddenly to screams as a woman and two children went down beneath flailing hooves. By the time Dewett had brought his troop back to order, ensured that none of the injuries was life-threatening, caught and penned the pigs and with the flat of his sword made a way through the press, it was well past midday.

A few miles further they found the bridge over the River Axe was blocked by an overturned wagon of logs. Huffing with impatience, Dewett brought his men to a ragged halt. With twenty soldiers at his disposal it would have been a simple matter to clear the road and ride on had the wagon master's boy not chosen that moment to fall over the parapet. With a bubbling scream he disappeared into the swirling water beneath the bridge. Moments later, the luckless urchin's head reappeared several yards downstream, his mouth a black hole in a face white with terror.

To shouts of encouragement from the bridge, Dewett's men abandoned their horses, scrambled along the bank and plunged to the rescue. The lad, shivering and vomiting river water, was eventually hauled like a skinned rabbit to safety while on the bridge the growing crowd of spectators cheered and clapped. A tapster emerged from the adjacent inn, his potboys carrying brimming mugs of cider for the dripping rescuers, and once again Dewett had to get his troop into order and beat a path through the crush.

Some time later, just as Dewett was beginning to feel he was making headway, the road was blocked yet again, this time by the largest flock of sheep he had ever seen. The tightly packed ribbon of bleating wool came towards him like a bore wave. He gestured widely to his men, shouted, 'Get round, get round.' But here, with high banks on either side, the road was at its narrowest. Halting in confusion, some of the men turned back to search for a passing place. Others, including Dewett, pressed on, only worsening the situation as sheep at the front panicked and tangled with those behind, the flock being driven relentlessly onward by a distant besmocked figure carrying a crook and accompanied by two dogs. The cacophony of distressed bleating sparked the horses and it was all Dewett could do to keep his seat. Getting his animal under control with whip and spur, he turned in the saddle to see most of his men disappearing at full gallop back the way they had come – a bevy of bucking backsides.

By the time all this had been sorted out and the hapless shepherd, still quivering from the venom of Dewett's frustration had taken his unusually large flock on its way, it was well into the afternoon. Recalling the mention of sheep stealing, a worm of suspicion crawled into Dewett's brain. One or even two such delays he might have expected on these dreadful roads, but three? He looked surreptitiously at the sombre faces of his men once more riding tidily in column, but could detect no glimmer of amusement, no sign of treachery. He dismissed his suspicions as fanciful, for how could anyone have known they would be coming this way?

The remainder of the journey passed without incident, but it was early evening, the light beginning to fade and their horses to founder by the time Dewett and his troop came at last to Tiverton.

On the North Devon coast, as the sun was westering and the bats flitting out of Instow's church tower, a pigeon flew over the ancient windmill – its sails stilled these many a year – and fluttered down from Mutton Hill to the cote at Tawford Barton.

Ned saw it coming, but having been warned by Lady Ellen that on no account was the Master to be disturbed, he left it until he had finished tending the horses. Catching up a lantern and calling by way of the cowshed to fetch a pail of milk for the house, he retrieved the capsule and took it to her Ladyship.

'Er arrived 'bout an hour gone, my Lady.' He handed the tiny cylinder to Ellen. 'But you said not to disturb, so I left it 'till now.'

'Thank you Ned, I will see to it.' Hiding her irritation, Ellen took the milk through to the kitchen and lit the lamps as Ned trudged away into the gathering dusk, his lantern attracting a following of moths. Sliding out the curl of paper, Ellen held it to the light and decoded the cipher, her face tightening with anxiety. Lord Bath must be warned. There were two tiny sets of initials, so the message had been relayed, even now it might be too late. Dropping the message on the kitchen table, she went hastily to the stairs, paused at the bottom to listen. All was quiet. Alexander so badly needed sleep. Who else could she send? Ned? Quicker to go herself! Not bothering with a lantern, for she could find her way to Tawstock blindfold, she retrieved her cloak from a hook in the hall, quietly let herself out and hurried across the yard to the stables, selected a placid, sure-footed mare, bridled it and led it to the mounting block. Scooping up her skirts, Ellen scrambled astride the animal's warm back – this was not a time for niceties; she didn't give a fig for them anyway – and was soon on her way.

At Tawstock Court, Rachel Fane, Countess of Bath, was bidding goodnight to the children. Descended from John of Gaunt, Rachel's paternal grandmother was a Neville, her brother, Mildmay Fane, was the Earl of Westmorland, and she was wed to Henry Bourchier, the fifth Earl of Bath. With such illustrious connections, the Countess was a naturally authoritative figure and some found her daunting. In fact, though always conscious of her position – as those who crossed the line of propriety were quick to find out – she was kind and generous to a fault. Just shy of her thirtieth birthday, tall and slender, with a mop of dark brown ringlets, Rachel had thin features, rather austere until you noticed the twinkle in her eyes. Clever she certainly was and it had often been remarked she was educated to a degree unseemly in a woman.

It had been this very trait – and her connections, naturally – that had attracted the Earl of Bath, himself a bookish man. Henry was considered ungracious, sour-tempered and unsociable by many of the King's courtiers, who – when they thought he was out of earshot – referred to him unkindly as 'the Colossus'. Big he certainly was and often clumsy and irritable, plagued as he was by indigestion, haemorrhoids and kidney stone, and undoubtedly he was more at ease with his horses than at a social gathering, but it had taken Rachel no time at all to discover that beneath her husband's crusty shell was a shy, affectionate, gentle man who loved the arts and was possessed of a sharp wit and a dry sense of humour much like her own. Though they made an odd couple it was a good match for them both and they were seemingly contented for all he was twenty years her senior.

Wed four years, the Countess had suffered three miscarriages and as yet had no children of her own, but her household teemed with fosterlings. Each evening they were lined up in the nursery in their nightshirts, hands and faces reddened by vigorous cleansing from attentive nursemaids, and marched to the upper drawing room adjoining her Ladyship's bedchamber. Here, Rachel would take the youngest on her knee as they gathered around her, their ring of eager faces lifted to hers. Sometimes she would read to them from *The Faerie Queen* or *Aesop's Fables*. At other times she would show them her daybook and they would look in awe at her tiny drawings: a robin redbreast, an old badger, a family of fox cubs, before she led them in bedtime prayers.

As Ellen was ushered into the room, Rachel relinquished the baby to a waiting nurse and watched with a smile as the children, bobbing their heads like inquisitive chickens, were hustled reluctantly to bed. Rachel greeted Ellen with an affectionate hug, her brow wrinkled with consternation. 'My dear, this is a surprise. How lovely, but whatever is the matter that you come at this hour unannounced?'

Tensely, Ellen returned the hug, 'I have received a message that could not wait. Your Lord husband is in danger and must leave Tawstock immediately.'

Rachel smiled, her expression quizzical, she bent to move her pet cat, which had seized the opportunity to curl up on her cushion the moment she vacated it, and drew Ellen to the settle. 'Sit down, my dear. Now, tell me, what danger?'

'The Earl of Bedford has sent a troop of horse from Dorchester to arrest his Lordship.' Ellen fidgeted in agitation. 'We must get him to safety, there is no time to lose, the enemy soldiers cannot be far away.'

'Hush, my dear, be calm, My Lord husband is not here. After we received your nephew's warning yesterday, our men-at-arms loaded everything onto wagons and took them to Stow. They left early this morning and Henry went with them. I do not expect him back tonight.'

'Alexander sent you warning *yesterday*?'

'You seem surprised? Yes, he did. We received two messages yesterday; the first concerning Sir Ralph Hopton's flight from Minehead – but surely you knew? Your steward brought it over in the afternoon. It was to ask if we would send a guide to meet Sir Ralph at Chittlehampton. My Lord sent his manservant, Peter Bold.'

Ellen pressed her lips together. Her steward, Robin Gubb, had been out when she returned home yesterday afternoon and she had not seen him since – that was not unusual – but he had left her no word of this. She quelled her irritation. It was likely he had thought it too dangerous to trust the information to another. She became aware that Rachel was looking at her, curiosity sparking in her eyes.

'I can see you had no knowledge of it? I'm surprised, but no harm done, my dear. Sir Ralph and his men will be safe in Stow with Sir Bevill Grenville by now or I would have heard,' the Countess reassured, patting Ellen's arm. 'Tawford's message came later, by way of a colossal gentleman, bald and rather florid looking.' She smiled, put her hand to her mouth and gave a little cough. 'He was embarrassingly large for his clothes, but reliable I am sure. He told us Tawford had reason to believe the Earl of Bedford would despatch a rebel troop here today to arrest My Lord husband. He also said they would be delayed on the road to give us time to get our plate and weapons away and take whatever evasive action we deemed necessary for our safety.' The Countess smiled. 'I rather suspect your nephew has arranged for the enemy soldiers to meet with some difficulties on their journey.'

Ellen's jaw dropped. How could Alexander possibly have known they were coming, never mind done anything about it? She thought rapidly, her mind going over what little information she had gleaned from Dickon. The messenger Rachel described could only be Cobb. Alexander must have learned of Lord Bath's arrest before he went into Ilminster to get himself captured. He could not have known he would escape in time to warn Lord Bath himself, so had sent Cobb. Why was she so surprised? It was typical of him, not only to anticipate what might happen, but also to say nothing about it.

'I fear you have had a wasted journey,' the Countess was saying. 'But it is so good to see you, I cannot help but be glad. Come, let us go downstairs, Voysin will be as delighted as I.'

Rachel got up from the settle, tucked Ellen's hand under her arm and led the way downstairs to the great hall. 'I wanted to prevent the house from being ransacked, so I persuaded Henry to go to Stow without me. If Tawford is right and we are to be raided tonight, the rebels will find us amenable and will have no excuse for hostility. I have even arranged for the gates to be left unbarred, lest they think to burn them down. I think my presence will be enough to deter them from harming us, don't you?'

Ellen gasped. 'Can you be sure of that?'

The Countess smiled. 'Oh, they may shout and stamp about for a while when they realise Henry and his weapons have gone, you know what men are like, my dear, but I doubt I am in any real danger. Apart from my steward, we are merely a household of women, and what do women know of the important affairs of men, eh?' Her eyes twinkled. 'Besides, you forget, Lord Bedford is our cousin.' The Countess arched an imperious brow, 'And even were he not, I think the rebels would not dare to lay a finger on me!' She patted Ellen's hand. 'So, my dear, we shall remain calm, have some refreshment and play a hand or two of loadum, and later, I will ask my steward to escort you home. Such troubled times we live in, you should not travel alone in the dark. So tell me, how are your hot beds coming along and is Lewin still proving satisfactory?'

Ellen, preoccupied, answered without her usual enthusiasm as they descended the stairs. Lord Baths' steward, Richard Pollard, was waiting in the hall to speak with the Countess. He looked up with a smile, bowing slightly. 'Lady Ellen, how nice to see you; you are unattended? May I take your cloak?'

Sliding it from her shoulders, Ellen shivered, but whether from the chill of the great hall, with its high moulded ceilings and marble-tiled floor, or from the sudden swirl of tension between Lady Bath and her steward, she could not have said.

Pollard addressed the Countess, 'All is quiet, my Lady. I have sent young Kit to keep watch at the crossroads and your visitors have been taken to…' With a glance at Ellen, he hesitated.

With an imperceptible shake of her head, Rachel cut across him. 'Thank you, Pollard. Have the fire lit in my bedchamber if you please, it is chilly tonight, do you not think? I would not be surprised if there is frost in the air.'

With a nod at her steward, the Countess drew Ellen towards the parlour. 'Come, I told you we were a houseful of women: you know Voysin, of course, but have you met my niece? My sister, Eliza Cope, has sent her from Oxford to stay with us for a while – she thought Bess would be safer with me than at home, there is so much activity in the Midlands.' Rachel gave a wry grimace. 'Goodness knows what Eliza will say when she hears of this!'

The parlour was scented with apple-wood from the fire, warm and welcoming, at the windows, blue baize curtains had been drawn against the night. Gilded candelabra cast their glow on walls hung with pictures, maps and colourful Turkey carpets. Books were scattered on various surfaces and at one end of the room stood a set of virginals and a viol that Rachel was learning to play. It was here she and her Lord indulged their pleasure in gaming: there was a billiard board, numerous chairs and baize-covered tables and another, inlaid with squares of ebony and ivory, set with chessmen. Most surprising of all was the parrot. It sat beady-eyed on its perch in the corner; it had amused the Earl to present it to his wife as an anniversary present. As the Countess pushed open the door, the parrot flew squawking to the extent of its silver chain, gave a passable imitation of the Earl's rare, barking laugh and mumbling obscenities, settled back on its perch to preen its ruffled feathers. It provided a welcome release of tension and Ellen could not help but laugh.

At first glance the room was a picture of calm domesticity: a girl of about thirteen, whom she assumed to be Bess Cope, sat by the fire reading. Sara Voysin was busy with her needle, a tablecloth laid across her knees, a tumble of coloured silks at her elbow. Ellen liked Sara – she was French-Swiss and had been lady-in-waiting to Rachel's mother before accompanying Rachel to Devon. The dowager Countess of Westmorland had thought to make her daughter's married life in darkest

Devonshire a little more like home! Sara had been happy with the arrangement, even more so now, having recently accepted a proposal of marriage from Richard Pollard. She looked up at Ellen and gave a bright smile, setting her work to one side.

Ellen observed that her first impression had been mistaken, the calm naught but an illusion: Sara's smile was too bright and the book Bess was supposedly reading was upside down, but they greeted her delightedly nonetheless. Normally Ellen would have enjoyed spending time in their company, but tonight she was distracted and impatient to return home. Had Alexander intended to stay overnight at the Barton? He could surely not have anticipated his own sorry state whatever else he had managed to arrange, and if the rebels were cheated of their expected prize at Tawstock might they not turn their attention elsewhere? Since her nephew's alleged involvement in the Army Plot, Tawford Barton was an obvious target. And she had left him there, dead to the world. Her mind in a whirl of anxiety, Ellen extricated herself as soon as she politely could, easing her guilt at abandoning her friends with a promise to return soon. Richard Pollard, armed with a brace of pistols and a lantern, was duly summoned to escort her home. Her mare, she noted wryly, had been saddled.

James Dewett took the only course open to him and rested his weary men at Tiverton while the constable, roused from his fireside, insisted on hearing all the news before he could be prevailed upon to procure fresh horses. No easy task, he explained, since no fewer than fifty men from the town had ridden to join the Earl of Bedford's army and taken the best that were available. But he sent a man to see what could be done and plied Dewett with wine, engaging him in small talk while they waited. Drumming his fingers, Dewett answered the constable's questions in increasingly clipped tones. The sounds of a commotion in the street sent him rushing to the door.

A weasel-faced labourer in smock and floppy hat stood without, shouting. 'Constable, Sir, I have news.'

'What's that you say? Who are you?' From the doorway the constable held a hand to his ear and held up a lantern to peer over Dewett's shoulder.

'Tom Bowman is my name. The carter, Sir, come by way of Chittlehampton. A body of Cavaliers rode in last night and the Earl of Bath's man from Tawstock met them there this morning. I thought you'd want to know. I'd have been here sooner, but my cart lost a wheel.'

Dewett started, his handsome face lighting up at the carter's use of the derogatory term. 'Cavaliers, you say! Are they still there?'

The carter directed his gaze uncertainly from the constable to Dewett and back again, took off his hat, twisting it in his hands.

The constable beckoned him inside. 'Come in, man. This is Captain Dewett. The Earl of Bedford has sent him to apprehend these very men and arrest the Earl of Bath, so your news is most timely.'

'Ah.' The carter nodded. 'Then I fear he may be too late. A shepherd over to Bittacot said he saw them leave on the back road and head for the river.'

'Where would that take them?' Dewett spoke harshly, impatience barely controlled, his nose only inches away from the carter's face. 'Answer me, man!'

The carter took a nervous step backwards. 'That depends, Sir. The shepherd didn't wait about to see what direction they took after, and I can't say as 'ow I blame him neither, there were a good many on 'em, he did say.'

The constable raised his brows. 'Did you not say they might be making for Cornwall, Captain? They'll most likely have gone that way to avoid Barnstaple's garrison. It's an

JO FIELD

alternative route to the border,' he explained, his voice light with relief. 'You can stop worrying, Captain Dewett, as can we all. They will be in Cornwall by now and no longer our concern.' He smiled at the carter. 'Thank you for bringing this warning, Bowman – it is as well to be alert. These are troubled times, gentlemen, troubled times. Who knows, but there may be more enemy soldiers on the way?'

He turned back to Dewett. 'I doubt you will want to continue to Barnstaple now, Captain? I assume the Earl of Bath's arrest can wait until morning? I daresay I can find you and your men a billet for the night.'

Tom Bowman was clearly agitated. 'Beggin' your pardon, Constable, but they could've been going to Tawstock.'

Dewett's head came up sharply. 'Is that likely?'

'It's not the way I'd go.' The carter sucked his teeth. ''Tis a narrow track and part flooded, but it's quicker than the main way. Like I did say, the Earl of Bath's man collected them from Chittlehampton, so they must've been expected.'

'Why would they want to go to Tawstock?' The constable's features screwed up with renewed anxiety. An enemy force in the vicinity was not good news, Tiverton castle had no garrison, the best of the volunteers had all gone soldiering, and while the townsfolk were strong for Parliament, they would not be able to put up any serious resistance. Fact is, he thought gloomily, an enemy troop could walk into the town and take it if they'd a mind.

Dewett, his stomach churning, gave a grim smile. 'The Earl of Bath has a stockpile of weapons and at least two hundred men at Tawstock, Constable. Lord Bedford believes Hopton is planning to join forces with him. Who knows, they may intend to attack Barnstaple.'

The constable blenched. 'I'd no idea Lord Bath had so many men. In which case, you should take warning to George Peard with all haste. I will go see if your horses are ready.' He scuttled away, a worried man. Barnstaple was altogether too close for comfort.

Dewett thought quickly. Lord Bedford had indeed ordered him to Barnstaple for reinforcements before taking any action, but if there was even a chance that Hopton was at Tawstock, he was disinclined to waste precious time. He had too few men to mount an attack, certainly, but he could keep watch until Peard's reinforcements came up. At least he would be there, ready and waiting. He was damned if he was going to let that Irish scum slip through his fingers twice. Dewett looked at the carter and smiled. 'You have done well – what did you say your name was?'

'Tom Bowman, Sir, but they do call me Carter, as often as not.'

'I am obliged to you, Carter.' Dewett reached into the pocket at his belt and jingled some coins. 'Could you guide me to Tawstock by the same way?'

'Aye, Sir, I surely could.' Carter's narrow eyes gleamed.

'Right, come with me.' Dewett strode through the streets to the town centre where his men waited, fresh horses milling around them, singled out a trooper and called him over.

'I want you to find a guide and ride for Barnstaple with all speed: kill the horses if you have to; our lives may depend on it. When you get there, ask for George Peard.' Dewett pulled Bedford's note of authority from his coat and handed it with a flourish to the attentive trooper. 'Give him this and tell him we believe Hopton and a troop of enemy horse have joined forces with the Earl of Bath and may be planning to attack the town. Tell him he is to send reinforcements to Tawstock as soon as he gets this message. We will attempt to hold the enemy there until he arrives. Tell Peard they have around five hundred men between them, so we need at least that number – more if he can spare them. Now repeat that back to me.'

It was almost full dark by the time Dewett had got his men together, explained where they were going and why, found a mount for the carter and extricated himself from the constable. Fortunately it was a clear night, the full moon lighting their way rather better than their smoking torches, but the going was rough, the horses half starved and to Dewett, in a fever of impatience, their progress seemed agonisingly slow. Deep in thought, his vengeance so near he could almost smell it, Dewett was blissfully unaware that a horseman was shadowing them, nor did he observe the rider take his chance under the cover of woodland to overtake the column and spur ahead.

Ellen's journey home from Tawstock was uneventful. As she rode, she pondered on the brief exchange between the Countess and her steward. She knew Rachel's covert activities were a closely guarded secret. Since the start of the troubles, the Countess had courageously assisted persecuted Anglican clergy, taking their infants into her ever-expanding nursery, sheltering their wives and ensuring their children received an education. Given her position, these charitable acts did not excite too much attention, but hiding Papist priests was quite another matter. That she did so Ellen knew only because Alexander had occasionally helped get them to safety, usually concealed on boats bound for Ireland or France, often via Lundy. She could only assume the visitors Pollard had been so reluctant to mention in her hearing were similarly bound. Such dangerous activities were conducted in the utmost secrecy, so much so even Lord Bath was unaware of them. Nor was he aware, as Ellen also knew, that his steward was one of a growing body of West Countrymen pledged to remain neutral and protect their homeland by obstructing and hindering marauding soldiers, no matter for which side they fought. They were becoming known as Clubmen, for they had precious few weapons but clubs and staves, but they used guile, quite often carrying ale by the wagonload and tempting soldiers to drink themselves incapable. There were too few of them, as yet, to make a difference – but one day there might be enough. Ellen hoped so.

Pollard helped her to dismount, brushed aside her gratitude with a smile, politely refused her offer of refreshment and waited, holding up the lantern to light her way to the stables. When he had ridden away, she unsaddled and settled her mare, pausing with a pang of anxiety to glance in the adjacent stall at Tweed and her new foal. What would become of them if the rebels came here in search of plunder? Should she rouse and arm her labourers? They were too few. What chance would they stand against a troop of soldiers? Better to leave them in ignorance, that way they might not get hurt. More important was to get Alexander away – Todd could take him in the boat to Lundy, he would be safe there.

Hurrying across the yard to the house, a part of her mind noted there was not a breath of wind, the black sky studded with stars, the yard bathed in moonlight. Rachel was right, there could well be a frost come dawn. Ellen wondered how the cucumbers would fare, were the straw mats thick enough? Goodness – how could she be worrying about cucumbers at a time like this!

Letting herself into the house, she heard the murmur of women's voices; Wilmot and Rose had returned. Not wanting to alarm them, she quietly ascended the stairs to Alexander's bedchamber. His door stood ajar. Biting her lip, Ellen agonised outside it for a moment, there was not a sound from within. Should she disturb him? Was she panicking unnecessarily? Maybe the rebels would not think to come here, but could she take that risk? She gently pushed open the door.

The bedclothes were rumpled where he had lain, but the bed was empty and his clothes had gone.

Chittlehampton was in darkness when Dewett and his men clattered into the square. Conscious of eyes peering out of windows, his face sheened with sweat, grey in the moonlight, Dewett drew rein and turned to face his men. 'We are almost at our destination.' He held up his hand to stem the nervous buzz, adding, 'Keep your match alight and your muskets primed, and keep your wits about you. Have courage lads. There will be rich pickings for all of you when this night's work is done.' Signalling forward, he spurred his horse into a trot. The murmurings subsided as the column fell in behind.

At about this time, having as instructed all but killed his horse, Dewett's messenger arrived breathless at the gates of Barnstaple and was taken to George Peard. Alarmed to learn that a large company of Cavaliers was in the vicinity, Peard glanced cursorily at Dewett's note of authority before tossing it apologetically to one side. He was disinclined to weaken the garrison by deploying men to Tawstock – Barnstaple would be a sitting duck! The Earl of Bedford was not an unreasonable man, would surely understand the town must be his first priority. Captain Dewett, whoever he was, would have done better to bring his men to Barnstaple – the man was either mad or a fool. 'Return to your Captain,' he instructed the trooper. 'Tell him I regret I cannot oblige. He would be advised to bring his men here and leave the Earl of Bath alone until we know what the enemy intends.'

The exhausted man took directions to Tawstock and on a fresh horse rode fearfully away.

Below Chittlehampton, Dewett and his men had reached the river. Bringing the column to a slithering halt he peered at the bridge, fingers of anxiety prickling his spine. It was narrow – perfect for an ambush. 'Quiet,' he hissed pointlessly, straining to hear above the noise of the water. 'Put those torches out!' Cautiously nudging his mount forward, Dewett peered the length of the bridge, scanned the shadows, gazed at the trees on the far bank, tried to see through the bushes clustered thick and dark beside the water. Nothing moved. Satisfied, he waved his men forward, observed the carter was hanging back, and whacked the man's horse on the rump. 'Go to it man, look lively.'

His spirits lifting with relief, Dewett brought up the rear and clattered over the bridge. His relief was short-lived. He had no sooner negotiated the far bank than an explosion ripped open the night sky directly behind him. The bridge went skyward, disintegrating in a dazzling display of fireworks.

As the burning timbers descended, Dewett panicked, dived from his horse and let go of the reins. 'Take cover! Shoot on sight!' An instruction, he realised belatedly, face pressed into the mud, as pointless as it was dangerous, for as the bridge subsided hissing into the river a billowing cloud of smoke and steam made it impossible to see anything at all, much less recognise friend from foe.

Cursing roundly, Dewett waited for the rattle of musket fire. When none came, he rose cautiously from the sticky morass and looked about him. The bewildered men, having followed his example, rose muddily in the moonlight like a bunch of disfigured apparitions and watched helplessly as their screaming horses, tails held high, reins trailing, disappeared into the night.

Dismayed, Dewett sought to cover his mistake, screamed, 'Stop them!' Anger rose in his throat like bile. 'No, wait, bring me the carter.' The man was brought to him and forced, quaking, to his knees. Grasping Bowman's jerkin, Dewett, his face suffused with rage, half lifted the cringing carter from the ground and said between gritted teeth, 'Who knew you would bring us this way?'

'Nobody,' the man gasped, his eyes bulging. 'Aside from the constable, that is.' The carter's voice rose to a squeak. 'Beggin' your pardon, Captain, Sir, but it were you yourself asked to come this way and I've not left your side since.'

Dewett's eyes narrowed. Releasing his grip so abruptly that the carter toppled over, he hissed, 'If I find you had anything to do with this you will hang!' He turned to look back at the river. 'Get those torches alight and bring one over here.' He strode down the bank as a trooper hurried to obey, holding the flaring brand aloft for Dewett to examine the smoking remains of the bridge.

'There, Sir, look,' a trooper pointed. A length of fuse was clearly visible dangling from a blackened spar. Dewett swallowed, his throat suddenly dry. Had they been but a few moments later...

'There is nothing more to see here.' He addressed the men who had gathered behind him. 'The murdering cowards who did this have scuttled back to Tawstock without bothering to check their handiwork. I don't doubt they think we are dead. Praise the Lord, He is on our side, lads.' Dewett paused, his lips drawn back from his teeth in the semblance of a grin. 'Before we hang the bastards, we will give them reason to consider their incompetence!' He waved the troopers away as they gave a ragged cheer. 'Go catch the horses. See about it. You,' he pointed at the carter, 'Go with them.'

As the troopers ran to do his bidding, Dewett turned once more to stare at the smoking bridge, unable to suppress a shiver.

Lying numb under the water in the shadow of the bank, lungs bursting, Alexander held on to the roots of a tree and fought the current. He had intended to be here much earlier, had not expected to spend the day in an opiate-induced stupor. When the sound of Wilmot and Rose cheerfully returning home had woken him, it was already dark. Afraid he had left it too late, he had gathered up a substantial length of fuse cord, selected a bay gelding from the stables and ridden fast to the Bassetts' house. With hurried explanations and a quantity of coin sufficient to make good any damage to the bridge, he had retrieved the two kegs of gunpowder left there by Cobb the day before, borrowed a lantern, hidden his mount under the trees by the river and made his way back to the bridge. With the water so high it had been a struggle to keep things dry, but eventually everything was in place. He had withdrawn to the bank to wait, beginning to wonder if his intuition had failed him, that this whole circus had been a claybrained idea after all, when Cobb's man, Zach, breathing hard had arrived on the bridge.

'They're about two miles behind, give or take.' Zach had reined in his sweating horse. 'Twenty troopers and their captain – name of Dewett.'

'Dewett? You're sure? *James* Dewett?'

'Aye.' Spare of frame and sharp of feature, Zach looked down at Alexander, his seamed face hidden beneath the brim of his hat. 'I've been following them since Axminster. The delaying tactics worked a treat. They think yon Cavaliers are at Tawstock and have sent a message to Barnstaple asking for five hundred men.'

Alexander's face split in a wolfish grin, fresh blood springing to his lips. 'Have they, by Jove. The Countess was expecting visitors, but not quite that many. It seems almost a shame they're going to be disappointed.'

Zach's eyes gleamed with amusement. 'Your birds have flown, then?'

'Long ago! Have you seen Cobb in your travels?'

'Aye, he went back to help with the shepherding. Still at it I wouldn't wonder, what with so many beasts to return. They'll be forgetting which came from where and getting their yows mixed up with their wethers, like as not. That'll be a fine to do.'

Chuckling, Alexander wiped his sleeve across his bloody mouth.

Zach peered down at him. 'You need any help here? You've bin in a fair fight already by the looks of you.'

'No, I'll manage, but thank you, Zach – as always.'

'Aye.' Zach had touched the brim of his hat and ridden away, leaving Alexander rapidly calculating. Ideally he wanted the bridge to blow just as the rebels came to it. Not only to give them the fright of their lives, but also to further delay their arrival at Tawstock – not that it was any longer necessary; Cobb and his men had done him proud. But hell and the devil confound it: Captain Dewett! He could never have anticipated that in a million years. Almost he could have kissed the Earl of Bedford. It was just too good an opportunity to miss; for a moment he pondered killing the lot of them just to get back at Dewett for the beating he had condoned. But no, the rebels were only following orders – poor sods – good men probably, most of them. He might so easily have been one of them. Resisting the temptation and judging the length of cord, he had cut and lit the fuses and hidden in the water beneath a clump of low growing willows to watch, cursing as one of the fuses sparked and died. The other had kept going, the flame flickering steadily towards the hollowed stick he had let into the barrel of gunpowder – one would be enough.

The fuse had not yet reached the barrel when he had heard the rebels coming down the hill. Godamme! He had misjudged it and was going to kill the bastards after all. Short of revealing himself there was nothing he could do. He held his breath, exhaling with relief as the troop trotted over the bridge in the nick of time, but it was a close call.

He had watched in disbelief when the greenhorns had dived into the mud and loosed their horses. Stifling his laughter – God it hurt – he had filled his lungs with air and still spluttering, had slid under the water just as Dewett came striding purposefully towards the smouldering remains of the bridge.

Alexander stayed under for as long as he could. When he broke the surface Dewett was alone on the bank staring at the river. Trying to still his chattering teeth, Alexander watched the rebel captain turn away, forcing himself to wait a few more moments, until, chilled to the marrow, he knew he had to move or drown. He pulled himself out of the water and crawled shivering onto the bank. Wrapping his arms about his chest, he stumbled through the trees away from the river, working his way laboriously to where he had left his horse.

As always after a megrim, his head felt as if it was filled with cotton wool and his eyes refused to focus: the poppy had a lot to answer for!

His horse was where he had left it, but something felt wrong. Instincts screaming, Alexander stopped short and dropped to a crouch. He was reaching for his knife when the club smashed into his head from behind.

7

In the early hours of Sunday morning Henry Bourchier, fifth Earl of Bath, had arrived at Stow with a wagon load of muskets and another of powder, bullets, match and quantities of his best plate, along with two hundred and eighty men, well armed and mounted at his expense. Satisfied with the generosity of his contribution – he had already given the King a huge loan – Henry was soon overflowing the Grenvilles' largest chair, placed for him by the fire in their cosy downstairs parlour, and relating what he knew of recent events at Sherborne, which was not a lot. The disreputable great oaf of a gypsy, who had brought warning of his impending arrest, had been singularly uninformative.

Henry Bourchier and Bevill Grenville were both approaching their half-century, but there the similarity ended. Bevill, whose illustrious grandsire was the fabled adventurer, Admiral Sir Richard Grenville, was of small stature and blessed with a cheerful, optimistic disposition. An ardent Member of the House of Commons for twenty years or more and immensely popular with his neighbours, he bounced around the countryside devoting himself to the affairs of his beloved Cornwall. His loyalty to his Sovereign had never wavered and though he had campaigned vigorously against Ship Money – who in the South West had not? – his generosity to the King's cause in the Bishops' Wars had all but beggared him in recent years. Since his appointment in July as a Commissioner of Array he had been energetically raising men and money for a Cornish army and, like Henry, he had been declared a malignant traitor by Parliament, his impoverished estates marked for the attention of John Pym's Sequestration Committee. Beyond this and their devotion to their respective wives, Bevill and Henry were as different as chalk and cheese.

Now, waiting in eager anticipation for Sir Ralph Hopton to arrive, they roasted their toes by the crackling fire, warmed their fingers on tankards of mulled ale and speculated on how the war in the South West would be won for the King. That it might be lost never entered their heads. Nodding sleepily, the Earl of Bath agreed in principle to everything his friend suggested, but Henry was no soldier. Concealing a yawn as Bevill enthusiastically expounded his theories on military strategy, Henry's drifting thoughts returned to his wife. The anxiety, which had been gnawing at him since he had left Tawstock was beginning to interfere with his digestion. How could he possibly have allowed his darling girl to persuade him she would be safer at home without him? What had he been thinking of? As the day wore on, both he and his bowels became increasingly agitated. By the time Peter Bold rode into Stow with Sir Ralph and his men, weary but unscathed and looking forward to a few days' well-earned rest, Henry was in a state of acute discomfort and unable to contribute much to the prolonged Council of War that followed.

In the late afternoon, when he was taking yet another turn around the Grenvilles' delightful garden, escaping for a moment the amused glances of his colleagues, Henry convinced himself he should not be here. Farting like a horse, the mixture of relief and pain making his eyes water, he arrived at a decision: whatever his cousin Bedford's orders were concerning the safety of his person – confound the man, how dared he presume, devil take him – the rebels would be expecting plunder at Tawstock. Henry knew only too well how soldiers behaved when their blood was up. He shuddered to think what they might do when they discovered their prize had gone. His mind was made up: he would return home. Rachel's safety was paramount. The rebels could arrest him if they must – God rot their black souls – so long as they left his wife alone.

As soon as Hopton and his officers had retired for the night, Henry tentatively excused himself. Better he return to Tawstock than go with them to Cornwall, he gruffly informed his host. He was not a military man and his present ailments precluded long hours in the saddle. He could be of more use keeping an eye on things in Barnstaple.

Hiding a smile Bevill was inclined to agree, but being a kindly soul he affected disappointment, saying only that he quite understood. Relieved, Henry sought out his hostess to take his leave. Somewhat puce about the gills, his buttocks tightly clenched, he bowed awkwardly over Lady Grenville's perfumed hand and thanked her for the stomach powders she pressed on him.

'Take one in warmed milk before you go to bed,' she whispered kindly. 'It never fails.'

Leaving his men under Bevill's able command, the Earl of Bath mounted his huge, sway-backed cob and with Peter Bold in attendance, lumbered out of Stow.

Some two hours before midnight, as Henry was greeting his startled wife, Captain Dewett's footsore men at last caught up with their horses a few miles from Tawstock.

When Ellen had recovered from her shock at finding Alexander was not in his bed and discovered a horse was missing from the stables, she assumed her nephew had gone to Stow, though God alone knew how in his condition, she thought irritably, fear for him making her angry. She would like at least to have been privy to his plans. Wretched boy!

The more Ellen thought about the approaching rebels and the possible consequences, the more concerned she became. Even with Alexander gone, Tawford Barton may be unsafe. In the past few weeks there had been dreadful tales of soldiers raping and pillaging up and down the country, doubtless they were exaggerated, but suppose they were not? There was no smoke without fire. In the end, Ellen decided to err on the side of caution: she would get her people away from the Barton and take them to her brother's house, they would be safe enough there. Robert had so far managed to remain neutral in this abysmal quarrel and was known personally to the Earl of Pembroke who was John Pym's right-hand man. The rebels would be unlikely to sack Marley Court without direct orders from Parliament.

Having made this decision, Ellen set about achieving it with quiet efficiency. She alerted Wilmot and Rose, sent them to rouse the farm labourers and their families, sent Todd on ahead to warn her brother of their imminent arrival, organised getting her best plate and valuables brought out of the house and put into a cart packed tightly with straw, and tried with some success to keep everyone calm and quiet. Ned took charge of the womenfolk, herding them into a hay wain with the smaller children and Tweed's foal, and everyone who could ride was given a horse to lead, they would have to leave three behind, but it could not be helped. Within the hour, to the distressed wailing of cold, over-tired infants, the cavalcade set off for Marley Court.

It was only as Ellen was dismounting into her brother's anxious arms that she remembered with a cry of guilt that she had completely forgotten about Dickon. She sent Todd back to the Barton to look for him, just in case the boy had somehow slept through the commotion and was still there. She thought it more likely he had gone to Stow with Alexander – he must have taken one of the little Exmoor beasts from the orchard – but she could not rest until she knew for certain. If there was any sign of the soldiers at the Barton, under no circumstances was Todd to approach, but hide, watch to see what happened and bring back news.

An hour or so later, when Ellen had just finished sorting out accommodation for her people, had her belongings carried into the house and seen that Tweed and her foal were settled into her brother's stables, Todd returned leading two horses. The Barton was deserted, he said; the two moorland beasts were still in the orchard, but the black gelding had gone from its stable. Perplexed, Ellen could only assume that Dickon had woken to find the house empty and had taken the horse. She hoped fervently he had gone home to his parents, but there was nothing more she could do about it tonight; she would pay the Chichesters of Hall a visit in the morning. Too weary to give Robert more than a cursory description of the day's events, she stumbled to bed only to lie awake into the small hours, worrying.

Dickon had woken from a deep sleep feeling warm and comfortable and lain for a moment looking at a shaft of moonlight on the wall, wondering what had woken him and trying to work out why the window was on the wrong side of the room. He listened to the silence – not quite silence, he could hear the sea.

He sat up with a start as everything came back to him. Whatever was the time? Devil take it! He must have slept the day around. His stomach knotted as he remembered what he planned to do. Fully awake, he felt anxiously for his clothes.

Swiftly and silently he dressed, retrieved his sword and holding it tightly against his chest, crept along the corridor. There was not a sound from Tawford's room. For a moment, feeling like a Judas, Dickon hesitated outside the half-open door. He hated walking out like this, but what choice did he have? The alternative was to face the ignominy of being sent home to his parents. Resisting the temptation to look in lest it weaken his resolve, he stole past, prayed his feet would not land on a creaking board and gingerly negotiated the stairs. A sudden pang of hunger reminded him he had fallen asleep before he could eat his dinner. Trying to remember the layout of the house, he felt his way to the kitchen. A single candle burned there pooling wax onto a scrubbed table. He quickly found some food, cramming a slice of cold meat into his mouth while hacking off another for the journey, along with some bread and cheese, which he wrapped in his neckerchief and stuffed into the pocket at his belt. He thought longingly of the whortleberry pie, but there was no sign of it. There was a pitcher half-full of milk though – he drained it. There was still no sound in the sleeping house. Holding his breath, Dickon tiptoed through to the back kitchen and out into the yard, surprised at how light it was, the moon almost full and riding high. Quietly pulling the door closed, he crept to the stables, wincing as his feet crunched on the frosty ground.

Most of the stalls were empty – there were but three horses from which to choose, which was odd. There must be another stable block somewhere. No matter, he needed only one. The tack room was adjacent. Waiting for his eyes to adjust to the gloom, he selected what he needed, saddled and bridled the best of the beasts – a quiet black gelding – and feeling like a thief in the night, led it unresisting away from the Barton. He could only hope Ellen would understand, thought she probably would, deliberately closed his mind to what Tawford's reaction might be. Nearing the top of the track, his bladder uncomfortably full, Dickon relieved himself in the hedge, took one last look at the sleeping Barton, adjusted the leathers and mounted up. It was eerily quiet in the moonlight, a ghost world. 'Struth, it was cold! Shivering, he drew his cloak tight about him and hoped he would remember the way. The last time he had ridden to Burrow Mump it had been with his cousin James – heavens, was that only four days ago?

The river crossing seemed much further than Dickon remembered; surely it had not taken so long before? But at last there it was, he recognised the break in the trees. When he saw the burned out remains of the bridge, he stopped, confused. What had happened here? Nervously peering into the shadows, his hand resting on his sword, he swivelled in the saddle and strained to hear above the noise of the river. Glaring at the swirling water, his mind in a whirl, Dickon considered his options: he could attempt to swim the horse across, but what if it foundered? He could retrace his steps and go the long way round by Barnstaple, but what if he were seen? The safest alternative was to follow the Taw upstream and hope to find another crossing even if it took him out of his way. The decision made, he nudged the gelding towards the narrow track that ran through woods alongside the riverbank. Drawing his sword, his eyes probing the shadows, Dickon encouraged the gelding into a trot. He had ridden only a few hundred yards when he heard a body of horsemen coming swiftly towards him. Stomach churning, he kicked his mount off the track into a shadowed thicket of scrub, dismounted, grasped the gelding's head and held its nose tight against his chest, muttering soothingly into the flickering ear. 'Hush my lovely, don't give us away.'

There were about two-dozen men, armed and travelling fast, torches flaring. Most wore buff leather coats and one or two had breastplates – soldiers then – but whose? Friend or foe? It was impossible to tell. One was leading a horse, the body of a man slung across its back. In the brief moment as they galloped by, Dickon saw the man's hands were roped. His breath caught in his throat; there was something familiar about that head lolling against the horse's belly. Then they were gone.

Releasing his grip on the black's nose, Dickon waited until he could no longer hear hoofbeats then led his horse onto the track and stared after the riders, trying to place the spark of recognition, but it eluded him; the glimpse had been too fleeting. Whoever the poor fellow was, he had looked beyond anyone's help. Mounting up, Dickon rode warily on, but the image of the lolling head kept nagging at his brain. He had covered a few more yards when it came to him. He pulled his horse up short. No, it could not be. Calling himself all manner of a fool, Dickon kicked the gelding into a trot. The full moon was addling his head. He would be seeing pixies next! It was not possible. Tawford was back at the Barton, asleep in his bed. But the further Dickon rode, the more certain he became, until he knew he could not go on; he had to find out. Not stopping to think what he, alone, could do against so many, he wheeled the gelding and set off after the horsemen, riding as in a race, head low against the animal's neck. Afraid to consider that if he was right, his captain might be dead, Dickon galloped past the burned out bridge. As he did so, an image of Tawford flashed into his mind.

Tawford leaning out over the rails: 'Just looking,' he had said.

Dickon heaved on the reins, the gelding reared up, skidded to a halt. Hellsteeth! Had Tawford gone alone to blow up the bridge and been caught in the act, while he, Dickon, had been sleeping like the babe his captain obviously thought him? But if so, why? It made no sense. With a cry of frustration, Dickon kicked his confused mount back into a gallop.

Catching sight of flaring torches ahead he slowed the gelding just in time, saw the troop veer left into the trees, waited a moment then followed. The river dropped away on his right as he trailed the horsemen up a steep, winding, woodland track, a soft carpet of leaves deadening the sound of his gelding's hooves. At the top of the hill the soldiers drew to a halt by a high, castellated wall. A few yards further on he could see an imposing stone archway. Torches burned in brackets on either side, lighting tall double gates of solid wood. Though he had never been here, Dickon was fairly sure this was the entrance to Tawstock Court.

Nudging as close as he dared, he dismounted, led the horse behind a thick clump of brambles and peered round it hoping to get a clear look at the prisoner, but the troop had closed around him. They seemed to be hanging back. What were they doing? Puzzled, Dickon watched as one of them rode forward to the wall, clambered to his mount's back and hauled himself up to look over the top. After a moment the trooper jumped down from his horse, walked up to the gates and pushed against them. Dickon watched in disbelief as they yielded and the soldiers, moving slowly forward, rode through them unchallenged and disappeared from view.

Tethering the gelding in the shadows, Dickon crept cautiously forward. He was near enough now to identify the Earl of Bath's arms embossed over the archway – so he had guessed right, this was Tawstock Court. Why then was it undefended and the gates unbarred? Were these the Earl's men? If so, why had they not ridden straight up to the gates? And why had they captured Tawford – if indeed it was Tawford? His thoughts going round in circles, Dickon stood biting his lip, undecided what to do. He could hear horses clattering and men shouting behind the wall, wanted desperately to get another look at the prisoner. If he was mistaken and it was not Tawford, he would like nothing better than to leave here. And as quickly as possible! Dared he risk climbing the wall as the soldier had done to look over? Keeping it on his left, he ran alongside it away from the gates, looking for somewhere to climb. On his right, the woods dropped steeply to the river and far below him he caught glimpses of shining water. Owls were out and hunting, their ghostly cries shivering through the trees. Beneath his feet the ground was knotted with tree roots, he stumbled against one, catching his toe as an overhanging branch slapped him in the face. Cursing, he almost missed seeing the small wooden door let into the wall. It was overgrown with ivy and secured by a rusty chain and padlock, but the gatepost was rotten. Fumbling for his knife, Dickon prized off the hasp and pushed. The door did not budge. Using all his strength he tried again and got it open a crack. Gasping, he unbuckled and dropped his sword, flung his cloak on top of it, held his arms over his head and holding his breath, squeezed sideways through the narrow gap, tripped over a handcart propped behind the door and overbalancing, fell smack into a soft pile of wet, steaming compost.

Muttering obscenities that would have had Papa unbuckling his belt, Dickon picked himself up, brushed himself off and looked about him. He was in a walled garden. A central path between neat raised beds led to an archway in the opposite wall. Through it he could see a small apple orchard, the boughs heavy with fruit. For a moment Dickon had to pinch himself to ensure he was not dreaming, for in the moonlight everything was bleached of colour and looked strangely ethereal; not quite real. He shivered and wishing fervently that he had not removed his cloak he walked swiftly through the garden, his feet crunching on cinders. Now he could see beyond the orchard to an area of meadow, the ground rising to a row of yew trees that had been clipped into spheres like gigantic cannon balls. Behind were grassed terraces and a flight of wide stone steps ascending between ornamental balustrades to the manor house. It was built of stone, with curved gables and mullioned windows. Decorative chimneys clustered atop slate roofs, bright in the moonlight.

Keeping to the shadows, Dickon ran low under the apple trees and across the meadow, making for the shelter of the yews. He stopped there to catch his breath and study the back of the house; noticed one of the ground floor windows was dimly lit. He could hear men's voices coming distantly from the courtyard at the front. Sending up a swift prayer, he drew a deep breath and scrambled like a monkey up the steps and across the terraces in full view of the house, his shadow running before him, his senses screaming, alert for shouts to tell him he had been seen. None came. Weak with relief, breath rasping, heart thudding, he ducked beneath the lighted window and peered cautiously through a gap in the curtains.

Though Dickon had been only an infant when he had last seen the Earl of Bath, he recognised him instantly. Clothed in a colossal, fur-trimmed nightgown, his face like thunder, jowls purple and wobbling, he was gesticulating wildly. Beside him, white and strained, a woman who could only be the Countess clung to his arm in an attempt to restrain him. Dickon soon saw why. A man moved into his line of vision; a soldier, tall and darkly handsome. In his hand, pointing steadily at Lord Bath's chest, he held a pistol.

The soldier was speaking, but the glass was too thick to hear what he was saying – it hardly mattered. All the pieces fell into place: these were rebel soldiers and they had come for Lord Bath. Tawford had expected them, tried to stop them by blowing up the bridge, was captured before he could bring warning. A spike of anger surged in Dickon's chest as he dropped to his knees below the window. Why in God's name had the fool not said anything, asked for help? He swallowed, his throat suddenly dry as his anger turned to fear. Tawford! Was he even alive?

Backing away, Dickon crawled along the terrace beneath the windows until he reached the side of the house, his breath steaming and clouding the air. He was about to push himself to his feet when he caught a blur of movement out of the corner of his eye. He stopped short with a gasp. It was naught but a cat playing with a mouse. When it saw Dickon, it arched its back, but stood its ground, tail twitching. Ignoring it, he got up from his knees and flattened his back against the wall, the rough stones catching on his jerkin. He could hear men's voices clearly now. He edged slowly towards the front corner of the house, peered gingerly round it and looked into a cobbled courtyard. Dickon could smell the faint whiff of pitch from the smoking cressets that lit the yard. The doors of the coach house were wide open and two carts had been drawn onto the cobbles. Soldiers laden with plunder were streaming in and out of the house: trunks, rolls of carpet, tapestries, bundles of clothes, pewter, paintings, even small items of furniture, which they were piling into the carts. Others were leading the Earl's horses out of the stables, and two men were dragging out a boy and a young woman who must have been hiding there. As Dickon watched, one of the soldiers upturned his musket and smashed the butt over the boy's head, laughing as the lad dropped like a stone to the icy cobbles. The woman screamed and went on screaming as her captor caught hold of her bodice, ripping it to her waist to expose her breasts, one hand fumbling with his breeches. None attempted to stop him. Dickon, his fists clenched in a spasm of helpless anger, could do nothing but watch in sickened fascination, fleetingly aroused despite his abhorrence at what he was witnessing. Bastards! Parliament's soldiers were supposed to be Godly men, were they not? This was no better than Ireland. Dragging his gaze away, he at last located the prisoner. He was still tied face down over a horse, arms and head hanging motionless, hair darkly stained and matted with blood. Two rebels were guarding him, match glowing, muskets pointed steadily at his back. There was no question it was Tawford.

There would be no reason to guard a dead man. So intense was Dickon's relief, he started forward, slipped, lost his footing. Grabbing onto the wall, he jerked back into the shadows, hardly daring to breath. Saw a trooper look up, stare straight at him, walk slowly forward to investigate.

The cat saved him. Tired of its game, it shot out from behind the wall and streaked across the courtyard, the mouse dangling from its jaws. The trooper stopped, grinned, reached back into the cart, grabbed a candlestick and threw it at the cat, then turned and went back into the house, the candlestick bouncing harmlessly over the cobbles coming to rest only inches from Dickon's toe.

At that moment, the officer who had held the Earl at pistol point came out of the house to stand on the top step. 'You!' he shouted, pointing.

Dickon gasped, froze. He was done for. He was on the point of throwing caution to the winds and fleeing, when the man shouted again, 'Yes, you! Stop that right now,' pointing not at Dickon, but at the trooper who was forcing the woman to her knees. Her skirts were up over her head, her screams quietened to a low whimpering. With a muttered oath the trooper dropped her and laced up his breeches, venting his frustration with a vicious kick at the unconscious boy. Suddenly released, the woman scrambled to her feet, pulled her shawl around her nakedness and ran screeching out of the courtyard and off down the road. The boy lay still, like a heap of rags on the cobbles.

'Listen up, all you men.' The officer waited, tapping his foot until he had everyone's attention. 'The prisoners are to be held overnight in Barnstaple. At first light we begin our journey to London. I say again, Lord Bath is not to be harmed.' Drawing his lips back in a grin, he shot a malevolent glance at Tawford. 'I have no such instructions concerning that murdering son of a Papist bitch. Do with him as you will, but keep him alive – I want him to feel the hooks when he's drawn. Now get mounted, we will be ready to leave directly.' He turned and went back into the house.

Almost weeping with relief, his legs turned to jelly, Dickon backed away. What he had heard appalled him; he had to get help, but from where? He had been too long in Ireland to know where people's loyalties lay: Barnstaple was all for Parliament, that much he knew. There would be no help there. He could ride home and fetch his brother, but not without alerting Papa, who would abhor what the rebels were doing but would not lift a finger to help either Tawford or Lord Bath. Ellen had no armed men at Tawford Barton, so there was no point going back there, and he did not know her brother, Lord Westley, knew only that Tawford and he were estranged. Trying not to panic, Dickon decided there was only one thing to do: he would stick to his original plan and ride to St Michael's, get word to Tawford's men.

Retracing his steps, he fled down the terraces, through the orchard to the garden, struggled through the door, cursing as his jerkin caught on the latch, lost patience, tore it free. Chest heaving, he retrieved his sword and cloak, ran to where he had left the gelding, mounted and rode fast away from Tawstock. Back to the river crossing; there was no alternative now. He kept his mind busy forming a plan: the gelding was an old horse, it would soon tire, but if it would just get him to the Randalls' farm, he could retrieve Tawford's horses. They would be well enough rested by now. Dickon tried not to think about the responsibility resting on his shoulders, banished images of the fate that awaited Tawford if he failed.

Somehow – he was never sure quite how – he got himself and his horse across the swollen river, his sopping clothes soon stiffening with ice as he rode up the hill to Chittlehampton. He had lost his hat in the water and the bread in his pocket was a sodden, inedible lump, but he stilled his chattering teeth by chewing on some cheese and meat. He was forced to stop a time or two, racking his brains to remember which path to take. When he got to the woods above North Molton he drew his sword and urged the gelding into a canter, but if the footpads were still there, they left him alone.

The farm was in darkness. Dickon greeted the dogs, quickly silencing them with the remains of his food; he wanted to avoid waking Josh Randall, the old man would only delay him. He found Tawford's horses tethered in the barn, wondered fleetingly if he could manage all four, quickly rejected the idea; it would slow him down. It would also make him too rich a prize for thieves – or soldiers – to resist. It was a sobering thought; he would lead just the one as before. Dickon unsaddled the tired black gelding, whispered his thanks and shoved a pile of hay under its nose – there was no time to rub it down; the horse had done him proud, he hoped it would suffer no ill effects.

Tawford's halters, bridles, sheepskins and light saddles were hanging from nails in the barn wall. Dickon bridled two horses, threw a sheepskin and saddle over the back of one, discarded his cloak, stiff and heavy with ice, wrapped the other sheepskin round his chest and tied it in place with a halter. Spotting a pile of empty sacks and some twine in the corner, he tied one over his head and another round his shoulders. Feeling like a scarecrow, but a little warmer, Dickon mounted up and rode out of the farm, wondering as he did so what old Josh would make of it come morning.

Afraid of losing his way, he headed for the main Dulverton road, the way he and James had come with the horses on his first journey to St Michael's. Though a few miles further than Tawford's cross-country route, it was more straightforward, would most likely be as quick. He could only hope he met no rebel patrols on the road or if he did, they would take him for a humble servant and leave him and his horses alone. He certainly looked the part.

Tawford was alive, but for how long? The thought drove him on, changing over horses from time to time, riding as fast as he dared. Some hours into his journey, when nothing looked familiar and he had begun to worry he had missed the way, Dickon recognised the derelict barn by a stream where he and James had broken their journey. Sobbing with relief he stopped to water the horses and empty his bladder, unable to control his shivering as he watched the steam rise in the moonlight. He reckoned he must be about half way by now, felt muzzy for want of sleep, had no idea what hour it was, his feet were completely numb and his fingers not much better. Adjusting his clothes and pulling the sheepskin closer, Dickon tucked his hands under his armpits and stamped a few circuits around the barn. He felt no warmer, but it woke him up.

At dawn, just outside Taunton, he was challenged by the Watch. Protesting he was a groom taking the horses to the smith for his master, who was a captain in Lord Bedford's army and would not thank them for delaying him, he prayed they would let him pass. They did, but not before insisting he gave them news of the army. Trying to sound convincing he gabbled about the Royalists' escape from Sherborne, which seemed to satisfy them. Telling him he would be better off as a soldier than continue working for a master who could only afford to clothe him in sackcloth, they laughingly let him go. By then it was full light, the wind had got up and storm clouds were building on the skyline. Soon, to add to his misery, it started to sleet. People were getting about in the villages, heads down against the weather nobody spared Dickon a second glance as he trotted by.

By mid-morning the horses were no longer capable of more than a stumbling walk and Dickon kept nodding off, jerking awake to find he was half out of the saddle. He began seriously to doubt that he would ever reach St Michael's, so tired he was hallucinating, wanted nothing more than to sleep. The urgency of his journey ceased to hold meaning; he moved forward like an automaton, no longer sure where he was going or why. When he came at last in sight of Burrow Mump he sobbed uncontrollably like a child, hot tears scalding his cheeks. As his horses faltered to a halt by the bridge, Dickon toppled slowly over his mount's shoulder and passed out.

8

Monday 26ᵗʰ September, 1642

Looking for her brother, Ellen crossed the great hall and peered around the door of what used to be the servants' parlour, where Robert spent much of his time. It amused her that having had one side of the room shelved to hold his books he had taken to referring to it rather grandly as 'the library', but though small it was comfortable, and tucked between the kitchen and buttery overlooking the garden on two sides, it was nice and light even on a cold, grey day like today. A big oak table stood in the middle, stained with ink and candle grease and littered with an assortment of quills, sticks of charcoal and screws of paper, along with a pile of rolled-up manuscripts and an astronomical table-clock that Robert, fascinated by all things scientific, had brought back from his Grand Tour. The clock was by far the most handsome of the many artefacts and curiosities gathering dust about the room where the only feminine touch was a set of gaily-embroidered cushions strewn on a settle by the fire; a labour of love by the woman whose portrait hung above the fireplace – Robert's late lamented wife had hated needlework – her stern gaze staring at him possessively even from beyond the grave.

He was asleep on the window-seat, his long, boot-clad legs stretched out muddily in front of him, his chin resting on his chest. Reluctant to disturb him Ellen tapped hesitantly on the door. He looked up with a start, smiled sleepily and beckoned her in.

'Come in, little sister. You've caught me napping – I must be getting old.'

'Nonsense.' She returned his smile, wrinkling her nose at the mingled odours of horse and wet dog, beeswax, wood smoke and musty vellum that assailed her nostrils as she closed the door behind her. A log fire crackled merrily in the grate casting flickering shadows on the linen-fold panelling and reflecting warmly in the hearth. Stretched out in front of it, muddy-pawed and gently steaming, were Robert's favourite hounds, Chaser and Turk. Long-eared and wrinkle-browed, they jumped up to greet her, but at a signal from the window-seat dropped instantly to the floor, their tails fanning the flames.

'I thought I might find you in here.' Rearranging the cushions, Ellen plonked herself down on the settle and leaned forward to fondle Chaser's ears. 'Have you been writing? I don't want to disturb you.'

'You are not disturbing me.' Robert drew in his legs, clods of mud dropping from his boots to the polished floorboards. 'I've only just got back. I rode over to the Barton early, but all is quiet – not a soldier to be seen. It's chilly out, but rain is on the way I think. How did you sleep? Well I trust – you look a little better this morning.'

'Not at all badly,' Ellen lied, wishing she could spill out the fears that had kept her awake all night, but talking with Robert these days was like tiptoeing around in the meadow lest she step on a nest of lark's eggs. It had not always been like this, she thought sadly. They had been close confidantes once, but after Henry's tragic death her brother had changed. To lose a child was a sorrow beyond bearing, as Ellen knew only too well. Robert, stricken with grief and unable to speak of it, had distanced himself from anyone who might force him to acknowledge his loss, hiding his feelings behind a shield of small talk so that she no longer knew what he was thinking.

He looked down at his hand and picked at his fingernails. 'So tell me, sister, what of Alexander? Did I hear you say he has gone into Cornwall?'

The tense set of his shoulders belied his studied nonchalance and Ellen, undecided how much to tell him, for a moment did not reply. Looking past him and out of the window she could see Todd rhythmically wielding a besom in the garden. He was brushing leaves off the lawn, his footsteps leaving a trail of green in the frosted grass. He had wanted something to do. They all felt at a loose end away from the Barton, even she, for though she was born and raised at Marley Court it no longer felt like home to her; that had ceased on the day she married Edward. That had been a cold, grey day too, she remembered. She sighed, an ache of guilt and sorrow catching at her heart as it always did when she thought of her late husband.

'Ellen?' Robert's voice pierced her reverie. She got up from the settle and wandered restlessly to the table. 'Forgive me, I was thinking of my wedding day,' she smiled gently down at him. How careworn he looked, gaunt and hollow-eyed, his face etched permanently with sorrow since Ruth's death in childbed two years ago – the babe, a boy, had been stillborn – so cruel, just when Robert had begun to put the past behind him, but on top of that had come this rift with Alexander. She knew her brother had once held him responsible for Henry's death, but last year, when Robert had moved heaven and earth to obtain Alexander's release from the Tower, she had hoped they would be reconciled. Her hopes had been short lived for soon after Alexander's return it was apparent they were still very much at odds. Neither one would tell her why and Ellen, grieving over the estrangement between the two people she loved best and at a loss to understand it, felt like banging their heads together.

Whatever the reason, it was clearly taking its toll on her brother: once tall and slender, now stooped and painfully thin, his fair hair streaked liberally with silver, he looked a good deal older than his three and forty years and Ellen felt a sharp stab of pity. Giving herself a mental shake she collected her thoughts. 'I've already told you what I know. He arrived yesterday morning with a megrim having ridden from Somerset with a week-old gunshot wound in his thigh, but it was clean and will heal if he will only let it. I tended him and left him sleeping, but when I returned from Tawstock he had gone. I'd lay strong odds he has ridden to Stow to join Sir Ralph Hopton, but I cannot be sure.' She decided not to mention that he had been beaten half to death by rebel soldiers; there was no point in worrying her brother unnecessarily.

''Sdeath!' Robert cursed. 'I had hoped he would come to see me. I need to talk to him.' His mouth twisted in a lop-sided smile belied by the haunted look in his eyes. 'It seems he does not wish to talk to me.'

Ellen thought that was likely true, but forbore to say so.

'He was hardly in a fit state yesterday, but if you would only try to mend this quarrel, I am sure —'

'It is not for the want of trying, sister,' Robert cut across her. 'He ignores my letters, turns away my messengers, what more can I do?' Disconsolately he bent to pick up a crust of mud, balling it in his fingers and tossing it across the room towards the fire.

'What is it between the two of you? Surely it is not still because of Henry? You must know it was not Alexander's fault; Henry was a darling child, but he could be such a handful.'

'It has nothing to do with Henry,' he said shortly, refusing to meet her gaze.

'But you did blame Alexander,' she persisted.

'I did at first, but only because I lost my reason. When Alexander carried Henry's body to me on that dreadful day and told me what had happened, I could not understand how it was possible. Henry was a good horseman, despite his youth, but Alexander was exceptional. How could he not have prevented it? All I could see was my beautiful boy, bleeding and broken in his arms, and all I could think was that Alexander had intended it to happen.' Robert's voice sank to a whisper, 'I was wrong, God forgive me, but I was blinded by rage and grief. I called him a murderer; said I never wanted to see his face again.'

Not wanting even to think about the pain behind that desperate accusation, nor of Alexander's utter devastation on hearing it, Ellen listened in appalled silence, her chest so tight with pity she could scarcely breathe.

'By the time I came to my senses, he had gone overseas. Rumours of fratricide spread like wildfire, but what could I do? I could not unsay it. I wanted to cut my own throat – would have done were it not for Ruth.' Pushing himself up from the window-seat Robert moved unsteadily to stand at the end of the table, rested his hands on it, head bent. 'Henry was so young, so alive, the manner of his death unbelievably cruel. I was angry with God, Ellen. So angry I could not accept His will.' Of a sudden Robert balled his fist and slammed it down with such violence that the charcoal sticks bounced and shattered on the table. 'And to punish me He took my wife and babe as well.'

'No!' Ellen cried out, tears springing to her eyes. 'Do not think such a thing.'

He looked blankly at her and then in surprise at the blood welling on his knuckles, sucked at it and wiped his hand on his sleeve. 'After Ruth died I tried to find Alexander, wrote several letters begging him to forgive me and come home, but I heard nothing. I learned later that one of them found him, but by then he was embroiled in the Scots War and after that he was imprisoned, so I did not see him again until he came to thank me for negotiating his release. He said then that I could never blame him for what happened to Henry as much as he blames himself and he hoped I might one day be able to forgive him that it was Henry who died and not him.' Robert drew in a sobbing breath, his eyes glassy with unshed tears. 'God knows, even in my worst moments I had never wished for that. I did not know what to say to him, sister.'

'Whatever you had said he will go on punishing himself,' she murmured. 'He courts danger as though he has a death wish – and God knows there will be plenty of opportunities in this unspeakable war.' She fiddled absently with a screw of paper. 'I am so afraid for him, Robert. He could so easily be killed.'

'You think I am not aware of that?'

'Of course not, which is why you must mend this quarrel. I do so wish you'd tell me what it's about, I might be able to help.'

'I appreciate your concern, but I'd prefer you did not meddle, it is nothing to do with you.'

Stung, Ellen railed at him. 'How stupid of me, I was under the illusion that I was your sister! Do forgive me; the last thing I want is to pry into matters that do not concern me.'

'Sarcasm does not become you, Ellen.' Thrusting his fingers through his hair, Robert turned away from her and strode to the window.

'Perhaps not, but you should put it right. Dammit, Robert, Alexander is your son!' So easily said, instantly regretted, Ellen inwardly cursed her wayward tongue.

Her brother stopped in mid-stride. 'Alexander is not my son, and even if he were, I do not need you tell me what I should and should not do,' he said coldly.

'Oh, for God's sake, brother! Of course he is. I've known it for years. You surely cannot imagine it is a secret just because nobody ever says it to your face?' In a surge of frustration Ellen reached over the table and swept the pile of manuscripts to the floor. They fell with a clatter, skittering over the floorboards and disturbing the sleeping hounds. Raising their heads they looked at her reproachfully from sad, red-rimmed eyes.

White with anger, fists clenched, Robert swung round to face her. 'I see you have not yet learned to control your temper, sister. Calm yourself, do.'

'I am perfectly calm,' she retorted between gritted teeth, aware she was anything but. 'Is that what is wrong between you, this persistent refusal to acknowledge Alexander's paternity?'

'I do not wish to discuss it further,' Robert warned. 'The subject is closed.' He turned back to the window and sank onto the seat.

Too tired and worried to heed his warning, Ellen burst out shrilly, 'God's bones, I could understand it while your sainted wife was alive, but what can it possibly matter now she is dead?'

Robert flinched as if she had struck him, his face a mask of pain.

'Oh Lord, I should not have said that,' she said, remorsefully. 'I'm sorry. I don't mean to hurt you, it is just that I cannot bear it when you and Alexander quarrel.'

He looked up at her and, making a visible effort, acknowledged her apology with a stiff smile. 'I know our estrangement pains you, sister, but it is between Alexander and me – hard as that is for you to understand.'

'Don't patronise me,' she retorted, her remorse dissipating. 'What's not to understand? That you are so ashamed of your adultery you must deny it? Oh, I understand – better than you know, brother. What I fail to understand is why Alexander should be made to suffer for it. He thinks you do not name him as your son because he shames you.'

Robert frowned. 'He has said so?'

'He does not need to. You really have no idea how the stain of bastardy plagues him, do you? And for that Ruth is to blame, may God assoil her, for she rubbed his nose in it at every opportunity. Oh, do not deny it, brother,' Ellen cried as Robert buried his head in his hands. 'Don't let Alexander go to his death thinking you are ashamed of him. Acknowledge him – I beg you – before it is too late.'

'Do you think I would not do so if I could? Alexander is not mine, I tell you.' Robert was not patronising her now; the anguish in his muffled cry was all too clear.

'But I have always thought...' The words stuck in her throat. 'Please tell me you are lying,' she whispered.

He lowered his hands and met her gaze, his mouth twisting in a wry grimace. 'I may have many sins to repent, sister, but adultery is not one of them. In all the years since I brought him here, have you once heard me claim Alexander's paternity?'

'No, but nor have you denied it. Why not when you must have known it is what everyone believed – even your wife!'

Mutely he shrugged, lowering his gaze to the floor. A log snapped, hissing in the fire. Ellen could hear the soft whirring of the clock, the hounds snoring. Outside it had started to rain, washing away the frost from the lawn. Undeterred, Todd was still sweeping leaves. It seemed strange to her that everything was still the same, as if in some way it must be changed. She stepped backwards and grasped the edge of the table, feeling the wood warm and solid beneath her fingers. Her foot came up against a roll of manuscript and turning, she bent to retrieve it. As her thoughts reached out to Alexander she gasped in sudden, horrified understanding. Dropping the manuscript on the table she swung round to face her brother. 'You have told him?'

Robert's mouth tightened and he nodded. 'I have now.'

'Dear God!' She had thought they had quarrelled, but this was infinitely worse. With startling clarity she recalled the day that Alexander had gone over to Marley Court. He had come storming back to the Barton, drunk himself into a stupour and ridden off without a word. When he returned days later he was uncharacteristically short with her, responding to her anxious queries with such biting sarcasm that reluctantly she had been forced to admit defeat. She had blessed the day when Adam and Hugh had come looking for him. Almost she had blessed the war, for it had thrust Alexander into activities that demanded he stay focussed – and sober. She had always known the stigma of illegitimacy was hard for him; it was why he strove to excel, ever goaded by the need to prove himself worthy of the man he thought was his father. To learn that he was not must have cut Alexander to the quick.

Sadly, Ellen looked down at her brother. 'What about his name – is that a lie too?'

'Of course not, he is related on the spear side – as I explained to you at the time. If you remember, I asked you to be kind to him because he was distant kin and an orphan.'

Distractedly, Ellen nodded, but she had forgotten. It was a long time ago and she had not believed it anyway. Scarcely more than a child herself, she had been jealous of Alexander. A winsome little boy with a mop of yellow hair and big green eyes, he had followed her big brother around like a puppy and the gossips had had a field day. When Robert had done nothing to deny rumours that Alexander was his bastard it was taken as tacit admission they were true, particularly when he assigned Tawford Barton to the boy. Ellen had never doubted that Alexander was her nephew.

Feeling as if her legs would not hold her up she moved away from the table and sank to the settle. 'Did you explain that to Alexander too?'

A flush staining his cheeks, Robert shook his head. 'He was too young to understand why I was taking him away. His foster-mother was kind to him and he loved her well – he had no memory of his parents. When he asked if I was his Papa it suited my purpose to say yes, but I did not want him upsetting Ruth, so I told him he was to keep it a secret lest it sadden my wife that she was not his Mama. Barely three years old he accepted that readily enough and a far as I am aware, he never told a soul. Naturally I told Ruth he was not mine, but she preferred to believe her gossips.' Robert gave a hollow laugh that turned into a sob. 'She forgave my infidelity at the last!'

Astonished, Ellen bit back the caustic remark that sprang to her lips. Ruth had certainly been saddened, but not in the way Robert implied. A possessive woman, she had been so resentful at having her husband's by-blow foisted on her that she had made Alexander's life a misery – until Henry was born. After that she had ignored him, which was why Ellen had stopped being jealous and instead gone out of her way to befriend Alexander. It was largely thanks to Ruth that their relationship had blossomed into one of such close understanding and affection.

'I cannot believe you have only now told him the truth,' she murmured. 'Small wonder he has no wish to talk to you – he must feel as if his whole life has been a lie.'

'For pity's sake Ellen, I am burdened enough by guilt as it is. I had always intended to tell him when he turned sixteen and was old enough to understand and could deal with it, but that was when Henry was killed and after that Alexander was gone for nigh on eight years; there was no opportunity until he came home this year. In fact, I had made up my mind not to tell him at all. It seemed kinder after all these years to let him go on thinking he was mine – and I could love him no more if he were.'

'I know; he loves you too,' Ellen said absently, certain from her brother's edgy demeanour that he was lying about something, but not sure what.

Robert sighed. 'He did once, but not any more, I think. That day, when he came to see me after his imprisonment, he said the experience had given him too much time for reflection. He wanted to know about his mother. I suppose I should have seen it coming. What could I say? Naturally I had to confess that I was not his father after all.'

Trying to make sense of it, Ellen's gaze was drawn to Ruth's portrait. 'I cannot help but think it would have been kinder for everyone if you had left Alexander where he was – you say he was well cared for. Surely you could have met your kinship obligation simply by financing his upbringing?'

As she was speaking, something her brother had said nagged at the corner of her mind. Suddenly it came into focus and she looked across at him. 'What do you mean, it suited your purpose?'

For a moment Ellen thought her brother was not going to reply. She noticed his hands were shaking and seeing the direction of her gaze he had laced his fingers to still them. She was about to repeat the question when a log shifted in the grate sending a shower of sparks into the hearth. Yelping, the hounds leapt under the table, the smell of singed fur pervading the room.

Abruptly Robert spoke, hugging his chest and thrusting his hands into his armpits. 'I was sworn to conceal Alexander's identity and asked to protect him. The practical solution was to raise him as my own. I thought if he believed he was my son it would foster the gossip. I could scarcely openly acknowledge his paternity, but people love a scandal. I knew if I said nothing they would think Alexander was my by-blow and not question who he is.' He held up his hand as Ellen opened her mouth to speak. 'And before you ask, sister, I cannot tell you that – or anything else. I have already said far more than I should. Please, no more questions, I beg you.'

Astounded, Ellen was momentarily silenced. She clicked her fingers at Turk as he sidled out from under the table to lean against her knees, followed warily by Chaser. Their hangdog expressions would ordinarily have made her laugh, but she was too distressed. 'I trust you have told Alexander?'

'No, I have not, nor do I intend to.'

It had been a rhetorical question and Ellen gasped in disbelief. 'You surely cannot mean to keep him in ignorance,' she exclaimed. 'It is unsupportable!'

'Yes, it is, but nonetheless that is my decision.' Robert's gaze slid away as Ellen, seething with agitation, jumped up from the settle.

'Why? And why did Alexander need your protection? Is he tainted in some way? What dreadful secret are you hiding – and for whom? Who sired him, Robert?'

'I assure you he is not tainted – not in any way- and no dishonour attaches to his sire,' Robert said quietly, looking down at his feet.

'No? Then what is his name? You must tell Alexander that at least. I cannot let you do this to him, it isn't fair.'

He looked up at that, distressed, his face ashen. 'Fair or not, it is too dangerous for him to know. If they find out Alexander is alive, they will kill him. That is why I lied to him and even were I not held to an oath of secrecy I would not tell him, and nor will I tell you.'

Her hand to her mouth, Ellen cried out. 'Who? Who will kill him?'

Robert shook his head and plucked at his knees with trembling fingers. 'Please, Ellen, no more,' he begged hoarsely. 'It is a burden I must carry alone.' He gave a racking sob and the tears long held in check spilled down his haggard cheeks.

'Oh my dear,' Ellen rushed across the room to him, wincing as she caught her hip on the corner of the table; later she would probably not recall how she had come by the bruise. Fear for Alexander choked her in a wave of nausea. Forcing it down she held Robert to her, whispering endearments until his shuddering subsided, her mind a turmoil of thoughts she could not voice: oh my brother, what in God's name have you got yourself into, and what are we to do about Alexander?

Looking over Robert's shoulder at the rain splattering on the window Ellen noticed Todd had stopped sweeping. He was standing hands on hips, staring towards the drive. Suddenly he dropped his broom and broke into a run. Moments later there was an urgent knocking on the library door.

The hounds jumped up barking. Moving away from Ellen's arms Robert stood, cleared his throat and wiped his hands across his face. 'Down,' he commanded the hounds, and in the same breath called, 'Enter.'

It was the Earl of Bath's steward, Richard Pollard, looking ill at ease, his cloak wet, boots muddied. 'Forgive this intrusion, My Lord, but I fear I am the bearer of bad tidings.' He nodded to Ellen, dislodging a shower of raindrops from the brim of his hat. 'My Lady.'

'Come in, Pollard.' Robert gestured to the fire. 'Don't stand in the doorway, man. Come and get warm. What is it? Has something happed to Sir Ralph Hopton?'

'No, My Lord – that is, I do not know. My news concerns Lord Bath. He returned unexpectedly from Stow last evening and has been arrested by a troop of rebel soldiers. They held him in Barnstaple overnight. I very much regret to inform you they have also captured Master Tawford.'

Ellen gasped, swayed, reaching out a hand to her brother. Robert put his arm about her, his face ashen. 'Where in Barnstaple?'

Pollard grimaced. 'The gaol, My Lord, but I fear they have already left. They are under orders to take both men to the Earl of Pembroke, in London. I was not there when they came to Tawstock. The scullery maid managed to escape their foul attentions and came to alert me. I rode immediately to Barnstaple to plead with George Peard, but there was nothing he could do. It appears their Captain is acting for the Earl of Bedford, though I feel sure it was not Lord Bedford's orders to ransack Tawstock. It is fortunate that Lord Bath had moved most things of value to Stow. The rebel officer – name of Dewett – had expected to find weapons, plate and money, but was disappointed. He held me for questioning, but I was unable to enlighten him.' Pollard's expression was wry. 'Dewett must have been persuaded I was of no account, for he let me go this morning. The Countess asked me to come straight here with the news and to ask if she may borrow a team of six. She intends to journey to London straight away, but the soldiers have emptied the stables of horses.'

'Poor Rachel,' Ellen murmured. 'I trust her Ladyship was not hurt?'

'No, Lady Ellen, the Countess and her ladies are naturally distressed, but nobody was hurt apart from the stable-boy, Kit, whom they knocked unconscious and left for dead. He is young and resilient and will soon recover, pray God.'

Agitated, Ellen looked at her brother. 'I must go to her.'

'Of course you must. I will arrange an escort.' Robert turned back to the steward. 'Can you tell me if Master Tawford was badly hurt?'

'No, My Lord, I was not permitted to see either him or Lord Bath.'

'Did you hear anything of a young man by the name of Richard or Dickon Chichester?' Ellen asked suddenly. 'He may have been with my nephew.' She said it without thinking.

That he was not her nephew at all seemed hardly important just now.

'No, Lady Ellen, I heard of nobody by that name. I believe the rebels had only the two prisoners.'

'Praise God,' Ellen breathed. 'Dickon must have returned to his family. He at least is safe. Oh Robert, what are we to do?'

'Hush, little sister.' Robert took her hands to still them. 'I will ride for London immediately and petition for Alexander's release.' He turned back to the steward. 'At what time did they leave?'

'I understand it was a little after first light, My Lord. If I may, I will accompany Lady Ellen to Tawstock. I must return and attend to arrangements for her Ladyship's departure.'

Robert nodded. 'Of course, and thank you for bringing us this grave news so soon, I am obliged. Take your pick of the horses and whatever men you need.'

'Thank you, I am only sorry I am the bearer of such ill tidings.' With a slight bow, the steward left the room.

Ellen turned anxiously to her brother, her face chalk white.

'Will a petition help?'

'I am not without influence, Ellen,' Robert said, gently. 'I will go to Lord Pembroke. He is not an unreasonable man. You know I will not rest until I have secured Alexander's release. As for Lord Bath, the Countess will plead his case infinitely better than can I. They won't hold him for long, I am sure.'

'I expect you are right.' Ellen twisted her hands, her mind in a whirl. 'You will leave soon?'

'Within the hour and I will ride post. If you want to reach me, I shall be at my lodgings. Don't worry, dear heart, Pembroke will listen to reason, I am certain of it. I will send news as soon as I have any.'

Ellen reached to kiss her brother's cheek knowing he lied for her sake. There was every reason to believe Alexander would not cheat the hangman this time. She could not bear the thought of returning to the Barton, inactive, waiting for news. Patience was not one of her virtues. There must be something she could do. A worm of an idea crept into her mind. A petition could easily fail, but there might be another way. Money could sometimes open locked doors if you knew whose hands to put it in. She would ask for Cobb's help. He had friends in London among the pickpockets and cutpurses who inhabited the alehouses and stews along the waterfront. They might know who could be bribed. It was a slim chance, but it was better than doing nothing. She said none of this to Robert.

'God keep you safe, brother.'

'And you, sweetheart.' He hugged her briefly, snapped his fingers and strode from the room, Turk and Chaser at his heels.

Shortly afterwards, Ellen gathered her people around her in the great hall and broke the news. There was a buzz of concern: they all liked Master Tawford. Taking Ned aside she asked him to take charge of the proceedings. Now the rebels had gone it was safe for them to return to the Barton. Tweed and her foal could stay at Marley Court for now, but the rest of the horses should be returned. Ned listened gravely to her instructions.

'Leave it to me, m'lady. You don't need to be worritin 'bout us. You'll be seein' bout the Maister. I'll see to they. You bring him home safe. Uz'll all pray for 'ee.'

For Ned it was quite a speech and Ellen was taken aback. 'Thank you, Ned.' She turned away, hesitated, turned back. 'If I were to write a message to Cobb, could you send off a bird for me?'

'I reckon as 'ow I could, though 'tis not a safe way of messaging, thou dost knaw, m'lady? Mister Gubb do zay they birds can't be relied on.'

'I know that, Ned.' She smiled. 'But it's worth a try. Please wait, I'll be back directly.'

Hurrying to the library, she wrote a brief note in cipher.

Carefully initialling the bottom, she rolled it tightly and returned to Ned, who was in the courtyard overseeing the loading of the women and children into the wain.

He took it gingerly in his soiled hand. 'I'll see to it for ee, m'lady.'

Robert, with only two men to guard him, had already gone when Ellen rode out of Marley Court with Richard Pollard, a groom, six carriage horses and four of her brother's men to escort her. The hounds, leashed temporarily in the stable-yard, were still giving vent to their misery as she left.

On her way to Tawstock, Ellen was rehearsing in her mind what she meant to do. If Rachel asked for her company to London she could hardly refuse, but having decided to enlist Cobb's help, she wanted to ride to the gypsy's encampment straight away, impatient to put her plan into action. Hoping fervently that Rachel would have no need of her, Ellen thought it through. As a lone woman she would attract attention, but not if she were dressed as a boy. She had often donned Alexander's clothes in the past once she had discovered the freedom it gave her. At first he had laughed at her impropriety, but had quickly made sure she knew how to defend herself. She could use a dagger and shoot a pistol as well as any man, and he had also taught her a number of tricks, among other things, how to throw an unsuspecting man to the ground, or jab her fingers into an attacker's eyes to blind him while she got away. She smiled, remembering how it had amused Alexander to teach his aunt – Lady Seymour, no less – the tricks of a street fighter! Except she was not his aunt, as he had known for a full six months. Why had he not told her – and would she ever be able to think of him as anything but her nephew?

Ellen arrived at Tawstock to find Rachel standing in the courtyard directing operations amidst a flurry of people and packing cases. Outwardly she seemed calm; this exodus from one house to the other was commonplace for the Countess since she and her husband divided their lives between Tawstock Court and their residence in Lincolns Inn Fields, but Ellen knew from Rachel's uncharacteristic irritability with the servants that her calmness masked a fever of anxiety. Thanking Ellen for her concern, she gratefully refused her company to London; there was no need, she said. She would have Voysin with her, and her niece too, at least for part of the way – she was taking her home since they must pass through Oxfordshire.

Hiding her relief and feeling more hindrance than help, Ellen took her leave. She knew Rachel would do everything in her power to obtain Alexander's release, but held out little hope that the Countess would be successful. There could be only one outcome for a captured Royalist spy. He would be interrogated and put to death in a way that Ellen could not – would not – allow herself to think about. As she rode out of Tawstock, the Baths' emblazoned carriage was being pulled from the coach house and harnessed to the borrowed team of six.

Ellen hastened home under the watchful eye of Robert's guards. It was early afternoon. Where was the rebel troop now? Had they gone by way of Exeter? She dreaded to think what state Alexander would be in. How had he been captured? What had caused him to leave the Barton? Had he been on his way to Stow and in his drugged state ridden straight into the rebel troop? She would never have administered laudanum had she known his plans. Why, oh why had he not taken her into his confidence? Because he knew she would try to stop him? Probably! All his life, it seemed, she had been making excuses for him, rescuing him from the consequences of his wild behaviour, and God help her – here they were all grown up and she was *still* doing it! Ellen gave herself a mental shake; there was nothing to be gained by dwelling on it.

As soon as she arrived home she sent her brother's men back to Marley Court and went in search of Ned. He was in the stable yard.

'The bird's gone off to Cobb, m'lady and us be all settled and tidy like.' He handed her down from her mare.

'Thank you, Ned – has Mister Gubb returned?'

'No m'lady, he's sent word he's bin delayed over to Hartland, but he's bought three Dorset rams and should be back with them vor dark.'

'Good.' Ellen nodded. Of course, she had forgotten. Robin had said last week he needed some new blood in the flock and was going to buy some rams. She had wondered at the time if it was wise to buy them now; the tup was over for February's lambing and fodder was always scarce in the winter months. On the other hand, for that reason they could be bought more cheaply and Robin usually knew what he was doing, so she had not interfered. 'I will be going out later, Ned, and I may be away for a few days. I will write a note for Mister Gubb.' Ellen ran her hand down her mare's shoulder. 'She seems a bit lame in her right fore. I think the shoe may be loose. Could you look at it for me? I'll take the bay gelding.'

'Aye, m'lady, I'll get'un ready for ee. Be you gwain back to Marley Court? Will ee take Todd?'

'No, I won't need him.' She avoided the question, but Ned persisted.

'Thee disn want to be abroad by yourzel', m'lady.' He looked at her curiously. It was unusual for Ellen to leave the Barton for any length of time. 'Be you gwain after the Maister? He'll be mad if he knaws I let ee go wi'out a man to keep ee safe.'

Ellen did not to enlighten him; the fewer who knew where she was bound, the better. She smiled. 'Don't worry, Ned. I will not be on my own for long and he knows me too well to hold you responsible.'

She went in search of Wilmot who was in the kitchen with Rose and Lucy, the scullery maid who came in each day from the village. They each bobbed a curtsey as Ellen hurried in, the smell of baking making her mouth water. It had been some while since she had eaten. No time to think about that now. She took Wilmot to one side, explained she was going away for a while, rattled off a list of things that needed seeing to and handed over the keys that always dangled from her belt. Before the cook had a chance to ask the questions that brimmed avidly in her eyes, Ellen hurried to the parlour to write a brief note for Robin. She scribbled various items of news about the Michaelmas rents and heriots for collection, included brief details about Alexander's capture and that she could be reached through Cobb, but only if absolutely necessary and he was to keep this to himself. Finally, she instructed him to increase Wilmot's wages commensurate with her added responsibilities. Sealing it, she propped it on the side-table in the hall and ran upstairs to Alexander's chamber. They were of similar build and most of his garments would fit her; his boots were on the large side, but they would serve.

She rummaged through the press, selected the plainest, oldest and warmest clothes and took them back to her room to change, fumbling with the unfamiliar points and laces in her haste. She found a battered old hat, realising as she did so that she would have to cut her hair. She found her sewing shears, twisted her long hair into a rope, pulled it forward over her shoulder and with only a moment's hesitation, chopped it roughly to the nape of her neck. As the shining, coppery tresses slithered to the floor Ellen felt a pang of regret, but upbraided herself smartly. It would soon grow again. Scooping the hair from the floor, she shoved it into a drawer. From her cabinet she retrieved a pistol, powder cartridges, spanner and shot, and her dagger. Alexander had given it to her some years ago, a pretty thing in a shagreen case, she had not yet had occasion to use it. Ellen ran her thumb across the blade, wincing as the blood welled. It was still honed razor sharp. She tucked it into her belt together with a priming iron. Grabbing her saddlebag, she pushed in a purse of silver shillings, five gold sovereigns and some small change, added one or two things she might find useful, including stool paper, bandages and salve, needle and thread, a quantity of lint, two pairs of woollen stockings – there was nothing worse than having wet feet – a clean shirt, a change of undergarments. Fortunately, she had just finished her flux. As an afterthought she added a stick of charcoal and some writing paper. Finally, she pulled on a pair of gloves and for Wilmot's benefit, tucked the hat and pistol under her arm and covered herself in her long, hooded cloak.

Ned was on the other side of the yard, the mare's leg held firmly between his knees. The horse was nuzzling his backside and she could hear him grumbling as he prised off the loose shoe. He had saddled and bridled the bay gelding and left it tethered by the mounting block. Ellen checked the leathers and swiftly mounted before he could come to assist her, raised her hand to him and set off up the track. She usually rode astride; it would cause no comment and his eyes were not good enough to see what she was wearing. Once out of sight, she shrugged off her cloak, rolled it up, secured it behind her saddle and plonked the hat, now squashed as well as battered, on her head. Her pistol she pushed into the calfskin holster at her saddlebow. With a quick glance behind, she turned her face towards Exmoor and set off across country.

9

When Dickon came to, he was wrapped in warm blankets and lying on Tawford's truckle bed in the side chapel. He struggled to get up.

James was sitting on the end of the bed, his chubby face serious for once, his eyes showing his concern. 'You gave us a scare, Coz. As well I was watching the bridge.'

'The horses…?'

'They've been looked after, don't worry.' James helped Dickon to sit up. 'Do you feel any better? Well enough to talk? We didn't expect to see you back here so soon. Can you tell us what has happened?'

'Give him a minute, James.' Adam Hartley came into the room. 'Here, try this.' He held out a cup of steaming broth.

Dickon took it gratefully. It scalded his tongue but tasted like nectar. 'What day is it?'

'Monday.' Hartley smiled.

Monday. Only Monday. Everything came back to him in a rush. 'Tawford's been captured,' he gasped. 'He needs help. They are taking him to London. They have taken Lord Bath too. He – Tawford – is in a bad way. They had him tied to a horse, his head was bleeding, they mean to kill him, he might already be dead.' The words spilled out of him.

'Steady, lad, take a few deep breaths,' Hartley said, kindly. 'Now, slowly, who has taken him?'

'I don't know – rebel soldiers – about two dozen of them. They took him to Tawstock. I was at Tawford Barton asleep. We went there once we knew that Sir Ralph Hopton was safe across the river, but Tawford must have gone back to destroy the bridge. He didn't tell me. I wish he had. I could have helped him.' Dickon pulled a glum face.

James nodded sympathetically. 'You'll get used to that, Dickon. He always keeps his cards close to his chest. He knew they were coming for Lord Bath. He'd already sent a message to Fane telling him which way to send them. He must've guessed Bedford would take the opportunity to look for Hopton at the same time. He will have blown the bridge to delay them.'

Hartley studied the boy's face. 'Tell me, Dickon, if you were asleep at the Barton how did you come to find out what happened?'

Dickon flushed to the roots of his hair. 'Tawford said I couldn't stay with him if my father objected and I knew he would, so —' He glanced up as James snorted.

'You were doing another moonlight flit, were you cousin?'

Dickon blushed. 'Yes. I'd planned to come back here before Papa learned I was with Tawford. I crept out while everyone was still abed, borrowed a horse and got away without anyone seeing. It was only by chance that I saw the rebels had got Tawford. I followed them to Tawstock. There was no resistance – Lord Bath had no men at arms – they just walked in. I watched them plundering the house. They had the Earl at gunpoint – Tawford too – so I think he must have been alive still, but their captain told his men they could do what they wanted, as long they left enough life in him to feel the hooks when he's quartered.' Dickon sobbed. 'You've got to help him.'

'When was this, Dickon?' Hartley spoke with studied calm.

'Last night. It was last night. I would guess from the moon around midnight, but I couldn't be sure.'

James started. 'Good God, man! You have ridden here without stopping? That's the third time you've made the journey in as many days. I wouldn't want to try that myself.

No wonder you passed out.'

Dickon grinned. 'They're good horses,' he said weakly.

'Well of course they are, they're mine, though you've damned near killed them.' His cousin laughed ruefully.

Hartley looked up as a short, nimble man entered the room. 'Ah, good, you're back.'

The man looked down at Dickon and gave a slow smile. It deepened the many lines about his eyes and mouth. 'Hello, what's happened to you? I'm Hugh Lyddon.' His eyes twinkled as he held out his hand.

'Richard Chichester, your servant, Sir.' Dickon shook the proffered hand. He remembered there were others too whom he'd not yet met. Lyddon must be one of the men who had gone to rescue Tawford from Barrington Court – barely three days ago – it seemed impossible.

'What news?' Lyddon turned to Hartley.

'Tawford has been taken by the rebel troop who went to arrest the Earl of Bath.'

'Dewett?'

'I assume so, yes.' Hartley turned to Dickon. 'He was the Roundhead who questioned Tawford at Barrington. He will be disinclined to be kind.' His smile was without humour.

'I thought our illustrious leader had a plan to get Lord Bath away,' James said.

Lyddon nodded. 'He did. Cobb was to take a warning. He must have failed. Dewett will take them to London. The Gatehouse almost certainly.' He frowned. 'When did they set off?'

'They held them overnight in Barnstaple.' Hartley turned to Dickon for confirmation.

Dickon nodded. 'That's what their captain said. They were to leave at first light.'

'So they'll be well on the way.' James scratched his nose. 'Likely approaching Exeter by now.

'Right.' Hartley turned on his heel. 'Gather in the tower room. We need a plan. I'll fetch the others. Acland and Basset have gone to Hinton St George, but they should be back by noon.'

Dickon scanned the room. 'Where are my clothes?'

Hartley looked down at the boy's flushed face 'Not you, Dickon.' He felt for his pulse. 'You're exhausted. I don't want to have to cup you. Stay there for a while, eh?' He walked to the door, turning back as Dickon protested. 'Rest assured, lad, we'll let you know what we plan to do.'

James got up to follow. He winked at Dickon. 'They're hanging in the linhay to dry,' he whispered. 'But I do believe Tawford keeps his spares in there.' He gestured to the chest. 'Or did you want me to fetch your beautiful doublet?' He grinned.

Dickon pulled a face at him. The relief at handing over responsibility for Tawford made him feel light-headed. As soon as he was alone he got up from the bed. He was not going to be treated like a child, not after what he'd been through. He looked in the chest. A pile of clothes lay neatly folded in the bottom. Tawford was taller, but not enough to matter. It took him only moments to find what he needed.

Eight men were crowded round the table in the tower room. He knew most of them from the other night: Francis Sydenham was the tallest of the group; everything about him was long and fine, from his sandy hair to his narrow, pointed chin. Will Mohun, by comparison, was shorter and chubby with a shock of carroty hair and china-blue eyes, his brow peppered with freckles. He was the only one of the group to wear an unshaped beard. It was an unruly fiery bush of which he was inordinately proud. Rob Pollard too was of stocky build, but fair. His eyes were set close together and he spoke with slight stammer. Jonathan Southcott, like Lyddon, was short, but his chest bulged with muscle. His hair was prematurely grey. It looked odd against his youthful, acquisitive face.

Hartley looked up as Dickon joined them. He shook his head with mock gravity then smiled. 'I believe you know everyone here except our gunner, Hal Gifford? He may look like a Spanish pirate, but I assure you he's not, though he is part French – but we don't hold that against him.' Hartley's eyes twinkled. 'And what he doesn't know about guns is really not worth knowing.' He spoke to the man beside him who did indeed look like a buccaneer; his hair was a mass of black curls and his skin the colour of tobacco. His lips beneath the thin moustache were full and dark and his narrow pointed beard turned up at the tip. He wore an earring in one ear, which twinkled as he moved his head. 'Hal, this is Dickon Chichester. He has risked life and limb to bring us this news. I think we can take it he's one of us now.'

'Welcome. That was well done.' Gifford nodded to Dickon, whose heart swelled.

Hartley looked round at them. 'However much we may want to, we can't all go riding like demons to the rescue.'

'It's certainly getting to be something of a habit,' Lyddon observed dryly.

'Can't somebody tie his legs together?' Pollard grumbled. The others chuckled.

Their levity surprised Dickon. It was as if nobody was taking it seriously. He opened his mouth to voice his concern, but Lyddon caught his eye.

'Don't mind us, Dickon, despite appearances to the contrary, we are mindful of the urgency.'

Hartley leaned a hand on the table, waiting until he had their undivided attention. None questioned his authority as he now took control of the meeting.

'We have to get the arms out as soon as possible and go to the aid of Prince Rupert. Those are our orders and with reason. Essex is marching to confront the King. If it comes to a battle – and there is every reason to believe that it will – the army will be in desperate need of them.' He paused, his expression grim. 'Tawford's standing orders are that we should never allow sentiment to get in the way of duty. He would not expect – nor would he approve of – a rescue attempt. But I for one have no wish to leave him in rebel hands. Who is with me?'

There was a chorus of assent. 'Oh Lord.' Southcott pulled a face. 'I feel another tongue lashing coming our way.'

This time Dickon joined in the laughter.

'Right.' Hartley nodded. 'I think we can spare four of us to go to his aid and for obvious reasons I had better be one.' He addressed Dickon. 'Dewett had about twenty men, you said?'

Dickon nodded. 'Yes.'

'So four won't be enough.' Hartley turned to Mohun. 'Do you remember if Lord Poulett left some men at Hinton?'

'Most of them went with the Marquis of Hertford to Wales, but he'll have left a few to guard the arsenal, maybe a dozen or so. Bassett and Acland will be able to confirm how many if they get back in time.'

'We'll call in on our way past and hope Lady Poulett will spare us some at least. Bassett and Acland will have cleared the arsenal so she'll not need much of a guard. Since she's your cousin, Mohun, you'd better be one of the four.'

Mohun's face lit up. He rubbed his hands together. 'As long as she'll spare us six; ten of us should be more than a match for twenty of them.'

'Who will ride with us?' Hartley looked round at the tense, eager faces. 'No Dickon, not you – I most certainly don't doubt your courage, but with the best will in the world, you would be a liability just now.' Thoughtfully he looked at Lyddon. 'Cobb's men know you better than the rest of us, Hugh, and we could use their ingenuity.'

'I'll get a message off soonest.' Lyddon nodded.

'You can't,' Southcott said. 'We have none of Cobb's birds left. The last one went off two weeks ago.'

'Godamme!' James swore.

'I wonder what's befallen Cobb,' Mohun said thoughtfully. 'Something must be wrong or he'd have got Tawford's warning to Lord Bath.'

'For all we know, he did,' Gifford said. 'His Lordship may not have heeded it. He had three hundred men at Tawstock, he may have decided to stand and fight.'

'True.' James nodded.

'Not true,' Dickon said. 'I told you – there was no resistance at all. The place was virtually deserted. There were certainly no men at arms.'

'There's no point in speculating,' Hartley said. 'Will you come with us, Hugh? Who will be the fourth?'

'Let me.' Francis Sydenham smiled. 'I'd like to try my sword on Dewett's neck.'

'You'll blunt it, man,' James grinned.

'Snap it, more like,' Pollard teased. 'He's had it on the stone every day for a week – it's thin as paper.'

'What would you know,' Sydenham snorted. 'You wouldn't recognise a good blade if it cut you.'

Hartley held his hand up to stem the jeers. 'Right then, saddle up. Speed is of the essence. The rest of you carry on with the job in hand. Remember, the *Gabriel* is to sail on Friday evening's tide, so we don't have much time.' He turned to Jonathon Southcott. 'Will you go with her? The Welsh miners are mustering for the King so you should have plenty of help getting the arms to Shrewsbury.'

Southcott nodded. 'Will the army still be there?'

'The King was preparing to march this week. I doubt they'll have gone far by the time you get there.' Hartley looked at Gifford and Pollard. 'Our orders are to clear out of here by the end of the week and go to Prince Rupert. If you've gone when we get back, the others will catch up with you. We do not know the extent of Tawford's injuries, but if we succeed in getting him back here alive I will stay with him until he's fit enough to ride.' He looked around at each of the men in turn. 'That's the plan, then. We're all agreed? Does anyone have any alternative suggestions?' He waited a moment. Nobody did.

Mohun grinned. 'What shall we do about Lord Bath?'

'Put him on a heavy horse and send him back to his wife,' Hartley retorted. 'Best get to it then.' He pushed back from the table. 'Dickon, go and rest, and that's an order. Tomorrow, when you are recovered you must think about what you mean to do. It is no small thing to go against the wishes of your father and there is no guarantee that any of us will come out of this war alive. Think carefully; you may never see him or your family again. If you are still sure you want to join us, you will ride with the others to Prince Rupert. Before you do so, I will have to ask you to swear a sacred oath, as we all have done, binding you in loyalty and secrecy to Tawford and St Michael's.'

Dickon nodded. 'Yes, Sir. I understand, but I will not change my mind. I will gladly take the oath.'

Hartley smiled down at him. 'I know you will, but it had to be said.' As the men got up to go, he put his hand on James Chichester's shoulder to stay him. 'I will hold you responsible for ensuring your cousin is familiar with our ways, James. Perhaps you could also talk him through the ciphers and the pigeon codes? Pollard will see he has all the equipment he needs. Right, Dickon, back to bed!'

Obediently, Dickon made his way to the chapel. He was asleep before the four men had ridden away from St Michael's.

On the road just outside Hinton St George, Hartley, Lyddon, Mohun and Sydenham met up with Kit Bassett and John Acland, on their way to St Michael's with a tumbrel of steaming muck. Both men were clothed in soiled smocks, woollen caps and baggy britches and hoping the ripe stench would afford them so wide a berth that nobody would notice the drayhorse was working harder than was merited by the load. Acland, walking beside it, his cheerful face even more florid than usual, was using his cap to swat at a cloud of dung flies. Basset, balanced with a foot on each shaft and looking thoroughly miserable, was singing a mournful ballad at the top of his lungs and flicking the reins at the straining horse.

After a quick exchange of ribald comments, Hartley, his hand over his nose, brought the two men up to date. It transpired they had just left Lord Poulett's house. In the bottom of the stinking tumbrel were half a dozen kegs of powder, eighty muskets and two small field guns. With her husband's arsenal now off her hands, a relieved Lady Poulett had decided to take the children to stay with relatives in Hampshire and had already left, taking all her guards with her. There would be no help from that quarter.

It took all of Hartley's powers of persuasion to prevent Acland and Bassett from unhitching the horse, abandoning the cart and joining the rescue expedition, but eventually they agreed and grim-faced, took their leave.

When they had gone, Hartley moved off the road and crossed a stubble field to a narrow belt of trees, beckoning the others to him. 'Without Poulett's men we are done for, unless we can think of some trickery to shorten the odds. My guess is the rebels will be travelling slowly, especially if they are carrying plunder, but in any event, I think the presence of Lord Bath will slow them down. They can't treat his Lordship like a common felon no matter how much they may want to. He has too many friends in high places for Dewett to risk harming him.'

Lyddon nodded. 'If they left Barnstaple at first light, they may stop in Exeter to change horses and let the great man rest, which will give us more time.'

'More time for what?' Mohun growled.

'To dance a jig, what do you think, jingle brains.' Lyddon clicked his fingers at Mohun. 'Time to work out how we can extricate Tawford without getting ourselves killed, numbskull.' He stood up in the stirrups to scan the road, saw a lone horseman moving along it at a steady pace. The man did not look in their direction. The sky was overcast, wind buffeting the trees depositing eddies of leaves at their horses' feet. Lyddon sat back in the saddle. 'We should not tarry here. Enemy patrols use this road.'

'If you say so,' Mohun grunted, turning up his collar.

'We need to work out what we are going to do,' Hartley said.

'I agree with you, Hugh, the rebels will likely change horses at Exeter, but they'll be jumpy. Lord Bath is well respected thereabouts. Dewett won't want to leave it to chance to find a suitable inn, nor risk camping in the open. I think he will make for the garrison in Yeovil for the night.'

'Even with fresh horses that's a fair ride,' Lyddon said. 'They won't get there in daylight. We could lie in wait and catch them after dark, create a diversion and snatch Tawford in the confusion.'

'It's too risky,' Hartley said. 'Besides, we don't know Tawford's state of health. Suppose he can't ride? Snatching him may be enough to finish him off.'

'Standing here talking about it is getting us nowhere,' Sydenham grumbled. 'Whatever we do, it needs to be quick. Are we to head for Yeovil or what?' He flicked the reins impatiently, causing his horse to dance forward. It cannoned into Lyddon's mount, which tossed its head, laid back its ears and squealed.

Lyddon let out a curse. 'For God's sake, Francis, keep that animal under control! I imagine Dewett knows who Tawford is by now. Peard will have told him.'

Mohun let out an exasperated oath, turning his horse back to the road. 'Then he won't be alive for long, if indeed he still is. I agree with Sydenham. What are we waiting for? I'm for riding to meet the bastards, and fast.'

'And do what?' Lyddon put out a hand to stay him. 'Four of us can't take on twenty men in a straight fight.'

'We could if we can work out a way of splitting the troop,' Sydenham said. 'We can manage a dozen Roundheads between us, can't we?' With a wolfish grin he fingered his sword.

Hartley looked thoughtfully at Mohun. 'I think you're wrong, Will, I think it more likely Tawford's identity will save him. He is quite a prize for Dewett. I fancy the bastard will want to get him to London alive, but in any event, we can't act until we are sure what road the rebels are using and how fast they are travelling. And as I said, we need to know the extent of Tawford's injuries,' he grimaced. 'To put it bluntly, there is no point in risking our lives for a dead man.'

There was a grim silence as the four men looked at each other in despair. Hartley lifted his hat, repositioned it and pulled the brim low over his brow. 'I propose we get a message to Cobb, ask him to track the rebels from Barnstaple, find out where they are, get round them and bring us news. At least we'll know what we're dealing with. Are there any of Cobb's people round here will take a message for us, Hugh?'

'There's a man at Honiton, used to work with Cobb, landlord of the "Angel" now – it's on the London road. We can hole up there while we wait.'

'God's blood!' Mohun exclaimed, pulling at his fiery beard. 'There's no time for that. Can't one of us find out where the godammed rebels are? Let me go.'

'No, Will. I don't think it wise to split up, we're too few as it is,' Hartley said.

Mohun scowled. 'I say we look right now for a likely spot to ambush the bastards. Suppose Dewett hasn't stopped at Exeter? If we don't act soon there's every chance he'll slip by us and be safe in Yeovil while we're still sitting on our arses in Honiton waiting for Cobb.'

Lyddon glared at Mohun. 'Dammit, Will! Do you think we don't know that? But what choice do we have? We can't be in two places at once. We can't be sure Dewett still intends taking his prisoners to London. He may have changed his mind if he's learned who Tawford is, decided to take him straight to the Earl of Bedford. In which case he won't be on the London road at all, he'll have gone by Tiverton to pick up the Bristol road and head north. Cobb can find out more easily than we can, Will.' Lyddon slammed his fist to his thigh, his face drawn with anxiety. 'If we do as you suggest, we could be sitting like clods by the side of the London road till kingdom come.'

'Calm down, Hugh,' Hartley said. 'I grant what you suggest is possible, but I think it unlikely. Tawford is a bonus for

Dewett, his primary target was the Earl of Bath, remember, and Pym's Committee want his lordship in London. I take your point though, we need to be sure.' He turned to Mohun. 'Come on, Will. I know what's driving you, but it's the same for all of us. Quarrelling amongst ourselves is not going to help Tawford. I think we should ride fast to Honiton, get a message off to Cobb and take it from there. And if we meet the rebels on the way, so be it, we'll cross that bridge when we come to it.'

'Bridge!' Lyddon and Sydenham exclaimed in unison.

Hartley's eyes twinkled. 'Quite so – and a keg or two of powder with a dash of trickery thrown in – we can set about that while we wait for Cobb. What say you, Will?'

Mohun looked back at him and then at the other two. Slowly his scowl was replaced by a grin. 'You win, hell and the devil confound you!'

Inwardly sighing with relief, Hartley gathered his reins and led the way back to the road.

Alexander tasted blood on his tongue. He studied the blurred ground. He seemed to be seeing it from an unusual angle and it appeared to be moving. It came to him only slowly that he was looking at it upside down and that he no longer felt cold. In fact, he could not feel his limbs at all. He wondered idly if his head had been struck from his body and was hanging suspended from a saddlebow. The thought made him want to laugh. Was it possible to laugh without a body? The urge died in his throat. He had been wrong. He could feel his limbs after all. He would rather not. He was just getting round to thinking that Captain Dewett was not so careless after all, when mercifully, he slipped back into unconsciousness.

Riding at the head of the column, Dewett was imagining the approbation he would receive from the Earl of Pembroke. He had long since torn Colonel Strode's damning letter to shreds and dropped the pieces in the mud. Even if Sir Ralph Hopton had got away, Lord Bath had been arrested as ordered, and what is more, he had captured an important enemy spy. Lord Pembroke would surely reward him with a commission. Dewett grinned happily. It had been sheer chance he had glanced back at the burned out bridge and caught a movement by the riverbank. Acting purely on instinct, he had walked purposefully away from the river as though going after his men, waited a moment, doubled back and worked his way silently through the trees. Finding the tethered horse he had lain in wait. Moments later, the shadowed figure had stumbled past him almost close enough to touch. It had been simple to bring the man down and sling him across his horse. Dewett had led the animal back to the road and in a patch of bright moonlight, pulled his captive's head up by the hair to look at his face. For a moment Dewett had not been able to believe his eyes. This man was slim, his colouring fair, but the scar and bruising were unmistakeable, as were the vestiges of blacking in the hair. Dewett had shouted his elation, viciously letting go of the prisoner's head and fastidiously wiping the blood from his hands onto the man's wet clothing.

Once reunited with his men and the horses, arresting the Earl of Bath had been child's play. Dewett's surprise at finding Tawstock undefended had turned to disappointment when Lord Bath's cache of arms could not be found. Despite threatening the Earl and his Countess at pistol point, neither would say where it was hid. After a fruitless search, Dewett assumed the Earl's men at arms had cleared out the arsenal and gone to join Hopton, were doubtless in Cornwall by now. Still elated, drunk on power, Dewett had been tempted to teach the Countess a lesson, imperious bitch. He had casually fingered his groin, watched her flinch, seen the fear and contempt in her eyes. It had inflamed his lust almost beyond the point of control, but common sense had prevailed. Lady Bath had important relatives, not least the Earl of Bedford. Dewett had contented himself by allowing his men free rein to plunder – not that there had been much of value easily transportable – but it had kept them happy. The horses they had taken were very fine and would fetch a high price in London. One, a mettlesome grey, he quite fancied keeping for himself.

When they had arrived in Barnstaple he had sought out George Peard and made arrangements for what was left of the night. The Earl of Bath, after his first angry protestations, had kept silent. The other prisoner had not regained consciousness, but Peard had identified him: Alexander Dynam of Tawford, reputedly the estranged, illegitimate son of Lord Robert Dynam, Viscount Westley, a local dignitary who had yet to show his colours, but was acquainted with the Earl of Pembroke. According to Peard, Tawford was a bad lot, he had not only plotted with the French Queen to turn the army's guns on Parliament, he had also killed his own half-brother, Viscount Westley's heir, though on either count there was insufficient evidence to hang him. Dewett was not surprised; the man was cunning as a fox, got on some Irish peasant no doubt and very likely a Papist too. Well, thanks to James Dewett, his days were numbered now!

Before leaving Barnstaple that morning, Dewett had detailed four men to find sumpters to carry the plunder. They were to bring it, along with the horses from Lord Bath's stables, and follow the column at their own pace. Four men were hardly enough to protect such an inviting pack train, Dewett reflected, but he dared not spare more. Placing the prisoners under close guard in the centre of the column, he had mounted up and left the town, but not before taking George Peard to one side and soundly berating him. Despite Lord Bedford's authority, the man had seen fit to ignore his request for help. As it had turned out, it had not been necessary, but it might have been, by God, and for that he would make sure Peard was called to account.

By the time they had ridden away, it was later than Dewett

had planned, but they were making good time despite the persistent rain. The Exeter road was under water in places and fetlock-deep in mud, but it was well travelled and better than many in this accursed part of the country. By Dewett's reckoning it would take six days or so to reach London – five if his luck held. Turning to look over his shoulder, Dewett saw with a grin that the Earl of Bath looked extremely unhappy. His hands were tied behind his back and he was fidgeting in the saddle as though he sat on a bur. Lord Bedford's orders had been carried out to the letter; the great oaf had not been harmed, but Dewett saw no reason to make him comfortable. The Royalist spy was tied across a horse as before, his arms and head hanging loose below the horse's belly, swaying to its gait. Apparently the man was still unconscious. Dewett frowned. It had been too long, dammit. He wished he had not struck the Irish turd quite so hard. Lord Pembroke would be less than pleased if such a valuable prisoner was dead on arrival. A man like that would have many secrets: Dewett hoped fervently that he might be permitted to make the bastard spill them.

The prisoner's state of health began to prey on Dewett's mind. Raising his hand, he signalled the troop to halt and walked his horse back along the column. The spy was breathing shallowly, his face waxen, pale as death. Alarmed, Dewett instructed two men to put the prisoner astride his horse and rope him into the saddle. As they did so, Tawford's eyes flicked open. Like a dead man he stared blankly at Dewett's face. Leaning over, Dewett passed his hand in front of the unblinking eyes. There was no reaction. Dewett felt the hairs rising on the back of his neck. Fumbling for the man's wrist, he felt for the pulse. Barely discernable, it flickered unevenly.

'Is anyone carrying aqua vitae? See if you can get some of it down his throat,' he instructed as one of the men reluctantly handed over a leather flask. 'Have a care not to choke him.'

He waited for a few moments while they attempted to do as he said. The prisoner coughed and spluttered, his eyes snapped shut and he slumped forward onto his mount's neck.

'Lash him tightly and make sure he doesn't fall,' Dewett said. 'Let me know if there is any change.' He returned to the front of the column, unaware of the buzz of comments at the back.

'One minute he wants the sod half-beaten to death and the next he's treating him like a lover with his lass. Why can't he make his mind up?'

'Like he said, he wants the sorry bastard to feel the hooks when they quarter him.'

'I saw it done once. I'll swear when the heart came out it was still beating. It's an art keeping them alive that long.'

'It's all about timing. You have to judge it exactly.'

'And the drop. It's no good if the rope's too short.'

''Sblood! Nobody deserves to suffer that.'

'Well, this one does. Or had you forgotten he tried to blow us to kingdom come? A pox on the bastard Cavalier, a pox on 'em all, I say.' There was an angry murmur of agreement.

'Hey-up, we're moving.'

Preoccupied, Dewett had kicked his mount into a canter and was waving them forward. The reward he had been anticipating was slipping from his grasp. He would get nothing for his pains if the prisoner died. The disappointment was too great to contemplate. When he got to Exeter he would have to seek out a physician and put up with the delay.

Ellen rode up through Bratton Fleming and out onto the moor. Cobb's men inhabited a collection of ruined cots in a deep combe, once the home of monks and hermits, but long since deserted and overgrown by scrub: thorn trees, gorse and bramble. Anyone stumbling across them – not that many came up here – might think the cots little more than a heap of old ruins, but behind the façade, set well back in the combe,

Cobb's men had restored the best of them and used the stones to build a longhouse and outbuildings. The gypsies called it the 'Warren' and it made a habitable refuge for themselves and their womenfolk. The place was so well hidden it was almost impossible to find unless you knew the way, but last summer, when Cobb had come seeking Ellen's advice about an outbreak of the bloody flux, he had taken her there. Her healing skills had served her well on that occasion and although two of the smaller children had been beyond her help, the rest had recovered. Ellen knew she would be welcome.

Climbing the track to the ridge, she aimed for the distant swell of Dunkery. She often rode up here. On a clear day the view was spectacular. It stretched all around as far as the eye could see – as far as Dartmoor and Bodmin and across the Severn Sea to the Black Mountains of Wales – but not today. Low clouds mantled the moor, it was already getting dark and the mist, cold and clammy, was rising from the boggy ground. Along the ridge was a series of ancient barrows, haunted by spirits whose bones had lain here since time began, so it was said. Folk crept up here to leave votives for their ancestors and pray to the Mother, a pagan practice that had long been outlawed, but still they came.

The wind sighed in the reeds and grasses and keened through outcrops of stunted trees, their branches pointing inland like skeletons' fingers. Ellen kept her mind busy, but her skin prickled as she rode by the burial mounds. Shivering, she picked her way along the narrow path and concentrated on avoiding the bogs on either side. The mist was thicker now and in the half-light it was difficult to see. Afraid she might stray off the path, Ellen travelled slowly, searching the ground as she rode. When the path forked, she hesitated. The last time she had ridden this way it had been full light, but now Dunkery was no longer visible and the moor was closing in around her, wild and lonely.

Hearing hoofbeats, Ellen looked up and saw a rider coming fast towards her out of the mist. She tensed, reached for her pistol. As the man neared, he raised his arm in salutation. With relief, she recognised the spare frame of Cobb's man, Zach. He stopped short in surprise, tipping his hat. 'Lady Ellen?'

'Yes, Zach, it's me.' Ellen grinned at him delightedly.

He grinned back. 'You had me fooled for a minute, my Lady.'

Zach's seamed face reminded Ellen of a walnut shell.

'Good!' She beamed at him. 'That was my intention. Did you get my message?'

'Yes, I was coming to meet you. We've had one from Hugh Lyddon too. One of our people brought it in a short while ago. They know about Tawford.'

'But how could they?' She was perplexed.

'That I cannot say, but some of his men are already on their way from St Michael's to see what can be done. We'll get yon lapwing away from the rebels, my Lady, never fear, he'll not be captive long.' Zach spoke reassuringly.

Despite herself Ellen was amused. The lapwing was a bird that diverted attention from its nest by guile – a deceiver. It was a good name for her nephew – no, not her nephew – with a pang of sadness, Ellen put the thought swiftly to one side. 'Do you know how he was taken?'

'He was firing the bridge below Chittlehampton. They must have caught him after.'

Ellen gasped. So that's what he'd been up to – brave and stupid as ever – her eyes filled with tears to think what it must have cost him.

Not noticing her distress, Zach was grinning. 'By God, Lady Ellen, we made they rebels a merry journey though. Had them falling over themselves more than once.' His grin widened. 'Tawford arranged it all with Cobb on Saturday. He knew the soldiers were coming for Lord Bath, and Cobb was to delay them. Tawford said he'd take out the bridge and he'd wait there for me. I'd been on their tail most of the day, you see. It was my job to warn Tawford when they were through Tiverton, so he could set the fuses. He's a canny rogue that lad of yours, it all worked out like he said it would.'

'Not quite all, apparently,' Ellen said tartly. 'How did they happen to catch him?'

Zach shrugged. 'I left him on the bridge, my Lady. I don't know what happened after.'

Ellen cried out. 'What! But he was wounded. Surely you must have noticed? Did you not see he was sick?' She grasped Zach's arm, shaking it in her distress. 'How could you have left him like that?'

Gently, Zach prised away her fingers. 'He was bruised about the face, but he seemed his usual self, Lady. He said naught about being wounded. He'd plenty of time to set the fuse and get away. I don't know what went wrong. He must have left it too late, misjudged it. He said he didn't need my help and I was to go on home. I was but following his orders.'

Ellen was stricken with remorse. 'Of course. Forgive me. I am so afraid for him.'

'Don't take on so, my Lady. We'll get him away, never fear. Come, we leave the track here. Stay close. It will be full dark in an hour and no moon tonight to light the way. Cobb's just got in, he'll be able to tell you more I daresay.' Zach turned his horse and trotted into the mist.

Riding close behind him Ellen tried to regain her composure. Why had Alexander been so foolhardy? He must have known Sir Ralph Hopton and Lord Bath were safe in Stow – well, not Lord Bath as it happened, but Alexander could not have known that. Why then had he gone back to the bridge when there was no need? Because, Ellen answered herself, when he and Cobb arranged the 'merry journey', as Zach called it, Alexander could not have been sure it would create enough delays, and anyway, once he had given his word, he would stick to it no matter what. She shook her head in exasperation. It would have amused him, despite the risk, to blow up the bridge in the rebels' faces. But why had he so uncharacteristically misjudged it and got himself captured? Because he had been befuddled with laudanum and in the aftermath of a megrim, the stupid, stupid boy. Had he only taken her into his confidence, Ellen sighed. There was no point in wishing. He would never change.

Exasperated, she turned her mind to the message from Hugh Lyddon. How was it possible St Michael's had already learned of Alexander's capture? The answer stared her in the face. Dickon! He must have gone with Alexander after all, hidden by the bridge, seen the rebels take him and knowing there was nothing he could do on his own, the courageous, sensible boy had ridden overnight to St Michael's. And Adam Hartley was there. He would know what to do. Adam. Ellen's breath caught in her throat as the familiar ache welled up inside her. For the second time in two days, thoughts of him flooded through her, thoughts she had struggled so hard to overcome, sure at last she had succeeded, but no, they lurked beneath her skin, waiting only to catch her unawares. Firmly, she put Adam from her mind. Now was not the time.

Within the hour they came to the standing stone that marked the entrance to the Warren. Ellen could hear the noise of the stream coursing down the length of the combe. As they passed the stone two black shapes rose out of the bracken. Ellen's mount shied. Taken completely by surprise, she lost her stirrup, slipped sideways in the saddle.

Zach let out a string of virulent curses. 'Confound you, what be doing, claybrained clodpoles, it's me with the Lady Ellen.'

Shamefaced, the two men hastened to help her. 'We didn't know 'twas you, m'Lady.'

Graciously accepting their apologies, Ellen followed Zach as he picked his way through the trees to the ruins and round behind them to the longhouse. Cobb was waiting by the door with a lantern. He came forward at once to greet her. It never failed to surprise her how swiftly this big man could move. Helping her to dismount, he searched her face, his own splitting from ear to ear. Everything about Cobb was big and round, from his balding head and grey-whiskered face, to his great belly and enormous thighs. At first glance he looked simple, a bumpkin. It was an illusion, as those who failed to observe the intelligence in Cobb's eyes learned to their cost. They gleamed at her now, filled with laughter.

'It is good to see you again, Lady Ellen, though I had not thought to see you looking like this.' He chuckled. 'You do make a good lad, for sure.'

Ellen dismissed her appearance with a quick smile 'It gives me more freedom and I want to help.'

'Aye, as to that, come, we will talk.'

Zach leaned across and took her horse. 'I'll see to him, my Lady. You go in with Cobb and get warm.'

She allowed Cobb to help her into the longhouse, the noise bursting on her ears as she walked under the lintel. The crowded room was thick with smoke. Prickets of tallow candles stood on every available surface and appetising smells wafted from a skillet bubbling over a blazing fire. Men and women laughed and talked, pots brimming with ale in their fists. Most were seated on benches at a long table that had been pushed against a wall to clear a space. Two men were playing counterpoint with fiddle and whistle and a young woman danced, her skirts kilted up around her knees while others stood around her, stamping and clapping. Children played on the dirt floor getting under people's feet, and in one corner a woman was seated on a stool, an infant stuck contentedly to each ample breast.

As Ellen followed Cobb into the room the music stopped in mid-flow with a shrill squeak on the whistle. Everyone fell silent, turning to look at her.

'Cat got your tongues?' Cobb roared, looking round at them. 'You all know the Lady Ellen Seymour. Where's your manners, clodpoles?'

Sweeping off her hat, Ellen gave a gallant bow. 'Good evening.' Her voice was mellow.

With a sudden burst of laughter, they chorused a respectful greeting.

'Thee do cut a fine figure of a man, m'Lady.'

'Aye, us thought t'were Master Tawford's brother himself.'

'He 'aint got no brother now, thee bist claybrained.'

'I knaws that, clodpoll.'

'Then why say so, ye daft bugger?'

Before their banter could become even more unseemly, Cobb's woman, Sarah, came hurrying towards Ellen and bobbed a curtsey. 'You'm looking brave, m'Lady. We be sorry 'bout Master Tawford. The menfolk are ready to go after him, you only have to say the word.'

There was a buzz of agreement around the room.

'Thank you.' Ellen smiled. 'That's why I am here.'

'I know, m'Lady,' Sarah said, drawing her to the fire. The fiddler took up his fiddle and the talk and laughter resumed.

'You must be hungry after your journey. Will you have something? It's naught but coney stew, but 'tis warming. There now, and we've a deer hanging too. If I'd known sooner you were coming I'd have had a haunch on the spit ready for you, but that great oaf didn't say naught about it till 'twas too late.' She looked fondly across at Cobb.

'The stew smells wonderful, I'd love some, thank you.' Ellen's stomach growled in anticipation.

Behind her the table was being pulled away from the wall. Cobb raised his voice above the din. 'I'll have all the womenfolk and children out. Now. Off to bed, the lot of you.' He turned to Ellen and gestured to the only chair – his own, a carver – at the head of the table. 'Please be seated m'Lady.'

Ellen, thus exempted from her womanhood, hid a smile and sat down as Sarah placed a manchet of steaming food in front of her. The women rounded up the grumbling children while the men took their places at the table, joined by Zach, who had come in with Ellen's saddlebag over his arm and was shaking out her hooded cloak to hang by the fire. Cobb, having placed a pot of ale at her elbow, stood by her and waited, his hand resting on the back of the chair.

Ellen listened to the muffled wailing of the departing children. The silence lengthened. Nobody spoke. A log shifted in the fire. Under the men's avid gaze she self-consciously ate her stew, surreptitiously glancing at their faces. Many she recognised from her previous visit. One or two had called at the Barton from time to time with messages from Alexander. Most of the faces were lean, weathered and seamed. These men were vagrants, thieves and felons, most – but not all – driven to this way of life through poverty. A few, like Cobb, had eked out a living from their packhorses, turning to thieving when people had less and less money to spare for their merchandise. Others had been strolling players, drummed out of villages where once their frivolity had been welcomed; likewise the fortune-tellers and the keeper who looked after the bear and fighting cocks. Another had been a mariner, a muscle-bound, bald-headed thug who went by the unlikely name of 'Mouse' and had killed a man in a brawl. One or two were minor gentry, men who had lost once too often at the gaming tables – Zach was one such – and a former merchant whose ships had fallen prey to Turks. The life Cobb held out to these men was infinitely preferable to being hounded by their creditors – or worse.

There was even an Anglican clergyman. Unlikely in the midst of such company to find a man of the cloth, Ellen thought, but she knew why. He had refused to dispense with his vestments. For his defiance he had been stripped, thrown out of his living and kicked naked onto the streets, his wife and children left to starve. There were hundreds in like case – many less fortunate, she thought grimly. Looking at the man now, indistinguishable from the rogues around the table, she wondered how he made his peace with God. She supposed that even here there were souls worth saving. She didn't envy him his self-appointed task.

The people of the moor knew of their presence here – some of the men still had family in the villages around – but either through fear or from gratitude for the gifts that appeared on doorsteps overnight, their hideaway was not betrayed. So generous were their bribes that even the Forest Verderer turned a blind eye. Masters of disguise, the men moved about the country selling information to whoever paid the most. It had once been a sideline, but in the present climate was rapidly becoming their mainstay. Ellen had always wondered about Alexander's wisdom in using these men. It was a dangerous game he played, for they had no allegiance – King or Parliament, it made no odds to them – they were a law unto themselves. Cobb ruled them with a fist of iron and if any had ever crossed him he had not lived to tell of it. Cobb was clever, like a fox. He sheltered them and kept them alive and to him they were fiercely loyal. And because Cobb told them to, they gave their loyalty to Alexander. For that alone, Ellen could forgive them much, whoever or whatever they were or had been.

She knew she had somehow to break the tension and gain their confidence if they were to treat her as one of their own. With a quick smile she pushed the half-eaten manchet away from her, belched loudly and wiped her mouth on the back of her sleeve. 'Godamme!' she used Alexander's favourite swear word, smacking her lips. 'That were the best coney stew I've ever eaten.' Pulling out her dagger she plunged it into the table. As the sound resonated in the room, she took a long pull on the ale, cleared her throat and spat a gob of spittle roundly on the floor before announcing to nobody in particular, 'I think it might be wise if you stop calling me your Lady and use some other name, don't you?' She seized on the first one that came into her head, 'Master Simms, perhaps?'

There was a stunned silence, broken at length by Zach. He looked across at her and smiled. 'Tis easy to tell you're Tawford's woman.'

There were loud guffaws from around the table, none louder than Cobb's. 'Aye, by God!' he roared. 'Master Simms it is then.'

Looking at their grinning faces, Ellen gulped. Is that what

they thought? That she was Tawford's woman? She supposed she shouldn't be surprised. She and Alexander had ever been close and their affection plain to see. There were but nine years between them and their close blood ties had never been publicly acknowledged – not that they had any, as she now knew. And even if they had, these people would not think twice about it. Perhaps it was wise to let them continue to think it – as a chattel of Alexander's she would receive the same loyalty as he. She grinned weakly back at Cobb and said nothing.

'Young Jonas brought the message from Lyddon about an hour gone.' Cobb indicated a spotty-faced youth with a red nose at the other end of the table. 'Wat sent him. Wat used to be one of us till he met up with a tapster's widow. She's turned him all respectable. He runs the Angel over to Honiton now. Jonas here's her boy.'

Jonas looked down and examined his bitten fingernails.

'Come on, lad,' Cobb prompted. 'Tell her la...,' he coughed. 'Tell Master Simms here what you told us.' He turned to Ellen. 'Jonas fell over a bridge yesterday, so don't mind if he sniffles, he got a gutful of river water and caught a chill.'

The boy flushed as the men guffawed. He looked up at Ellen who gazed at him attentively unsure what the joke was, but smiling her encouragement.

'They said they'd drown me else.' He sniffed. 'The water were bloody cold.'

Ellen raised her eyebrows at Cobb.

'Jonas was part of our delaying tactics. Mouse blocked the bridge over the Axe and pushed him in just as the rebels were approaching. He squealed like a mating sow and the troopers came to his rescue, him not being able to swim and all.'

'I cad so,' Jonas cried. 'Bouse said I bust pretedd dot to.'

Cobb grinned at the boy's efforts to speak through his blocked nose.

Ellen frowned. 'I'm sure Mouse wouldn't have let you drown, Jonas.'

'Do you say so?' Mouse squinted up at her from the other side of the table. He made a face at the boy, opened his mouth to display the yellow stubs of his teeth and growled.

Ellen raised her voice to be heard over the jeers. 'Never mind him, Jonas – Cobb would have saved you, wouldn't you, Cobb? I think what you did was exceedingly brave.' The youth's pimpled face lit up.

'It weren't up to me,' Cobb said blithely. 'I was away shepherding at the time.' There was another gale of raucous laughter. Ellen decided not to ask. She would doubtless hear all about this merry journey in due course.

'Aye, well, never mind about that now.' Cobb echoed her thoughts. 'Give us the message again, boy.'

Jonas leaned away from the table and blew his nose through his fingers, carefully wiping his face on his sleeve. Ellen was glad she had already finished her stew. 'It were Master Lyddon,' he said. 'Him and three others, but I only knows Master Lyddon.'

'Only four?' Ellen gasped. 'They had no others with them?'

Jonas shook his head and struggled on. 'Master Lyddon said they thought the rebels would go by Exeter and may stop there to change horses, it being a safe garrison and them having Lord Bath with them and not being able to treat him like a common felon and all. But they weren't sure. And they didn't know how long they'd stop for, or even if they'd go that way. They might have gone by the coast and be headed for Bristol.' He sneezed.

Ellen nodded, her gaze never leaving the boy's face.

'So they sent me to ask if Cobb could set a man on their tail and find out what way they were headed. They also need to know if Master Tawford is still alive.' Seeing Ellen's wince, he flushed, dropped his gaze, mumbled, 'Master Lyddon said they'd wait for news at the Angel and they'd have powder and match ready in case the rebels came by.' Jonas finished his message with a juicy sniff.

'Thank you, Jonas,' Ellen said. 'I think you should go find Sarah and ask her for a dose of fennel and barley water. I have some salve in my bag that would soothe your nose.'

As Jonas pushed back from the table she looked at Cobb. 'What do you intend to do?'

Cobb pursed his lips. 'I know for a fact they've not gone by the coast road, they've been seen going through Chulmleigh. It is likely they are headed for Exeter as Lyddon believes. If Zach and I cut across country, we'll soon pick up their trail and if they're bound for London they will eventually pass right by the Angel, it lies directly on the London road. One of us can cut round and let Lyddon know where they are and how fast they're travelling. Though with only four men against twenty it'll be a risky business. I am guessing Lyddon means to lay a trap.'

'I will go with you.' Ellen glared at Cobb, daring him to argue.

'Of course, Master Simms,' he grinned, 'I would not expect otherwise.'

Captain Dewett had arrived in Exeter a little after noon and was taken straight to Rougemont Castle. The officer in charge of Exeter's Trained Band, a Major Richard Saunders, was taken aback to learn that the august Earl of Bath was without and under close guard. He eyed Dewett nervously. Lord Bath had long been an important magnate in Devon and was known to be a close confidante of his Majesty. If this unholy conflict went the King's way Saunders did not want to be associated with this business at all. He was slightly mollified by Lord Bedford's crumpled note of authority, which Dewett – having retrieved it from Peard's floor – flourished under his nose. After some argument, Saunders agreed to allow the captain to rest his men, change their horses and seek help for the sick prisoner. However, he insisted, Lord Bath was to be made comfortable for the duration of their stay, which he hoped most sincerely, would be no longer than was absolutely necessary. Although Exeter was predominantly for Parliament, there were men of strength and ability in and around the town who were well affected to the King. They could cause trouble if Lord Bath's arrest became known. The militia were already stretched – more than half the volunteers had gone to assist Lord Bedford in Dorset. Such men as were left in Exeter had enough to do carrying out Sir John Bampfield's orders to repair the walls and build new fortifications, without having to deal with rebellious malignants into the bargain.

Reassuring the harassed Saunders that he intended to reach Yeovil by nightfall and they would resume their journey the moment the sick prisoner had been revived, Dewett had the Earl of Bath brought into Major Saunders' quarters while a physician was found for Tawford.

They carried him into a nearby lodging house and laid him on a bed. Dewett was still haggling with the landlord when a Doctor Stevens arrived. He was a gaunt man. Under his roundel hat his hair was white and his face pale. Clad in the long black robes of his profession, he looked more like the angel of death than an angel of mercy, Dewett thought.

Opening his bag, the physician pulled out a urinal together with a selection of gruesome-looking instruments and laid them neatly on the bed, before turning his attention to its occupant. Pursing his lips he examined the patient closely, opening Tawford's slack mouth to sniff his breath and probing the wound on the back of his head. As he worked, Stevens rapped out questions: What instrument had caused the injury? How long had the patient been like this? Had there been any signs of awareness? Had there been occasion to observe his urine? Had he vomited and if so, what colour was it? How had he received the wound in his thigh and who had treated it? Did Dewett by chance know in what month the patient was born?

No, Dewett did not know, nor did he care, but he answered as best he could, describing how the prisoner's eyes had opened, how he had felt the man's pulse, which had been weak and uneven. He wasn't aware the prisoner had injured his thigh. The physician looked down his nose – a magnificently long and pointed organ and one of his principal tools – and deigned to explain to Dewett that unless he could say how the patient's pulse was normally, this information was of no use to him whatsoever.

Thus put in his place, Dewett fell silent. The physician was all too self-important and would likely present an outrageous fee to match, he thought sourly, having already dug deep into his purse for the lodgings. Soon afterwards he left the room to go in search of food. When he returned, Doctor Stevens was packing his instruments away and Tawford's eyes were open, unfocussed, but not corpse-like as before. Dewett smiled with relief and looked at the physician with new respect.

The Doctor quickly wiped the smile off his face. 'The patient is not to be moved.'

'For how long?' Dewett was alarmed.

Stevens looked at Tawford, then at the ceiling, then back at Dewett. 'He has had a severe blow to the skull. As far as I can see, the bone has not fractured, but it is impossible to be sure until the swelling subsides and I cannot say what damage has been sustained to the brain. It could take several weeks.'

Dewett's mouth dropped open. He was appalled. 'Weeks? How many weeks?'

'Such cases differ and it much depends on the vigour of the patient, it can take six weeks or more.' He caught sight of Dewett's horrified expression. 'However, if the wound does not fester and is tightly bound it may be possible to move him a little sooner than that.'

'I am afraid that will not be possible.' Dewett frowned. The charlatan was obviously trying to push up his fees. 'We must resume our journey today. You will bind the wound as necessary and make him ready to be moved, if you please.'

'In which case I will take my fee now,' the Doctor said peremptorily. 'But I caution you, if this man is disturbed, within hours he will be dead and you will have no further use for my or anyone else's services, apart from those of the sexton. In addition to his head wound, he has lost a great deal of blood from his thigh. He has two cracked ribs and I would not be surprised if he has internal bleeding judging by the discolouration and swelling on his chest. Indeed, it is a wonder to me he is still alive. Were he not so young and of such a strong constitution, that would certainly not be the case. Even if he does survive, he may never fully recover his wits.'

Dewett was in a dilemma. The longer he stayed, the more it would cost him and the greater the chance that Exeter's Royalists would secure the release of Lord Bath, which would not go down at all well with the Earl of Pembroke. On the other hand, if Doctor Stevens spoke the truth and he moved the prisoner, he would be cheated of his prize. So whatever he did, he stood to lose. He thought for a moment and had an idea. 'That will not be necessary. I will make other arrangements.'

'A wise decision, Captain.' Stevens handed to Dewett three empty bottles, a funnel and a lengthy prescription. 'Have someone collect this from the apothecary. It is to be administered every hour on the hour. See the patient's urine is collected three times a day – morning, noon and night – and the time clearly noted. I will also require to see his stools. Have someone cleanse his head wound with water of ivywort and dress it with a linen cloth steeped in a seethe of sage and honey. The next two days are critical. I will call again on the morrow.' He nodded at Dewett and picking up his bag swept from the room, almost colliding with lodging keeper's wife. The woman had found an excuse to linger by the door and was simpering at the grinning guards, both of whom snapped to attention as they saw Dewett.

He looked with ill concealed distaste at the tendrils of lank hair escaping from the woman's soiled bonnet and the sheep-eyed gaze she was now casting in his direction, but he lifted her reddened fingers to his lips and treated her to his most charming smile – anything to keep the price down; it rarely failed. He handed her the prescription and asked if she would be good enough to see it was taken to the apothecary. And was it possible she could arrange for someone to nurse the prisoner or even do so herself? He could tell she was as accomplished as she was beautiful. Hiding his amusement at her pathetic eagerness to oblige, he casually patted her ample backside, smirked at her pretended outrage and leaving her giggling, went in search of his men.

He would have to split the troop. Ten could take the Earl of Bath under guard and proceed on their journey. He looked up at the sky. It was now well into the afternoon and still raining. They would have to ride fast to reach Yeovil before dark. He mulled over what Major Saunders had said. Suppose his men were attacked on the road. If he lost Lord Bath and Tawford did not survive he would be left with nothing at all. It was a chance he would have to take. It meant he would have only six men to guard the prisoner overnight, but they should be safe enough here under the garrison's nose. His lips drew back in a snarl. The Irish bastard could not move anyway – he was not going anywhere. And tomorrow the four men with the pack train should arrive. They would have to sell the plunder in Exeter. It would not fetch as much as in London, but he could not afford to be hampered by a string of pack animals once he resumed his journey. Major Saunders might be persuaded to buy the horses, except the handsome grey, he would take that one with him.

He sought out Major Saunders and explained his dilemma, why the prisoner was so valuable and the urgency of the situation. The Major sympathised, but wanted nothing to do with it. Dewett must act as he saw fit, but yes, he could billet the men for the remainder of their stay. Dewett again dug into his purse and paid a notary to write a letter to the Earl of Pembroke. He then gave orders to the men, singled out the most experienced – a corporal – told him to take command and gave him the letter, promising to see he was made up to Sergeant if he succeeded in delivering the Earl of Bath safely to London.

When they were ready to leave and had pushed and pulled the big Earl back on to his horse and trotted away, Dewett worked out a guard rota for the sick prisoner. Finally, before retiring for the night, he looked in on Tawford again. Praise God, the man had a little more colour and appeared to be sleeping normally, though his breathing was still shallow. The lodging keeper's wife was sitting near the bed. She looked up at Dewett and smiled a bold invitation. In the dim glow of candlelight she looked almost attractive. He moved to stand behind her, his hand sliding down her neck to cup her breast, the nipple springing into his palm as she leaned against him. She turned up her face, lips puckered for his kiss. For a moment he was sorely tempted, but his accursed lust had got him into enough trouble as it was. He withdrew his hand and put his finger to his lips. 'Later,' he whispered. Giving her a broad wink he backed out of the room.

True to his word, Doctor Stevens returned the next morning and again in the evening, this time with an assistant carrying his bag: a lissom, clean-shaven young man who, as he entered the room and saw the prisoner, gave a small cry and dropped Stevens's bag.

The Doctor swung round impatiently. 'As you can surely see, the patient is quite harmless.' He frowned as his assistant mumbled an apology and stooped to retrieve the bag.

Taking Dewett to one side, Stevens explained his usual man was indisposed and he had only this very afternoon found a temporary replacement, but the young man seemed proficient and carried admirable letters of commendation. And so it proved, for under Stevens's watchful eye, the assistant cupped and bled the patient with a minimum of fuss. When he had done, he stood aside while the Doctor inspected the prisoner's wounds and sniffed and tasted his urine – as yet, there had been no stools. Declaring himself to be well satisfied with the patient's progress, he said the crisis seemed to be over, but the treatment should continue. He might now be offered a little warm gruel and they would call again tomorrow to administer a clyster. After they had gone Tawford seemed considerably brighter. Dewett took heart.

Two days later, observing that the prisoner, although very weak and apparently not able to speak, appeared to be much improved, Dewett ran out of patience. Ignoring Doctor Stevens's warnings that appearances in these cases can be deceptive and the patient should be given time to fully recover or he may regress, Dewett paid the physician's fee, dispensed with his services, organised a litter for the prisoner and made arrangements to resume his journey on the following morning.

10

Friday 30th September, 1642

Dewett had been leading his men along the twisting lanes for about an hour when he rounded a bend and came to the River Otter. He signalled the troop to halt and prime their muskets, dismounted and went cautiously to inspect the narrow wooden bridge. He was not going to be caught out again, by God! He took some time to look underneath, but the structure had not been tampered with and appeared sound. He was about to beckon the troop over when, coming from the opposite direction, he heard the tinkling of a bell. Stiffening he looked up. A bent figure had emerged from the far bend and was approaching the bridge. The man – Dewett assumed it was a man – was garbed head to foot in a hooded robe and walking with the aid of a staff, the bell hung loosely from his fingers. At the sound of its melancholy warning, Dewett strode back to his horse and hurriedly mounted. His men averted their faces and covered their mouths with their cloaks. Shrinking into the hedge, they waited while the leper shuffled over the bridge and hobbled past them.

Dewett was about to proceed when he saw three women toiling with a handcart towards the bridge and behind them a man on a donkey. The handcart was steaming, full to overflowing with scavengings. The women heaved, pulled and pushed and eventually got it part way onto the bridge, but no further, it was firmly stuck. Their master, a swarthy fellow, clattered backwards and forwards leaning from the donkey's back to strike them ineffectually with his crop. It did nothing to help, Dewett noticed sourly, seething with impatience as behind him, the troop started sniggering. He was about to send one of them across to help, when the handcart came free with a rush depositing part of its stinking load on the bridge. In a flurry of underskirts one of the women sat down with a surprised shriek. It was too much for Dewett's men. With loud guffaws they shouted ribald encouragement as the other two women hastily moved in front of their companion to shelter her from the troopers' lascivious gaze, and pulled her to her feet.

His lips twitching, Dewett shouted at the women, impatiently beckoned them over the bridge and promptly wished he had not. Flustered, they picked up their skirts and ran towards him in their haste to do his bidding, leaving the handcart behind. They clustered round Dewett's restive horse and gazed up at him from under their bonnets in unabashed admiration, to the sheer delight of his men.

'You're well in there, Cap'n.'

'Shall us wait for ee, Sir.'

'We'll hold your horse for ee, Cap'n.'

'Thee disn't want all three do ee, Cap'n? Spare one for us.'

'Us don't mind if 'tis the ugly one, Sir.'

'Which one be that, then?'

The men fell about laughing, their comments coming thick and fast, each one more ribald than the last.

They were raw-boned, these big peasant women, Dewett, wrinkling his nose, had to agree, as ugly a bunch as he'd seen and they smelled of the midden. Flushed, he swung round yelling at his men to come to order, just as the man on the donkey, cursing and blaspheming, looked down at the handcart, looked up again, shook his fist at his charges and whacking the donkey with his crop, brought it trotting over the bridge.

'Beggin' your pardon Captain. They be scatty as a coop o' broody hens.' He raised his crop to strike at his charges. 'I'll have them out of your way in no time.' As he spoke, the donkey pulled its lips back from its yellow teeth and seized the corner of Dewett's cloak. Apoplectic with rage he struck out at the beast with his fist and tugged his cloak, ripping it away. The troopers shouted with laughter as the donkey, a mouthful of torn cloak clutched between its teeth, put its nose in the air and let out a screaming bray of outrage. Above the cacophony, its rider addressed the women at the top of his lungs. 'Gidout the Captain's way, ye brazen trollops. Hellsteeth, ye lazy good-for-nothing strumpets, I'll take the whip to ee.'

Humiliated, Dewett swung round in the saddle snarling with rage. 'Silence, you men! Come to order!' He looked severely down the column until the noise subsided. Trying to hold onto his temper, he crossly inspected the tear in his cloak, shoved the women roughly aside, stared down the fool on the donkey until he moved out of the way, collected his horse and waved the column forward.

Trying to summon up some dignity, Dewett rode smartly onto the narrow bridge. Still sniggering, the troop followed. As Dewett squeezed past the abandoned handcart he let out an oath of frustration, momentarily he had forgotten it. The prisoner's litter was strapped to two horses abreast. There was not enough room. Turning, he stood up in the stirrups to look over the heads of his men and saw that three troopers were hanging back on the far bank with the litter.

'You and you.' Dewett indicated two of the men behind him. 'Clear that handcart off the bridge.' They jumped off their mounts and handing the reins to their comrades, ran to obey. He noticed that the women and their master had stopped to watch and that his three troopers had their muskets trained steadily at the litter. It was hardly necessary; the prisoner was weak as a kitten. There was no cause for alarm. Sitting back down in the saddle, Dewett trotted off the bridge, his men leading the two riderless horses, followed. They waited on the bank, shouting jocular encouragement to the two soldiers struggling gamely with the steaming handcart.

In that moment a burst of smoke shot up from the scavengings. As it did so, the women, swords flashing suddenly in their hands, overpowered the three troopers from behind while the man on the donkey pulled the litter back from the bridge. It happened in a trice. White with fear, Dewett drew breath to scream a warning.

He was too late. The handcart erupted in a burst of flame. It was a big explosion. The two unfortunate troopers were blown to pieces. The middle of the bridge collapsed into the swollen river and Dewett and his men were catapulted backwards, their horses screaming.

Momentarily stunned by the blast, his ears ringing, Dewett brought his frightened horse under control. Helplessly watching the far bank he saw the women – who were not women, but men – leap onto his three troopers' mounts. Their 'master' had abandoned the donkey and jumped up behind one of them. He then saw the leper had returned, had abandoned his staff and was climbing astride one of the litter horses. Only he was not a leper. He was Doctor Stevens' assistant.

With a mist of red rage behind his eyes, Dewett reached for his pistol and loosed off a shot across the river. It went wide. His men followed his example, fumbling with their ramming irons and firing to little effect. The enemy were already disappearing round the bend in the road. Screaming orders at the top of his voice, Dewett drew his sword and drove his horse into the water. It was chest high and the current strong. By the time he had reached the bank where his three troopers lay groaning, the prisoner and his rescuers had gone from view. Recognising Dewett, the donkey, quivering with indignation, lifted its head, opened its mouth and let out another ear splitting bray.

Dewett gave chase, spurred on by tantalising glimpses of his quarry, always just a bend in front. Convinced the enemy could not outride him – not if they wanted the man in the litter to stay alive and with two of them doubled up – Dewett mercilessly thrashed his mount, his men struggling to keep up with him. They were half way back to Exeter when it dawned on Dewett he was following a decoy. Somewhere along the way the litter must have left the road. Cursing, he drew rein, his men skidding to a halt behind him. Gripped by panic, he retraced his steps, pushed through every gap in the hedge and cast about on the ground, found nothing until they were almost back to the river.

Waving to his men to follow, Dewett picked up the trail. It led away from the river and into a patch of woodland. Sick to his stomach he saw women's petticoats strewn on bushes, the garments stirring in the wind as though luring him onward. With an oath, Dewett grasped a skirt and flung it to the ground. On the other side of the wood the mud was churned with many more hoof prints. Had there been accomplices waiting or was this where they had hidden their own mounts? Beyond the trees the ground started to rise. Here the going was firmer and littered with shale. The tracks were less easy to follow. As Dewett reached the summit of the rise, they petered out altogether. He looked round in despair at the rolling, wooded countryside.

Suddenly, the troopers shouted. Dewett screwed up his eyes to see where the men pointed. They had picked up the trail again, more clearly defined than before. Dewett could see where two of the horses had trotted abreast and there were footprints, as if someone had dismounted and run alongside. It had to be the litter. Despite himself, Dewett began to feel more hopeful. Swiftly he and his men followed the trail down the other side of the hill, across a level stretch of country and on into another outcrop of trees.

It was there, in a clearing, they came upon the troopers' three horses. One of them wore a lacy bonnet tucked jauntily into its headband. Exclaiming in rage, Dewett dismounted, seized the bonnet and ground it under his heel into the mud. He cast around the clearing, but the tracks stopped right here.

They had played him for a fool. He had been led deliberately along a false trail and by now his quarry could be anywhere. Sick at heart, Dewett was forced to accept that his valuable prize, his promise of advancement, his sweet revenge, had gone from under his nose and there was nothing he could do about it.

Disconsolately he and his subdued men led the three horses back to the river to retrieve their wounded comrades and gather up what bits they could find of the two dead men for decent burial. There wasn't much.

Looking up at the lowering sky, Dewett pulled his cloak tight around his hunched shoulders and plumbed the depths of depression. What made it even worse was that deep within himself there crawled a traitorous worm of admiration. The bastard! The clever Irish bastard had outwitted him at every turn. Alexander Dynam of Tawford. The name went round and round in Dewett's head. He hoped fervently that the man would stay alive. If it took as long as he lived, one day he would find and match this clever adversary. One day, by God.

Riding behind Lyddon, Hartley, Mohun and Sydenham, Ellen, on the back of one of the litter horses, concentrated on keeping it steady. Bringing up the rear were Cobb and Zach, leading a spare horse. Had they not been so anxious about Alexander, Ellen thought, they would have been cock-a-hoop. Their plan had worked like a dream.

Waiting in the Angel late on Monday afternoon, Lyddon had seen the rebels ride by with Lord Bath well guarded in their midst. Seeing there were but ten of them, Mohun and Sydenham had been eager to take them on, but Hartley, sure that Dewett and the rest of his men would be close behind, had restrained them. It was too much of a risk. Lord Bath would come to no harm and the Countess would soon obtain his release.

When Dewett had not appeared, their fear for Tawford had mounted. On Tuesday, frustrated by inactivity, Mohun had been on the verge of riding towards Exeter when Zach had clattered into the Angel's cobbled yard. Grinning with relief, they heard how Ellen, in the guise of a man, had ridden with Cobb and Zach from Exmoor, and that Tawford was alive and receiving treatment. It was as they had hoped; Dewett had not wanted to lose his captive to the grim reaper. They had laughed to learn Cobb had bribed the physician's assistant and Ellen was to take his place this very evening. It was even better than they had hoped. Dewett's troop was reduced to ten and they had plenty of time to arrange an ambush. Sitting round a table in a small back room of the Inn, they had laid their plans.

Eager to help, the merry-eyed mistress of the Angel had busied herself with her needle, inserting panels into bodices, letting out seams and taking down hems. She had laughed until the tears ran down her face as she had watched the dress rehearsal. Her husband, Walter Balch, had somehow acquired the powder and match Hartley asked for. It was he who had suggested the Otter crossing as a likely place to spring the trap, and told them of his cousin, Jacob, who lived only yards from the bridge in Ottery St Mary. The Ottery folk were loyal to the King, they would not interfere and Jacob could be relied upon to shelter them while they waited for Dewett to leave Exeter. Jacob was a scavenger by trade, so for a price could supply them with a handcart of filth – that had been Wat's idea too – and a donkey, though it was an evil-minded beast.

Zach had returned to Exeter. Ellen was staying in lodgings found for her by Cobb. The choice was limited and he had opted for safety and convenience rather than cleanliness and comfort. The house was in St Stephens, one of the few parishes in Exeter where sympathies, like those of the Dean and Chapter, were largely for the King. It was but a short walk to the lodgings where Alexander lay, but it was needful to be cautious. Rumours of Royalist sympathies had caused the city watchmen to step up their patrols.

Having made sure Ellen was as comfortable as she could be, Zach had gone to find Cobb. The two men had spent the intervening days quartering the city, moving from place to place posing as out-of-work journeymen, frequenting the taverns and alehouses, listening to the gossip and asking veiled questions. They learned of Major Richard Saunders, the officer in charge of the trained bands, and of the elected Mayor, a staunch Puritan by the name of Christopher Clarke. They were told how people were being imprisoned for speaking out against Parliament. Only the other day a fiddler, John Gollop, had been arrested in the Bear Inn for composing a scandalous song about John Pym, but not before he had sung it all over town! It was clear which way the wind was blowing in the City Chamber. By the end of the week, Cobb and Zach had a good idea where Exeter's weaknesses lay, both within and without the walls. They also had news of Cornwall. Sir Ralph Hopton was evidently creating a stir.

On Wednesday, Jonas had returned from Exmoor, coughing and sneezing, his nose still red. His mother had sent him unresisting to bed with a hot posset. The same afternoon, Tawford's men had left the Angel and followed Wat and his cart to Ottery, the powder kegs, match and several flagons of his best cider concealed beneath a load of split logs. By the time Wat was ready to wend his way home that night – fortunately his horse knew the way – Jacob would have agreed to sell them his mother.

In Exeter, Zach had taken alms to the hospice and come away with a monk's hooded robe and a leper's bell for Ellen.

On Thursday Hartley and Sydenham had set off on foot to examine the bridge and the surrounding countryside, while Mohun reluctantly shaved off his beard, collected up the various things they needed and attempted to make friends with the donkey.

A little after dark, Cobb and Ellen had arrived with news

that Dewett planned to leave Exeter in the morning. Too mean to hire a wheeled litter for his prisoner, Alexander was to travel in a sheet of sailcloth on two poles slung like a hammock between a pair of horses. Ellen, horrified by the thought of so much jolting, had tried not to dampen the convivial reunion that took place in Jacob's tiny cottage. They had talked through the night, only too well aware of the many things that could go awry. Adam had tried to persuade Ellen to stay out of the action – he might have saved his breath. Zach was still in Exeter and would follow the rebels when they left, get round them and bring warning.

Friday morning had dawned damp and overcast. Hartley and Cobb had buried their weapons under a heap of dead bracken by the bridge, borrowed a length of rope from Jacob and gone off with all the horses to lay false trails. Their plan depended on their being able to secure at least some of the rebels' mounts to make their getaway. Ellen, doubled up with nervous laughter, had helped Sydenham, Mohun and Lyddon don their women's garb. By the time Zach had arrived – blowing almost as much as his horse – to tell them Dewett was within half an hour of Ottery, the handcart was loaded with two barrels of powder beneath Jacob's stinking scavengings, and the rescue party were ready to take up their places. It only remained for Hartley to give hurried directions to where he and Cobb would be waiting with the horses. Finally, Mohun had lighted the slow match and concealed it as best he could without setting light to his skirts, and the stage was set.

It was Lyddon who had taken the tumble on the bridge to distract the rebels while Mohun lit the fuse. Dewett's impatient beckoning had played right into their hands. The unfortunate demise of the two troopers had not been part of the plan. Ellen had been appalled, but her concern for Alexander had quickly overridden her dismay. As the handcart exploded they overpowered the surprised guards and galloped away with the litter, leaving the road as soon as they rounded the bend while Zach, having abandoned the donkey, had ridden on to lure Dewett as far away as possible before taking cover and doubling back across country.

With Sydenham leading the way, tearing off the hampering skirts as he rode, Ellen, riding with the litter, one leg hooked uncomfortably beneath the other, and Mohun and Lyddon, doubled up on one of the trooper's mounts, bringing up the rear, they had fled to the woods where Cobb and Hartley waited with the horses. Mercifully, Alexander had fainted. When they reached the clearing and Ellen felt anxiously for his pulse, he had opened his eyes, grinned weakly at Mohun and in a voice hoarse with pain had whispered, 'By God, you make ugly maids,' turned his head and vomited.

'Not that ugly, surely?' Lyddon's murmur had raised a smile.

Standing protectively around the litter, pistols primed and swords in their hands, the rescuers had waited tensely for Zach, all of them praying Dewett would be too blinded by rage to realise he was chasing a decoy. To Ellen, holding her breath to listen, it had seemed an age before they heard a lone horse approaching and Zach, laughing and breathless, came crashing through the trees. The fools had followed him almost as far back as Exeter, but they would soon be on to the false trails and there was no time to lose. Leaving the troopers' three horses, they had pulled the others well back into the wood and waited while Sydenham and Mohun covered their tracks with armfuls of dead leaves and branches. Then, ears straining for sounds of pursuit, they had mounted up and leading Ellen's bay, for at her own insistence she was still riding with the litter, had set off.

When they had laid their plans they had thought to take Alexander to the Warren rather than returning to St Michael's. The distance to travel was much the same and he would be safe in Cobb's hideaway for as long as it took to nurse him back to health. But now, increasingly concerned by his deteriorating condition, Hartley drew rein and called the others to him. 'It is too far. I fear he will not survive the journey. Can anyone suggest somewhere nearer where we can hide until the morrow?'

'Could we not return to the Angel?' Ellen bit her lip. 'It is but five miles.'

Observing the distress she was trying so hard to hide, Hartley's eyes softened. 'No, it is too dangerous.'

'Besides, we'd have to get the litter back across the river, which could prove a mite difficult now,' Lyddon murmured dryly.

Alexander's eyes flickered. Ellen bent to stroke the hair back from his face. 'What is it, dear heart?'

'Luppit.' His whisper was barely audible.

'Of course!' Mohun exclaimed. 'Sir Popham Southcott. His house is at Luppit. It is but twelve miles away – and it's fortified.'

'He's with the King,' Hartley said.

'Yes, but Lady Southcott will be there – she's Jonathon's aunt. Pity he's not with us, but she will welcome us without him I am sure and there's no need to cross the river if we go by Broadhembury. I will ride ahead. If there's a problem I will come back to you.' He turned to go.

'Mohun, wait.' Hartley stayed him. 'Who else knows the way?'

'I do.' Cobb nudged his mount forward to take the lead and beamed at them.

'Then let's pray Dewett doesn't,' Lyddon said grimly.

'It's unlikely, he isn't familiar with this area, nor his troop or they wouldn't have followed Fane's cockeyed directions to Tiverton.' Mohun grinned. 'He's probably never heard of Luppit.'

'Then what are we waiting for?' Sydenham gathered his horse.

Hartley nodded. 'Onward then and Godspeed, Will.'

Already on his way, Mohun looked back and raised a hand in farewell.

Ellen kicked her mount forward, leaning across the litter

to pull up the horse on the other side. Alexander looked up at her and grimaced. Even more than the pain, she knew he hated this helplessness. She made a face at him and was rewarded with a weak lopsided smile.

'Easy, my Lady.' Riding up on the other side of the litter, Zach took the reins and led the horse gently forward.

The road to Broadhembury was poor; nothing more than a deeply rutted cart track leading from one farm to another. In places it was impossible to travel faster than a walk. Ellen, her hand resting on the litter, felt every bump tenfold. Trying to remain calm she looked about her. It was pretty country, the earth red as henna and the pasture lush and fertile. Ahead of them were the Blackdown Hills, their lower slopes dotted with sheep, fat as butter. Looking up, Ellen saw a buzzard hovering high over the heath. Suddenly it dropped like a stone. Her senses heightened, she felt a twinge of anguish for its prey.

As they approached Broadhembury it started to drizzle. Hartley drew rein and came back to check on Tawford. Slipping off his oiled cloak he laid it across his captain's supine body.

'Is he conscious?'

Before Ellen could reply Alexander opened an eye. 'Was ever a man plagued by so many nursemaids. I'm not dead yet, but if you don't get a move on I will soon die of thirst.'

Meeting Hartley's eyes, Ellen raised an eyebrow and shrugged. 'Would you prefer it if he wasn't?' She smiled despairingly.

Reassured, Hartley grasped her shoulder giving it a gentle squeeze. 'Not much further now. Cobb tells me we are within two miles of Luppit, which is by Dumpdon Hill.' He pointed ahead to a curious knob-shaped hill in the distance. He looked down at Tawford. 'And if he thinks he's getting anything stronger than warm milk when we get there, he can think again.' Adam returned her smile and went forward to ride at Cobb's side as they continued on their way.

The grey, castellated house stood on rising ground overlooking the great bowl of the Otter valley. It had been built by Will Mohun's forbears and though it had belonged to the Southcotts for more than sixty years, it was still known as Mohun's Ottery. Loitering impatiently by the gatehouse for sight of his comrades, Mohun could not help but feel a little proprietorial. It was a fine house.

Lady Margaret Southcott had been delighted to see him; she knew Lord Mohun, his brother, very well for he was often at court, was he not? She was glad to have news of her nephew, whom she had not seen in over two years. She knew of Tawford from her husband, who had never believed the rumours about that brave young man – traitor indeed. If there were more like Tawford fighting for his Majesty, this dreadful quarrel would be over in no time at all. She had plied Mohun with sugared figs and wine, listening with bated breath as between succulent mouthfuls he had described Tawford's rescue. When he had come to the bit about the donkey tearing Dewett's cloak, she had put her hand to her mouth and laughed like a trooper.

At last his comrades straggled into view. Mohun leapt through the gatehouse and ran unsteadily to greet them. 'How is he?'

'He lives.' Hartley grinned. 'But we need to get him out of this litter. He says he is thirsty, as it appears were you.'

Mohun laughed. 'Lady Southcott is nothing if not generous. Her cook is preparing a feast for us. Her Ladyship has a bed ready for Tawford and she is eager to greet Lady Ellen. She wants to see her in her man's garb and cannot wait to tell her gossips about it. She is much like her husband – every bit the wag.'

'She might contain herself until after we have gone,' Lyddon said dryly, riding up behind Hartley. 'Or we'll have Captain Dewett here in no time. Have you left us anything to drink, Will, or have you poured all of Lady Southcott's wine down your gullet?'

Mohun pulled a face at him. 'If you go on through to the courtyard, there are men waiting to help. I will tell her Ladyship that you are here.' He ran back up the carriageway.

With relief flooding through her, Ellen looked down at Alexander. 'We are here. It is over.' She had met Margaret Southcott only once; it had been on her first visit to court. So excited had she been to meet the tiny King and his equally tiny and very vivacious Queen that most of the introductions had blurred into a sea of faces and soon forgotten names, but not Lady Margaret. She was Margaret Berkeley then, before she wed Sir Popham Southcott. Ellen remembered her as short and attractively plump with a mass of golden curls, eyes of sapphire blue, a flawless complexion and an enviably small, cupid's bow mouth from which had uttered a loud, gurgling laugh as incongruous as it was infectious. Not only was she very pretty, but daughter of the celebrated old Lord Fitzharding, she was a considerable heiress. Under the benevolent eye of the Queen, she had been surrounded by a throng of eager young men, and Ellen, unfashionably tall and feeling gawky and terribly plain, had been wrung with envy.

She smiled at the memory – it was all so long ago. Time had not been kind to Lady Margaret; her plumpness had run to fat, she had lost several teeth and her hair was thin and faded, but the bewitching eyes and infectious laugh were just as Ellen remembered. Bending to greet their hostess, legs wobbling like a newborn calf, Ellen found herself enfolded in a warm, suffocating embrace that made her want to weep. For the first time in almost a week she felt safe.

Much later, when Hartley had tended Alexander's hurts and administered some warm milk laced with a sleeping draught, and they had eaten steamed perch, roasted duck and apple pie, washed down with Sir Popham's best French wine, they retired to the drawing room to sit in comfort. Ellen laughed in delight to see a heap of spaniels drowsing in the firelight by the great hearth. They raised their heads reluctantly, eyes melting and dewy. A pug struggled out from under them and bounded to his mistress's feet.

'They keep me company while My Lord husband is away.' Lady Margaret apologised, reluctantly pushing the pug to the floor and making to eject her pets from the room.

'Oh please, don't disturb them, they're lovely.' Ellen seated herself on the settle and put her hand down to the pug, which snuffling, wagged its entire sturdy little body and delicately licked her fingers. 'I had a greyhound who was my comfort too and I still miss him sorely. He died in January.'

'I know how you feel, my dear. So sad. The best thing is to have another straight away. I have some hound pups in the barn; you must take your pick. They have been weaned a week. They're not pure I'm afraid, but the dam has a wonderful character.' Brushing aside Ellen's thanks, Lady Margaret sat beside her. The dogs, seeing they were to be left undisturbed, relaxed contentedly and the pug leapt onto his mistress's lap, where she fondled it absently. After a moment she took Ellen's hands in her own.

'Now, please tell me, I want to hear all about your adventures again. What is it like to ride like a man? So unseemly! Is it not dreadfully uncomfortable? And how do you manage when...?' She cast a quick glance at the men and flushed. 'You know,' she whispered nudging Ellen's arm.

Ellen laughed. 'With some difficulty; it is a little inconvenient,' she whispered back. Full of food and warmed by the fire she felt her eyelids pricking, but Lady Margaret was looking at her so eagerly. With an inward sigh, Ellen sat up straighter and making an effort to stay awake related the events leading up to Alexander's rescue, the men chipping in from time to time.

When she came to the end of her story, Lady Margaret clapped her hands delightedly. 'How brave you are, my dear – and they say we are the weaker vessels.' She wagged a fat finger at Adam who was warming his backside by the fire.

'You do me an injustice, Lady Margaret.' He smiled down

at her. 'Lady Ellen is as courageous as any man I know. I would never dare to call her weak.'

'Spare my blushes, Adam,' Ellen retorted, a flush staining her cheeks. She quickly changed the subject. 'Do you have any news of Sir Popham, Lady Margaret?'

'Oh please, my dear, do call me Meg. Indeed, I must tell you. Wait, I have a letter.'

As she bounced up from the settle, the pug transferred itself to Ellen's lap. Adam grinned at her. 'Do you know, that animal reminds me of Cobb.'

Cobb looked up sleepily from his chair. 'And I would be wagging my tail too were I sitting where he is!'

They were still laughing when moments later Meg returned, triumphantly waving her letter. 'Did you hear about the Marquis of Hertford? He is with the King again. Such courage! He escaped by boat from Minehead, don't you know, he had to fight the rebels off almost single handed while that odious Earl of Bedford pursued him half across the sea.' She spoke breathlessly her eyes shining.

'Really? That's amazing,' Lyddon said smoothly.

'The Marquis told Popham that were it not for the cowardice of the Somerset men – so many of the vulgar sort being fainthearted and inexperienced in martial discipline – he would have won the day. How proud you must be, my dear.' She looked at Ellen. 'Was he not related to your poor, dear husband?'

Ellen nodded, mute.

Sydenham gasped. 'Cowardice? They were outnumbered five to one! Hertford is a...'

'Very courageous man indeed,' Hartley cut across Sydenham's words and shot him a warning glance as Lady Southcott looked up to hear what he was saying. 'What news of the army, my lady? How does the King?' he added quickly to distract her, knowing she was a personal friend of Lord William Seymour, the Marquis of Hertford.

'It is all good news.' She smiled looking back at her

letter. 'My husband writes that Lord Strange, Sir Thomas Salisbury and Sir Edward Stradling have raised four thousand men between them and the Welsh have been coming over the border in their thousands. Nobody doubts the King will prevail, though Popham says his intentions are not yet known. Some say he thinks of wintering in the Midlands, but others that he will hazard a battle quickly and be done, and we will all come back to Whitehall for Christmas. Is that not the finest thing?'

'Indeed it is.' Ellen managed a smile. Somehow she doubted it. To be reminded of her husband, Edward Seymour, had cut her to the quick. Glancing at Adam from under her lids, she felt again the twist of guilt that had plagued her marriage. Poor, dear Edward, it was not his fault her heart had belonged to another. Had things only been different... Ellen bit her lip, her fingers straying to the pug's silky ears. She had tried to be a good and dutiful wife. Perhaps love for Edward would have grown in time, but time they had not been granted. The great pox had taken her husband and then her baby daughter. Was it retribution? Was God so cruel? The loss of her little girl had left an aching void that time did nothing to assuage. With an effort she put such thoughts away and listened to the conversation.

When Lady Southcott at last retired, having insisted they stay at Mohuns Ottery until Alexander was well enough to travel and offered them the use of her gig to replace the litter, the six men discussed in undertones what they would do.

'It is kind of Lady Southcott to offer us a refuge.' Hartley frowned. 'But we should not stay here. We are too few to defend the house for long and it would place her in a very awkward, if not dangerous position if word gets out she is harbouring us.'

Lyddon nodded. 'I agree. We should go on to Exmoor as planned.' He turned to Cobb. 'Which is the shortest way from here?'

'Through Tiverton to Dulverton and over Hawkridge.'

Cobb pursed his lips. 'But you won't be able to use the gig or a litter beyond Tiverton, the moorland roads are only fit for pack animals.'

'Then one of us will have to double up behind Tawford and support him in the saddle.' Hartley helped himself to some more wine from the table, waved the decanter around.

'Anyone?'

Sydenham frowned. 'Is there no way to avoid Tiverton? The town is strong for Parliament.'

Zach nodded. 'True. And the Sheriff knows Dewett was on his way to arrest Lord Bath. He might even know of Tawford's capture by now. His suspicions will be easily aroused by a group of armed strangers carrying a wounded man.'

Cobb stood up and wandered over to the fire. 'Only by going miles out of your way and it will be a slow enough journey as it is. You won't want to travel faster than a walk.'

'No, he's been jolted enough,' Hartley agreed.

Ellen looked thoughtfully at the fire. 'If we were fewer, we might not be so noticeable. Can we not split up?'

'I was coming to that,' Hartley said quickly. 'The *Gabriel*, God willing, will have sailed by now. If all is well, the others will leave St Michael's tomorrow. Someone should take them news of Tawford. In fact,' he looked at his colleagues, 'I think it best if you three return to the Mump and go with them to join Prince Rupert. There's little point in us all going to Exmoor. I cannot say how long it will take Tawford to recover. It could be at least three weeks before he is well enough to ride, possibly longer.'

'You'll never keep him off a horse for three weeks,' Mohun grinned.

'Rather you than me,' Sydenham said dryly.

'What about Nick Slanning?' Lyddon asked suddenly.

'What about him?' Hartley said.

'Didn't Tawford say he had a message for him?'

Hartley smacked his hand to his head. 'Yes, of course. In all the excitement I had forgotten. And anyway, we should probably let Sir Ralph know what's going on. Would you go to Cornwall, Hugh? We can ask Tawford about it when he wakes.'

Ellen looked up anxiously. 'Do you think it would be possible to get a message to Lord Westley? My brother must be sick with worry.'

Mohun nodded. 'I'm sure Lady Southcott will have someone reliable.'

'There's no need,' Cobb said suddenly. 'You don't need both me and Zach to guide you to the Warren. I'll take it for you, Lady Ellen.'

'That's very good of you and I'm grateful for the offer, Cobb, but I can't ask you to go all that way. You do know he left for London on Monday last?'

'Yes, my Lady, I do, but it is no trouble.'

The others looked curious; it would take the best part of two weeks there and back, quite a lot of trouble in fact, but beyond muttering he had some personal business to attend to in London – which served only to increase their curiosity – Cobb gave his usual beaming smile and said no more. It was always impossible to tell what the gypsy was up to unless he wanted you to know. Whatever it was, he was keeping it to himself.

'In which case, I will write a letter for you to take to him. Thank you, Cobb, it is a weight off my mind.' Smiling her relief, Ellen looked up at Adam. 'That leaves you, me and Zach, then.'

'There is still the problem of hiding Tawford,' he pointed out.

Slowly Ellen smiled. 'We do not need to hide him. On the contrary, we can make him more prominent.' Her smile widened. 'I am sure Lady Southcott can lend us a fat cushion and I will ask her if she can spare some women's clothes. She will be only too pleased to see me properly dressed!' The men gazed at her quizzically.

Hartley asked the question. 'Whatever is the cushion for?'

'For Alexander.' Ellen looked smug. 'My brother and I – that's you, Adam – are taking our sister home, that's Alexander in women's garb. You, Zach, if you don't mind, will be my groom and will ride up behind him. Should anyone stop us we will say our poor sister has recently lost her husband and is so overcome with grief she cannot ride unsupported. What is more, as anyone can see, she is great with child and about to give birth to a poor, fatherless babe and we are in a hurry to get her to…'

'Bethlehem?' Mohun suggested, as they all cracked out laughing.

'I was going to say Dulverton,' Ellen retorted primly, her eyes glistening.

'Pity we left the donkey behind,' Cobb wheezed, tears shining on his florid cheeks.

Zach, gasping, shook his head. 'Aye, lass, like I said, it's not hard to tell you are Tawford's woman.'

At his words, Cobb went into another paroxysm of laughter, but the others, their mirth quickly stifled, looked sharply at Ellen. Mockingly she gazed back at them, one eyebrow raised, her eyes brimming with amusement. She was past playing the blushing maiden.

'You had best shave him close in the morning, Adam.' She got up from the settle. 'Well, gentlemen, I am for bed.' They shot to their feet, their faces a picture of embarrassment. She had no doubt they would put Zach right as soon as she had left the room. Tawford's woman, indeed!

It was coming dusk as Robert Dynam rode up Ludgate Hill, his men watchful at his back. It was a while since he had been to London. The streets were not as busy as they used to be, he reflected, what with theatres and alehouses either closed down or going out of business for want of customers. People walked with hunched shoulders and averted their gaze as though afraid of attracting attention. Everyone he saw seemed to be in a hurry, nobody out for a stroll stopping to pass the time of day, no chairs or hackneys picking their way through the noxious amalgam of mud and ordure the scavengers never quite managed to clear, no sounds of merriment, just an air of sombre weariness and anxiety.

He turned into the Bell Savage Inn, gave his men some money for livery, food and lodging and left them there with the horses. He then called for a linkboy and with the light swaying before him, set off for his rooms in St Martin's Lane, relieved to find that Ludgate was still open. Not sure what to expect he kept his hand on the hilt of his sword, but saw little evidence of rioting. As he passed by the grand new portico of St Paul's, where even the booksellers had packed up and gone home, he saw a gang of rowdy apprentices being dispersed by the Watch. They had not long been released from the day's toil and were in high spirits, exchanging playful insults with a handful of uniformed soldiers. It sounded good-natured enough, but such encounters could turn quickly to bloodshed. Robert quickened his pace.

From the top of Paternoster Row it was but a short stride past the Saddlers Hall to his lodgings. For a while after his father's death he had maintained the Westley's town house in Arundel Street, but he had so rarely made use of it – Ruth had never liked London – that he had eventually acquiesced to his widowed stepmother's incessant pestering and agreed to lease it to her and her odious son, George Dynam, his half-brother, and since Henry's death, his heir. Having done so, he avoided Arundel Street like the plague, and had instead found lodgings in an area that abounded with immigrant craftsmen. These were mostly Flemish and Italian jewellers whose presence was a constant source of irritation to the nearby Company of Goldsmiths, but troubled Robert not at all. It obviated the need to make polite conversation with neighbours. He rented the two rooms on the first floor, modest but adequate for his needs and blessedly quiet, the ground floor being used as business premises and the garret as a storeroom.

His visits to town were rare. He had never enjoyed attending the court, preferring to live quietly in Devonshire in between his journeys to Cork and Dublin. When Henry had died, even those had become less frequent. They had ceased altogether when Ruth's death had rendered him too melancholy to stir himself. Since then he had left things to his Irish agent, Art O'Neill. He sighed. It must be thirty years since his father had appointed Art, the agent would be getting on in years by now. Robert knew he should think about pensioning him off and finding a replacement, but there were complications and he couldn't face the prospect. Had things been different, he would have asked Alexander to deal with it for him. He intended anyway to transfer a third of the Irish holdings to the boy – not that they had yielded much revenue since the rebellion, but they might prosper again one day.

Alexander knew nothing of this; Robert had told nobody apart from his lawyers. He had wanted it watertight before the widow got wind of it and took the matter to Chancery. The loathsome woman had almost prevented him from signing over Tawford Barton, so protective was she of her son's inheritance. Had she not considered it a mean tract of valueless marshland she might well have persisted, but happily she had let the matter drop. Robert grimaced. Anne Dynam was a greedy woman and not without influence. Through the marriages of her sister she was related to three extremely powerful families who would doubtless rise to her defence in anything that concerned property. Well, he thought with a grim smile, the widow would never get her hands on Tawford Barton now, even though Alexander had turned it around and made it profitable – as Robert had known he would.

Alexander… had things only been different… Trudging disconsolately behind the wavering pool of light, Robert sighed heavily. Unable to broach the subject of Ireland when last they had met, his plans for the boy had come to naught. The deed of transfer, however watertight, lay unsigned at Marley Court, and there it would remain if he could find no way to bridge this gulf between them.

Robert paid off the linkboy, scraped the filth off his boots as best he could and let himself in, shutting the door behind him with a relieved sigh. Dropping his saddlebag he felt for the taper and tinderbox. They were in their usual place in a niche by the door, together with a branched candlestick. Fumbling to light the taper Robert cursed with irritation as it slipped through his shaking fingers. He had made the journey in only four days; he had every reason to feel exhausted, he thought, bending to search for it on the floor. When he had learned that Captain Dewett and his troop had stopped to change horses at Exeter and found they were still there, Robert had ridden on to the next posting house, determined to reach London – and Earl Pembroke – before them. Tomorrow morning he would seek an audience. For now it was as much as he could do to drag his weary bones up the stairs to his rooms. Nor did he have the energy to disrobe. He should have brought his manservant, but had left Marley Court in such haste it had not even occurred to him. He supposed it would have been wise to take some supper at the Bell Savage while a message was sent to rouse his landlord. His rooms had not been prepared, not even cleaned by the look of them. The place smelled dank and stale, the wretched man had not even laid a fire; the blackened ashes from his last visit lay there still, gathering dust and bird droppings, and everything covered in a film of thin black soot. It didn't matter. Robert was too tired for anything much to matter – except Alexander.

Robert walked through the parlour to his chamber, put the candlestick on the side table, lowered himself gingerly on to the bed, eased off his boots, pulled the coverlet over his lower body and sank back against the damp bolster. He lay there shivering, willing sleep to come, but his mind would not let him rest. He pondered on what he would say to Lord Pembroke and tried not to consider the possibility of failure. He was fairly sure Alexander was spying for the King. If Pembroke had proof it would go ill with the boy, unless he was playing a double game. Was he? Robert had wondered about it when Parliament had been so unexpectedly amenable to Alexander's release from the Tower. It would be like the boy to hold two hands at once; he had always courted danger. If it were true, this time it might just save his skin. Please God.

Robert's thoughts led him to Ellen, seeing again the contempt and pity in her eyes. How he had longed to tell her everything, to share the burden he carried, the anxiety that lay like a tape worm in his belly eating away at his strength. But he must not weaken. If the truth became known, what then would be unleashed? He had already lost one son, could not bear to lose another. Robert drew a sobbing breath. But you are not my son, Alexander. You are not my son. The boy's face loomed before him as it had looked when they had last met: green eyes glittering, cold and unforgiving, his hurt so apparent in their depths and yet so quickly masked. Robert sighed heavily, whispered, 'If you knew the truth, could you ever understand why I did what I did? Could you ever forgive me, or would you be lost to me and I to you, forever?'

The candle grease puddled on the table and one by one the wicks spluttered and went out. Eventually, Robert slept. In his dream the woman returned to him.

Defenceless and alluring she lay before him, her huge eyes swimming with tears, her hands outstretched, beseeching. He looked down at the parchment burning in his fingers, watched it curl and blacken, faded words consumed by flame, ashes drifting to the floor. When he looked up, her face had gone. In its place was a grinning death's-head seething with maggots. A crow had alighted on her pillow and was picking them off one by one. It turned its head towards him, eyes glowing like burning embers. Crying out in horror he raised his hands to his face. When he lowered them he was standing by his father's grave. The crow was sitting on the tombstone. It put its head on one side and watched him. He saw that in its beak it held a strand of silken, yellow hair. As he made a move to grab it, the bird flapped its wings and rose into the air. And suddenly he was the crow, soaring above the earth feeling the wind beneath his wings, the hair in his beak flowing about him like a veil. The land dwindled until he could no longer see it and he was lost in a great white expanse of sky. Then he was a man again, falling, falling... the ground rushed up to meet him and everything went black.

As the cold, grey light of dawn stole into the chamber, Robert slipped into a dreamless sleep.

11

It was noisy in the Anchor and Dickon was enjoying himself. He was watching Billy Baines balancing a pot of ale on his head, so full it was slopping into Billy's hair, sending streams of amber liquid down his face. Sticking out his tongue, Billy started walking unsteadily over the stone-flagged floor. The betting was fast and furious and the tables scattered with coins. His audience were mostly foremast hands, but there were a few old mariners with red-rimmed eyes and sad, nostalgic faces. As Billy reached the halfway point, the pot began to slide. The men stamped their feet and jeered at him, none louder than James Chichester who, having already lost his wager, was soaking wet and stinking like a brewery. Billy, holding his head at an impossible angle, neatly sidestepped the feet thrust into his path and successfully negotiated the length of the room. Whereupon he lifted the pot from his head, downed the contents, replaced it upside down, and beaming sat down suddenly on the floor.

Chuckling, Dickon joined in the raucous applause. He felt warm and relaxed and not a little drunk, despite Bassett's warning to go easy. They had cause to celebrate; they had successfully loaded the *Gabriel* without attracting attention, and with her lights dowsed she had slipped out on the ebb. But as Bassett had pointed out, there were still the two empty barges to take back up the Parrett and with Southcott gone with the arms, they were a man short. If the Wharfinger reappeared they would have some explaining to do.

There had been no news of Tawford. Dickon knew it was too

soon, but his fears for his captain's life were increasing by the day. He wished he could share the men's unshakeable belief in Tawford's invincibility, but they had not seen him as Dickon had, lifeless, head hanging down, matted with blood. Dickon kept these thoughts to himself, however. These men lived in ever-present danger, but rarely did they voice their concerns or allow their tension to show. After only three days in their company, he had come to realise their constant ribaldry and horseplay were but a ploy to mask their underlying anxiety. Dickon had soon fallen under their spell, could not remember a time when he had laughed so much.

On Tuesday he had taken the oath. The six men, their faces unusually solemn, had led him into the chancel. On his knees before the altar, he had sworn before God to defend his country from her enemies, pledged his loyalty to the King and to Tawford, promised to uphold the secrets of the company and defend his brothers in arms, if need be unto death. For Dickon, it had been an awe-inspiring moment, binding him irrevocably to St Michael's. Afterwards, with much back slapping, the men had drawn him into their circle, described how the company worked, reeled off names of the men he had not yet met, explained the role of Cobb and his men, the ciphers – which he had to learn by heart – and the colour coding of the carrier pigeons. But there had been little time for lengthy discussion about cavalry tactics. It had taken all the time they had left to bring in three more cartloads of weapons, finish loading the barges and take them downriver to Bridgewater.

It was late afternoon when they had moored the two barges up to the wharf. The port was unusually quiet. The blockade had stifled trade and all but the smaller boats had been commandeered by Parliament, but there were a few yawls and ketches used for ferrying supplies to the blockading ships. The *Gabriel* stood out like a sore thumb, but with carpenters apparently busy on her decks and no crew or cannons to be seen, she had – for the time being – been left alone.

Only once had they been challenged. As they tied up to the harbour wall, the Wharfinger had come striding over, demanding to know their business. While Acland explained they were victualling and gestured vaguely towards a Yawl bobbing on the incoming tide, Southcott had quickly loosened the two uppermost barrels and nudged them with his knee. They had rolled from the stack and crashed spectacularly onto the quay, bursting asunder. Out of one had streamed a slither of stinking fish and from the other a dense cloud of flour, which splattered the suspicious Wharfinger from head to foot. As he hopped from one foot to the other, his expression one of shocked indignation, the inevitable had happened: his foot had landed in the fish and slipped from under him. Screaming invective, his arms flailing like windsails, he had sat down, a ghost on the quayside.

Dickon, tears streaming down his face, had watched as Southcott had leapt from the barge and with humble and profuse apologies, hauled the man to his feet and attempted to brush the sticky mess from his robe. Gifford, meanwhile, had jumped off the second barge and was gathering up armfuls of fish into a basket, which he pressed into the irate Wharfinger's arms by way of compensation. When the horrified man held up his hands to push the offending basket away, Gifford had shouted at Dickon. 'You clumsy, good for nothing addlepated clodpoll, fetch a broom and clear up this mess.' He had then asked the Wharfinger if he wished to examine the barges, though it would be dark soon and perhaps it could wait until morning? Coughing and spluttering, the poor man had waved them angrily away and flounced back to his house, leaving a trail of white footprints in his wake.

The roars in the Anchor indicated that someone else had been persuaded to rise to the challenge. As Dickon craned to see, he noticed Bassett signalling him to the door – he also noticed the serving wench coming towards him. She was the prettiest girl Dickon had ever seen. For some time he had been surreptitiously watching her progress round the room as she squeezed between the cheering men, a full jug of ale in each hand. Nodding to Bassett, Dickon reluctantly pushed himself to his feet and saw the girl was bending towards him, refilling a proffered tankard. Treated to a full, uninhibited view of her breasts straining voluptuously over her bodice, Dickon was transfixed. She looked up suddenly, catching his avid expression and giving him a mocking smile, her gaze moving meaningfully to his bulging crotch. Flushing to the roots of his hair, Dickon turned quickly away, his discomfiture heightened by the girl's sudden peal of laughter. Across the room, he could see that Gifford, Acland and Pollard were making their way to the door and that everyone was laughing at James who, clowning abject misery, had flung a handful of coins on the table. Sweating with embarrassment, Dickon pushed his way around the back of the room to the door, glad to be out in the keen night air.

Despite Bassett's warnings, they were all considerably less than sober and it was nothing short of a miracle that at least one of them did not end up in the river as they hoisted the sails and manoeuvred the big, flat-bottomed boats upstream. In the end they had to resort to poling and it took some hours to reach Burrow Bridge. By the time they had climbed up the Mump, Dickon was all but dead on his feet, but he made his way unsteadily to the linhay to check the pigeon loft. One new bird had come in. On its breast was a dab of yellow. Disappointed, he removed the capsule, took it to Bassett and stumbled off to his mattress.

He woke next day to find James standing over him grinning, a tankard of small beer in his hand. 'Get this down your throat, it will help.'

Dickon, who had woken with a raging thirst and a head that felt as if it had been used for kick ball, struggled to sit up and took it gratefully. As he came fully awake, he remembered with a sickening lurch that today he was riding to war. He handed James the empty tankard. 'Have you ever killed a man, cousin?' He tried to keep the question nonchalant.

Understanding what had prompted it, James's rubicund face was serious for once. 'Yes, lad, I have, in the last Scots War. I was so afraid I shat myself and all but fainted away.

But the worst time is before the fighting starts. It's the waiting that curdles your blood; once you're in the thick of it you don't have time to think about it, it's only afterwards that your guts turn to water and your legs to jelly. You'll not disgrace yourself, no more than the rest of us, never fear.'

'I am not afraid, cousin, never think it.' Dickon threw off the blanket and swung his feet to the floor.

Chichester smiled at the boy's bravado. 'It is only a fool goes into battle without fear in his heart, coz, and we are none of us fools, not even Tawford, for all he turns mad in battle!'

More comforted than he cared to admit, Dickon grinned.

'So what is planned for this morning?'

'You mean what's left of it?' James teased. 'As soon as you have eaten – there's some bread and cheese in the tower room. I should force some down if I were you – we are to muck out the linhay. The others have gone down to Burrow Bridge to help carry up some of the Churchwarden's things and see if there's anything else we can do for the villagers before we leave.'

'What was in Fane's message?' Dickon scrambled into his breeches as James turned to the door.

'An update on Bedford's strength and to tell us the army's reached Gloucester and expects to meet up with the Earl of Essex within a few days. Come on lad, we must get on. We aim to leave before noon.'

On his way to the tower room, Dickon saw the church had been cleared out and swept clean while he lay abed. Feeling guilty, he gulped down the bread and cheese and still chewing, went out to the linhay. His cousin had tethered the horses outside and was wielding a dung fork. Looking up at Dickon, he pointed to another. They worked companionably until the muck was neatly piled round the back and the linhay scrubbed out and filled with clean, fresh straw.

Stopping to lean on his fork, his shirtsleeves rolled up to the elbow, Dickon looked about him. Although overcast, the view from up here was magnificent: away in the distance he could see Glastonbury Tor. The land in between seemed almost entirely under water. It was like being on an island, Dickon thought, putting a hand to the small of his back. He eased himself upright, yawned and stretched. He had done more physical labour in the last few days than in his entire life. It was thirsty work. Bending to retrieve his jerkin, he thrust the fork into the straw and turned back to the church to fetch a drink.

'Whoa, lad.' James nudged Dickon in the ribs. 'We haven't finished yet. There's that lot to split and stack round the back.' James pointed to a pile of timber with a great axe stuck in the top. 'But first, nip up into the loft and tally the birds for me.'

'Twelve red, eight yellow and nine green, only one blue,' Dickon called, climbing down from the loft and transferring fluff and bird droppings from his hands to his backside. 'Do we take them with us?'

'All but the yellows, we have no way of returning them to Fane and there won't be an opportunity to retrain them. Likewise the blue, that's a London bird. The villagers will probably eat them. You'll find a hamper somewhere – try the porch.'

Dickon found it, partly concealed under a pile of sheepskins, dragged it out and carried it back to the linhay. 'Once we're gone from here we'll be out of contact, won't we? With Tawford, I mean.'

'By pigeon we will be, yes. But if there's any news worth hearing you can be sure someone will bring it to us.'

In the end, James decided to release the older birds. 'We will take only those most recently fledged, just in case we are in the same place long enough to retrain them,' he explained. 'The greens are Cobb's, but they will probably tag along to Tawford Barton with the reds. Tawford's steward will know when they arrive that we have left St Michael's.'

Dickon had watched the small flock flutter confusedly above him, then, as if at some invisible signal, they had wheeled away to the West. 'How do they know where to go?'

'They will always head for home, but how I don't know. It may be by smell,' James said. 'Some say it's by the position of the sun, others that they recognise the lie of the land, the rivers, mountains and roads. We've a man breeds them for us in London, by the name of Nab. He reckons they can read the force of the earth and follow the ley lines. But it's a mystery to me, lad. It takes about four weeks to train them and it's best if you start as they fledge, but if you keep them in one place for too long they get confused and have to be re-trained. Some never will accept a new home. They can't travel at night and if the weather is bad they can be blown miles off course and tire. Some come down and lose their way or get hurt, especially if they are not in prime condition. But as you have seen, for the most part it works quite well, as long as you don't rely on it. For important messages we always try to send a man as well, but the birds can travel in an hour what it takes a man the best part of a day.'

Dickon was fascinated. Marvelling, he had watched the birds until they were tiny black dots in the sky. 'Is it possible to train any sort of pigeon?'

'No, a common woodpigeon is no good. These are a particular strain. Tawford brought the original breeding pairs back from the Continent; they use them more over there. I'll have to introduce you to Nab some time, he knows everything there is to know about pigeons. Ask him and he will talk your ears off.'

They had just finished splitting wood and stacking logs when Gifford, Acland, and Pollard staggered up from the village weighed down with chattels: pots and pans, lanterns, a small table and several stools. There was even a clock – the Churchwarden's prized possession – a long mirror and a roll of moth eaten tapestry. Bassett was leading a donkey, its back piled high with bundles of green withies. In the other hand he carried a crate of moulting hens. Behind him ran three children, squealing and laughing, catching feathers.

'There are five families in the village,' Chichester explained as Dickon watched the cavalcade in amazement. 'They live off the commons and spend the winter weaving baskets and hurdles to take on the barges to Bridgewater and Taunton. They harvest the withies right through the winter, getting about on rafts and stilts or skates and sleds when it freezes. It's amazing to see, they make it look so easy. I had a go on stilts once and fell flat on my face.'

'Do they actually live up here?' Dickon asked.

'If they have to – usually when the rivers flood, and from the look of them this morning that'll be soon.'

It was well past noon before the men were ready to leave. They were in the tower room having a last minute bite to eat when they heard a great bellow. "Sdeath, if that doesn't sound like Mohun!' Acland leapt to the door.

They all rushed out, roaring with delight when they saw Mohun's fiery head as he came running up the path waving his hat.

Dickon's face fell. 'I can't see Tawford.'

'Don't assume the worst, coz,' James said in his ear.

'Praise the Lord,' Mohun gasped. 'I feared you'd be gone. I've left my horse in the village, nearly killed the poor beast to get here in time.'

'What news, man?' Bassett said urgently.

'He is safe.' Mohun's grin widened. 'Well, he was when I left Luppit. He is grievous hurt, but will mend, Hartley says, given rest and nursing.'

'Thank God,' Gifford breathed fervently.

'And the others?' Pollard asked.

'All well. We took him from under the rebels' noses with barely a shot being fired.'

Bassett slapped Mohun on the back. Everyone was grinning like a lunatic and for a moment nobody spoke, their relief palpable.

Gifford craned down the path. 'Is Tawford not with you? Where is everyone? What were you doing in Luppitt?

'And what happened to your beard?' Acland added.

Mohun put a hand to his chin. 'Thereby hangs a tale.' He

grinned. 'We dressed as maids and ambushed the rebels at Ottery St Mary, then stayed the night with Southcott's aunt at Mohuns Ottery. Hartley's taking Tawford to Cobb's place today; he'll be safe on Exmoor till he's recovered. Tawford's countermanded Hartley's orders, that's why I'm here. We're not going north – we are to go to Sir Ralph Hopton's aid. Lyddon and Sydenham are already on their way to Cornwall.'

'Why? Is there news?' Chichester asked.

'Zach picked up some gossip from a Plymouth carter in Exeter. Sir Richard Buller has called for the militia to muster at Bodmin and means to confront Sir Ralph before he has a chance to rally the Cornish. Tawford wants us to be there.' He grimaced. 'Hartley thinks he can keep Tawford off a horse for three weeks – I'd be surprised if he manages three days. When I left they were already arguing about it. Our Captain was not in the best of moods this morning.' Mohun grinned. 'But he is great with child and you know how that affects a woman's temper.' He slapped his knees and cracked out laughing.

The others gazed at him, perplexed. 'Are you going to share the joke, Will, or do you mean to keep us guessing?' Acland clapped him on the shoulder.

Before Mohun could reply, Bassett broke in. 'Come on in, get yourself a drink and you can tell us all about it in comfort. In fact, we have cause to celebrate, why don't we broach a barrel?'

They piled back into the tower room. It took quite some time to tell the tale, Mohun's graphic descriptions occasioning a good deal of raucous laughter. When they finally saddled up and led their mounts down to the village, it was well after noon. The Churchwarden, looking distinctly relieved, appeared at his door to wave them goodbye. Dickon was feeling happy. He glanced back at the Mump wondering if he would ever see it again; it seemed he had been there forever. With a shrug, he turned his face forward and kicked his mount into a canter.

Mounted on Chichester's fine horses there was no point in pretending to be peasants, but the clothes the men habitually wore: knee-length boots, woollen stockings, worsted breeches, linen shirts, buff leather jerkins, hats and oiled cloaks, were much as any regular soldier would wear, whatever his allegiance, so long as his master was wealthy enough to clothe him. Each man was armed and led a second mount to carry his saddlebag, his spare weapons, powder flasks and ammunition concealed in a rolled up blanket strapped to its back.

Riding beside his cousin, it surprised Dickon to see so many people going about their business as if everything was normal. He saw lines of ponderous oxen drawing ploughs across fields of stubble, the turned earth behind them flocked with screaming gulls. The further west they rode, the redder the earth became. He saw children herding sheep and cattle onto fresh autumn pasture, farmyards busy with men flailing barley while women winnowed the grain and small children got in the way. The only sign of the times was where villagers had blocked the road with ramshackle barricades, but these were largely unmanned and although Dickon and his six companions received many a fearful sideways glance, they were allowed to pass unchallenged. They spent the first night at an isolated farm, where the farmer, pleasantly surprised by their offer of payment for horsemeat and shelter, took them for Godly men and gave them use of his barn.

The following morning they skirted Exeter and crossed the river Creedy on the outskirts of Crediton. There they saw a column of foot soldiers marching towards them led by a man on horseback.

'The town's Posse Comitatus I would guess,' Chichester said to Dickon out of the corner of his mouth, drawing rein. Pulling their mounts to the side of the road, the St Michael's men waited for the Posse to approach. Most places of any size had a trained band to defend the town in times of emergency and Dickon had expected this, but his stomach clenched in anticipation. As the column neared, he saw a few of the soldiers wore odd bits of hand-me-down armour. Many carried staves and pikes. Some had fowling pieces or ancient muskets, one even carried a longbow, but only their captain was mounted. Dickon relaxed, they were a rabble. If it came to fight, none was a match for Tawford's men.

'Leave them to me,' Chichester grinned, moving forward to meet them. He stood up in his stirrups. 'Are you for Parliament, lads?' When they noisily assented, he waved his hat – from which he had earlier with some reluctance torn the bedraggled feathers – and cheered.

'Good day to you.' Their captain drew rein bringing the column to a halt. 'Captain Thomson, your servant, Sir,' he addressed Chichester. 'Might I ask who you are and whither you are bound?'

'Good day to you, Captain, we are under orders from the Earl of Bedford and bound for Cornwall. The enemy surrendered Sherborne a week ago, but some of the Godless bastards escaped with that turncoat Sir Ralph Hopton. He is raising the Cornish against us, had you heard?'

'I had not,' Thomson replied. 'This is grim news indeed.'

Chichester nodded. 'General Sir Richard Buller is at Bodmin mustering the militia. We are sent to his aid.' Chichester replaced his hat.

Thomson's gaze slid enviously to Chichester's horse. 'We receive little news in these parts. What else can you tell us?'

'Portsmouth has surrendered to our brave General Waller and we have secured Somerset and most of Dorset. The King raised his standard at Nottingham last month – you did know that?'

'That much at least!' Thomson looked indignant.

'Well, Lord Bedford has taken his army north to join our Lord General, the Earl of Essex. They say the King is at Shrewsbury and it is rumoured he plans to march on London. If so, a confrontation is inevitable.'

Grimacing, Thomson shook his head. 'This war is a foul matter.'

'Without a doubt, Captain, but with brave lads such as yours and with the good Lord on our side, we will soon wrest the King from his enemies and restore him to Parliament.'

'I pray God that it may be so, Sir...?'

'Lieutenant James, at your service, Captain.' Chichester made a small bow, gesturing to the others still waiting at the side of the road. 'We are under orders from the Earl himself.'

The man was obviously impressed. Dickon sniggered and looked down, fiddling with his reins. 'Control it, lad.' Bassett whispered. Chastened, Dickon straightened his face.

'I am happy to meet you, Lieutenant,' Thomson was saying. 'Will you do us the honour of inspecting the town's defences? I have been putting these lads through their paces this morning. Brave they may be, but they are mostly ploughboys, herders and shepherds and as you can see, our equipment is sadly wanting. I fear we are ill prepared for war. We would welcome the benefit of your experience.'

'I am honoured, Captain, but alas, we must make all speed.' Chichester smiled apologetically. 'If all goes well in Cornwall we will return this way and call in to see you then. God keep you and your lads safe meantime.'

'And you, Sir. I am obliged to you.' Thomson saluted and turning in the saddle shouted to his men. 'Advance your weapons!' Those who had arms to present did so and the column stood raggedly to attention while Chichester kicked his mount forward. 'For God, the King and Parliament,' he shouted. 'Death to the Cavaliers!'

Falling into place behind him, Dickon looked at the sea of cheering faces. The soldiers' enthusiasm was infectious and he found himself carried away by it, cheering with them at the top of his lungs. It was only as he quickened his pace to leave the posse behind it dawned on him what he was doing. These men were the enemy. If it came to battle, he would have to raise his sword against them. The thought sickened him and for many miles, he rode in sombre silence.

It took the rest of the day to journey to Okehampton, and all of the next to reach the Tamar at Polston Bridge, from whence they crossed into Cornwall.

12

Sunday 9th October, 1642

In urgent need of solitude and frustrated by his enforced inactivity, Alexander took up a flintlock carbine, loaded it and crept from the sleeping Warren. It was just before dawn. He climbed slowly towards the ridge, stopping to rest against an outcrop of rocks. Behind the distant swell of Dunkery the sky was beginning to lighten. Wind rustled through bracken. A fox barked, the cold air pungent with its scent. Settling the carbine in the crook of his arm Alexander pushed himself upright and scanned the hillside looking for the deer. Ellen would be less than pleased to find he had gone out alone. For nearly ten days he had been smothered with kindness. He knew they meant well and had borne it with unusual patience, but enough was enough. His wounds were all but healed and though his head was still sore, his vision was no longer blurred. The dizzy spells and headaches, fewer now, he had learned to hide. It was time he got back on a horse. True, he felt damnably weak, but the longer he waited the longer it would take to regain his strength. He needed to be free of mollycoddling. Tomorrow he would insist Hartley escort Ellen home and since the news from Cornwall was good, Hartley could then return to Prince Rupert. He would brook no more arguments.

Yesterday a letter had come in from Lyddon, brought by Dickon. The boy seemed to have grown in stature, his chest was broader and he now wore a carefully nurtured line of hair on his upper lip. He hadn't stopped talking until bedtime. Sir Richard Buller's call to arms had yielded only seven hundred men, while Hopton and Grenville had gathered close on a thousand. When they arrived in Bodmin, it was to find Buller had circumspectly retreated to Launceston in the hope of obtaining more men from Devon's Trained Bands. Cornwall's frightened officials had meanwhile issued indictments for illegal war-mongering and sent out the High Sheriff and his posse with orders to disperse both armies. Hopton, wanting the local magistrates on his side, had immediately postponed a confrontation with Buller and ridden to Truro to attend the Michaelmas Assizes and answer the charge in person. They had been astounded by his effrontery, but nonetheless much mollified.

Lyddon had written:

'His defence was nothing short of brilliant. He argued his case within the framework of the law and the jury soon acquitted him. They even expressed their gratitude to the King for sending Sir Ralph to their aid and gave him leave to muster the Cornish Trained Bands and drive Parliament's soldiers out of Cornwall. By Monday last, the High Sheriff had assembled some 3,000 foot on Moilesbarrow Down for our inspection. They were a poor lot, but all eager and cheering for the King. We sorted them into regiments and marched them to Launceston, but by the time we got there Buller had taken fright, dispersed his men and fled to Plymouth. Sir Ralph lost no time in securing Saltash and we now hold most of Cornwall without a shot being fired, which is just as well, for the Trained Bands (so called!) are as rusty as their weapons and undisciplined as children. They have been plundering and burning in the town. We have had to make an example

of the ringleaders and put twenty men in jail to cool their heads for it is doing the King's cause no good whatsoever. Sir Ralph has in mind to disband them and raise an army of volunteers before he attempts to cross the Tamar (he thinks it unlikely he will be permitted to take them out of Cornwall anyway). To that end, Sir Bevill Grenville has been entreating his friends and men are arriving every day. John Arundell (him they call Jack for the King), Jonathan Trelawny, John Trevanion and Sir Richard Vyvyan have brought nearly a thousand between them and say they will pay their wages out of their own pockets! There are many of like ilk and all generous to the cause, so it augurs well. As soon as he has enough men, Sir Ralph plans to attack Plymouth.

Nick Slanning says to thank you for the intelligence from Ireland. His privateers continue to run the blockade under the noses of the two men-o'-war stationed in the Roads. The rebels dare not venture in range of the guns at Pendennis and if they give chase, our ships go close in to the Channel Islands and are protected by the guns at Castle Cornet and Castle Elizabeth. Also, Sir Francis Bassett has found a master gunner to get the cannons working on St Michael's Mount, so we can land supplies more safely at Penzance in addition to Falmouth. Slanning is trading tin in Dunkirk for weapons and powder got by the Queen and according to our old friend George Goring (he is helping Her Majesty in France, as is Henry Jermyn, but I daresay you knew that) we can expect a shipment of ten thousand musketeers before long, also several companies of horse and possibly some heavy artillery (I wish!).

Mohun and the others arrived safely (Lord

Mohun is here so Will is having to behave himself.
You would scarcely know him!). We are all engaged
in recruiting and training volunteers until you
should send further orders. We have no news of
what is happening with the King. When will you
join us? Mohun says if you tarry too long, it will
all be over. I think he is overly optimistic.

Alexander was inclined to agree. He had no quarrel with
Hopton's strategy, but even with the help of the esteemed
Cornish gentry it could take weeks to raise an army capable of
taking Plymouth. Lyddon had scrawled a postscript:

Sir Ralph asks me to thank you for your efforts
on his behalf and bids me wish you a speedy
recovery. He is convinced Parliament will send an
army against us in short order once they receive
news of Cornwall. It would help to know how
much time we have and the numbers we must face.
I have decided to send Dickon with this – the lad
is coming on well and I would stake my life he
is trustworthy. We hope you may have some news
from Fane for Dickon to bring back to us. H.L.'

No. He had no news from Fane or anyone else, dammit.
Continuing his climb, Alexander pondered on Lyddon's words.
Certainly Parliament would mount a campaign against Hopton,
they could not afford to leave Cornwall in Royalist hands.
They would know by now the King had a ready supply of arms
and men coming from the Continent, they may even suspect
from Ireland too. It would not take a military genius to work
out that Exeter, Plymouth and even Bristol were increasingly
vulnerable to attack and if Hopton were successful, the war
in the South West would be over indeed. But the strength and
speed of Parliament's response would much depend on what
was happening in the Midlands. Alexander had sent a couple

of Cobb's men to find out, but neither had yet returned and there had been no word.

Alexander bunched his fists. To be so cut off from news at such a time was unsupportable. Like some naïve greenhorn, he had under-estimated James Dewett: how could he have been so careless? It was a question he had asked himself repeatedly since recovering consciousness to see Dewett's face leering over him. And where the devil was Cobb when he needed him? Still in London dancing attendance on Lord Westley, no doubt. A sharp stab of resentment rose in Alexander's throat. He still could not think of his erstwhile guardian without feeling angry and hurt. Part of his problem was having too much time to think about things best forgotten. Ignoring the rabbits skittering in his path Alexander quickened his pace and tried to empty his mind.

The stags had begun fighting yesterday. Their roars had echoed across the valley until late afternoon. When it was over, the forest had fallen strangely silent. Now, as the first rays of sunlight cast a hazy mantle of gold over the moor, guttural bursts of sound again carried on the wind. Searching the ridge, Alexander spotted the young stag high above him, its head thrown back proclaiming its triumph. A few hinds popped up from the bracken and cursorily viewed their new lord to see what all the noise was about before returning to their grazing. Amused by their nonchalance, Alexander quartered the ground until he found the scene of the battle. It had been a bitter struggle. The bracken was flattened for several yards and the ground deeply scored. Picking up the slots of the defeated animal, he followed them round the side of the hill into a skirt of oakwood.

He was an old fellow, this Lord of Exmoor, with all his rights and three atop his magnificent head, the twelve points of his wide black antlers worn shiny white at the tips. No longer able to support their weight, the dying beast had fallen to his knees. The drab, russet coat covering his thin body was grizzled like an old man's beard and the coarse greying ruff that fell about his thickened neck was stained and flecked with blood. Scenting Alexander the stag turned its head towards him, the once bright eyes sunk dully in their sockets.

Alexander raised his carbine and easing back the dog catch aimed for the beast's heart. As his finger tensed on the trigger there was a flurry of movement. A child shot out from the trees and flung herself across the stag's body. Alexander jerked his arm upwards and the ball sped harmlessly wide of its mark. A cacophony of crows rose from the treetops. The stag tried to rise, kicked out, knocked the child backwards. She crumpled and lay still.

In three strides Alexander reached her and pulled her away from the flailing legs. The animal's hooves had caught her on the temple. Blood trickled from under her hairline. Pressing his hand to her neck Alexander felt for her pulse. It beat strongly under his fingers. Relieved he reached for his hunting knife and turned back to the struggling stag. With a swift downward thrust he severed the beast's throat, watched its lifeblood, scarlet as the toadstools, gushing onto the forest floor. Alexander wiped his blade on the beast's rump and returned to the child, dropping to a crouch beside her.

She was a plain little girl, small, unkempt and painfully thin. Her dirty elfin face was framed by a lank tangle of dark red hair and across her tip-tilted nose was a smatter of freckles, repeated on her bare, skinny arms. He judged her to be about seven or eight. Her shift was torn, her legs smeared with blood from numerous scratches and her bare feet crusted with mud. She murmured restlessly and opened her eyes. Alexander caught his breath; they were extraordinary; the colour of woodland violets. As the child saw the knife in his hand she gasped, clasped her arms around her legs and rolled into a ball.

Quickly dropping the knife, he tried gently to prise them away. 'Hush, little one, do not be afraid. I mean you no harm.' He smiled down at her. 'I thought you were a maid, but now I see you are a hedgehog. Let me look at your hurts.'

Flinching away from him she turned her head towards the stag. It lay still, its eyes open, already glazing. Her lips trembled. 'You have killed him.'

'No. It was his son who killed him. I but eased his passing.'

'My mother could have made him well and I would have looked after him.' Angry tears coursed down her pale cheeks. Her voice had a slight Welsh lilt.

'You would have done him a disservice.' Alexander sat back on his heels making no attempt to touch her again. 'He was far too noble a creature to live as a pet, outcast from his tribe. He would not have thanked you; he knew his time was past. There is a new King now. That is the way of things.'

Defiantly she met his eyes. 'Is his spirit on its way to heaven, then?'

Alexander recognised a challenge when he heard one. 'How can you doubt it, kinchen?'

She unclasped her legs and sat up. 'The preacher says that beasts don't have a spirit and cannot go to heaven and to say so is blasphemous.'

'Does he now? Then why does our Lord trouble to know when every sparrow falls if not to make a place for it in heaven?' As Alexander spoke he remembered having had this conversation before. He saw another young, inquisitive face looking up at him hoping he would give the right response. Deliberately he forced down the memory, unaware of the shadow that passed across his face.

She looked at him curiously. 'Don't worry, I won't tell. Mama says that too.'

Apparently he had passed the test. 'There you are then. But others are not so wise as your Mama. Perhaps it is best to keep this wisdom to yourself lest she be blamed for leading you into blasphemy. Come, let me help you, you have a very large pigeon's egg on your head.' He held out his hand.

Pushing it aside she felt the lump on her head and winced. 'Have you got one too?' She looked at the bandage still swathing his head.

He laughed. 'Something like that, little one, but nowhere near as big as yours.'

She sat up straight and stared at him. 'I am not little. I am twelve years old and my name is Jennet.'

Alexander's mouth twitched. 'I do most humbly beg your pardon.' Moving up onto one knee, he bowed his head and taking her grubby hand in his brought it to his lips. 'Would the Lady Jennet allow me to assist her?'

Suddenly her mouth curved upwards and she let out a peal of laughter. 'Mama only calls me Jennet when she's cross. Usually it's 'Pixy'. You may call me Pixy if you are to be my friend.'

She was a captivating child. Unable to keep a straight face, Alexander laughed with her. 'That's a good name and I'd wager your ears are pointed under all that hair.' He put out his hand to see, dropping it as she started away from him.

'Supposing I had killed you. What would your Mama have said then? You will most certainly be 'Jennet' when she hears of it.'

'But you didn't.'

'No, thanks to you, young lady.'

She shrugged. 'What are you called?'

He smiled. 'Many things, not all of them complimentary, but Alexander is my name. One of my friends sometimes calls me 'Lapwing' if you like it better'.

She looked at him quizzically. 'Yes, it's a nice name, but why? You don't look like a lapwing, your beard is the wrong colour.'

'You will work it out if you get to know me better. Come. We should find your Mama and see if she can mend your head. Will you let me help you?' This time she nodded and grasping his proffered hand pulled herself upright. 'Can you stand or must I carry you?' She swayed against him. 'Whoa. I think I had better, don't you?' He swept her into his arms and winced.

'Is it far?'

'Not far, but what about him?' She looked down at the stiffening carcase.

'What would you have me do with him?'

'Bury him.'

'Do you not think your Mama might like to eat him?' The child bit her lip, her face crumpling. 'No,' he said hastily. 'Of course, he should be buried as befits a King, but I will have to come back and do it later.'

'Promise?' Tears trembled on her lashes.

'I promise. Look, I will even leave my carbine here. Now, which way do we go?'

Reassured, Jennet pointed through the trees. 'That way.'

Alexander carried her to the edge of the wood stopping when he came across a spring that bubbled out from bright green cushions of moss. Carefully putting her down, he knelt, cupped his hands and drank thirstily. The water was pale amber and tasted earthy. Pulling up a handful of moss he moistened it and carried it back to Jennet. 'You have some blood on your cheek. No, here.' He guided her hand. 'How does it feel?'

'It hurts.'

'I expect it does.'

'I feel sick.'

He gently rubbed her back as she vomited, bringing up a stream of yellow bile. 'Better?' She nodded miserably. He held his hand in front of her eyes. 'How many fingers?'

'Three.'

'How many now?'

She giggled, 'One.'

'That's alright then.' He bent to pick her up.

'I think I can walk now.' She scrambled to her feet.

'Very well, if you're sure.' His head itched. It would be good to be rid of Hartley's bandages. He put his hand up to scratch, thought better of it.

'What's really wrong with your head?'

'Someone hit me.'

'Why?'

'He thought I had tried to kill him.'

'Had you?'

He considered her for a moment and decided to opt for the truth. 'No, but I might have done.'

Her head on one side, Jennet looked into his eyes, nodded and grasped his hand, giving a little tug. 'It's this way.'

She led him out of the wood, picking her way up the hill through clumps of spiky grass. Pausing at the top to get his breath, Alexander looked about him. Dark clouds were gathering on the skyline. With the sharp clarity that precedes rain the Forest stretched like an artist's palette into the distance. Shafts of sunlight turned the bracken into swathes of fire, quickly dowsed by blue shadows chasing across the moor. Here and there were outcrops of grey stone and clustered round them dark patches of gorse spangled with knobs of butter yellow. The lower slopes were stained muted purple, drifts of faded heather colonising land that had been deforested and cultivated by a people long gone. A buzzard sailed high on the wind. Of the deer there was no sign.

Letting go of his hand, Jennet set off down the hill towards a low wall. Slithering on the scree-littered ground he clambered after her. The wall was encrusted with lichen, the crumbling stones held together by clumps of heather and gorse. Behind was a deep track, worn to bedrock by the water coursing down its middle. The sparse grassland beyond was dotted with sheep. Jennet scrambled over the wall and slid down the bank to wait for him. Feeling suddenly old, he followed.

'We are nearly there,' she said.

'I don't believe you. I think you really are a pixy and any minute now you will lead me through a hidden doorway into the hill and I shall sleep for five hundred years.'

She grinned. 'But only if you eat of the faerie feast.'

'So I'm right. You are one of the little people.'

She laughed. 'Papa used to tell me about them. He was the best storyteller in all of Wales.'

'But not now?'

The child's lips tightened. 'No.'

From her expression, Alexander knew better than to probe. The track dropped steeply into a narrow gorge. In silence they negotiated fallen boulders almost hidden by tall grasses and brambles. Weeds trailed out from fissures in the rock face, which was hung with moss and trickling with water. It smelled dank and musky. Suddenly Jennet spoke.

'I was in the barn with my brother. We were playing hide and seek and it was my turn to hide. I wanted to be by myself for a while, so I crept out and ran down over the fields. I knew it would take him a long time to find me. I shouldn't have left him, he was only little and I was supposed to be looking after him. I waited and waited, but he didn't come, and then I smelled the smoke. He'd climbed up to the ledge where Papa kept a tinderbox for the lamp.' She swallowed. 'I heard him screaming and I ran back, but the flames had caught the stack and the timbers were already on fire. Papa tried to save him, but the beam came down on top of them. Mama pulled them out, but my brother died and Papa nearly died too, he was so badly burned and his legs were broken.' She paused. 'He cannot walk now and he doesn't tell stories any more.'

Alexander was appalled. The silence stretched on while he tried and failed to find words of comfort. 'Thank you for telling me, I can imagine how hard that was.' He stopped walking and put a hand on her shoulder turning her to face him. 'But Pixy, it was an accident, it was not your fault.'

She stared up at him, her big, beautiful eyes glistening with unshed tears. 'Yes, it was.'

'How old were you?'

'Seven. Owen was only four, so you see I should never have left him on his own, but Mama says it doesn't matter because it was the Lord's will. She says we should not question His divine purpose, but be thankful that we had Owen in our lives, even for so short a time.'

Alexander frowned down at her. 'Your Mama is right, of

course. But it does matter, doesn't it? It matters terribly. You lie awake at night and see your brother's face. You live what happened over and over and imagine how it might have been if you had acted differently. But you can't turn back time and little bits of you shrivel up inside because you know there is nothing you can do to change things and the guilt tears at your soul.' Abruptly he stopped speaking, his breath caught in his throat. Whatever was the matter with him?

Jennet studied his face, her eyes wide. 'How do you know it is like that?'

'It happened to me too, except that Henry wasn't my brother, but I thought he was then, and we were close like brothers. Like your Owen, he was killed and it was my fault.'

She didn't seem to find this strange. 'What happened to him?'

'I let him ride my stallion. It was much too big for him and I knew I shouldn't, but he'd gone on pestering until in the end I lost patience and we swapped mounts. We'd not been riding long when something sparked the horse and it bolted. Henry was only a little boy and he couldn't control it. I was riding ahead of him. I heard him shout and turned back, but I was too late.' Alexander stared down at the track, his eyes distant, unseeing. 'I saw the horse fall, it seemed to happen very slowly.' He stopped speaking. He felt drained. In all these years he had never spoken of it, not to a living soul. Somehow this child had got under his skin, broken down his defences. Behind his eyes the pain started to throb.

Jennet put out her hand and grasped his arm giving it a little shake. 'Then what happened?'

Alexander started, raised his eyes to look at her. 'The horse broke its leg. Henry was crushed beneath it. There was nothing I could do. He died very quickly.' The horrifying scenes unfolded behind Alexander's eyes: the struggling stallion, Henry's face contorted in agony gasping for help; the sound of the breath bubbling from the animal's windpipe as he drew a knife across its throat; somehow pulling the supine body off the screaming, whimpering boy. Alexander felt again the sick, overwhelming grief, the utter helplessness he had felt as he had seen the extent of Henry's injuries and known there was nothing he could do but hold the boy close and watch him die. Then he had carried Henry's broken body home and Robert had called him a murderer.

Alexander shook his head, dashing his hand across his eyes in an attempt to wipe the image away. Jennet was looking at him, her eyes filled with sympathy. He forced himself to smile at her. 'But it was different for me, Pixy. I was a man grown, responsible for my actions. You were scarcely more than a babe. You must believe me; nobody could or should hold you responsible for Owen's death. It was not your fault.'

'I know,' she said simply. 'And I am sorry about Henry.'

Catching hold of his hand, she tugged at him and they continued walking. He became aware that it was raining, a persistent clammy drizzle that crept under his shirt and trickled down his neck.

Jennet pointed to the end of the gorge. 'We're here.'

Alexander looked to where she pointed. The track curved around a flat piece of ground gouged out of the hillside. Behind it the scarp rose sharply to the heath. Below, scattered with clumps of sedge and stone, the windswept land dropped steeply to a rivulet. Built into the scarp from the stone it had yielded was a longhouse. It faced a yard of embedded shale. The thatch, reaching almost to the ground, was rotting and green with moss. A drift of smoke wafted from the chimney. Butted on to the house was a shippon, beside that a linhay and on the other side two swine-cotes and a stable. The barn – what remained of it – stood on the far side of the yard. It was open to the sky, the skeletal timbers scorched and blackened, the collapsed walls covered in weeds and rubble.

Jennet led Alexander through a gateway into the yard. He looked down the length of the valley beyond, wondering as he did so how anyone could survive in this wild remoteness, least of all a woman with a small daughter and a crippled husband.

A few hens pecked desultorily in the yard and two hat-rack cows with stringy udders stood outside the linhay, one was cudding contentedly, the other was scratching its tail against a post, uttering little groans of ecstasy as it swayed from side to side. A black pig was wallowing in a pool of mud. It sat up and plodded snuffling to meet them. Careless of the mud, Jennet scratched its ears affectionately.

'This is 'Mochyn.'

'An unusual name.' Alexander surveyed the animal as it leaned against Jennet's hand.

She giggled. 'It's Welsh for pig. We used to have a horse too, but he died. He was very old.' Letting go of Alexander's hand she ran across the yard, pushed open the front door and disappeared into the house.

Hesitantly he followed, ducking under the lintel into the gloom of the parlour. The room smelled of peat smoke drifting from the smouldering fire and the flags were strewn with rush matting. There were two small windows both overlooking the yard, neither letting in much light. Against the back wall was a cupboard stairway. In one corner a hound was suckling a mewing litter of pups. She growled a warning deep in her throat as he moved into the room, his head grazing the uneven beams. The furniture was sparse: a table, a settle, a chest and four rough-hewn back-stools. Leaning against one was a lute. As Alexander brushed past it the strings shivered with sound, making his fingers itch to play. A black cat dozed on the settle and by the hearth a fox cub lay curled in a basket, a bandage on one of its paws. Jennet was not there and Alexander could hear no voices. He walked towards a door that stood ajar at the end of the room. Gently pushing it open he saw Jennet. She was standing behind a table fiddling with her hands and looked agitated.

At the end of the table stood a woman her head turned away, her gaze on the child. She was working with a pestle and mortar, her face flushed with effort, the sleeves of her shift pushed up to her elbows. He saw that one of her hands was misshapen and her wrist covered in ugly scars. The table was cluttered with an assortment of small clay pots, bunches of lemon balm, feverfew and garlic. The acrid smell caught in Alexander's throat. The woman's dark, auburn hair was plaited into a thick shining rope that fell from beneath her coif to the small of her back and was tied with a slip of red ribbon. She was not much taller than Jennet, and slender. He could have spanned her waist with his hands. She wore a white apron over her nettle-green petticoat, the thick woollen fabric unevenly faded and many times darned, but clean. Her berry-red bodice was tightly laced over her shift and a white neckerchief modestly covered the swelling curve of her breasts. Her ankles were bare of stockings and on her feet she wore wooden clogs. From her demeanour it was clear she did not know he was there. Not wanting to startle her, Alexander stayed in the doorway and rattled the latch. 'Good day to you, Mistress.'

She ignored him and went on pounding with the pestle, but Jennet looked up and flashed him a smile. Taking hold of the woman's arm she shook it and pointed. The woman started, hastily pulled down her sleeves to cover her wrists and turned her face to him. 'Forgive my unseemliness,' she murmured, bobbing a curtsey, 'I was unaware of your presence or you would not have found me so.'

Dumbfounded he stared at her, unable to hide his horror. One side of her face was cruelly swollen and blotched purple with bruising. Under his startled gaze her flush deepened. Quickly recovering his composure he moved into the room shook his head and gave a short bow. 'It is I who must apologise for my intrusion, but I happened across Jennet on the moor. She has had a slight accident and I thought it best to escort her home. I am Alexander Dynam of Tawford,' he added as an afterthought, not sure what Jennet had told her.

She transferred her gaze from his lips to his eyes. 'No, please don't apologise, you have been very kind.' Resting the pestle, she wiped her hands on her apron. 'I am Bethan Morgan,

Jennet's mother. How can I thank you? Have you eaten? May I offer you a drink?' Her voice was low and husky.

He shook his head. 'Thank you, no, I do not wish to intrude upon you further. I just thought you should know your daughter somewhat impetuously thought to hug a dying stag and in so doing collided with its hind legs. She was unconscious for a few moments and has a nasty bruise on her scalp. Nothing too serious – as far as she will let me see – but you should perhaps take a look at it.'

From behind her mother Jennet stuck her tongue out at him, quickly retracting it as Bethan, with an expression of puzzlement, turned back to face her daughter's gesticulating hands. 'Ah yes, the Lord of the Forest, you have put him out of his misery,' she said after a moment. 'It is for the best. His teeth had gone. He would not have survived another winter. I am sorry if my daughter got in your way, I am afraid she wants to rescue every hurt creature in the forest.' She looked at Jennet in exasperation. 'Though she has never brought me a young man before,' she murmured.

Alexander's eyebrows shot up. 'But I am not in want of rescuing, Mistress, and besides, she was not in my way at all. If anyone is to blame, it is I.' He winked at Jennet and was rewarded with a grin.

Bethan continued as if he hadn't spoken. 'You will have seen the fox? We have a young hind in what is left of the barn, also a hare and a squirrel, not to mention the numerous rabbits she has rescued from traps. You may be forgiven for thinking Jennet an imp, but despite appearances to the contrary I can assure you I am not a witch.' She gave a hesitant smile.

'No? How disappointing.' Alexander made a face at Jennet, who giggled. 'And I was so certain of it when I saw the cat.'

He had expected Jennet's mother to look careworn, indelibly marked by the tragedy that had befallen her, but her eyes winked merrily back at him. She reminded him of a Jenny Wren. He returned her smile. 'If it is no trouble, may I change my mind about that drink?'

'Of course, but I fear we have run out of cider and the choice is limited to buttermilk or elderflower wine.'

Alexander gestured to his head and grimaced. 'I had best confine myself to the buttermilk, thank you.'

'You are hurt? It troubles you? Do you wish me to look at it?'

'Thank you, no. It has been looked at more often than I can bear of late.' He grinned. 'I have two nursemaids who vie with each other to care for me. It itches, that is all.'

'That is a good sign.' Her gaze was again focused on his lips. 'If you like, I can give you something for your headache.'

He shook his head. 'I had hoped it wasn't that obvious. Please don't worry, it will soon pass.'

She shrugged. 'As you wish.' Retrieving an earthenware jug from a stone shelf, she poured a cup of frothing buttermilk and handed it to him. 'Jennet, please take Mister Dynam through to the parlour then come back here so I can see to your head.'

'Call me Alexander, please, or Tawford if you prefer.' He paused awkwardly as things fell into place. He waited until she was looking at his face. 'Forgive me, but am I right in thinking you do not hear?'

She cast a vexed look at Jennet. 'Did my daughter not warn you? She should have done. I have some hearing on one side and can read your lips. If I concentrate I can understand most of what you say, but Jennet acts as my ears, which makes me lazy. I am sorry if I have embarrassed you.'

'Goodness, you have nothing for which to apologise.' Alexander took the cup.

Biting her lip, Jennet walked meekly round the table and led him back into the parlour. She pushed the cat off the settle and indicated he should sit. The cat gave him a malevolent stare, stretched, strolled towards the fire and proceeded nonchalantly to clean itself.

Sitting in its place, Alexander stretched out his legs gratefully. 'Why did you not tell me your Mama cannot hear, you minx?'

Jennet turned down her mouth. 'I'm sorry, I forgot.'

He wondered if that was true or if he had again been challenged and if so, whether he had passed the test. 'You speak with signs?'

'Yes.'

'That's clever. Who taught you to do that?'

'Mama. She made it up. Each finger is a sound, depending on how you move it, where you touch it and which hand you use.' With her right hand she touched the fingers on her left. 'Sometimes it is a whole word, like this.' She cupped her elbow.

'Can you teach me?'

Jennet smiled. 'It would take a long time, but yes, if you want me to.'

Putting down the cup he held up his hands and waggled his fingers at her. 'Have I said something rude?'

Shaking her head she laughed at him. 'No, but you do look funny.'

'I do?' Tucking his hands out of sight, he grinned. 'I shall have to be more careful, I can see. Has your Mama always been deaf?'

'No, it was after father started...,' the child faltered, dropping her gaze in dismay. As if on cue, there was a muffled shout from above. She looked up. 'Father, I must go to him.'

At the bottom of the stairs she hesitated and turned back, her hand on the newel post. 'He doesn't mean to hit her,' she said quietly. 'Sometimes he can't help it. He is in dreadful pain.'

Alexander watched her run up the stairs, two at a time. A loose floorboard creaked over his head and he could hear the muffled sound of a man's voice. He wondered how Jennet juggled her burdens of guilt and loyalty without seeming bitter. He had detected not a shred of resentment in her, just a curious mix of childishness and maturity. At least she knew who she was, he thought sourly. She was not some whore's get spawned in the gutter – or something unspeakably worse.

His lip curled in self-disgust. Gulping down the buttermilk he went back to the kitchen.

'That was delicious, thank you.' He handed Bethan the empty cup. 'I really must go. Please say goodbye to Jennet for me. She has gone up to her father.'

'You are welcome. Morgan would want to greet you himself, but I am afraid he is not well enough to come downstairs today. It is a struggle, he has lost the use of his legs.'

'But not his fists evidently.'

Her eyes dark, Bethan looked at him steadily and said nothing. Alexander felt like a small boy caught with his finger in the flummery. 'Forgive me. I should not have said that. Jennet told me about the fire and your son. I am sorry.' He framed his words carefully.

She nodded, putting a hand up to her face. 'I am afraid you have caught us on a bad day. It is not always so. Some days are worse than others. He is in much pain.' She dropped her gaze. 'And he blames me,' she added softly.

'For the fire?'

She looked up sharply. 'Lord, no! For his surviving it.'

'Dear God!' Compassion welled in his throat. 'But if he cannot walk, why can't you…'

'Get away from him?'

He nodded.

'Because I am his wife,' she said simply. 'I am all he has left that he feels able to control. How can I take that from him too? Besides, there is Jennet… she dotes on him.' She shrugged, looked away, 'It is hard for you to understand.'

She was right. He did not understand that kind of sacrifice.

'Do you have any help?'

'Most folk hereabouts think I go about on my broomstick after dark, so they keep well away from us, but some are kind. The Minister comes to see us sometimes.'

He laughed. 'And do you?'

'I only wish I could.' She smiled and gestured to the pots

on the table. 'I exchange potions for food and we have a neighbour down the valley who helps with the sheep.' She shrugged. 'We manage, though it is hard sometimes for Jennet. She is a wayward child.'

'She is delightful.' Standing close to her, Alexander looked into Bethan's eyes, they were slate grey and webbed with laughter lines. She regarded him calmly, her unmarked cheek was pale as alabaster, her mouth full and soft. Strangely moved, Alexander wanted to reach out and touch her. He took her scarred, twisted hand and raised it to his lips. 'I know from your daughter that you are wise, I see that you are also brave.'

Her fingers fitted snugly into his. He felt strangely comforted. Reluctantly he released them and turned to go.

Her lips curved in a slight smile. 'We will see you again.'

He hesitated, turned back, a polite denial on his lips, but before he could utter it she said softly, 'It was not a question.'

The hairs stood up on the back of Alexander's neck. He gave Bethan a searching look, but she said nothing more. At the front door he looked back. She stood watching him as though turned to stone, her twisted hand curled at her throat.

By the time Alexander had trudged back to the Warren it was past noon, still drizzling and he was cold to the marrow. Coming up the track towards him were Zach and Dickon. As they neared, Alexander scowled.

'Don't tell me, it's the wet nurse and the infant come looking for me.'

Dickon stared at him indignantly, but Zach's face creased in a relieved smile. 'It be the Lapwing himself and sour tongued as usual. Your lady sent us. I warn you, she's chizzly as old grit.'

'Why does that not surprise me? Since you're here, you can do something for me. I left the old stag in the oak wood over yonder.' He gestured towards the ridge. 'If you ride on up the hill you'll pick up his slots. You'll find a carbine by the body.'

'He's gone then, poor old bugger. Aye, I'll fetch'un back for you. Stringy as old boots I wouldn't be surprised. He'll need a deal of hanging.'

'There's not enough meat on him to make it worth the trouble. Take a spade and bury him.'

'Bury him?'

'Yes, bury him. Go shake your ears, Zach. Do I have to say everything twice?'

'If he's no good for eating why not let the crows have him?'

Under Zach's curious scrutiny, Alexander felt faintly uncomfortable. It annoyed him. 'Because I made a promise to a young lady.'

Zach let out a cry, his eyes watering. 'Do you say?' he wheezed, winking at Dickon. 'I knew it, he's tight as a tick in a mattress. You didn't have to go out looking for it, my friend. There's many a moon-faced wench back here would've obliged had you but asked.' Dickon snorted.

Alexander scowled up at them. 'You can stop that right now. She is but a child, name of Morgan.'

Zach's laughter stilled. 'The witch's maid?' Dickon, still grinning, looked suddenly interested.

'Balderdash!' Alexander fumed. 'Her mother's a respectable young woman. She's no witch.'

Zach scratched his nose pensively. 'That's not what I heard tell. They do say she turned her man into a toad and gives him suck with her devil's titty. Fletcher's seen him when he was over to Hore Oak. Hopping about he was, all hairless and warty and hollering like a beast.'

Alexander raised a contemptuous eyebrow. 'And I suppose he also saw Mistress Morgan flying on her besom.'

'He didn't say nothing 'bout that.' Under Alexander's mocking gaze Zach shifted uncomfortably in the saddle.

'It's naught but superstitious twaddle, Zach and I'm surprised at you.'

The gypsy's face stiffened. 'That's as may be, but I'm

telling you they sort's best left alone. They'll put a murrain on your cattle as soon as look at you.'

Alexander shook his head wearily. 'Fletcher is a numbskull, but I had you down as a man of some intelligence. I see I was mistaken. Have you never seen a face badly scarred from burning? The man was trapped under a beam trying to rescue his son when their barn caught fire. His wife got him out, but he can't walk. He only survived because of her healing skills. Their boy died. Enough to make any man holler, wouldn't you say?'

Zach dropped his gaze and flicked the reins at his mount's wet mane. The horse snorted, shaking its head. Behind it, Dickon's horse pawed restlessly and danced sideways towards Alexander. He stepped back quickly, almost falling over the verge. 'Can't you keep that animal under control, idiot boy?'

Stung, Dickon kicked his horse forward and rode off up the track, his departing back speaking volumes.

Alexander cursed under his breath.

Zach shook his head. 'If I were you, I'd be more careful with that boy.'

'Fortunately you're not,' Alexander retorted. 'I want you to get hold of some timber, take a couple of men and rebuild the Morgans' barn, and before the winter sets in you can also renew their roof, the thatch is rotten in places. And while you're at it, load up a cask of ale, some sacks of flour and a side of cured beef. The family is barely surviving and from the look of her, the child is close to starving.'

The gypsy huffed and mumbled, but under Alexander's steely gaze, inclined his head.

'Do it, Zach. You'll change your mind about Bethan Morgan when you meet her.' Alexander turned away. 'And don't forget to pick up a spade for the stag.'

The following morning, after much tiresome wrangling, Alexander finally got his way and Ellen, having closely inspected his wounds and made him promise to keep her informed of his whereabouts, mounted up and left, with Hartley in courteous attendance. Earlier, he had sent Dickon back to Cornwall with a reply for Lyddon. The boy had gone readily enough, but had barely spoken two words since yesterday. Alexander knew he should have found time to mend Dickon's hurt pride, but he lacked the patience for it right now. There would be time enough.

A little after mid-morning, Zach, Mouse and Billy Ridley left the Warren carrying axes and trailing a string of sumpters loaded with mallets, chisels, a coil of rope, bags of nails, bundles of reed and the food Alexander had asked for. Sarah had wept to hear of the Morgans' plight and had included a tub of lard, a cask of salt, some apples and a small box of her precious sugar. Finally she had bundled up some of the children's warm hand-me-down clothes for Jennet and a shawl for Bethan. Alexander had written a short note to Jennet, as an afterthought wrapping it around the gillyflower trinket, found lying forgotten in his pocket, and tucked it into the bundle. He thought it might please her. The amethyst would match her eyes. He wondered briefly how Bethan would react to the help he had so impulsively arranged for her. He doubted she would refuse it, however hurt her pride. Alexander had warned Zach about her deafness, which he had discussed with Hartley. As he suspected, regular blows about the head were quite likely to have damaged the delicate membranes in her ears. Hearing was rarely recovered in such cases, Adam had confirmed.

When they had all gone, the first thing Alexander did was to remove his bandages and scratch his head. The relief was exquisite. The pain made his eyes water. He then packed his saddlebags, picked out an oiled cloak, selected a hat and placed it gingerly on his head, buckled on his sword, stuck a pistol in his belt and thrust a dagger into his boot. He could hear the rumble of men's voices overlaid by the clattering of pots, a baby crying and women shrieking with laughter. Leaving a handful of coins on his bed, enough to pay for the Morgans' gifts and more, he quietly let himself out at the back and went round to the stables, picked out a fleet-footed chestnut gelding and saddled it.

By chance it was Fletcher who was on watch at the standing stone. Alexander reined in his horse and looked down at him. He was a skilled cutpurse; a cunning, wiry little man, the dross of the gutter in which Cobb had found him. Under Alexander's gaze he shifted uncomfortably, his eyes flicking from side to side. Alexander leaned down, spoke softly, his voice menacing. 'Bethan Morgan is not a witch and her husband is not a toad. I don't care what you thought you saw, if I hear that you've spread any more tittle-tattle about that family, I will whip the flesh off your backbone. Is that clear?'

Fletcher shrank back, nodded and looked resentfully down at his boots.

'I said, is that clear?' Alexander contemplated him for a moment and manoeuvred his mount to push against the little cutpurse.

Fletcher stepped back, came up against the standing stone and gasped. 'Aye, it be clear.' He gazed sullenly at Alexander who nudged forward. Pinned to the stone by several hundredweight of horseflesh Fletcher cried out. 'Stop! You be crushing me.' Ignoring him, Alexander leaned the full weight of the horse against him. Fletcher's voice rose to a breathless shriek. 'I'll not say another word about them. I swear it on my Mother's grave.'

Alexander nodded. 'Good.' Reining back, he set his horse up the track without a backward glance, leaving the frightened little man doubled up and glowering, his arms about his ribs.

The sky was overcast, it looked as though a storm was brewing. Alexander pulled his collar up against the drizzle and settled into an easy canter. It felt good to be on a horse again. Once off the moor, he turned his horse towards the London road. Largely thanks to Jennet, he had reached a decision. It was time he faced his demons.

13

Although Ellen's anxiety about Alexander hovered over her like a grey cloud, she was pleased to be leaving the Warren, riding astride, dressed once more as a man. Grateful as she was to Cobb's people, particularly Sarah, the lack of privacy had become increasingly onerous. The name of the encampment was, Ellen thought wryly, entirely apt. She had hoped for an opportunity to talk privately with Alexander, particularly about what Robert had told her, but he was so rarely alone. If it wasn't Zach it was Adam, or Sarah – and the children, always the children. Alexander attracted them like a magnet. And even had there been an opportunity, Ellen was not entirely sure he would welcome her intrusion into what was, for him, so personal a matter. Alexander had never spoken of it to her, never revealed why he and Robert had quarrelled and perhaps she should let sleeping dogs lie and not assume he would be glad of her sympathetic ear. And so she had kept her counsel, but as the days dragged by, Ellen had become uncharacteristically irritable. If she was honest with herself, much of it stemmed from her close proximity to Adam. It had been difficult for them both and Ellen felt she needed to clear the air between them, but now she could talk freely, she was finding it impossible to think of the right words. She was sharply aware of the glances Adam stole at her, riding attentively at her side. For a while they rode in silence, then both spoke at once.

'No, you first,' Ellen smiled.

'I was only going to say you must try to stop worrying

about him. We succeeded in keeping him quiet for a good deal longer than I ever thought possible. He is young and fit and his wounds will soon be fully healed.'

'Is it so obvious? I'm sorry. I must learn to cut the leading reins, but it is easier said than done. I forget he is no longer a mischievous boy.'

'And old habits die hard?' Adam smiled.

She inclined her head in wry acknowledgement. 'Aside from divesting himself of his bandages at the first opportunity, do you know what he will do now?'

Adam chuckled, but his face was grim. 'He'll go in search of news. We need to find out the state of play and what Parliament intends to bring against Cornwall, if indeed they have not already done so. Eventually he means to rejoin Sir Ralph Hopton, but I would hazard a guess he will go first to London and depending what he finds there, may well head north towards Shrewsbury, assuming the King and Prince Rupert haven't moved south by now. We are so cut off from any news here. For all we know, his Majesty may already have been brought to battle, with God knows what outcome.'

Adam stopped speaking and drew in behind her as the road narrowed. It descended sharply to a stream, the slippery shale giving way to thick mud. Their horses' hooves sucked and squelched. As they approached, two ducks flew squawking from the reeds.

'They at least are enjoying the weather,' Ellen said over her shoulder, splashing through the stream and starting up the hill on the other side.

Adam grinned, resuming his place at her side. 'This lack of news is frustrating in the extreme. It was the one disadvantage of hiding out at the Warren. Apart from Lyddon and now Dickon, not even our own men know exactly where we are,' he paused thoughtfully. 'Lord knows what's happened to Cobb, we had expected word from him before now.' He shrugged. 'Whatever, you can be assured Alexander will keep in touch with you since he gave you his word.'

'Which he tries never to break, I know. We must be thankful for small mercies, I suppose.' Ellen kicked her horse into a canter, her thoughts turning to Robert. She had twice sent to Marley Court for news. Her brother's steward had received a note of Robert's safe arrival in London, together with a recent copy of the *Mercurious Aulicus*, but aside from passages concerning the massive fortifications going up round London, which evidently the whole town had turned out to build, the newssheet contained little of interest. Robert had ringed a graphic account of Sir Ralph Hopton's 'triumphant escape across Exmoor', which had obviously been written by someone with no knowledge of the area for the route Hopton was supposed to have taken was a nonsense. Aside from that, there was a brief account of the skirmish at Powick Bridge in which 'our dashing young Prince Rupert won the day with consummate skill and outstanding heroism.' Gratifying as it was to read, it was not difficult to tell where the writer's sympathies lay and required a heavy pinch of salt.

Reining back her mount to negotiate a boulder in her path, Ellen waited for Adam to catch up with her. 'I wonder if Robert is still in London. I wish I knew how he fares.'

'Cobb will have told him by now that Alexander is safe. His Lordship is doubtless on his way home, unless he means to stay and help Lady Bath petition for her husband's release. Did he say anything about it before he left?'

'No. I'm afraid our thoughts were solely on Alexander at the time. It would be like him, though. How selfish I am. I had not thought of Lord Bath in all this time. Poor Rachel, she must be at her wits' end. Parliament surely will not harm him though, will they?' Ellen looked at Adam for reassurance as they walked forward, keeping their horses in step.

'Lord, no! They will probably keep him in comfortable captivity until he agrees to pay the sequestration fine and gives his word not to bear arms against them, then they'll let him go.' Adam smiled. 'Don't worry. Her Ladyship is more than capable of holding her own in any negotiations with the likes of Lord Pembroke. Did you want to call at Marley Court on the way? There may be some news.'

Ellen shook her head. 'If there is news, they will bring it to the Barton.' She drew her mount to a standstill. It dropped its head to nose the verge, the reins pulling wet and slippery through her fingers. Ellen hated this persistent drizzle. If it was going to rain, let it rain properly. She shivered.

'Adam?'

He drew rein at her side. 'Yes?' He waited patiently, his brown eyes regarding her steadily, their warmth bringing a slight flush to her cheeks. Flustered, she dropped her gaze.

'There are things I have wanted to say to you,' she said at last. 'There has been no opportunity and now I am not sure how to begin.'

He looked at her thoughtfully, a slight frown creasing his brow. 'Sweet Ellen, there is no need for words between us. I know what you are going to say. I understand that you cannot possibly return the feelings I have obviously failed to hide from you. You do not need to spell it out for me, nor imagine you need to show me any kindness. I am no longer a callow youth.' He smiled faintly. 'In my own defence, I can say only that it has been difficult to be so near to you. I would have avoided it these past days if I could. I would only ask that you forgive me if I have embarrassed you.'

His look of misery brought tears to Ellen's eyes. 'But you have not,' she gasped in surprise. 'You do not embarrass me. How could you when I love you so dearly? I have never stopped loving you, Adam. You must surely be aware of it,' she cried.

Adam's mouth dropped open. If Ellen hadn't felt so torn with conflicting emotions, his expression would have made her laugh. Instead she managed a weak smile. 'As well for you there are no midges about, you'd have a mouthful by now.'

Adam shut his mouth quickly, his expression one of stunned disbelief. 'I thought... that is, when you married Lord Seymour, I was so sure...'

'I married Edward because I had no choice,' she said tartly. 'Oh Adam, why? Why did you leave me? I was so unhappy, so afraid.'

He leaned towards her putting out a hand to touch her arm.

'Sweetheart, don't weep, please. I had no idea. But this is wonderful. I never dared to hope even for a moment...' He gazed into her eyes. 'Of what were you afraid?'

'That I had lost your respect.' Her tears ran unchecked. 'I let you roll me in the hay like some lusty trollop impatient for the marriage vows. When you suddenly went away and didn't respond to my letters, what else was I to suppose?'

'But my dear, nothing could be further from the truth. The memory of what passed between us is one I treasure above all others, no less now than I did then.'

'Why then?' Ellen stared at his face as he struggled for words. 'Why did you leave me?'

'It was wrong of me to go without a word, but you must believe it was out of my respect for you that I did so,' Adam said gently. 'We were so young, Ellen. Even had it been a suitable match, I had nothing to offer you. Lord Westley would quite rightly never have agreed to it. I knew that if I allowed it to carry on, sooner or later there would be a scandal and your chances of ever finding a suitable husband ruined. I could not have lived with the guilt of it. I had to let you go. It was the most painful thing I have ever had to endure, but I felt it was the only honourable thing to do.'

Adam's eyes pleaded with Ellen to understand. In the distance, a flock of curlews rose from the heath, their plaintive fluting in tune with her anguish. She cried out, 'But why did you not tell me how you felt?'

Adam sighed heavily. 'I just wish I had been strong enough at the time, but I was so afraid my resolve would weaken if I saw you again. When I eventually found the courage to return and face you, explain why I had acted as I did, I learned you were betrothed to Edward, a man far more suited to be your husband than I could ever be. Hard as it was, I knew then that I had acted for the best and no explanation was necessary.'

Ellen looked up sharply, unable to hide her anger. 'For the best? The best for whom? It didn't occur to you that I might have liked a choice? Was I so stupid a creature that my opinion was judged of no importance?' She breathed deeply, trying to stem her flood of exasperation. What use in being angry now?

A sudden squall of wind made Ellen look up. The heavens had responded to her wish. Black clouds were gathering on the horizon. A faint flicker of lightening in their midst was followed by a distant rumble of thunder. A few large drops of rain smattered onto her upturned face.

'Of course I never thought you were stupid, it wasn't like that.' Adam glanced at the sky. 'We should take shelter before this breaks.' He stood up in the stirrups scanning their surroundings. 'Look, a cattle shed, over there, quickly.'

Collecting his horse, Adam seized Ellen's reins and led the way across the fields.

Ducking their heads they rode under the eaves and dismounted, looping their reins over a gatepost. The cattle shed was dark, empty but for a heap of mouldering straw and reeked of stale cow dung. Adam wrinkled his nose. 'It's leaking I'm afraid, but will afford us some shelter while this passes.' He searched the thatch over their heads, pointed to the far wall. 'It's drier over there.'

Ellen shrugged, pulling off her sodden hat and cloak and flinging them away. 'No matter, I can't get any wetter.' She looked at Adam's face. It was etched with misery. 'Please don't look like that. I cannot bear it.'

'Like what?' He was startled.

'Sad. I didn't mean to be angry with you. I was then, but not any more. It is gone, past; there is no profit in dredging it up now. Forgive me.'

'You have every right to be angry. We may be older and perhaps a little wiser, but in some ways nothing has changed.

Not a day goes by I do not regret my weakness and wish I had acted differently.'

Ellen bit her lip. 'Nor I, but it is easy with hindsight. When you went away and the weeks went by with no word from you, I thought you had forgotten me, that I meant nothing to you. I was convinced I had been naïve, failed to recognise your words of love as a ploy to satisfy your lust – and how well they succeeded!' She grimaced. 'I fell for them hook, line and sinker. Oh Adam, I loved you so very much and I was so ashamed. Then, not long after you had gone, Robert brought Edward home to meet me. I knew he wanted the match and I felt I had nothing to lose.' Ellen faltered, her eyes distant. 'Edward was so kind, so gentle, such a comfort to me, and I did him such a very great wrong.'

'How can you say that?' Adam protested. 'You were a dutiful wife, I am sure. You gave him a child and had he lived would doubtless have given him more.' Adam bent to retrieve Ellen's hat and cloak, shook them out and laid them over an empty manger. The horses were standing together, heads drooping companionably close. There was a rumble of thunder, sounding closer now. Adam glanced towards the doorway; the rain so heavy he could hardly see through it, the water puddling and splashing up from the muddy ground, swamping the entrance. He turned back to Ellen, who was leaning against the far wall, her face deep in shadow. He walked towards her. 'I don't doubt you made Edward happy. He could have asked no more of you.'

'You think not? He might have asked for honesty!' Ellen retorted. 'He deserved more than a miserable chit of a girl dreaming of her lover. I came to him only half a person, but worse than that... With a sharp gasp, she stopped speaking, blood suffusing her cheeks. Dear God, what would he think of her. And yet, did he not deserve to know the truth?

Adam had not noticed. 'I thought in time you would forget me. I never dreamed...,' he shrugged, helplessly. 'I kept your letters, I have them still, but I could never bring myself to write back. You were so far above me and I was so afraid I would weaken and flee to your side, beg you to live as my wife. Never mind I had no money, was not yet qualified and had no prospects beyond those of a country physician. Never mind if your brother disowned you, society shunned you, so long as I had you at my side. Sweetheart, how could I be so selfish? I could never have kept you in the manner you were born to and deserved. I would have taken from you everything you held most dear.' Adam's voice cracked. 'How long would it have been before you hated me?'

Ellen let out a cry of frustration at his words. 'But that's the whole point, Adam. Don't you see? You were everything I held most dear. I never cared a whit for the trappings of wealth, I never would have minded living a humble life so long as we lived it together, and as for the approval of society, for goodness sake, surely you know me better than that?'

'I do now, but not then.' He grimaced. 'I thought I was doing what was expected of me, what was right for you. So puffed up with self-righteousness and honourable sacrifice I failed even to consider your right to make a choice. Can you ever forgive me?' he whispered. 'Is it too late for us now?'

Ellen dropped her gaze. 'If anyone should plead forgiveness, it is I of you.'

Reaching towards her, Adam stretched out his thumb to brush the tears from her cheeks. 'In the name of all that's holy, what can there possibly be for me to forgive you, sweet girl?'

She swallowed. Closing her eyes, she leaned her cheek into his hand feeling the warmth and strength of it. For a moment her courage faltered, then she drew back and faced him squarely. 'I am no sweet girl, Adam. You do not know me, of what I am capable.'

He studied her face. 'Perhaps not, but I cannot imagine there could be anything that would change how I feel about you.'

Ellen arched her eyebrows. 'No? Not even that I am a cheat and a liar?'

He sighed, a faint look of amusement in his eyes. 'Ellen, my Ellen, don't torture yourself so. You could never be either, not knowingly. What is it that distresses you so? Tell me.'

Adam's gentle expression was one of kind concern. He looked at her as he would at an innocent child and some devil in Ellen wanted to wipe it from his face. Her mouth twisted.

'I might have been a whore so well did I spread my legs for Edward.' She heard Adam's gasp, went on regardless. 'I took what you and I had learned together in that soft, sweet hay and cheapened it, used it to ensnare him.'

Adam was not patronising her now. His face was a mask of pain. Ellen, tears flooding her face, did not spare him.

'Edward stood no chance. But even had he not loved me, I knew he was too honourable to walk away. I used him coldly and calculatedly, Adam. What made it worse was that he was so happy, so full of plans. I should have stopped it. I knew you had returned, but when you didn't come to me, I was so afraid your love had been a sham. Afraid you would reject me if you knew the truth, or worse, that I would tie you to me out of duty. So I acted the coward and I lied to Edward. I put my hand on the Holy Book and swore to love and honour that good, selfless man and in so doing, bound us to him until death. And I tried to love him, God knows I tried...' Ellen's voice tailed away, spent.

'Us?' His face paled.

'Yes, Adam! I was carrying your child, our beautiful daughter. She was yours and mine, not Edward's. Don't you see? I cheated you both. Not only did I deceive my husband, I stole from you your daughter. By keeping you in ignorance I took away your right to make a choice even as you had taken mine. It is for that I beg your forgiveness.'

Adam stared at her, tears starting to his eyes. His hand dropped lifeless to his side. Unable to bear it, Ellen looked away. 'Do not punish me with silence, Adam, please. I have been punished enough. Our little girl was the light of my life, she was all I had left of you and the Lord took her from me.

It was no more than I deserved, but I miss her so badly. I miss her, I miss her...' The strain was suddenly too much. In deep, shuddering sobs, Ellen's control gave way and she swayed towards him.

'Dear God,' Adam whispered. 'My love, my poor love.' Blindly he reached for her. 'Oh my dear, I'm sorry, I'm so very sorry. Hush, sweetheart, hush.'

Ellen moved into his arms, his breath felt warm against her cheek as he murmured words of comfort, rocking her gently while she fought to bring her grief under control. At last she fell silent, drained, lifted her head to look into his eyes. 'How I have longed to tell you, to feel you close, but I don't deserve this comfort, such weakness is sheer self-indulgence.' Ellen smiled up at him through her tears. 'And here's me, supposed to be a man!'

Adam returned her smile. 'Never, not even in those dreadful britches and shorn like a Roundhead.' He teased back a wet curl from her brow, his face suddenly drawn with tension.

'Ellen, sweet Ellen,' he murmured. 'Tell me it is not too late for us.'

'It is not too late for us,' she whispered. Shivering, she reached up, her lips seeking his with all the hunger of their wasted years.

Lifting her against him, he carried her to the pile of straw and laid her gently down.

'Our first bed of hay smelled a good deal sweeter than this,' she murmured wrinkling her nose.

The sound of his laughter was lost in a crash of thunder as the storm broke over their heads.

On his way back to Bodmin from the Warren, Dickon was smarting with hurt and resentment. He recalled how eagerly he had ridden from Cornwall, pleased that Lyddon had trusted him to take a message to Tawford. He had been so looking forward to seeing his Captain again. Huh! More fool him. Remembering that dreadful ride through the night from Tawstock, Dickon knew he had done more than was expected of him, had not failed Tawford as he had feared.

Riding from Cornwall, following Lyddon's careful instructions to the gypsy encampment, Dickon had proudly imagined how it would be when he got there: Tawford clasping his shoulder, man to man, gratitude standing in his eyes. Himself, nonchalantly waving his Captain's gratitude away with a shrug. 'It was nothing,' he would say, as Tawford looked at him with undisguised admiration. So excited was Dickon by this imagined greeting, he could hardly wait to get to Exmoor.

When he had arrived at the Warren, Tawford, with an expression of mild irritation on his sardonic face, had simply held out his hand for Lyddon's message and listened, stony-faced, to news of Cornwall. He had said nothing at all about the ride from Tawstock, the part Dickon had played in his rescue. Not that Dickon had expected gratitude – or even wanted it – but he had hoped at least for some recognition, above all, to be treated like a man. After all, were it not for him, Tawford would be in some gaol awaiting the most unimaginably awful death by now. But no, all Tawford had done was to dismiss him as though he were a mere servant, treat him like a child, call him an 'idiot boy'. Well he was damned if he was going to let it get to him. Whether Tawford liked it or not, he was a St Michael's man now – he had bloody well proved it. Tawford could go hang. The man was no better than Papa; devil take them both!

Kicking his horse into a canter, Dickon left Exmoor behind and wished he had not remembered his father. It made him feel decidedly uncomfortable. He knew he should have sent a message to say he was safe, but he had still not been able to find the right words. He also felt guilty about his brother;

Edmund had doubtless been at the sharp end of Papa's anger. There would have been a row for sure. Last time they had quarrelled, Dickon had feared they would actually come to blows. It was when Edmund had mentioned his intention to visit James. Papa had exploded in a burst of vitriolic invective against their cousin's friend, Tawford. Curious, Dickon had eavesdropped.

He remembered Papa pacing the floor of the parlour, limping a little from his gouty knee and working himself up into a blistering rage. 'I don't care if you are a man grown,' he had fumed at Edmund. 'You are still my son and will do as I say. Your conscience is your own affair, but I will not have you gallivanting around the countryside with malignant incendiaries, inciting men to riot and breaking the law like your cousin James and that den of traitors, thieves and cutthroats he consorts with. I am not in your uncle Chichester's mould, never think it! He has no control over that grout-headed whippersnapper son of his – if it were up to me James would be locked up to cool his heels until he comes to his senses.'

Papa's whiskered face had turned purple with spleen as he had continued pacing, thumping his stick on the floor and brushing off their mother's brave attempts to pacify him. 'Get off me, woman. I will not be gainsaid. It is beyond belief that a member of our family stays with that profligate Dynam bastard whose misguided loyalties – should he have any unless they suit his own devious purposes – lie with the enemy. The man is guilty of treason – and that is the least of his crimes. Beggar me! What about young Henry, eh? His own brother, for pity's sake – he killed his own brother,' he had spluttered. 'Westley must have been deranged to take him back – the shock must have rendered him senile. In his shoes I would have the bastard hanged from the highest tree – and I will not have James set foot in this house while he remains under Tawford's influence, and as for you, Edmund, I will have no son of mine consorting with the enemy. If necessary I shall lock you up – and there's an end to it.' And he had stomped from the room, leaving their mother in tears and Edmund, fists clenched, white-faced with frustration.

Afterwards, Dickon had sought his brother out, eventually tracking him down in the stables where he'd returned from a hard ride to cool his anger. It had been raining and the smell of wet earth had filtered into the stables mingling with horse-sweat and leather.

'Why does Papa say James' friend is guilty of treason?' Dickon had picked up a twist of hay to rub the sweat from Edmund's steaming horse.

'Tawford? He was allegedly involved in a conspiracy,' Edmund had explained. 'It was a couple of years ago when the King's army was defeated by the Scots Covenanters. The men were in a rebellious mood because they'd had no pay. Parliament would give the King no money, so he had to use the men's wages to buy off the Scots. When they were on their way home, the officers plotted to march the army right up to Westminster and petition Parliament for their pay, but it all got out of hand when the Queen found out what they intended. She wanted the army to turn its guns on the mob and on Parliament, force them to submit to the King so he could rule with absolute power, like her brother does in France. Most of the officers balked at that, but some weren't sure and while they argued about it, those who supported the Queen lost patience and tried to break Earl Strafford out of the Tower. Someone alerted John Pym and he caught the plotters red-handed, called out the militia and had the ringleaders rounded up and charged with treason. As far as the Londoners were concerned it proved what John Pym had been saying all along: the King meant to use the army against his people. Tawford was implicated as one of the ringleaders, but there was no proof and they let him go. Mind you, that too caused talk. It was rumoured he turned traitor and gave the names of the plotters to John Pym in return for his release. Others say he is a Papist, being part Irish, and it was he who leaked the plot to the Queen. One way or another, Tawford seems to have made a lot of enemies. I would certainly keep a pistol primed under my pillow if I were he.'

Dickon had been intrigued to know more about Tawford and had asked whether it was true he had killed his own brother. 'If gossip is to be believed, Henry was his half-brother,' Edmund had said. 'Tawford would have been about six when Henry was born, so about sixteen when he died. As to whether he meant to kill him,' Edmund had shrugged. 'I suppose he might have done. As far as I know, he has never denied it. He was alone with the boy at the time. Nobody knows the ins and outs of it and the family never speak of it, but it was given out that Henry lost control of his horse. The boy was mounted on a stallion far too big for him and known to be hard-mouthed. He should never have been allowed to ride it – he was only a little lad, small for his age. It was rumoured Tawford put him on the horse deliberately and led him on a gallop over rough country. At best it was an extremely foolhardy thing to do, at worst, well, it only takes one person to whisper "murder" and soon everyone believes it. Some thought with Henry out of the way and Lady Westley unlikely to have another child – the poor woman was always ailing – Tawford stood to inherit the Dynam lands and title.

'It's unusual for bastards to inherit, of course, but not impossible if there's no other heir, but in this case there is. Lord Westley's father, Cleve Dynam, married again quite a long time after his first wife died. There was a son from that marriage. The boy must be much the same age as you by now, Dickon, maybe a few years older, lives in London with his mother. Cleve Dynam died before the child was born and his widow never stayed long at Marley Court, which is why people forgot about him I suppose. I've never met him, but he is Lord Westley's half-brother and his present heir, so Tawford had no motive for killing Henry for the inheritance, but I have sometimes wondered if he was driven by jealousy. He and Lord Westley were very close before Henry was born, but afterwards, well, Henry was Westley's legitimate heir, it was only natural the boy would come first in his father's affections. Tawford was left very much to his own devices and he ran wild getting into all sorts of scrapes before he was packed off to Oxford. He was popular with his friends and damnably bright. Papa used to say he was Chanticleer personified and far too clever for his own good. Could have been a top-rate lawyer if he hadn't interrupted his studies, but he went off soldiering on the continent and when he came back he took over Tawford Barton. Henry was killed not long after and Tawford disappeared. He didn't even stay for the funeral, which fuelled the rumours of course; it seemed like an admission of guilt at the time. The talk was that Lord Westley had banished him. Some said he'd run off to Lundy and taken up with pirates, others that he'd gone back to Ireland. Then, later, he was said to be fighting in France and we know from James that he fought in the Scots Wars.'

'Whatever the truth might be,' Edmund had concluded, 'Tawford and Lord Westley are still estranged. Anyway, Dickon, I would caution you to forget about it. It is never wise to listen to gossip, far less add to it, and it has caused Viscount Westley troubles enough, poor man.'

Remembering this conversation with Edmund, Dickon maintained a steady pace, head down against the weather, his horse eating up the miles effortlessly. Little had he realised then how important to him Tawford would become, but he had been agog with curiosity, and when Edmund had said he was going to see James, had badgered to go with him.

Predictably, they had found their cousin in the stables at Raleigh. Bluff and hearty, a great bear of a man, his rubicund face beaming and his wayward, mousy hair only barely confined by a flamboyantly feathered hat. To Dickon he was like a younger version of Papa and the irony of the thought had struck him with a surprised jolt as James roared his delight at seeing them.

'Cousins, you're like two peas in a pod. Dickon? Can this great, strapping lad be little Dickon – no, surely not! Do I have to call you Richard now then, eh? For I doubt I could get you up onto my shoulders any more.' He had lunged at Dickon to have a try. It was impossible to take offence and Dickon had joined in their laughter as James staggered a few steps before depositing them both sprawling in the mud. Still laughing, arms about their shoulders, he had taken them into the house and plied them with mulled ale and lardy cake. They had exchanged news, talked a little of Ireland and shaken their heads in mutual gloom over the situation here at home. Dickon had hoped to learn more of Tawford, but all too soon Edmund had got up to go. Dickon had pleaded with his brother to let him stay a while longer. Fortunately, their cousin had added his own gentle persuasion, for he wanted Dickon to see his stallion: there was nothing James liked more than showing off his horses. Giving in to them both with a wry smile, Edmund had reluctantly agreed, urging Dickon not to tarry long. 'You know what Papa will say to me if he learns where you are, lad, and Lord knows, I can do without another row!'

Dickon had gasped with delight at the fine black stallion – a Barbary, James had told him – running with the mares. 'We need a lighter-boned animal,' he had explained. 'We are hoping his foals will retain the strength and stamina of their heavier dams. Then we will have an animal that can travel faster yet still cover the distances, but it's very much an experiment at this stage, though these fine yearlings are showing much promise as you can see.'

Dickon had seized the opportunity. 'We? You mean Tawford and your band of cutthroats?'

James had put his head back and roared with laughter. 'Well, yes, I suppose so, in the first instance,' he had gasped. 'Cutthroats? Who told you that? No, don't tell me, it was your Papa. We're not cutthroats, Dickon, just men who have chosen our own master and want a say in how and when we fight and for what. We none of us want this war, no more than any man, but we all believe that if it must be, then our duty lies with the King – as I think at heart so does Edmund. I guess your Papa

accused Tawford of treason, did he? Called him a traitor?
He is entitled to his opinion and I would not want to gainsay
him. Nor would I want to lead you from filial obedience, but
did he also tell you how Tawford distinguished himself with
great courage in the field against the Scots? Or that he has
been acting as Sir Ralph Hopton's scout since the King raised
his standard? Did he tell you he has frequently risked his life
performing acts of bravery in the King's service? No? Fact is,
Dickon, I trust Tawford with my life and I am proud to be a
member of his company. He is no traitor, lad, believe me, but
why not judge for yourself? I am returning to our camp with
some horses tomorrow, I could use some help. It goes without
saying you must tell Edmund; gain his permission before you
leave,' James had smiled. 'But if it helps, you can tell him I'll
make sure you come to no harm. Best if your father doesn't
know. You'll have to think up some plausible excuse for your
absence or he might take it into his head to have you followed
and bring me back in chains.'

They had both laughed, but then James had gazed at him
and frowned, his expression uncharacteristically grave. 'I am
placing my trust in your honour, Dickon. If you do choose to
accompany me you will have to take an oath of secrecy, as we
all have done, for we have a job to do and there are men's lives
at stake here. It's not to be taken lightly, you understand?'

Dickon had lain awake for most of the night wrestling with
his conscience, but such an adventure was all too tempting.
Since he had been big enough to carry a sword he had learned
from Edmund how to use it and use it well and he was no
mean horseman, nor was he a milksop. He was not prepared to
sit back and finish his schooling while there was a war going
on, which was what his father would have him do. No, he was
nigh on fifteen and it was time he joined the company of men
to fight for his King and his country. And what better way
than at the side of his cousin, James? But to tell Edmund of
his plan would put his brother in an impossible position. Best
he remained in ignorance. So Dickon had risen well before

dawn, dressed proudly in his richest clothes – for now he was a Cavalier, which name to him was not an insult as some would have it, but an honour – packed a few essentials in his saddlebag, hastily written a note absolving Edmund of any knowledge of his actions, propped it where his father would find it and crept out of the house to meet with James.

And now here he was, a man grown and a sworn member of that very same 'den of thieves and cutthroats' his father despised, riding to Cornwall to take up his place in Sir Ralph Hopton's army and fight for the King. He would show Tawford, ungrateful bastard. He'd show Papa too. He'd show them all he was no longer a child; damned if he wouldn't.

Urging his mount into a gallop, Dickon headed for the Tamar.

14

Wednesday 12ᵗʰ October, 1642

Absorbed in what he was writing, Robert failed to hear his ward's lurching footsteps on the stairs.

'Why you continue to stay in these dismal, poky rooms is quite beyond me,' Alexander drawled, leaning against the door. 'Is it out of meanness? Or no,' he laughed, 'don't tell me you have been unwise with the Dynam fortune? Shame on you, Sir.' He surveyed his benefactor with sardonic amusement.

At the sound of the familiar voice Robert started, looked up from the table and gasped, momentarily speechless. With a delighted smile he rose hurriedly from his chair, his discarded quill scattering blots of ink across the page. 'I received a message to say you'd escaped, but I hadn't dared hope… Please, Alexander, come in.'

'Indeed, I suppose I am that still.' Alexander cut sharply across Robert's faltering welcome. 'Tell me, did you wish me to drop the Dynam? I forgot to ask in our last exchange if I had a claim to your family name. What about Tawford Barton, do I get to keep that?' His face was flushed, his clothes dishevelled. The candlelight picked out the sheen of sweat on his brow. 'I cannot imagine why you gave it to me. A sop to your conscience, perhaps, or was I always to be an object of your pity?' His tone was scathing, his eyes cruel.

Robert sat down again heavily, disappointment shadowing his face, his lips drawn into a thin line. 'There are matters to discuss, I agree, but much as I have wanted to see you I would suggest it might be wise if you return when you are sober.'

Alexander ignored him and moved unsteadily into the room. He flung himself down on the one comfortable chair sprawling his legs towards the fire, raised an eyebrow and contemplated Robert's taut face. 'You will not be rid of me until you tell me who sired me or confess you do not know.'

'You know that I am not prepared to do that, nor will I lie to you.'

'Why not? It never troubled you before,' Alexander sneered.

'I'm sorry if that is what you believe, but taunting me will make no difference.'

'Then maybe this will.' Alexander leapt from the chair, his dagger suddenly appearing in his hand. In a trice he had leaned across the table, the narrow blade held at Robert's throat. 'Perhaps I can persuade you to change your mind,' he hissed, his breathing deep and ragged.

Robert regarded him calmly. 'Or what? Put it away and sit down.'

Alexander, his lips drawn back in a snarl, exerted pressure on the dagger; a trickle of blood ran down Robert's neck. Without flinching, he met Alexander's gaze. 'Kill me by all means, but if you do, you will learn nothing.'

For a moment, his eyes glittering dangerously, Alexander stared Robert down. Suddenly his shoulders sagged and with an obscene oath, he flung the dagger from him. It caught against a cupboard and rattled spinning to the floor.

Shakily Robert stood up, retrieved from the table a discarded napkin and holding it to his neck, crossed the room to the sideboard and poured a glass of wine. The red liquid slopped over the rim and pooled on the polished wood. Dropping the napkin, Robert lifted the glass and drained it. Drawing a deep breath, he picked up another glass and took it with the decanter back to the table, his movements slow and deliberate. Filling both glasses he handed one to Alexander. 'Sit down, I pray you. There are some circumstances about your birth I am prepared to discuss with you, but not while you threaten me.'

Alexander took the glass and returned to the chair, hooking his leg over the arm. He twirled the stem watching the firelight through the wine, red as blood. 'So tell me. You do not have to spare my feelings, My Lord.' He made the title sound like an insult. 'It matters not to me that I am of lowly birth, I have never craved nobility, but I am interested to know what manner of a man spawned me and what unspeakable taint attaches to me that you cannot bring yourself to tell me. And why in God's name did you claim me as your own?'

Failing to hide his relief, Robert sat down at the table and with trembling fingers reached for his glass, took a sip of wine. He pushed his ruined papers to one side and leaned on his elbows. 'In the first instance I can assure you that your father was a noble and honourable man.' He ignored Alexander's snort of derision. 'Secondly, you were not born of rape, nor are you the product of incest if that is the taint you fear. Thirdly, as you will recall, I have never acknowledged you as my son. I freely admit I was wrong in allowing you to think it. I have already begged you to forgive me. I do so again.'

Alexander inclined his head. 'Perhaps if you can explain why you brought me from Ireland I might find it easier. It seems a little unusual for a man of your station to collect stray bastards from the gutter, unless... but no, pretty boys hold no appeal for you, do they.' His lip curled. 'I should be thankful for that at least.' He got up and walked over to his dagger, bent to retrieve it.

Flushing, Robert emptied his glass, poured another and held out the decanter. Alexander shook his head. 'As you have pointed out, I am already drunk. Were I not, I would not be here.' Balancing the point of the dagger on his outstretched palm, he went back to the chair, tossed the blade into the air and caught it deftly. Beads of blood welled in his hand. 'Not drunk enough, perhaps.'

Robert put the decanter down with an angry thump. 'God

knows, you have cause. Were I in like case I would probably behave no differently. It's damnable. The position in which we find ourselves is not one I sought. It was through no choice of mine I brought you from Ireland.'

'Ah, a grain of truth at last!' Alexander's mouth lifted in a mocking smile. It didn't reach his eyes. He stopped playing with the dagger, thrusting it into his boot.

'No, you misunderstand me. You must believe me when I tell you I have always – and still do – hold you in the fondest regard. I just felt that it would have been best for you to stay where you were. Not in the gutter, as you put it, but in the care of your nurse, at least until you reached maturity. But I had no choice in the matter. Before he died, your father extracted a promise from me. It was not a careless whim – as I said, he was an honourable man. He was concerned for your safety. He felt that if I raised you as my own and kept the circumstances of your birth secret, you would be in less danger. And he wanted to protect your mother.' Abruptly Robert stopped speaking as if aware he had said too much.

'My mother?' Alexander leaned forward. 'You knew her? So that was a lie too. Does she live?'

Robert dropped his gaze. 'Yes, I knew her. I do not know if she still lives, but I have reason to doubt it.' He shuddered, remembering the nightmares that plagued his sleep. 'She was very beautiful,' he added, almost to himself.

'She was Irish? And my father? Was he Irish too?'

Robert shook his head.

'Is that a "no" or a refusal to answer? From whom did my mother need protection?' Alexander's eyes narrowed, 'Was she a planter or perhaps a planter's wife?' He looked into Robert's eyes for any sign of reaction. There was none. Robert declined to answer.

Alexander tried again. 'Is that why she abandoned me, because their union was an aberration? If he was so anxious to protect her it must have been something more than a casual acquaintance. Was she his mistress? Did he have a wife? Or

267

she a husband?'

Robert made to speak, changed his mind. He held up his hands, his eyes pleading with Alexander to stop. He looked haunted.

Stubbornly Alexander persisted. 'Why did I need protection, and why did my father select you of all people to carry the burden of my upbringing? Moreover, why did you agree? What was there between you? He must have had some hold over you. What was it? Surely there is *something* you can tell me?' In his frustration, Alexander sent his glass spinning with a crash into the fire. It exploded into fragments, scattering into the hearth.

Robert pressed his lips together. 'I have said all I am prepared to say. There is no point in continuing in this vein.'

Alexander ran his fingers through his hair. 'You speak of danger. Why? What kind of danger?'

'That I cannot disclose.'

'For God's sake, man.' With an exasperated cry, Alexander lapsed into silence. The fire shifted in the grate, a glowing coal fell to the floor, singeing the threadbare carpet. From the street below, the sonorous voice of the watchman called the time. 'Ten of the clock, the night is clear and all is well.'

'It is getting late,' Robert said. 'There are other matters we need to discuss but perhaps it would be wise to continue this conversation another time? I feel there is no profit in going on with it now. Can you return tomorrow?' He looked at Alexander's bent head, the boyish hair ruddy in the firelight, the despondent set of his shoulders. 'I am sorry, it is not much, I know, but I cannot break my word to your father.'

Alexander's mouth twisted. 'Heaven forfend you should be forsworn for my sake!'

'You do me an injustice. If it were that alone I would be twice damned and gladly if it would mend this rift between us and satisfy your curiosity, but it wouldn't. You would never let it lie and only harm would come of it. In this you have to trust me.'

Alexander buried his face in his hands. 'I did once.' His voice was muffled. 'And look where it got me.'

'Alexander, look at me.' Robert waited. Slowly the minutes dragged by, the silence heavy. At last Alexander raised his head and turned reluctantly to face his guardian. Robert's eyes were sunk in dark hollows, his face etched with exhaustion. For a brief moment Alexander felt an unwelcome stab of pity.

'A man is what he makes of himself no matter what his parentage,' Robert said gently. 'You have the potential for greatness. Don't let bitterness destroy that. You are a born leader, clever, skilled and compassionate, everything I ever hoped for in my son. Does it really matter you are not? It is one reason why I gave you Tawford Barton. I did not intend to speak of this now, but there is something else I want to do for you. Among my papers at Marley Court there is a document transferring the Munster holdings to your name. It wants only your witnessed signature to make it valid. The land has yielded well in the past and will do so again. Use it wisely and the income will keep you in comfort all your days. Come home with me now. Be my son in every way that really matters. Can you not be content with that? It is what I have always wanted.'

Alexander looked up in surprise. 'No, you cannot do this,' he cried. 'I will not be used to compensate for your inadequacy. If you cannot manage to get a new wife and fill her belly, go trawl the stews. Find another bastard more willing to be bought than I, for you will never buy me.' Suddenly he exclaimed, his voice sharp with pain. 'Godamme! You cannot make me into Henry, no matter how much you want it.'

Robert uttered a cry as if he had been struck. After a moment he drew a shaky breath, speaking with quiet dignity. 'I would rather you held your dagger to my throat than cut me with those words.'

Alexander shrugged. 'As you said, I should not have come to you drunk.' He made to push himself from the chair, changed his mind and sank back. 'If I do not know who my enemies are, how can I protect myself? Tell me that much at least, please, I beg you. Then I will leave you alone.'

Robert shook his head. 'I cannot,' he said helplessly.

Alexander's gaze was coldly compelling. 'I ask it for a reason,' he hissed, 'to do with Henry's death.'

Robert's eyes widened in alarm, 'Why? What do you mean? What reason?'

Alexander gave Robert a considering look. 'You know I have never denied responsibility for it and we have settled it between us – as much we ever can – and maybe it is a mistake to raise it now, but at the time I was convinced it was not the accident it seemed.'

'Whatever do you mean?' Robert started, knocking over his glass. A pool of wine spread across the table and dripped to the floor.

'You will remember it was my stallion he was riding – and yes, it was much too big for him, but I felt the risk was minimal. Even so young he was a skilled horseman and it was a steady animal, not given to bolting for no apparent reason. I never understood what sparked it that day and it seemed too cruel a coincidence that it should happen on the roughest stretch of our ride, what is more, the only place that afforded cover. I began to wonder if someone had mistaken Henry for me. God knows, even then I seemed to attract enmity and it was a route I often took. Anyone wanting to harm me could have known that, somehow got at the horse, I don't know, tainted its food maybe. Unlikely, I know, and until it bolted it had not seemed unusually skittish...' Alexander's voice tailed away, his eyes distant. After a moment he continued. 'The stallion's body was unmarked beyond the cuts and bruises it took when it fell. I even examined the leathers to see if I had missed something, some irritant, burrs maybe. I found nothing, and yet...' He paused, his eyes on the fire.

'Go on,' Robert looked at him intently.

'It troubled me so much that before I left for France I went back over the ground. On that occasion, quite by chance, I found something. Ellen's hound dug it up in the woods and brought it to me – a length of hollow cane. It put me in mind of a blow tube, such as the natives use in the Indies to spit poisoned thorns at their prey. Laughable, I know, but such was my state of mind, I was convinced I had found the answer. I questioned every known felon in the district, put it about that I was offering a substantial reward for information, but nobody came forward. There was nothing to confirm my suspicions and eventually I was forced to conclude that in my desperation to lay blame, I had let my imagination run away with me, that what I had found was of no significance. So I dismissed it. But now you speak of danger, I wonder if my instincts were right; maybe someone was trying to kill me and used that outlandish weapon to make it seem like an accident.' He stopped speaking, his mouth twisted in a grimace of remembered pain. After a moment, continued, 'Only they missed and hit my horse instead. The poison from one dart would not kill a big animal like that, but it would have sparked it, even brought it down – and I wasn't on its back, Henry was.'

Robert's face was ashen. 'There is a flaw in your thinking. Henry was but a small boy, nobody could have mistaken him for you.'

'Not normally, no, but it was a dull wet day and we were swathed in heavy cloaks.' Alexander shrugged, his expression bitter. 'But you're right, of course. It is wishful thinking and I should not have mentioned it. Even yet I find I need to assuage my guilt.' His mouth twisted, his voice was raw. 'My God! Not a day goes by that I do not wish it had been me on that horse.'

'I know.' Robert spoke hoarsely, his emotion barely controlled. 'And I know how fond you were of Henry and he of you. It may be poor consolation, but I believe what you are suggesting may be true, except for one thing: it was not a mistake. Had Henry been riding his own mount it may not have succeeded as well as it did, but it would have happened anyway, whatever horse he was on. Alexander, don't you see?

They were not trying to kill you. It was Henry they waited for that day. My son; my little boy.' With a strangled cry Robert covered his face with his hands. 'Why didn't I see it? God in heaven, I should have known, I should have protected him.'

Alexander gave a snort of derisive laughter. 'Oh please! Who in God's name would want to kill a small boy whose worst crime was to steal the honey cakes? You really do not need to go to such lengths to fob me off. I accept you are not prepared to divulge the source of danger to my life and since there is obviously nothing I can do to change your mind, I will relieve you of the need for playacting.' Alexander stood up. 'I will endeavour to ensure we do not meet again, but if we do, don't expect me to be civil. As for your land in Munster, thank you, but no. Use the income to get some better rooms!' With an ugly look of contempt he turned and walked to the door.

'No!' Robert called urgently. 'Wait. Think, man. Who might benefit from Henry's death if I have no other son?'

Alexander hesitated, turned, walked slowly back into the room. He wiped a hand across his face, sank his fingers into eye sockets. 'I cannot imagine… unless…' He looked up. 'No, surely not; not even she would go so far.'

'You think not?' Robert raised his eyes helplessly to Alexander's. 'But how can it be proved? It is too long ago. Had you only voiced your suspicions at the time.'

Alexander gave a humourless bark of laughter. 'And you would have listened? As I recall, you were convinced I was a murderer.'

'No!' Robert flushed, dropped his gaze. 'Yes, I blamed you, but I never thought it was deliberate. You know I did not mean it – you cannot believe that of me.'

Alexander shook his head impatiently. 'Then face her with it.'

'If I accuse her without proof she will beggar me. You do not know her. She has powerful friends.'

'And if you had proof?'

'If she believed it, I might be in danger of my life.'

Alexander nodded. 'Then let it lie.' Compassion sparked briefly in his eyes. 'Nothing you do will bring Henry back.'

He turned to the door and leaving Robert staring blindly after him, hurried down the stairs. As he reached the street he felt a hand grasp his shoulder. He twisted out from under it, dropping suddenly to a crouch, his dagger glinting in his hand. Before he could launch himself, Cobb's solid frame blocked his arm.

'Alexander, hold hard, it's me.'

Alexander relaxed. 'You shouldn't make a habit of creeping up on people like that, one of these days you might not live to regret it.'

Grasping his arm, Cobb pulled him upright and peered into his face. 'You have a megrim? Can you see?'

'As much as I want to of your ugly features.'

Cobb grunted. 'Have you left him alive or dead?'

'Alive. How did you know I was here?' Cobb gave a sly grin and tapped his nose with his finger. It was lost on Alexander, who shook off the gypsy's hand and stumbled away from him.

'You'll not get far like that, my boy.' Cobb reached into his voluminous coat and withdrew a flask. 'Here, this will put fire in your belly.'

The strong spirit made Alexander gasp. 'You want to poison me?' He coughed hoarsely, made to hand the flask back, changed his mind and took another long pull. He wiped his mouth with the back of his hand, his eyes watering. 'If this be poison I shall die right gladly.' He grinned weakly.

'Well there's more where that came from and I have what else you need waiting in the Mermaid. She's clean and comely and not much used I would wager, and I have paid for her services till morning.' Taking hold of Alexander's elbow, Cobb steered him round a heap of horse dung, kicked the bloated body of a dog out their path and guided him into an alleyway.

'The chains are up at Aldersgate and Ludgate and Skippon's

Roundheads are all over the place,' Cobb murmured in his ear. 'I've a boat waiting. Come quietly.'

They threaded their way along deserted alleyways into Cheapside, past the stocks, empty for once, past St Mary le Bow – whose bells had long since rung the curfew – and into Bow Lane, all the while moving silently towards the river. With Cobb's guiding hand at Alexander's elbow, they climbed up to the leads and down again into low, narrow passages, dodging in and out of courtyards to avoid the Watch. They crept past the Livery Halls and the tightly packed tenements in between and arrived eventually in Thames Street. A few more yards and they had reached the Old Swan Stairs to the river.

Cobb cupped his hands to his mouth and gave a low whistle. A wherry glided out of the shadows and bumped against the bottom step. Alexander stuck out his foot and swayed towards it scraping his hand on the slimy wall. The gypsy grabbed him from behind and with the help of the boatman, lifted him in. He sank gratefully on to a coil of rope and bent his head between his knees, aware of the murmur of voices, the gentle chuckle of water beneath the boat, the smell of tarred rope, dead fish and more besides.

Suddenly there were shouts and the sound of running feet on the quay above them. 'Who goes there without a light? Stop and show yourselves.'

Cobb hesitated, one foot in the boat, the other on the bottom step. Swearing under his breath, he called up. 'Us be but two poor watermen on our way home across the river and the lantern's run out of wick. Did you want a ride, Sirs? Us'll take ee for a penny each.'

There were six of them, Philip Skippon's soldiers in their fine new uniforms. They clustered at the top of the steps, their muskets rammed and ready, match smoking in their hands. One came halfway down with a lantern, holding it up to peer into the wherry. 'What's the matter with him?' He looked suspiciously at Alexander huddled in the bottom of the boat.

'Well, if I'm honest I can't rightly say.' Cobb scratched

his head. 'Damn me if he wasn't pulling at the oars all day, but suddenly he's complaining and 'afore you know it he's puking blood and I've to hire a replacement, as if I didn't have enough to worry about with the wife sick at home,' Cobb grumbled, gesturing to the boatman who nodded and tipped his hat. 'He's got a fever I should say, for one minute he's hot and the next he's shivering, but it wouldn't be the plague, not this time of year, and he's got no spots last time I looked, so most likely 'tis the ague or could be the sweating sickness, but if you'd bring that light and step down into the boat, you could have a look at him for yourself. If it's the great pox he'll be showing it by now.'

Alarm written all over his face, the soldier backed hurriedly up the steps. He slipped and sat down with a bump at the top, managing to hang on to the lantern but not his musket, which cart-wheeled out of his hand, caught the wall, narrowly missed the wherry, slipped through Cobb's outstretched fingers and disappeared with a splash into the river. Chortling, his comrades hauled him unceremoniously to his feet. Cobb's expression was sorrowful. 'Oh dear, now there's a pity.' The boatman coughed and examined his oars.

'Come on my bonny lads, how's about it?' Cobb wheedled. 'A penny each? You'll not get a better rate this time of night.'

Recovering his dignity, the soldier looked down at him with a scowl. 'Go on your way, we've no business in Southwark. Get that man to a doctor. And get a light.'

Cobb shrugged his great shoulders. 'If you say so, Sir.' He climbed into the boat, shoved off and took up the other pair of oars. 'Lie still,' he muttered.

Alexander grinned in the direction of Cobb's voice and with the stink of the river in his nostrils, settled back and closed his eyes. By the time the boat bumped against the opposite bank his headache had receded and his vision was as much restored as the contents of Cobb's flask, now empty, would allow. Leaving the boatman with a generous fee for his trouble, they climbed out of the wherry and wended their way to the Mermaid.

Sprawling along the south bank of the Thames, Southwark, with its wide open spaces and sweet country air, yet so convenient for the City, had at one time been a fashionable place of residence for those who, like the Bishop of Winchester, could afford to build their houses here. Not any more. Damned by the Puritans as a haunt of vice and sinful pleasures, it was lately deemed the poorest and most disreputable quarter of London. Because the livery companies' regulations were less strictly controlled in the suburb, the overcrowded streets teemed with artisans and traders not qualified or too poor to set up shop in the City. It also attracted strangers: hundreds of continental craftsmen, mostly in the furniture trade, lived here in the tightly packed tenements. So too did apprentices – especially apprentices. It provided a refuge for vagrants, criminals, Papists and spies, and was a favourite meeting place for radical thinkers and dissenters. It was also a breeding ground for rats along with most ailments known to man. The Bishop of Winchester's successors had long since moved out.

Most of the Mermaid's clientele were drawn from among those who serviced Southwark's many delights – not all of them illicit: watermen, link boys, tapsters, ostlers, victuallers, brewers, players, animal keepers and such like, people whose work made them largely invisible. Anything that was worth knowing found its way to the Mermaid, which was chiefly why Alexander came here. Located between the Globe and the Rose – both theatres silent and empty these many months – at the end of a passage off a lane leading to the bear gardens, the brothel was distinguished from its neighbours by a crude painting on the door of the mythical sea creature for which it was named, and which numerous inebriate visitors – with vivid imaginations and not a little wishful thinking – had accentuated until the creature's breasts had spread from the door to the wall.

The Mermaid was not licensed and continued to exist only

through the guile and generosity of its owner, Beth Dogget, whose breasts were as vast as those of her trade sign. She was a magnificent woman of indeterminate age, her cornflower-blue eyes lost in rolls of fat that quivered when she laughed. Her hair was her finest feature: bright blonde – kept so with lemon juice and camomile – it fell in corkscrew ringlets about her ample shoulders. Her tiny hands and feet were cuffed with fat like a babe's and her enormous buttocks were constrained in a gown of amber taffeta that rippled and shone as she waddled from table to table keeping a proprietorial eye on proceedings. Once – and in many of her customers' eyes, still – a great beauty, these days she reserved her personal favours for one or two old favourites, of whom Cobb was one. For the rest, she prided herself on the deserved popularity of her establishment and the cleanliness of her girls and woe betide any man who mistreated them. It rarely happened, there were few men brave enough to cross Beth Dogget. Those who did were usually found face down in the Thames next day.

Through the eruption of noise and jollity that was the Mermaid, Beth advanced on Alexander, her face split from ear to ear to display her not quite so successfully brightened teeth. Even lemon juice must have its limitations, he decided. Flinging her arms around him, she drew his head to her bosom and for a moment he was smothered in mounds of soft, perfumed flesh. 'You have stayed away from Beth too long, naughty boy, where have you been all this time?'

He came up gasping for air, spluttering with laughter, his brow imprinted by the string of garnets glittering at her neck. Cobb, having safely delivered his charge, had circumspectly moved away and was lost in the thick blue haze of tobacco and smoke from the hundreds of candles that glittered and danced about the room, overlaying the stink of men's sweat, stale urine and vomit. The Mermaid was heaving: long tables piled with steaming food and frothing tankards, men in various stages of drunkenness, their arms clutching at women in various stages of undress, some of whom led their captives up the staircase to the gallery and disappeared into one of the many discreetly curtained alcoves thereon. Others, their faces intent, their hands nervously fingering their money, contented themselves with games of dice and cards. At one end of the room, two men had come to blows. Several more had formed a ring around them and were yelling encouragement. Four hapless musicians had moved out of harm's way under the gallery and judging by their inflated cheeks and industrious scraping were playing a lively tune. Only in snatches was it audible.

Grinning at Beth, Alexander held her away from him and taking her podgy hand to his lips swept her a low bow.

'Sweet Beth, your beauty overwhelms me. Only by force have I been kept from your side these past months. My eyes are gladdened by the sight of you and my heart is held captive to your unsurpassed charms.' He had to shout to make himself heard.

'Lah! Such pretty ways and such a pretty boy.' She beamed at him, fingering her necklace.

'It grieves me that I have not yet brought you something to replace those poor beads.' Alexander turned his mouth down. 'But I will, next time, I promise.' He unpinned from inside his shirt a large oval brooch. It was made of pale blue enamel, painted with cherubs and set in whorls of gold shaped like acanthus leaves. A pretty thing; he'd won it at Tarot somewhere. 'In the meantime, I hope you will accept this trinket as a small token of my esteem.' Careless of modesty, he selected what little of her gown he could find beneath her cleavage and pinned it there. It took him a while.

Roaring with laughter, Beth seized him by the shoulders.

'If I was twenty years younger I'd keep you all to myself.'

Pursing her cupid's bow lips she smacked him a kiss full on the mouth and keeping a firm hold of his hand led him to a table, at the same time beckoning to a young woman who stood holding a tray of food at the side of the room. 'This is Katherine. I have been saving her for you since Cobb told me to expect you. Now sit yourself down and make yourself comfortable. She will attend to all your needs and I will come and see you later.' With another beaming smile, Beth waddled away.

Katherine came forward smiling shyly. She was tall and unquestionably pretty with a curtain of dark brown hair falling about her shoulders and halfway down her back. Her face was oval, her eyes dark grey and her mouth was of the kind that invited a kiss. She bent provocatively forward and placed the tray in front of him on the table. The smell of cooked beef was so good, for a moment Alexander wished he felt hungry. Katherine took up a small piece and held it to his lips. He shook his head. She popped it into her own mouth and reaching across for a tankard, filled it from a jug of beer on the table and handed to him. He took it with a smile. She sat on the bench beside him, her eyes downcast, her hand curled lightly on his thigh. His interest quickened, but conversation was impossible.

Downing his beer Alexander grinned at Katherine, patted her hand, removed it from his thigh and stood up. Indicating she should hold his place for him, he walked unsteadily over to the musicians, capered in front of them for a moment, frowned, shook his head and proceeded flamboyantly to conduct them, his gestures becoming increasingly crude. Taking it in good part, they grinned at him. Behind him people started to laugh. One of the musicians shrugged and offered up his fiddle. Alexander took it, whispered in the ear of the man with the whistle, drew off his doublet, kicked off his boots and bounding onto the nearest table, started to play. Avoiding the many hands that reached out to grasp his ankles and sidestepping the bowls and platters of food, Alexander paused, reached down to grab a jug of beer, took a long pull, poured the remainder over the nearest head and resumed playing. Beckoning to the other musicians to follow him, he capered on down the table. By now he had everyone's attention.

Standing at the back of the room, Beth Dogget was holding

her sides and crying, tears of mirth disappearing into the folds of her wobbling cheeks. Leaping to the next table, Alexander continued on his way, leading his accompaniment on a merry dance around the room to the shouts and cheers of his delighted audience. It all came to an unsavoury end when he slipped, lost hold of the fiddle and landed in a large tureen of stew, at which moment those who had received a dowsing of beer happily returned the compliment. With a beatific smile, beer streaming over his head, Alexander sat in the stew for a moment, then rose in a single fluid movement and with lumps of beef and gravy sticking to his breeches, bowed deeply to all four corners of the room and climbed unsteadily to the floor. He returned to Katherine, reached for her hand and led her to the stairs, stopping at the top for a final bow. From across the room Beth, mopping her cheeks, gave an approving smile and pointed to the far end of the gallery. He raised his hand to her and grinned.

Ignoring the curtained alcoves, he led Katherine to a room with a door. This was Beth's personal domain, rarely used by her clientèle. Inside it was comfortably furnished and lit by sconces that hung on the walls. A small fire burned in the grate and the tester bed was made up and clean. On a chest by the bed was a bottle of wine and two pewter goblets. Alexander shut and bolted the door and smiled at Katherine. She stood in front of him, her slender body taut as a bow. Hesitantly she stepped out of her shoes and proceeded to pull at her bodice, loosening the fastenings. He saw that her feet were bare and clean and her fingers were trembling. He put out a hand to stay her. 'How old are you Katherine?'

'Turned fifteen, Sir.'

Alexander doubted it. He strolled to the chest, poured a goblet of wine and handed it to her. 'And how long have you been at the Mermaid?'

'Since July, but I have not yet…' She looked up at him and quickly down again, a flush staining her pale cheeks.

Alexander sighed. Much as he loved Beth, she was nothing

if not an astute businesswoman. By reserving for her wealthier customers the youngest, prettiest and least used of her girls, she encouraged the return custom of men able to afford the highest prices, who would not only continue to patronise her business but would increase its reputation. It gave her the edge in a profession that was keenly competitive. Alexander supposed he was considered a prime target.

'Are you a virgin, Katherine?' He smiled gently.

She studied her feet and nodded. 'But I know how to pleasure you, Master Tawford.' She looked up quickly, her eyes filled with childlike anxiety.

Of a sudden he felt very tired. 'I am sure you do. May I call you Kate?'

She nodded.

'So, Kate, would you be offended if I declined your obvious charms for tonight? It is not that I do not find you attractive, quite the reverse.' Alexander smiled. 'Indeed, you are very pretty, but I am very drunk and very tired.'

'If you turn me away, Mistress Dogget will think I have not pleased you,' she said in a small voice. 'She said I was to be especially kind to you and remember all she had taught me, and that I ought to know how lucky I am to have such a special gentleman my first time.'

'Did she now. Then you had better stay with me while I sleep and Mistress Dogget will be none the wiser.' He grinned conspiratorially. Supporting himself against the bedpost, he picked off the worst of the mess from his clothes, put a hand to his points and sat down on the bed. About to draw off his breeches he caught sight of her flushed face and stopped. 'Should I close the curtains round me or would you prefer to turn around? Tonight I am harmless as a puppy, I promise you.' Kate visibly relaxed and smiled at him, his manner and the wine having an obvious effect. Alexander swung his legs onto the bed and with a contented sigh lay back and closed his eyes. The last thing he felt were her fingers easing off his sodden shirt, filthy breeches and stockings.

When he woke some hours later it was to find Kate curled naked beside him. Her long hair was spread across his chest, her face turned towards him flushed in sleep, lips slightly apart. Aroused, he pondered his predicament. How long would it be before this lovely girl was taken, who knew how roughly, by another of Beth's 'special gentlemen'? How did such a girl come to be in this situation? It was a foolish question, he knew only too well. Doubtless she had a family bordering on starvation at home. Gently he moved away from her. She had not closed the bed curtains. His disgusting clothes had been neatly folded and placed beside hers on the chest. The candles still flickered, low in their sconces, but the fire had died to a dim glow. The Mermaid had fallen silent, the satisfied snores from its unconscious customers barely penetrating the room from the floor below. Outside, a pair of tomcats began to screech in discordant serenade; a dog barked.

Resting his head on his hands, Alexander kept his mind busy. His guardian had given away a good deal, more perhaps than he was aware, certainly more than he had intended. Now at last he had something to go on, a trail to follow, however cold. The answers he sought lay in Ireland, as he had known they must. He had only distant memories of his foster-mother; extraordinary how someone so central to his infancy should have faded almost beyond recall – even her name. He frowned. Shoonah, that was it, and she was the wife of Westley's agent, Art O'Neill. Were they alive still? He would find out – but not yet. His first priority was to get back to Sir Ralph Hopton with as much information as he could glean about what Parliament intended for the South West. Alexander's lips tightened. Before he did so, he would pay a visit to Lady Anne Dynam, Westley's stepmother. Why had he not thought of her before? She was the one person who might benefit from Henry's death should Westley fail to produce an heir.

Momentarily forgetting Katherine, Alexander shifted restlessly. The movement woke her. Moving closer, she propped herself on her elbow and smiled sleepily down at him, one of her breasts brushing softly against his ribs, the nipple springing against his skin. Alexander gritted his teeth.

'I usually keep my promises,' he whispered. 'But you are not making it easy for me, sweet Kate.'

'You are as handsome a gentleman as ever I have seen and like Mistress Dogget said, I must start somewhere.' Kate placed a finger on his chin, playfully exploring his dimple with her fingertip. 'And I am glad it is with you,' she murmured, bringing her lips softly down to his.

With a groan he reached for her, everything forgotten but the urgency of his need. Kate pulled suddenly away from him, her body going rigid. It was a timely reminder of her inexperience. Cursing himself under his breath, Alexander lay perfectly still for a moment, then proceeded to caress her, lightly running his fingers down the small of her back to cup her small buttocks, nibbling at her neck, running his tongue around her ear and whispering nonsense, until she squealed with laughter. Feeling her relax against him, he moved his head until he could kiss her breasts, gently sucking, nipping and teasing with teeth and tongue, bringing her to the edge of intense pleasure until she mewed with impatience, her hands entwining in his hair, pushing him downwards. Taking his time, he gently raised himself onto her and judging the moment, entered her, his patience rewarded by only the smallest gasp of pain. For a moment he lay still, forcing his mind to consider the problem of prime numbers. Raising his head he looked at her face, his eyebrow lifted in a query. He saw in her eyes her awakened delight, the urgent movement of her body answering his unspoken question. Then, even mathematics failed him.

After Alexander had left him, Robert sat for some time watching the door, seeing again the spark of contempt in those cold, green eyes. Reaching for the decanter he systematically emptied it, but the oblivion he sought eluded him. His mind in turmoil he stumbled blindly to the fireside chair. As he sat there unmoving, going over and over what Alexander had said, the embers glowed dully then turned white; one by one the candles guttered and went out. Robert sat on in the darkness, unseeing, his mind numb with anguish. How could he have been so blind? He had known his stepmother was greedy for the Westley inheritance for her son, but surely not even she, vile as she was, would stoop to the murder of a small boy to get what she wanted. Was it possible? Even as he asked the question he knew the answer.

Anne Dynam was from rotten stock. Her father, Sir John Fisk, had been minor gentry: a drunken brute who had foully abused his wife and two daughters and terrorised his neighbours with bouts of drunken violence. One night he went too far, killed a man in cold blood. Maddened with drink, he killed again, this time committing suicide by falling on his blade to avoid the hangman's noose. Small wonder Fisk's daughters were morally destitute. Ambitious for wealth and a title, the youngest, Anne, had ensnared Robert's father, Cleve Dynam, who, at more than twice her age, had been captivated by her beauty. Robert's lip curled at the memory. His father had not been the only one to fall under Anne's spell. He too, a callow youth not yet bedded, had been driven almost to madness by vile, incestuous thoughts of her, forced to assuage his hot, urgent desire alone, in the shadows, eaten up with guilt and self-disgust. She had known, of course, it had amused her to seduce him. When his father had sent him to live in Ireland, Robert had been in despair, yet at the same time relieved. Had his father guessed what was happening between his wife and son? If so nothing was ever said and later, when Robert had met and married Ruth and come to understand the difference between lust and love, any feelings he had harboured for Anne Dynam had turned to bitter loathing, both for her and for himself.

Instinctively Robert knew beyond doubt his stepmother was responsible for Henry's death, but if he sought retribution without proof he would face financial ruin – Anne Dynam had powerful friends, not least her brother-in-law, Richard Grenville – and as Alexander had said, it would not bring Henry back. Nothing could do that. And what of Alexander? Would anything bring him back? Robert doubted it. Sinking into a pit of abject misery, he wrapped his arms tightly round his body and tried to stem the racking sobs that tore at his throat, but his unhappiness defeated him and in the end he gave vent to it, howling like an animal in pain.

15

Thursday 13th October, 1642

The following morning – having with some reluctance struggled free from the sweet mountain of flesh that was Beth Dogget – Cobb went to see Nab. The wizened little Yorkshireman was in the loft over the stables at the back of the Mermaid cooing to his birds. Covered in feathers and birdlime, oblivious to the reek of ammonia, Nab was sitting cross-legged on the floor holding a pigeon in each hand. A bird sat on his head, another on his shoulder, a dozen or more clustered noisily at his knees stretching up their necks for the corn he always carried in his pocket. As Cobb's face appeared in the hatchway, Nab grinned, the one remaining tooth in his head a beacon in the black cavern of his mouth.

'Did ever I see a man with a sore ade?' Nab said to the pigeon on his shoulder. 'Poor man, says I. But then I says to myself, don' ee feel sorry for un Nab, for tha naws ee deserves it.' The pigeon swayed, moved its head up and down, its black eyes winking. Nab addressed Cobb, 'Bin up boozin' all night I see.'

'Ho, Nab!' Cobb put up an arm to shield his head from the sudden uprush of beating wings as he heaved his bulk into the loft. 'Still talking to the birds I see. They haven't carted you off to bedlam yet then.'

Nab stuck up a rude finger. 'Hush my beauties, don't take on so, ee won't hurt thee, ee's nubbit a clumsy great ox, tha's all ee be.' Responding to Nab's soothing voice, the birds fluttered down around him.

'I need some more birds, Nab. Good ones, mind. Have you got any ready?'

'What you bin doin wi' 'em all Cobb?' The little man grumbled. 'Puttin' 'em in the pot like as not.'

'You know better than that. Come on, old man, I only need a couple. You must have some you can spare,' Cobb wheedled, eyeing the two fat birds nestled in Nab's hands.

'Mebee I do, mebee I don't.' Nab lifted his hands to his lips, planted a kiss on the head of each bird in turn and carefully putting them down, rose effortlessly to his feet. 'But you can take your eyes off they beauties, them's me breeders. Wait there an I'll see what I got.' Tipping some corn from his pocket, Nab stepped round the chuckling birds and walked towards the stack of wooden cages at the far end of the loft. Cobb made to follow, cracked his head on the beam that Nab had walked under with ample clearance, and momentarily stunned, sat down in a whirl of startled pigeons.

Hearing Cobb's cry, Nab turned to look. 'Now didn' I tell ee to wait there? Oh my Lor,' he spluttered with laughter, slapping his knees, tears streaming down his seamed cheeks. 'An just look at your poor ade. That'll larn ee, stubborn great ox.'

'Bastard!' Wincing, Cobb put a hand to his bald pate and uttered a stream of obscenities. 'I'll leave you to your birds, you old bugger. Just sort me out two or three good ones into a travelling hamper by this afternoon.' He crawled backwards to the hatch, his hands and knees slimed with bird excrement, struggled through the hole in the floor and felt with his feet for the ladder. As he reached the ground he could hear Nab still wheezing with laughter. The sound was infectious and ruefully, still rubbing his head, Cobb grinned.

At about the same time, dressed in the neatly pressed uniform of one of Philip Skippon's captains of the guard, who had unwisely visited the Mermaid one night with insufficient funds and been parted forcibly from his clothes, Alexander presented himself at the Westley's town house in Arundel Street. It was a pretty house, small in comparison to its neighbours on the Strand, those great mansions of the nobility whose forbears had built their houses with more care for status and utility than beauty. This one was of pleasing proportions, a façade of Portland stone with decorative bands of dark red brick, and gardens sloping down to the river.

Giving his name as Captain Pickering, Alexander was admitted by an elderly manservant and kept waiting in the hall for nearly an hour. He was pacing irritably beneath gloomy portraits of Dynam ancestors when Anne Dynam, the dowager Lady Westley, deigned to make an appearance. She swept down the imposing staircase, her hand lifting the skirts of her blue velvet gown to display her dainty jewelled slippers. Even in her late forties Anne Dynam was a ravishingly handsome woman. Still slender, her narrow waist emphasised by a tight, low cut bodice, her shapely bosom barely concealed by an elaborate lace collar pinned together by a large sapphire brooch. It was not difficult to see what had captivated Cleve Dynam. Dark ringlets, without a trace of grey, framed her delicate, unlined features. Her face was pale, a touch of rouge highlighting her cheekbones, her eyes almond-shaped and deep blue.

At the bottom of the stairs she paused, her face alight with curiosity, her perfect mouth curving in a provocative smile. With a flourish Alexander swept his hat from his head and made a low bow. 'My Lady.'

Anne Dynam came forward with a smile, hand outstretched.

'To what do I owe the pleasure, Captain?' Her voice was as richly husky as he remembered it.

Plainly the widow had not recognised him. Hardly surprising; he had been only twelve years old when they had last met on one of her rare visits to Marley Court – visits, now he thought of it, that had always coincided with Robert's absence.

'Forgive me for disturbing you, my Lady, but is there somewhere we can talk in private? My business is personal and concerns your family.' Alexander looked up to the top of the stairs where two giggling maidservants were leaning over the banister gazing raptly down at him, their hands over their mouths.

The widow looked up sharply and the women hurriedly disappeared from view. 'Leave your sword and pistol if you please and come this way, Captain.'

Alexander did as he was bid and followed her into the parlour, a delightful room, its windows overlooking the gardens and the river, busy now with traffic. Seating herself gracefully on a settle she looked up at him. 'My family, you say? Of what concern can my family possibly be of yours, Captain... Pickering?'

Replacing his hat, he wandered over to a window and stood for a moment looking over the garden, then turned. Appreciatively he stared at her. Saying nothing, he let his gaze rest lasciviously on her cleavage and travel slowly up her neck to her face, his lips lifted in a mocking smile.

She caught her breath, a flush staining her cheeks. Giving him look for look, she lifted a hand to finger her brooch. 'You are impertinent, Sir. Kindly explain what brings you here or I shall have you removed.'

He raised an eyebrow. 'I think that would be unwise, Madam. First, allow me to apologise for a slight deception, but I felt you would be unlikely to admit me did you know my identity. Indeed, we have a common interest in the Dynam family. My name is Alexander Dynam of Tawford and I suppose in some tenuous way we must be related, though I hesitate to work out how. Let me see now, if I am not mistaken you would be my grandmother by marriage?' He emphasised the 'grand' and smiled.

She gasped, speechless, her lip curled in an expression of cold contempt. 'Most certainly I would not have received you. I am not in the habit of entertaining traitors, particularly a murdering bastard who has stolen from my son what is rightfully his.'

'Is that so? I assume you refer to Tawford Barton? You do not think it a little hasty to lay claim to the Dynam inheritance for your son? Last I heard, Lord Westley was alive and well and perfectly capable of getting another heir. How is dear George, by the way?' He cast an exaggerated glance around the room. 'Not here? What a pity. I am sure he would be intrigued to hear what I have to say.'

Once more Alexander had rendered Anne Dynam speechless, until at last her curiosity got the better of her.

'What brings you here?'

'Ah, as to that, Madam, I have a small business transaction to discuss with you. It concerns my dear departed brother, the late Henry Dynam.' Ignoring her sudden start, Alexander continued speaking. 'Something has found its way into my possession that indirectly belongs to you.' His mild tone was belied by the coldness of his gaze. 'And I have information concerning his death that, were it to be made public, it might… shall we say, damage your reputation – it may even stretch your neck! I am prepared, for a small consideration, not to speak of it.'

Anne Dynam's eyebrows shot up. Without a trace of fear she laughed at him. 'Blackmail? Come now, Master Bastard, can you do no better than that? Whatever it is you think you know will, I feel, be of little moment.' The smile she gave him was no less mocking than his own. 'For impersonating an officer alone I can have you taken to the Gatehouse. For threatening me, I can have you hanged.' The widow rose from the settle and started for the door.

Before she was halfway across the room, Alexander reached her, his hand closing over her wrist like a vice. 'Just so, my Lady,' he smiled. 'But perhaps you might be wise to hear me out. I imagine your various protectors may consider the murder of Lord Westley's son and heir to be something rather more than of little moment, don't you?' He was no longer smiling. 'I have to assure you, Madam, I will not go silent to the gallows.'

For a moment the widow held his gaze. He could see she was considering alternatives, unsure exactly what he knew. She made no attempt to free herself, rather, she leaned against him and for a moment the musky scent of her was in his nostrils. Briefly he found himself admiring her poise. Eventually she lowered her gaze and gestured to a chair. 'Very well, I will listen to what you have to say. Kindly unhand me and sit down. Would you care for some refreshment?'

Alexander burst out with genuine laughter and released her, his fingers leaving ugly marks on her wrist. 'How kind, but I prefer to discuss business on an empty stomach, don't you?'

Rubbing her arm, Anne Dynam returned to the settle and composed herself. 'What makes you think I had anything to do with Henry's death? As I understand it, everyone knows you killed him yourself. Why do you come here with this accusation and how can you possibly imagine that anyone would believe you?'

He removed himself to a chair and sat down, stretching out his elegant legs to cross one ankle over the other. A lump of mud fell from his boot onto the pale green carpet. 'You mean, what proof do I have?'

'That is not what I said,' she snapped.

Alexander regarded her calmly. 'No?'

The widow turned to face him, her expression calculating. 'Let me be sure that I understand you correctly. You imagine you have some sort of proof connecting me to the death of Westley's son who was, I will remind you, my own grandson, as indeed – and as you have made pains to point out – are you.'

'But, thank God, not by blood, Madam!'

'I assure you, the feeling is entirely mutual.' Anne Dynam, gazed at Alexander with contempt. 'Can you imagine for a moment that anyone would heed you – *you*?' She laughed. 'Come now, sirrah, I had thought you a lying cheat, a rogue and a traitor, but never a fool. Yet you seem to think I would be willing to pay for your silence. Whether or not you are correct – and whatever is said in this room I can assure you I will emphatically deny – by paying you, I would merely affirm your accusation. Why should I do that? Why should I not simply have someone dispose of you, as you seem to believe I am capable?'

Keeping his eyes blank so she would not see his repugnance, Alexander shrugged, 'Naturally I have evidence of your guilt. You surely do not suppose I have come here without taking steps to ensure it will be published if anything happens to me?'

Her eyes narrowed. For the first time Anne Dynam looked uncomfortable. 'What evidence?'

'I am not prepared to divulge that at this time.'

'Lah!' She trilled, relieved. 'Then how am I to believe you?' She shrugged. 'You are lying.'

Alexander raised a languid hand and fingered the new growth of whiskers on his upper lip. 'Can you afford to take the risk that I am not?' He spoke softly, almost nonchalantly.

Anne Dynam regarded him in silence. For the first time Alexander caught a flicker of fear in her eyes. He waited. Suddenly she spoke, her voice brittle.

'Who else knows you are here? Westley?'

'I am not in the habit of taking Lord Westley into my confidence.'

She looked at him thoughtfully. 'The rumours are true, then? You are estranged from your father? Why is that, I wonder? Few of his station raise their bastards so handsomely as he has raised you. Surely you owe him much?'

He grimaced, directing his gaze out of the window. 'A poxy stretch of marshland fit only for seabirds – so poor even you didn't want it, as I recall?' Alexander's tone seethed with resentment. 'I owe him nothing. He cannot even bring himself to publicly acknowledge me. He is nothing to me. No more was his son and had you not hired someone to kill Henry, I would have done so myself.' Alexander shifted his gaze to study the widow's expression. Like everyone else, she plainly believed he was Westley's son. He wondered what instinct led him to perpetuate the myth. 'You saved me the trouble, that is all,' he added.

'So,' she breathed. 'The bastard boy's true colours will out.' The widow gave a small, satisfied smile. 'If this is so, it would seem to me we might be useful allies. Pray, do tell me, is it only money you want? Or is there something else I can offer you?' She looked pointedly at Alexander's crotch, slowly raising her gaze to his mouth, her own slightly open, breathing quickened. 'You always were a pretty boy,' her smile broadened coquettishly.

Suppressing the responsive twitch in his groin, Alexander returned her gaze. Godamme! The woman was almost irresistible. He wondered idly what she would do if he were to reach for her. He drew his lips back in a sneer, his eyes cruel. 'Money will suffice, Madam.' He let his gaze linger on her body, his contempt plainly visible. 'You surely cannot imagine there could possibly be anything else? I prefer my meat a little fresher.'

She flinched as if he had struck her, the coquettish smile wiped from her face, her breasts heaving with the effort of controlling her anger. Her fingers splayed towards him and for a moment Alexander half expected to feel the sharp drag of her nails on his face, but she clenched them, trembling, to her lap. 'How dare you!' The words came out in a ragged hiss.

Alexander laughed. 'Did I misunderstand your offer? Do forgive me, Madam, I am but an ill-mannered bastard – as you have so often pointed out.' He shrugged. 'I am interested only in money.'

Anne Dynam visibly brought herself under control. 'How much money?'

'One thousand pounds.' Alexander uncrossed his ankles and sat forward.

She gasped. 'That is a great deal of money. For that you

will have to produce your evidence.'

'Oh, be assured, I will.' He got up from the chair and stood looking at her. 'But for two thousand more, I will remove the final obstacle to your son's advancement. How say you, Madam? Three thousand pounds and a small income for life and George can come into his inheritance right now, this very day.'

It took her by surprise. She looked up at him sharply. 'You would go that far? And what makes you think that even had I such a fortune I would part with it, when all I have to do is wait?'

Alexander nodded, his expression faintly bored. 'You may have to wait a very long time... ah, I see you have not heard. My father plans shortly to remarry. Did I not mention? The lady is young and well connected.' He smiled mockingly down at her. 'And I hear she has broad hips. Westley will soon have a legitimate furrow in which to plant his seed. And with a good deal more care than he took begetting me,' he said acidly.

Anne Dynam's face had suddenly paled. Her breath escaped in a hiss, her hand rising involuntarily to her throat. 'Who?'

'Does it matter? You will learn soon enough,' he drawled. 'So, Madam, can it be that my proposition is of interest to you after all?'

'Supposing it is. How could I be sure you would do this without implicating me?'

'Ah.' Alexander smiled his satisfaction. 'So, you do not deny that it interests you.'

'Even if it did, I do not have that sort of money.' She shrugged, her face hardening. 'You are wasting your time.'

'Perhaps – but let us leave that to one side for the moment, there remains the matter of Henry Dynam. Or shall I take what I know to your erstwhile brother-in-law – the cuckolded one?'

'Richard Grenville?' she gasped.

Alexander's eyebrow shot up. 'Of course Richard Grenville

– but no wonder you have to ask, how tactless of me – your sister cuckolded all her husbands, didn't she? And now I gather she has taken up with her groom. What an embarrassment she must be for you.'

'You would not dare. Grenville will kill you.'

'Oh, I don't think so,' Alexander said mildly. 'I do believe Sir Richard has troubles enough of his own without yet another scandal. I am sure he will pay for my silence if you will not. On the other hand, I could take it to his brother. True, Sir Bevill would not countenance blackmail, not even to protect his family, certainly not when it concerns the cold-blooded murder of a small boy, but at least I should have the satisfaction of knowing you will pay for your crime – if not in one way, then another.'

'How dare you,' she hissed. 'You sanctimonious hypocrite.'

'Ah! Not so useful an ally then? And look,' he glanced down, 'there's a shame, when we might have grown to enjoy one another.' His mocking smile broke into mischievous laughter as despite herself the widow's gaze was drawn to his groin, his physical reaction to her evident in his breeches.

She flushed scarlet and at last her resistance crumbled.

'Very well, bring me your evidence. When I am satisfied you speak the truth, you shall have your thousand pounds.'

Alexander nodded. 'And the other?'

'I shall think on it,' the widow said shortly.

'Very good.' Alexander gave a brief nod. 'Until then I shall bid you good day. Please don't trouble to get up. I will see myself out.'

She stared at him, her face a mask of cold hatred, all illusion of grace and beauty shattered. He turned on his heel and without a backward glance, made for the door.

Feeling conspicuous in his uniform, Alexander walked along the Strand. He had been acting on a hunch and risked a good deal, but it had paid off: the widow was guilty as hell, he was certain of it. Now all he had to do was prove it. Cutting through to the Fleet Bridge, intent on retrieving his clothes – cleaned and pressed, if somewhat stained – which he had left in a room at the Bell Savage, he was about to turn into the courtyard when he was forestalled. A uniformed officer was attempting to bring to order a large group of foot soldiers in front of Ludgate, but the attention of those at the rear had strayed to a flustered young woman hurrying towards the Inn, her arms full of bread. From the head of the wavering column, looking decidedly harassed and obviously delighted to see another officer, the captain hailed Alexander and pointed to the rear. It was too good an opportunity to miss.

With a responsive nod, Alexander stemmed the catcalls and gestures with a few curt commands and took his place at the back of the column. The soldiers were apparently some of Major-General Skippon's new recruits about to set out for drill and target practice in Finsbury Fields and not yet allocated to a regiment. The Common Council had mobilised London's Trained Bands earlier in the year, and without a doubt, Skippon was fast transforming them into a force to be reckoned with. Alexander tramped along at the rear for a while, drawing the stragglers into conversation. Being greenhorns and still in training, they were only too eager to display how much they knew. He soon learned that London's four regiments had been increased to six and there were now forty companies, with two hundred men in each. He took careful note of everything they told him.

The column forced its way through the crowded streets towards Moorgate. Even with war imminent and the impressive fortifications around the city nearing completion, life seemed to be going on as usual. The volume of noise was, as always, ear-shattering: the markets in full swing, hawkers shouted, carters getting their vehicles stuck and cursing, streams of sheep, cattle and geese being driven willy-nilly through the streets on their way to Smithfield and Leadenhall. Master masons, busy with their hammers, yelling at apprentices struggling with scaffolding poles and blocks of stone – war or no war, there was always building work going on in London. At an opportune moment, Alexander slipped away and walked back to Ludgate, his mind going over the bits and pieces of information he had gained in the last few days, rejecting some as irrelevant, tucking other snippets at the back of his mind for possible future use – such as who was making clandestine visits to whom – and bringing to the fore anything he needed to pass on. It appeared the Earl of Bath had been removed from the Gatehouse to the Tower and was visited almost daily by Lady Rachel. It also appeared Lord Westley had spent some hours closeted with the Earl of Pembroke, which was puzzling, but Alexander had been unable to find out the purpose of his visit. He grimaced as the thought brought with it the usual twist of resentment and betrayal. He could not bring himself to believe Westley's protestations of affection; if it was not a blood tie that bound him, what was it? Alexander shrugged impatiently, his thoughts returning to the house in Arundel Street. Bluff and counter bluff. He had needed to know if Westley's suspicions were well founded and now he did. He had undoubtedly unnerved the dowager Lady Westley; it would be a shame not to take advantage of it; prove her guilt and be rid of the rumours once and for all that he had murdered his brother. A half-conceived idea began to take shape in his mind. Preoccupied, he passed without incident through the Ludgate and down the hill. By the time he had reached the Bell Savage, where Cobb was waiting for him, he knew what he wanted to do.

Sitting at a table in a private room at the Bell Savage, a full jug of ale between them and pewter tankards in their fists, the two men put together what they had learned. Since Cobb had departed Luppit, he had spent much of his time visiting friends and colleagues, trawling the stews, inns and taverns all over London. Alexander had been similarly engaged. Between them, they now had a considerable amount of intelligence, though – as always – it was hard to sort rumour from fact. According to Fane, no sooner had the Earl of Bedford met up with Lord

Essex than he was ordered to turn tail and go to the defence of Plymouth. If rumours were to be believed, Bedford had seven troops of horse and one thousand foot intended, it was said, as the nucleus of Parliament's Western Army. Alexander knew Parliament had given overall control of their South West campaign to Lord Philip Herbert, the Earl of Pembroke, tasked to engage with and destroy Sir Ralph Hopton and his Cornish Royalists. He doubted Pembroke would entrust the command to the Earl of Bedford, still suspected of fainthearted loyalty to Parliament's cause. A more immediate threat to Sir Ralph came from Sir George Chudleigh, actively recruiting an army in Devon to resist invasion from Cornwall. Alexander had also heard from his informant, Sidney Hawley, still with the Earl of Essex now in Warwickshire. The gap between the two main armies was fast closing. It appeared Lord Essex was surrounding himself with continental consultants: experts in gunnery and cavalry tactics – typical of 'Old Robin', as the Earl's men were calling him these days. With a wry grin, Alexander tucked the information away.

Before he could leave for Cornwall there were things he needed to do. He called for writing materials and penned a note to Lord Westley, signing it baldly, 'Tawford', which he gave to one of Westley's men still lodging at the Bell Savage, instructing him to ensure it was placed into His Lordship's hand within the hour. He then wrote in cipher everything he and Cobb had learned concerning London's defences, addressing it to Adam Hartley. By now Adam should be with the King's army, which, according to latest intelligence, was on its way south and nearing Bridgnorth. This he gave to Cobb to arrange for a reliable courier. Finally, he wrote to Ellen, assuring her he was fully recovered and departing London for Cornwall. He told her he had been to see her brother and they had parted on good terms. It was not quite true, but they had at least talked and it would please Ellen to think they were reconciled. He added such news as there was concerning Lord and Lady Bath and one or two bits of gossip he knew would amuse, adding an affectionate postscript. About Anne Dynam he said nothing.

'Have Westley deliver it when he returns to Marley Court,' he said, handing the letter to Cobb.

That done, Alexander recounted to the gypsy most of what had transpired in Arundel Street, outlined his plan regarding Anne Dynam and what he hoped to achieve, and gave Cobb explicit instructions to set it in motion. In this respect, two matters needed to be arranged straight away: Lord Westley was to be protected at all times and Anne Dynam was to be watched and followed. No matter where she went, what she did or to whom she spoke, however trivial, Alexander wanted to know about it.

'You leave it with me, my boy,' Cobb said.

'I intend to, just as I always do.' Alexander placed a heavy leather purse on the table. 'This should be enough to see you through.'

With a nod, Cobb pushed back from the table, picked up the purse and tucking it away under his coat turned to go. Alexander shot out a hand and grasped his arm to stay him.

'I may not always show it Cobb, but for what it's worth, you have my gratitude.'

The gypsy regarded him steadily. 'Aye, well it would've been a bad death for me had you not slit that devil Saleeman's throat. Besides...' He closed his eyes in pretended ecstasy and jingled the purse beneath his coat. 'Think what I'd have missed were it not for you.'

Releasing Cobb's arm, Alexander laughed. 'Indeed. Well don't go giving all my money to Beth Dogget, you'll never get home and then what would Sarah have to say to me? I'd as soon face a charge of cavalry single-handed – and on foot what's more. Which reminds me, did you find me a horse?'

Clapping him on the back Cobb shouted with laughter, beckoned and still grinning led the way out to the courtyard, signalling to the ostler. The bow-legged man nodded, scuttled into the stables and emerged a few moments later leading a horse. Alexander's jaw dropped.

It was a magnificent animal, a mare, not much above fifteen hands, but powerful, its buff-coloured body sturdy and well muscled. Along the centre of its back, extending from mane to tail, was a dark brown line, the colour repeated in the legs, darkening almost to black below the knees and marked with the characteristic stripes of the dun. The dished nose, eyes slightly protuberant and bright with intelligence, proclaimed Welsh ancestry. With her tail held high, the mare arched her neck, tossed her head and snorting, side-stepped away from the ostler, shod black hooves slipping and sliding on the cobbles.

'Gidover yer gurt flibbertgibbet!' The man puffed out his cheeks and turned the horse in a tight circle to bring her under control.

'Where the devil … ?' Alexander swung round to Cobb who stood, hands on hips, face lit up with delight at his reaction.

The gypsy winked and tapped a finger against his nose.

'Let's just say I was owed. She's six years or thereabouts and she answers to "Biscuit" on account o' her colour, but you'll call her what you will, I daresay.'

'I shouldn't think so, too much of a mouthful – though I suppose I could shorten it to Wat…,' Alexander murmured. Seeing the gypsy's furrowed brow he laughed. 'You're alright Cobb, Biscuit it is.'

Cobb's brow cleared. 'Aye, well… she's freshly shod, but not bin out for a sennight and according to Tom there she's bin eating enough for two, so is a mite fresh. You might want to ease her in a bit gentle like.'

'You don't say.' The sarcasm was lost on Cobb. With a grin Alexander gently approached the horse and taking his time, examined each of her legs and feet in turn. The hard, bony swelling on her off fore had happened in her youth, probably the result of a kick or being worked too hard, too young, but there was no trace of warmth in it and though unsightly, it was slight and would cause her no trouble.

The gypsy watched in amusement. 'The splint is cold.

You'll find nought wrong with her. I've already checked her over – she's sound as a bell.'

Ignoring Cobb, his lips pursed in a silent whistle, Alexander nodded at the ostler. 'Tom, isn't it? Take her round, will you?'

He viewed the animal from all angles as it was led at a walk and then a trot around the yard, the puffing ostler eventually bringing it skidding to a halt in front of him. Placing one hand on the mare's shoulder, Alexander gently ran the other under her belly, stroked across the ribcage to the flank, felt the flesh quiver beneath his fingers as they encountered the telltale ridge of scars. At one time or another the horse had been cruelly – and unnecessarily – spurred. 'Easy, lass,' he soothed, moving to Biscuit's head, a shade darker than her body and marked beneath the forelock with thin black streaks like a spider's web. Holding her nose, Alexander ran his fingers along her throat, gently probing around and under the jaw to the chin, looked into the mouth and smiled as the soft, whiskered lips nuzzled at his hand but made no attempt to nip him.

At length satisfied, he turned to address Cobb standing behind him. 'As you say, she's sound as—' he got no further. The mare suddenly dropped her head and gave Alexander a firm shove. Caught off balance he gasped in surprise, lost his footing and arms flailing, sat down with a bump on the cobbles.

Cursing vituperatively, he remained where he was for a moment glaring at the mare as she nosed innocently at his boot. 'Trained her to do that, did you, you bastard?' He looked over his shoulder at Cobb, who was bent double, hiccupping. Accepting the grinning ostler's outstretched hand, Alexander pulled himself to his feet, ruefully rubbing his buttocks and eyeing the horse. She stood docile as a donkey and eyed him back, a glint of amusement in her eye. Sharing the joke with her, Alexander smiled wryly. 'Butter wouldn't melt, eh? You'll do, Biscuit. You'll do very well. Give her some meat and water then saddle her up for me, will you, Tom? A lightweight saddle and a plain snaffle bit.' Still grinning, the ostler nodded, picked up the halter rope and led the animal away.

Alexander turned back to Cobb, quirked an eyebrow. 'I can't imagine where you found her, you old rogue, and since you're not going to tell me, I won't ask, but just so's I know, I'm not likely to be hunted for a horse thief, am I?'

Cobb, wet-cheeked, still gasping with laughter, shook his head. 'No lad, you're alright, 'tis all legal and above board. I've a bill of sale to prove it – and there's a man who'll think twice afore he rolls another loaded die with me!'

Shortly after noon and satisfyingly replete after a plateful of hot food, Alexander, now sombrely clad in his usual worsted breeches, plain shirt, buff jerkin, thigh length boots and swathed in a warm oiled cloak, settled his bill, retrieved his mount, adjusted his saddlebags and led Biscuit away from Ludgate. Man and mare occasioned little interest as they threaded through the traffic in Fleet Street, the horse, though watchfully alert, walking calmly at Alexander's side. Once past Temple Bar, he checked and tightened the leathers, mounted up and set off at a gentle trot along the Strand to pick up the Bath Road, pleased to find the horse soft-mouthed and responsive despite the carelessness of her previous owner. Reaching open countryside at last, he held Biscuit back for a while, but eventually gave in and let the impatient animal have her head.

It was well after dark when they arrived at the Greyhound in Maidenhead, having stopped at various points along the way for water and to rest. Chary of trusting his horse to an ostler he did not know and wanting to ensure Biscuit was not allocated a stall where she would be kicked or bitten by restless neighbours, Alexander followed as the mare was led away. He stayed to watch her watered, stabled and rubbed down, and just in case anyone had a mind to steal back half her corn as soon as his back was turned, waited while she fed.

From the moment he had first seen the dun horse, Alexander had decided not to travel post. He did not hold with the view that mares were inclined to be temperamental – bloody-minded, maybe, but he liked that spirit in a horse. A mare needed to be managed, certainly, but to counter that inconvenience was a native intelligence lacking in her male counterparts. Cobb had done him proud; Biscuit was in fine fettle and barring accidents should take him all the way to Cornwall. Even so, he did not want to push either of them too hard – he was not at all sure he was yet fit enough anyway – and he could afford to take his time. The information he had for Sir Ralph Hopton was not so urgent as to necessitate breaking his neck. Whoever was assigned command of the enemy's Western Army, it would take the Earl of Pembroke's regiments of foot some weeks to march to Plymouth, particularly if they were lugging heavy ordinance, which was likely.

Sitting in the lamplight on a heap of straw, Alexander let his thoughts stray to the long journey ahead. He would aim to cover another thirty miles or so on the morrow, which would get him to Newbury. After that, Marlborough and if all went well he should be in Bath by Monday night. There were people he could do to see along the way and he would rest the horse a day or two. God willing, he would make Bodmin in a little under ten days. Alexander cast his mind back to Lyddon's letter, had he said Bodmin or Launceston? No matter, he would find them soon enough.

The sound of Biscuit chomping and blowing into her corn was soporific. Feeling himself drifting off, Alexander yawned. His thigh, though well enough healed, was aching and he was suddenly aware he was ravenously hungry and more than a little thirsty, though not for want of water. With a rueful grin at Biscuit, he got stiffly to his feet and stretched, massaging the dull ache that had settled in the small of his back, flexing his legs and rubbing at his bruised backside. The mare stopped munching and turned her head to watch her new master's curious antics. Giving her neck a playful slap, Alexander smiled. 'Goodnight, old girl, we're going to get along just fine, you and I.'

16

Friday 14th October, 1642

Making his way back across the river on the morning tide, Cobb thought through what he had achieved since Tawford's departure the previous afternoon. A trustworthy messenger had been despatched north with a sealed package, a basket of two pigeons and instructions to seek out Adam Hartley and place them into his hands alone. If he ran into trouble, the birds were to be released and the package destroyed.

That done, Cobb had sent a man and boy in the guise of beggars to Arundel Street, and another similar pair to St Martin's Lane – the men to watch and tail, the boys to bring him word of anything untoward. There was never a problem in hiring people to work for him, he paid them well and his reputation was such that none dared to double-cross him.

Cobb had then sought out the Frenchwoman, contracted her services and agreed her fee. His next visit was to an old friend whom he knew could supply as many hard men as he might need and would ask no questions. Finally, he had called to see an inky-fingered pamphleteer of his acquaintance and passed on a piece of hot gossip. His business at last concluded, and satisfied that he had carried out Tawford's instructions to the letter, Cobb had returned to the Mermaid. Now he was on his way to see Lord Westley: the next stage of Tawford's plan.

The beggar in St Martin's Lane was sitting like a heap of rags across from the entrance to Westley's rooms, a pair of crutches at his side, his leg swathed in filthy bandages and stuck out before him. The boy loitered nearby, picking his nose with one grubby finger, the other hand held out plaintively to irritated passers-by. Cobb smiled to himself; he was a bright lad, that one. The beggar covertly gestured towards Westley's shuttered windows and gave a slight nod. Cobb raised his eyebrows and made his way up the stairs, rapped the door and waited. There was no sound from within. He rapped again. Still he waited. Increasingly concerned, he tried the door. He was on the point of forcing entry when at last he heard a bolt slide back and Lord Westley opened the door.

Cobb was shocked by the man's appearance. Westley's face was sallow and haggard, his eyes blearily bloodshot, his clothes crumpled and stained with vomit, his hair and beard matted and unkempt. Robert looked blankly at Cobb, shook his head with a gesture of dismissal and made to shut the door. The gypsy thrust out his foot, appalled. 'My Lord, it is I, Cobb. May I come in? You don't look at all well. Is aught amiss?'

Robert backed into the room. 'Cobb, so it is. No, nothing is amiss. I am a little tired that is all. You have a message for me?'

'Yes My Lord.' Cobb closed the door carefully behind him and divested himself of hat and cloak. 'I am to put myself at your disposal should you need any help with Tawford's plan, and I have the letter for you to take to Lady Ellen.' He held out the package.

Robert ignored it. 'Plan? What plan? He spoke of no plan.'

Cobb frowned. 'But did you not receive his message, My Lord? He sent it from the Bell Savage; your man should have brought it to you yesterday.'

'Yes, no, it's over there.' Robert wearily indicated a package lying unopened on the table behind him. Turning, he reached for his chair and held onto the back of it, his knuckles white.

Suppressing an oath of frustration, Cobb contained his impatience. 'My Lord, forgive me, but you should read it. Tawford has set events in train that might compromise you.

His note will tell you most of what you need to know, but he advises you return to Devon within a few days.'

Robert swung round, aghast. 'What has he done? For God's sake man, tell me!'

'As I understand it, he has made himself known to the dowager Lady Westley, Anne Dynam, My Lord, and intimated to her that he is privy to some information that could cause her deep embarrassment.'

'What!' Moving round the chair, Robert sat in it with a bump and spread his fingers over his face. 'What else did Alexander tell you, Cobb?'

'That he has satisfied himself your suspicions regarding the Lady's involvement in your son's death are well founded, My Lord.'

Robert caught his breath, withdrew his hands and interlaced his fingers to still their shaking. 'What does he want me to do?'

'He wants you to partake in a small deception. He has informed the Lady that you are to be married and that your betrothed is a young woman capable of bearing you a son. He asks you to go along with the lie.'

Robert looked up startled. 'Why in God's name has he done that? What does he hope to gain by it?'

'He is hoping the widow will panic and take some kind of action that will lead us to her accomplice and the evidence you seek. Tawford expects her to call on you to see for herself if what he says is true and—'

'Accomplice?'

'At least one, possibly more; the lady could not have acted alone, My Lord.'

'I suppose not,' Robert said wearily. 'I would that Tawford had paid me the courtesy of coming to tell me about this himself. The idea is preposterous, a waste of time; my stepmother will see through it immediately.'

'As to that, My Lord, I think I might be able to help you convince her.' Cobb moved to the table and placed Ellen's sealed letter beside the other, unopened package, noticing the empty decanter, the glass lying on its side in a stain of pooled wine. Some half eaten bread and cheese had attracted a stray bluebottle; it buzzed fretfully away as Cobb righted the glass. The room was stuffy, felt damp and cold and a foul smell emanated from a full chamber pot in the corner. Dismayed, Cobb swung round. 'Do you not have a manservant, My Lord? Why did your man not stay and see to your needs? Please, let me call for one.'

'Eh?' Robert unlaced his fingers, glanced distractedly round the room. 'No,' he said shortly. 'I sent him away. I can manage. Leave it Cobb. I will not go along with this ridiculous idea of Tawford's and I am not returning to Devon. My men can take the letter to Lady Ellen. You will find them at—'

'The Bell Savage, yes I know.'

'So you do. I am a little confused.'

'I can see that, My Lord. When did you last eat?'

Robert waved his hand absently towards the mouldering cheese. 'Yesterday, I think. Please go, Cobb. You have delivered your message – now leave me be.'

'At least let me see to your immediate needs.' Cobb ignored Robert's plea. 'I will call for some hot food and ale and set your rooms to rights. Forgive me for saying so, My Lord, but I think you need help. I do not know exactly what transpired between you and Master Tawford, nor do I care to, but whatever you may think, I know he is concerned for your welfare and would never forgive me were I to leave you like this. Nor would the Lady Ellen – even less so – as well you know.'

The gypsy moved towards the fireplace as he spoke, reached for the irons and began riddling the grate. There was some kindling, a few bits of coal and a couple of logs in the box; it would do for now. He continued to talk about nothing in particular, keeping his voice low and soothing as he laid a fire, found a spill and tinderbox and blew on the flames until the kindling caught. That done Cobb heaved himself to his feet. 'Please, My Lord, at least let me help you change your clothing.'

When Robert shook his head and waved him away, Cobb persisted, hardening his tone much as he would with an uncooperative child. 'Neglecting yourself is injurious to your health and no way to be going on. It is plain to see you are not yourself, but Tawford has risked much. Are you prepared to throw it away out of pique? Do you not wish to see this woman brought to justice? Pull yourself together, man!' That at least got through to him. For a moment Cobb held his breath, afraid he had gone too far. It was no way for a gypsy to speak to a peer of the realm!

Robert's head came up with a start and he looked full at Cobb, his eyes cold with anger. 'How dare you speak to me in that tone about matters that do not concern you – who in God's name do you think you are?' He pointed to the door. 'I should have you whipped. Now get out.'

Cobb stood his ground. 'I know full well who I am, and I dare because anything that threatens Tawford concerns me. What lies between you is nothing to me, I make no judgement nor do I ask questions. You can trust my discretion in this as in any other matter.' The big man looked down at Robert kindly and held out his hand. 'I do not mean to offend you. I speak out of concern for you, My Lord. I pray you, don't let Tawford's efforts go for naught. Let me help you.'

After a moment the tension left Robert's body; he nodded, took the proffered hand and pulled himself to his feet. 'My son is to be envied—' He stopped short, his mouth twisting wryly. 'But I imagine there is no point in perpetuating that lie with you is there. Tawford must have told you that he is not my son?'

Cobb inclined his head. 'I have known it for some time.'

'Is there any of my business to which you are not privy, Cobb?'

The gypsy smiled. 'How would I be knowing that, My Lord?'

'No, I suppose not.'

'As I said, I do not ask questions. It is of no moment to me who or what Tawford is, nor what he is to you.'

Robert looked at the gypsy curiously. 'He is fortunate indeed. What binds you to him, Cobb?'

'You know, My Lord.' Cobb shrugged. 'I owe him a life. It is a debt of gratitude not easily repaid.'

'You think not? Perhaps you are right.' Robert eyed the gypsy for a moment, turned away with a sigh. 'Would I could command such loyalty.'

'As to that, my loyalty extends to you, My Lord, and of course, to the Lady Ellen, whom I hold in deep regard.' Cobb broke off, a twinkle in his eye. 'I and many another, it has to be said.' He was rewarded with a smile.

'So, my sister has you wrapped round her little finger too, does she, the minx. Do you have news of her, Cobb?'

'No more recent than you I think, My Lord. She was in good health last I heard.' Relieved to see Robert turning towards his chamber and shrugging out of his filthy doublet, Cobb let himself out and went swiftly down the stairs, beckoned to the beggar boy, pressed coins into his hand and gave him instructions in an urgent undertone. He then returned to Robert's rooms.

Within minutes, Lord Westley's two men had arrived from the Bell Savage with a barber in tow and carrying between them a tub of hot water and a basket of logs. In less than an hour the rooms were clean, the shutters open to fresh air, the bed made up with clean linen, the chamber pot replaced with a fresh one and pushed out of sight beneath it. The fire, now crackling brightly, was at last throwing out some heat, the table was laid and Robert, freshly washed and dressed, his beard trimmed and his hair combed, was looking much more like himself. A maid arrived from the Bell Savage carrying a pan of steaming beef and a jug of ale, a stick of bread tucked beneath her arm. Thanking and dismissing them all while Lord Westley sat himself down, Cobb returned to the table to serve him, his stomach responding with reverberating growls to the appetising smells wafting from the pan.

Hearing them, Robert hid a smile. 'I am in your debt, Cobb. Won't you please share my table, there is plenty here for two, get yourself a plate man.' He gestured to a court cupboard on the far wall.

Cobb's face split in a beatific grin. 'I confess I am hungry. I thank you, My Lord.' He selected what he needed and returned to the table, pulled out a chair, sat on it and reached for the jug, his mouth watering in anticipation as ale frothed into his tankard. Taking a long pull Cobb smacked his lips in noisy satisfaction, wiping his whiskers with one hand while helping himself to a ladle of stew with the other, pleased to see Westley eating hungrily.

'So Cobb, supposing I were to go along with this nonsense.' Robert picked at a piece of gristle caught in his teeth. 'You say you can help me? How?' A ghost of a smile played across his drawn features. 'Who is it I am supposed to be marrying? Did Tawford mention? I would make a sorry bridegroom, that's for sure.'

His mouth full, Cobb grinned back at him. 'I'll own I've seen you looking better, My Lord, but there's plenty worse than you make a trip to the altar.'

'Mm.' Robert looked sagely at the gypsy. 'It is plain you need no lessons in flattery, Cobb.'

The sarcasm was so unexpected, Cobb laughed out loud and choked on a mouthful of food. When he had stopped coughing he straightened his face. 'In all seriousness, My Lord, you know full well you would be a fine catch for any young woman – as indeed does Anne Dynam. You can be sure she will make it her business to find out if the betrothal is genuine, so it has to be believable.'

Robert gave a short barking laugh. 'Believable? Look at me, man. I live like a monk. It might be just a little more believable if there was a bride in the picture.'

Cobb gave an answering smile. 'As it goes, there is: a widow by the name of Arabella Béjart. She's an actress who—'

'An *actress*!' Again Robert laughed, but without humour. 'French of course,' he said disparagingly.

Cobb nodded. 'Half French, My Lord; her mother was English. She has performed for King Louis himself and is quite sought after so I understand – though I don't hold with it myself,' he added hastily, amused by Westley's horrified expression.

Robert's lip curled in distaste. 'My stepmother would never believe that I would entertain *marriage* with such a woman however comely she may be. Tawford will have to do better than that.'

Cobb hid a smile. Westley would not be the first to be beguiled into marriage by just such a woman, but he let it pass. 'Rest assured, her credentials are quite fitting, My Lord; she is the only child of the late Claude de Bourdeille, Comte de Montrésor.'

'Never heard of the poor fellow. How does the daughter of a count come to fall so low?'

'She took up with a strolling player when she was just fifteen. He was from a theatrical family in Paris, name of François Béjart. They eloped and she bore him a child. Her father disowned her, but when Béjart was killed in a brawl barely a year later, the Count forgave her and took her and the child back to live with him at Montrésor. She was there until quite recently, then she came to London to seek out her English relatives, it appears she is her father's sole heir, the Count has so neglected the estate in his later years it is worth very little – his family is impoverished, My Lord. She is penniless.'

Robert nodded. 'I see. And the child is with her?'

Cobb shook his head. 'No, her daughter did not survive infancy.'

'Poor woman.' Robert was silent for a moment, his face etched with sympathy. 'So what is her situation?'

'She is renting a house in Lincoln's Inn Fields – is a neighbour of Lady Bath's, in fact, and has been received by her, though is not yet well known in society. Anne Dynam will know of her, but they have not met. Mistress Béjart is not without poise, My Lord, and she is, of course, an actress. Tawford believes she will appear eminently suitable a match for you. She has spirit, but I fear she is less than comely,' he added.

Robert shrugged. 'It is of no moment to me if she is hag-faced and warty as a toad, it is a ruse, Cobb, I am not actually going to marry the woman.' He gave a wry smile, 'Though if she is plain, I imagine my stepmother might wonder what the attraction is.'

Cobb grinned. 'Not for long, My Lord; I have ensured details of Mistress Béjart's considerable fortune will soon occupy the gossips. People always believe what they see in print. None will doubt she is an heiress of some means.' Cobb smiled. 'And by the time Anne Dynam discovers the truth, hopefully she will already have incriminated herself.'

'It appears Tawford has thought of everything,' Robert said dryly. 'And this actress has agreed to this? Why?'

Wondering how much to divulge, Cobb examined his jerkin and scraped off a morsel of food with his fingernail, decided to keep it simple. 'She owes Tawford a favour, My Lord.' The less Westley knew about why, the better.

'Hm!' Robert grunted with distaste. 'I might have guessed.'

'You misunderstand me, My Lord. It is purely a business arrangement. Mistress Béjart will be handsomely paid for her services.'

'Will she indeed. Does she know the reason for this mummery?'

Cobb nodded. 'It was necessary, but Tawford trusts her discretion implicitly.' And with reason, he thought, but did not say.

Pushing his plate to one side, Robert leaned his elbows on the table and tented his hands. 'She understands it might be dangerous to her reputation?'

'Yes, My Lord. As I said, she has spirit.'

'And if I refuse to go along with it?'

'Naturally it is your decision, My Lord, but Tawford believes the widow, your stepmother, will soon give herself away if she thinks her son's inheritance is about to slip from her grasp. There may never be a better opportunity to trap her. I need hardly remind you why he wants you to do this.'

Shocked into silence, Robert buried his head in his hands. After a moment he sighed, looked up, the lines about his mouth cut deep. 'You never knew Henry, did you, Cobb?'

The gypsy shook his head. 'Only by repute, My Lord, but I know how he died.'

Robert's eyes glimmered. He dashed his hand across his face, cleared his throat. 'I suppose I will have to meet this Arabella... what did you say her name was?'

'Béjart, My Lord; it would be advisable – and soon if you are to convince your stepmother she is genuine. Bella waits only for my word and she will arrange to call on you to discuss details of how to proceed, for naturally you will have to be seen together a time or two. There is one other matter we should discuss.'

Robert nodded. 'Go on.' He leaned forward.

'If Lady Anne is convinced of your betrothal, Tawford believes she will stop at nothing to prevent your marriage from taking place – nothing, My Lord,' Cobb repeated, emphasising the gravity of the warning. 'You will be safer in Devon. Tawford urges you to go home as soon as your stepmother has taken the bait. A week should give us enough time and I have already arranged an armed escort for your journey.'

'Then you had better unarrange it.' Robert, who still looked drained, but now at least had some colour in his cheeks, gave the gypsy a wry smile. 'Can it be that for once there is something Tawford has failed to discover or anticipate? Much as I would like to, I cannot return to Devon just now.'

'Cannot?' Cobb frowned.

'Regrettably not – I have accepted a commission from the

Earl of Pembroke. I am to serve as a captain of horse under
Colonel Sir William Waller. I fear the machinations of my
stepmother are the least of my worries,' Robert added dryly.

For once Cobb was at a loss for words. He would have
wagered his life on Westley being the King's man.

'I have shocked you?' Robert's mouth twisted. 'I can
assure you it is not by choice. It was my part of the bargain
for Tawford's life – I was committed before I learned of his
escape.'

Quickly recovering his composure, the gypsy felt a spark
of compassion for Lord Westley. It was no odds to Cobb who
fought on which side in this unholy war, but he could foresee
only anguish here. 'You surely don't mean to go through with
it, My Lord?'

'I have little choice. I must leave to take up my post on
Monday or be placed under guard in the Tower.' Robert shot
the gypsy a grim smile. 'I suppose I might be safe from my
stepmother there, eh Cobb? But yes, I mean to go through
with it. Apart from anything else, I have given my word. It is
a question of honour you understand.'

Cobb gave a small grunt of frustration. God's Bones! He
knew it was futile to try to persuade Westley to flee. The gentry
clung to their notion of honour like leeches to a vein. 'Can you
not at least delay your departure?'

Robert shook his head. 'I dare not. Unless this trap of
Tawford's can be set within the next couple of days, I fear his
plan will have to go along without me. Do you know where he
is? I had hoped to see him before I leave. We still have much
to discuss.'

'He has already left for Cornwall, My Lord. He is carrying
intelligence for Sir Ralph Hopton. I fear you will not see him
again for some while.'

Robert's shoulders slumped. Outside the sky had turned
dark with rain clouds and though not long past noon, the room
was shadowed and gloomy. He got up from the table and
walked to the window, pulling the shutters closed against the

draught. Moving to the fireplace, he reached into the firebox and threw a log onto the spitting fire, stamping out the sparks that showered onto the singed hearthrug. From the mantelpiece he took a fresh candle, pressed it into a holder and held it to the flames until the wick caught. Cupping it with his hand, he carried it to the table and stood looking down at the gypsy. Cobb waited in silence.

'Very well,' Westley spoke at last. 'If my stepmother calls to see me before I must leave, I will do what I can to convince her I am happily betrothed to your Mistress Béjart. But why is Tawford so sure Anne Dynam will fall for it? My stepmother is a clever woman. If she guesses I am playing her for a fool, she will never show her hand as Tawford hopes. Might it not be better to forget the whole idea? Surely if the woman has admitted her guilt it is enough to bring her to justice?'

'She has not, not in so many words, My Lord, as you say, she is a clever woman; she has simply demanded Tawford bring her proof, but your son's death is too long ago and the trail long gone cold. Tawford wants her to panic, act without her usual guile. He believes this ruse to be the only way.'

'I see. If she does swallow the bait, what does he mean to do exactly? Indeed, what can he do from Cornwall?'

Cobb shifted in his seat, a small bubble of trapped wind making him wince. Noisily he cleared his throat and let the fart escape, his expression a mixture of apology and relief. 'In case the ruse should fail, Tawford has put a proposition to her, My Lord, one he believes she will be tempted to accept. If she does, he will have ample proof of her perfidy. He means to return as soon as she has had time to reflect on it.'

Robert snorted. 'Assuming the small matter of a civil war does not get in his way, eh Cobb?'

Cobb shrugged. 'He will do everything humanly possible, but naturally we cannot predict the fortunes of war.'

'Indeed we cannot.' The candlestick still clutched in his fingers, Robert gestured impatiently, the flame stretched and guttered, hot wax splattered to the floor. Suddenly his eyes narrowed. 'A proposition you say?' He put up a hand as the gypsy made to speak. 'No, wait. Let me guess.' His mouth twisted into a grimace. 'Has Alexander by chance persuaded my stepmother that he too wants me dead? – God in Heaven, it may even be true.' Robert gasped, dazed.'

Cobb's brow wrinkled. 'Odslife! Whatever there is between you, My Lord, you cannot possibly believe that of him. It was necessary to convince Anne Dynam he is prepared to kill you, yes, but it is a calculated and preposterous lie. You surely don't imagine...'

Robert shook his head as though to clear it. 'No. Forgive me, I am not thinking straight.'

Cobb nodded. 'Tawford thinks it would help his case if your stepmother believes the enmity between you to be mutual.' The gypsy gave a half-smile. 'He said he did not think you would find it difficult to give that impression, and she is more likely to believe his proposition is genuine if she thinks you are at daggers drawn.'

Robert put the candlestick on the table and fingered his beard. 'Enmity is one thing, Cobb, but patricide? In heaven's name, why, if she believes like everyone else that Tawford is my son, would she imagine he would go so far as to kill me?' Robert leaned his hands on the table and stared tensely at the gypsy, his eyes glistening with anxiety. 'Unless... do you know if he has told her otherwise?'

Cobb shifted uncomfortably under the intensity of Westley's gaze. 'He didn't say – though I doubt it – it is not something he speaks of, not even to me.' He shrugged, 'I have told you everything I know. If there is anything more, Tawford has not divulged it to me.'

A log shifted in the grate, breaking the tension between them as both men glanced towards the fire. A spurt of flame shot up the chimney, shadows danced in the hearth. After a moment, Robert relaxed. With a nod he seated himself at the table. 'If he is to gain evidence against Anne Dynam that will stand up in a court of law, he will need witnesses.'

'I imagine he will have thought of that.'

'Yes, of course.' Thoughtfully Robert considered Cobb's words, looked up at him and frowned. 'Tawford places a very great deal of trust in you. Where do you come from, Cobb?'

The question was so unexpected, Cobb started. He evaded it. 'Here and there – I travel about a lot – I fear I am too long in the tooth to recall where exactly I was born. Why do you ask, My Lord?'

Robert eyed Cobb with curiosity. 'Methinks you were not always a gypsy?'

'I have lived as one for too long now to remember otherwise, though I was a soldier once.' Cobb shrugged and lapsed into the vernacular. 'I do live as wit and fortune take me. How else be a plain man to fare in such haggling times? I'll rather be unmannerly than troublesome for sure, but I do not shame to say I love yon brave boy as my life – an' that's rightdown gospel true and no gainsaying.'

For a moment Robert held the unwavering gaze of Cobb's clear grey eyes, nodded and reached into a drawer. He drew out a sheet of notepaper, a small knife, a quill, a bottle of ink and a silver pounce pot. 'I have decided I will not wait on the whim of my stepmother to call on me,' he looked up briefly from sharpening the nib.

'My Lord?'

'I want you to take this to her.' Robert bent his head to write, the nib scratched and spluttered on the page. 'It is to ask if she will receive me on the morrow as I have some happy news to impart.' Robert looked up, one eyebrow quirked, his lips lifted in a wry smile.

Cobb was stunned into silence. Westley's whole demeanour had changed; the marks of exhaustion masked by a look of purpose and decisiveness reminiscent of Tawford.

Quickly reading through what he had written, Robert gave a small grunt of satisfaction and lifting the pounce pot, shook sand over the wet ink. He replaced the writing tools in the drawer, pushed it shut, blew on the note, folded it still gritty and handed it to Cobb. 'Be good enough to wait on her reply.'

'Certainly, My Lord.' Cobb took the note held out to him and pushed back from the table, the legs of his chair shrieking with noisy protest on the floorboards. Getting to his feet he belched. 'If you will allow, I will accompany you to Arundel Street on the morrow.'

'There is no need. If my stepmother means me harm it will not be in broad daylight, nor will it be by her own hand. As we have seen, that is not her style.'

'As you say, My Lord.' Cobb acquiesced. Westley was probably right, but he would follow him to Arundel Street even so, and he would go armed.

'While you're about it, find a post-boy for Ellen's letter if you will. Also, send your message to Mistress Béjart – I will see her this afternoon – I assume it will be convenient? Though I fear I am ill equipped to entertain a lady here – even if she is an actress,' Robert added with a smile, glancing round the room as he spoke.

His sardonic expression was disturbingly familiar to Cobb. It was only natural, he supposed, that Tawford would have modelled himself on this man. 'Bella will not be expecting to be entertained, My Lord, and I think you will not dislike her, despite her former profession.' Cobb smiled, picked up Ellen's letter, retrieved his hat, shrugged into his cloak and turned to go. With his hand on the door, he turned back, made to speak, hesitated.

'What is it Cobb?'

'Forgive me, My Lord, I don't mean to insult your intelligence, but when you meet with the Lady Anne it is imperative she remain convinced of your ignorance, both in respect of her crime against your son, and also of her meeting with Tawford.'

'Apology accepted. Have no fear, I do understand that, Cobb. Was there something else?'

'I will likely be gone for some while, perhaps you will take some rest, My Lord?'

Robert smiled at the gypsy's apparent concern. 'Perhaps I will, Cobb, perhaps I will. And thank you.'

Raising a hand, the gypsy let himself out and descended to the street. Once again he beckoned the boy over, gave him instructions, watched for a moment as he scampered away. Indicating to the beggar he was leaving, Cobb set off purposefully in the direction of Arundel Street, his head bent against the sudden squall as the heavily laden clouds released their promised burden.

Robert settled down in his chair by the fire and thought about Cobb, convinced he was keeping something back, certain he was not what he seemed. Cobb's intelligence and manner of speech belied his simpleton's appearance and were not those of a gypsy. Robert wondered suddenly if Alexander was wise to trust the big man as much as he obviously did. Watching the flames, he began to analyse everything that had taken place and to think through the forthcoming, distasteful activities with which he had been forced, reluctantly, to agree. After a while, he dozed.

Some three hours later, Robert was disturbed by the sound of men's raised voices and a carriage coming to a halt in the street below. He went quickly to the window, but the overhang obscured most of his view and despite the flare from a linkboy's torch it was now too dark to make out who was alighting. He did, however, recognise the livery as that of the Earl of Bath. Confound it! Why was Lady Bath visiting unannounced? It was highly inconvenient just now when he was expecting this Béjart woman to arrive. Firmly closing the shutters, Robert glanced quickly round the room, shut the door to his chamber, folded Cobb's chair and pushed it back under the table, cleared the remains of the meal to the sideboard, using his arm to brush the crumbs to the floor, shoved some papers into the drawer, lit a few more candles, plumped up a cushion on the chair, threw another log on the fire, and went breathlessly to the door, a branched candlestick clutched in his fingers.

Hoping he might have been mistaken Robert waited on the landing, heard women's voices, footsteps on the stairs, trilling laughter. Resigned to the inevitable, he moved to the top of the stairs and held the candles aloft to light the stairwell. The first to appear was Sara Voysin, the next he did not recognise; it was certainly not Lady Bath.

'Lord Westley, isn't this exciting? How lovely to see you.' Sara reached the top of the stairs and held out her hand. 'Forgive us, but is it convenient, My Lord? May we come in?'

His heart sinking, Robert bowed over the neatly gloved hand. 'Sara, this is an unexpected pleasure. To what do I owe the honour? Please... do come in.' Lighting the way into his rooms he attempted to hide his exasperation, wondered how the devil he was going to seat the two women comfortably. What a pickle. 'May I take your cloak? And your companion, Mistress... er... I don't believe I've had the pleasure...?'

'Lah!' Gazing at him raptly, Sara gave a peal of laughter, put out a hand and gave his wrist a slight tap. 'Come now sir, don't tease. Surely you recognise your own betrothed?' She again trilled with laughter. 'You don't have to pretend with me. Arabella has told me everything. Such thrilling news.'

She flung off her cloak, thrust it into his waiting hand, swept past him and plonked herself down in the chair, stretching out her boots to the fire. 'What a lovely fire – such a wretched afternoon don't you think? But how could you keep such an exciting secret from us all? Shame on you, My Lord.' Sara turned and smiled up at him.

Robert put down the candlestick and stood awkwardly to one side, Sara's cloak still clutched in his fingers, completely at a loss, unsure what she knew.

Her companion moved quickly forward from the door, relieved him of the cloak, placed it with her own on the back of the chair and took hold of both his hands. 'My Lord, please forgive me, I know you wanted to give Lady Anne Dynam our news before anyone else heard of it, but Lady Rachel and Sara happened to be with me when your message came and, well, I have so wanted to tell everyone, it was impossible for me to hide it. Her Ladyship kindly insisted I take her carriage and Sara offered to come as my chaperone, and here we are. You don't mind too much, do you, my dear?' Raising her face to his, she kissed his cheek.

Cobb had been right: she was not at all comely; more horse than toad, Robert thought sagely. He could well imagine she would pass for a boy on the stage. Arabella was much too tall for a woman, the top of her head almost level with his. She was stick thin, her high cheekbones prominent in her strong square face, her nose too long, her mouth too wide and her skin too dark. Her hair was undoubtedly her redeeming feature. It fell from beneath her little lace cap to the small of her back, in lustrous ringlets. Neither blonde nor brown, but the colour of freshly spun honey, it was complemented by the rich russet of her gown. And then there was her voice: low and musical and with a captivating accent – and her eyes, an unusual shade of amber, which now gazed into his with stark amusement at his discomfiture. Strangely he felt as if he knew her. There was something about her that reminded him of Ellen. God knows why for they were completely unalike, and yet she put his sister so much in mind Robert almost laughed out loud. How Ellen would have loved this!

Sara smiled up at them. 'There you are, Bella, what did I tell you? I knew your Lord would be delighted to see us and wouldn't give a fig about your telling us the news first. I cannot imagine why you were so anxious about it.' She settled herself into the chair and turned her face deliberately to the fire. 'Now, you two must have lots to talk about so take no notice of me, I will sit quiet as a mouse and you will hardly know I'm here.'

Flustered, Robert led Arabella to the table. 'Forgive my humble accommodation. I so rarely entertain that I lack the proper furnishings.' He pulled out a chair and unfolded it for her. 'May I offer you a glass of wine?' He retrieved the refilled decanter and three glasses from the sideboard and brought them to the table. 'I am sorry it is so dark in here. I seem to have run out of candles and I fear I have nothing to offer you for supper.'

Bella shrugged, leaned her elbows on the table and smiled up at him. 'It is dark? I had not noticed. A glass of wine will be just the thing.'

Feeling decidedly awkward, Robert poured three glasses while wondering what the devil they were going to talk about with Sara listening so avidly by the fire. He signalled to Bella with his eyes, his brows quirking in frustration. She grinned at him and with a slight shake of her head put her finger to her lips. 'Thank you.' She reached for a glass and took a sip of wine. 'I have been telling Sara how we met, My Lord.'

Her rich, musical voice captivated him and it took a moment for Robert to realise what Arabella had said. 'You have?' He was acutely embarrassed and could see she was laughing at him as he carried a glass of wine to Sara.

Sara took it with a smile. 'Such a romantic story – and so brave of you, My Lord.'

'It was?' Robert felt as if he was fumbling in the dark.

'Oh Bella, no wonder you love him. Such modesty!' Sara gave a small shiver of pleasure. 'To take on four men like that when you were unarmed, and to lift Bella into your arms and carry her to safety without a care for the wound you took, knowing at any moment you might be pursued. I think that was terribly brave.'

'Any man would have done the same,' Robert said helplessly, running his fingers through his hair.

Sara shook her head. 'Not so many as you might think, Lord Westley, and I have explained to Bella she should take more care. It isn't the same here as in France – Montrésor sounds delightful, not at all like London. It isn't safe to go out unaccompanied when the streets are so dangerous, especially now with all the soldiers about, and everyone shouting and quarrelling and throwing things at each other – don't you agree, My Lord? And the language! I have to block my ears they blaspheme so.' Sara pouted. 'But you don't want to listen to me. I really will keep quiet from now on, I promise.' With a coquettish smile, she turned her back on him.

Robert doubted it, but returned to the table, retrieved his glass and took a gulp of wine. After the excesses of the last two days it made him feel slightly queasy, but he decided it might help him to enter into this fantasy. He pulled out another chair and sat down.

'Sara is right,' he ventured. 'It was foolish of you, Bella.' It was the first time he had said her name; it felt strangely familiar on his tongue. 'But you have promised not to do it again, haven't you, my dear?' He wondered for how long he could keep this up; began fervently to pray that Cobb would return.

Bella's mouth framed an exaggerated pout. 'But if I had not, we would not have met and I would not be the happiest woman in the world, knowing you cannot wait to be my husband, but must rush me to the altar so soon and with so much still to arrange. I am in, how you say... a whirl?'

'As indeed am I.' How true! 'So which date have you decided on, sweetheart? And do you wish the ceremony to be here in London?' Two could play at this game, Robert thought, taking another gulp of wine.

'Oh I think a Christmas wedding, don't you?' Behind them Sara gave a rapturous little sigh. Robert hid a smile behind his hand as Bella arched her brows at him. 'And of course here – where else? Unless... you do not mean us to travel to France, *mon chéri*?'

The term of endearment took Robert by surprise. He cleared his throat. 'We will if that is what you want, my dear, but I was thinking of Marley Court. You might like to see it before you decide. Devon is so beautiful at this—' he stopped short. Whatever was he thinking of? Just for a moment he had almost begun to believe this was real. Again he cleared his throat, frowned at the woman sitting opposite him, her mannish face softened by candlelight and her cat's eyes brimming with laughter. 'I think we will have to discuss these arrangements some other time. It is getting late and as Sara has pointed out, the streets are dangerous, especially after dark. I should not have asked you to come, it was selfish of me, but I needed so much to see you.' That also was true, he thought. Behind them Sara gave another little sigh and wriggled in the chair.

Bella smiled. 'It gladdens my heart to know you are so impatient you could not wait until our assignation tomorrow.'

Robert looked at her blankly. Now what the devil was she talking about. 'Our assignation... yes, of course,' he murmured, his eyebrow shooting to his hairline.

'Surely you have not forgotten? Come now, My Lord. Our meeting with the lawyers to finalise my portion and settlement?'

Robert was impressed. The woman was as cool as one of Ellen's wretched cucumbers. 'How could I possibly forget such an important matter, my dear,' he responded dryly.

'Is two o'clock still convenient for you, My Lord? I could rearrange it if not.'

'There is no need, that is fine.'

Bella nodded, finished her wine and placed the glass carefully on the table. 'Then, when we have done, you will take me home and we can talk about the invitations, yes?'

'Yes,' he said weakly. Rising to his feet Robert moved round the table to her side. 'Is Lady Bath's carriage waiting for you?'

Bella inclined her head. 'Yes, and with two footmen. We will be perfectly safe. I am sure you have no need to worry about me, my love, though it gladdens me that you do.'

'But I do... I am extremely worried about you, my dear.' Robert found he was almost enjoying the ambiguity of their conversation – almost! He handed her from her chair, noticing how gracefully she moved, despite her height. As Cobb had said, she had poise, was not at all vulgar. But, of course, she was an actress, he reminded himself – little better than a courtesan. The thought made him tingle. It was a totally unexpected response and it alarmed him. He had not sought the company of a woman since Ruth died.

Bella leaned towards him, her hand still grasped in his, once again lightly kissed his cheek. He caught the scent of her in his nostrils, a seductive mix of musk and gillyflower. 'I am sorry,' she breathed in his ear. 'This was unavoidable – but you really should consider a career on the stage, My Lord.' She treated him to a broad wink.

Shocked, Robert dropped her hand like a hot coal and started away from her, a flush staining his cheeks.

Getting to her feet, Sara smiled across at them indulgently. 'What sweet nonsense is she whispering that is making you blush so, Lord Westley?'

'Sara, please!' Bella smiled. 'Leave the poor man some semblance of dignity. I was merely telling him how handsome he is and how much I adore him, no?'

Both women laughed as Robert, flushed scarlet, turned hurriedly away to retrieve their cloaks, at which moment there came an urgent rap at the door. His prayer had been answered – if a little late.

'Ah! Cobb, come in do.' Robert could not hide his relief. 'My visitors were just leaving. Be so good as to help them out.' He turned to Sara, once again bowing over her neat little hand. 'I should have asked if there is any news of Lord Bath. Most remiss of me – I apologise if I seem all of a dither.'

'Of course you are – understandably so.' Sara smiled warmly. 'My Lord of Bath is in good health and as comfortable as her ladyship can make him in that dismal place, but he is impatient to be free. She goes to see him every day and takes him gossip to amuse and books to read, but you know how he suffers so with his health and as yet there is no agreement as to when he may be released. It is not easy for them.'

'I can well imagine,' Robert said, his face grim. 'It is a wretched business.' He bowed again, 'Thank you for coming to see me, Sara. Please give my warmest regards to your mistress. Will you ask if I may call on her tomorrow? There is a matter I need urgently to discuss with her.' He turned to Bella. 'I imagine we will be done by about four o'clock, if Lady Bath could see me then?'

Bella looked at him, curiosity sparking briefly in her eyes. 'Whatever you say, My Lord.'

Robert bowed over her hand. 'Thank you my dear; until tomorrow then. And let us hope we may get everything sorted out to our mutual satisfaction.'

'Indeed, My Lord.' Bella gave him a wide smile, but he noticed it did not reach her eyes.

Cobb's rubicund face split with pleasure as he bowed smartly to each woman in turn. 'Mistress Voysin, how lovely to see you; Mistress Béjart, allow me.' He helped them on with their cloaks, picked up a candlestick and led the way downstairs.

When they had gone, Robert poured himself another glass of wine, walked over to the fire, absently threw on a log, leaned on the mantelshelf and stood looking into the hissing flames. The actress had skilfully engineered another meeting, embellished the fiction with talk of lawyers, provided him with a story of how they had come to meet and suggested the timing of their supposed matrimony – and all without giving herself or him away. She was good; too damned good. Almost he was thankful he would soon be out of it, which thought led him to Lady Bath. He needed to explain about his commission from Parliament. He did not want her to learn from anyone else of his apparent betrayal; could only hope she would understand why he had accepted it. Dimly he heard the coach clattering away and Cobb's feet on the stairs.

The gypsy burst breathlessly into the room. 'Forgive me, My Lord, I had meant to be here – I was unavoidably delayed. Why was Mistress Voysin here? I trust she doesn't know the truth of the matter?'

Robert, his gaze distant, looked up from the fire. 'No, it

appears not. They arrived together. I gather her company was impossible to avoid.'

Cobb threw up his hands with a muttered oath. 'So you and Bella haven't had a chance to talk?'

'Not really, though in fact Bella was able to achieve far more than I would have believed possible without actually giving the game away. She has arranged for us to meet tomorrow, hopefully in privacy.' Robert smiled ruefully. 'She is an actress of some ability, I will grant you that. And it is an ill wind, as they say, Cobb. At least it afforded me the opportunity to practise my skills in duplicity!'

Cobb relaxed, grinned. 'Tawford said she'd do it well, My Lord.'

'What news, man? Did you see my stepmother?'

'No, My Lord, only her manservant, but I have her reply. She will see you at eleven o'clock and hopes you will take dinner with her.'

'Does she indeed. Very well, then that is what I will do. Thank you, Cobb. Leave me now. I bid you goodnight.'

'My Lord.' The gypsy bowed in acknowledgement and left, closing the door quietly behind him.

For a long time after he had gone, Robert remained where he was, staring into the flames.

17

Saturday 15th October, 1642

Robert woke the next morning to the sound of rain; he could hear it bouncing off the leads and spattering in the mud below. It reflected his mood. He was not looking forward to this day. The irony of the thought did not escape him; he could not recall a single day he had looked forward to in the five years since Ruth died. Forcing himself to leave the warmth of his bed he took extra care with his toilet, shivering as he found a cake of soap and sluiced his body from the bowl of clean water that someone – presumably Cobb – had thought to leave for him. He thought longingly of the comforts of home, wishing himself back in Devon. Alexander was right; he should look for less primitive accommodation for the times he spent of necessity in London. He selected his finest, lace-trimmed shirt, a matching collar, a pair of long, pale fawn breeches and his new doublet of blue velvet – it was in the latest cut, his tailor had assured him; shorter and more tightly fitted at the waist. He supposed he would soon get used to it and he had to concur, with the fashionably long breeches it accentuated his trim figure. Everything, apart from the doublet, smelled mouldy with damp as he pulled it from the press in a cloud of moths, but there was nothing he could do about that. There was a time when he'd taken a pride in his appearance, but since Ruth had gone it had not seemed to matter. Robert sighed; gave himself a mental shake. As Cobb had so candidly suggested – outspoken rogue – it was time he pulled himself together.

Fully clothed, Robert looked down at himself: trim maybe, but he knew he looked careworn and older than his years; not at all like a prospective bridegroom. But again as Cobb had said, there were far worse than he. Robert smiled at the thought, casting around for a pair of buckled shoes, changed his mind and pulled on his soft, wide-top leather boots. A plumed hat, kid gloves, an embroidered pocket and a long cloak completed his apparel. Since he was signed up as an officer in Parliament's army, it seemed hardly to matter if he looked overtly Royalist – which of course he was, at heart. Satisfied, he primed a pistol and stuck it into his breeches, changed his mind and leaving it on the table, tucked a dagger into his boot instead. Finally he searched for and found his cane: a pretty thing; Malacca and mounted in silver, the knob was of opaque amber. Ellen had given it to him three years ago – a gift for his fortieth birthday. He smiled. She never forgot.

Reaching the street, Robert glanced up at the sky and ducked as a stream of rainwater cascaded from above, quickly bedraggling the plumes on his hat. He took it off and shook it, as he did so looking around for a chair. Usually he preferred to walk, but it seemed foolish when he had taken such care with his appearance. Spotting a beggar boy sheltering on the opposite side of the street, he beckoned him over. Finding a shilling to be the smallest coin he had, Robert gave it with a shrug to the disbelieving boy, watching amused as the lad, skipping for joy, sped away to find him a chair, the coin clutched tightly in his grubby hand.

It arrived soon enough, the bearers squelching through the mud, their hard-bitten faces pinched with misery. Giving them directions, Robert climbed aboard bending to brush from the seat a scrap of torn paper that lay there creased and muddy. As he did so, his attention was caught by the words: *Open up your purse strings or else!* He picked it up and smoothed out the creases. It was from a pamphlet bearing yesterday's date.

His lips compressed as he read: *... and the House of Lords are to vote tomorrow on the dastardly bill that will authorise Parliament to imprison anyone refusing to give money to their cause. Gentlemen, be warned! If you support your King against these rebellious peers you will be forcibly stripped of title and property and your revenues used by Parliament to raise arms against His Majesty while you languish in chains...*

The remainder had been torn away. Screwing it into a ball, Robert flung it away. He had heard of this outrageous bill, though had not expected it to get by the Commons in quite this form. He did not doubt the Lords would give their assent; the way things were, they had little choice. Would Marley Court be safe? Would his enforced allegiance to Parliament make a difference? Somehow he doubted it. They would all be beggared by this accursed war. Where would it end? The whole order of things was being turned on its head and it frightened him.

The rain had stopped by the time Robert arrived at the top of Arundel Street. He halted the chairmen, gave them a generous tip and waving aside their obsequious gratitude went the rest of the way on foot, sidestepping the puddles and attempting to avoid the worst of the filth. It had been a while since he had been here. The house looked in need of some attention. The creeper his father had planted completely covered the end wall now, its tentacles wrapping around the guttering and disappearing under the eaves. The wind and rain had knocked most of the leaves to the ground; they lay like a pool of blood across the carriageway. Momentarily he wished he had kept the house for himself and not so weakly given way to the demands of his father's widow. He shuddered. The woman sickened him. He would decline her invitation to dinner. He simply could not face it. At precisely eleven o'clock he presented himself at the door and rapped it with his cane. He was kept waiting for only a moment. The sour-faced manservant bowed, mumbled 'My Lord,' relieved him of his cane, hat, cloak and gloves and ushered him in to the parlour.

Anne Dynam was standing by the window. His breath caught at the sight of her, she seemed hardly to have changed, as beautiful as he remembered her, like some poisonous, exotic plant whose scent cannot be resisted and whose oil is lethal to the touch. She regarded him imperiously with her impossibly blue eyes, her face wreathed in a smile that went only as far as her lovely mouth. The gorge rose in Robert's throat. He had forgotten just how much he loathed her. To cover his confusion he bowed low over her hand. 'Madam, I trust I find you in good health?'

'Stepson! What a joy it is to see you,' she responded. 'But such a naughty boy to have neglected me so sorely – what would your dear father have said?' She smiled in amusement at his obvious discomfiture. 'But my dear, how weary you look; come, sit down do.' She indicated a settle cushioned in plush red velvet. Uncomfortably aware that even now she had the power to reduce him to a tongue-tied youth, Robert did as he was told.

She assumed an expression of curious amusement. 'To what do I owe this unexpected pleasure? It's been such a long time and we have so much to catch up on. I am afraid George is still up at Cambridge – how sorry he will be to have missed you. I have been on tenterhooks since receiving your message. Come, tell me your news, I can wait not a moment longer, and then you shall dine with me.'

Unable to meet her eyes Robert fixed his gaze at a point just above her head and cleared his throat. 'I thank you, but I regret that a pressing prior engagement forces me to decline your kind invitation.'

She gave a delighted laugh. 'Oh Robert, my dear, so formal – and you were ever a poor liar. What nonsense is this? Of course you will stay.' She picked up a small bell from a side table. Her manservant summoned by its tinkling chimes came quickly to the door. 'Tell the cook that Lord Westley and I will take dinner in fifteen minutes.' She waved her hand in dismissal and turned back to Robert, moving to seat herself gracefully on a stool opposite him, the folds of her blue silk gown riffling about her like water. 'May I offer you a glass of wine?'

It was useless to argue. Robert resigned himself; everything depended on his keeping calm and delivering the lie in as convincing a manner as he could. He sat back, forced a smile, shaking his head. 'No thank you, My Lady.' The title stuck in his craw like a thorn. Again he cleared his throat. 'I wanted you to hear this from my own lips, for I know it may come as a surprise to you, though indeed you could be no more surprised than I am myself.' He paused, studied her face hoping she might give herself away, for of course she already knew from Alexander what he was about to say.

She waited on his words, the smile hovering on her lips, her brows arched quizzically. 'I am all agog, Robert. Such mystery. Whatever can it be?'

He could detect not a shred of anxiety in her, knew she was toying with him – or was it that she could not bring herself to believe it and was even yet hoping Alexander had lied? He pursed his lips. 'I had not intended it to be a mystery. This is the first opportunity I have had to speak with you. I am to be married,' he finished abruptly.

The smile remained frozen on her lips. She reached for a fan from the side table, her gaze never leaving his face. He shifted uncomfortably on the cushion, his hands flat beneath his thighs, the rich velvet clinging to the sweat on his fingers. 'I had hoped you would be pleased for me,' he ventured softly.

She snorted in derision and snapped open the fan. 'Come now Robert, you know better than that. Surprised you say? Shocked more likely. Even you, it seems, cannot keep your prick in your breeches – but then,' she shot him a mocking smile, 'You never could, could you?' She paused. 'Ah, my poor Robert – you were such a handsome boy, but oh, so inadequate, why should I imagine anything has changed? But marriage? What manner of a woman can it be who has inveigled you into so rash a promise? Surely you need not go to such lengths? Or is it that she will not let you into her bed without it?' She arched her brows. 'And there was I thinking you, of all people, would remain faithful to the memory of your dear, sweet, useless little wife.' The words dripped like venom from her tongue. 'Obviously you have found another such? So, who is she?'

This was the woman he recognised; her vileness disgusted him. In that instant Robert could easily have put his fingers around her milky throat and squeezed. He clenched his fists, gritted his teeth, struggling to maintain control. 'As I recall,' he said icily, 'You did everything in your power to belittle my wife when she was alive. I will not have her undoubted sweetness sullied by your vulgarity now that she has gone. How dare you, Madam!'

Anne Dynam's face crumpled. She dropped her fan, put out a hand to him, the other she held to her throat. 'Oh Robert.' She gasped, her eyes bright with unshed tears. 'Please forgive a feeble, jealous woman. I do not know what I am saying. It is the shock. You are to be married? I cannot bear it. You must surely know I have always harboured feelings for you. I had once hoped you might have returned them; indeed, for a time it seemed you did...' She faltered, allowed the tears to fall. 'But no, you are right. It was sinful and unnatural. I am so sorry.' Her face was a picture of supplication and distress. 'Naturally I am happy for you.' Her bosom heaving, Anne Dynam drew a handkerchief from the folds of her gown and weeping, dabbed at her cheeks.

To think this consummate display would at one time have fooled him! But he was older and wiser now. He knew this creature only too well: this creature who had seduced her husband's son and killed a small boy – his own son – to get what she wanted. Robert swallowed, his need to accuse her raw in his throat. But if he did, all this would be for nothing. He had to bring it to an end, and quickly, or he would throw caution to the winds and cry out what he knew, no matter what. He regarded her tears with contempt. 'Desist woman!

You no longer have the power to control me with your beauty nor deceive me with your lies.' Suddenly, Robert was aware it was true. A surge of relief flooded through him. Springing up from the settle he raised a hand as if to strike her, gratified to see her flinch away from him. 'I am no longer a callow youth panting for a sight of your cunny. Your behaviour then was unspeakable and I pray God may forgive you, for I never shall, nor do I forgive myself, but if you think to disturb me with your wiles now, you are sadly mistaken.'

Spinning on his heel, Robert turned his back on her and strode to the window, looked out at the garden and the river beyond while he got himself under control. The skies had opened again, the driving rain hiding the traffic on the river. It was miserable weather; he hated this time of year. Summoning his reserves, Robert swung round to face his stepmother, his features set in a grimace of distaste. 'I came here today in good faith, Madam. I did not expect you to receive my news gladly, but nor did I expect to be treated to your foul mockery. You will kindly conduct yourself in a seemly manner or I shall be forced to leave.'

For a moment Anne Dynam regarded him coolly, no vestiges of distress remained on her face. Acknowledging defeat, she bowed her head. 'Very well; so do tell me, who is the fortunate creature?'

'It is I who am fortunate, Madam. Her name is Arabella Béjart.'

Anne Dynam lifted her head in surprise. 'The Frenchwoman? But she is so…' Seeing the warning in his eyes, she coughed. 'That is to say, as I understand it she has been in England but five minutes. How do you possibly come to know her?'

'As to that, Madam, how and where we met is not your concern, though I do not doubt your gossips will bring you the tale soon enough. It is of no moment and I will thank you to keep your nose out of my business,' Robert said coldly. 'It is enough to know Arabella Béjart has gladly accepted my offer of marriage. We are to be wed in December.'

'December?' She echoed in disbelief. 'Not *this* December?'

Nonchalantly flicking an imaginary speck from his doublet, Robert nodded. 'Indeed.'

'So soon! But why such unseemly haste? It is not like you at all, Robert. You must know what people will say. Are you so besotted you are careless of her reputation? Surely not, but if not that, then why?' Her eyes narrowed. 'Unless—' She took a sharp intake of breath, for the first time her composure slipped. Biting her lip, she raised a hand to her breast, a flush suffusing her throat. 'Can it be that she is breeding? You have bedded the slut already? That is it, isn't it?'

Thinking on his feet, Robert stared at her in silence, ignored her vulgar jibe and masked his disgust with a smile – a slow, pride-filled smile – reflecting as he did so that Bella was right and he should have chosen a career on the stage. The thought broadened his smile. If his stepmother thought he had already fathered a child, so much the better. 'Think what you will, Madam. Mistress Béjart's reputation is not, nor will ever be, in question. If we are blessed with a child he will be legitimate, of that I can assure you.' Robert paused to let the point sink in, changed his tone. 'I have said what I came here to say. I can think of nothing more we have to discuss. For form's sake you will naturally receive an invitation to the wedding. I urge you to be otherwise engaged.'

She curled her lip. 'And if I am not?'

'You will find the lease on this house will not be renewed,' Robert said succinctly, 'and your allowance from my father's estate will be drastically reduced. Indeed, you cannot expect to continue to enjoy indefinitely the privileges you have hitherto enjoyed. The circumstances have changed. The new Lady Westley may be disinclined to be so generous as was my first wife. If Arabella chooses to live here, I will naturally grant her wish. Indeed, how could I do otherwise?'

Anne Dynam's face paled. 'You do not have the power,' she snapped furiously.

'You think not? I would not be so sure, Madam.' Robert eyed her disdainfully. 'Naturally, you must not expect your son to remain as my heir. Arabella is more than capable of providing me with sons of my own.' Quirking an eyebrow, he looked down at her with a mocking smile. 'A whole nursery full of them – I fear George will go to the bottom of a long line.' He moved towards the side table, grasped the bell.

Anne Dynam flinched as though he had struck her. 'The graveyard is full of sons, Robert, one of them your very own,' she hissed. 'I think you would be wise not to count your chickens.'

He stopped in his tracks. 'Are you threatening me, Madam?'

Recovering, she laughed at him. 'You deceive yourself, sirrah. How could I, a mere woman, possibly threaten *you*?'

Robert did not trust himself to reply. Even though he had tried to push the woman to the edge, that he had almost succeeded sickened him. He rang the bell sharply, looking up in some surprise as the manservant immediately opened the door. Frowning, Robert addressed him curtly. 'Fetch me my things if you please, and inform Her Ladyship's cook that I will not after all be dining.' He waited while the servant went to do as he was bid. 'I find your manservant's manners wanting, Madam. I do believe the man has been eavesdropping.' Robert regarded his stepmother coolly for a moment, but it seemed for once he had silenced her. The man returned quickly with cloak, hat, gloves and cane. Robert took them. 'Thank you – you may go. I will see myself out.' With a curious glance over Robert's shoulder at his mistress, the manservant bowed and backed away.

Stretching out his fingers Robert pulled on his gloves. 'I see no reason for us to meet again. My lawyers will act on my behalf should there be a need.'

'You overreach yourself, Sir,' she snapped. 'You are a Royalist, are you not? I will have you arrested as an enemy of Parliament. Then we shall see who has the power! Your revenues and title will come to me.' She smiled triumphantly. 'And whatever sons you may get on this French slut will have naught to call their own.'

Robert regarded her coldly, gave a slow mocking smile, watched her triumph turn to uncertainty before he spoke. 'I think in the present climate that is unlikely, Madam, but in any event, had you not heard? I am commissioned by the Earl of Pembroke; I go to fight for Parliament.'

She gasped. 'Then you are a traitor, Sir, and guilty of treason against His Majesty.'

For the first time, Robert was surprised into laughter. 'Come now, you cannot have it both ways. Can it be you are a little confused, Madam? Treason it may be, but I rather fear there is nothing you can do about that.' His stepmother was speechless, her face twisted in spasm, her eyes filled with murderous rage. He wondered how he could ever have thought her beautiful.

'How like your bastard whelp you are – could anyone have doubted it? He is cast in the same mould.' Anne Dynam's voice grated in frustration. ''Tis no wonder he is fit only for the hangman's noose.'

'You refer to Alexander?' Robert raised an eyebrow. 'It seems for once we are in agreement, Madam. The boy was a chance begetting I infinitely regret and could I deny him, I most certainly would. Should he chance to end up on the scaffold it would be nothing but a relief to me. So there too, I fear your jibes are meaningless. I bid you good day.'

With a mocking bow, Robert placed his hat firmly on his head and without another word swept from the room, leaving Anne Dynam staring after him, fists clenched, angry tears flooding her face.

Once out of sight of the house, Robert, sickened, leaned on his cane, bent towards the gutter and retched. Wiping his mouth on a fold of his cloak, he bent his head against the driving rain and forced his leaden legs to move forward. Gradually the reaction lessened. He quickened his pace, failed to notice Cobb, and two men whom he would not have recognised, watching from some yards away. He was unaware they followed him as he reached the end of the street and turned towards Lincoln's Inn Fields.

The business was accomplished; the trap set. The loathsome woman was convinced, of that Robert had no doubt. Sickening as it was, the meeting had gone better than he might have hoped. How far would his stepmother be prepared to go to prevent this marriage? He was acutely aware that by insinuating his betrothed was already breeding, he had endangered not only Bella's reputation, but also quite possibly her life. About his own safety he was less concerned. He would doubtless stop a musket ball before he was much older. From whence it came seemed unimportant, the result would be the same – and then it would all be down to Alexander. Robert shrugged; he had done all he could and now he needed to get his affairs in order. He had two days – he knew Pembroke's spies were watching him – two days before he must leave to seek out Lord Essex's army and take up his commission. Again he quickened his pace, careless now of the wet seeping through his clothes, the mud splashing up his breeches. 'Dear God, Alexander,' he whispered beneath his breath. 'What is it you have made me do and where in God's name will it end?'

In the ten days since Alexander and Biscuit had arrived in Bodmin after an unpleasantly wet but uneventful journey, he had scarcely had a minute to himself. The St Michael's men with their customary ribaldry had masked their delight at seeing him again and quickly brought him up to date with the state of play in Cornwall. Sir Ralph Hopton had long since dispersed the Cornish trained bands, but now had approaching two thousand men: volunteers lured by the promise of regular work, food and pay, or tenants pressed into reluctant service by the landed gentry who controlled their lives. It was an army of ploughmen, shepherds, fishermen and miners, a rank and file that could just about tell its left foot from its right, but few could load and fire a musket or shoulder a pike without wounding their neighbour. Nonetheless they were equipped from arms fetched by the wagonload from all over Cornwall, allocated to regiments and drilled each morning on Bodmin Moor.

It was proving an uphill struggle to turn them from a brave and enthusiastic rabble into a disciplined and efficient fighting force. The pikemen and musketeers continually vied for supremacy and squabbled constantly with inevitable results. The only way to keep them from killing each other was to tire them out, so the training had been stepped up to a punishing schedule, which kept the St Michael's men busy from dawn to dusk overseeing mock battles, strenuous games of kickball and long chases of 'hare and hounds' over Bodmin moor. If nothing else, these activities instilled a sense of camaraderie among the new recruits, as well as presenting Alexander with an opportunity to familiarise Biscuit with the sights and sounds of exuberant men and exploding gunpowder. He had grown fond of his new horse, so much so he would allow none other to ride it. The mare was responding well – he only wished he could say the same about Dickon.

Recalling how it felt to be treated like a child when one considered oneself a man grown, Alexander was uncomfortably aware he had been unusually thoughtless with the boy and was not unduly surprised to find Dickon sulkily avoiding him. He had attempted to make amends and chivvy him out of it a time or two, but was too busy to pay him much attention and having received favourable reports on his progress decided to let time heal.

The problem of Dickon had slipped from his mind when, two days ago, a scout had run breathlessly into Hopton's billet with news that thirty-six boatloads of rebel soldiers out of Plymouth had crossed the Tamar. They were occupying land on the Rame Peninsular around Mount Edgecumbe, but though on the Cornish side of the river, by dint of a bulge in the border it was on Devon soil and the Cornish posse would do nothing to hinder them. Sitting as it did on Plymouth's doorstep, the Mount was of strategic importance to Sir Ralph Hopton's campaign. Having already ascertained that its owner, Piers Edgecumbe, was well affected to the King he had put a garrison in place at nearby Millbrook. He now sent immediate orders to its commander, Colonel Walter Slyngesby: 'Go to Edgecumbe's aid, drive the rebels back to Plymouth and secure the west bank of the Tamar.'

Alexander, slightly bored with training raw recruits, had seized the opportunity to give some of them a taste of real action. He picked out thirty musketeers, took a few veterans along to keep them steady, and force-marched them to join Slyngesby, relieved to find the Colonel had not yet mounted an attack. He was waiting for daybreak, drawn up on the hill above Maker Church out of sight of the enemy, with a troop of cavalry and fifty dragoons. Volunteering his company as a forlorn hope, Alexander left Biscuit with a dragoon's horse-holder well behind Slyngesby's lines and led his men stealthily down through the woods below the church. His plan was to get as near to the Roundheads' position as possible without being seen and at a given signal charge into the camp and distract them, allowing Slyngesby's cavalry to sweep down and take them by surprise. The dragoons – who generally dismounted and fought on foot – would bring up the rear.

Shivering with suppressed excitement, which he tried to conceal lest it be taken for fear, Alexander brought his musketeers to a halt at the edge of the trees. The grey light of dawn was beginning to steal through the bare, mist-hung branches that dripped onto their heads. Had he come far enough? Too far away and they would be shot to pieces before they could reach the rebels' camp and Slyngesby's charge would lose its impact. He untangled the odours hanging on the still morning air: the salt tang of the sea, the stink of the unwashed men at his back, the scent of rotting leaves and mildew and the acrid stench of smouldering slow match. Was he imagining a faint drift of wood smoke and the unappetising smell of burning fat from below the woods? Straining to see, he peered through the trees.

Aware of a sudden stir at his back, he turned sharply, shook his head and frowned at the men jostling nervously behind him. God, they were a rough lot, despite his having greased several palms to see they were issued with army clothes, still in short supply and keeping tailors and seamstresses busy all over Cornwall. They wore blue coats, brown kersey knee britches, canvas doublets, white calico shirts, woollen stockings, canvas leggings, brown leather shoes, and black, wide-brimmed hats with blue hatbands – blue being Hopton's regimental colour. Despite this resplendent uniformity, most of the men looked as though they had been pulled through a hedge backwards. Hardly surprising, Alexander thought with a sudden grin; he had marched the poor sods twenty-five miles over rough, hilly country in under two days. He cast his gaze critically over their weapons. Each man carried a sheathed sword from a belt at his waist, in one hand he clutched his musket rest and in the other a matchlock musket, the stick for ramming and scouring clipped under the barrel. Matchlocks were not much use for this kind of work when so much depended on speed; almost five feet long and heavy, they were desperately unwieldy and fiddly to load. Flintlocks would have been better, but being easier to manage on horseback they were reserved for the dragoons and as yet there were simply not enough to go round. Ah well, matchlocks made useful clubs and with surprise on their side his men would confuse the enemy just the same, which was all that was required of them this morning.

He put his fingers to his lips, pointed out of the trees and drew the edge of his hand across his throat, waiting until the men fell silent – or as silent as a company of musketeers could ever be with the discordant rustle and clunk of the powder cartridges dangling from their bandoliers, the chinking flasks of priming powder and pouches of shot that hung from each man's belt and the rattling canvas snapsacks slung across their backs, ostensibly to carry their food, horn cup, spare shirt and stockings, bullet mould, firing pan, pincers, flint and striking iron, along with whatever they had managed to plunder as they marched. Not that these men had yet had the opportunity for looting – nor would they if Alexander had his way, though he could hardly blame them for trying when they had yet to see a penny piece in wages. But Hopton was adamant; all provisions must be paid for and looters would be severely punished. It was a question of discipline.

Suddenly, from beyond the woods came a crackle of musket fire. Signalling the men to wait, Alexander dropped to his belly and squirmed out of the trees into the long grass of the deer park, sliding down the hill until he had a clear view of Mount Edgecumbe, the magnificent, turreted manor house some four hundred feet below him. A century ago, Piers Edgecumbe's illustrious ancestor had made a judicious marriage to acquire this land. He had certainly picked a very fine spot to build, adjacent to the Tamar with far-reaching views of Plymouth and the Sound, though this morning they were hidden by a thick sea mist.

It was not the house that claimed Alexander's attention, but the ground before it, where three hundred enemy soldiers were breaking their fast behind scantily erected barricades of freshly cut timber. There was not a breath of wind; in ghostly columns the smoke from their cooking fires rose and hung. Alexander could see no picquets; the rebels seemed unaware of Slyngesby's presence to their rear. He snorted with contempt – the greenhorns! They were from Plymouth's Trained Band and should know better. Most were armed much like his own men with ancient swords and matchlocks, though he could see some pikemen among them. The musket fire was coming from the house. Now that it was light enough to see, Piers Edgecumbe's guards were loosing off shots from the top floor windows. It was a gesture of defiance for they were too few to do much damage and were barely in range.

As Alexander watched, clear across the deer park came the sound he had been waiting for; the rat-tat-tat of Slyngesby's drummers. The enemy heard it too. Suddenly the camp came alive; men scurrying about like headless chickens forming into files of eight as if it were a drill practice – pike-men in the centre flanked by musketeers – their attention focused towards Maker Church, way above the heads of Alexander and his men. It was what he had bargained on. Backing away, he got to his feet, signalled to his men, drew his sword, yelled at the top of his lungs, 'Now! To me...', and set off down the slope at a loping run.

His musketeers burst from the trees and came roaring in his wake, close on his heels as he jumped the nearest barricade, his blade catching the light as he set about him like a whirling dervish, oblivious to all but the dangerously intoxicating thrill of dicing with death. Inspired by his example, they followed, slipping and sliding, thrusting and clubbing, they split the rebels' formation into a surging mass of hand-to-hand confusion. Taken completely by surprise, the Plymouth men were barely aware of how small was the attacking force and for a brief time the forlorn hope held their own, but by sheer weight of numbers they started to go down.

Had Slyngesby's cavalry not then appeared, hooves drumming across the deer park, riders screaming invective and brandishing their swords, Alexander and his men would have been lost in that maelstrom of spilt blood and guts. As it was, the terrified rebels dropped their weapons and fled, streaming past the house towards the boats they had left at Cremyll harbour, pursued by jubilant Royalists cheered on by Piers Edgecumbe's relieved guards.

By the time the dragoons arrived, there was nothing left for them to do beyond tend the wounded and bury the dead. Alexander, miraculously unscathed, had lost five men killed and eight wounded. For the time being the west bank of the Tamar was secured, as indeed was Alexander's reputation: his

Cornish recruits thought him a charmed maniac. Leaving them with Slyngesby's men to help strengthen Mount Edgecumbe's defences, he returned to Bodmin with dispatches for Sir Ralph Hopton, unaware that as soon as his back was turned some of the men, flushed and cocky with the success of their first action, had slipped away to go plundering. Worse, they were using Hopton's name as their authority to demand money and plate from local inhabitants. When news of this came to Bodmin, Sir Ralph was infuriated – not least by the slur on his reputation – and ordered the miscreants rounded up and flogged, which they were, within an inch of their lives, but the damage had been done. The incident was held up by Parliamentarians as an example of Royalist perfidy and several hundred local people – mostly fisherfolk – retaliated, armed themselves with clubs and stones and went on the rampage, skirmishing with any group of Royalist soldiers they happened to meet. Beacons were lit on the hills and people sent fleeing from their homes in terror. Alexander, on his way to Saltash with messages for Lord Mohun, was caught up in bringing the ensuing riots under control.

He was still in Saltash when news came that a company of enemy soldiers had landed on the beach, their ship forced in by heavy seas. Expecting it to be an easy night's work, Alexander rode with a troop of raw dragoons sent to apprehend them. As it turned out, the enemy were experienced mercenaries out of Ireland, hired by King Louis and on their way to France under the command of Colonel William Ruthin, a seasoned Scottish Covenanter, so it was far from being an easy night's work. Refusing to be intimidated, Ruthin lined up his seasick soldiers on the sand and challenged the dragoons to best them. The stiff and bloody skirmish that followed was Biscuit's first experience of hand-to-hand fighting, as it was for many of the dragoons, but to Alexander's relief the mare responded to his slightest touch, not baulking as he drove her forward and laid about him with his sword. The dragoons performed equally well; Ruthin and his Scots were beaten back and sent with bloodcurdling jeers and profane insults running for

Plymouth.

Next day, Alexander and Biscuit – weary but unscathed – returned to Bodmin.

On All Saints' Day came the joyous news of a great victory for the King at Edgehill, but a lengthy and sorrowful letter received a few days later from Adam Hartley soon dampened the celebrations.

> *'Contrary to what both sides are claiming, neither has won a victory and nothing is resolved. It was an ill-considered confrontation lacking order and discipline and with great and tragic loss of life on both sides. I fear eight of our men were killed, including Sidney Hawley who was discovered bringing intelligence to Prince Rupert's scouts and shot for a spy. I will endeavour to retrieve his body and ensure he is buried with full honours. Southcott has taken a nasty wound to his sword arm. He should recover, but will not be able to fight again, at least not for some time – though I am to tell you he can still write! The rest of our men are unhurt beyond minor cuts and bruises, but I have no recent news of Fane. I assume he is still with Bedford's army, which our intelligence tells us is marching to Plymouth.'*

Adam's letter went on to give a grim account of the battle. Reading the names of the dead Alexander was sickened. So many brave men lost, including Sir Edmund Verney, the King's standard bearer, of whom Hartley had written:

> *'... they found his severed hand the following day, rimed with frost and still clutching the staff. Both sides are shocked and saddened by their losses – the brutal reality of civil war is far removed from the threats and posturing of the last few weeks. Essex has withdrawn to Warwick leaving the*

road clear to London, but despite Prince Rupert's urgings to press on, His Majesty is too stricken to act and has fallen back on Banbury thus losing any advantage he might have had. Now there is talk of negotiating a peace, which I pray fervently will go forward that this desperate sacrifice might not have been in vain – but I do not see how their differences may now be settled until one side or the other has won a decisive victory. I fear this is not the end, but only the beginning.'

It was devastating news and not surprising that Hartley was so despondent. He had included a postscript, which Alexander read with startled dismay.

'You will be pleased to know your guardian has taken but small hurt, though you may be surprised to learn he has sided with Parliament and is serving as a Captain in General Sir William Waller's regiment. I have not been able to find out any more, I am kept entirely occupied with the wounded, but will send to you when I do. God keep you. AH.'

There was a further postscript on another sheet that looked as though it had been added on the move: *'Prince Rupert has won his way and we are to ride for London.'* Alexander had almost missed it, so stunned had he been by Hartley's news. His mouth twisted in angry contempt at Westley's disloyalty. Why in God's name had the man sided with Parliament? Perfidious bastard! It explained his visit to the Earl of Pembroke at least. Alexander wondered briefly what had happened about Anne Dynam, but no message had come from Cobb and he was forced to assume Westley had refused to co-operate. So be it. His plans for that wretched woman would have to wait. Swept up in events he had little time to dwell further on Adam's perturbing news.

18

Jennet had been out on the moor since dawn looking for late blackberries. Most of the fruit had gone over now or failed to ripen at all. It had taken her until mid-morning, braving the fat bellied spiders that clung to the web-strewn brambles, and still the bottom of her basket was barely covered. Scampering home to the farm, she heard the raised voices as she came through the front door: her father's angry shouts, her mother's cries. With a sob she crept past the bottom of the stairs, ran into the kitchen, dropped her basket and crawled into a corner pulling her shawl over her head, but she could not block out the sounds. She heard a bumping dragging noise on the floor above, heard her mother scream, her father cry out; a strangled agonised cry that chilled her to the marrow. There was a dull thud, then silence. Dreading to see fresh bruises on her mother's face and pretend as usual that nothing was wrong, the anguished girl left her corner and tiptoed out of the kitchen, intent on fleeing back to the moor. At the bottom of the stairs she held her breath, paused to listen, wished she hadn't. Her mother cried out. 'Jennet, are you there? Help me please.' Her voice sounded strange; high pitched and filled with fear. Jennet looked longingly towards the front door, but the habit of obedience was too strong. Her stomach knotted, she climbed the stairs to her parents' chamber.

Time froze, the sight that met her eyes printing indelibly on her brain: her mother bending over her father, a bloodied knife clutched in her clawed hand. Her father lying twisted at her feet, blood welling between his fingers. Blood soaking through his shirt, blood smeared on her mother's gown, blood pooling on the floor. Rooted to the spot, her face stark with horror, Jennet cried out. 'No! No! No!'

Her mother saw her standing there, saw the pinched, tear-streaked face, a child's face stained about the mouth with blackberry juice, saw the chilling accusation in her eyes – an adult's eyes. Bethan dropped the knife with a clatter to the floor, grasped her husband's shoulders. 'Help me, please,' she gasped. 'Jennet, please, now. I beg you.' Bethan screamed helplessly at her daughter. 'Take his legs.'

The urgency in her mother's voice got through to her. Jennet moved quickly into the room, caught hold of her father's wasted legs. Half dragging, half lifting, they got him onto the bed and rolled him on his back. He groaned, his fingers plucking at the wound in his chest. Bending over him, Bethan pressed her hands to it. 'Fetch me some cloths, the jar of red plaster, some oil of rosemary, lichen and lint, hurry, child.'

As Jennet sprang to the door her father drew a shuddering breath, cried 'Jennet, no!' Uncertain she stopped, turned back, saw his gaze slide to her mother, heard his whisper. 'For the love of God, no, not this time. I beg you, as you love me, not this time.' The anguished pleading in his eyes rendered the words redundant. Bethan's face crumpled. She released the pressure on the wound and with a gesture of helplessness moved backwards, her bloodied hands held out to him, her bruised face gaunt with pain. 'I'm sorry, I'm so very sorry.'

Jennet turned on her, her body rigid, eyes dark with shock. Scarcely aware of what she was doing she seized her mother's arm and shook her. 'Don't let him die; he is dying; please don't let him die.' Bethan shook her head, made no move to stop her. In a paroxysm of weeping, Jennet tugged at her mother's arm, cried out, 'Mother, please!'

'Pixy!' her father's cry brought Jennet to her senses. He struggled to speak; raised his hand, beckoned weakly. Letting go of her mother's arm she moved to the bed, caught hold of his fluttering fingers and bent towards his lips, straining to hear his hoarse whisper.

'Forgive me, Pixy, I would have spared thee this.' The breath rasped in his throat. She bent closer. 'Do not blame your mother.' His eyes looked into hers, pleading. 'Find forgiveness in your heart, *cariad*,' he gasped as a trickle of blood escaped from his lips, 'and know I have always loved thee, now go, sweetheart, leave us.'

Shaking her head in an agony of disbelief, Jennet released her father's fingers and backed slowly away from the bed. Rounding on her mother, she looked at her as at a stranger, her stricken face a white mask of horror. A shrill cry tore from her throat. 'Murderer!' Spinning on her heel, she jammed her fist into her mouth and fled.

With the image of her father stark behind her eyes Jennet did not know how far or for how long she ran, was unaware of brambles tearing at her legs, branches catching in her hair, the painful sobbing in her chest. When a pair of strong arms grabbed her she struggled against them, but they merely tightened about her. 'Let me go, let me go.' She screamed, unseeing, kicking and biting, straining to be free.

'Hush, child, what be wrong? Hush now, be still, stop your blethering, I 'int going to hurt you.' The man transferred his grip to her wrists and held her away from him looking at her kindly. 'It's the Morgans' maid, b'aint it? What be wrong with you, girl?'

The calm voice soothed her, she saw the fowling piece strapped to his shoulder, the leather jerkin and badge of office, the bundle of rabbit pelts strung from his belt, recognised the verderer and sank against him. In racking sobs she told him, then fainted dead away.

Jeptha Lythal was a kindly man. He knew what they said about the Morgan woman and her husband and felt not a little afraid, but this was naught but a chit of a girl. He had seen her on the moor a time or two, poor mite to be caught up in this evil doing. He picked her up and carried her to his house, cradled in his arms he took her upstairs and placed her unresisting on his late wife's bed. The child was conscious but said nothing more. He covered her with a blanket, fetched a cup of water, but could not rouse her to drink. She lay motionless, the pupils of her eyes shrunk to pinheads, a far-away unseeing look in them that frightened him. He put the cup on the floor where she could reach it. 'You stay there, maid, I'll be back soon.' Shaking his head in pity, he turned away, hesitated, took one more look at her white little face then left her, closing and locking the door behind him and pocketing the key. With a heavy heart he fetched his horse from its shed, saddled up and rode for the village to fetch the constable.

It was mid-afternoon when Zach rode into the Morgans' farm. He had taken to calling every so often with whatever could be spared from the Warren – today it was a sack of flour. His initial fear of Bethan Morgan had turned to liking over the past weeks, just as Tawford had said it would. He smiled to see the tumble of pups playing in the yard, their watchful dam thumping her tail as he spoke to her. He glanced up at the new barn with satisfaction. They had done most of the work that needed doing, though there was still a bit of thatching to finish on the house. Zach looked up at the sky; he would deal with that today if the light held. Dismounting, he hitched his horse by the water butt, loosened the leathers and carried the sack of flour to the house to let Bethan know he was about. The front door stood ajar. Jennet must be out on the moor or she would have come running to greet him by now – like as not with the deer as usual. He smiled; she was fey that one, but endearing nonetheless. He stuck his head round the door and called, was met with silence. He cocked his head to listen.

Ducking under the lintel Zach walked inside. The house had an empty feel, even the cat was not in its usual place and the fire had gone out. He went through to the back kitchen to leave the flour, saw the basket on its side, blackberries strewn across the floor. Feeling a tingle of apprehension between his shoulder blades Zach came back to the stairs. 'Hello?' He called again, listened. Putting his hand on the newel post he noticed a smear of blood on the banister. There was another on the stairs. Drawing his knife he climbed slowly to the top; saw into the bedchamber, the mess of bloody footprints on the floorboards. What had gone on here? Cautiously he entered the room, gasped at the sight of the blood-stained sheet on the bed, beneath it the shape of a body.

Someone had put pebbles on Morgan's eyes and folded his hands across the ugly wound congealed in his chest; a prayer book was clutched in his stiffened fingers. Replacing the sheet, Zach ran back down to the yard and went into each of the buildings in turn, but the farm was deserted. The cart was still in the shed and he could see the horse he had loaned to Bethan grazing in the meadow beyond. Wherever Jennet and her mother had gone, they had either walked or been taken there. His eyes creased in anxiety, Zach sheathed his knife, returned to his horse tightened the leathers mounted up and rode out of the yard examining the ground around the gateway. There were several fresh prints but not those of a child. Knowing where Jennet habitually walked on the moor, he quartered the ground, saw a scrap of red cloth where her shawl had caught on a bramble, found her tracks, knew she was alone and that she had been fleeing.

Used to tracking deer, Zach was a practised hunter and Jennet's trail led him at length to the verderer's house on Shoulsbarrow Common. It was a substantial house of stone and slate with a lookout turret built into the roof. There were a few outbuildings and a neat garden surrounded by a low wall. A wisp of smoke curled from the chimney; beside the door was a stack of freshly cut logs. Zach pieced together what had happened. Thieves had chanced upon the Morgans' farm. Not locals – they were too afraid of the witch to go near; strangers then. Soldiers maybe – there had been a few stories recently of deserters pillaging in the area. Yes, that was more likely. And finding nothing worth the stealing, they had killed Morgan and taken Bethan away for their evil sport – God in heaven. But why had they not taken the horse? And who had closed the dead man's eyes and left the prayer book – had Jennet hidden and seen it all, tended her father after they had gone? The thought sickened him. No wonder she had fled. She must have come here for help. Was she still here? He hesitated; did not want to draw attention to himself unnecessarily – it was too close to home. Tethering his horse to a branch out of sight of the house, he moved uncertainly towards it. The light was beginning to fade, the air smelled sharp and earthy.

Zach was still thinking what to do when he heard horses approaching. Ducking behind the garden wall he heard the murmur of voices. Peering over he saw it was the verderer and with him was the Churchwarden. He watched them tether their mounts and disappear into the house. He crept closer. After a moment he saw lamplight glowing at the windows. He had to find out where Jennet was. Moving round to the side of the house he resigned himself to wait.

He waited for maybe half an hour before he heard the door opening. He strained to hear what they were saying. What he heard made his blood run cold. Chilled to the bone he forced himself to stay where he was while the Churchwarden took his leave; watched while the verderer attended to his mount. Not until he had gone back inside and closed the door did Zach run back to his horse.

It was full dark by the time his tired mount clattered into Tawford Barton. Ned, still working in the stables, heard him arrive and came out with a lantern. He nodded at Zach, looked curiously at the lathered horse, but merely grunted and held its nose while Zach, dismounting, asked breathlessly, 'Is Her Ladyship within?'

'Aye. Be she expecting you? Er didn't zay nuthin.'

'No, but I must speak with her.'

Ned handed Zach the lantern and took the horse. 'Ee'll be needin' rubbin' down looks like. Do ee want' un fed?'

'Please.' Zach was already on his way to the front gate. Wilmot opened the door to his urgent knocking, held up a lamp, cast a withering glance at his muddied boots and told him to go round the back. He was about to argue when Ellen herself came to see who it was. He smiled with relief. 'My Lady? May I speak with you?'

'Of course. It's all right, Wilmot.' Ellen drew him into the parlour where she had been going through the steward's accounts, her papers spread across a table. Candles burning in their sconces threw flickering shadows around the room; a coal fire glowed warmly in the grate. Wilmot, her lips thinning, relieved Zach of his hat and cloak and loitered by the door.

'Thank you Wilmot, that will be all.' Ellen waited while the cook, muttering, went back to the kitchen. When she had gone, Ellen closed the door and turned to Zach, her face tight with anxiety. 'What brings you here at this hour? Is it Alexander?' She searched his face, her hand clasped to her throat. 'What has happened?'

'No, My Lady.' Zach hastened to reassure her. 'He be safe so far as I know.'

'Then what?' The tense expression left her face. 'Is someone ill at the Warren?'

'No, My Lady – it's about the Morgans.'

'The Morgans?' Ellen's brow furrowed. 'Do I know them?'

'Possibly not, My Lady. They live on the moor not far from the Warren. Master Tawford may have spoken of them?'

She shook her head. 'I don't recall his having done so.' She indicated a joint stool by the fire, waited while he sat.

'Thank you, My Lady.'

She smiled gently. 'Zach, please call me Ellen. I shall not be in the least offended – quite the contrary. I infinitely preferred Master Simms!' Her face alight with curiosity, she perched herself on the settle where she could see his face. 'I can see you are agitated. What is it? Tell me.'

Zach inclined his head, cleared his throat and launched into the reason for his agitation. 'It's a dreadful pickle. The verderer is holding Jennet. She must be terrified and quite beside herself.' He leaned forward wringing his hands. 'I don't know what to do for the best. Master Tawford would want us to help her, he was well taken with the child, but I don't see how I can do anything short of taking her by force, but then I'd have the constable after me and it be too close to the Warren for comfort, and anyway if she be sick I'd not know what to do and then I thought of you and—'

Ellen held her hand up to stop him in mid-flow. 'Whoa, Zach, slow down. Who is Jennet if not a female donkey and what has she done that the verderer is holding her – has she been caught poaching? If so, I cannot think what you expect I can do.' Her brow furrowed with concern. This was not like Zach. She got up from the settle. 'But before you tell me, I will get us some spiced ale and then you can begin at the beginning, eh?' Ellen smiled encouragingly.

It had the desired effect. By the time she returned with two steaming mugs smelling pungently of cinnamon, Zach seemed calmer. She listened as he settled back and recounted what he knew of Bethan, her husband and Jennet, of the fire in the barn and its tragic consequences.

'The poor souls.' Ellen's face was stricken. 'How does Tawford come to know them?'

Zach told her about the king stag, about Tawford's brief meeting with Bethan and the work they had done for the Morgans at his behest. Then Zach told her of Bethan's deafness, her skill with potions, her reputation as a witch and of his growing liking and respect for her. 'She talks with her hands, though one of them be twisted – and she is skilled at healing;

has a way with wild things, takes in the wounded creatures that Jennet brings her off the moor and makes them right again – but she's no witch, Ellen – though there've been complaints against her and such tales as you wouldn't believe. There's many swear she's cast the evil eye on them and a plague on their cattle.' He hung his head. 'To my shame I were no better than they before I got to know her.'

Ellen nodded, warming her hands on her mug, sipped the sweet liquid thoughtfully. 'There's no shame to you Zach. We all entertain such fears, especially when someone is different from the rest of us – as is your Bethan from what you say. But tell me, why are they holding her daughter? What has she done, and what is her mother doing about it?'

'That's the dreadful thing. There's nothing she can do about it. She's locked up in chains. Constable Bowden had to go to Exeter today and he's taken Bethan with him.'

'What?' Ellen started forward. 'But why?'

Zach swallowed, the horror standing in his eyes as he described what he had found at the farm that afternoon, how he had followed Jennet's tracks to the verderer's house and overheard the two men talking. 'Bethan has killed her husband; stabbed him with a knife. Jennet saw it happen and told the verderer.'

Ellen caught her breath. 'Dear God in Heaven.'

Zach nodded. 'It don't bear thinking about. From what I could gather, Jeptha Lythall – he's the verderer – fetched the constable from the village and they went over to the Morgans' place, then when the constable had taken Bethan away, Mister Lythall must've gone to fetch the Churchwarden back to Jennet, but he couldn't get her to speak. I heard him say she'd been struck dumb and her mother had like as not laid a spell on her.'

Ellen's eyes widened in horror. 'That's nonsense; the poor child is in shock, it often happens that way. It will pass in time if she has proper care.'

'Aye, well that's as may be, but the Churchwarden told

Mister Lythall to keep her close and he'd have Morgan's body fetched back to the village tomorrow.' Frowning, Zach bent to put his mug on the floor. 'It'll likely be a pauper's grave for him.'

'I can certainly do something about that.' Ellen grimaced. 'I don't see what I can do for Jennet though, at least not until she has recovered and is able to go home, then of course I will do whatever I can. You don't think perhaps you are worrying unnecessarily? It sounds to me as though they are taking care of her.'

Zach shook his head. 'No, you don't understand. They don't mean to let her go. I heard the Churchwarden say that he don't want no trouble in the village and the verderer must keep her locked up till Constable Bowden gets back and that may not be for a week or more.'

'But why? What sort of trouble? Are you sure you didn't mishear, Zach? Unless... surely they don't think she had any part in her father's death?'

'Who knows what they numbskulls think?' Zach shrugged. 'I'm sure I heard aright, but I confess I don't understand it. I would never have thought Bethan capable of killing, there's not an ounce of spite in her.' He grimaced. 'Though Lord knows she's had cause enough, could you but see what she has suffered these many years. Morgan beat her cruelly – that's what took away her hearing according to Master Tawford – yet all I've ever seen is her gentle kindness towards him and it is clear there was deep affection between them once.' He sighed, picked up his mug and took a gulp of ale. Replacing it on the floor he looked up at Ellen. 'But much as I don't want to believe it, she's confessed to it. I heard the verderer say so.' He shook his head in despair. 'And they've accused her of witchcraft into the bargain, the daft buggers.' He gave Ellen a look of apology. 'They think Bethan used the evil arts to kill her man. They'll burn her, Ellen.'

Ellen gasped. 'God forbid! What will happen to Jennet?'

Zach's brow creased in a worried frown. 'I don't know.

To lose her father like that, and then her mother and in such a way, I fear the little maid will be driven to madness. I know Master Tawford would want us to look out for her. If only he were here – or Cobb, but he's still in London and I'm not sure what to do for the best.'

Ellen, her eyes dark with sympathy, tried to unravel everything Zach had told her. 'From what you say of Bethan I do not understand what can have happened. If she could no longer suffer her husband's cruelty why kill him? Why did she not just leave him? He could hardly have followed her.'

'She'd never have done that, not when he needed her care. He was mazed with pain much of the time, that's why he hit her, he didn't mean to hurt her or so she told me.' He shrugged. 'Besides, where would she have gone? She's all but deaf, has no money, no family hereabouts and who would take her in thinking she's a witch? And there is Jennet. She and her father were very close. Bethan would never have taken her from him, nor left her behind. Fact is, Ellen, she had little choice but to endure it.'

Ellen bit her lip. 'What a dreadful plight, the pity of it.' She gazed at Zach intently. 'But if she meant to kill him she could surely have used an easier way, you say she is skilled with potions.' She frowned, pursed her lips. 'And if she was driven by some dreadful impulse, for all he's a cripple he could surely have overpowered her, prevented her from striking a mortal blow?'

'That's what the Churchwarden said. That's why they think she used witchcraft to take away his wits and his strength.'

'Nonsense!' Ellen shrugged impatiently. 'Could it have been an accident?'

Zach shook his head. 'It was an unlikely wound for an accident, and anyway, like I said, she confessed to it. Why would she do that if she were innocent?'

At a loss, Ellen's hand strayed to her mouth. In her head she heard Alexander's voice. *Always put yourself in the other man's shoes, look at all the angles, think beyond the obvious.*

'Are you sure that Jennet actually saw it happen?'

'So the verderer did say.'

Ellen turned to the fire, stared at the glowing coals. She tried to imagine how it must have been for this poor woman, her struggle to survive in such pitiable circumstances, enduring her husband's cruelty for the sake of her daughter. Her thoughts turned to Morgan, the desperate bid to rescue his son from the fire that had rendered him a cripple; his humiliating helplessness and acute sense of loss, the constant pain and frustration that had driven him to hit out at the woman he loved. His guilt and self-contempt must have been unbearable. *Think beyond the obvious.* She looked up at Zach. 'Could he not have stabbed himself?'

Zach started forward. Frowned.

'Is that not possible? You say he was often melancholy and in much pain. Could he have taken his own life?'

'Yes, it's possible.' He thought for a moment. 'But Jennet would not have lied.'

'Maybe she was mistaken in what she thought she saw. Suppose Bethan had actually been trying to stop her husband from harming himself, was wresting the knife away from him when Jennet came upon them. The child must have been beside herself. Imagine her distress. Whatever she said to the verderer would not have made much sense.'

He shook his head. 'That can't be, or why would Bethan have confessed to it?'

'She must have been no less distraught than her daughter, Zach. She may not have known what she was saying.' Ellen's eyes filled with tears. 'Or maybe it was out of love for him.'

Zach stared at her. 'I don't see...,' he faltered as the implication struck him. If Morgan had taken his own life the Church would deny him a Christian burial. 'You think she means to sacrifice herself so they'll bury him proper like?'

'I think it's possible,' Ellen said gently. 'Or maybe she seeks atonement. Even if she did not kill him, she may feel she is to blame for his death. By confessing to his murder she is taking his sin upon herself.'

Bending his head, Zach pressed his fingers into his eyes.

'I don't know what to think.' His voice was muffled. 'It is beyond pity.'

'We should not jump to conclusions, Zach. I only offer an alternative explanation for what might have happened. Bethan may indeed have killed her husband. If she is guilty I fear there is nothing we can do for her. Nor should we try, however moved we are by pity. It is the gravest of crimes. In the eyes of the law there are no circumstances to justify petty treason of that magnitude.'

Zach took his hands away from his face, his eyes glistening with tears, held Ellen's gaze. 'Everything I know of Bethan tells me she is innocent. I think it happened as you say. She did not kill Morgan. She could not have done so. I am certain of it.'

Ellen was taken aback by Zach's intensity. Bethan must be special indeed to arouse such emotion in this calm, self-effacing little man. He was not the kind to be taken in by a woman's wiles. She nodded. 'Then we must find someone to speak in her defence. And we need to get Jennet away from the verderer and find out exactly what she saw.'

'How?'

'It may not be easy.' Ellen frowned. 'If they believe her mother is a witch they may also believe that Jennet has been taught the evil arts. It is the only reason I can think of for their holding her captive. They may mean to keep her locked up until they have established Bethan's guilt.' She paused, grimaced. 'For I doubt they will be looking to prove her innocent, Zach. And you know the lengths to which they will go.' Ellen shivered. 'Bethan would not be the first woman to admit giving suck to the Devil to appease her torturers. You must face the fact, even if they find her innocent of petty treason they may still hang her for a witch.'

Zach nodded glumly. For a moment he pictured Bethan chained up in some dark cell. She would be terrified; fraught with anxiety about Jennet and stricken with grief about Morgan. Would she be able to understand her inquisitors – hear what they asked of her? Probably not – until it was too late. He clenched his fists, looked up at Ellen. 'We cannot let it happen. What can we do?'

'Nothing at this moment I fear. For one thing it is too late. I would suggest you stay here for tonight and tomorrow we will get a message to Tawford.' She gave a tight smile. 'He may know someone who will speak for her, someone with enough authority to make a difference. As for Jennet, I will call on the verderer in the morning and demand to see her.' She frowned. 'She does not know me; has no reason to trust me – you will have to come with me, Zach. Does the verderer know who you are?'

'Not exactly, though he's seen me a time or two and he knows about the Warren, but he leaves us alone. He's handsomely rewarded for his silence – I doubt he'd want that to end.' He shrugged. 'It's a chance we'll have to take.'

'If you don't mind playing my groom again, he may not place you.' Ellen arched an imperious eyebrow. 'And if I act the grand lady and don my silks and furbelows, I think he will not refuse me leave to speak with Jennet and—' She broke off. 'What is it Zach?'

Zach's eyes had crinkled in genuine amusement. 'You'd be best to go drab, My Lady. One look at your silks and furbelows and old Lythall will close the door in your face and reach for his prayer book!'

'He's a Puritan?' She quirked an eyebrow. 'Then I shall do as you suggest. What kind of man is he? Will he give way to browbeating do you think?'

Zach shrugged. 'He's a simple God fearing man; keeps himself to himself. He lost his wife to the sweating sickness not so long ago. I heard tell she led him by the nose.' He gave a wry smile. 'He's not taken another so far as I know.'

'Has he not? Then it is highly improper that Jennet remain with him, as I will point out in no uncertain fashion.' She paused, her brow wrinkled in concentration. 'He might wonder how I come to know she is there or indeed why I should concern myself with her. I will have to think up a convincing tale. We don't want him thinking I'm a witch too.'

Zach smiled at the thought. 'Could you not have met Constable Bowden on his way to Exeter this morning?'

Ellen nodded. 'Indeed I could. And could I not also be the Morgans' kin? Who would know any different? It would explain my interest in Jennet and I daresay the Churchwarden will be so relieved to find someone willing to pay for Morgan's burial he'll not question it deeply.' As she spoke, the candles in one of the sconces sputtered and went out throwing half the room into shadow. She made a face at it, got up from the settle and smiling down at Zach put her hand lightly on his shoulder. 'I think that is all we can do tonight. Try not to worry. Things will look brighter in the morning – they always do.'

Zach got hurriedly to his feet and gave a small bow. 'I do not know how to thank you.'

Brushing aside his gratitude with a small shake of her head Ellen leaned forward and kissed him lightly on the cheek. 'I bid you a good night, my friend. Wilmot will show you to your room.'

Surprised and a little flushed he stood looking after her, starting for the door when he heard her call Wilmot to attend him.

19

Monday 14ᵗʰ November, 1642

Waking from a nightmare in the early hours and knowing further sleep was impossible, Ellen got dressed in the dark and donned the clothes she habitually wore for gardening: a plain gown of grey kersey, a linen apron and about her shoulders a dark blue woollen shawl. Her hair – still too short to put up into a bun – she covered with a starched white cap. She had not slept well. Rehearsing what she would say to Jeptha Lythall, her thoughts had drifted anxiously to her brother. According to Alexander's letter of nearly a month ago, Robert should be home by now. Where was he? And what of Alexander? Should she be troubling him with the Morgans' plight at such a time? She had received a brief note to say he had arrived safely in Bodmin, but nothing since. What was now happening in Cornwall? Whatever it was, she knew Alexander would be in the middle of it – and they must by now have heard the dreadful news.

It had come to Barnstaple last week. The town had been full of jubilant gossip about a great battle on the edge of a hill somewhere in the Midlands. They were saying many thousands had been slaughtered, but the brave Earl of Essex had won the day and chased the King and his Godless Cavaliers from the field. Appalled, but knowing to take such talk with a pinch of salt until she heard it from a reliable source, Ellen had not allowed herself to dwell on it. But each night in restless sleep she dreamed she was floating over a misty battlefield fruitlessly searching for Adam amongst the twisted limbs and grey faces that stared up at her with sightless eyes.

Trying to dispel the lingering horror of her nightmare, she felt her way down to the kitchen where she always kept a single large wax candle burning overnight. She knew it was extravagant, but it was so much easier than having to fumble with flints and steel when her head was still thick with sleep, and wax lasted so much longer than tallow – and smelt a good deal sweeter! Using the flame to light a lamp, Ellen carried it through to the parlour, found her writing materials and settled herself on the window seat to write to Alexander. She would send it with Lewin's boy, Todd. He was a bright lad and strong, and he had a married sister in Launceston so knew the roads. Not wanting to burden Alexander too greatly she worried about how much to tell him, deciding not to use a cipher – it would take too long.

Choosing her words with care she wrote: '*I know from Zach you have concerned yourself with the Morgans in the past and would want to know about this, or I would not be troubling you with it. By some sorry mischance Bethan's husband has met with a violent death. I do not yet know how, but that Bethan was with him at the time seems likely. She has been arrested, accused of petty treason and witchcraft and taken to Exeter to stand trial. Zach is convinced she is innocent of this heinous crime and from what he says I am inclined to believe him. Can you suggest anyone with sufficient authority in these troubled times with whom I might plead on Bethan's behalf? I cannot think what else I might do for her.*' Ellen chewed the end of her quill. What should she tell him about Jennet? In the end she wrote simply, '*Be assured Jennet is safe.*' Certain he would know more than she of what had happened in the Midlands, she added, '*I would be grateful to receive any news you may have of recent momentous events and to know everyone is safe.*' She knew he would read between the lines. Finally, she told him Robert had not yet returned from London and she had no news of him or of Lord Bath. She closed: '*Send Todd*

home with your reply – he is a good boy and can be trusted.
As always you are in my thoughts. May God keep you safe.'
She read it through, could see nothing incriminating should it
fall into another's hands, initialled and sealed it. By the time
she had finished she could hear the murmur of voices in the
kitchen.

Ellen had decided to take Wilmot and Rose into her
confidence – or as much of it as she deemed necessary – for
fear they would tittle-tattle if she did not, and was pleased
that both were filled with concern for 'that poor lamb' who
needed proper care while she recovered from the untimely
death of her father. Ellen did not explain the circumstances of
Morgan's death, only that the verderer was presently holding
the child because her mother had been wrongfully accused
of some dreadful misdeed and taken away by the constable.
Ellen told them she hoped by a small deception to bring Jennet
back to the Barton until her mother was proved innocent and
released, as of course she would be. Also, she said, she needed
to send a message about it to Master Tawford because Mistress
Morgan had been a friend to him and he would want to know
of her misfortune. Ellen knew as soon as she uttered those
magic words she would have Wilmot and Rose on her side,
both were devoted to Alexander.

Rose, her eyes sparkling with excitement, went to fetch a
bleary-eyed Todd and made up a snapsack of food for him
to eat on the journey. It was still dark when puffed with self-
importance he was despatched to Bodmin on Ellen's strongest
horse. By which time, she noticed with some amusement,
Wilmot appeared to have forgotten her disapproval of Zach.
Not only had she found him a smart coat and hat to wear – as
befitted his role as 'Her Ladyship's groom' – but had also
given him an enormous breakfast of fried hogs puddens, eggs
and chitterlings, discomfiting him with an uncharacteristic
wink as she plonked the plate in front of him.

It was still early, though full light, when Ellen and Zach
set off in the unrelenting drizzle for Shoulsbarrow Common,

Ellen wrapped in a warm, hooded cloak and seated sidesaddle on a small and rather plump grey mare. The horse was a heriot willed to her by a tenant, and because it was so placid and sweet natured she had kept it as a companion for Tweed. It seemed eminently suitable for the role she had to play today. Ned had saddled it for her with some surprise, but characteristically merely grunted and touched his hat when she thanked him; the ways of the gentry were passing strange, but in his eyes Her Ladyship could do no wrong.

Jeptha Lythall was attempting to harness his frustration, chopping kindling outside his front door. He had endured a trying morning. The witch's maid seemed more aware of him for her gaze had followed him around the room, but he could get no sense out of her. She did not speak at all, just lay on the bed trance-like. The food and drink he had left for her were untouched and the chamber pot had not been used. There was an air of innocence about the maid that appealed to Jeptha, he found it hard to believe there was any evil in her, but the Churchwarden had warned him to be careful and he was a little afraid. Even more than usual he missed his wife. True they had not always seen eye to eye, but she had been a good woman. She would have known what to do about the child. As always, he tried not to question why the Lord had chosen to take his wife from him, but it was hard at times to bend to His will. That this poor maid had come to him was just another cross he had to bear. He knew he should welcome it and suppress his feelings of resentment, but it was not fitting when he had no woman in the house, it just was not fitting. If the Churchwarden had wanted the maid locked up he should have taken her back to the village and kept her in the vestry, as they did with other miscreants before they could be taken

into town. He sighed. As it was, he supposed he would have
to fetch a woman from the village for the duration of Jennet's
stay. He did not relish the prospect; he was not a sociable
man.

Resting his axe and straightening his back, Jeptha watched
the woman riding towards his gate. He did not recognise
her, but her companion, who by his deference was likely
her groom, was vaguely familiar. Leaning on his axe, Jeptha
waited, looking with curiosity at his visitor and approving her
humble mount and sombre clothing. The woman drew rein
and waited while her groom helped her to dismount, then
walked gracefully up the path towards him.

He frowned. 'Good morrow to you, Mistress. What brings
you here? Have you lost your way?'

'Mister Lythall? Mister Jeptha Lythall?' She was well
spoken and though humbly clad had an air of the gentry about
her. She was tall – an unattractive woman.

He nodded cautiously. 'Yes, I am he.'

'Then I am not lost. I wonder if I might speak with you,
Sir? It is a matter of the gravest concern.'

Jeptha's stomach lurched. Who was she? He stared at her
while he went over in his mind the few small misdemeanours
of which he was guilty and for which he daily begged the
Lord's forgiveness. 'You'd best come inside,' he said a little
ungraciously, ushering her into his front room.

She removed her wet cloak and held it out to him, her
expression unsmiling, haughty even. He hung the cloak on
the back of the door and waited while she settled herself on
the bench, her back straight as a die, her hands resting neatly
in her lap. He noticed they were rough and reddened. She was
no stranger to hard work then for all her airs and graces.

'Allow me to introduce myself. My name is Hannah Peard.
I am come from Barnstaple.' She said it as if it explained
everything. Perhaps it did. Even he had heard of George Peard.
The man was strong for Parliament, that much Jeptha knew.
He wondered if she was kin, shook his head. She shrugged

impatiently. 'You do not know me. It is of no consequence and I will come straight to the point. I understand from Constable Bowden that you are holding Jennet Morgan. She is my kin – a cousin of my late husband's – and I wish to speak with her.'

Jeptha started, jaw-dropped. 'The witch is a Peard?'

The woman looked down her nose at him. 'No, indeed she is not. Fortunately the kinship is on the other side. The aunt of poor Mister Morgan, who was yesterday so sadly and treacherously done to death, was married to my husband's cousin twice removed.'

'Ah.' Jeptha nodded assuming an expression of sympathy while racking his brains in an effort to work out the degree of kinship. He gave up. 'It is a terrible thing.'

'Indeed it is. Wicked beyond belief. In the circumstances I am extremely grateful to you for your kindness to the child and I thank you for it, but I am sure you will be glad to know I have come to relieve you of the responsibility.'

Although that was certainly true, Jeptha was not sure about this at all. He shook his head. 'I can't—'

Mistress Peard cut across him. 'You are right to be concerned, Mister Lythall. You have, I believe, been told to hold her captive? It is a sorry state of affairs when a poor innocent child is tainted by the wickedness of her mother, don't you agree?'

Jeptha nodded helplessly. About to protest, he was again interrupted.

'However, whilst I agree with Constable Bowden it is necessary to keep Jennet close until her mother's trial, it is highly unsuitable that she remains here in your home.'

Her expression discomfited Jeptha. There was something about Mistress Peard that made him feel like a small boy caught scrumping apples. He looked down at his feet.

The woman went on regardless. 'I understand your good wife passed away quite recently and you now live alone? Jennet may yet be a child, but she is not far from marriageable age.'

Jeptha gaped like a fish. The implication was embarrassingly clear. All the more so since the same thought had occurred to him not an hour ago. Trying to suppress black thoughts about the Churchwarden for putting him in this position, Jeptha cleared his throat and attempted to summon up some dignity. 'You don't have to tell me that it is not fitting Mistress. I was going to fetch a woman from the village to tend the maid. It is hardly my fault that—'

Mistress Peard held up an imperious hand. 'Please, Mister Lythall, I quite understand what you are trying to say and I am not blaming you. I am sure you have been presented with a set of circumstances quite beyond your control and I do not for a moment believe you would take advantage of poor Jennet, but the fact remains she is here alone in your house and in an extremely vulnerable condition. I dread to think what people will say. I do not wish her to be so compromised. I am sure you will agree this state of affairs should not be allowed to continue. Now, if you will let me see her, perhaps we can discover precisely what ails her? She is ailing, is she not?'

At a loss, Jeptha nodded, 'Aye Mistress, something ails her. She has not moved since yesterday, nor will she speak.' A worm of suspicion squirmed into his mind. 'But how do you know that? I was not aware of it myself until after the constable left yesterday so he could not have told you. And how did you come to see him? He was going to Exeter.'

'Constable Bowden and I are well acquainted. It fortuned me to meet him on the road – not that it is any business of yours,' the woman said curtly. She looked at Jeptha with barely veiled contempt. 'I hardly need to be told the child is ailing Mister Lyhthall. As I understand it she witnessed her mother stabbing her father to death. Is that not correct?'

He nodded, shuffled his feet. 'Aye, so the little maid did tell me before she were struck dumb.' He shivered. 'Her mother's doing I don't doubt.'

'Precisely. Do you not think, Sir, even without her mother's evil practices, to witness such a dreadful thing is enough to make anyone ill, let alone a girl of Jennet's tender years? May God have mercy on her soul – I cannot imagine how this might have affected her mind or indeed if she will ever recover from it. To have seen such wickedness...' The woman gave a small sob and dabbed at her eyes. 'Can you be surprised she is unable to move or speak? Who knows what evil has been done to her? It is quite possible she is possessed.'

Jeptha gasped in horror. It would explain why the maid had behaved so strangely. He shuddered to think of it.

Mistress Peard was staring at him. 'Yes, I see you understand what I am saying.' Her face softened. 'With the Good Lord's help we must do what we can for the child, Mister Lythall. Did He not say, "Suffer the little children to come unto me?"'

Jeptha took off his hat and twisted it in his hands. 'And forbid them not for such is the Kingdom of God – the Gospel of St Mark.'

Nodding, she smiled. It changed her face completely. 'Indeed Mister Lythall: Chapter ten, Verse fourteen.'

Jeptha was impressed. The woman knew her scriptures.

'Such comfort the Good Lord brings to us poor sinners,' the woman was saying, 'a comfort I fully intend Jennet shall have. Pray God it is not too late and she is untainted by her mother's wickedness. We must go down on our knees and pray for His divine guidance to bring her to the light. Now then, Sir, be good enough to take me to the child.' Mistress Peard rose from the bench and looked at him expectantly. 'And since she cannot walk, I am sure you will allow my groom to help me?'

The temptation to be rid of this whole situation was too much for Jeptha. He nodded dumbly. The woman was God fearing. She was clearly well connected and was obviously concerned for the maid's wellbeing and anyway, she was kin. And given she knew the constable, he could see no reason to stand in her way, but Jeptha was a cautious man. 'The people hereabouts are much afeared of Mistress Morgan, and not without cause. We thought they might try to harm the child thinking she'd been taught her mother's evil ways, and who is to say otherwise until she can be questioned? It was the Churchwarden told me to keep her locked up. For her own safety, you understand, at least until she comes to her senses. I am not sure I should let her go without his say so, Mistress Peard.'

'I applaud your caution Mister Lythall, but I am sure the Churchwarden would not object.' From the folds of her damp gown the woman drew a purse and held it out to him. 'Be so good as to tell him I will keep Jennet safe until her mother is brought to trial and that Constable Bowden knows where to find me in the meantime. This should more than cover the expenses for Morgan's funeral, God rest his poor, tortured soul. You will tell the Churchwarden he is to see it is properly done. I will not have my husband's kin buried as a pauper.'

Jeptha took the purse, felt its weight and gazed at the woman with new respect. The Churchwarden would surely be delighted at this unexpected turn of events. 'Very well, Mistress, I will do as you say. It is perhaps for the best.'

Carrying the purse to the other side of the room, he placed it carefully in the ironbound box that he kept under the stairs, aware as he did so the woman was tapping her foot. With an apologetic glance, he went to the front door, opened it and beckoned to her groom who was loitering outside. Jeptha noted the fine quality of his coat; Mistress Peard was undoubtedly well to do. 'How is your man called? I am sure I have seen him before.'

'I doubt it,' she said curtly. 'He is not from around these parts. His name is—'

The groom sidled through the door, 'Makepeace Rivett, at your service Sir, you need me, Mistress?' Jeptha did not recognise the name.

'Ah...Makepeace...?' The woman's sudden, wide smile was a little too familiar in Jeptha's view. 'Yes, if you will. Mister Lythall here tells me Jennet is too ill to walk.' Turning to Jeptha, who was still staring at the groom trying to place him, Mistress Peard was suddenly taken with a fit of coughing. 'Forgive me,' she spluttered, her hand to her throat. 'Might I have a drink?'

Alarmed, Jeptha went quickly from the room and fetched a cup of water from the butt outside the back door. When he returned, Makepeace Rivett was standing respectfully at his Mistress's side, his face partially concealed beneath his wide-brimmed hat.

The woman took a few sips of water and smiled her gratitude, said hoarsely, 'Thank you. I fear I must have caught a chill. I don't feel at all well. This wretched weather.' She handed Jeptha the cup. 'Be so good as to take us to Jennet and we will be on our way.'

Jeptha nodded, took the cup. 'She's in my late wife's bedchamber.' He led the way upstairs, unlocked the door and was about to open it when of a sudden he was pushed from behind. Mistress Peard gave a small cry. Swinging round, he saw she had stumbled and fallen against him. Distractedly he bent to help her and as he did so, her groom brushed past them and walked into the bedchamber. Appalled by the man's want of manners and apparent lack of concern, Jeptha waited while the woman recovered herself.

'Thank you, Mister Lythall, how clumsy of me, but no harm done.' Mistress Peard maintained her grip on his sleeve, bending to brush the dust from her gown. 'Though you'll own your stairs are a little dark,' she added tartly.

Jeptha found himself stammering an apology as she let go of his arm and he moved aside for her to enter the room. Makepeace Rivett was standing a little way from the bed, his head bent respectfully, his face still concealed. Jeptha frowned, was about to rebuke the man when Mistress Peard gave a cry of distress. With her hand to her mouth, she approached the bed. 'Oh! The poor child!'

Distracted from the groom, Jeptha watched the child intently hoping to see some reaction, but the maid's pinched, little face was devoid of expression. She lay as he had left her, unmoving.

Mistress Peard bent to feel Jennet's brow, pushing back the tumble of dark red hair that so accentuated the child's pale skin. The freckles on her nose stood out like a pox. 'Oh my dear cousin – that I should find you in this unhappy condition. What a dreadful thing to have happened, but you must not be afraid, child, I have come to take you home with me. Makepeace will carry you for Mister Lythall tells me you cannot walk, but can you speak to me, Jennet?'

Craning over Mistress Peard's shoulder, Jeptha felt the hairs lift on the back of his neck as the witch's maid looked full at him. Her eyes were sunken, their pupils huge, her expression haunted. Slowly she turned her head towards the groom.

'That's right, Jennet,' the woman said. 'You remember Makepeace, don't you?' Of a sudden Mistress Peard rounded on Jeptha, her voice raised in anger. 'I do not like what I see Sir.' Startled, he stepped back. 'It is far worse than I had imagined. Why has this poor child been left in this condition? She should have been seen by a physician.' Mistress Peard glanced at her groom. 'We must take her home – and quickly. Be so good as to wrap her in the blanket and carry her downstairs – I assume Mr Lythall you will not mind if we take it?' She gasped suddenly. 'Forgive me. I am distraught. To see her like this is more than I can bear.' Putting her hand to her head, Mistress Peard swayed against Jeptha.

He put his arm tentatively about her waist to support her and was unable to suppress a twinge of pleasure. Lord, forgive me, he thought, women are lustful, dangerous creatures. They tempt a man from virtue and he was but a man, a man who had not felt the touch of a woman for many months. Thus exonerated, he kept his arm about Mistress Peard's slender waist and helped her down the stairs to the bench.

'More water, I pray you.' She sat with her face in her hands while he hurried once more to the water butt. When he returned, slopping water on the floor in his haste, Makepeace Rivett was already outside the front door, holding the child's thin, motionless body cocooned in the blanket.

Jeptha knew he had seen the man before. Where had it been? Handing the cup to Mistress Peard he made to follow, but she held him back. 'You have been extremely kind, Mister Lythall. I feel a little better. I am sorry to have caused you so much trouble. Rest assured I shall have your blanket returned to you.' As he stammered that it was of no consequence, she plucked at his sleeve. 'My cloak if you please and be so good as to help me to my horse.'

Jeptha had no choice but to wait while she finished her drink. He held out her damp cloak and gave her his arm as they walked to where her drab little mare was tethered. Rivett, already mounted, was waiting at the gate, the witch's maid cradled in his arms. Jeptha frowned with concentration, the elusive thread of recognition hovering just within his grasp. Mistress Peard gathered her reins, placed a hand on his shoulder and lifted her foot, nudging it against his knee. Shaking his head in frustration, Jeptha bent and linked his hands for her, hotly aware of the feel of her leg beneath her gown as he lifted her into the saddle.

She smiled down at him, a warm, wide smile. 'Once again I thank you, Mister Lythall. I shall remember you in my prayers and give thanks to the Lord for your kindness. Rest assured with His help I shall fight Jennet's demons and bring her to a state of grace. Good day to you, Sir. God be with you.'

Her smile illuminated her face. Jeptha had thought her unattractive; he saw he was mistaken. He watched as she kicked her mare into a shambling trot and rode after her groom. When they were lost to sight, he went back inside. He had to admit Mistress Peard had unsettled him. Perhaps it was time he thought about taking another wife. A man needed a woman. It was the natural way of things. Had he done right letting the witch's maid go with her? He wondered what the Churchwarden would have to say about it.

Moving to the stairs, Jeptha crouched down by his ironbound box and lifted the lid. It creaked back on its hinges. Retrieving the purse, he took it to the table and spilled the contents onto the polished wood. His eyes lit up. With all thoughts of Makepeace Rivett gone from his mind, he started to count.

20

Tuesday 15th November, 1642

By mid-November, having secured most of Cornwall, the Royalists were making inroads into Devon: a garrison of foot remained in Tavistock, Sir Bevill Grenville and his regiment were in possession of Totnes and Sir Ralph Hopton and his forces were at Plympton, sitting outside Plymouth in a fruitless attempt to weaken the city with a landward blockade, but while Parliament controlled the navy there was little the citizens of Plymouth could not obtain by sea. Meanwhile, the rebels were growing stronger by the day. Parliament had authorised the Deputy Lieutenant of Cornwall to raise one thousand men and sent two troops of horse to aid them. They had also ordered the Committee for Devon to allot five hundred dragoons to Parliament's Cornish forces. Hopton, in desperate need of men to counter this threat was hoping to link up with the Devon Royalists and was delighted to receive a message from Sir Edmund Fortescue, newly sworn in as the King's High Sheriff of Devon, who proposed to call a muster at Modbury and hoped Sir Ralph would join him there. With high hopes of obtaining several hundred, if not thousands of well-armed foot soldiers capable of helping him mount an assault on Plymouth, Hopton, in an uncharacteristically cheerful mood, set off for Modbury with a company of horse and a few of his officers, Alexander among them.

Their hopes were sorely dashed. No orderly ranks of infantry were lined up at Modbury to greet them. Instead, to Fortescue's acute embarrassment, the place resembled nothing so much as a fairground: a joyful throng of inebriated Devonians happily enjoying a rare day out with barely a horse or a musket between them. It was a bitter blow, but Hopton and his men tried to make the best of things. They were searching through the festive crowds for likely recruits when a message was brought with great urgency. A scout, holding his ribs and gasping for breath, stuttered out what he had seen: an army out of Plymouth fast approaching Modbury, no more than half a mile away.

Fearful that the defenceless, panicking mob would be cut to pieces, Hopton refused to flee. Instead, cursing the ineptitude of his picquets, he drew up his meagre force ready to fend off an attack. This, it transpired, came from none other than Colonel Ruthin, who had been persuaded to donate his mercenaries to Parliament's cause instead of continuing his journey to France. Still smarting from his ignominious defeat at Saltash it took the Scot no time at all to exact vengeance, his men quickly routing the Royalists and taking several prisoners, Sir Edmund Fortescue among them. Hopton himself only narrowly avoided capture when Nick Slanning and Alexander pulled him forcibly from the field while Ruthin's troops were focused on dispersing the frightened revellers with the butt ends of their muskets.

Safely back in Plympton, Sir Ralph spent the next few days regrouping and calling in his scattered forces, he then brought his senior officers together for a Council of War. As things stood, they simply did not have enough troops to mount an attack on Plymouth. They could stay where they were in the South Hams and hope to recruit loyal Devonians, or they could call an end to the year's campaign and retreat back across the Tamar. After the debacle at Modbury, Hopton's men were unanimously loath to return to Cornwall with their tails between their legs, but prolonging their stay was increasingly risky. A large enemy force was gathering at Lifton under the able command of Sir George Chudleigh. Marching to join them at the head of Parliament's new Western Army was the Earl of Stamford – as Tawford had suspected, the command had not gone to the Earl of Bedford – which, according to recent intelligence, had already reached Gloucestershire.

There was another alternative: Exeter. Encouraged by Fortescue's few remaining Devonians, who were certain the city remained weakly garrisoned and was likely to succumb to a surprise attack, and that in any event, once they knew of the plan, loyalists in the South would flock to help him, Hopton eventually agreed. It was a bold stratagem, but there were distinct advantages: properly strengthened Exeter would provide a good defensive position to overwinter and would be an ideal base from which to bring North Devon under Royalist control. If they were to be successful, it had to be now, before Stamford could come to the city's aid.

Though a cautious man by nature, once having made the decision, Hopton quickly put together a plan of attack: he would lead it from the west, occupying the outlying villages of Powderham, Ide and Alphington. From these positions he would cross the Exe upriver, dig in and mount culverins to bombard the city walls. At the same time, Grenville, who had been recalled from Totnes with most of his regiment, would occupy Topsham and lead an attack from the south. Additionally, five hundred men would be despatched north under the command of Colonel John Acland to secure Torrington, which was known to be covertly sympathetic to the King's cause, and from where Acland could watch for and send back word of any potentially threatening activity out of Barnstaple and Bideford.

Signalling Alexander to stay behind while the officers piled enthusiastically out of his quarters to go and prepare their men, Sir Ralph poured them both a glass of claret and with a heavy sigh, thrust a map of Exeter across the table, stabbing it with his forefinger. 'I am not sure about this enterprise, Tawford. It is against my better judgement that I have allowed myself to be persuaded. If Fortescue's men are wrong and we get no more support from Devon, or if Exeter is stronger than they would have us believe…'

He left the sentence unfinished, his brow creased in an anxious frown. Alexander waited patiently, fairly sure he knew what was coming.

After a moment, Hopton continued. 'We can but put our trust in the Lord, but I would be obliged if you would take what men you need and spy out Exeter's defences in advance. Also, Grenville and his regiment will need a boat to ferry them across the river to Topsham.' Hopton looked up at Alexander and slowly he smiled. 'I know I ask much of you, but if you could find a way to arrange it for him…?'

'Understood, Sir. I will do what I can.' Returning Hopton's smile, Alexander complimented him on the wine, emptied his glass, scooped up the map and headed back to his billet, his mind busy. It was now Tuesday. It would take the army five days with foot soldiers and heavy ordinance to reach the Exe and be in position, which gave him until Sunday night to find a boat for Grenville, but if he could send back intelligence in the meantime, so much the better.

After supper, in the huge stone-flagged kitchen of his billet, Alexander spread out the map of Exeter on the wax-spattered table and was mildly irritated to be disturbed by a knock on the door. Looking up, he observed a boy swaying on his feet in the doorway. For a moment, his head full of numbers, he did not recognise him. When he did, his first thought was of Ellen. Alarmed, he started forward from the table. 'It's Lewin's boy, isn't it?'

'Aye, Master.' the boy took off his cap and held it under his arm. 'Todd,' he added.

'Of course, Todd, forgive me, I did not expect to see you here. Is aught wrong with your Mistress? You have a message for me?'

The boy reached into the pouch at his belt and held out Ellen's letter. 'The Lady Ellen were in good fettle when I left yesterday mornin' an 'er said I were to deliver this to ee wi' all haste. I'd have bin 'ere afore now, but I did go by Tavistock.'

He flushed as his voice moved through several octaves ending on a squeak. '

Alexander took the letter with a smile. 'You have done well indeed to find me so soon. I doubt the King's couriers could have done any better.'

Todd grinned with pleasure as Alexander unsealed the letter, held it to the candlelight and glanced with a frown at the contents. After a moment he looked up at the boy's white face, noticed the shadows under his eyes, the mud splashed on his breeches and the jagged tear in his jerkin. 'You look in sore need of a rest, lad.' Moving to the door he called to the guard on duty outside then turned back to Todd. 'Go with Sergeant Threthick now, Todd, and when you have rested I will have a reply for you to take back to Lady Ellen.' He addressed the soldier who had come hot foot to his summons. 'See that this man has some beer and hot food inside him then find him a comfortable bed for the night, will you? And have someone see to his horse. When you've done, be so good as to send Lieutenant Lyddon to me.'

'Aye, Sir.' Threthick nodded at Todd and held open the door for him. The boy, glowing with pride, pushed his way outside.

When he was alone Alexander re-read Ellen's letter with dismay. He cast his mind back to his meeting with Bethan remembering her courage and how strangely he had been drawn to her. Could she have had a hand in Morgan's death? It was unthinkable, unless... He recalled her anguished words: *He blames me that he survived.* Had it been an act of mercy? Appalled, Alexander's thoughts turned to the passionate child with the violet eyes. Jennet's devotion to her parents had been painfully apparent. Dear God, had the family not suffered enough? If Bethan was found to be a witch – the imbeciles, it would be laughable were it not so serious – she would surely hang. But if they found her guilty of murdering her husband by witchcraft, they would burn her at the stake. He imagined the flames licking at her hair, the sickening stench of scorching flesh, her wisdom and spirit extinguished on a pyre of ignorance. Shuddering, he banished the thought, reached for paper and graphite to scribble a note in cipher to Ellen:

> *Thank you for this news, you were right to send it to me. Do what you can for Jennet and leave Bethan to me. Tell Zach to put a man in the Morgans' house to keep their property safe from plunder meantime.*
>
> *Edgehill yielded no victory either for the King or Parliament and I fear there were many losses. Both sides have retired to lick their wounds and there is talk of peace. I think it unlikely, but I doubt there will be another major confrontation this side of Christmas.*
>
> *Your perfidious brother is no longer in London, but with Parliament's army serving under Sir William Waller. I imagine he is looking to safeguard his property. I understand he survived the battle with small hurt.*
>
> *I am still with Sir Ralph Hopton. We are to mount an attack on Exeter within the next few days. I go to spy out the defences in advance. I will seek news of Bethan at the same time. Try not to worry. Affectionately yours, etc.'*

He glanced again at Ellen's letter, frowned, added:

> *Adam is safe and remains with Prince Rupert. Be assured I will recall him soon.*

He was folding the page when Lyddon strode into the kitchen. 'You have news?'

'Yes. Is everyone back from Totnes?'

'All but the Chichesters, but they are on their way I believe.

Should be here by this time tomorrow.'

Alexander nodded thoughtfully. 'We will have to do without them for now.' He indicated the map spread out on the table. 'There is some urgent business to which I must attend in Exeter.'

Sensing Alexander's mood, Lyddon's saturnine face quickened with interest. 'Official?'

'Yes and no.' Alexander grinned. 'Fortuitously I have been ordered to penetrate the city for intelligence – that at least is official.'

With a surge of excitement Lyddon grinned back. They would all welcome some action after these tedious weeks of drilling illiterate greenhorns. 'So what is it then? Are you going to tell me or do I have to guess?'

'Patience, Hugh, I don't want to have to say it all twice. Get the others in here, will you? Tell them to come quietly. And would you give this to young Todd Lewin and tell him there is no need to break his neck over it?' He held out the note. 'Threthick will know where to find him. The lad should rest himself a day before he attempts to leave – tell him that's an order. Tell him also I would like him to take my mare back to Tawford Barton and I do not want her exhausted. She picked up a flesh wound at Modbury, nothing serious, but she needs to be rested and I want Ned to care for her meantime.'

Still grinning, Lyddon nodded and went to do as he was bid. When he had gone, Alexander reached for a stool and sat, leaning his elbows on the table. Given the severity of her supposed crime, Bethan would be held either in the South Gate Gaol or the dungeons at Rougemont Castle. He could only hope it was the former. Rougemont housed the garrison and would be much more difficult. He turned his attention to the map checking the positions of the city gates – all would be guarded, but some less well than others. Getting in should not be a problem. Getting out might not be so easy. Thoughtfully he sketched in the route of the underground passages trying to remember where the various entrances were.

The passages had been dug out centuries ago to take piped water to the Cathedral Chapter from a great spring in St Sidwell's outside the city to the east. The tunnel started in the outer ditch and carried the pipes underneath the walls, beneath the physic garden of St John's Hospital and along under the High Street. There were other access points within the city to allow engineers to mend leaking pipes. The outer entrance had surely been blocked – the rebels would be fools to leave it open – but there was a slim chance it had been overlooked. Alexander pursed his lips. Too slim! Even so, the passages might afford a useful hiding place. Lost in thought, he gazed unseeing at the candle flame. When Hopton attacked there would be a good deal of confusion in the city, which should work in his favour. After a few moments he reached again for graphite and paper and scribbled a list for Rob Pollard, his quartermaster.

The flame guttered in a sudden draught. Alexander looked up to see Lyddon holding open the door, the men filing quietly inside: Will Mohun, whose beard had re-grown though was not yet restored to its former glory, closely followed by Francis Sydenham, Kit Bassett, Rob Pollard and Hal Gifford, with John Acland bringing up the rear. They crowded in silence around the table and looked at him expectantly. With a sudden pang Alexander thought of Hartley, missing his steadying influence – not that Adam would believe it!

'Thank you for coming, gentlemen, and I apologise for disturbing your evening, but we have work to do.' He handed the list to his quartermaster. 'I know you like a challenge, Rob.' His lips lifted in a dry smile.

Pollard's eyebrows shot up as he glanced at it. 'By when?'

'By mid-morning if you can.'

'A challenge indeed,' Pollard murmured doubtfully. 'It'll cost you.'

'I know it will.' Alexander reached into the saddlebag he had earlier kicked under the table, threw a purse at Pollard who deftly caught it, weighed it in his hand appreciatively and grinned. 'I trust the dice weren't loaded.'

Alexander grinned back. 'Cards. And before you ask, they weren't mine.'

Pollard shook his head despairingly. 'You've the luck of the Devil. I'll see what I can do.'

'We also need some boats – or better still a ship.' Alexander looked round at the tense faces. 'Any ideas?'

Acland nodded with a smirk. 'Captain Nutt is back in Lympstone. Last I heard he was on a pot walk in the Black Swan. He'll likely not be conscious yet, rarely is when he's on dry land.'

'Ideal. Find the old pirate; get him sober any way you can then remind him he owes me a favour. You'd best take someone to watch your back. The Prideauxs own the land all round Lympstone and they're strong for Parliament.'

Acland raised his eyebrows at Kit Basset. 'I'll take Basset,' he said as Kit nodded. 'Assuming we find Pirate Nutt, and assuming he has a ship and is amenable, when and where do you want it?'

'Oh, rest assured he'll be amenable.' Alexander smiled wickedly. 'It was a very big favour! Have it lying in the Exe by Saturday night. If you fail to find him, beg, borrow or steal as many small boats as you can. Anything that floats will be better than nothing.'

It was too much for Will Mohun. He gave a sudden exasperated growl, bunched his fist and slapped it into the palm of his hand. 'Come on, Tawford, you fox, tell us what the devil's going on.'

Silencing Mohun with a lift of his eyebrow, Alexander tilted back his stool, linked his hands behind his head and proceeded to outline Sir Ralph Hopton's plans.

And then his own.

21

Wednesday 16th November, 1642

The sun had dipped below the horizon a half hour since. The suffusion of ruddy orange, which had lit up the roofs and reflected fiery tints in the sluggish waters of the Exe, was now just a trace in the darkening sky. Lieutenant Arthur Green was on guard duty on the bridge. He stamped his feet and cupped his hands round his match, wishing he had a warm pair of gloves and a knitted scarf like those of his sergeant who was stationed at the West Gate end of the bridge. They had positioned eight young guards between them at intervals of twenty-five feet. From time to time he turned to stare at them. Not that he could see them clearly in the half-light and with the torches just lit and all smoking – but they didn't know that.

It was quiet. The last of the seabirds had gone to roost and though not yet time for the curfew, the bridge was clear of traffic. The workers had all gone home and the revellers – for there were still a few – had not yet turned out. Bored, Lieutenant Green craned his neck to look at the emerging stars. It was going to be a clear night. Was it better to be cold and dry or warm and wet? He was debating this issue with himself, coming down on the side of warm and wet, when he caught the sound of men's voices carrying on the crisp air. Peering into the gloom he saw a small body of mounted soldiers approaching the bridge. He knew they were soldiers because he could see the glint of their helmets and breastplates, but was not unduly alarmed. They were too few to be a threat and they were riding at a leisurely pace, talking, laughing and making no attempt to conceal themselves. He shouted to his men to advance their weapons and waited while the strangers drew near. As they came closer he counted five of them. They wore buff leather coats under their steel and each man had a sash round his waist. He could not see what colour. As the leading horseman clattered onto the bridge, Lieutenant Green moved, blew on his match and settling his primed musket in its rest, blocked the rider's path. 'Who goes there? Halt in the name of the King and Parliament.' He waited for the password. It was not forthcoming.

The horseman drew rein, dismounted and removing his helmet walked forward leading his horse. His short hair was dark with sweat and he was clean-shaven. 'I commend your vigilance, Lieutenant, but put up.' Extending a gloved hand the stranger gently moved aside the end of Green's musket and smiled pleasantly, one eyebrow raised. As a torch beside them flared, Green noticed a wicked-looking scar slanting from the soldier's hairline, puckering his eyelid. Slightly mollified and ready to be impressed, he wondered if the man had been wounded in action.

'We come on official business from the Earl of Essex,' the stranger was saying. He reached into his coat and pulled out a sheet of folded paper. 'See here.' His breath clouding the air, he waved it under Green's red nose, half-turning to indicate his companions. 'And as you can surely see, we wear His Lordship's colours.' He fingered the wide, tasselled scarf tied about his middle, which the Lieutenant now saw was orange. 'I am Captain Oliver Blewitt and those four men are my guards. Have you not been warned to expect us?'

Green, not wishing to display his ignorance about what colour the Earl of Essex happened to have chosen for his troopers – presumably it was orange, but how the devil was he supposed to know that – was on the point of replying that no, he had not and unless they knew the password he could not let them pass, when a sudden movement caught his attention. A sixth horseman, whom he had not noticed until now, had emerged from behind the group of mounted men still clustering at the entrance to the bridge and was riding forward. As the man rode into the light Green saw he was not garbed as were his companions in leather and steel, but wore a black velvet doublet, frothing at neck and cuffs with flounces of lace. He also wore lace-trimmed boot hose. From his shoulder his dark blue cloak was turned back to reveal a lining of pale blue silk, the facings laced with intricate knots of gold and silver thread. The pattern was repeated in his hatband, which sparkled in the torchlight. The Lieutenant gazed at this display of finery with ill-concealed distaste. The popinjay brought his mount to a halt a yard or two away from him and stood up in his stirrups to survey the length of the bridge, observing as he did so that nine rested muskets were pointed at his chest. His handsome face darkened with spleen.

'*Qu'est-ce que c'est?*' He sat back in the saddle, a sneer curling his lips. '*Que signifie ce délai? Pourquoi ce benêt bloque-t-il notre chemin? Est-ce normal que je reçoive un accueil pareil quand je rends service si librement?*' As he spoke the pitch of his voice rose higher and higher until he was almost screaming, flecks of spittle spraying onto his black pointed beard. '*Suis-je venu jusqu'ici pour être insulté?*'

Gaping at this stream of unintelligible invective Lieutenant Green took an involuntary step backwards and looked uncertainly at Blewitt, who shrugged, raised his eyes to the sky in a gesture of amused resignation and whispered conspiratorially. 'He's French.'

Sensing an ally, the Lieutenant whispered back. 'What is he saying?'

'He says he has come a long way to be of service to this city and feels insulted by the delay. He asks that you be so kind as to let him pass.' Blewitt smiled. 'Don't worry, I will tell him I am dealing with it.' He called over his shoulder to the Frenchman. '*Je suis désolé mon capitain. Permettez-moi le traiter lui, Monsieur.'*

'Who is he?' The Lieutenant, uncomfortably aware Blewitt's translation was most likely censored, added, 'just give me the password and I can let you through. I have my orders you understand.' Hearing muffled sniggers from behind he swung round to see the guards had gravitated to the centre of the bridge and were gawping at the Frenchie, their comments becoming increasingly ribald. 'Get back to your positions,' he snapped, waving them away.

Blewitt shook his head sympathetically. 'Youth today eh? He is Monsieur Henri Lafitte, gunnery consultant to the Lord General the Earl of Essex, and—' He got no further. Hearing his name the Frenchman shifted his gaze to Lieutenant Green and pointed an elegant finger encased in a white kid glove, the cuff of which, Green noted sourly, was also trimmed with fancy lacing.

'What eez zis mans letting not me to pass? He eez imbecile, yes? *J'ai fatigué, froid et faim. Ayez cet homme stupide enlevé de mon chemin immédiatement.'*

With a glance of mute apology at Green, Blewitt whispered, 'He says he is tired, cold and hungry and begs you let us pass immediately.' Blewitt turned back to Lafitte. 'The Lieutenant is naturally concerned to protect the bridge, Monsieur, and he has his orders. I am sure he will let us pass if you will allow me to explain our business.'

The Frenchman looked at him blankly. '*Pardon?*'

'*Il est naturellement concerné pour protéger le pont, Monsieur et il a ses ordres. Je suis sûr qu'il nous laissera passer si vous me permettrez seulement d'expliquer nos affaires.*' Blewitt translated patiently.

Monsieur Lafitte looked a little mollified. 'Ah, so, eet ees, ow you say…' He screwed up his eyes, fingered his nose and looked heavenwards. 'A stupeed meestake, no?' He smiled triumphantly, adding peevishly, '*Ainsi pourquoi ne poursuivez-vous pas avec lui?*'

'*Oui Monsieur.*'

Green, able to tell from Lafitte's tone and Blewitt's visibly gritted teeth that the Frenchie had told him to get on with it, hid a smile.

'I am sorry, Lieutenant,' Blewitt was saying. 'I do not have the password – I fear our communications are not good – but we have reports from Sir George Chudleigh that enemy forces have crossed the Tamar. We are come hither to inspect your city's defences in advance of the Western Army, which I am sure you must know is on its way here under the command of the Earl of Stamford. The Lord General wants to ensure Exeter does not fall into enemy hands before Lord Stamford is able to arrive. I think you had better let us through, Lieutenant.' He nodded towards the West Gate. 'Is my friend Major Saunders still in command here?'

Lieutenant Green breathed a sigh of pure relief. 'You know Major Saunders? Why the devil didn't you say so... er, Sir,' he said, remembering belatedly that he was outranked. 'That is to say, had I known...'

'No matter, Lieutenant.' Blewitt dismissed his indiscretion with a terse smile. 'I would have done the same in your position. Where will I find him – at the castle?'

'Yes, Captain, with the garrison; I will have my sergeant take you there.'

'Thank you, Lieutenant.' Blewitt mounted up and waved his party forward while Green shouted an order to his men to stand down and to get the gates open.

In Rougemont Castle, Major Richard Saunders yawned and poured himself another goblet of sack. He had just sat down, pulled his boots off and with a contented grunt stuck his stockinged feet in front of the fire, when he heard the commotion outside. With a sigh of resignation he reached for his boots and had just managed to ease them back over his swollen ankles when there was an urgent knocking at his door. Calling to the man to enter he listened with increasing frustration to the message. Communications in this godforsaken army were no better than the smoke signals of savages – if as good, he thought with a grunt. How the devil was he supposed to operate effectively when he never received information? It was too bad. He had not heard of either of these men, though it appeared that one of them professed to know him. Blewitt? He supposed he might have forgotten the name. It happened increasingly these days. But he knew the Lord General employed foreign advisors in his train. They had all laughed about it when they had heard. Typical of Essex – always puffing away at that damned pipe of his.

'Very well, Sergeant.' He motioned the man away. 'Be so good as to explain to my visitors that I most humbly beg their pardon, but I cannot possibly receive them just now. Ensure they are properly fed and housed. I will meet with them in the morning when they have rested and refreshed themselves.'

With some trepidation the sergeant repeated Major Saunders' words to the two visitors whom he had left waiting in the guardroom, their four guards having gone with a groom to stable the horses. He was relieved when the storm of words he had anticipated was not forthcoming. The Frenchman muttered darkly to himself, but said nothing more and Captain Blewitt accepted the arrangement quite amicably. He had not expected they would arrive so late, he said, and his party were hungry and tired. It was eminently sensible to postpone their meeting with Major Saunders until morning. Pleasantly surprised, the sergeant showed them to the rooms set aside for visitors to the castle and ordered their supper to be brought to them on a tray.

The following morning Saunders duly examined the credentials handed to him by Captain Blewitt, whom, for politeness' sake he pretended to remember – the man did indeed seem familiar, though try as he might he could not place him. Satisfied that everything was in order, he took both men on a tour of the walls and ramparts while their guards, who had been excused duties for the day, went off eagerly to see what the city had to offer by way of entertainment. Saunders showed Lafitte around the fortifications, pointing out the repairs that had been made to the city wall, and both men commented favourably on what had been accomplished. They tramped around the gun emplacements inspecting the twenty-five pieces of ordinance mounted on gun platforms along the one and a half miles of wall. Saunders then walked them to vantage points from where they could see areas without the wall where buildings had been demolished and cleared to allow for widening and deepening the main ditch and throwing up a secondary bank of earth. As they could see, he pointed, work was underway on an outer ditch and he had positioned outlying small gun batteries to defend the main roads into the city. He would soon have almost five thousand men at his disposal, he explained proudly – it was a only a slight exaggeration – comprising members of Exeter's Trained Band, a regiment of foot soldiers left by Colonel Bampfield, several hundred volunteers and the reinforcements he expected to arrive within the next few days from Plymouth, under the command of a Colonel Ruthin, whom he understood was an experienced soldier – a Scot, evidently. Saunders could see from their expressions that both men were impressed.

Despite Captain Blewitt's skills as a translator, it was a laborious and tiresome process and took much longer than it should. Saunders was forced to admit, however, that it was a worthwhile exercise. The Frenchman clearly knew what he was talking about and was able to suggest a number of improvements to the gun mountings, talking haltingly with the gunnery teams, inspecting the shot and tinkering with the elevation quoins. When at last they came down from the walls the two men insisted on walking the perimeter to take a closer look at the gates. Passing the East Gate, Saunders mentioned the engineers had been taken off the ongoing work on the underground passages and plans to extend the aqueduct beyond St Stephens to the Great Conduit had been abandoned. The St Sidwell's water supply had been temporarily cut off and some of the lead piping was being melted down for shot. He wished he had kept his mouth shut for Blewitt then insisted on walking along the ditch to inspect the outer entrance to the tunnel. Yes, Saunders knew it was vulnerable; he had ordered it blocked with rubble – it was the next job on the engineers' list. When at last they were satisfied and he trudged them back to the castle, Saunders knew he was going to have the devil's own job getting his boots off.

Later that day, after he had wined and dined his visitors with the best that Rougemont's kitchens had to offer – poor fare, but Saunders made no apology; there was a war on after all and the city's defences had severely disrupted trade – he picked their brains for news of London and they discussed the state of affairs up country. The news of Edgehill was a little dampening. In Exeter, word was that it had been a decisive victory for Parliament. Not so, Blewitt assured him; it was regrettable, but the battle had ended with no advantage for either side. Saunders then retired to take his ease as he customarily did after dinner, leaving his visitors to their own devices for an hour or two while he gratefully soaked his feet in a bowl of warm water. Blewitt had said he needed to write a report for the Lord General the Earl of Essex, and the Frenchman wanted to visit the cathedral to see how it compared with the fine architecture of Nôtre Dame. Lafitte declined the offer of an escort; said he would be perfectly happy to wander incognito – though quite how the Frenchie expected to remain incognito when he strutted about like a peacock in full display, caused Saunders not a little amusement – but before they left the Major made a tentative request. Would Monsieur Lafitte be prepared to meet with his officers and engineers later? Perhaps give a short talk on defence strategy and bring them up to date with new developments in gunnery? He was sure they would all derive great benefit from Monsieur's obvious expertise. His request was duly translated and the Frenchman expressed effusive delight to be of service. It was arranged for five o'clock in the Great Hall immediately following their four o'clock meeting at the Guildhall with the Mayor and City Chamber, which Saunders had arranged with some difficulty that morning – getting people together at such short notice was never easy.

Shortly before the appointed hour, Mayor Clarke and his officials gathered expectantly in the Guildhall. Shortly after the appointed hour, they still waited. Some time afterwards a man was sent to Rougemont Castle to fetch Captain Blewitt, but he was not in his room. At five o'clock the members of the City Chamber dispersed and Saunders sent out a search party. The mayor was irate; the officers and engineers disappointed and Saunders embarrassed. It was most disconcerting. Imagining all the dreadful things that might have happened to his valued guests, he tried to contain his anxiety. At half-past five when there was still no news and it was almost dark, he sent a man to fetch Blewitt's guards – they at least should by now have returned to the castle. They had not, neither, it seemed, could they be found. They had apparently left the city by the West Gate in the early afternoon. Their pass had seemed in order he was informed. There was no sign of Monsieur Lafitte or Oliver Blewitt. Were it not for their two horses in Rougemont's stables, the two men might never have existed.

Reflecting on this curious state of affairs, Major Saunders was forced to conclude it was a mystery he could not easily explain. When some days later an explanation presented itself to him – by which time it had come to him when and where he had last seen 'Blewitt' – he was filled with chagrin, a good deal of humiliation and, if he was honest, not a little admiration. But happily the incident passed off with no apparent ill consequences and in the ensuing momentous events people had apparently forgotten. It seemed prudent not to remind them of it thereafter.

Todd took Tawford at his word and rested a day at Plympton. Watching the bustle of the camp and enjoying the cheerful camaraderie of the men, he decided he wanted nothing more than to be a soldier. He made up his mind to return just as soon as he had delivered Tawford's message and horse to the Barton. He left the billet on Thursday morning, stopping the night at his sister's in Launceston and arriving home the following evening. It was suppertime and raining when he led Biscuit limping into the yard at Tawford Barton. He had hardly dismounted when Ned pushed past him and eyed the dun appreciatively. 'I'll see to they, you giddon up to th' house.'

'Tis the Maister's horse,' Todd said proudly. 'He told me to bring un home. Er be called "Biscuit" an er took a wound at Modbury so er's to be cared for special like, the Maister said.'

Pausing only to make sure Ned had understood the import of his words, Todd hurried across the yard to the back door to announce his arrival. With his new status as a messenger and conscious of his dignity, he was much discomfited to be greeted with a hug by Wilmot, who pulled him inside, sent Rose to fetch her ladyship and placed a tankard frothing with ale into his fist. He drained it and forgave her.

When Ellen came hurrying to the kitchen Todd transferred his white moustache to his sleeve, bowed and reached into his snapsack. The letter was creased and splotched with grease where it had nestled against the cheese his sister had given him for the journey. He tried to clean it with his thumb and only made it muckier. Embarrassed, he handed it to Ellen with a murmured apology. Her Ladyship seemed not to notice. She asked him about Master Tawford and Todd dutifully related every detail he could recall. Thanking him with a warm smile, Ellen gave Todd a half-crown and told Wilmot to buy him a new jerkin when she went next to Bideford market. Flushed with pleasure and squeaking out his gratitude, Todd, with a cocky grin at Rose, bade them goodnight and went home to tell the tale to his father.

Ellen took the letter to the parlour, opened it, smoothed it out and quickly deciphered the contents. Holding it tight to her chest she closed her eyes and uttered a quick prayer of thanksgiving. Alexander was safe and so was Adam. The news of her brother perturbed her greatly. Knowing Robert as she did Ellen was certain he had been coerced. Sequestration and imprisonment would not have been enough to turn him against the King. With what had they threatened him? She frowned. There was little point in speculating. At least she knew he was safe meantime, for the moment nothing else mattered. Please God keep him that way – all of them. She sighed. How she hated this wretched war. She wondered what Alexander intended to do about Bethan, '*leave Bethan to me*', he had written, which led her thoughts to Jennet.

For the time being she had put the child in Alexander's chamber. It was such a nice sunny room and from the window there was a lovely view of the sea. Not that Jennet seemed aware of it. In the five days since they had brought her away from Shoulsbarrow her condition had improved but little. Unresisting, she had suffered Wilmot's clucking administrations, her thin body washed, the scratches on her arms and legs salved, her hair combed and braided and one of Rose's nightgowns pulled over her head. It was much too big for her. On Wednesday she had sat up unaided and was persuaded to take a little warm bread and milk, but she remained mute and showed not a spark of interest in her surroundings.

Only with Zach did the child's haunted little face seem less tense. Ellen had seen a gentle side to the gypsy she had not hitherto suspected. This morning he had sat on the bed and talked to Jennet for an hour or more. All the while the child had gazed at him with those amazing eyes, silent and intense, but her only reaction had been yesterday when he had broached the subject of her mother. Jennet had gasped and turned her head away, body rigid, cheeks flooding with silent tears. Zach hadn't tried again. Instead he spoke of the wild things on the moor and today had brought her a cutting of flowering gorse and a spray of scarlet dog-rose hips wrapped into a posy with a stem of ivy, which he had laid on the chest by her bed. When he had left her, promising to return on the morrow, the infinite sadness etched on the child's face had made Ellen want to weep. She knew it could take many months for the mind to heal after such a shock, but it worried her nonetheless. However, as hard as it was, Ellen was determined not to treat Jennet as an invalid; she had no physical injuries. When Wilmot went shopping for Todd's jerkin she could buy the child some clothes. There was no reason why Jennet should not get dressed and come downstairs. It might help her if she was distracted by the normal goings-on in the Barton.

Ellen found she was looking forward to sharing Alexander's letter with Zach. She had invited him to stay at the Barton to be close to Jennet, but he had declined. Instead he was journeying to and from the Warren each day. He had anticipated Alexander's instruction – had already put a man into the Morgans' farm to care for the stock and finish off the thatching. The other thing he had done, which delighted Ellen's heart, was to bring the hound and whelps back with him to the Barton. They had taken up residence in the barn and she had quickly made friends with the dam. For what seemed like the first time in weeks she had been brought to helpless laughter by the antics of those energetic bundles playing in the straw.

In Exeter, as they had agreed beforehand, Tawford and Gifford made their separate ways to the underground passages, accessing them by an entrance adjacent to St Stephen's Church. Since plans to extend the aqueduct beyond St Stephens had been shelved and the water supply temporarily disrupted, there was little cause for anyone to be down here. Pollard had left a bundle of clothes and two pairs of clogs for them to find, before he, Mohun, Lyddon, and Sydenham had ridden out of the city to return by a circuitous route to a loyalist's house in the outlying village of Ide. They had been forced to leave Tawford's and Gifford's mounts behind in the Rougemont stables. It was regrettable, but taking them would have aroused suspicion. Two more would be found for them in Ide.

Given its antiquity, the vaulted passageway was in surprisingly good repair; made of local stone and big enough for a man of moderate height to stand comfortably, though Tawford's head brushed the myriad spiders' webs that clung there in the dank, musty dark.

Containing their high spirits with difficulty, the two men divested themselves of their outer garments and changed quickly and quietly by the dim glow of the rush light Pollard had left burning in a niche in the wall. With the peasants' garb, he had also left two bundles of reed for them to carry, changing their appearance effectively to that of itinerant labourers.

Suppressing a chuckle, Alexander grasped Gifford's arm. 'That was well done Hal. You almost had me convinced you are a French popinjay, never mind Major Saunders – I began to feel quite sorry for the poor bastard! I wonder how long it will take him to remember Captain Dewett's sickly prisoner and work out he and Oliver Blewitt are one and the same!'

Gifford's answering snigger turned quickly to a grimace, 'I fear Sir Ralph was right to be cautious. Exeter is much better defended than we thought and the ordinance well set up and in good condition. My adjustments to the elevation quoins won't throw them for long I fear!'

'I agree. Saunders and Bampfield have done a good job between them. Taking the city is not going to be as easy as Fortescue's men would have us believe.' Alexander looked critically at Gifford, reached across and pulled the brim of the shapeless felt hat lower over his brow. 'You'll do. You should get a move on or Lieutenant Green will be back on duty.'

Gifford grinned. 'I doubt he will recognise us like this.'

'Not us, Hal, I am not coming with you. When you get to Ide, you and Lyddon are to take all we know about Exeter's defences to Sir Ralph. If he asks where I am, tell him I am seeing a man about a boat.'

Gifford started in surprise. 'Why the change of plan?'

'I have some other business to attend to in the city. It is a personal matter.' Alexander held up his hand to stop Gifford from interrupting. 'Tell the other three they are to make contact with Acland and Basset who may need help with Captain Nutt. If they have not found him by tomorrow they are to acquire as many boats from other sources as they can – the bigger the better. Grenville may come under fire taking his men across the river to Topsham. He will sustain fewer losses if he can get them over in one go. Tell Pollard to watch for me at the Black Swan in Lympstone. If I am not there by Sunday evening they are to wait for Sir Bevill and assist. You, Lyddon and the Chichesters are to stay with Sir Ralph. God keep you, my friend.' He gave Gifford's arm a little shake. 'Now go.' Gifford hesitated, but knowing better than to question his captain, he nodded, picked up a bundle of reeds and made for the steps leading up and out of the tunnel.

Alexander waited for a few minutes after Gifford had gone then taking the light walked up the tunnel, his hat soon festooned with cobwebs. The concave floor sloped upwards in a gentle gradient and was slippery with algae where water had leaked from the pipes before the supply was cut; rats scurried and squeaked in the shadows accompanied by the indignant croaking of toads. The walls were crumbling here and there, the tunnel littered with fallen masonry, but generally it was in good repair.

When he could see daylight ahead, he extinguished the light and edged forward, listening. He could hear men talking; there were soldiers in the ditch outside. The engineers had not yet filled in the entrance then, but clearly it was guarded. He smiled grimly; the guards would not be looking for people to come *out* of the tunnel and when Hopton commenced bombardment they would be kept fully occupied. Turning he retraced his steps, feeling his way along the wall, his mind busy. He had discovered by dint of skilful questioning that as he had hoped, Bethan was not being held at Rougemont, which left the South Gate. As foul as it was, the gaol would be easier to access.

Before leaving the tunnel he sat for a while his back against the wall, staring into the darkness and devising a plan. He could not achieve it alone; needed help. Thanks to past conversations with Cobb, he knew where he would most likely find it. Picking up the other bundle of reeds he turned towards the steps.

22

Friday 18th November, 1642

The head turnkey at the South Gate Gaol had been expecting Matthew to arrive since first light as usual and it was now getting on for mid-morning. The old man and his son brought the parish coffins and bolts of calico winding sheet to the gaol and took away the unclaimed bodies for burial in Bartholomew's Yard, a grassy haven in the northwest corner of Exeter, used as a cemetery since the Cathedral Yard was declared full to bursting five years ago. Bartholomew's lay just inside the city walls in an area once known as 'Britayne', named, it was said, for the Britons who lived hereabouts in ancient times and who, according to old Matthew, were here still! After only five years, the Yard already billowed with grave mounds and teemed with restless spirits.

Whenever there was an outbreak of gaol fever in the South Gate – more often than not in this godforsaken place – Matthew and his son came most every day. Condemned men were always cheating the hangman, though from the look of them hanging might be kinder. The turnkey did not dwell on it – the miserable buggers were destined to burn in hell either way.

When Matthew eventually arrived, he had a stranger with him; ill favoured he was too, carroty-haired, his pasty face a mass of pimples, a nasty looking boil on his chin and a patch over his eye.

Giving the stranger the once-over, the turnkey nodded up at Matthew. 'You're late. What's up? Where's Luke today?'

'He's took sick and a lot 'o trouble I've 'ad about it too, runnin' around for someone else to help me.' The old man sniffed. 'I'd do it on me own but I can't 'ardly, not at my age. An I don't feel too good myself neither.' He gestured with his thumb at the stranger. 'This ere's Isaac. He'll be helpin' me a day or two till Luke be on his feet again. What you got for us?' He sneezed vigorously.

The turnkey was used to the old man's grumbling, but just in case he had cause for once, kept his distance. 'Four signed off and two waiting for the coroner, one a woman – hardly bin ere five minutes too.'

Isaac lifted his head and stared intently at the turnkey, but said nothing.

'A woman?' Matthew looked curious.

'Aye, and her babe; came in last week unwed and great with child – wanton hussy – she were caught thieving from her mistress.'

Matthew spat on his hands. 'Aye, well, 'tis the Lord's justice.' He shook the reins and the cart creaked forward into the yard.

Isaac, sitting on a coffin in the back of the cart, looked up one-eyed at the ancient bastion of stonework. There were two round towers on either side of the deep arched gateway. In one a small door opened to a flight of steps, which ascended past a storeroom to the apartments over the arch. Here the coroner had an office and the city officials a meeting room. Did they care to peer through the arrow-slits they would come face to face with St George – though the statue carved over the gates was now so weathered the saint's face was a featureless blob, and the dragon he was in the act of decapitating more closely resembled an earthworm. On the other side of the archway was a lodge for the head turnkey and his two deputies, and the guardroom. The steps in each tower spiralled up from the dungeons to castellated ramparts and off each landing were tiny windowless cells where the more dangerous prisoners were held. The gaol was notoriously harsh. Few of the felons incarcerated here for any length of time survived. Of those who did many were rendered witless by the experience.

The dead were carried from their cells by two of their fellow prisoners selected at random by the turnkey's deputy, chained together by the ankles and watched by two armed guards. They took the bodies to the storeroom, where two hags employed for the purpose wound into shrouds those unfortunate wretches who had no next of kin to claim them. Once signed off by the coroner – a formality, he rarely inspected the dead – they were taken away in re-usable coffins to be checked in by the parish clerk and buried in their winding sheets, often by the sexton and his helpers, who not only dug the graves, but stood in as pall bearers. The parish priest sometimes said a few words, but more usually declined since there was none to pay him his fee.

As the cart rolled to a stop in the yard, the turnkey unlocked the storeroom door. It was a foul and risky business this; gaol fever was not selective. He stood well back jangling his keys while Matthew and his helper got on with it. Within half an hour, the cart was loaded. Matthew huffed onto his seat and took up the reins. 'What about the woman and her babe?'

'The coroner's gone for today. They'll wait on the morrow. There'll be some more by then I daresay.'

'Aye.' Matthew nodded. 'On the morrow then.' He shook the reins and the cart rumbled away to deliver its grisly load to the sexton in St Bartholomew's Yard.

Ellen was seriously concerned. Far from being well enough to come downstairs, Jennet seemed to be slipping away. Though she had drunk a small cup of warmed milk, she had refused the food Rose carried up to her and turned her face away when Wilmot had tried to spoon it down her throat. Nor had she shown any interest in the new gown selected for her in Bideford, but had mutely resisted all attempts to persuade her to leave her bed, curling up her legs and sticking her thumb in her mouth like an infant. The child was painfully thin, her cheekbones seemed more prominent, her eyes huge in dark circles. She was apparently not as young as Ellen had at first thought, for on top of everything else and despite the trauma, Jennet's flux was upon her. Giving her some tincture of willow bark to ease her discomfort, this morning Ellen had lingered, sitting on the bed talking about the mischief Alexander used to get up to as a boy, hoping against hope it might bring a spark of interest, but nothing she said made any difference. Jennet's face was devoid of expression.

At length Ellen gave up and went downstairs, remembering as she did so how Blue, forbidden the bedchambers, used to wait for her on the bottom tread and how often she had almost broken her neck as a result. How she missed him. As she found herself out of habit stepping high over his imaginary form she was struck suddenly by an idea.

Hurrying to the barn Ellen selected the boldest of the pups, carried it plump and wriggling to Alexander's bedchamber and placed it carefully on the bed. With its tiny tail circling like wind sails it squirmed towards the pillow, snuffled in Jennet's hair, sat on her face and deposited little wet kisses on her nose. With a mewing cry the child's arms came round it, she squeezed it tightly to her, held it away and looked at it, then tentatively she smiled.

The transformation took Ellen's breath away. Kicking herself for not having thought of this before, she put her fingers to her lips, whispered, 'Don't tell Wilmot!' and with a conspiratorial smile straightened the bedcovers. As she turned to go, the child was holding the pup close, her face buried in its silken coat, her chest heaving. Instinctively Ellen knew Jennet needed to give vent to her grief in solitude, had barely reached the top of the stairs before she heard the muffled, heartrending sobs.

Ellen ached with compassion and yet was relieved: the child was weeping normally at last and would be the better for it. She had to face her loss before she could even begin to come to terms with it. Only then could Ellen explore the manner of Morgan's death and help Jennet understand what she had seen. It wasn't going to happen overnight, but this was a start. Wanting to share the good news with Zach, Ellen waited impatiently.

When he arrived she almost pulled him into the parlour. First she told him about Jennet and watched his face light up with a slow smile. Then she told him what Alexander had written and Zach's smile turned to a worried frown. 'They mean to attack Exeter?'

'So it would seem.'

'When, did he say?'

'Within the next few days he said – that was four days ago – it might be happening as we speak.'

Zach shook his head. 'The army can only go at the pace of the foot and the ordinance will slow them down. It will take them the best part of a week to journey from Plympton, and then they will have to dig in outside Exeter. I would be surprised if they could mount an attack before Sunday at the earliest.'

'But Alexander is already there. Sir Ralph sent him ahead to spy out the defences. He writes that he will seek news of Bethan at the same time.' Ellen looked at Zach in consternation. 'What can he possibly do for her in the circumstances?' She bit her lip. 'I was hoping he might persuade someone in authority to plead for her, but obviously he can't do that now.'

'What exactly does he say?'

'He just says "Leave Bethan to me" – nothing more.'

Zach nodded, wrinkling his brow. 'Master Tawford will have a plan, of that you can be sure. And I rather doubt it will have anything to do with pleading!'

Ellen raised her hands to her mouth as she took in the

implication of Zach's words. 'You think he will try to break her out of gaol?' She gasped in agitation. 'Dear God, he will be killed or captured. And what of his men? Will they help him?'

Zach looked at Ellen thoughtfully. 'He will do nothing to risk his men on this I think, nor will he jeopardise Sir Ralph Hopton's plans. We can be fairly sure he will choose to operate alone. If he means to get Bethan out he will use trickery. He may be hoping for an opportunity while the city is under attack.' Zach seized Ellen's fluttering fingers and looked into her eyes. 'Don't distress yourself, Lady Ellen. Tawford is a clever young rascal. If anyone can do it, he can and it may be Bethan's only chance.' Suddenly embarrassed, Zach released her hands.

She moved away from him her eyes bright with tears, reached out to steady herself on the back of the settle, whispered, 'Yes, I suppose you may be right. Oh Zach, what will become of him?'

His eyes crinkled as he smiled at her. 'They'll have to get up early to catch that one, lass – 'tis why I call him Lapwing, remember? Better than anyone I know at deceiving – better even than Cobb. He shuffled his feet awkwardly, distressed by her tears. 'There now, don't weep, my lady. I will go to Exeter and see what I can find out. I might be able to help him – if nothing else I can watch his back. At the very least I can bring you news.'

Ellen gazed at him, her tears forgotten. 'No, Zach! You must not. It is too dangerous – you will be caught up in the fighting.'

He shrugged. 'So I may. But I would rather that than sit around here wondering if I might have made a difference to Bethan.'

Ellen looked at him with ill-concealed curiosity. She was aware from the way Zach had spoken of Jennet's mother that he had a fondness for her, but now she wondered if his feelings ran deeper than that and the thought took her aback. But why should it? Zach was clearly a sensitive man and as far as she knew he had no other attachment. 'You are prepared to risk your life for Bethan?'

He flushed. 'Aye, for Bethan and for Jennet – and for Tawford too.'

Ellen crossed the room to him and as she had done once before, kissed him gently on the cheek. 'And for me too I daresay,' she murmured. 'Then selfishly I will not try to dissuade you. You're a good man, Zach. I pray God will keep you safe.'

In St Bartholomew's Yard, his head hot and itching beneath the ginger wig, Alexander gave Matthew a gold crown, being one third of the money they had agreed; he would get the rest when the job was done. Having helped the old man unload the cart, he made his way back across Exeter to the cellar of a condemned house in St Stephens, where a group of six strolling players had taken up temporary residence. He had eventually tracked them down last night after engaging in a seemingly innocent conversation with a potboy at the Bear Inn. One of the players he knew by repute; a skilful tumbler by the name of 'Jelly', the friend of a friend of Cobb's – who wasn't!

As soon as Alexander had made himself known to them, the players welcomed him with the open-handedness characteristic of those who have little to share. These were grim times for entertainers and though they continued to risk the wrath of the constable, narrowly avoiding arrest on more than one occasion for disturbing the peace and encouraging the pursuit of sinful pleasures – 'We're not so much strolling as running these days,' they told Alexander with wry smiles – the six young men were forced to supplement their income by picking up casual labour when and where they could. Only those jobs nobody else wanted were easily come by, which gave the players a working knowledge of, among other things, piss pots and close stools – urine was highly sought after for the making of gunpowder, especially now – offal tubs, middens, gutters and graveyards: the odours in the cellar were indescribable.

In the course of the evening Alexander had discovered that one of the players – the one they called 'Cat'- had been convicted of thieving the year before and was held for a short time in the South Gate Gaol – a short time only because he had escaped. He always landed on his feet, Jelly told Alexander with a smile, hence his name, though Cat was fast running out of lives! Hardly able to believe this stroke of good fortune, by the time Alexander rested his head he knew the layout and daily routine of the gaol, as importantly, who could be bribed. As he drifted into sleep that night, he remembered someone telling him he had the luck of the Devil – who was that? He wondered idly what he might be asked to pay for it.

Cat went off first thing to suborn Matthew. It had not been difficult – his son would have settled for a few days off if the truth were told – it was doubtful if either of them had ever seen a gold crown, never mind possessed one. He had promised them three! While Cat was gone, Jelly rummaged in the players' box of tricks and set to work on Alexander's appearance: lightened his skin with powdered lead, used hide glue to fix the ginger wig and with great artistry and considerable amusement, covered Alexander's face with pimples of red cinnabar, fashioning with beeswax and gum a suppurating boil on his dimpled chin. To hide the puckered eyelid, he cut out a patch from an old felt hat and tied it on with catgut. 'There! Now not even your own mother would recognise you.' Grinning, Jelly had stood back to admire his handiwork quite unaware of the effect of his words on his subject.

By the time Alexander was ready, Cat had returned to tell him 'Isaac' was expected and he had better cut along as

Matthew was waiting to leave for the gaol. Cat next went to see what could be done to bribe the deputy turnkey, warning he would not be bought cheaply, but having already assisted Cat's own escape, was wide open to blackmail and could hardly refuse. The hags, he explained with a wink, would give no trouble!

True to his word, Cat returned that afternoon with news that the turnkey had agreed, though had demanded two gold sovereigns, but the hags were content with a couple of groats each, which was just as well – Alexander's purse was fast getting lighter.

'They'll have drunk it afore the day is out,' Cat grinned. 'Your woman is in one of the tower cells. They were chary of putting her in the dungeon with the rest, what with her being a witch an all. The deputy turnkey will tell her to play dead on the morrow. It'll have to be then because he's already done the rounds for today, but on Saturdays he does them late then goes off duty till Monday morning, and he won't change his routine lest it arouses suspicion. So you'll not get her out on the morrow I fear. He says for the money he'll get her into the storeroom before he goes, but it's no odds to him if she lives or dies and we can take it or leave it. I've told him we'll take it. I dare not try bribing the other deputy; he's not the sort to be bought. I know it's not ideal because Matthew never goes into the gaol on Sundays, which means your witch will have to lie two nights with the dead instead of one, but at least nobody will pay her much mind once she's in the storeroom.' Cat shuddered. 'There are three others with the fever not expected to last above a day, so she'll not want for company! Rather her than me, but it's the price she'll have to pay. I'm sorry; it's the best I could do. You'll just have to take in some food and drink for her to find when you go on the morrow – and hope she survives the ordeal.'

Alexander nodded, frowning. It was far from ideal. He had hoped to take Bethan out when he went with Matthew on the morrow, not only to minimise the horrifying time she must wait with the cadavers, but also, by Sunday the city would have got wind of Hopton's approach. Routines in the gaol may well be disrupted and the guards watchful and jumpy, but it seemed there was no alternative. He shrugged. 'And the hags?'

'They'll put her in a shroud first thing Monday, then it's up to the coroner, but he's not usually tardy with his paperwork when there's fever about.'

Thanking Cat, Alexander delved into his purse, but the player shook his head and grinned. 'You keep it, my friend. I'd as soon you owed me in kind – it might be useful one day, what with me running out of lives an' all!'

That night under cover of darkness, his face clean of makeup, but still wearing the wig and eye patch, Alexander made his way back to the tunnel under St Stephens. Feeling for his soldier's clothes and boots, he quickly changed, picked up the steel plates, hesitated, decided against them. Not many men in Exeter's Trained Bands had yet been issued with armour – he would stand out like a sore thumb. He buckled on his sword, took off the eye patch, rolled it into the smock and shoved them under his coat. He would have to carry the clogs.

With his hand on the tunnel wall he walked up the passageway, passed under the city walls and out into the ditch. A great pile of rubble had been tipped there – he stumbled, all but fell over it – by tomorrow the entrance would be filled in. Alexander listened, waiting for the challenge, a vulgar excuse springing to his lips concerning a doxy in the suburbs and his need to get out of the city unseen by his sergeant – and his wife! But though he could hear the low rumble of voices, none shouted. The moon had waned, it was very dark tonight and as he had suspected, the guards were not paying much attention to what was going on behind them. When news came of Hopton's approach it would be a different story – their heads would be swivelling then.

Like a wraith Alexander crept along the ditch until he saw

the four guards; they were crouched by a fire, a flaming brand stuck in the earth beside them, a pool of light flickering in the ditch. From their muttered laughter and curses he guessed they were rolling dice. He backed away. Flattening himself against the earth and rubble of the bank, he clamped the clogs under his arm and started to climb. One of the guards shouted. Alexander froze. Seconds later there was a guffaw of laughter: someone had thrown a six. He relaxed. Once out of the ditch he started to run.

Bent almost double Alexander ran beside the bank, stopping from time to time to ease his back and get his bearings. As he had expected, most of the soldiers were concentrated in the ditches outside the South and West gates, their torches and fires lighting up the night. Praying the guards on the ramparts would be looking into the distance rather than beneath their noses, he left the protecting cover of the bank and set off at a tangent towards the river. It was both a blessing and a curse that the weather had closed in; neither moon nor stars to light his way. Fortunately he knew the way and there was a strong wind, which covered the noises he made each time he missed his footing and stumbled in the darkness. He needed a boat. There was a canal that cut from the quay by the Water Gate to below the weirs on the river, but he dared not go there. Though not much used – most of the ships offloaded their merchandise at Topsham and brought it by road to the city – it would be well guarded. He had no excuse to be on the canal, if he were spotted there he would likely be taken for a spy or a deserter and shot either way. With this grim thought in mind, Alexander set off to walk the three miles to Topsham.

The suburbs, where they had not been cleared as part of the defences, were deserted. Even the alehouses were closed and shuttered. Alexander saw not a soul and was thankful for it. It was the same at Topsham, though he did not doubt that mariners would soon be spilling out of the inns by the quay under the nervous gaze of the Watch. He avoided it and made for the church. Beneath the tossing branches of an ancient yew he left his smock and clogs then felt his way through the graveyard to the wall. On the other side was a steep drop to the foreshore. Unbuckling his sword he threw it down and climbed after it. At the bottom he peered into the blackness wishing there were just a glimmer of starlight, but the sky was thickly overcast. Above the noise of the wind he caught the sound of water slapping on wood. His feet sliding and sticking in the stinking mud of the estuary, he waded towards the sound. A small rowboat; exactly what he needed. Heaving himself aboard he picked up the oars and slid them into the rowlocks. The tide was on the ebb and the going was easy.

There was nobody about in Lympstone and few of the cottages showed any light. Alexander supposed it must be quite late; he had no idea how long it had taken him to get here.

It was quiet in the Black Swan. On a bench seat by the fire were three men, one of them wearing the leather apron of the tapster. They looked up in silence as Alexander pushed open the door. Their expressions, he noted, were both fearful and sullen. They disliked strangers, even if they were Parliament's soldiers. On the other side of the room Pollard and Sydenham were seated at a table in a wavering pool of candlelight. As they jumped up grinning to welcome him he silenced them with a warning shake of his head and beckoning, backed out of the door. The locals looked relieved to see he was not staying. He waited for the two men to follow and led them some distance away until he was sure they would not be overheard.

'I am not at all sure those ginger locks favour you,' Pollard murmured.

'You haven't seen the worst of it.' Alexander scratched his head; it felt hot and uncomfortable under Jelly's wig and he was sweating so much he feared the glue would dissolve. 'Did you find Captain Nutt? Where are the others?'

'Yes. They've got him aboard the *Porpoise*. She's a brig; two-masted, square-rigged and carrying sail fore-and-aft with gaff and boom. She's lying off Exmouth. Had the devil's own job to get Nutt sober – well, relatively sober, it'd take a week – we've poured so much salt water down his neck he's goose-turd-green, poor sod. We decided it was best to keep him from going back ashore.'

Alexander grinned. 'He'll live. Has he got enough men to crew her?'

'Aye – enough to sweep her if they have to and they'll manage on the flood. They're going to bring her up as far as Powderham on the morning tide and wait there until someone brings us news of Grenville.'

'Good. Whatever you do make Nutt understand that once Grenville's men are over the river he is to keep the boat lying off Topsham. The city is much better defended than we'd been led to believe. If Grenville is forced to retreat he'll have need of her. And for God's sake don't let Nutt or his crew drink anything stronger than water. You can tell the old barg-pitcher from me that I'll personally keelhaul him if he doesn't stay sober till his work is done.'

'You're not coming with us?'

'No. I am returning to Exeter.' He could hardly see their faces, but he knew from their silence they were unpleasantly surprised.

Sydenham grunted. 'This personal business of yours – it is not yet finished? Gifford told us.'

Alexander raised an eyebrow. 'Did he now.'

'Can we not help you?'

'No, I would prefer to keep it personal, thank you.'

'You must surely know you can trust us?' Sydenham sounded offended.

'It is not a question of trust, Francis. I do not want your help in this and that being so there is no need for you to know about it. Find some safe cover and wait for Grenville. That's an order. I'll catch up with you as soon as I can.'

Sydenham shrugged. 'As you will.'

They walked with him in silence to the foreshore, treading softly over the shingle to where he'd left the boat. In turn he gripped each man by the hand. 'Until we meet again, God be with you and don't forget to keep your heads down. Gifford has fiddled with the gun alignments – there is no knowing which way the bastards' balls will fall!'

Grinning at the deliberate ambiguity, they helped him push off. The tide was still on the ebb and it was hard work going back. He left the boat as near as he could to the foreshore and climbed into the churchyard to retrieve his clothes. He then made his way into the church. There was no candle burning; the place was pitch black. By feel he changed his clothes and put on his eye patch, felt for a pew and using his leather coat as a cushion, made himself as comfortable as he could and set himself to wait.

He woke with a start, cold as ice and stiff as a board. It was still dark. Leaving his coat and boots under the pew with his sword – regrettable, but no peasant carried a blade – he let himself out of the church and set off to walk to Exeter. His plan was to mingle with the traffic that streamed into the city when the West Gate was opened at dawn. Pulling his hat well down over his face he hoped fervently that Lieutenant Green was not on duty on the bridge. It was a risk he would have to take since getting back in by the tunnel was a greater one.

Happily Green was nowhere to be seen as Alexander tagged onto a group of day labourers and walked into Exeter. He went quickly to the cellar in St Stephens and re-applied his makeup. None of the players was there but on the table they had left him bread, cheese and a jug of small beer, which he swallowed gratefully. Somebody, presumably Cat, had thought to leave some food wrapped in a cloth, together with a leather bottle of what he guessed to be cider. Picking them up and conscious of the time, he hurried to Matthew's house in Milk Street, not so much a street as a ramshackle arrangement of cow-sheds, cottages and milk sellers' shops, where the old man rented a room for himself and his son and a shed for his horse and cart. Matthew was waiting for him and looked hard done by. 'You'm late. Us thought you'd changed your mind,' he grumbled.

The visit to the gaol passed off as it had before, except today Alexander secreted the food and drink into the storeroom and tucked it out of sight on a ledge behind the door where the hags kept their shears, needles and thread. Even as he did so, he knew the rats would most likely get to it before Bethan did – but at least she would have the drink. He could only hope she was strong enough not to lose her wits and that the Lord would keep her safe from infection. There was nothing more he could do but pray.

It did not take them long to load the cart; there was only one other body beside the woman and the pitiful tiny bundle that was her babe. Bleakly Alexander did what he had to do and was never more thankful than to leave the place. They were not expected back until Monday.

With nothing better to do for the remainder of the day but wait, he returned to the cellar and got steadily drunk. When the players came home from work he set himself to entertain them. Towards mid-evening they ran dry. With a beatific smile, Alexander held his purse upside down and shook out the last of his coins – apart from his reserve, which he had wisely stowed away lest he forget he still had bribes to pay. They drew lots and Jelly lost. He duly went off to purchase more supplies, came back rolling a cask of cider, a keg of wine hoisted on his shoulder and his face split from ear to ear. 'Look what I found loitering outside the Bear!'

Looking up, Alexander squinted, shook his head, rubbed his eyes and tried again. It took him several goes to identify with foolish delight Zach's several beaming faces. For the remainder of the evening they got out the Tarot cards and sang increasingly inventive ribald songs. None of them remembered the words next day.

The city was full of churches. Alexander woke to the sound of bells, which the Puritans had not yet managed to still. It was extremely unpleasant. He pulled himself from prone on the floor into a crouch and stayed there for a moment, his head in his hands, wondering what the hell he had been drinking that had made him blind. It slowly dawned on him that he was still wearing Jelly's wig and it had slipped over his face. He pulled it off and levered himself to his feet, uncomfortably aware of three things: a pressing need to empty his bladder, a raging thirst, and five men standing looking at him. They were dressed in relatively clean black coats and each wore a black sugar-loaf hat – they were Puritans – no, they were not, Puritans did not grin. For a moment Alexander was convinced he was still asleep and dreaming. Jelly spoke first.

'We assumed you would not wish to come with us to morning service so we did not wake you. Help yourselves to bread and beer, we will say a prayer for you – you look as if you need one! We will be back later. Cat has gone to find us meat pie for dinner.' So saying, Jelly straightened his face and led the way as they filed solemnly out of the door and closed it behind them.

Bemusedly, Alexander looked around the room. Zach was curled up motionless on the floor against the wall. Zach! Dimly it came back to him. He moved, winced and pressed his fingertips into his eyes. At last the bells stopped ringing. Stirring Zach with his foot and getting no response, Alexander climbed the steps out of the cellar. The house was at the end of a row that had been partially destroyed by fire. It had escaped the worst of the flames; the walls were still standing, but most of the roof and the upper floors had collapsed inwards. Everywhere was littered with scorched timbers and chunks of lathe and plaster. He negotiated his way to the small yard at the back, to the open drain they used as a privy. Moments later, feeling decidedly more comfortable, he splashed water over his face from the rain butt against the wall and returned to the cellar. When the houses were knocked down to make way for re-building, the players would have to look for somewhere else, Jelly had told him. Meantime, though it was a comfortless place, there was no rent to pay and they were grateful for a safe haven while it lasted. They slept on straw pallets on the floor; there was a table, two cupboards, a chest and not much else. Each piece was falling apart having been rescued from some rubbish tip or another. The cellar was cold and dark – the only natural light came from gratings at ceiling height in the front wall. It was also very damp. How the players could be so cheerful about it Alexander could not fathom.

Eventually, helped by a dowsing of rainwater, Zach roused himself and the two men talked. The gypsy had left his horse at an inn in St Davids and come into the city through the North Gate. He had arrived just before they closed it, convincing the guards he was but a poor labourer visiting his mother who had been taken sick. There had been no trouble getting in.

Alexander was appalled to hear the full story of what had happened to the Morgans, but the manner of Jennet's rescue made him smile. He could almost feel sympathy for Jeptha Lythall. When Zach came to the end of his tale, Alexander in turn outlined the state of play in Cornwall, ending with a description of Gifford's 'Monsieur Lafitte' and their guided tour about the city's defences, and it was Zach's turn to smile. He then listened carefully to Alexander's plan to extricate Bethan, which now – thankfully – included him.

When the players eventually returned they had news. Scouts had come in with reports that the enemy had been sighted. The city was abuzz with it. The Royalists were but eight miles to the southwest at Dunsford. The townsfolk were nervous; the soldiers too, though they did not admit to it. It was still not certain if Hopton planned to attack Exeter. There were rumours he meant to march his Cornishmen right on by and was on his way to Oxford to join the King. Jelly had other news: a regiment of foot soldiers had come in this morning by the East Gate to help defend the city; they were under the command of a Colonel John Wear. Alexander knew the name. Wear had been attached to Bedford's army at Sherborne.

Alexander, Zach and the players spent the rest of the day quietly, enjoyed the food Cat brought triumphantly home, too hungry to mind that the pie was stale and the windfall apples bruised. After they had eaten they dozed and conversed, played cards and dozed again. In the early evening Jelly and Zach went out to see if there was any further news. There was: Hopton's vanguard had been sighted approaching Alphington and the main army was but three miles behind.

A Royalist messenger had come in under a white flag: Sir Ralph Hopton urged the city to surrender peaceably, for he had no wish to spill Exeter's blood in this unnatural war. There was now no question of his intent. All patrols had been called in, the guards doubled on the South and West Gates and the Exe Bridge, and the Mayor had called an emergency meeting of the City Chamber. Not one member was in favour of surrender. A defiant message had gone back to Hopton to the effect that he and his Cavaliers should quickly depart from Exeter's walls or they would be sorry.

Alexander knew Sir Ralph would be disappointed – his desire to avoid confrontation and spare lives was sincere and typical of the man. Had Exeter been less well defended the Mayor might have taken advantage of Hopton's humanitarian stance and surrendered the city. As it was, Alexander, who knew Hopton would attempt to take Exeter by force, had begun to doubt he would succeed.

For the moment, however, he had other things on his mind: there was no way of knowing if the deputy turnkey had held to his word. Alexander tried not to imagine how it must be for Bethan if he had – or worse, if he had not. Equally, there was no way of knowing how the news would affect his plans, could only hope the collection of the dead from South Gate Gaol would proceed as usual.

Both Zach and Alexander knew that tomorrow, one way or another, they intended to bring Bethan away or die in the attempt. They may die anyway, of course; there might be crossfire to contend with.

It was a sobering thought on which to go to sleep.

23

Monday 21st November, 1642

The small hurt Robert took at Edgehill was in fact a glancing sword cut to his upper arm. In his efforts to avoid killing anyone and careless of his own safety he had been unhorsed when Prince Rupert's cavalry charged, sweeping all before them. He was not aware as he fell, lost his helmet and was struck unconscious by his mount's flailing hooves, that the Royalist officer had recognised him and deflected the stroke. Consequently the cut was not as deep as it might have been, but for a while it had bled profusely. Though not seriously wounded, when he came to, Robert had stayed where he was wrestling with his conscience as the battle veered away from him. He lay there for much of the day, unable to comprehend the terrible carnage, blocking his ears to the groans and screams of the dying. By dusk, concussed, dehydrated and weak from loss of blood, his clothes stiff with frost, he was dimly aware of a man bending over him. Not wishing to be taken for dead and stripped naked, for looters were already at work in the fading light, he had struggled to move. Seeing he was alive the trooper had helped him to his feet and taken him back to the surgeons. Robert did not know the man, a well-favoured, dark-bearded fellow, his clothes splashed and splattered with gore. Neither did he notice the trooper turn to stare as he gave his name and that of his commanding officer to the weary, blood-drenched surgeon, who stitched him up, gave him aqua vitae and sent him back to his regiment. But by then, the Earl of Essex had ordered disengagement and both sides were leaving the field.

Had Robert's wound not festered he would by now be on his way to Surrey to attack Farnham Castle with Sir William Waller – now being dubbed William the Conqueror by his admiring soldiers – to whose regiment he had been attached. As it was, a few days after the battle he was loaded into a wagon and taken with other severely wounded men to a makeshift military hospital in London. That he survived the journey at all was due largely to the fact that his throbbing, swollen arm quite soon burst open, the poison draining out of him in a sickening stench of pus, but by then he was fevered and remembered little of it, only that he had been faintly surprised to recognise, riding beside the wagon, the trooper who had helped him from the field.

The hospital physician – who rarely sullied his own hands but deigned to instruct the nursing staff – had prescribed maggots. After their work was done, the wound was to be cleansed daily with a seethe of sage and garlic in honey and vinegar, and tightly bound. Whether this treatment would have effected a cure was never discovered for within a day of Robert's arrival the news was quite naturally brought to his betrothed, the Lady Arabella Béjart. As soon as she received it, she contacted Cobb and set arrangements in hand to have Lord Westley removed to his lodgings. That done, she had a porter carry various of her belongings and a truckle bed to St Martin's Lane where, careless of her reputation, she moved in to nurse the patient. Bella had a good deal of experience in tending sword cuts and none of it included the deliberate application of maggots. She had chosen Lord Westley's lodgings rather than her own in order to remove herself from the caring but inquisitive eyes of Sara Voysin and Lady Bath. Bella doubted she could maintain the pretence under close observation for any length of time, and it was still necessary. Even more so now she had discovered with whom the widowed Anne Dynam had associated in the past.

Cobb, having carefully considered the situation, had reasoned there was little point in sending for Ellen. She would not be able to get here before the crisis of Lord Westley's condition was reached, and if he survived it they would take him home to Marley Court – indeed, would take him home whether he survived it or not. The gypsy did, however, despatch a message to Tawford, along with various other items of news, including what Bella had told him concerning Anne Dynam. That done he made sure the widow was watched with even greater vigilance, reinstated the beggars in St Martin's Lane and went there thrice daily to see to Lord Westley's personal needs and whatever else Bella needed him to do. She sent him frequently to the apothecary.

Bella nursed Robert with calm efficiency, not leaving his side as he tossed and turned, laying cloths soaked in lavender water on his brow, soothing him when he cried out and holding his hands away from the wound, which she cleansed with oil of sage – old-fashioned maybe, but it had worked well for her in the past – and left open to the air. To bring down his fever she spoon-fed him an infusion of feverfew and camomile. Much of what he said was unintelligible, but at the height of his fever he repeatedly cried out two names. The next day she broached this with Cobb.

'Who is "Eithne"? His mistress? He keeps calling for her. Perhaps we should send for her? He calls for Alexander too, but even supposing he was able, the lapwing will not come.'

Cobb, looking a little shocked, had replied curtly. 'I do not know anyone of that name and Lord Westley does not have a mistress. As far as I am aware he has not had a woman since his wife died. He was most probably calling for Ellen and you misheard.'

Bella shrugged. Perhaps he was right, Robert's cries had been strangled and indistinct, but attuned as she was to picking up signals, she had noticed Cobb did not meet her eyes and wondered why, decided she was probably being overly sensitive. The crisis passed, the cries ceased and she thought no more about it.

Ten days after Cobb had sent the message to Cornwall he learned his messenger had been killed in crossfire outside Reading. Tawford, then, remained unaware of his guardian's condition, but by then Lord Westley was on the mend.

News of Robert's wounding inevitably reached the ears of Anne Dynam. Not daring to hope for the worst, she called for a chair intent on finding out for herself how bad it was. Cobb's tailing beggar had to run to keep up with the puffing chairmen. He watched the woman alight in St Martin's Lane and sent his runner to the Mermaid to find Cobb.

Anne Dynam ascended the stairs to Westley's door and waited to be admitted. Both women were momentarily speechless as they came face to face, but both were past masters at dissembling. It was Bella who broke the silence.

'My Lady, how kind of you to call in person, Lord Westley will be delighted when he learns of it, but I fear he is not yet well enough to receive visitors. Perhaps I could send to let you know when he is stronger?'

Brushing her aside the widow swept into the room in a rustle of silk. She wasted no time on preliminaries. 'He will live?' She looked towards the bedchamber, but the door was closed and Bella, more than a head taller than she, had swiftly positioned herself in front of it.

'I do not wish him disturbed. As I said, he is not yet strong enough for visitors, not even you. But yes, he has survived the crisis and will recover with rest and nursing. I am sure you must be as happy and relieved as I.'

'I doubt it,' the widow snapped. But disappointed as she was, she realised not much was to be gained by antagonising this horse-faced woman. Nor was she prepared to enter into an unseemly tussle to access the bedchamber. She was, however, unable to resist looking pointedly at Bella's waistline. 'I understand you are to be congratulated?' She looked haughtily around the room, saw the truckle bed pushed against a wall, the bundle of Bella's clothes and personal belongings scattered over various surfaces, gasped as she took in the implication.

'Though now I think of it, perhaps congratulations are a little premature. You are staying here? Alone with my stepson? But my dear, have you no care for your reputation? Or are the morals of the French aristocracy so lacking you are not aware of the impropriety? I should warn you, we do things differently in England. I fear you will be dismissed as a wanton. Lord Westley will not be moved to wed you, my dear. He would not wish to wed a wanton, however skilled she is at... ahem, nursing.' She gave a mocking smile. 'It seems you are destined to bring yet another Dynam bastard into this cruel world. How unfortunate.'

Bella gazed at her coldly. 'Why do you bait me, Madam? Can it be you are jealous of Lord Westley's happiness? Or is it just my nationality that offends you?'

Aware of her mistake, the widow attempted to retrieve the situation. 'I hasten to assure you I have only your best interests at heart, Mistress Béjart.' Her voice broke. She dabbed delicately at her eyes with a gloved finger. 'And of course those of my poor, dear stepson. My intention was only to caution you, my dear, not as you say, bait you. Forgive me if I have given that impression. I am only disappointed that I shall not after all have occasion to welcome you into the family as my daughter.'

Bella gurgled with laughter in sheer delight at the woman's effrontery. 'Then you will be pleased to know Lord Westley cares even less about my reputation than I, My Lady. We will indeed be wed, though 'tis true it will have to be postponed until he is stronger.' She laid her hands provocatively on her stomach and looked down. 'And since you have so indelicately pointed it out, I can assure you the ceremony will be in good time for there to be no question of our child's legitimacy.' She lifted her head and smiled. 'So, Madam, your disappointment is misplaced. I shall be your daughter after all. Does that not please you? Now, if you will forgive me, much as I would like to, I regret I do not have time to discuss it further just now.

Be so good as to take your leave. And in future perhaps you will send warning of your intention to call that I may be better prepared to receive you?'

The widow gasped and stared at her for a moment, but Bella coolly held her gaze. Anne Dynam knew when she was beaten and she did not like it one bit. Resolved to make the Frenchwoman pay for her insolence, she nodded, gathered up her skirts and swept from the room without a backward glance.

From across the street James Dewett saw her leave and followed.

In the aftermath of Edgehill Dewett's regiment had been detailed to search for wounded and at the same time discourage looting – a fool's errand; might as well try to stop a tidal wave. It had been sheer chance he had stumbled over Robert Dynam, though at the time had not known it was he. Overhearing the name in the surgeon's tent had jolted him. Not because the man had sided with Parliament – many families were divided in this war, and not always on principle. It was considered prudent by some to have at least one member of the family on the winning side. No; his surprise had been because of all the names he might have heard, that one had been the least expected. While he had fantasised about meeting his adversary in battle he knew it was unlikely while Sir Ralph Hopton was in Cornwall. But that would not always be so. It was inevitable that one day they would meet for he, James Dewett, would make damned sure of it.

He was elated by his good fortune; had no doubt at all that the father would lead him to the son and he was not going to let Robert Dynam out of his sight, which was why he had volunteered to escort the wounded to London and thereafter kept a careful, seemingly casual eye on the comings and goings in St Martin's Lane.

Watching the handsome woman leave Westley's rooms, Dewett followed her chair to Arundel Street and made a careful note of the address. He spent the next two hours making discreet enquiries as to her identity. What he discovered exceeded his expectations. He had assumed she was Westley's mistress. To have found yet another member of the Dynam family increased his elation to the point where he could almost taste it. He would have no difficulty in browbeating a woman. Maybe he could use her to bring his quarry to London. He presented himself at the door in the late afternoon and informed the manservant that he was enquiring after Alexander Dynam of Tawford and would Her Ladyship be kind enough to receive him?

She most certainly would. Anne Dynam had been tempted by Tawford's proposition concerning his father, but after much thought had decided to go with her instincts. Whether or not the bastard boy wanted Westley dead – and it seemed likely that he did – she could not trust him. Nor did she have any intention of negotiating with him over the supposed proof of her involvement in Henry Dynam's death. She was fairly sure such proof did not exist – she had been too careful. There was but one other person who knew of it and she was certain he would never reveal her secret, apart from anything else she knew too much about him. Odious little man – but he had proved useful at the time. It had been nine long years and never a whisper until now. She was not even sure if he was still alive. No. There was no proof. Tawford was guessing and she meant to call his bluff.

With these thoughts at the forefront of her mind Anne Dynam composed herself for an unpleasant confrontation with Tawford's messenger. It was thus with considerable and mutual surprise that she viewed Dewett's handsome features and discovered in fairly short order that his hatred of Alexander Dynam was no less than her own. The man posturing before her was undoubtedly a fool, but he was an undeniably attractive fool. He would be useful and she might as well enjoy him. She allowed her gaze to linger on his thighs as he stood, legs apart, making no attempt to hide his obvious admiration. Oh yes, she would certainly enjoy him! She patted the red velvet of the settle and smiled up at him invitingly.

'Come, Captain, sit by me. Perhaps we may be able to help one another?' Her laugh was low and throaty. 'What is it you want to know?'

Outside, deep in the shadows, Cobb's man waited.

He had to wait a long time.

Bella was aware of Robert's gaze following her around the room as she picked up her swabbing cloths and various medicaments, straightened the bedcovers and tidied away his books that had slid to the floor. He was so much better now the fever had gone. His wound was as clean as a whisker, healing nicely and no longer paining him as it had, but he was not a strong man. The illness had devastated him and Bella had insisted he remain in bed while he regained his strength. She knew he was getting restless and she would not be able to keep him on his back much longer. Yesterday she had discussed it with Cobb and they had agreed that within a few days Lord Westley would be well enough to travel.

Bella tutted with irritation; she wore her hair piled on top of her head and trapped it there with lace cap and pins, but it would keep escaping down her back, as now. She put her cloths and bottles down on the chest and raised her arms, reaching to twist the offending strands back into place, unaware of the effect this fetching sight had upon her patient.

Robert was no longer as embarrassed and uncomfortable as he had been when he had first become aware of Bella's presence at his bedside. Covertly watching the movement of her breasts as she attended to her hair, his imagination straying increasingly pleasurably, he became aware she was scolding him again.

'It is bad for your eyes to read so much by candlelight. Can you not wait until morning?'

'Stop bullying,' he smiled up at her, his expression wry. 'If I cannot read I shall die of boredom. Unless – will you play another game of chess with me? It is only fair you allow me the opportunity to take my revenge,' he wheedled.

Bella shook her head, speaking to him as she would an errant child. 'Not now, it is late and you should rest. Perhaps tomorrow, but only if you behave.'

And as a child, he attempted to delay her. 'Who came to see you today?'

Bella hesitated. Decided it would do no harm to tell him.

'It was your stepmother. I think she was a little disappointed to learn you are not going to die.'

His eyes widening in consternation, Robert pushed himself up from the pillow. 'What happened? What did she say?'

Bella arched her brows. 'What do you imagine happened, My Lord? We talked, that is all. She told me how concerned she is for my reputation and warned me you will not countenance marriage with a trollop – no, a wanton – with no regard for, how you say – English propriety – and that she is most disappointed, for I will not after all be her daughter.' Bella burst into a peal of laughter at Robert's horrified expression. 'When I said she need not concern herself and I would indeed soon be able to call her "Mama", I fear she was not best pleased!'

'The woman is a disgrace. I most humbly apologise that you have had to endure her foul tongue. You should have let me deal with her.' Robert grimaced. 'If she returns you must leave her to me.'

'Oh I think you can be assured she will not return.' Bella's tawny eyes sparkled and she gave a grim smile of satisfaction. 'I rather enjoyed the encounter, My Lord. She is, how you say, a challenge? It is a while since I was able to sharpen my wits on so worthy an adversary. Your stepmother should be in theatre – she is a consummate actress. Perhaps I should suggest it?'

Despite his misgivings, Robert was forced to laugh. He had come to know Bella quite well in the last two weeks and if anyone was capable of besting Anne Dynam it was she. Not thinking, he shrugged, grimacing as the pain stabbed through his shoulder.

Bella wagged her finger at him. 'That was silly, but if you are forgetting it enough to shrug, it must be getting better, which is good for Cobb wants you to go home. Do you feel well enough to face the journey?'

He gazed at her and frowned. Part of him longed for Marley Court and to see Ellen again, but part of him did not want this interlude to end. He had tried to deny it to himself, but his initial attraction for this strong, unusual woman had blossomed into genuine liking. He was becoming too fond and had to keep reminding himself that Bella was playing a part. That she had taken it upon herself to nurse him so attentively had surprised him greatly, until he remembered Alexander was paying for her services. He had to assume she was merely fulfilling a professional obligation – and yet he dared to hope her concern for him was genuine. Impulsively he said, 'I think so, but I would feel more confident if my nurse came with me.' He had meant it as a joke, but as the words were spoken he realised they were true and he would like nothing better than for Bella to go home with him to Devon. He cocked an eyebrow. 'Will you come with me, Bella?'

She took him at face value. 'Lah! You will have nurses aplenty, My Lord. You do not need me any longer, your sister will look after you as well if not better than I.' Bella patted her stomach and smiled. 'Your stepmother is convinced I am carrying your child and we will be wed before it becomes noticeable, so there is no need for me to come with you. I feel you will soon have proof of her wickedness – and that is what this charade is for, *n'est ce pas*? My job is done.'

Robert was disconcerted. 'Then there is even more need. I do not want you meeting with an accident for my sake, Bella. I beg you to consider my suggestion. You will be safer at Marley Court – and anyway, I would like you to meet Ellen. I think you will enjoy her company and she yours.' His eyes pleaded.

She moved towards him to brush a strand of his hair back from his brow, smoothing it over his head with her fingertips. It was an intimate gesture that brought a flush to his cheeks. He trapped her fingers and held them against his cheek. 'I do not want to lose you, Bella. I need you in ways that have nothing to do with our professional arrangement.' He looked up at her and grimaced. 'Forgive me. I have embarrassed you – I have embarrassed myself.'

Making no attempt to withdraw her hand she smiled down at him. 'Embarrassed? *Non mon chéri.* Touched, not embarrassed, and how can I possibly refuse such an eloquent request? Very well, I will come with you. But there are things I must attend to first. Tomorrow you will get dressed and I will ask Cobb to stay here with you until it is time for us to leave.' Gently she withdrew her fingers from his grasp. 'Will you spare me for a day or two, My Lord?'

'You think I imagine you do not have a life that does not include me?' He turned his mouth down in a rueful smile and met her gaze. 'I am not quite that selfish. Of course you must have people to see and arrangements to make. I have monopolised your time, I know it. Please forgive me.'

'I forgive you. Now you must get some rest. *Bonne nuit mon Robert doux.*'

Liking the sound of her husky voice calling him her 'sweet Robert', he smiled as she extinguished the candles, picked up her bundle from the chest and left him in darkness to his thoughts.

Bella had not been surprised by his plea, had known Lord Westley was becoming attached to her. It happened that way sometimes between a nurse and her patient and she had been prepared for it; nursing a sick man was a necessarily intimate affair. She knew from experience it would fade as he became stronger and less dependent on her. What she had not been prepared for was her own reaction to him. She had discovered him to be delightful company; intelligent, well read, able to converse on almost any matter authoritatively. He was also a sensitive man, which she liked. And they laughed a lot, about little things. She smiled at the thought. But it would not do, she reprimanded herself. Only grief could come of it. He had no idea of her background apart from what he had been told. She was quite sure he would not approve were he to discover what had really brought her to England – or that Alexander had at one time been her lover. Would that matter to him if he knew? Given the nature of his relationship with his bastard son, probably yes. So was it wise to accompany him to Devon? On one level, probably not, but on another it would serve her purposes admirably to get away from London. Her work here was done and Cardinal Richelieu was ill – close to death, she had heard – and unlikely to need her services again. She had no wish to work for his successor, however much King Louis might want her to. In Devon she could lose herself for a time. She smiled to herself, so long as she did not lose herself in Robert Dynam! But a brief dalliance? Now that was a pleasing thought.

In Arundel Street Anne Dynam was consuming James Dewett. He was completely captivated by her. Here at last he had met his match. He had not really believed such a woman could possibly exist beyond his wildest dreams.

Drawing on all his reserves, he allowed her to arouse him yet again while wondering idly what he had done so right as to deserve this gift that had fallen into his lap. The appropriateness of the thought made him laugh.

Tantalisingly, she stopped what she was doing, leaving him gasping in exquisite agony, the tips of her breasts slid up his sweating body as her soft, beautiful lips moved by degrees to his mouth, stifling his laughter.

24

The situation in Exeter was as tense as it was noisy. When Sir Ralph Hopton had received the Mayor's impolite refusal to surrender, he had set his men to digging. Cornishmen were miners, as handy with shovels as they now were with muskets, they quickly entrenched on the west side of the city. Downriver, Grenville's men had commenced boarding the *Porpoise*; it took most of the night to get them all across the Exe and moved up from Topsham to dig in on the south side, but by morning, the King's Western Army sat in a semi-circle of trenches outside the walls of Exeter, just out of range of Saunders' batteries, and all traffic to and from the city ceased.

As soon as it was light enough to see, Major Saunders directed his gun crews to commence firing. Hopton's guns replied; he had half a dozen brass sakers, and three iron demi-culverins – not as effective as mortars at battering down walls, but each one capable of throwing a twelve-pound ball of iron up to eighteen hundred paces. It could severely weaken the fortifications and pulverise any man or horse unlucky enough to be in its path – though it was more by luck than judgement if it did either. Most of the gun crews at Exeter that day had yet to gain experience. It would be some hours before either side did any significant damage – if then – but the noise was shattering.

Alexander, once more looking like a one-eyed, ginger-haired labourer in the final stages of chicken pox, had woken Zach before dawn. The players were sorry to see them go, extracting a promise that one day they would return to Exeter, hard as it was to imagine when that one day might be. They took with them some food and aqua vitae, a woman's shift and petticoat, a shawl, another pair of boots and a leather coat, all courtesy of Cat who seemed no less canny than Pollard at acquiring things. The only item he had been unable to procure was a sword – but he had got hold of a halberd. Would that do? It most certainly would. Alexander knew better than to ask Cat how he came by these things, but this time insisted he accept a sovereign for his pains. Cat had also brought welcome news: the turnkey's deputy had played his part as agreed; the witch had been taken to the storeroom late on Saturday afternoon and as far as he knew had not been discovered, nor would be. Nobody looked too closely at the corpses, apart from the shroud hags. If Bethan still lived, she would be safe from the turnkey, if not from the infection that had killed her macabre companions.

It was a dark morning, overcast and drizzling as they ran through the streets of St Stephens, Alexander wondering if the rain would make his pimples run; the thought both amused and alarmed him. Leaving Zach to make his way down the steps to the tunnel where he was to wait, Alexander, carrying the clothes and clogs bundled under his arm, his knife strapped within easy reach to his leg, hurried unnoticed through the wet streets. They were empty of all but a few townsfolk, the stench of sulphur in their noses, cannon fire ringing in their ears, scurrying fearfully to barricade themselves into their homes.

Having the gypsy's help – as welcome as it was unexpected – had lifted a weight from Alexander's mind. Abandoning his men at such a time had been playing on his conscience. Now Zach could take Bethan out of the city. The beauty of it was she would not be missed – as far as the head turnkey was concerned, she was dead – and if all went according to plan, there would be no hue and cry. Once she had been delivered into Zach's hands, Alexander could forget about her and concentrate on getting himself out of the city. He wondered what state she would be in, whether she would be able to walk, refused to entertain the possibility that she might not be alive. Zach could carry her if he had to and he had a horse waiting in St David's; hopefully he would have ample opportunity to get her out by the North Gate in the confusion of Hopton's attack.

Alexander arrived in Milk Street to find Matthew had not yet hitched his horse to the cart. The old man was peering out of the stable, visibly quaking. He backed nervously away, shaking his head when he saw Alexander walking purposefully towards him. 'You didn't say nuthin' bout any of this,' he had to shout to make himself heard above the noise of cannon-fire and the bawling of frightened milch cows. 'I can't do it, not now, 'tis more than my life be worth. The head turnkey'll not be expecting us, not wi' all these goings-on. He'll know there's summat queer 'bout it an' they'll hang us both for sure. An' even if they won't, 'appen they'll turn us away from the gaol.'

With difficulty, Alexander contained his impatience, kept his expression neutral. 'Then you will have to explain to the turnkey how these goings-on are going to make you so busy shifting dead, South Gate will have to whistle for you and if he don't let you clear his corpses out today, they'll lie there stinking in his storeroom, most likely for a very long time.'

As he spoke, Alexander held out a sovereign. Matthew, his face creased with fear, eyed it sadly shaking his head. With a sigh, Alexander palmed his last sovereign. The old man's eyes gleamed as he saw the two coins glinting there, far more than the three crowns he had been promised, and even that had been more wealth than he could imagine. Unable to resist, he reached for the sovereigns just as Alexander closed his fist. 'As soon as it is done, old man, they are both yours.'

Matthew huffed and hesitated, his gaze on Alexander's fist. After a moment he nodded grudgingly. 'Aye, well, mebee 'tis true what you say. Us'll go on now then.' With that he led out his horse and backed it between the shafts. 'They cows won't be givin' nary a drop of milk today what with all this noise going on. What's the world coming to? 'Tis the Devil's work, that's what. And where's Luke? You might well ask. Daft young bugger's gone up onto the wall to watch, that's what. He'll get his head blown off like as not and then where will I be? As if life weren't hard enough.' Matthew grumbled in this vein all the way to the South Gate.

The old man was right: the turnkey was surprised to see them, but he took the point; it was going to be a busy time for sextons and gravediggers. The thought of having the victims of gaol fever lying around stinking for several days was not something he cared to dwell on. There had been only four deaths since Friday; it seemed the infection had almost run its course – till the next time. Best to get them removed while he could. He let the cart rumble into the yard while from above, excited youngsters sneaking up to watch from the walls and being roundly cursed by the harassed gun crews, gave a running commentary between the boom of the guns and the distant rattle of musket fire.

Hopton's chances of taking Exeter were slim: the Devon Royalists' promise of volunteers had again failed to materialise. Without them he lacked the manpower for an effective siege; supplies and reinforcements would be able to enter Exeter by the North and East Gates, which he could not cover. His only hope lay in throwing everything he had into an assault, but that would not be today. Alexander knew he would be hoping to frighten the city into reconsidering his demand for surrender before he committed men's lives. Equally, Major Saunders would be hoping with a superior show of strength to frighten Hopton away. Like a pair of circling dogs, hackles raised, neither side would do much more than growl and snarl today.

The coroner had other things on his mind than paperwork this morning and none of the dead had been signed off, but in the circumstances the turnkey was prepared to let it go. Who knew what was going to happen in the next few days? It would not be the first time the records had been penned retrospectively. He scribbled a pass and grinned up at Matthew. 'Be careful, mind, one o' they's a witch. Murdered her husband they do say. Mind you, she weren't much of a witch when all's said and done or she'd 'ave turned 'erself into a toad and 'opped away, 'stead of letting the fever take 'er!'

The turnkey was gratified, if a little taken aback, when Matthew and Isaac roared with merriment at his witticism, prompting him to add, 'They've not 'ad a chance to question 'er yet neither and 'tis a while since we 'ad a burning too. Shame.' He spat at the ground. 'Aye, well she's a higher court to answer to now.' He unlocked the door and stood well back as the two men unloaded the coffins into the storeroom.

She was alive. Alexander could not tell if she was conscious, but her mouth felt warm. The hags had left a crack for her to breath through the shroud. He did not dare speak to her or look too closely for though the turnkey was standing back, he was watching nonetheless. They lifted Bethan into the coffin where the clothes and clogs were concealed, and loaded her onto the cart. They did the same with the other three. The business was soon done. Alexander sat on the lid of Bethan's coffin and tried to look bored as Matthew took up the reins and gestured in the direction of the gunfire. 'I'll not be back vor this lot be o'er one way or 't'other.'

The turnkey nodded. 'Aye. I'd not expect it. God keep you, Matthew. God keep us all.'

As the cart rolled forward there was a sudden deafening roar and they all ducked: a cannon on the wall by the South Gate had overheated and exploded, the blast of broken, twisted shards of hot metal killing two of its crew and maiming the rest – horribly.

Screaming and crying, splattered with gore, the watching youngsters took to their heels. So did Matthew's horse. Almost thrown from his seat, the old man hauled ineffectually on the reins as the cart was pulled swaying, rattling and bumping over the wet cobbles, its macabre load bouncing up and down within a whisker of sliding from the cart. Alexander flung himself across the four coffins, hung on grimly and prayed as they careered with unseemly haste through the city, arriving at the gates of St Bartholomew's Yard in record time.

Normally, the dead were taken to a small side chapel to be checked in by a parish clerk and left in their coffins to await burial later in the day. Numbers were important for each corpse attracted a fee and even were it waived, as was the case with unclaimed dead, it still had to be entered in the account books as a loss. Sometimes, if he was busy, the parish clerk left it to the sexton to tally the corpses and tell him later. Since the man could neither read nor write, nor count beyond his fingers, it was hardly an exact science.

As Alexander had hoped, nothing in Exeter was normal today, but though the Yard was deserted, the parish clerk or the sexton – or both – might appear at any moment and Alexander knew he would have no choice but to knock either one unconscious while he and Bethan made their escape. Were that to happen, the authorities would soon question what had occurred and Bethan's escape from the city would be in serious jeopardy, as would Matthew's life. He continued to pray.

In order not to arouse suspicion should they be observed, the two men had to follow their usual routine. With his heart racing and all his senses tingling, Alexander helped Matthew slowly and with due respect unload each coffin from the cart, carry it into the chapel and cover it with a mortuary cloth from the charity pile left neatly folded by the bier, which was propped against the back wall. They then retrieved and loaded the empties – only the wealthy could afford to be interred in their coffins. When all four bodies had been safely transferred, Alexander gave Matthew his two sovereigns, thanked him and wish him God speed.

When the cart had rattled away he glanced quickly around the deserted Yard and ducked back into the chapel, drew the mortuary cloth from Bethan's coffin and spread it on the floor, raised the lid, lifted her out and laid her on the cloth, reaching for his knife to cut off her shroud. She had been lying with the dead since Saturday and swaddled in a winding sheet since first light. It surprised Alexander not at all that she looked as dead as she had pretended to be. Naked, her skin was grey, her limbs rigid with cramp, but as the shroud fell away, her lips parted and she opened her eyes. Trying not to rush, his senses prickling, alert for footsteps, he put his finger to his lips, knelt down and vigorously rubbed her feet, legs and arms. When she was able to move them he supported her into a sitting position, retrieved the shift and petticoat, easing them over her head and pulling them down to cover her nakedness. He concealed her red hair beneath the shawl, wrapping the garment about her shoulders and tying it tightly at her breast. She was shivering uncontrollably. He knelt behind her and put his arms tightly round her waist, holding her hard against him, rocking her and all the time murmuring into her good ear. 'Be strong sweetheart, just a little while longer. The worst is over.'

When her shivering lessened, Alexander went to the doorway and looked cautiously around, sending up a prayer of gratitude. The noise of cannon-fire seemed to have increased as the gun crews got into their stride, but the cemetery was still and deserted. No sign of parish clerk or sexton, nor scurrying clergy. The latter were doubtless on their knees – Exeter needed all their prayers this day. He turned back to Bethan, mouthed, 'Can you walk?' When she nodded, he bundled up the shroud and gave it to her to carry, fitted the clogs onto her feet and helped her to stand, supporting her, almost carrying her out of the Yard.

At last Alexander was able to breathe more freely. The streets were teeming with panicky people carrying bundles, pushing handcarts and leading wailing children by the hand. Two constables were attempting to calm things down with little success. On one corner stood a black-clad minister, arms held open to the heavens, he was shouting a prayer, his voice lost in the cacophony of gunfire and people screaming as the occasional ball missed its mark, whistled high over the city wall, smacked into a building and fell with a crash of crumbling masonry. As Alexander half carried Bethan through the streets to the tunnel entrance, nobody cared or paid them any attention, but he was relieved to see Zach's saturnine face peering anxiously from the steps. Between them they carried Bethan down and along the tunnel to where the gypsy had a rush light burning; it cast their shadows huge upon the streaming walls. The sound of the guns was muffled down here. Only when they stopped and set Bethan gently to her feet did she speak, looking round at the tunnel in wonder and then at their shadowed faces.

'I will never be able to thank you for what you have done,' her voice hoarse and broken. 'I want you to know you have not saved the life of a murderer. My husband did not die by my hand.' A sob tore from her throat, tears spilling from her eyes.

Zach shook his head. 'There, there, hush my lovely, we know.' Alexander's eyes widened in surprise, not only at the endearment but as he realised the gypsy was signing as he spoke. 'Don't try to talk,' Zach said. 'You are cold. We have some food and aqua vitae for you. When you are feeling a little better, we will leave the city and I will take you home to Jennet.'

'Jennet?' The name burst from her lips as a cry of pain.

Zach nodded. 'She is safe and waiting for you at Tawford's home. God willing, you will be with her by tomorrow.'

Tears flooded down Bethan's face as she reached out to Zach, almost falling against him. He put his arm about her waist to still her violent trembling and looked over her shoulder at Alexander. 'It's only reaction,' he said unnecessarily. 'She'll be better directly. You go. I'll manage.'

Alexander nodded. 'You will be safe down here until you're ready to leave. Any townsfolk who think to use the tunnel for shelter will not take it amiss to find you are doing the same.'

Reaching for buff coat and boots he changed swiftly, this

time donning back and breastplates, for while they might make him more conspicuous, they might also save his life. Adjusting the straps at his shoulders he cast around for his helmet and jammed it on over his wig. Grinning, he pulled off the eye patch and offered it to Zach, who returned the grin and shook his head. Alexander dropped it with a shrug and picking up his discarded smock, spat on it and scrubbed at his face for fear his dissolving make-up would arouse curiosity.

'Here, let me.' Zach's grin broadened. 'You look like a ghoul.' Easing Bethan away from him, the gypsy tore off a piece of shroud, moistened it with aqua vitae and cleansed Alexander's face of pimples and boils. Within short order he was ready, the halberd glinting wickedly in his fist.

'Do not try to get out by any but the North Gate, Zach. If they won't let you through, go back to the safe house and wait. Remember, you have no pressure of time. Nobody is going to know Bethan has gone and if the parish clerk checks the paperwork and finds he is missing a body, he will get no sense out of old Matthew and will probably assume the turnkey made a mistake. It is my belief Hopton will be looking to mount an attack tomorrow, before Colonel Ruthin and his Scots arrive. I do not think he will prevail. Even without Ruthin, Exeter is too strong and will beat him back. If you cannot get out before the attack starts, wait in hiding until it is over. Jelly and the others will help you care for Bethan meantime and sooner or later you will be able to walk out of the city, no questions asked.' Alexander smiled encouragingly at Bethan who was anxiously searching his face.

Zach frowned. 'Are you sure you know what you are doing? Would it not be better if you came with us?'

'No. Dressed like this I would attract too much attention. They would think I am trying to desert in the face of the enemy.'

'Then could you not stay in the guise of a labourer and wait with us?' Zach's seamed face was creased with concern.

Alexander shook his head. 'You know I must get back to

my men, Zach, stop fretting.'

'How do you plan to manage that without being seen?'

'Dressed like this it doesn't matter if I am seen – unless I come face to face with Lieutenant Green or Major Saunders, both of whom would probably shoot me on sight – but there are fairly long odds against that happening,' Alexander grinned. 'I will attach myself to the next troop ordered out of the garrison and into the ditch. They won't be counting heads today and there is bound to be an opportunity sooner or later.'

Zach nodded and slowly he smiled. 'Aye Lapwing, you'll manage it if anyone can. Do you have a message for Ellen?'

Alexander thought for a moment. 'Tell her, God willing, I will come home soon and she is not to worry, and if anyone comes looking for Jennet meantime, or there is any trouble about Bethan, she is to go to Richard Pollard. He will know how to get them away to safety and will help her – but keep that information under your hat.'

Zach grinned. 'I will not tell a soul. God keep you, Lapwing.'

'Thank you,' Alexander lightly grasped Zach's arm, 'and you, my friend.'

Bethan smiled up at him and as she had done once before, whispered, 'I will see you again.'

He raised a teasing eyebrow. 'Then I feel safer already!'

With a laugh, he turned towards the steps.

If he was being honest, he had not given much thought to how he was going to get out of the city and back to his men; his mind had been focussed on Bethan. While still in the tunnel he had been tempted to walk along it and try forcing his way out into the ditch, but soon dismissed the idea. Even if he could – and judging by the pile of rubble he had come up against the other night it would not be easy – it was too risky. It would be the supreme irony if after all this he really were shot as a deserter. He had to find another way. Walking smartly in an effort to look like a soldier hurrying to carry out an order, and feeling very exposed, he made his way through the streets in the general direction of the castle. He had told Zach he would attach himself to a troop from the garrison, but he had said it off the top of his head. He very much doubted if Saunders had any men left in the castle beyond the usual guards. By now they would all be on the walls or in the ditch returning enemy fire. He was still thinking about it and trying to come up with a credible excuse that would get him out through the gates, when a harassed looking captain appeared round the corner directly in front of him, two musketeers marching smartly behind. Alexander instantly recognised the man as one of Saunders' engineers. There was no time to avoid him, so he removed his helmet and stood to attention, thanked God he had kept on the ginger wig, screwed up his eyes to minimise the effect of his puckered eyelid, and prayed.

The captain paused, stared at Alexander's breastplate and halberd, and snapped, 'What regiment?'

Thinking rapidly, Alexander remembered Colonel Wear and his men had arrived in Exeter only yesterday, there was a good chance they would not yet be known and it was likely that at least some of them had armour. Wishing he had a sword instead of a halberd and keeping his fingers crossed behind his back, he said, 'Colonel John Wear's, Sir. I am sent to ask about supplies of powder for the west side. They're running a bit short, Captain, Sir.' Alexander knew from experience it was a safe bet; gun crews were always running out of powder.

The captain, distracted, had not recognised him as Lafitte's translator – not yet. He nodded, 'Well, never mind that now. Know anything about cannon, trooper?'

'A little, Sir.'

'Good. They are short of a gun crew on the south wall.' He gestured to the two musketeers at his back who shot Alexander rueful grins. 'Go with these men, trooper. I will go back and see about the powder supplies. Fall in now. Look sharp. Quick, march.'

Alexander had no choice but to do as he was told. He

marched set-faced with his two companions, through the city and up to a platform on the southern ramparts; apparently another gun had exploded. A demi-cannon had been brought to replace it, but only two of the crew were fit for duty, all the others had been severely wounded in the blast. Ideally there should be six men to each crew: the master gunner, his right-hand man to hold his ladle, rammer and sponge and pass him shot, his left-hand man to hand him powder and wadding while ensuring that none of the charge escaped from the touch hole during ramming, and three assistants, two to stand by with linstock, scourer, and handspikes – the latter to lever the cannon and adjust the elevation quoins after recoil, and the third – the lowest in the pecking order – to keep the crew supplied with wadding, powder, shot, wet cloths and sponges. It was a complex and highly dangerous operation and most of the unpractised gun crews were all fingers and thumbs, the explosion of overheated guns an occupational hazard. Having learned gunnery aboard a pirate vessel, Alexander could have done it in his sleep.

After snapping out a few choice questions, the master gunner allocated positions to the two musketeers and relegated Alexander, who clearly knew next to nothing about gunnery, to fetching and carrying. They were still a man short and he was kept busy doing the work of two. He was in fact kept busy for the rest of the day and since none of the crew was particularly experienced, they did not notice how slow he was nor did they know that his extreme clumsiness was out of character. He was roundly sworn at for committing the cardinal sin of spilling powder on the ground and he kept forgetting to replace the cloths in water and clean the sponge. When they ran out of powder or shot, he took as long as he possibly could without arousing suspicion, to fetch more. The master gunner, increasingly short-tempered as the firing interval got noticeably longer and the adjacent gun crew started to howl with mocking laughter, took to cuffing and swearing at Alexander at every opportunity, which made him even clumsier.

Alexander was decidedly uncomfortable with the situation in which he found himself. Not only because he was forced to assist the enemy in bombarding Hopton's trenches – and therefore his own men, dammit – but also, from time to time, Major Saunders did the rounds to see how the gun crews were coping. So far Alexander had managed to avoid being seen, but even his luck would surely run out sooner or later. He kept his head down and prayed. As the light at last began to fade and bombardment to cease for the day, he was light-headed with relief. Musketeers arrived to replace the gun crews and keep watch on enemy lines, and the weary gunners were marched back to the garrison for sustenance, salve for their burns and a well-earned rest.

Alexander, not daring to go with them into the castle, fell back to the rear and at an opportune moment slipped into a side street. At a loss, uncertain what to do next, eyes gummed up with gun smoke, throat parched and sore, head pounding from the continual, ear-splitting roar of cannon fire, he made his way to St Stephens and down into the cellar, half expecting to find Zach and Bethan there. They were not and he could only pray that in all the confusion they had found their way out of the city.

He received an uproarious welcome from the players and a draught of cider that was as close to drinking nectar as he had ever come. He also received two items of news: Colonel William Ruthin had already arrived, having force-marched five hundred foot from Dartmouth, slipped round Hopton's lines and entered the city by the East Gate. There was nothing Alexander could do about that, but the second item of news set him alight. With Ruthin's support, the Mayor was planning to lead a night sally out of the East Gate. His men were to creep round the back of Hopton's trenches and fall on the enemy from the rear, while at the same time, Major Saunders was to launch an attack from the West Gate. It was planned for an hour after midnight when the Royalists would be unsuspecting and exhausted, bleary with sleep and quite probably drunk. The Exeter men were to wear white kerchiefs tied where they could easily be seen so they did not kill each other in the darkness – and they were to carry grenades, which the engineers had been busy making all afternoon. The Mayor had called for volunteers to help, promising a penny for each grenade, which was how the players came to know so much about it – they had managed to make two crowns between them. Alexander could not blame them; he would most likely have done the same in their position.

The proposed sally was a mixed blessing, for though it was grim news, it did at least provide Alexander with an opportunity to get out of the city, and if he could only take warning to Hopton, the attack might not be quite so devastating. The players found him a piece of white cloth to tie to his shoulder straps and wished him luck – for he was going to need it – and towards the appointed hour, he once more made his way through the empty streets. He retraced his steps towards the castle, keeping to the shadows wherever he could. The night sky was glowing from the hundreds of fires and flares outside the walls and there was still the odd rattle of musket fire, but after the bombardment the city seemed eerily quiet.

As he heard the column approaching, he flattened against a wall and waited until the first few ranks had tramped by him, match smoking, muskets shouldered, swords, halberds and poleaxes clanking, white kerchiefs clearly visible. Making a great show of fastening his breeches, Alexander stepped out of the shadows, his features set in a sheepish grin. He was not the only nervous trooper forced to leave the column or wet himself. The nearest guffawed, moved with an obscene gesture to make room for him and seeing that apart from his halberd Alexander's hands were empty, offloaded two grenades. They did not notice he was not carrying lighted match.

And so he marched out of Exeter. All he had to do now was to seek an opportunity to slip away and give warning, but it was not to be. Carried along in the tightly packed troop, there was nothing Alexander could do. Ruthin's mercenaries, afire with nervous enthusiasm, were keenly alert for treachery, swords drawn, watching for cowards to slip away and cuffing anyone who made a noise. Not that the enemy would have noticed, for as Major Saunders had correctly surmised, few in the Royalists' trenches were sober. The Mayor led his men out of the East Gate, stole over the cleared ground of the suburbs, moved south until he was behind Grenville's trenches, turned west behind Hopton's trenches, waited for his men to spread out and signalled forward.

The night erupted; the Royalists taken completely by surprise.

Alexander dropped to his knees as the alarm went up and all around him unseasoned, frightened Cornishmen leapt from their trenches and fled towards the river. Exploding grenades lighted up the night, men shouted, screamed and died as Exeter's troopers beat their way through Hopton's lines laying about them with their halberds, poleaxes and the butts of their muskets. But now they were meeting resistance as fierce as it was desperate.

Bending double, Alexander ran along the trench making for the thick of the fighting where he knew he would find Sir Ralph Hopton. Dropping his grenades, he flung off his helmet, tore off his wig and was trying to rip off his white kerchief, when he came face to face with Dickon.

Alexander stopped dead, shouted, 'Dickon, no!'

The boy, face stark with the shock of recognition, tears of disbelief starting to his eyes, saw only betrayal. Opening his mouth he screamed, raised his pistol, aimed for Alexander's face and fired.

At such close range he could not miss, but one of Ruthin's men running in the trench behind Alexander saw what was about to happen. In one fluid movement he shoved Alexander to one side, swinging the butt end of his musket with a sickening crack against Dickon's head. Dickon, the pistol still smoking in his nerveless fingers, collapsed. The ball burst through the straps of Alexander's breastplate knocking him backwards and seaming his left shoulder. Still running, the trooper hauled him to his feet and with a hand under his elbow pushed him past Dickon's inert body and along the trench.

Stumbling forward Alexander succeeded at last in divesting himself of the kerchief. His left arm was completely numb, but his right appeared to be in working order. Turning on the trooper who had saved his life, he swung his halberd and felled him. It seemed cruel recompense, but he had no time for regret for in that moment two more of Ruthin's men, running up behind him and armed with poleaxes, forced him backwards along the trench and he was fighting for his life. He was filled with the bitter irony of it. As he had run towards the Royalists' positions he had been aware of the risk that he would be taken for a Roundhead. It had not occurred to him that he might be recognised and taken for a traitor. Godamme! Why, oh why did it have to be Dickon?

Alexander did everything he could to get back to where the boy lay, but he was caught up in the press of fierce hand-to-hand fighting. His eyes streaming, coughing up the thick, sulphurous smoke that filled his lungs, he focussed all his efforts on wielding a halberd one-handed until he could discard it for a dead man's sword. No time to think, only to react; to let instinct for survival take over. Ignore the brains and bowels that splattered in your face, the obscene stench of burning flesh and spilled viscera that made you retch. Close your ears to the blood-curdling screams of agony and fear. Ignore the pain – especially ignore the pain. Kill or be killed. Stay alive.

Sir Ralph Hopton and Sir Bevill Grenville drew together and rallied their forces again and again, standing back to back, holding out against Major Saunders' troopers on one side and Ruthin's on the other. Bravely the Royalists held on until the early hours of the morning, but their losses were appalling. Still lying off Topsham – quite literally – was the *Porpoise,* on her side in the mud, her crew drunk and incapable. Cornishmen who had fled hoping to escape by boat were found face down and bloated in the Exe for days afterwards.

As daylight dawned on the devastation outside Exeter, the gates opened and townspeople came streaming out in their thousands to chase the hated enemy away. Cheering for the Mayor, they grabbed whatever weapons they could find. The Royalists, heavily outnumbered and desperately short of ammunition and powder, had no alternative but to admit defeat and flee.

Will Mohun and Hal Gifford, who had been fighting at Hopton's side, searched for and found the bodies of John Acland and Kit Basset. Hugh Lyddon, who had seen Alexander go down, found him alive but unconscious beneath a pile of enemy dead, covered in gore, his hand still clutching his bloodstained sword. Francis Sydenham and Rob Pollard, who had both taken wounds, though not life-threatening, helped James Chichester, unscathed barring cuts and bruises, hunt for Dickon. They spotted the boy moments before they were forced to run from the field, and could only watch helplessly as he and several others were taken prisoner and at musket point herded roughly towards the South Gate.

The defeated army withdrew from Exeter to Crediton, pursued by Ruthin and threatened by a force from Barnstaple – sent by George Peard on receipt of Ruthin's jubilant message – intent on capturing Hopton's guns and cutting off his retreat. They were too late: the Royalists slipped past them and made for Bow, where the St Michael's men sought and were granted leave to take their dead home and care for their wounded.

It was a sombre group of men who turned their horses away from Hopton's fleeing, dispirited army, none more so than Alexander who, until he returned to his senses, had to be forcibly restrained to prevent him from going back for Dickon.

Sir Ralph Hopton and Sir Bevill Grenville – their battle-weary Cornishmen anxious to return home and increasingly mutinous – made for Okehampton. Here they rallied one more time, beating off Ruthin's pursuers, before continuing by slow stages to Bridestow and thence to the Tamar.

By the time they had crossed into Cornwall, the Earl of Stamford had arrived in Exeter at the head of three regiments of foot. For the time being, Sir Ralph Hopton's hopes of wresting Devon away from Parliament were in pieces around him.

25

Monday 5ᵗʰ December, 1642

For Zach and Bethan, getting out of Exeter could not have been easier. In the early afternoon, by which time Hopton's gunners had at last got their eye in and were beginning to do some serious damage to the south and west of the city, the trickle of frightened people queuing at the North Gate became a threatening flood. The terrified guards at last gave way and opened the postern gate. Zach and Bethan were not challenged – or even noticed – as they mingled with the escaping crowds. It was only when they got to St Davids that their troubles began. Zach's horse was not where he had left it and there were no fresh mounts to be had in the vicinity since anything and everything on four legs that could move had been stolen or was jealously guarded. Bethan, weak from shock, grief and the effects of imprisonment was in no fit state to walk far and although there was nothing to fear from pursuit, Zach knew they were easy prey for padders, deserters and marauding soldiers. Tales of atrocities were growing by the day; it was not a time to be out on the roads, defenceless. They had travelled but three miles when he knew she could go no further. He had the money Ellen had pressed on him before he had left Tawford Barton, which was not enough to purchase a horse, even supposing he could find one, but it would at least buy them somewhere to rest. On the other hand, he might as well carry a banner proclaiming: 'I have money – rob me!' He wrestled with the problem as he half-carried Bethan towards

Upton Pyne. In the end he compromised, selected the poorest looking hovel he could see, crossed his fingers and knocked on the door.

Ellen had not expected Jennet's recovery to happen overnight, but since her brainwave with the puppy the child's condition had improved in leaps and bounds. She ate everything that was put in front of her and though her elfin face remained haunted by sadness, the dark circles around her eyes receded, colour came into her cheeks and her red hair took on the lustre of copper, much like Ellen's own, though a darker shade. 'Witch's hair,' as Lucy had muttered and received a clout round the ear from Wilmot.

The day after Jennet's cathartic storm of weeping, she had allowed herself to be dressed and had come downstairs. Over the next few days, they had quickly established a routine. When the child was not helping Wilmot and Rose in the kitchen or with the household chores, she was to be found in the barn – to where her pup had been banished since her recovery – or in the stables watching Ned tending the horses. Jennet had fallen in love with Biscuit, whose slight wound had healed with barely a trace, and who was growing fat and sleek under Ned's care.

Not having imagined Jennet would be able to read, Ellen had been surprised one morning to find her immersed in the books that cluttered the surfaces in Alexander's chamber. Delighted, Ellen encouraged it, selecting some of her own books and chatting about the magical worlds between their covers. She knew the child listened, for sometimes she would nod thoughtfully and just occasionally her lips would curve in the shadow of a smile. But still she did not speak. It was indeed as if she had been struck dumb. Sooner or later, Ellen knew, she would have to broach the subject of Morgan's death, but each time she spoke of Bethan, Jennet's wild-eyed reaction was as a rabbit mesmerised by a stoat. Ellen contained her impatience and waited for time to heal.

As a week went by and then another with no news, Ellen's anxiety increased to fever pitch, but she endeavoured to keep it hidden. In an effort to carry on as normal she set preparations in hand for Christmas. With Jennet's help she decked the house with greenery: bay, rosemary, holly and ivy garnered from around the Barton, and in the kitchen she busied herself with the mincemeat, plum puddings and sweetmeats that she always made for the farm workers' families and took to them with a cut of beef a week before Yule. She was up to her elbows in this mindless but not unpleasant task when a message arrived by word of mouth. The young lad who brought it was on foot. He had come from High Bickington, he explained. He was to tell her the gentleman and his lady from Exeter were there and safe. The lady was in good health but weak so they could travel but slowly and would arrive on the morrow. He was also to tell her the King's soldiers had withdrawn from Exeter and were being chased back to Cornwall.

With her heart in her mouth Ellen asked the boy the gentleman's name. He did not know, though was able to describe him. She thanked him, gave him a mug of ale, a fistful of currants and a shilling and sent him on his way. She knew Zach had sent her this message so she could prepare Jennet; the shock of seeing Bethan without warning might addle her wits completely. Ellen, her relief tempered by anxiety, took Jennet by the hand, led her into the parlour and sat her down on the settle. The child, sensing something was wrong, looked up at her, eyes wide with fear.

Ellen, deciding there was nothing to be gained by dissembling, came straight to the point. 'Do not be afraid, Jennet. Your mother is safe. She is with Zach and he is bringing her home. They will be here tomorrow and you and she will be able to make your peace.' For a moment the child stared at Ellen as if she had not understood, then, with a heartrending cry, leapt from the settle and fled. Ellen let her go. Later she would find her, most likely in the barn with the pups, and would offer what comfort she could. She did not doubt that once Jennet was reunited with Bethan her mother would know how best to deal with her and would be able to explain what had happened on that dreadful day. For the rest of the afternoon, Ellen remained in the parlour busying herself with her accounts and trying to contain the wild imaginings that filled her mind. Apparently Sir Ralph Hopton had been defeated outside Exeter, but what of Alexander?

Travelling only at night and keeping away from roads that by day clattered with Roundhead troopers scouring the countryside to mop up Hopton's fleeing Cavaliers, Alexander and his men rode slowly north from Bow. With heavy hearts they came eventually to Torrington. The town, its garrison commanded by Colonel John Acland, still held for the King and it afforded them a respite, a place to bury their two brothers-in-arms, which they did, in the parish church dedicated appropriately to St Michael.

Ten days after leaving Bow, by which time their wounds were beginning to heal, Alexander called the men together, waited until they were gathered in the front room of the cottage where he was billeted, and he had their attention.

'As you know, Sir Ralph means to return to Launceston to regroup and as you would expect, Plymouth is his next objective. He cannot make a move in that direction until he has raised more volunteers, replenished supplies of powder and ammunition, and the troops we expect from Ireland have arrived in Cornwall – all of which will take some weeks. Indeed, he is unlikely to be ready before mid-January. That being so, I believe this is a good time for you to go home. Spend Christmas with your families,' he paused, his expression grim, 'it is probable you will not have another opportunity to see them for many months.' He could tell by their faces they had heard the words he did not say: *if at all.*

Alexander indicated two sealed packages on a side table.

'I have written letters to John and Kit's parents and would be grateful if you would deliver them for me. It is the worst time of year to receive such dreadful tidings. I think their families would appreciate hearing from you who knew them so well, how courageously their sons lived and died. It may bring some comfort. Little enough, I know. Will you do that for me? I must go to the Chichesters of Hall and tell them about Dickon.'

'No!' James shook his head. 'Let me. It is too dangerous. My uncle will be beside himself. He will kill you.'

'It is my responsibility, James, not yours. I should never have let the boy remain with me.'

Chichester frowned. 'Had you not done so, you would doubtless be pushing up daisies by now and your skull decorating the London Gatehouse.' He gave a tight smile. 'Besides, if you remember, my cousin was on his way back to St Michael's to take the oath despite you. I doubt you could have prevented it and it was my fault he came to us in the first place.'

'That is no excuse,' Alexander murmured. 'As your Captain, it is still my responsibility.'

'On this occasion I beg leave to gainsay you,' Chichester said, shaking his head. 'I appreciate it is your honour that drives you, but this is a family matter. It will be better coming from me.'

Alexander held Chichester's sombre gaze for a moment, aware that what he said was true. If he went to break this dire news of Dickon to Richard Chichester, who hated him and everything he stood for, it would only make matters worse for Dickon's family. He nodded. 'Very well.'

He had not told any of the men how he had come by the wound in his shoulder, nor how narrowly he had escaped death at Dickon's hands. Indeed, only recently had he explained what he had been doing in Exeter, had deliberately kept it from them, knowing had he told them beforehand they would have risked their lives and neglected their duty to help him. The story of Bethan's rescue, its lighter aspects deliberately embellished, had provided a moment's relief in their otherwise unhappy ride from Bow. He had not, however, disclosed his meeting with Dickon at the height of the attack and saw no reason to do so now. They would be appalled at the boy's lack of faith, would not understand how he could have made so grave an error of judgement. Alexander, who blamed himself for not taking more care with the boy, did not want Dickon diminished in their eyes.

Pollard, who had been the most severely wounded, scratched at the bandaging on his chest. 'Will they hold the lad in Exeter do you suppose?'

Alexander shook his head. 'It is unlikely. They have little enough room. They will most likely ship the prisoners to London: the Gatehouse or the Tower, or possibly to Windsor if it still holds for Parliament. It'll be wherever they have the space; they might even use the Clink or the Fleet. God forbid, stinking hulks in the Thames.' He shrugged. 'Whichever, it is a sorry case for Dickon, I fear.'

James looked thoughtful. 'I think my uncle may persuade the Committee for Safety to release Dickon into his custody. He is only a boy after all, and Richard Chichester has stood firm for Parliament since the outset. He will argue the lad was made to act under duress. They will let him go.'

Alexander doubted it, but nodded. 'I hope that may be so.'

The following day they packed up their meagre belongings, took their leave of Colonel Acland and having agreed to meet up in Launceston – or wherever Sir Ralph Hopton's headquarters happened to be in the first week of January – left Torrington. None questioned where Alexander was going; all assumed he too was going home for Christmas.

Zach had at last been able to borrow a mount, so they were able to ride the last leg of their journey, Bethan wearing a long hooded robe and cradled in his arms as once her daughter had been. They arrived at Tawford Barton in the late afternoon and were met by Ellen, who came running up the track to meet them.

Zach's smile of greeting froze as he saw her agitation. 'Lady Ellen, this is Bethan Morgan, Jennet's mother – but what is it? Is something wrong?'

Ellen, her face taut with anxiety, shook her head. 'Not here, Zach, come into the house where Bethan can sit in comfort and I will tell you.'

Zach nodded, hurriedly dismounted and reached up to lift Jennet's mother from the saddle as Ellen, trying to remain calm, held out her hand. 'Bethan? How thankful I am to meet you at last, but you must be exhausted.'

She saw a short, slender woman, who drew back the hood of her robe and was smiling up at her, saw that beneath the escaping mass of dark, auburn hair, Bethan's eyes were slate grey and her face marked with fading ugly bruises. Ellen gasped, becoming aware that Jennet's mother was bobbing a curtsey, reached out and seized Bethan's hands. 'No, please, I beg you.'

Bethan inclined her head. 'Lady Ellen, you can be no more thankful than I. Zach has told me about you and what you have done for Jennet. I owe you a debt of gratitude that I will find hard to repay.'

Ellen shook her head, her eyes bright with tears.

Bethan observed her calmly. 'I think you should tell us what troubles you. It is Jennet? My daughter has gone, has she not? That is what is distressing you so?' Gently she withdrew her hands and lightly grasped Ellen's arm in a gesture that was almost a caress. 'You must not blame yourself, My Lady.'

Even as she felt strangely comforted, Ellen was astounded. It all came out in a rush. 'Yes. I am so sorry. I cannot forgive myself. It never occurred to me – she has seemed so much better of late. She disappeared yesterday.'

Suddenly remembering Bethan did not hear, Ellen directed her gaze to Zach. 'It was after we received your message. She was unsettled by the news and I thought it best to leave her for a while, but when I came to look for her I could not find her. I have searched everywhere. I do not know where next to look. I am so afraid for her.' She returned her gaze to Bethan. 'But how did you know?'

'I know my daughter, Lady Ellen,' Bethan gave a small shrug, her face white, her voice low and taut with pain. 'She believes I murdered her father. The wound is tearing her apart. It is too great for her to bear and she is frightened. Rather than face me she will seek solitude in a place where she feels safe. Short of keeping her captive there is little you could have done to prevent her from leaving. Jennet will have gone to the moor.' Bethan swayed, put out a hand. Zach shot out an arm and caught her as she fell.

The Royalist prisoners taken at Exeter, together with those captured at Modbury and held meantime in Dartmouth, were carried by ship to the Clink Prison beside the old Bishop's palace in Southwark. At one time the Liberty of the Clink had been under the jurisdiction of the Bishops of Winchester and the prison had been there for as long as anyone could remember, its cells echoing with the screams of ages past when both Catholics and Protestants had been held and tortured here. These days the inhabitants were mostly thieves and vagrants, misbehaving actors, prostitutes and drunks dragged from the taverns, theatres and brothels that abounded on the south bank of the Thames. Now it seemed the Clink was also to house prisoners of war. News of their arrival came to the Mermaid, no distance from the Clink as the sparrow flies. Cobb, to whom it might have meant something, was not there. Beth Doggett, who only ever expected the gypsy when she saw him, tucked the information away in case it might be useful.

Throughout the long, miserable journey from Exeter, Dickon had plumbed the very depths of depression. He scarcely noticed the harsh treatment he received at the hands of his captors; almost he welcomed the aching pangs of hunger and thirst, the unspeakable stench of human ordure that enveloped them in the closely packed hold. It suited his mood. The pain from the deep cut in his head, which refused to heal, the groans of men awash with shit and vomit and the stink of putrefaction helped to take his mind away from the anguish that lay cold like a stone in the pit of his belly. When he had seen Tawford running towards him, hands full of grenades, white kerchief fluttering from his shoulder proclaiming his allegiance, the bottom had dropped out of Dickon's world. Quick as thought, the shock of Tawford's betrayal rising in his throat like bile, he had aimed his pistol to obliterate that loved face. He told himself he had no regrets that he had killed Tawford; turncoat traitors deserved to die, so why did he ache so with emptiness? As he was herded with his fellow prisoners into the Clink, Dickon could not stem his bitter tears. The memory of the oath he had taken in St Michael's Church was like ashes in his mouth. His father had been right; he knew that now, but he would rather face death than acknowledge that truth. As the stink and despair of the prison closed around him, Dickon knew he would most likely be granted his wish. The thought held no fear for him. It was better so. He made his peace with God and waited for the end.

In the days since Lord Westley had set out for Devonshire accompanied by Bella – who had graciously but firmly refused his offer to hire a maidservant – his two men from the Bell Savage and four additional men hired by Cobb to guard them,

Cobb had been endeavouring to solve a puzzle.

His watchers had informed him of a stranger who had arrived in Arundel Street on the day Anne Dynam had been to see Lord Westley. Cobb had not seen the man himself, neither had he recognised the description: a tall, dark, well-favoured soldier would fit many another in London just now. Cobb had left no stone unturned, but the man's identity remained a mystery. The gypsy had been further discomfited to learn the stranger had also been seen in St Martin's Lane, but when his enquiries drew a blank in various quarters, he concluded it was a coincidence.

Receiving reports some days after Lord Westley's departure that the stranger had at last emerged from Anne Dynam's house, Cobb was not unduly concerned. They had observed a succession of young men going in and out of the widow's house over the last few weeks – indeed, her apparently voracious appetite had occasioned many a lewd comment from Cobb's watching men. Finding nothing whatever to connect the stranger to Lord Westley, Cobb eventually dismissed it as not meriting his further attention.

More significant was what Bella had discovered about Anne Dynam. It appeared she had a past association with a certain Oliver Woods, whom Bella knew to be have been engaged in undercover activities for France. She had told Cobb that Woods, whom she knew to be a vicious, unprincipled, lecherous bully, had some years ago been dismissed from his job at the East India Company's trading post in Madras, accused of embezzlement. Woods, maintaining his innocence, had resentfully turned to spying for Cardinal Richelieu. That Bella knew so much about him through her own covert association with Richelieu came as no surprise to Cobb. Tawford had told him she carried messages from France to England, principally to the King's Secretary of State, Sir Edward Nicholas. He had known too that Tawford had had similar dealings in years past, which was when he had met, helped and dallied with Arabella Béjart. None of this was of any consequence to Cobb, but he was concerned to find out more about this associate of Anne Dynam's, particularly given Tawford's find in the woods where Westley's son was killed. The significance of the spy's former life in the Indies did not escape Cobb. He set out to discover as much about the man as he could and soon learned Woods was back in England and working for Sir Samuel Luke. This information came as no surprise: Samuel Luke had recently been appointed by the Earl of Essex as a scoutmaster-general and was fast gaining a reputation as an effective spymaster. He would attract men like Woods as bees to a honey pot.

Armed with this information, Cobb set further investigations in train. He put Matthew Rudge onto it, or 'Weasel' as he was known: Weasel by name and weasel by nature, he was the best man Cobb knew for this kind of work. Eventually, Weasel tracked Woods to London. Sir Samuel Luke's spy was as slippery as an eel, he reported: moved about a lot, rarely frequented the same tavern nor slept in the same place twice and it was impossible to establish a pattern, but Weasel lived up to his name. Unobserved, he weaselled his way into Woods's domain and was able to report that at no time did the spy communicate with Anne Dynam. It seemed that his association with the widow was long past.

Cobb, after a week's absence from the smothering arms of his mistress, returned eager to the Mermaid and did not hear Beth Doggett's news until some time after they had retired to bed. He pricked up his ears. Royalist prisoners from the South West might carry news of Tawford. Since two of the turnkeys at the Clink were Mermaid regulars – a relationship Beth had fostered deliberately, given the proclivities of her clientele – it would not be too difficult to find out.

It wasn't. Cobb soon had the names of the prisoners. He had never met the young Dickon Chichester, but from Hartley he had learned of the boy's brave ride to St Michael's and his loyalty to Tawford. Arrangements were made, a considerable sum of money changed hands and within days Dickon was carried after dark from the Clink to the Mermaid. Knocked unconscious to keep him quiet – he had evidently been unwilling to co-operate – he was done up in hessian and passed to Cobb like a sack of marrowbones.

Dickon recovered consciousness to find himself in a soft bed lit by mellow lights and smelling sweetly of rosewater. As expected, he had died and was in heaven. Looking up he observed St Peter was waiting to address him. It was disappointing that there were no wings in evidence, but perhaps they were tucked behind – St Peter was as big a man as he had seen – only fitting for an angel. Dickon gulped, wished he had not been quite so sinful in his short life, observed the big man was about to speak and was not, after all, quite what he would have expected of so august a heavenly body – at which point his head exploded with pain and he knew he was alive.

'Hello Dickon, you have had a rough ride. I am sorry, but it was necessary. You are safe now.'

Dickon licked his lips. 'Who are you?'

'My name is Cobb. You will have heard of me I daresay?'

It was Tawford's man. Dickon's heart thumped in his chest. He looked warily up at the gypsy wondering what he knew.

'Yes, I have heard of you.'

'I won't keep you long, my boy, you need time to recover, but before I let you sleep, can you give me news of Tawford?'

God's wounds! So he did not know. For a moment Dickon was tempted to say nothing, but Cobb would soon find out what had happened and then would probably kill him. He grimaced, wished he did not feel so sick. 'He is dead.'

The big man's florid face went white. He sat down with a thump on the side of the bed, the tester swayed alarmingly.

'What did you say?'

'He is dead.'

Looking old and sad, Cobb's usual jovial features were set in a tense mask as he studied the boy's face. 'When – and how?'

'At Exeter, I am not sure when it was. I've lost track of

the time; maybe four weeks? We – that is, St Michael's, were with Sir Ralph Hopton and Sir Bevill Grenville when they marched from Plympton to take the city.' Dickon faltered as the horrifying sights and sounds filled his mind. He put his hand up to his eyes.

'Go on.'

'Tawford was not with us. Lyddon said he had some business in Exeter.' A sob rose in Dickon's throat. 'Well I know what that was now,' he cried, his voice harsh with bitterness. 'The rebels attacked us at night. Came round behind us, took us completely by surprise.' Scalding tears fell unchecked. 'Tawford was with them, leading them. He betrayed us and I killed him.' Dickon's voice dropped to a whisper. 'Shot him in the face with my pistol. It was what he deserved.'

Cobb started, his mouth dropped open, the sweat glistening on his bald head. 'You did what?' Grasping Dickon by the shoulders he pulled him half up from the bed. Gone were the kindly eyes, the gentle expression, of a sudden he looked mean and cruel and Dickon gasped with fear. Careless of the boy's injury the big man shook him backwards and forwards, rattling the teeth in his head. 'You did what?'

Unable to speak or resist, Dickon bit his tongue; blood spurted from his lips. Cobb flung him down, stood up and turned away from the bed, his mind in a whirl. It was a dreadful mistake, but nothing would be gained by taking his distress out on the boy. Controlling his emotions, he reached for the aqua vitae Beth had left by the bed and took a long swig, then, supporting Dickon's head, held the flask to his lips. The boy swallowed. The fiery liquid stung his tongue, coursed down his throat. He coughed. Cobb let him gently back onto the pillow. 'Now, tell me exactly what happened.'

'We were betrayed,' Dickon sobbed. 'Tawford had gone ahead with some of the others to spy out the city's defences. He sent the men back with the intelligence and he stayed behind. He was there all the while we were approaching. Lyddon said he had some personal business to take care of and would catch us up as soon as he was able.' The boy broke off, his face hot and angry. 'It was a foul lie. His personal business was betrayal. He was leading the rebels when they fell on us with grenades. There was no mistaking it. I saw him, as close to me as you are now. He was laying about with a halberd, carrying grenades and wearing the white kerchief they all wore. I s-s-shot him. I saw him fall. He is dead. He was a t-t-traitor; he deserved to d-d-die.' The boy's stammering voice sunk to a whisper and he burst into a storm of uncontrolled weeping.

Cobb sat heavily on the bed his head in his hands. After a moment he rubbed his face and looked again at Dickon. The boy was flushed with fever, his eyes wild with distress. Cobb, who knew Tawford of old, could imagine that he had been careless with this lad. Had won his devotion without even thinking about it and then neglected him. That Tawford had been engaged in some personal business in Exeter was not hard to imagine – it was just like him to keep whatever it was to himself. But whatever that might be, if they all lived till kingdom come, he would never have betrayed his men no matter what happened to him. He would die first. Any one of them would know it – but clearly not this boy. Well now he had died. Cobb's belly lurched as he took it in. Alexander – dead. Despite all his efforts to watch over him all these years, he had not been there for him when it mattered most. It could have happened at any time; Alexander was a law unto himself. He had died as he had lived, recklessly. It were ever thus and Cobb had always known he might not be able to keep him safe, but knowing it did not lessen the bitter anguish of his failure.

His heart heavy, he waited for Dickon's sobbing to subside, addressed the boy as gently as he could. 'I fear you have made a dreadful mistake. It is probably not your fault, you have not known Tawford long and in the heat of battle our normal senses desert us, there is no time to think. We react instinctively. But whatever you thought you saw, lad, I can assure you he was no traitor. There will have been a good reason for his guise as a rebel. He would never have betrayed you, not in a thousand years. You will understand that one day and I fear it is something you will have to learn to live with. For now you must allow yourself to grieve, for despite believing Tawford deserved to die, I think you are grieving, are you not?'

Dickon was undone by Cobb's gentleness; tears scalding his face, he nodded dumbly. If it was true and he had been mistaken, he had broken his sacred oath and killed Tawford in cold blood. He was a murderer, foresworn. If it was not true and Tawford was a traitor, then the man whom he had loved so dearly had betrayed his trust and the oath meant nothing. Whatever he chose to believe, Tawford was gone and all he could feel was an aching emptiness. Dickon knew it would haunt him forever. He could not think. He closed his eyes and swallowed, the gorge rising in his throat. He had thought he was dead. He so wanted to die.

Cobb stood. 'I will send someone to you to tend your wound. Try to rest. We will talk some more on the morrow.'

Leaving Dickon sobbing, Cobb sought the comfort of Beth. With Alexander dead his job was done. He could go home. Home at long last. Home to Ireland and the woman who was his only reason for being; home to confess that he had failed her. But first, he owed it to Alexander's memory to deal with Anne Dynam and remove the threat to Lord Westley.

James Dewett was singing. Not just humming, but singing at the top of his voice. After Edgehill, when he had volunteered to escort the wounded, he had been granted a week's leave of absence. By the time he had eventually torn himself from the arms of his most beautiful, his most accomplished, his most unparalleled, his most – words failed him for how could he possibly describe her – mistress, he had outstayed his leave.

It no longer mattered. He would not be missed. His regiment had been victorious at Turnham Green, beating back Prince Rupert's Cavaliers and sending them packing, along with the big white dog that followed the foreign Prince into battle and which folk said was his familiar – an imp of Satan – Dewett snorted at the thought.

On learning from Anne that Lord Westley and his betrothed had left London and were returning to Devonshire, instead of rejoining his regiment, Dewett had gone to Westminster, presented himself to the Committee for Safety and volunteered to be an agent for Parliament. He had information that would lead him to Sir Ralph Hopton's aide, the man whom he had so regretfully failed to secure following the arrest of Lord Bath. He was now confident he could redeem himself, recapture this Royalist spy and at the same time gain intelligence concerning the enemy's movements in the South West.

It was a lie, of course. His prime intention was to find and kill Alexander Dynam of Tawford, not just for himself, for Anne. He intended also to kill the bastard's father, Lord Westley, because she had asked him to. And when he had done for them both, he would return triumphant to her bed. He neglected to mention any of these facts to the dour man who granted him audience – a minion of the Committee – and who gazed at him with quickening interest. Hopton was a thorn in their sides and Dewett was confident his proposal would meet with approval. He had been kept waiting for quite a time, kicking his heels in an antechamber, but eventually the minion returned and handed to him a commission. He was now officially a scout under the command of General Sir Samuel Luke, and his orders were to discover Hopton's strength and plans, and take the information to Lord Stamford in Exeter. If at all possible, the Royalist spy, Alexander Dynam of Tawford, was to be captured alive and brought to London. Bowing acknowledgement, Dewett tucked away the all-important piece of paper. Now he had it in his hands, he intended to do neither.

Dewett had changed his appearance, following at a leisurely pace in Westley's footsteps and leading a packhorse, he looked more like a gamekeeper than a soldier. He had cut his hair short in Puritan fashion and let his beard grow out of shape. He wore a floppy hat pulled well down over his face and he had exchanged his belted leather coat for a jerkin. For warmth he had secured a sheepskin round his shoulders. Underneath it all, on a leather thong around his neck, he carried a soft pouch of money. It was far more than he needed – he smiled remembering how Anne had insisted – it made a comforting bulge under his shirt. Folded in his saddlebag, to hand in case Parliament's soldiers should challenge him, was his commission. He had made it his business to find out that there was not much Royalist activity betwixt London and Devon. So long as he avoided Marlborough, which was currently under siege by the delinquent Lord Wilmot and his bastard Cavaliers, and Oxford, for that is where the King had established his court and quartered his army for the winter, he should have no difficulty. Dewett was in no hurry. There had been little point in making an attempt on Westley's life on the road. The man was too well guarded and Dewett did not want to fail. Not prepared to take the risk, he had dropped right back. Anne had given him detailed directions to Marley Court, he could afford to take his time, pick his way and stay out of trouble.

As he rode he rehearsed in his mind what he was going to do when he got there. At the first opportunity he would kill the father – that would bring the son running. He laughed exultantly. He would be waiting for him. He longed for the moment. Afterwards he would return to Anne; she had promised him much. His chest swelled; he had not done badly for a country lad from a small village in Bedfordshire. His father, a ploughman, had died when he was three and his mother married again, to a smith. Dewett had been only four years old when his stepfather had put him to work in the forge – he remembered how upset his mother had been, but too frightened of her husband to help him. Denied the opportunity to go to school, he had spent all his daylight hours working with metal – except on Sundays, which he had spent largely on his knees praying for forgiveness for sins he was not aware he had committed. He had hated the forge: the stultifying heat and stink, the grinding labour, his hands and arms always smarting from burns and covered in calluses, his shoulders constantly bruised and his backside always sore. It was either that or a beating. Every time his small fingers fumbled, which they often did, his stepfather would stand over him undoing his belt. Dewett never knew if the belt would come stinging down onto his shoulders or if he would be thrown to the floor, his breeches yanked down, forced to bend over and submit to the unspeakable things his stepfather did to him. He was not even sure which punishment he abhorred least; he had never told his mother for fear she would stop loving him. The shameful thing that happened must be his fault; he was a bad boy, his stepfather told him so continually. Eaten up with fear, guilt and pain, Dewett had endured each day of his childhood in a welter of misery.

One day, not long after his mother had gone to the Lord and he had lost the only thing in his life worth living for, the worm had turned. Aged only twelve and strong as an ox – his musculature was the one thing for which he had to thank his stepfather – Dewett had waited until the belt came off, seized a hammer, laid into his tormentor and beat his brains out. He had not meant to kill him, but when he saw that he had, he was not sorry. He had left the body where it lay and set the forge on fire. When the flames began to eat into the timbers he had run into the house, found his stepfather's savings and fled. He had not stopped running until he reached Somerset. There he had lied about his age and joined the Militia. Determined to be the best at every physical sport he had constantly practised with sword and musket and had soon risen through the ranks. He had blessed the day when the King and Parliament went to war; it had opened up opportunities he had hardly dared hope for and he had seized them. The Lord helps those who help themselves. His mother had told him that and it was true. Dewett burst into another song; he had done well, but he was going to do even better. The future was golden.

Once Ellen had got used to Bethan's strangely direct gaze and unsettling way of seeming to know what she was going to say before she said it, she warmed to her. While Zach was out quartering the moor, they had sat by the fire in the parlour and Bethan described what had happened to Morgan. It had been exactly as Ellen had surmised. He must have concealed the dagger beneath the bedclothes, Bethan said. He had been in much pain that morning and had hit out at her even more than usual, bruising her face so badly she had almost lost consciousness. Appalled by what he had done – he always was afterwards – he had seized the blade and plunged it into his chest. She had tried to prevent it, but the strength in his arms was too much for her. The force of it had thrown him to the floor. Jennet had entered the room as she was trying to help him and in her agony of shock had mistaken what she saw. In her daughter's eyes she had killed him twice over, not only by plunging the blade into Morgan's chest, but by making no attempt to save him. Jennet was too young to understand how it had been for them since that dreadful day the barn caught fire taking their son – their only child – too young to comprehend what Morgan had suffered. When the constable and the verderer had come to the farm to arrest her on that dreadful day, Bethan had believed Jennet was lost to her forever. She had confessed to murder because it seemed the only thing left she could do for them; to ensure Morgan had a Christian burial. She had hoped one day Jennet would understand and thank her for it.

Even though Ellen had guessed most of what Bethan told

her, listening to her soft voice describing the horror of it wrung at her heart and it took her a while to hear what Bethan had actually said. As it dawned on her she was about to query it when Bethan spoke.

'Yes, you heard aright. Morgan and I had only one child, our son, Owen. Morgan was not Jennet's father. I tell you this only because of your kindness and generosity of spirit – and because Morgan is dead and it can no longer hurt him to hear it said, though naturally it would devastate Jennet. I have never told anyone before.'

Ellen felt as though Bethan's steady gaze was piercing her soul. Framing her words slowly and with care, she clasped Bethan's hand, gave it a quick squeeze. 'You need have no fear that I would break any confidence, least of all one so potentially damaging.'

'I know,' Bethan said at length. 'And I thank you for it. I was pregnant when Morgan married me. I did not conceal it from him. He knew I did not love him; I had already refused his proposal of marriage twice before. He raised Jennet as his own and loved her dearly and I would have forgiven him anything for that alone, but he had a sweetness and gentleness about him that I grew to love. But he was never able to forget I had granted to another the favours I had at first refused him, though his jealousy did not become apparent until after he was so badly injured. Only then did his ugly resentment come to the fore. It was as if his impotence and helplessness had negated everything we had come to mean to each other. All that was left was his mad jealousy. But by then we were trapped by our circumstances – and I suppose I felt guilty. I could not have left him. And at the last I knew he had never stopped loving me. We were able to make our peace and I thank God for it.'

Listening to this, Ellen had the strangest sensation that it was her own story she was hearing – though not its dreadful outcome. She too had been forced by pregnancy into a marriage with a man she did not love. But unlike Bethan, she had not been honest with Edward.

'Jennet's father – did you love him? Why did he not marry you?'

'For a time I thought I did. When I told him I was carrying his child he offered to marry me, but I knew he didn't love me. We had come together in the heat of the moment, but I knew his heart could never be mine. He was consumed by love for another; a woman far above him who was already married. I realised that he had used me to assuage his bitter wanting. I wasn't prepared to live like that and though he was a good man at heart, I did not believe he would stay with us.' Bethan shrugged. 'I wanted Jennet to have a father, not an empty name. I went to Morgan and told him what had happened. I promised that if he would be a father to my child, I would make him a good wife.'

'Did he know who it was?'

'No. I have never told a soul. Had he known he would have tried to kill him – he may even have succeeded, though I doubt it. More likely he would have died in the attempt. He tried to wring the name from me – it was something we quarrelled about constantly, it was one of the reasons he beat me.' Bethan grimaced. 'It is a secret I shall carry to my grave, except… that is, unless…'

'Jennet should ever need to know?'

Bethan met Ellen's steady gaze and nodded. 'Yes. I knew you would understand. Should anything ever happen to me and she is in need, then of course – it is her right. Which is why I am telling you. I had always meant to tell one other person; someone I could trust to keep the knowledge safe. As I lay among the dead in Exeter and came face to face with my own mortality, I realised I may have left it too late. I had thought perhaps Alexander…, but his life is as uncertain as mine. And so I am asking you because I sense in you the same sweetness of spirit that I see in him.'

Despite the gravity of what she was being asked, Ellen smiled. 'Few people know him that well, let alone after so brief a meeting. "Sweetness" is not a word that many associate with Alexander. Your intuition astounds me. But yes – he is the gentlest and most vulnerable of men, though he conceals it most carefully.' She paused to be sure Bethan understood her, the smile gone from her face. 'What you ask of me is a heart-rending responsibility.'

'I am aware that I ask a very great deal of you who hardly know me, but I ask it all the same. Will you bear it for me?'

Ellen looked at her gravely. With her own memories brought so near to the surface came the cruel image of her own baby girl whom she had not been allowed to see grow to maturity, she could feel only sympathy for Bethan; understood what she was being asked and why. With tears spilling down her cheeks she inclined her head, said. 'Of course.' Keeping her face neutral, she listened as Bethan revealed her secret.

When Zach returned after dark, his face bleak and weary, the two women were sitting side by side on the settle in silence, their thoughts turned inward, their anxiety shared.

Zach continued to search for several days, but Jennet was nowhere to be found. If she had indeed gone to the moor, it had probably swallowed her up – claimed her as one of its own – and perhaps that was what she had wanted. Who was he to question it?

Eventually, his heart heavy, Zach stopped searching.

26

Friday 9th December, 1642

Two weeks after leaving London, Dewett reached Marley Court. He waited until after it was dark, left his horses concealed in adjacent woodland and crept along the hedgerow until he came to the side of the lawns sloping down from the front of the house. He forced his way through the hedge, cursing as his foot slipped and he caught his hand on a bramble. Sucking the blood from his fingers he looked about him. It was as usual drizzling, but there was enough moonlight behind the scudding clouds to see the carriageway; it was lined with trees, the wind soughing through the bare branches. Away on his left was an arched gateway with a lodge. The big house was to his right; brick built from what he could see and well proportioned with a wing at each side. It was in darkness and he could detect no signs of habitation. He followed the line of the hedge and worked his way round to the back. A track led on presumably to the home farm; he decided not to venture down it to find out. Cautiously sliding along a wall he found the entrance to a cobbled courtyard surrounded by stables and coach houses. Nothing moved. He crept into the stables; they were empty. Disappointment lurched in his stomach. He went again to the front of the house and peered through some of the windows. He could just make out the dustsheets. If there was a caretaker he was not in evidence; probably lived in the lodge. It was apparent that not only was Lord Westley not here but he was not expected. Somehow, even though he had been behind and travelling slowly, he had overtaken him. No; that was impossible – Westley and his guards must have stopped off somewhere. Either that or something had happened to them. It occurred to him then that they might have stopped at Oxford, which he had so assiduously avoided. Devil take it! Cursing softly he retraced his steps.

By the time he returned to his horses he felt better. It mattered not. All he had to do was wait. Westley would turn up sooner or later. For tonight he would find somewhere to sleep. He did not want to stay at an inn; strangers always led to talk. He wanted nobody to know of his existence. He was used to living by his wits; had many times camped out in the open. There was sure to be a derelict barn somewhere in the vicinity. He would find one and tomorrow he would steal what he needed to subsist. The situation had not changed. He could be patient.

While Dickon lay at the Mermaid, nursed by Katherine, his head wound healing but not his heart, Cobb sent a messenger to Oxford where the King had reportedly established his court and where Adam Hartley was likely to be found with those of Tawford's men who had survived Edgehill. It was possible that Hartley had already received the heart stopping news from Exeter, but he could not be sure. Dickon had been unable to tell him if any of the others still lived. They might all be gone; it was a sad and chilling thought.

That done, he set about planning a trap for Oliver Woods. He singled out a young woman – known in the Mermaid as 'Angel' on account of her exquisite appearance – and gave her explicit instructions. Part of her attraction lay in her look of childlike, almost virginal innocence, which appealed to some men – she did indeed look like an Angel. Given the enthusiasm with which she went about her work, it was as incongruous as it was erotic and she was usually reserved for only the most favoured of customers. Cobb had a feeling that Woods would be easy prey. Beth, who almost always let Cobb have what he wanted but enjoyed being persuaded, eventually agreed to it for a fat fee. A lad was duly assigned to Weasel as a runner. He came for Cobb and Angel some days later. Woods had at last chosen to dine out and was to be found at the Star Inn on Fish Street Hill. They hurried over the river and met Weasel outside the Star. Woods was still inside, but had finished his dinner; they needed to make haste. With an appreciative grin, Weasel put his arm around Angel's waist, puckered his lips, gave her a smacking kiss and took her inside. Confident of the outcome, Cobb waited out of sight.

He soon heard the commotion. Angel had followed her instructions to the letter and as he had anticipated Woods was easy meat. She had lasciviously invited his attentions and once engaged, Weasel, playing the part of the jealous lover, was creating an angry scene. Not long afterwards Woods emerged with his prize on his arm. Cobb, joined a moment later by a breathless Weasel sporting a rapidly blackening eye, followed them to an adjacent lodging house. After waiting for a few minutes, with Weasel at his back Cobb followed them in. The landlord listening to what they wanted, taking in the gypsy's size and mean expression and noting that his hatchet-faced companion had been in a fight, looked around for an escape route, but when he saw the coins the big man was gently massaging in his fingers, his greed got the better of him. He gave Cobb a master key, directed him up the stairs, grabbed the money and beat a hasty retreat. Cobb located the room let to Woods, and waited outside the door listening. When the noises from within started climbing to a crescendo he unlocked it and strode silently across to the bed. Oliver Woods, his breath coming in hoarse gasps, his fleshy buttocks pumping obscenely over Angel's inert body, was beyond noticing anything. Cobb judged the moment to a nicety. As Woods cried out, only seconds away from the brief moment of ecstasy towards which he so vigorously laboured, Cobb cocked his pistol and put it to the back of the spy's sweating head. The man whimpered and froze. Angel scrambled out from under him and still naked rummaged around for his purse. She shook it, grinned with delight at Weasel who had appeared in the doorway, hastily flung her gown over her head, thrust her feet into her shoes and fled.

Like all bullies, Oliver Woods was a coward. Lifted from the bed by the scruff of his neck, his body screaming with anguished frustration, he offered no resistance. Shivering, he listened to what the big man wanted. Sitting in a chair with a pistol held to his head and a blade waving close to his moist, now flaccid penis, he would have agreed to anything. The job he had done for Anne Dynam, his mistress back then, was a long time ago, but he remembered it perfectly. She had paid him a considerable amount of money to make it look like an accident. It had been a filthy wet day. He had known he had only one shot and it was risky; the boy was a small moving target; he had feared he would miss and be seen. Had the fair-headed youth not been armed with a fowling piece it might not have mattered. As it was, he had been delighted to see Henry Dynam on the big, mettlesome stallion. He had deflected his dart to the horse's neck – a much bigger target – knowing it would bring the beast down. On that particular stretch and riding at such reckless speed, he would be unlucky if it did not mortally injure the boy. It did. And what's more, it had seemed like the accident he had hoped to achieve. From his perch in the tree he had seen the horse bolt and fall. He had watched the youth despatch it and carry the boy's body away. He had checked to ensure the dart was no longer in the beast's neck, buried his blowgun some way away – not that anyone in Devon would have recognised it for what it was, but he was a cautious man – and ridden away.

Racking his brains as he related these details to his tormentor, Woods tried to work out how they could possibly have connected him to this long ago crime. Shuddering in the chair, his hands clamped between his legs and his eyes watering, he concluded it could only be by witchcraft. Squeakily he directed Weasel to his saddlebag for writing paper, pen and ink as instructed. Shaking, he wrote, smeared and signed a confession stating that in 1634, he, Oliver Woods, had been hired by the dowager Lady Anne Westley, widow of the late Cleve Dynam, Viscount Westley, to kill Henry, son and heir of Robert Dynam, and that he had succeeded in so doing. He signed it and handed it to the big, bald-headed man who promptly insisted he produce two duplicates. He did so, watching helplessly as the two men attached their signatures as witnesses. That done the big man lifted the pistol.

Woods screamed. Bursting into noisy tears, spittle and snot dripping from his lips, a stream of urine splattering down his leg, he fell to his knees and grovelled, grasped Cobb's foot and pleaded for his life. Cobb kicked him away. 'I wouldn't waste powder or shot on you, you stinking, miserable old turd. But take note of this.' Cobb leaned close, his face only inches away, 'I will be watching you.'

He brought the butt of his pistol down on the spy's grizzled head and left him sprawled naked and unconscious on the floor. He then searched in the saddlebag, withdrew a number of closely written pages and a dagger, which he inspected and tucked into his belt. He took one last look around, nodded at Weasel to follow and left the room, locking the door behind them.

The following day, purporting to be acting on Lord Westley's behalf and having left a sealed packet with His Lordship's lawyer earlier that morning, Cobb went to Arundel Street and was admitted on the strength of Tawford's name. The widow looked him up and down with distaste and kept him standing by the door of her parlour. 'I imagine you have a message for me?'

'No. I do not. I have something else for you.'

Anne Dynam was taken aback. The slovenly man was very

large and extremely surly, his manner both impertinent and threatening. She felt a prickle of fear. 'Explain yourself.'

Cobb drew from his shirt a piece of paper and held it enticingly just out of her reach. 'It concerns the untimely death of the present Viscount Westley's son, Henry Dynam. You wanted evidence of Tawford's proof I believe? Well I have brought it for you.'

She snatched at the paper. He withdrew it and watched the colour spreading up from her neck, suffusing her cheeks. 'I will not pay whatever ridiculous sum you are going to demand unless I see it first,' she snapped.

Cobb waited for a moment, watching as she struggled to maintain her dignity then handed it to her with a mocking bow. She took it from him and read it quickly, tore it across and across, hissing, 'You think I would pay for this?' Her lips lifted in a smile of triumph as she flung the pieces into the fire and brushed her hands together. 'Tawford shows a distinct lack of wisdom in selecting his lapdogs these days. Do I detect a certain desperation in his methods?' She laughed.

Holding her gaze, Cobb slowly drew from his shirt another confession. 'Woods was not shaking quite so much when he wrote this one. It is much easier to read.' With an evil smile, he folded and replaced it in his shirt. 'I am not asking for your money, lady. Any agreement you made with Tawford is hereby withdrawn.' He moved towards her, saw her reaching for the bell, his smile broadened. 'The third copy is the best of all. Naturally I have it in a safe place. By all means call your guards, it will avail you nothing.'

Snatching back her hand, her eyes bright with angry tears, Anne Dynam glared at him. 'What do you want for them?'

'Nothing. I repeat, they are not for sale.' No trace of a smile remained on Cobb's face. His eyes were like chips of granite, his voice taut with menace. 'If you ever harm so much as a hair on Lord Westley's head, the third confession will be unsealed and presented in a court of law by His Lordship's lawyer, independent of whether or not I or Lord Westley are still alive. Do I make myself clear?'

Anne Dynam was speechless. She understood two things: one that she had been bested, which filled her with an anger so hot she could scarcely see, the other that this nightmare of a man was not going to use his evidence if she agreed to his terms. Sadly it was too late and there was little she could do about it. Summoning all her reserves of courage she gave him look for look.

'Pah! It is not worth the paper it is written on. It has clearly been given under duress and I very much doubt if the two witnesses are credible.' Her lip curled, mocking him. 'One of them is you, I assume. And pray, which one would that be – Barnabas Cobbart O'Neill or Matthew Rudge? The least you can do is tell me your name. Whatever, it will not stand up in a court of law.'

'Even if you are willing to take that risk, you should know that Oliver Woods will support his confession verbally if he has to. And he will have to.' Cobb paused, the evil smile once more flitting over his mouth. There was no humour in it. Added, softly, 'He is not a very brave man.'

At that her legs gave way. Trembling she fell backwards onto the settle. Cobb made no move to help her. She gasped.

'I fear you are a little late. How very unfortunate!'

Starting forward Cobb leaned over her, his hand opening to strike. 'What are you saying?'

She shrank back. 'I have given details of Lord Westley's probable whereabouts to a certain Captain James Dewett.' Anne Dynam paused as she saw Cobb's reaction. 'Ah. I see you know the name.' Afraid of Cobb as she was, she could not resist a mocking smile. 'He is even now on his way to Marley Court. He means to kill the bastard boy, but first he will kill Lord Westley – it is his gift to me. He believes it will bring Westley's son running. I neglected to tell him Tawford wants his father dead almost as much as I do. But never mind,' she attempted a laugh. It was strangled. 'They can kill each other for all I care. So you can take your worthless confession,

JO FIELD

sirrah. Be assured I will have no trouble in discrediting Oliver Woods. I will use everything I have at my disposal to fight you through the courts and if I succeed...', she looked him up and down, her lip curling, 'which I don't doubt that I will, I will see you hang. On that you can depend.'

She had regained her self-control. Cobb saw it and knew she spoke the truth. He did not tell her Tawford was already dead. He kicked himself that he had not taken the stranger, whom he now knew to be James Dewett, more seriously nor had him followed when he left Arundel Street. It had been no coincidence that Dewett had been seen in St Martin's Lane. The man must have tracked Lord Westley from Edgehill. Unable to contain his anger and frustration, Cobb shouted out loud and with the flat of his hand, smacked the woman hard across her mocking face, knocking her to the ground. She did not even cry out, she simply lay there looking at him, triumph and contempt warring in her eyes, the imprint of his hand flaming on her cheek. He left her lying there. He had thought he had won, but he had lost. Everything.

It was the end of the afternoon when he got back to the Mermaid. Beth Doggett met him at the door, her face wreathed in smiles, her chins wobbling in an ecstasy of delight. She seized him by the hand, led him to her room pulled him in and stood breathlessly in front of him. He gazed at her perplexed. He and Beth rubbed along quite well in their way; she was a satisfying mistress and they had enjoyed each other on and off for years, but he had never known her so eager for him as this. Inwardly he sighed; he was emotionally drained. He could no more accommodate her right now than he could fly to the moon.

Pushing her away apologetically, he opened his mouth to tell her so when from behind her bulk a voice drawled. 'What a shame; he is getting too old for you, my sweet girl. You will just have to come to me instead.'

It was a voice Cobb had thought never to hear again. His roar echoed through the Mermaid, put several of its clients off their stroke and started the curs barking in the street. Laughing, Beth stood to one side, left them to it, closing the door behind her.

Tawford was perched on the side of the bed, one sardonic eyebrow raised. In two strides Cobb had reached him, lifted him from the bed and enveloped him in a bear hug. 'You bastard boy; I might have known it would take more than a pistol shot to kill you. Hide like an elephant, always said so.'

'Unhand me, man. For goodness' sake.' Tawford pushed him away and brushed himself down, but he was grinning like a brewer's horse as he perched back on the bed, the candlelight throwing shadows on his boyish face and turning his hair rose gold.

It was only then Cobb remembered Dickon. 'There is a young man not so very far from here who will probably faint when he sees you.'

'I know. Beth told me. I understand he is mending under Katherine's lovely hands. Lucky boy. I imagine he is sufficiently recovered to be responding to her charms? I doubt he has any money and I am not at all sure I can afford her for as long as he is likely to want her. I suspect she may be his first. Best tell her to be gentle with him. Ah, the joys of youth.' He laughed. 'You have saved me a job, for which I thank you. Cobb to the rescue as always, eh? I will go and see him directly when I am not quite so drunk. I imagine the sight of me will be as welcome as snow at harvest. He tried to kill me, you know.'

Cobb nodded, his face suddenly grave. He had been right in his reading of the situation. It seemed Tawford had not the slightest idea of the boy's distressed mental state. 'He thinks he succeeded. You should tread a little carefully there, my boy. He doesn't know whether he made a mistake and is a foresworn murderer or whether you are a traitor and betrayed him. Either way he is unhappy about it and not even Katherine's charms can pull him out of the pit he's in right now.'

'Oh, for Lord's sake, stop your jabberment, you addlepated

old fool. Why the devil do you think I am here?'

Cobb grunted and ruefully smiled. 'And to think I was pleased to see you. There is something else you need to know – about Oliver Woods.'

'Woods? Can't say I know the name. What about him?'

'But you've heard of Samuel Luke?'

Tawford's eyes narrowed and he nodded, listened in silence, his unwavering gaze fixed on the gypsy's face.

'So it was a blow tube. My instincts were right,' Alexander murmured as Cobb came to the end of his story.

'Yes – Woods admitted it. He called it a blowgun. When Bella told me she'd discovered the widow had associated with Woods and that he had worked in the Indies, I put two and two together. Extracting a confession was not difficult. He won't be troubling anyone for a day or two. I lifted a list of ciphers that might interest you, but that's the least of it.'

'Go on.'

Cobb described his meeting with Anne Dynam and what he had learned from her. When he had finished, Tawford let out his breath in a long sigh. 'Dewett! Godamme! I should have killed him when I had the chance.' The string of oaths that loosed from Tawford's lips was inventive even by Cobb's standards.

Cobb hung his head, his round face wreathed in misery. 'I had hoped to make things safe. I was too careless and too late. I have failed Lord Westley. You cannot know how sorry I am about that.'

Alexander jumped up from the bed and clapped his hands to Cobb's arms. 'Good God, man; you cannot be in two places at once and you cannot keep us all safe. That you should think to try is worthy of more gratitude than I ever show you. Don't talk of failure.' He released Cobb and turned away, started pacing the room. 'Dewett may not have acted yet. There's many a slip twixt cup and lip. We may yet be in time. Is Dickon well enough to travel?'

Cobb nodded. 'What ails him is not physical.'

'Then I had best go and see him before I get any drunker – which is what I fully intend to do. Tomorrow I will recall Hartley, and then I will take Dickon home for Christmas and we shall see. Thanks to you, our work is done here. You may think you have failed, but if we can catch Dewett in time, Anne Dynam will be in no hurry to test the efficacy of those confessions. It is up to my guardian how he wishes to use them. Will you come home with us?'

Cobb grinned with relief. 'Yes. I will come. And I have already passed news of your death to Hartley.' He gave a wry smile. 'I wasn't sure if the others were able to do so. How did they fare? I gather from Dickon it was a heated confrontation at Exeter.'

Alexander grimaced as he brought Cobb up to date, told him about Cornwall, about Gifford's guise as a Frenchman and what they had achieved from it, though it all seemed pointless now; how he had stayed behind and why – he assumed Cobb knew of the Morgans? He related briefly what had occurred. He ended with the night sally, the wound he had received from Dickon and the death of Basset and Acland. He stopped pacing and looked up. While had had been talking Cobb had moved to sit down on the bed, his face was in shadow, his hand clinging white-knuckled to the bedpost. Alexander turned his mouth down.

'Their loss saddens me too, Cobb – more than I can say – and those we lost at Edgehill. God curse this damnable war.'

He slammed his first against the bedpost. The tester swayed over Cobb's head.

Eventually Cobb spoke, his voice strained. 'I had best go break the news of our departure to Beth.' He stood up and went to the door. Looked back over his shoulder. 'You will go to Dickon now?'

'Yes. I will go to Dickon now. And then, my old friend, we shall drink the night away and enjoy the delights of the Mermaid while we may. Tomorrow is another day.'

Cobb nodded, but did not smile. Alexander was not

surprised. Although Cobb did not know the men as well as he, he shared the same sense of loss and pity at the waste of it. He sighed, knew he must concentrate on the living. He had not had time to go to the Barton, all his efforts had been focussed on getting to London, finding and somehow rescuing Dickon. He could only hope Zach had got through with Bethan and that all was now well with Jennet. He had ridden to the Mermaid in a little under three days and damned nearly killed four horses to do it. He was swaying more from exhaustion than drunkenness if the truth be known – but he would soon fix that. That Cobb had already got the boy out of the Clink and kept him safe had been more of a relief than Alexander would own. For all sorts of reasons, he could not bring himself to think about Lord Westley just now. He squared his shoulders and went to find Dickon.

The boy had been out with Nab in the pigeon loft for much of the afternoon. The wizened old Yorkshireman had delighted in a captive audience and shared his knowledge gladly. The birds had soon quieted and come to Dickon's hand to take the corn he held out to them. It would have pleased him greatly had he not been so sick at heart. As darkness fell he had wandered disconsolately back to his room and flung himself onto the bed to wait for Katherine. He knew she would come to him – she was the only ray of brightness in his black world. That she was a whore plagued him, both with prurient curiosity and with jealousy; he could not bear the thought of old men pawing at her – or any man, come to that. The other evening she had kissed him gently on the mouth and then laughed as he had blushed. He found himself waiting all day for that kiss, his fantasies carrying his thoughts into places that made it difficult for him to meet her eyes. But even had he the money to buy her services, he wouldn't know how to begin and in his present state of mind he feared it would be a sad waste.

His arms behind his head, he lay back staring at the ceiling and thought about what he was going to do. He could never go home – not now. He could never go back to St Michael's, even supposing some of the men lived, how could he ever face them after what he had done? If they knew, he would be cast out; they might even kill him. He deserved no less. The more he thought about it, the more he became uncomfortably aware that Cobb might be right, that Tawford had been playing a part as he had done so often in the past. When Dickon had seen his captain running towards him as an enemy, he had not stopped to think, there had been no time; the heat, noise and smells – the fear – had addled his wits. Exeter was his first experience of battle; Tawford's men had kept him out of the skirmishes in Cornwall. He had never killed a man before; never heard the dreadful sounds of men screaming in agony as grenades dismembered them, turned them into unrecognisable lumps of meat. He had seen bloodcurdling sights in Ireland, true, but only ever in the aftermath, not in the appalling immediacy of battle. He shook his head in despair.

Feeling an echo of the terror that had gripped him in that trench as he had pissed himself trying to summon up his courage, Dickon shuddered. He had probably made a dreadful mistake and would carry the shame of it forever. There was nothing he could do to rectify it – he could not turn back time – but his sense of honour told him that he must, whatever else, go back to Devon and seek out Lady Ellen. He dreaded the thought, but he could not stay here living on Cobb's generosity for much longer. He had to face up to what he had done. Then he would go somewhere, anywhere, back to Ireland probably. He closed his eyes and tried to banish the image of how Ellen would look when he told her. He was drifting off into an unsettled sleep when he heard the door open. He kept his eyes closed, waited drowsily for Katherine's soft kiss, his lips puckering in anticipation.

'Well I will kiss you if you'd like me to, but I hardly think it appropriate. Whatever would Katherine say? Besides, I don't much fancy men with beards.'

Dickon's heart thumped in his chest as he heard the familiar voice. He couldn't breathe. He thought he knew fear, but never like this. Did ghosts speak? He opened his eyes to face the terrifying prospect before him and blenched.

Alexander cracked out laughing and grasped the boy's clenched fist. 'Feel me. I am warm. I am no ghoul, Dickon. Thanks to a Roundhead trooper, your shot but grazed my shoulder. I am sorry you received such a clout on the head for it though.'

Dickon knew not whether to laugh or cry. White-faced, mouth working, he swung off the bed and stood gazing uncertainly at his captain. 'I saw you fall. I thought I had killed you.' He put out a tentative hand and felt Alexander's arm. 'You are really alive.' A sob tore from his throat.

Alexander put his arms around the boy and held him close. 'Hush now. It is no matter. I am indeed alive and so are you and it is over.' He released Dickon and gave him a gentle push. 'Now stop weeping, or you will unman me, and that would never do.' He smiled gently at the boy's stricken face, which had gone through all shades of pale and was now flushed scarlet.

Moving to lean against the bedpost, Alexander waited in silence while Dickon, his chest heaving, sat on the side of the bed and spread his fingers over his eyes. After a moment the boy lowered his hands and looked up with a watery smile. 'I thought you had betrayed us. Can you ever forgive me?'

'I'm not sure,' Alexander teased, gravely shaking his head. Unable to keep his face straight at the boy's crestfallen expression, he chuckled. 'Yes, of course I forgive you, clodpoll.' He paused for a moment, grew serious. 'But first let me explain. I was in Exeter to break from gaol a personal friend who was wrongfully accused of murder and like to hang. It was necessary for me to pretend to be a Roundhead in order to get out of the city, which is why you saw me as you did. Had there been any other way, I would have taken it. Could I have warned you, I would have done so.'

He stopped speaking, meeting and holding Dickon's

troubled gaze, added, 'The oath we have all taken – yes, including me – I hold most sacred. It is not one I would willingly break and however it may appear to you at any time in the future, whatever else may happen I would never – not *ever* – betray either you or any other of my men. I would die first. You are a St Michael's man now, Dickon, you must know I speak true. Do not doubt me, not now; not ever again. There. Lecture over. It is said and we will put it behind us, eh?'

Still not quite able to take in what had happened, his heart swelling at Alexander's words, Dickon nodded, his face still running with silent tears. He swallowed, whispered, 'The others – do they live?'

'Your cousin James, Mohun and Gifford were unscathed. Pollard and Sydenham took wounds, not serious and they are recovering, but I fear Acland and Bassett gave their lives.' Alexander paused. 'We buried them at St Michael's Church in Torrington and Colonel Acland, who was John's cousin, gave them a guard of honour. They will be sorely missed.' He stopped speaking for a moment, his eyes distant. 'The others have gone home for Christmas. And that is just what we are going to do tomorrow. We will need to ride fast. Is your head healed? Can you ride?'

Miserably, Dickon nodded. He had liked Kit Bassett particularly. He did not know how to express his feelings. He looked down at his feet. 'I am sorry.'

'I know. They were the best of men. We must try to be thankful that we shared the privilege of knowing them. In time you will remember them as they would wish to be remembered – with laughter.'

As Alexander spoke a thought occurred to Dickon. He hardly dared to ask. 'The others… did you… do they…?' He stopped, shook his head, embarrassed. 'It doesn't matter.'

'No Dickon, I didn't tell them, if that's what is bothering you.' Alexander smiled. 'Only you, Cobb, Beth and I know what happened in that trench outside Exeter and that is the way it will remain, so you can stop worrying they'll hang you from the tallest tree, though I might do so myself if you don't stop weeping! Now, as I said, it is done and we need never speak of it again.'

Relieved, Dickon smiled through his tears and got up from the bed. 'Why do we have to ride fast?'

The habit of secrecy was hard to break and Alexander hesitated, but he needed to regain this boy's confidence and there was no better way than by being straight with him. 'You will remember Captain Dewett?'

'How could I ever forget? Vicious bastard!'

'As you say,' Alexander agreed, his expression grim. 'The man is driven by vengeance and wants my blood. He is on his way to Marley Court to kill Lord Westley in the belief that it will bring me running.' Ignoring Dickon's gasp, Alexander's mouth lifted in a humourless smile, his eyes hard. 'As it happens, I fear he is right.' He turned away. 'So gird your loins, my boy, and join me downstairs. I think it is time I begin your education in earnest for if Dewett has his way there may not be another opportunity.' He turned back to the boy and grinned. 'But a word of warning – don't follow my example and get too drunk. I have paid for Katherine to attend you until morning. It is a peace offering – though I rather doubt it will bring you much peace.' He laughed at the expression on Dickon's face and indicated the door.

27

Tuesday 13th December, 1642

Adam Hartley dipped his quill into the ink and yet again searched for words that would bring some measure of comfort to bereaved parents. This was the thirteenth such letter he had been forced to write and it sickened him. Of the nineteen St Michael's men under his command at Edgehill, only six remained. No fewer than eight lost that day; another four killed in a fierce and bloody struggle outside Reading when, learning the castle was under attack by the Earl of Essex, the King had taken his army to relieve the beleaguered Royalist garrison. Adam and his men had been among the cavalry sent charging down the hill from Caversham Heights. They had faced stiff cannon-fire from a battery guarding the bridge over the Thames. Getting past that, they had attempted to press on through the town when suddenly, seemingly out of nowhere, scores of Roundhead musketeers concealed in a barn had opened up devastating fire at close range. As if that were not enough to contend with, at exactly the same moment a fierce hailstorm had broken over their heads. To be assaulted on all sides and by the heavens too! It was too much: unable to see through the storm of lead and ice, they had been forced to withdraw and fight their way back up the hill. Their losses had been appalling and all to no purpose: Reading had surrendered and was now in Parliament's hands. Adam dipped his quill again, so deep in thought the ink had dried on the nib.

At least Jonathon Southcott was out of it. He had sent him home as soon as the wound taken at Edgehill was on the mend, and last week, when it became apparent the King had decided to stay in Oxford for the winter, Adam had sent the others home as well. It was many months since any of them had seen his family; they were long overdue some leave. Adam sighed heavily. He would go too, soon, but in his present mood the thought brought him no joy. Much as he longed to see Ellen, with so many of his friends dead he could take little pleasure in the thought of her.

He tried to bring sincerity to the oft-used phrases about courage and dedication to duty, that their son's death had not been in vain – all the usual things – it seemed a foul lie, but Adam knew it would not seem so to grieving parents. Was it a lie? He was not sure. At Edgehill, had they only been able to turn back Prince Rupert's men in their wild undisciplined chase after the enemy, so intent on plundering the baggage train they had returned too late to the field, the King might have won a victory and brought this dreadful war to an end. But had those men then not given their lives so bravely, the King may well have been utterly defeated and the cause lost – the cause! Even that had a hollow ring. Would it have mattered so very much? They were all Englishmen and Christians, were they not? What the devil were they fighting for anyway? In his darkest moments, Adam could not be sure.

He attempted to shake off his melancholy; to think in this vein was madness, but it was hard not to in the face of so much failure. They had tried and failed to take Windsor Castle, and though they had stormed and sacked Brentford, the Earl of Essex had been waiting for them at Turnham Green, along with Philip Skippon's soldiers and thousands of Londoners. Ordinary folk, armed to the teeth, facing them from behind hastily built barricades and jeering, daring them to charge. Incongruously, people from the city had treated it as a day out, crowding onto vantage points to sit with hampers of food and watch the entertainment. Entertainment! Adam's lip curled. What was it with people these days? What had happened to common decency and humanity? The Londoners must have been severely disappointed for not a shot had been fired. In the face of such heavy opposition, Prince Rupert had turned tail and led them away. Had the King only let him march on the capital immediately after Edgehill, it might have been a different story. As it was, it was all too late. And then, when Adam had thought he could be no more depressed, news had come from Exeter that Sir Ralph Hopton had been defeated and gone back to Cornwall. It seemed as though the King was going to lose this unnatural war. Despite all their sacrifices, the land was going to be ruled by a committee of zealots and only chaos would come of it.

There had been one ray of sunlight in all this dismal time. When Adam had returned to Oxford from Turnham Green, it was to find Viscount Westley waiting for him in his lodgings. Surprised and dismayed, Adam had greeted him coolly, unsure how to respond to Tawford's guardian whom he had last seen fighting with the enemy at Edgehill. But always ready to give a man the benefit of the doubt, he had listened to Westley's explanation.

Feeling that his honour as regards the Earl of Pembroke had been satisfied, Robert had torn up his commission and turned his back on Parliament. Knowing that word of his treachery would have reached the ears of the King he had stopped in Oxford on his way to Devon, to reassure his Majesty of his continued loyalty and beg forgiveness for acting as he had out of concern for Alexander's safety. As soon as he was fit, he would return to take up arms for the King.

Greatly relieved to hear this explanation and to learn he had not turned traitor, Adam, his trained eye noting the marks of illness that lingered on Westley's face, was surprised to see him looking so happy. He soon discovered the reason and liked what he saw. Arabella Béjart was delightful and Westley was clearly besotted by her. They had asked for his help to find lodgings while they waited for an audience with the King. It was not easy – Oxford was jam packed with all the paraphernalia of the court and the thousands of soldiers billeted there. There had also been an influx of Roundhead prisoners of war brought into the city to work on the fortifications; the streets were filled with clamour and clatter, not to mention drunken brawling and voluble disputes between soldiers and students. It was not a pleasant place to be right now, but Adam had eventually found them somewhere in a back street, not far from his own rooms in St Aldates. He dined with them a couple of times, but a day or two after their arrival, had ridden out in the train of Lord Wilmot to storm Marlborough and had not seen them since his return yesterday.

He had just finished the last letter, signed and sealed it and put it to one side when there was knock on his door. It was his landlady. It transpired a message had arrived for him almost a week ago while he was in Wiltshire, she had meant to give it to him when he got back yesterday, but what with one thing and another… she hoped it wasn't urgent. Thanking her he waited until she had gone and took it over to the window, his fingers tearing the paper in his eagerness.

His first emotion was one of keen disappointment that it was from Cobb and not Ellen. His second was sharp, heart-stopping dismay. In disbelief he read the words again: *'Tawford was killed outside Exeter…'* There was no mistaking them. He gazed from the window unseeing, the message slipping from his fingers to the floor. Filled with unutterable sadness he stumbled backwards to sit on the bed. They had shared so much over the years – he had been only ten and Alexander barely six when first they had met.

Adam's father was a country doctor and unlike most physicians who did little more than diagnose and left doctoring to barber surgeons, he believed in getting his hands dirty. On that day he had gone to treat Lord Westley's ailing wife at Marley Court and Adam had accompanied him. Young as he was, under his father's tutelage there were many things he could do to help, but not on that day. Lady Westley had once again gone into travail three months before her time and Adam had been banished from the sickroom. He had wandered out to the stables where he had almost tripped over a small boy lying face down in a heap of straw, his shoulders shaking with sobs. Not wanting to embarrass him, Adam, pretending not to notice, said cheerfully, 'Hello. I am Adam, who are you?'

'Alexander,' had come the muffled reply in soft Irish brogue. 'Go away.'

Adam had heard Lord Westley had brought a boy with him from Ireland – his bastard son, it was rumoured. Feeling sorry for the little chap, he had hunkered down in the straw and held out a tentative hand. 'Don't cry, Lady Westley will recover, my papa is the best physician in all of Devon.'

The boy had looked up, his green eyes huge in his thin, tear-streaked face, his unruly mop of hair barely distinguishable from the straw in which he lay. 'But she is losing her babe and it is all my fault.'

'Don't be silly.' Adam had retorted with lofty superiority. 'How can it be your fault?'

'Because I hate her – she says I am a bastard got on a witch.' He had flinched away from Adam's comforting arm. 'My mama was not a witch, she was a princess, but she is dead and I wish I was too.' Dashing the tears from his face he had jumped up from the straw and fled.

Perplexed, Adam had quizzed his father as they rode home later that day. 'What causes a babe to come too soon?'

'There are many reasons, son. In this case the infant was undernourished in the womb, the lady is not strong and her body could not sustain its growth. I only wish I knew why, for it was perfectly formed, but as physicians we can only work within the limits of our knowledge and I know of nothing I could have done to have prevented it. But we should pray that Lady Westley will recover and that, God willing, she will one day carry an infant to term.'

'It couldn't have been because of Alexander, could it?'

'The Irish boy? Good Lord no. What makes you say such a thing?'

Adam told him what Alexander had said. 'Poor lad,' his

father had murmured. 'Lady Westley has been less than kind to him and I can understand how he might feel that way. The added strain of having the boy under her roof may have increased her anxiety – but no, it would not have caused her to miscarry.'

'Why has it been a strain? He's only little and he seemed nice enough to me – is he really Lord Westley's bastard?'

Adam remembered that his father had looked down his nose. He had always discouraged gossip, but on that occasion had grudgingly replied. 'His Lordship has not denied it, but neither has he acknowledged it. In fact he has said very little about him, but it is not for us to question one way or the other. People love a scandal; it livens up their humdrum lives. There is probably no truth in the rumour and as I've told you before, Adam, you should not listen to idle gossip, but Lord Westley has spent a lot of time away from home and... well, son, let us just say that the temptations are very great for a man when removed from the comforts of his wife and home – one day you will understand. I am not excusing it and when you're a man grown you should pray to the Lord for the strength to resist; fornication is the devil's work.'

Adam had squirmed with embarrassment. He had a healthy curiosity about such matters; he knew all about fornication and what it entailed – his father had often tended its results.

'Even if he is a bastard, it is not his fault,' he had retorted. 'The lady is wrong to say he was got on a witch and wrong to be unkind to him.'

'It isn't a question of right or wrong Adam. Life isn't all black and white, especially when bad humours get into our blood as they do when we are distressed. We do not always use logic and reason then. You need to understand that if you want to be a good physician. Never condemn a person's actions without first considering the reasons for them. The lady has been struggling to give her lord husband a son, and now it seems he has produced one without her. Is it any wonder she is finding it hard? But she is not an unkind person – she has never been unkind to you, has she? So that should make you think, should it not? I have no doubt she will warm towards the boy once she has recovered and stops paying mind to gossip. In the meantime, he must be lonely and is doubtless homesick. Why not befriend him? I am sure he would welcome some company and things will settle down in time. Now tell me, what would you put with plantain to make a salve for an old sore?' And so his father – having made Adam see things differently, as he always did – had changed the subject, but Adam had continued to think about Alexander in the days that followed.

On their next visit to Marley Court he had sought him out, slowly winning his confidence. As the weeks went by he had learned something of the boy's life in Ireland, of his foster-mother who had raised him from a babe and whom he sorely missed. She it was who had told him his mother was a princess. He had spoken often of Lord Westley and it was plain to Adam the boy idolised him, but when he asked if Lord Westley was his father, Alexander had rounded on him, fists clenched. 'I cannot speak of it. Do not ask me!' Adam had been puzzled by this reaction, but had backed off and never mentioned it again, though like everyone else had come to believe it was true.

The following year, Lady Westley had at last carried to term the long-awaited Dynam son and heir, Henry, and from then on Marley Court had revolved around the babe's every whim. Alexander had been left very much to his own devices and was more often to be found in the Hartley household than his own. It was at about this time, Adam remembered, that Hugh Lyddon had come into their lives. An easy-going, likeable lad, he had dropped out of a tree onto their heads one day as they were companionably strolling by the riverbank intent on a day's fishing. In the ensuing scuffle he had gasped out that one of his father's hounds had just whelped and if they would stop punching him, he would take them to see. The three of them had soon become inseparable: they rode, fished, swam and fought together, gradually extending their friendship to other boys in the neighbourhood with whom they sailed the rivers Taw and Torridge and all around the coast, exploring every gully and inlet in search of buried treasure and arguing about whose turn it was to be Sir Richard Grenville – it was usually Alexander's, Adam remembered with a sad smile. Some of those loved friends had died at Edgehill.

Their idyll had ended when Adam had gone up to Oxford, but Alexander, though younger by almost five years, had soon followed and had benefited from an unusually enlightened tutor who stretched the curriculum beyond the traditional classics. The boy had excelled and his tutor had urged him to become a lawyer and go on to the Inns of Court, but that had not suited Alexander, who had taken himself off to join the army overseas.

Five years passed before the friends met again. By then Adam was a skilled barber surgeon, though not yet qualified to diagnose. Alexander had returned slim and taut as a whipcord, his skin a shade darker and his hair bleached almost white from exposure to salt and sun. He came back with a new scar on his face and was accompanied by a huge rogue named Cobb, who seemed rarely to leave his side.

Soon after Alexander's return Lord Westley had given him Tawford Barton and for a short time it had caused a resurgence of gossip, but it was old history and people soon lost interest. It was at around this time that Adam's father had died. Thinking of it now, Adam felt a surge of pain. Even after all these years he still missed his father's humour and wisdom. Determined to qualify as a physician he had gone to London. It had coincided with his decision to end his burgeoning relationship with Ellen and had been a wretched time. While there he had learned of the tragedy that had struck the Dynam family, though he had never for a moment believed the dreadful rumours. It was inconceivable that Alexander would have deliberately led Henry to his death. Adam heard that he had fled to France and did not see him again for many months.

Then had come the war against the Scots and the mad,

glorious experience of comradeship under Alexander's exhilarating leadership – until he was accused of treason. Returning to Devon, Adam had avoided becoming involved in the Army Plot and the next time he saw his friend was just after Alexander's release from the Tower. Adam had found him incapably drunk and ravaged by fever in the stews along Bideford's waterfront. Appalled, he had carried him to a safe house to treat him and listened as Alexander had talked in delirium of his infancy. Gradually Adam had pieced together the story and been astonished to learn what had occurred to cause his friend's distressed state. 'I always knew I was born a bastard, Adam,' Alexander had cried, weeping bitter tears, 'But at least I knew who I was. Now I am nobody – and God knows what unspeakable taint attaches to my birth that he will not speak of it.'

Eventually the fever passed and though waking dreams disturbed his nights and debilitating megrims – which only alcohol and vigorous exercise seemed to alleviate – his days, under Adam's skilful doctoring Alexander had mended. Becoming increasingly morose he had asked Adam to forget what he had learned and never to speak of it again, warning that if he did so their friendship was finished, he had then returned to Tawford Barton. Adam had been both hurt and offended and for a time the two men had shunned each other's company – until Hugh had propelled them into St Michael's.

St Michael's! Despite his misery, Adam smiled to think of it. It had seemed so exciting – God's Wounds, how naïve they had all been. Enthralled and inspired by Alexander's leadership they had thrown themselves with unbridled enthusiasm into the worst kind of war. And now, less than a year later, that brilliant young man whom they all believed was invincible, was dead. The waste of it tore at Adam's heart. Alexander; as close to him as a brother whom he loved more dearly than he cared to admit, was gone forever. He covered his face with his hands and wept.

The next day, because he knew he must, he went to see

Lord Westley and with great sadness watched Robert's newfound happiness dissolve as he struggled to contain his grief. Adam could do little to help him. In the end, it was Bella who persuaded the heartbroken man they should continue on their journey to Devon, for someone should take the sad news to Ellen and it would be best coming from her brother. Concerned for Robert's health, she asked Adam to accompany them, which he agreed to do. Closing the door quietly behind him he heard the sounds of muffled weeping and Bella's low comforting voice.

He took the news to the King and begged leave to return with Lord Westley to Devon. In granting it, the King's grace eyed Adam sadly, his mournful face marked by his own grief. King Charles was in some respects a distant, autocratic man, but he held a deep and abiding love for those who showed him loyalty, and his heart bled for the lives that had been sacrificed for his sake in this unholy war. He could not quite understand how it had come about, nor believe it was what his people really intended and he spent many hours on his knees each day praying for guidance. Charles was essentially a family man who missed his wife and children with a bitter, lonely anguish he was barely able to conceal. And now that the hoped-for peace negotiations with the parliamentary commissioners had irretrievably broken down, he was dismayed. The situation was worsening and he could not see an end to it.

Beckoning to his secretary, he dictated a declaration, signed it and handed it, the ink still wet, to Adam. 'We would be grateful if you will give this to our loyal servant, Viscount Westley. We hope it may be some small comfort to him in his great loss. We only wish we had done it sooner while we had the opportunity. Please tell Lord Westley that we forgive him unreservedly for his recent indiscretion, which we can only too well understand. Tell him also we are grateful for the courage and loyalty shown us by his ward and will be ever mindful of his sacrifice on our behalf.'

Bowing low, Adam took the scroll the King handed to him

and backed away.

It was a posthumous knighthood. Though he would never know it, the nameless bastard had made his own identity: he had died Sir Alexander Dynam of Tawford.

In the week since Bethan had arrived at Tawford Barton she and Ellen had become firm friends, both recognising a kindred spirit. Ellen's heart ached for Bethan, and knowing what she must be going through, had offered silent empathy; listening as Bethan talked of her son and daughter in happier times.

As Bethan grew stronger and for want of something to take their minds off their anxiety, most days they walked together, often strolling on the foreshore accompanied by the hound and her pups, which were growing apace and now chased after gulls, leaping into the sea and emerging to drench the two women in a cascade of droplets. As it turned colder and the wet ground hardened, they were able to walk more about the farm; sometimes they rode, but not often and they never strayed too far from home, not only because Ellen daily hoped for news of Alexander, Adam and Robert, but also because it was too dangerous. Bethan's presence might cause gossip if it were known. Ellen had asked all her people to keep silent, intimating that her visitor was sheltering from a vengeful Roundhead whose attentions she had spurned. It was a weak explanation, but all that she could think of at the time and she knew that despite their loyalty, tongues would inevitably wag.

None but Wilmot knew Bethan was Jennet's mother. Ellen had not been surprised by the cook's distress when the child had gone missing for Jennet had wormed her way into all their hearts. Zach, who called in to see them from time to time, brought no good news and though he had given up searching, they still hoped that by some miracle Jennet would return.

Ellen's hopes were beginning to fade when one morning, as they were picking their way as usual among the piles of wet seaweed, driftwood and dead crabs, their feet crunching on shells that decorated the sand, Bethan stopped and stood stock still as if listening, her gaze fixed unseeing on the ocean.

'She is alive!' Bethan turned to Ellen and smiled. 'I can feel it.'

Ellen hugged her and signed, 'Dear Bethan, I pray you may be right.'

It was probably wishful thinking and yet Bethan's certainty gave Ellen hope. A mother's instinct could sometimes feel these things. She had begun trying to speak in signs as Zach did. He had explained the rudiments to her, but it was slow and she could not imagine ever being able to express complex sentences by such means. Sometimes her efforts made Bethan laugh and for a brief moment they forgot their anxieties and felt the better for it. Bethan's lip-reading skills were such that Ellen occasionally forgot she did not hear, as when she had asked her about Zach. An expression of puzzlement had flitted across Bethan's features. Ellen had tried again; explained she did not wish to pry, but she feared for him for it was plain he was smitten. Clearly Bethan had affection for him, but was it merely gratitude?

Bethan, understanding at length what Ellen was trying so awkwardly to say, had smiled and reassured her. She was aware of Zach's feelings for her and would be careful not to hurt him, but she saw him only as a friend. Her state of mind and recent experiences did not allow for anything else. He was a dear, kindly man and perhaps it would come in time.

Ellen hoped so, for Zach's sake.

Dewett had found the ideal place to camp: not a barn but a tumbledown hovel tucked away near a gurgling stream in a wooded valley some two miles from Marley Court. The track to it was barely discernable and what had once been a garden was densely overgrown. With its lonely situation it suited his purposes admirably. The roof was partly fallen in and holed, but he was able to patch up a big enough area to keep himself and his belongings dry. There was even a fireplace. He did not dare to light a fire during the day, but after nightfall the smoke would not be seen.

He had changed his mind about stealing in case it should be noticed. Instead he had ridden into South Molton, which he considered far enough away to be safe should his presence be remarked on, and bought a couple of warm blankets, a roll of canvas, a tinderbox, a shovel, a few cooking utensils, a small sack of dried beans and one of flour, some fat and salt, a broad-bladed knife, some rabbit traps, a catapult and some meat for his horse – mostly grain; hay was too bulky to carry. He had also treated himself to a new pair of boots – they were thigh length and would be warmer. Armed with these purchases he had returned to the hovel. Fearing he had been a little extravagant he tipped out the pouch and counted the coins he had left. There were still plenty; Anne had been more than generous. The thought of her made him ache for her body; he smiled distantly, replaced the thong about his neck and nibbled absently at his fingernails. He did not have enough grain to keep the packhorse, but he no longer needed it. He thought about cutting its throat, but did not like the taste of horseflesh. He led it some distance away and released it to fend for itself. The other he kept tethered at the far end of the hovel, not only to keep it out of sight, but also because the weather had turned cold and a cold horse needs more to eat. He had gathered and dried some wood for the fire and some bracken and moss to make a bed on the dirt floor, using the canvas to wrap his saddlebag, sword, musket, powder and ammunition to protect them from damp. He had been overjoyed to find, buried in a sandy corner of the garden, a few potatoes that had obviously seeded themselves year on year. They were tiny, but tasty. He had also found a squirrel's hoard of nuts. By day he set traps and with his catapult shot woodpigeons; on one glorious occasion he had even brought down a small deer, which was meat enough for a couple of weeks or more even without the plentiful supply of rabbits. At a different time each day he cautiously approached Marley Court and observed the farm workers coming and going about the estate, but as yet there was no sign of Viscount Westley. Each night comfortable by the fire, wrapped in his blankets with a gutful of hot food inside him, his carbine cleaned and primed and a dagger at his hand, Dewett felt happier than he had in years.

The day after receiving news of Alexander's death, Robert, Bella and Adam, together with their six guards, left Oxford and headed towards Newbury. In grim silence they had been riding the ice-ridged roads for only three hours when they heard a small group of horsemen approaching at full gallop behind them. Adam pulled Robert and Bella quickly to the side of the road and stood with the guards, their weapons displayed to discourage attack. It seemed there were only three men and they did not appear to be threatening. They were still some distance away when they skidded their blowing mounts to a walk and came slowly forward.

It was Bella who recognised him first. She cried out and clutched Robert's arm. Adam could not believe what he was seeing, nor in his wildest dreams could he have hoped for it. He leapt from his horse and ran forward. Alexander did the same. They met in the middle of the road and gripped each other by the hand. 'Adam, by God – you should go to bed earlier, you look awfully tired.'

Adam was speechless. With tears in his eyes, shaking his head in wonderment, he studied his friend's features then looked up at Cobb and Dickon, both still mounted, looking down at him, stupid grins lighting up their faces. Slowly he smiled. 'Is he real or am I shaking the hand of a ghost?'

'Oh, I'm real enough.' Alexander released Adam's hand. ' I am also extremely thirsty as indeed are these horses I wouldn't wonder. Might I suggest we ride on to the nearest hostelry? We all have a lot to catch up on.' He looked over to where the others were waiting; the guards, having recognised Cobb, had pulled back and were chatting and laughing amongst themselves.

Alexander led his horse forward, bowed to Bella and gave her a beaming smile. 'How delightful to meet with you again, My Lady, and even more beautiful than I remember.' Ignoring her pleased but derisory snort, his eyebrow raised, he directed his gaze to Robert and bowed again, his smile gone, his eyes questioning.

'Lord Westley – I am deeply sorry you have been informed prematurely of my demise. I imagine it was something of a shock. It was a regrettable mistake. I can only apologise and lay the blame squarely on Cobb who should have known better.'

Behind him Cobb snorted and kicked his mount forward.

'Indeed, I should. It was wishful thinking on my part, My Lord. I do most humbly beg your pardon. As you see, the young rascal is very much alive and has been plaguing us to ride faster ever since we left London – which was but three days gone – but given that Dickon here was wounded at Exeter, I have tried to keep Tawford under control. It has not been easy. Fact is, we are beginning to wish the reports of his death had been true!' He quickly pulled his horse over as Alexander aimed a punch at his leg.

For the first time Robert, who had been shaken beyond words, smiled. He looked at Alexander's questioning gaze, the smile leaving his eyes.

'You have heard about Edgehill, I can see it in your face. I fear it is true, but I am no traitor. Pembroke coerced me in return for your life – it was before I knew your men had rescued you. I have repaid a debt of honour and made my peace with the King. He has forgiven me. I beg you, allow me to make my peace with you.'

Alexander held his gaze and nodded. 'I cannot tell you how glad I am to hear it. And yes, we have much to discuss, but not here, I think.' He turned back to his horse.

Bella, who had watched this exchange with interest, called after him, her eyes sparkling. 'Tawford, there is something you should know.'

He looked back at her. 'My dear Bella, I am quite sure there are several somethings I should know. Which one in particular are you clearly bursting to tell me?'

She laughed, a deep musical gurgle that was so infectious they all joined in. 'You are a knight of the realm, Sir.' She sketched a bow.

'Yes, it's true,' Adam said as Alexander's jaw dropped. 'The king has granted you a posthumous knighthood.'

Alexander laughed with delight. 'Isn't that just like him? It devalues the coin a little that I had to die first. Ah well. Do you think he will withdraw it when he learns I am alive?' He looked up at Dickon who was covertly studying Bella. 'Hear that Dickon? I am "Sir" to you from now on, and don't you forget it.'

Dickon, who these days knew when he was being teased, touched his hat. 'Yes, Sir, of course, Sir, I'll mind it, Sir. But if it's not too much to ask of your exalted personage, would you kindly introduce me to Lord Westley and his delightful companion – Sir?' Since his night with Katherine, Dickon's confidence had grown to a level that exceeded cocky.

Alexander held his hands over his ears. 'Oh Lord. Stop him somebody. It's enough to drive a man to drink.' Grinning, he turned back to Robert and Bella. 'However, he is right and I apologise for my lack of manners. Allow me to introduce Richard Chichester of Hall, commonly known as "Dickon" to distinguish him from the hoards of other Chichesters that plague us in North Devon.' He looked over his shoulder at

Dickon, who had nudged his mount forward, said dryly, 'This is my guardian, Robert Dynam, Viscount Westley and his betrothed, the Lady Arabella Béjart.'

Dickon was too busy bowing over Bella's hand to notice that both she and Robert, startled, had looked at each other, brows raised. Robert flushed and Bella gurgled with laughter. Hartley turned in surprise. 'You didn't mention... but this is wonderful news. We should celebrate. My Lord, may I be the first to congratulate you.'

'Almost certainly,' Alexander drawled. This time Cobb joined in the laughter. Hartley and Dickon were at a loss, but shrugged and laughed with them. Alexander mounted up. 'Enough of this jollity – we should move on. We are about three miles from an inn where I suggest we rest and feed our horses – and ourselves – and then we can talk.' He kicked his mount into a trot and led them off down the road.

Riding with Bella between the guards, Robert was amused at the way in which Alexander had peremptorily given them all their orders. He grinned. 'The boy doesn't change, but goodness, how it gladdens me to see him alive.' Her answering smile was full of tenderness. 'I know. Do you suppose he will persist in maintaining this story of our betrothal? I suppose there is still a need?'

'I fear so. It would not do for my stepmother to discover it is a ruse.' Robert paused, his eyes quizzed Bella, a flush staining his cheeks. 'Would you consider making it real, Bella? Would you do me the honour of becoming my wife?'

'You barely know me, My Lord.'

'I feel I know you well enough. You must surely be aware of my feelings for you. I have been singularly unsuccessful in hiding them.'

Bella gave him a gentle, teasing smile. 'You will have to give me some time to consider your proposal. Ask me again when this tedious journey is over.'

'Then it is not a "no"?'

'It is not a "no",' she agreed, kicking her horse forward.

Robert, a stupid grin on his face, followed suit.

By the end of the day they had all caught up on each other's news, which was considerable and took some time in the telling. Alexander had asked Cobb and Dickon to keep quiet about Dewett, whom he neglected to mention to Lord Westley. Dickon, still wide-eyed on hearing about Oliver Woods and Anne Dynam, had readily agreed. Cobb was not so sure that it was wise, but he could see that with the succession of shocks Lord Westley had suffered recently, still weak after his illness, still reeling from news of Alexander's death and discovering him alive, and now learning exactly how Henry had been killed, the added strain might all be too much for him, so he kept his counsel.

Later, Alexander had taken Adam aside and told him about Dewett. 'I thank God Westley elected to stop in Oxford. I could be wrong, but I believe our Roundhead captain will already be skulking in North Devon and that we have little to fear from him on the road. He may well know about Marley Court from Anne Dynam, but I very much doubt if the widow thought to mention Tawford Barton. Dewett will assume Lord Westley has broken his journey somewhere. He will be waiting at Marley, I am sure of it. I must somehow detain my guardian at the Barton, Adam, while you and I find and deal with Captain James Dewett.'

'Should we not bring Cobb and Dickon on board?'

'I think we can manage without them, don't you?' Alexander grinned. 'I want Dickon to go home to his family. He needs to make his peace with his father for though he would never say so, I know it troubles him. What about you, my friend? Will you spend Christmas with us? I fear Ellen will throw a tantrum if you don't.' Adam, throwing caution to the winds, accepted the invitation gladly. Did Alexander but know it, wild horses would not keep him from Ellen now.

True to his word, Alexander spent some time trying to persuade Robert to stay at Tawford Barton for a few days before going home to Marley Court. Though pleasantly surprised, Robert was reluctant. He wanted to go home, but Bella, attuned as she was to undercurrents, was fairly sure Alexander was hiding something. At an opportune moment she added her weight to the idea, saying how she looked forward to meeting Ellen and how nice it would be if she might have a few days getting to know her. Robert, unable to deny her anything, agreed. Alexander shot her a look of gratitude and breathed a sigh of relief. Given the way he felt about his guardian and the appalling tension between them it had not been an easy thing for him to do.

Adam, aware of the tension and Alexander's discomfort, wished they would make their peace. He alone knew what lay at the root of their problem. It was not his business, but he was concerned for his friend. It was painful to see the way he occasionally looked covertly at Robert, his face taut with longing. Adam doubted if anyone else was aware of it, though he saw Cobb watching Alexander sometimes, and wondered.

He helped Alexander bring pressure to bear on Dickon, shaming him with talk of honour and responsibility into acknowledging he owed his father an explanation and his mother a sight of him, especially at Christmas. At length Dickon gave way, saying that now he was a man grown, he no longer feared reprisals from his papa, but would go home only if they promised to fetch him should they need help dealing with Dewett. Straight-faced, they solemnly agreed.

It startled Adam when Cobb declined an invitation to the Barton, announcing his intention to go straight home. It was unlike the gypsy to leave Alexander's side when danger threatened, but Alexander merely shrugged, 'He has not seen Sarah and his boys in a while. He knows we don't need him. We are still two against one, Adam, and we have surprise on our side. I daresay Cobb will keep an eye from the Warren and come running if necessary.'

And so, a week after leaving Oxford, they came to the parting of the ways. Dickon took the road to Hall. Cobb paid off the four guards and sent them back to London before wending his way over the moor to the Warren, and Alexander with Robert, his two men, Bella and Adam, came at last to Tawford Barton.

28

Wednesday 21st December, 1642

Ellen was too excited to sleep. The people she loved best were all beneath her roof and she could hardly bring herself to believe it. Her heart swelling with gratitude she fell to her knees and thanked the Lord for bringing them home to her, safe: Robert, his face thin and marked by illness, but alight with love and laughter as he rested his gaze on Bella. How she liked Bella. And Adam, her love; solid, dependable Adam, the delight shining from his eyes as he watched her reaction to the stories they had to tell – and Alexander, her imp of mischief – her second self – his mobile features moulded into a mask of glittering amusement. And though the things he told them had caught at her heart, she had laughed until she cried, as before their eyes he became in turn a French engineer and his interpreter, a simpleton collector of dead bodies and a clumsy Roundhead gunner. Even Bethan had laughed, but she had soon left them to their joyous reunion, a smile playing about her mouth as putting her fingers to her lips she had slipped quietly from the room.

Pulling herself up from her knees Ellen stood by the window and pressed her brow against the ice-cold glass. She gazed out at the dark enormity of the ocean and the star-studded sky. Was Jennet out there looking up at the same stars? Or was her body lying somewhere on the moor surrounded by the wild creatures she had loved? The thought stained her happiness with guilt. Sighing she turned back from the window. She had lit a Solstice candle and placed it on the sill. She would leave it burning on this special night of magic and rebirth – a candle for the Goddess, may the Lord forgive her – a candle for Jennet. Closing her eyes she allowed her thoughts to drift to Adam lying only two rooms away, sharing with Alexander because the house was full.

Some hours after the household had retired for the night, Alexander and Hartley let themselves quietly out of the back door. They had agreed not to divulge their night sortie or its reason. They rode the crackling lanes to Marley Court, both jumping out of their skins when an owl screeched unexpectedly above and Biscuit, sleek and fat as an ox, reunited at last with her master, shied and skittered, her hooves sliding on the ice. Bringing the mare under control, Alexander gently scolded her; the horse was in dire need of exercise and a light diet! He would have to have a word with Ned, who should know better.

Leaving their mounts tethered some distance away from Marley Court, the two men circumnavigated the drive and ran low across the lawns towards the dark bulk of the house. As Dewett had done before them they found the stables empty and the house as still as the grave, its downstairs rooms swathed in dustsheets. Flitting like two ghosts in the shadows they quartered the grounds. Alexander was not sure what he had expected to find; if he had hoped that Dewett would be waiting there, an unsuspecting prey, he soon realised they were wasting their time; it would not be that easy. Dewett would not be tempted out of whatever hole he was hiding in while Marley Court was empty. He motioned Hartley to follow and they returned to the Barton.

The next morning, after they had broken their fast, Robert, looking refreshed and cheerful – more dapper than he had in years – announced he would take Bella over to Marley Court later that day. With a glance at Hartley, Alexander followed Ellen out to the back kitchen where Wilmot and Rose, their faces wreathed in smiles at the sight of him, were already preparing dinner. Grasping Ellen's arm, he murmured that he needed to speak with her. With a smile, she led him out into the garden, ostensibly to pick some rosemary for the roasting mutton. Alexander's sober expression alarmed her. 'What is it?'

'There is something I have not told you.' Ellen stared at him, her heart sinking as in a low voice he told her about Anne Dynam and Dewett. It filled her with blistering rage against her stepmother – her father's second wife – a loathsome woman whom she had barely known, but never liked and whom she had learned last evening was responsible for Henry's death. Now, it seemed, she wanted Robert dead as well to ensure that nothing could get in the way of her son's inheritance. The severity of Ellen's anger made her tremble. Clenching her fists she gazed at Alexander with tears in her eyes. She had thought they had a respite; that at least for the time being there was nothing to fear.

'Your brother is unaware of it and I think it best he remain that way.' Alexander smiled at her gently and plucked back from her cheek a wisp of hair that had escaped from her cap. 'Don't look like that, sweetheart. It is nothing Adam and I cannot handle, but it is imperative that until we have done so Robert stays here. Tell Bella and Bethan.' He grinned. 'Between the three of you I am sure you can use your wiles to keep him contained. If necessary you will just have to sit on him.'

Despite her fear she could not help but smile at the thought.

'He will be less than pleased when he learns he has been kept in ignorance like a child.'

'I know. But at least he will be a live child. I am afraid that if he knows, he will insist on returning to Marley Court to confront the danger. In his present state of health he is no match for Dewett and we cannot be at his side all the time. Don't worry; I daresay Bella will stop him from spanking

us when he finds out why we conspired to keep him here.'
Suddenly he laughed. 'Now is that not a surprise? I had no
idea, though maybe I should for Bella is in a class apart. She
has brought out a side to your brother I had not even suspected.
It seems he has a heart after all. I wonder if she returns his
feelings. I had never imagined it could ever be anything more
than a ruse for the benefit of the wicked widow. It seems I am
a matchmaker!'

She frowned at him. 'Don't joke about such matters. You
know full well Robert has a heart and that he loves you – and
I know what that means to you, Alexander, so you can stop
pretending that you do not care. He has told me why you
quarrelled and what lies between you.'

He started in surprise, the teasing smile leaving his face.
'So – you know I am not your nephew after all, that I am
nothing but a nameless bastard, the circumstances of my birth
so abhorrent he will not speak of it, nor tell me who I am.'
Alexander's mouth twisted as he searched her face. 'Are you
so favoured that to you he has divulged who sired me? If so
tell me, please. I beg you.'

She shook her head in pity and reaching her face towards
his, kissed him gently on the cheek. 'No, he would not tell me.
But he swore that no taint attaches to your birth and I believe
him. Robert loves you too well to keep this from you if there
were not a very good reason. Can you not learn to live with
it? Is your true identity so important you will split our family
asunder because of it? Does it really matter, Alexander? For
me, knowing you are not my nephew does not change a thing,
nor could it. You are yourself and I love you. I always have
and I always will. And if you will only let him, Robert will be
your father in every way that matters. Can you not be content
with that?'

He turned his face away from her so she would not see
his weakness, his voice rough with emotion. 'Perhaps you are
right to chide me. But yes, to me it matters – more than I can
say. For God's sake, Ellen! I could be from rotten stock; the

son of a traitor, or worse. I could have bad blood from either of my parents, even madness. Godamme! Wouldn't you want to know?' He stopped speaking abruptly, kicking the ground with the toe of his boot. Looked up, said, 'Keep him here until I tell you otherwise,' and swung away.

She watched him go, her heart clouded with sadness and anxiety. Hearing Bethan's soft voice behind her she turned in surprise. Bethan smiled. 'I am sorry if I startled you. I came to talk to Alexander, but I see this is not a good moment.' She turned to go.

'Please don't go,' Ellen caught her arm and signed to her. 'He is unhappy because he thought we were his family and now he has learned that we are not, he is like a child who has lost something precious and is angry and resentful because it has been taken from him.'

Bethan studied her face. 'But you *are* his family.'

'Not exactly, we are only distantly related. I don't know who he is. He was an orphan. Robert raised him as his own to protect him from I know not what. There is some secret that surrounds his birth. My brother will not tell me what, only that it is too dangerous to be revealed, but Alexander will not let it rest.'

Bethan held Ellen's gaze. 'He loves you,' she said gently.

'I love him too – we were children together – you are right, in that sense we are his family.'

'His love is not as yours I think,' Bethan murmured.

Ellen shook her head in frustration. Though her signing was getting better by the day, it was still slow and full of errors and Bethan frequently misunderstood. She would explain it later. She gestured to the house. 'It doesn't matter. Come. There are things I must tell you – and Bella too.'

Once again Alexander and Adam made their way to Marley Court. This time they called in at the lodge to see the caretaker. He was a faithful retainer of the Westleys, old and bowed. From the look of him he had barely the strength to remove the dustsheets. With increasing irritation, Alexander snapped out questions. Where were Lord Westley's men? Where was the steward? The servants? It transpired His Lordship had laid most of them off, apart from the cook, but she lived in the village and would return when His Lordship had need of her. Similarly the housekeeper, but she and His Lordship's manservant were away visiting for Christmas. The steward had taken up temporary residence with the farm staff at the home farm, and had moved the horses there thinking to take advantage of Lord Westley's absence to clean and repair the court stables. Naturally the grooms had gone with them. 'Taking advantage in more ways than one, I daresay,' Alexander muttered crossly to Adam.

With a hand to his ear, the old boy listened to the instructions he was told to pass on to the steward. The house was to be opened up and prepared for his lordship, the horses brought back from the farm and the servants to return or replacements hired. As they left the lodge, Alexander's face was creased in annoyance. 'Why the devil Westley doesn't sort out his servants is beyond me. His people should live in; the house is big enough, for pity's sake. He is always penny-pinching,' he retorted to Adam, who nodded but kept his counsel. He knew Lord Westley had impoverished himself giving a huge loan to the King, as had so many of the gentry when his Majesty had asked it of them. He had also paid a very large fine to get Alexander released from the Tower last spring and the family's estates in Ireland had yielded little income since the rebellion. Alexander surely knew this, but perhaps it had slipped his mind – not surprising in the circumstances – he and his guardian barely spoke, never mind discussed the state of Lord Westley's finances.

There was still no sign of Dewett; Alexander had not expected there would be. The two men split up to search further afield. It was Alexander who found him – or evidence of him – not entirely by chance, but because he forced himself to think about what he would do in Dewett's shoes. He would not want to be too far away, but far enough to remain unconnected with Marley Court should he be observed. He would avoid habitation so would camp out in the open, but at this time of the year he would need to find shelter – a barn or a linhay. It would need to be somewhere near a source of water. That narrowed it down only a little; this part of Devon had a myriad of springs and streams. And the man would need to eat, but would not want to use a firearm for fear of attracting attention. So he would be in an area of scrubland where there was a plentiful supply of small game to trap, somewhere with nearby cover; a wooded valley?

Alexander eyed the surrounding countryside and began systematically to search for a likely camp within a two-mile radius of the house. With his pistol primed he investigated numerous outbuildings and for some hours rode up and down tumbling streams, their mossy banks spangled with icicles. Towards mid-afternoon he stumbled across a pile of horse dung and the tracks of shod hooves. He followed them into woodland. Biscuit pricked her ears and whickered; there was an answering neigh and a small horse trotted out of the woods. It was sway-backed, rough-coated and almost certainly a pack animal. Alexander's eyes narrowed thoughtfully. He dismounted, loosened Biscuit's girth, slid up the stirrups and knotted the reins; he had trained the mare to respond to his whistle, there was no need to tether her. He left the horses nosing each other and searched the ground. Cautiously he followed the hoof-prints. The packhorse had not wandered far. Pushing his way through the undergrowth, Alexander eventually found the narrow track to the hovel. It was the ideal hideaway and instinctively he knew he had found Dewett's camp.

The place was still and silent. Raising his pistol he edged towards the doorway. The hovel was empty. With a soldier's eye he noticed where the roof had been patched; he observed the neat roll of canvas, the mattress of bracken and moss, the floor swept clean and tidy, the fire ready laid and the food raised on a makeshift table of logs to keep it from the floor. Beside it, stuck to a flat piece of slate, a candle with flint and steel. It was as he himself would have made it and deep within him there stirred an unwelcome curl of fellow feeling. Like himself, Dewett was a soldier. He was a stupid man, but not necessarily a bad one and like them all, was caught up in circumstances that were beyond his control: this unnatural war that pitted brother against brother; father against son; senselessly maiming and killing each other for the sake of what? Religion? Power? Wealth? Honour? What possible cause could justify it? Even now, though he condemned Parliament's actions in bearing arms against the King, Alexander could not bring himself to hate the soldiers who were his enemy. Dewett had been merely following orders at Barrington Court. In his position, Alexander knew he would have behaved no differently. Dewett's pride had been severely dented; it was only natural that he should want to redeem his self-respect by seeking to confront the man who duped him. Alexander knew that had circumstances been different, he might have been able to do something about that; given the man satisfaction, maybe even won him to his side; soldier to soldier. But it was too late for that now. Anne Dynam was like a spider; she had caught Dewett in her sticky web and poisoned his mind. Alexander knew he had no choice but to shoot Dewett down as he would a mad dog, but the thought of it troubled him.

Leaving the hovel he splashed over the stream, hid in the bracken behind a low outcrop of rocks and waited, his mind going over his conversation in the garden with Ellen. That she knew he was not her nephew had been a shock, but also an agonising relief. Of the few people he loved, she was dearest to his heart and he trusted her implicitly, yet so ashamed had he been, so afraid she would cast him off, he had been unable to tell her his secret. His lips lifted in a wry smile: it was an irrational fear – Ellen had always been kind to waifs and strays – but it was not her kindness he wanted and his overriding fear had been that she would scorn him.

Since Westley's revelation, Alexander had begun to look at Ellen in a different light, seeing her not as his aunt, but as a desirable woman. His affection for her had transformed into the deeper love of a man for a woman. Yet even though he knew there was nothing wrong in it, he could not overcome the feeling that his love was somehow besmirched. It set his mind somersaulting in a tumult of confused emotions, at times wanting her so badly he had been driven to seeking a release elsewhere. The fleeting physical comfort afforded him by whores, even those as sweet as Katherine, had done little to alleviate his torment. Why did he feel this way? This was not an incestuous infatuation. Godamme! Wesley was not his father – Ellen was not his aunt – so why, why, this intensity of guilt that persisted in haunting him?

He and Ellen understood one another so well that at times there was hardly need for speech between them and he had been forced to guard his thoughts, keep his feelings under tight control. It had not been easy. He shuddered; he could not have borne it had she guessed and found him abhorrent. He knew from her behaviour towards him that her love for him was as it had always been – that of an aunt devoted to her nephew – what else! He sighed, a low moan of despair. And now he must accept that her heart was given to Adam. He had always suspected it, but yesterday it had been so obvious from the way they looked at each other, the way they kept touching, their excitement and pleasure bubbling to the surface setting the room alight. Alexander groaned in frustration, buried his face in his hands. He loved them both and wanted them to be happy, but hell and damnation, how it hurt. He could never declare his feelings, not now, for even worse than not being able to love Ellen openly as he wanted was the thought of being the object of her pity. But dear God, dear God this morning her loving words had almost undone him.

With a megrim hovering behind his eyes, Alexander adjusted his position to get a better view of the hovel, slithering forward until he could rest his pistol on top of a rock. He looked up at the sky, it was heavy with snow clouds; what light there was would soon start to fade. Surely Dewett would put in an appearance soon? He squinted down the barrel, knowing that even were it full daylight his time was running out, for eventually the flickering aura of the megrim would begin to disturb his vision. Virulently cursing his disability, Alexander welcomed as a distraction the cold, hard discomfort of the rocks, the wind sighing through the bracken chilling his fingers and bringing tears to his eyes. He blew on his hands and tucked them into his armpits, started to calculate, forcing himself to think about complex numbers, but he could not stop probing the dark corners of his mind as a tongue will probe an aching tooth. Westley's words came back to him: '... a man is what he makes of himself no matter what his parentage... You are everything I ever hoped for in my son. Does it really matter that you're not?' Ellen had asked the same question. Irritably he asked it of himself. Why did it matter that he was not Westley's son, why could he not be content? He had no answer; knew only that the shock of losing his identity had almost unhinged him. He was driven to know who had sired him. Who had given him birth? Did people of his blood still live? What were the reasons for Westley's secrecy? Why was it so imperative to keep it from him? The questions went round and round in his mind. He was so preoccupied that Dewett had ridden into view before he became aware of him.

Banishing his tortured thoughts, Alexander sighted down the barrel of his pistol, his finger curling round the trigger as the Roundhead dismounted. Unable to get a clear shot Alexander hesitated, cursing under his breath as Dewett put the horse between them and led it into the hovel. A moment later, a flickering glow of light told him that Dewett had lighted the candle. Sending up a prayer that his quarry would come to the stream for water, Alexander waited, his legs stiffening with cramp, one arm tingling, growing numb; soon the megrim would progress to semi-blindness. He knew he had no choice; he had to act now. He was on the point of gathering himself to rush the hovel when Dewett reappeared. The man stood silhouetted in the doorway, looked around in the fading light, yawned and stretched. It was a gift; even in his present state, unable to clearly make out Dewett's features, Alexander could not miss. He aimed for the heart, squeezed the trigger and shot him full in the chest. Dewett, knocked backwards by the force of the ball, crumpled and lay still.

Alexander clambered unsteadily over the stream. Dewett was sprawled inside the doorway, one leg bent under him, his arms spread wide over his head. In falling, he had knocked over the candle extinguishing the flame, but though the hovel was in darkness there was enough light to see the dark stain of blood welling from his chest. Alexander looked cursorily at the body, stirring it with his foot – the man had not stood a chance. Sickened, his head bursting with waves of pain, Alexander leaned against the doorpost and vomited. Unable to stomach moving the body tonight even had he the strength, he left it lying where it was, loosed Dewett's horse, retrieved Biscuit and rode slowly home to tell the people he loved that they were safe.

Robert reacted predictably; shaking his head he gazed at Alexander in horror then erupted in a storm of anger, but after a while, with Ellen and Bella to calm him down, he grudgingly expressed his gratitude. Alexander regarded him coolly, one eyebrow raised, green eyes glittering, and he too acted predictably. Turning on his heel, with Adam hovering in anxious attendance, he rode to a tavern in Bideford, got horribly, mind-numbingly drunk and buried his raw emotions and frustration in an accommodating whore.

Dewett did not regain consciousness for some hours. The pain in his chest was severe, but the ball, deflected by the pouch of money hanging from his neck, had not killed him and the freezing temperature had stopped excessive bleeding. Dragging himself into the hovel, he did what he could to tend the wound while it was still numb. The ball had driven scraps of leather and coins into his flesh, gouged a deep furrow across the muscles of his chest and lodged under his shattered collarbone. With shaking fingers he took his knife, eased the ball from the wound, packed it with moss and fainted.

The following morning, suffering from his excesses, Alexander avoided Robert who was preparing to leave for Marley Court, and wandered out to the stables to talk to Ned about Biscuit's diet, but the little man was not there. As he turned to leave he saw Bethan. Looking at his face she grimaced and smiled. 'I can make up something for that head of yours.'

'No need; I brought it on myself. It will pass,' he mouthed, returning her smile, but his eyes were sad. 'I am so very sorry about Jennet. Ellen tells me you believe she is alive.'

Bethan, watching his lips, nodded. 'I feel it in my heart, yes. But I fear she may never come back to me. I have come to say goodbye. Bella has asked if I will go with her to Marley Court as her companion and chaperone, to stop tongues wagging. I tell her they will anyway, but I can never return to Exmoor. I don't yet know what I will do, but I like Bella and her lord. I cannot continue living on Ellen's generosity. For now it seems the ideal solution and I feel I will be safe under Lord Westley's roof.'

'Ellen would extend her generosity forever and will be sorely disappointed to see you go, but yes, you will be safe there.'

Bethan smiled. 'I know, but she has other things to occupy her now.'

Alexander grinned weakly. 'Ah yes, the noble Adam. They are both so besotted with each other it is hard to resist teasing.

I suspect there may be wedding bells before too long.'

Laughing, Bethan reached up and kissed his cheek. 'I do hope so. Ellen deserves some happiness, she is equally noble – they are well suited. But it is hard for you, I think?'

Alexander felt a frisson of emotion, stamped on it. 'You *are* a witch!'

'No – just a woman,' she smiled.

Catching her hands he held them to his lips. 'God go with you, Bethan. It is not goodbye.'

'I know.'

He gave a wry chuckle. 'Yes – of course you do.' He watched her walk away wondering what it was about this gracious, diminutive woman that so stirred him. It was not love, how could it be? He had no room in his heart for love. Nor was it lust; he had no desire to bed her. He could not identify what it was, knew only that he felt an intensity of emotion when Bethan was near, as though all his senses were heightened. He shrugged; whatever it was, there was one more thing he could do for her. He saddled up Biscuit and headed for the moor.

He went first to the wood where he had killed the stag and had almost killed Jennet. Sitting by the mounded grave, he leaned his back against a tree and as he had done so often in the past, tried to put himself into the other person's mind. With Jennet, it was hard. For one thing she was a child and a girl. But more than that: he had learned from Zach the full story of the horror to which she had been exposed and from Ellen that she had not spoken since that day. Even he, with his own horrifying experiences, could not imagine how hard it must have been for her. Fleeing to the moor rather than face her mother, Jennet would not have been reasoning; could so easily have stumbled into a bog and been swallowed up without a trace. If not that, then she might have been overcome by exposure, her body lying unseen beneath a pile of windblown leaves. He knew Zach had quartered the moor and found no sign of her. That could mean she had not wanted to be found, but it was more likely that she was dead.

And yet Alexander trusted Bethan's instincts. What would he have done? Would he have stayed near? Probably at first he would, even if he meant to move on later. Exmoor was the only home Jennet had known; given her state of mind and her fear of discovery, perhaps she would not have strayed far – not yet. If she was alive she must have sought food and shelter. In her shoes he would have gone to the farm at first. But Zach had put a man in there and Jennet would not want to be observed. Seeing him there, she would have hidden until he was out in the fields then taken what she needed: food and warm clothing; blankets maybe.

He rode to the Morgans' farm. It looked different from when he had seen it first. He noticed with approval the new barn, the longhouse neatly thatched. The yard was clean and free of weeds and some of the doors to the outbuildings had been mended. Amos, whom he knew by sight, came across the yard to greet him. Alexander chatted to him for a while. Given the circumstances, the Morgans' tenancy when it expired would not be renewed. He suggested to Amos that he remove the stock to the Warren – including Mochyn, Jennet's old sow, whose ears Amos was absent-mindedly pulling – and vacate the farm before Christmas.

Amos's face lit up – he had been lonely in this wild, isolated place and would be glad to go home. Alexander thanked him on Bethan's behalf, and rode away his mind busy, having learned that Amos had not seen the witch's maid and was not aware anything had gone missing. That didn't necessarily signify; Amos would be unlikely to have noticed the things Jennet would have taken. Once again Alexander tried to imagine what the child might be thinking and feeling. She had been gone for almost two weeks; afraid of being seen by the verderer, afraid of being found and dragged back to confront her murdering mother, where on the moor would she have looked for shelter?

The answer stared him in the face. Since ancient times the moor all around here had been mined for iron ore. Most of the mines had ceased to be worked when iron yielded its popularity to Cornish tin and copper, but Exmoor was littered with disused adits and mineshafts. Jennet could be hiding in any one of a number of these dark, dangerous places. It would take him forever to explore every disused mine in the vicinity and the longer time went on the less likely it was that Jennet would still be here – she would run out of food and be forced to move on – if she was not crushed beneath the earth or drowned. The thought chilled his heart.

Disconsolately, he turned Biscuit towards home. He was wasting his time: if Jennet did not want to be found then he would not find her, any more than Zach had. He was on a fool's errand. He picked up the track that ran around the bottom of Shoulsbarrow Common beneath the great mound of the ancient fort, which some said the Romans had built – or was it King Alfred? – 'twas ancient, either way. He shivered. The dark heavy clouds were shot with yellow from the sinking sun and the trees, bare of leaves now, clawed at the angry sky. A buzzard soared above him on its way to roost, and all around him was the sound of rushing, gurgling water from the streams that cascaded from the moor to flood the River Barle.

It was as he put his head back to look up at the great wingspan of the buzzard that he had an idea. He might as well act on his impulse – he was so near. Turning Biscuit he headed for Barton Town, one of the manors owned by the Chichester family, as was all the land around here. It lay by an ancient track-way that crossed Exmoor from the coast. A little way downstream was a busy flourmill, its great wheel driven by the River Barle. Because it was a natural gathering place and central to the cluster of hamlets that formed the parish of Challacombe, the church had been built here, high on the moor, right next to Barton Town; the church where they would have buried Morgan. It was towards this that Alexander headed, slithering and sliding down into the steep wooded valley of the Barle.

By the time he had persuaded Biscuit to take him across the river – not wide here, but full and fast flowing – the lower half of his body was wet through and the light was fading. Climbing out of the valley he came at last to the church. He left Biscuit concealed in a gateway and quietly let himself through the lych gate into the churchyard. There were a few new graves; none had headstones – few folk round here could afford them – but one mound in particular caught his eye. He hunkered down and saw the garland: it was a prickly posy of gorse flower, rose hips and holly wrapped around with stems of dried grass. Stepping back, he peered into the shadows and listened, but all he could hear was surging water. He walked to the porch of the church, leaned against the ancient wall and waited, clamping his teeth to stop them chattering. Was he still on a fool's errand? Somehow he did not think so.

He waited maybe two hours; lost track of the time. The sky had cleared off; he occupied himself by looking up at the heavens and naming the constellations. He started to count the individual stars; when that palled, he recited poetry. Looking at the grey billowing shapes of grave mounds he tried to remember suitably sombre poems; Donne could usually be relied upon:

> *As virtuous men pass mildly away*
> *And whisper to their souls, to go,*
> *Whilst some of their sad friends do say,*
> *'The breath goes now,' and some say, 'No'...*

But he had forgotten the next verse – and because he could no longer keep the thoughts at bay, he gave in to them and admitted the truth of Ellen's words, ' *...you can stop pretending that you do not care...* ' Yes. He cared. Godamme! He cared too much. And as he faced this truth and acknowledged to himself at last how important Robert's love and respect were to him, his anger began to ease and with it his pain. Another hour went by. He could no longer feel his feet and his clothes were stiff with ice.

And then he saw her.

Like a wraith she flitted to the grave and knelt beside it with her back to him. Her body was enveloped in a hooded cloak. He knew if she saw him she would be off like a startled deer. By sheer force of willpower he forced his cramped legs to move. Blessing the noise of the water he crept towards her and seized her from behind. There was no other way. She went rigid in his arms, her breath rattling in her throat. He held her close and murmured in her ear. 'Pixy, it is I, Alexander..'

Galvanised by the sound of his voice, she struggled against him pushing at him with her thin arms. He tightened his grip. 'Remember me? It is Lapwing, your friend. Do not be afraid. You promised to teach me how to talk with my hands; I have come for my lessons, but I am extremely cold and if you don't let me take you with me they will find us here in the morning, two statues of ice frozen together for all eternity, for now that I have found you I am not going to let you go.'

She stopped struggling and half turned to see his face. He smiled down at her, loosening his grip just a little. 'There now, you see. You remember me, don't you?' Her eyes closed, her head fell back and she went limp in his arms. While she was still unconscious, he picked her up and carried her to Biscuit, pushed her on to the mare's shoulder. Biscuit sidled and snorted, but it was only a token protest. Gentling the horse he mounted up behind Jennet, took her into his arms and rode away from the churchyard.

It was dark, he was frozen to the marrow, Jennet's slight body was no weight, but his hands were so cold he was afraid of dropping her. There seemed only one sensible thing to do; he would have to seek shelter for the remainder of the night. Nudging Biscuit into a fast walk he felt the child tense in his arms. Coming to, she turned her face to look up at him. He gave her a little squeeze, murmured reassurances and though he could not see her features, felt her relax against him, her head nestling into the crook of his arm. Pushing Biscuit into a canter, he rode to the Warren.

At the standing stone he was quickly recognised. He sent one of the lookouts ahead to fetch Zach, rode to the longhouse and waited in the yard. Zach came running with a lantern.

'Tawford?' He stood stock still as he saw Jennet.

Alexander grinned down at him. 'I tickled a speckled trout once that looked just like you, except it was prettier! I cannot move my arm; would you take her? Gently, man.'

Speechless, Zach dropped the lantern and took Jennet from Alexander's arms. He held her against him. 'Ah lass, my little lass. You are alive. Thank God.' She smiled at him faintly but said nothing. 'Where did you find her?' He looked up at Alexander who was easing his leg stiffly over Biscuit's back.

'By Morgan's grave.' Reaching the ground Alexander tried to rub life back into his thighs. He looked at Jennet and grinned. 'You see – I am a block of ice already.' Putting out a hand he cupped her chin. 'Pixy, now that I have found you, there are things of which we need to speak. I ask you – no – I beg you, give me a chance to talk with you. Do not run away from me. I promise on my life that when we have talked, if you still want to go I will not stop you and nor will Zach. Will you do that for me? Please?'

Motioning to Zach to put her down, Jennet reached out a hand to Alexander's arm and lightly touched it, looked into his face and nodded.

Zach bent to pick up the lantern. 'Come inside and get warm,' he said gruffly, his voice full of tears. He turned towards the longhouse, but Alexander stayed him.

'Is there a back way in? Can she have my old room? I fear the parlour will be a little bright and noisy for Jennet after the dark quiet of the mine.'

The child swung round, gasped, 'How did you know?'

Zach stared and Alexander laughed exultantly. 'She speaks! The child speaks! Ah Pixy, surely you have not forgotten? Did I not say you would lead me through a hidden doorway into the hill and I should sleep for five hundred years?'

'But only if you eat of the faerie feast,' she whispered.

'Well there, you see? You do remember. Come sweetheart, you go with Zach and get warm while I put my horse to bed, and then we shall have a feast indeed, and you shall tell me what the Little Folk have been saying to you and I shall tell you how I came by my mare; her name, by the way, is 'Biscuit' and aside from you, she is my best friend.'

Jennet nodded, her eyes huge in her thin white face. 'I know. We have already been introduced.'

'Of course you have, I had forgotten.'

Smiling, Zach handed him the lantern and taking Jennet's arm, led her round to the side of the longhouse. Watching them go, Alexander breathed a sigh of relief. The child had her voice back and he would encourage her to use it – all night long if need be. And when she was ready, he would talk to her of Bethan and of Morgan and of all those unspeakable things that had rendered her silent for so long.

He unsaddled and rubbed Biscuit down, gave her water and a pile of hay and whispered sweet nothings in her twitching ears, chuckling as the mare gave him an old-fashioned look and buried her nose in the hay. That done, he went into the rowdy warmth of the Warren and was greeted by Sarah and clapped on the shoulder by Cobb, who soon thrust into his fist a mug of hot, spiced ale and waited impatiently for answers to his stream of questions about Dewett. Alexander had to shout to make himself heard as a burst of laughter erupted from the other end of the room where a group of men were playing cards, he gave up, raised his hand. 'Later!' Beckoning Cobb and Sarah to the least crowded end of the room, he threaded his arms around their shoulders and pulling them close told them about Jennet.

'Zach has taken her in through the back to my old room,' Alexander spoke in urgent undertone. 'She has been living in a mineshaft for two weeks and has only just this minute got her voice back. I think all these folk will be too much for her just now. She needs space and quiet for a time. Could I avail myself of your generosity for the night? I need to talk to the child about her mother. Tomorrow I will take her back to Tawford Barton.'

Sarah put her hand to her mouth in consternation, her homely face flushed with warmth, brow creased with maternal concern. 'Of course you may. You surely know our home is yours. Oh, the poor child; I must go and see to her.'

As she bustled away, Alexander became aware that Cobb had fallen strangely silent, his round face was running with perspiration and he wore an oddly wary expression. 'What is it, Cobb? You look as though you've lost a crown and found a penny.'

Unusually for Cobb he did not smile. He started to say something, looked round, hesitated. He bent to Alexander's ear. 'Will you bear with me for a minute, my boy? There's something I think you should know.' He indicated the door at the far end of the room. Curiously, Alexander followed the gypsy through the Warren – aptly named, it was indeed like a rabbit warren, higgledy-piggledy with corridors leading off in unexpected places and steps up and down where levels changed.

Cobb stopped at a closed door, opened it and gestured inside. It was a small room; there was a table, a cupboard, an old carver chair and a joint stool. The table was heaped with papers and around the walls were shelves packed with books and strange-looking ornaments. In the corner of the room was an antique celestial table-globe. It was mounted on an elaborate wooden stand and was complete with printed horizon ring, dry compass and bronze meridian circle, the oceans decorated with sailing ships. It was a beautiful thing and must have cost a small fortune.

Alexander's mouth dropped open; he had never seen inside this room before. Even he, who knew Cobb so well and had always valued his intellect, was a little surprised. On the wall was a framed drawing of a woman's head and shoulders. His gaze was drawn to it. It had not been executed particularly well, but the artist had caught the subject's teasing expression, her face was flawless, her high forehead partially covered by a shawl so he could not see her hair. Her eyes seemed to look right at him and a small smile played about her mouth in a way that made him want to smile back.

Cobb shut the door behind them with a bang, distracting Alexander's gaze. 'This is my private room. Nobody comes in here, not even Sarah.' He indicated the chair.

Alexander sat down, crossed his legs and looked up at Cobb, eyebrow quirked. 'Then I am twice favoured.' It was quiet in here. A single rush light burned by a small window and a fire glowed in the hearth. He gestured to the picture. 'Who is she? She is beautiful.'

'Nobody.' Cobb spoke gruffly. 'Someone I knew once, a long time ago and yes, she was beautiful, more so than you can imagine or I can describe. The artist did not do her justice.'

'Was?'

Cobb gave an evasive nod. 'Glass of wine?'

Alexander smiled his thanks. 'She was special to you? I am sorry.'

Shrugging, Cobb reached into the cupboard and brought out two pewter goblets and a bottle, poured them both a drink and sat down, elbows on the table, chins resting on his hands.

'So – what is it you think I should know, old friend?' Alexander picked up the goblet and sniffed appreciatively. It was brandy wine. He waited, his gaze on the gypsy's face. At length Cobb cleared his throat and spoke.

'Years ago, when I first came to these parts, I met a woman who appealed to me and before I moved on we kept each other company for a time...' He cleared his throat again, a sheepish expression on his face.

Alexander was surprised into a grin. 'I'm flattered you should choose to tell me, Cobb, but can it wait, do you think? I am sure I would be vastly entertained to hear all about your past peccadilloes, but right now I am concerned about Jennet. I should go and talk with her. After that you can bend my ears with lustful stories all night, if that is your wish. This is excellent wine.' He took another appreciative gulp, replaced his goblet on the table and stood up.

Cobb frowned up at him, his expression hard. 'Sit down, my boy, and let me finish. It concerns Jennet, which is why I am telling you now.'

Taken aback, Alexander held the gypsy's gaze for a moment and sat down. 'Very well; go on.'

'As I was saying; I met this woman and I got her with child. I offered to marry her, but she turned me down and I was happy that she did so. Don't misunderstand me, I would have stood by her had she asked it of me, but she said we were not suited and I agreed with her. Not long after that I went to do some soldiering and met up with you.'

Alexander shrugged impatiently. 'What, pray, can this possibly have to do with Jennet?'

Cobb pursed his lips as though reluctant to speak, looked down at his fingernails. 'She is my daughter. The woman of whom I speak was Bethan. Her father was a Welsh miner – there were a lot still on Exmoor back then – she kept house for him. I was fresh come from Ireland and lodged with them a time.'

Alexander was dumbfounded. As he studied Cobb's face, little things clicked into place. He remembered how the gypsy had been strangely quiet and unresponsive at the Mermaid when he had talked of Morgan's death and Bethan's rescue. He had assumed it was reaction to the sad news from Exeter, knew now that it was not. When Cobb had chosen not to accompany them to Tawford Barton despite knowing of the risk from Dewett, it had seemed strangely out of character.

'That's why you didn't come with us to the Barton – because you did not want to see Bethan?'

Cobb flushed, nodded.

Alexander took another sip of brandy. 'Well! I confess that for once you have surprised me. Obviously Jennet is not aware of it. Did Morgan know?'

'Yes. Some years ago, when Jennet was only a wee lass and I was curious to see her, I called at the farm while Morgan was away. Bethan said she had told him, though not who had fathered her child. I had expected it. She is not a woman to be dishonest; would not have tried to pass Jennet off as his. We talked for a while. She was with child at the time, with their son, God rest his poor soul. She said she was content with Morgan and asked me not to come back again; it was not fair to him, she said. He was kind to the child, had given her his name and was raising her as his own. I offered her money, but Bethan is proud. Said she didn't want my help, made me promise to stay out of Jennet's life. It seemed the least I could do for her and I agreed. All these years I have held to it, but now through no fault of mine you have brought Jennet here. I want to do right by her, but Mother of God! Jennet is my daughter and I don't know what to do for the best. I do not want to break my word to Bethan.'

Listening to Cobb's halting words, Alexander's heart was wrung with pity for Jennet, but also for Bethan. Was that why Morgan had beaten her senseless all those years? He picked up the goblet, swirled the amber liquid around releasing the warm, pungent smell and took another gulp. How strange that Jennet's circumstances should be so like his own. Except Morgan was dead; could not lull her into a false sense of security, wait until she was grown then cut her feet from under her, denying what she held most dear, as Westley had done to him. There was no reason for Jennet ever to know that Morgan was not her father. Would that he had been similarly spared. Alexander banished the thought and looked up at Cobb.

'You have not broken your word as yet. There is no need for you to see Jennet while she is here. I will take her home in the morning to be reunited with her mother and...' Observing the expression on Cobb's face Alexander stopped speaking. He knew instinctively that he was asking the impossible. He shrugged. 'Look, Cobb, I think Bethan would understand your need to see your daughter since chance has brought her here. Indeed, I think she will be so overjoyed to have Jennet restored to her she would forgive you anything – well, almost anything. But there is one thing I suspect she would never forgive.'

'You don't need to say it, my boy. Jennet will learn nothing from me. She will have no cause to know Morgan did not sire her unless Bethan chooses to tell her so. I swear it by all I hold most holy. But if I might just talk with her a little – see her sometimes, maybe?' His voice subsided wistfully.

Alexander gave a brief nod. 'Now that Morgan is dead I see no reason why not. But I have not the right to give or withhold consent, Cobb. She is Bethan's daughter, not mine! You must sort it out with her.' A thought occurred to him. 'Does Sarah know?'

'Lord no. There is no need for her to know.'

'No, of course – but your other children….'

'Are Jennet's brothers, yes.

'A pity she will never know that joy. You know she bears the guilt of Owen's death? She was supposed to be watching him when he died, apparently – when the barn caught fire.'

Cobb shook his head, his face sad. 'I did not know. Poor little lass.'

Alexander shrugged. 'It is the Lord's will. They tell us we should bend to it.' He paused, added, 'It might have helped Jennet through her grief had she known she has other brothers. How many is it now, Cobb?'

'Three – and very possibly another on the way – though it is early days – best not mention it.' Cobb gave a tight smile and looked down at his hands.

'You randy old goat.' Alexander grinned. 'That is glad news indeed.' He finished his brandy with a gulp and put the goblet down on the table, pushing himself up from his stool.

'I will go to Jennet now. I have to talk to her about Morgan. It will go hard with her to learn he took his own life and she will be overcome with guilt and remorse about Bethan. But let us see how she is in the morning, eh? Maybe you will be able to spend a little time with her before we leave. And if you want something to talk about, you can ask her about Mochyn.'

Alexander smiled at Cobb's unspoken query. 'She's a black sow and Jennet dotes on her. Which reminds me, I have told Amos to bring the Morgans' stock back here and vacate the farm by Christmas. I dare say you will be able to accommodate it? There isn't much: a few sheep, one or two bullocks – some will go to settle the rent on quarter day – and a couple of old cows. The horse belongs to the Warren anyway. There is also a cat, but it will make its own mind up I daresay.'

Cobb nodded. 'If you think Bethan will not mind, I could perhaps buy them from her?'

'Good idea; they will cost you twice as much as they are worth. I shall make sure of it.'

'Then you are slipping, my boy.' Cobb grinned. 'I had thought three times at least.'

Alexander laughed. With a last glance at the picture of the woman on the wall, who still seemed to be watching him, he went to find Jennet.

Zach had lit a fire in the room while Sarah had found some clothes to replace those of Jennet's which, apart from the hooded robe that was much too big and had probably been her mother's, were threadbare, torn and filthy. Sarah, ever practical, had looked out some of her own children's clothes, for though they were younger than Jennet, the girl was so slight and small-boned, they would do.

The poignancy of seeing Jennet dressed in her brothers' clothes: breeches, woollen stockings, a belted shirt and a warm jerkin, saddened Alexander, but he gave her a cheery smile. She was sitting on a rag rug by the fire, her arms clasped about her legs. An empty bowl beside her witnessed she had devoured the stew Sarah had brought to her. She looked more as he remembered, except for the haunting misery lingering about her elfin face. The look of mischief he had found so appealing had gone. At some time she must have chopped off her hair for it stuck up around her head like a spiky dark red halo. 'I see you have followed Ellen's fashion.' He smiled. 'I am not sure I approve of women who look like boys. It makes me feel uncomfortable.'

She shrugged. 'It kept getting caught.'

'In the mine?'

'In the brambles growing around the entrance; I had to crawl through them.' She smiled at him shyly. 'I am sorry if I make you feel uncomfortable.'

He swallowed. He was glad of the childish smattering of freckles and the tip-tilted nose. He had once thought her plain. The short hair emphasised her high cheekbones, made her look older and drew attention to her glorious eyes. Her lips were full and soft and the signs were plain to see that before many more years had passed she would be quite lovely. The stress of the last few weeks had marked her face with a new maturity and though she was stick-thin, her body attested that her womanhood was just beginning to assert itself. As she gazed at him, her cheeks flushed, her eyes questioning, he knew he was going to have to tread carefully. A child's adulation was one thing; a young woman's was quite another. More than anything in the world, he did not want to hurt her.

He smiled at her gently and went to sit on the bed. It seemed a thousand years since he had vacated it – so much had happened since. 'You don't make me feel uncomfortable Pixy, just old.' He laughed. And then he started talking; told her of his first meeting with Biscuit; of their long journey from London and of his experiences in Cornwall. She became absorbed, began to ask eager questions, which he answered as best he could. He told her of dressing up to dupe the soldiers on the bridge at Exeter, and she laughed. The sound was like music to Alexander's ears. He told her of escaping down the tunnel to find a boat and of rowing to Lympstone in the dark and sleeping in the church at Topsham. He talked himself hoarse and stopped. He knew he had to bring her to talk of Bethan. He took the plunge. 'So now it is your turn. Why did you run away from Ellen?'

She looked away from him and quivered, her gaze going to the flames. 'I think you know why.' Her voice was small.

'Yes, but I want you to tell me.' He got up from the bed and hunkered down beside her. 'Tell me, Pixy. Speak to me.'

Haltingly, she began, her voice growing stronger as she began to release the appalling memories one by one: of her mother bending over her father with a knife, of her father's lifeblood draining away while her mother stood and watched, doing nothing to save him. All the while Jennet was speaking tears spilled from her eyes and flooded down her cheeks in an unending stream.

Alexander ached to take her in his arms and comfort her, but he forced himself to sit still and listen in silence, his gaze never leaving her face. When she reached the point of Ellen and Zach coming to her rescue, her voice faltered to a close.

'I know this is hard for you sweetheart, but will you think back to when your father was dying? Picture it for me now. You tell me that you and your mother got him onto the bed and he spoke to you. What were his words?'

Jennet shuddered as she relived the terrifying scenes she had tried so hard to forget, but never could. They remained behind her eyes all day and all night until she wanted to scream with the pain of it. 'He asked me to forgive him and told me I was not to blame my mother. He asked me to pray for him and said he had always loved me.'

'Do you know why he asked your forgiveness, Pixy?'

She shook her head dumbly. He tried another tack. 'What did he say to your mother?'

She stared at him, her eyes wide. 'He was begging her.'

'For what? To save him?'

She heard again those hoarse, gasping words: *For the love of God, no, not this time. I beg you, as you love me, not this time.* She shook her head. 'No, he said no.'

Alexander, with an effort, hardened his voice. 'No, she wasn't to save him?'

She started at his change in tone and nodded. 'She sent me

to fetch something to stem the bleeding.' Her eyes clouded with misery and she raised her hands to her neck. 'I had forgotten,' she whispered. 'He stopped me.'

'Why do you think he did that?'

Her eyes widened as she met Alexander's gaze. A harsh sob broke from her throat. 'Because he wanted to die.'

At last! Inwardly he breathed a sigh of relief. 'So think again, sweetheart; why do you think he begged you to forgive him?'

She gasped, her sobs juddering her chest. Alexander could bear it no longer. He moved towards her and pulling her into his arms rocked her backwards and forwards. 'Hush, sweetheart. I am so very sorry to make you talk about this, but it is so important you understand what really happened. What you saw was not your mother stabbing him, but trying to take the knife away from him. He killed himself, Pixy. Deep in your soul you must know your mother could not have done it, would not have done it even if she could, not just for his sake, for yours too. But you must not blame yourself for thinking so. The shock of what you saw took away your power of reasoning. It will get better, you must believe me, the pain will lessen in time.'

She moved out of his arms, predictably seeking refuge in anger. Alexander had been expecting it. Trembling, she jumped to her feet, her body taut, fists clenched. 'If what you say is true he committed a mortal sin and the Lord will never forgive him. He will burn in hell. Why did they bury him in the churchyard when he has no right to be there?' She burst into a storm of noisy weeping. 'Why did he want to leave us? Why wouldn't he let us save him? He told me to go away. I hate him. I hate him.'

'No, kinchen, you love him, which is why it hurts so badly. Try to understand. He was in so much pain. His suffering led him to hurt your mother and he hated himself for doing that. He couldn't bear it any more. He wanted it to end. It was his choice. You must allow him that choice and you must not judge him. Forgive him as he begged you to do, and pray for him. And never, not ever, imagine he is in hell. He was a good man. He loved you well and your mother too. And if you think the Lord will not forgive him then you must read again your Bible. It is our frailty that makes us human. There is no sin Our Lord will not forgive us if we repent of it. Your father made his peace with Him and it is because of your mother he is buried in the churchyard. Thinking she had lost you, she confessed to his murder so he at least would rest in peace in sanctified ground. Do not let her sacrifice be in vain, I beg you. She is the bravest of women and she is suffering so badly. Will you let me take you to her?'

Jennet stuffed her fist into her mouth and shook her head.

'She needs you, Pixy.' Alexander waited patiently.

Removing her hand from her mouth Jennet backed away and sat on the side of the bed. 'She must hate me,' she whispered.

'No! Not ever; not even for a moment. How can you think such a thing?'

'I told the verderer she killed my father. It is all because of me they took her away. I called her a murderer. How can she ever forgive me?' Jennet looked at him, tears welling again in her eyes and trembling on her lashes. 'When she needed me most I ran away from her. How can she not blame me?'

He smiled gently. 'She is too wise and she loves you too well to blame you. It is over now, sweetheart. There is no point in punishing yourself. Accept your grief; don't deny your anger, but never forget that your father loved you. As hard as it is right now to imagine, in time you will come to remember only that. We are all affected by what happens to us and we deal with it as best we can – sometimes in the only way we can – and we make mistakes. It is how we make amends that matters. You must forgive your father, but even more, you must forgive yourself. Your mother will help you if you'll let her. Now – I think we have talked enough and you should try to get some rest. Tomorrow, if you want to hear of it, I shall tell you how we rescued your mother from Exeter gaol – and then you will understand the extent of her courage.'

She gave him a watery smile. 'Will you stay with me while I go to sleep?'

He shook his head. 'No, Pixy; I have to go and talk to Zach and to Cobb who is Sarah's husband. You will meet him in the morning. He is another very good friend of mine. He will make you laugh I daresay. He does me. You are safe now, sweetheart. Face your demons and drive them away. They have no place in your heart, not now. Now it is time to mend.'

As he spoke, it came to him he should be speaking as much to himself as to Jennet. He stood, walked over to where he had last seen her, felt for her spiky head and dropped a kiss on it.

'I will ask Sarah to come and wish you goodnight.' He left her then, feeling his way to the door, closed it quietly behind him, and pressing one hand to his eyes and the other to the wall went blindly to find a drink that would numb the pain.

James Dewett was strong and fit. Were he not, he would not have survived the shock. As it was he lay all night shivering, wrapped in his blankets in the darkness of the hovel. The next day he forced himself to tend his wound, screaming as he picked out pieces of bone and cleansed it with ice-cold water from the stream, again packing it with moss. With slow, pain filled movements he cut strips of canvas and bound his chest and shoulder to keep the moss in place and support his collar bone. Everything took a very long time. He lit the fire, made himself some hot food and rested all that day and the following night. He did not know who had shot him. At first he had thought it must be padders for they had taken his horse. But his roll of belongings was untouched and he later found his horse had not been taken after all, for the next day it had wandered back to the hovel for food. He thanked God for that at least.

In the end he gave up trying to work out who it might have been and why. What mattered was that he was alive. Before he had been shot he had been returning from his daily visit to Marley Court. Had seen a bustle of activity, a steady stream of people coming and going from the house. Lord Westley must be coming home. Despite Dewett's care, the wound had gone bad, a fever beginning to burn in his blood. He knew he was weak and getting weaker. He would have to act soon if he was to keep his promise to his lovely Anne. And though he may not live to tell her of it, she would learn of his courage and know he had been worthy of her at the last. Even if he could not kill the son who had made such a fool of him, he could at least hurt him by killing the father. It would have to be enough. He primed his carbine and then his pistol, huddled in his blankets and waited for the afternoon – and while he waited, he prayed.

29

Saturday 24ᵗʰ December, 1642

The snow came stealthily in the night. By the time Jennet woke it had covered everything with a soft mantle of white. For a moment she lay looking at the ceiling and wondered where she was. It came to her in a great rush and for the first time in what seemed like forever, she was glad to find she was alive. She still hurt, dreadfully, but the pain was diminished in some way, as if her new understanding had blurred the edges. She thought of her Papa with mind-numbing sorrow. She would never see him again, never hear his voice or feel the touch of his hand as he gave her his blessing – but now she found she could think of him without dread. In the long, dark hours of the night she had begged his forgiveness because she had failed him, failed to comprehend the depths of his despair; despair that in the end had taken him from her. Weeping, she had forgiven him and prayed for him as he had asked her to. Now, in the core of her being she believed he was with God and with Owen and at peace. The belief was a salve and she knew it was Alexander she had to thank for it; her quicksilver friend who had brought her back from the dark pit of horror that had sucked away her soul on that dread-filled day. She was consumed with guilt about her mother, but despite Alexander's words, Jennet could not dispel her anger. Her mother should have known; should not have let it happen. Her mother was to blame.

Jennet's heart swelled as she thought of Alexander. She had not forgotten him, not since the day of the King stag. Even in the worst times, deep in the dripping blackness of the mine, she had sought the comfort of him in her mind, tried to conjure the strange, warm feelings he had engendered. But they had been lost to her. They flooded back to her now, her mind's eye roaming over his face: the dimple on his chin; his green eyes sparking with interest, hair clinging like a yellow cap to his head, teasing laughter deepening the lines about his mouth, eyebrow quirking. Her hand moved to feel the little amethyst brooch he had sent her. She kept it with her always, pinned to her shift. Remembered she was not wearing her shift, but someone else's and that Sarah had unpinned the brooch last night. Jennet sat up suddenly, afraid she had lost it, relieved to see it on the shelf where Sarah had left it.

Shivering, Jennet got out of bed to retrieve the brooch, heard children laughing outside and went curiously to the window. The thick, yellowed glass was opaque with frost, each pane rimmed with white. With her fingernail she scraped a small hole in the frost and peered out of it, her breath freezing on the glass as fast as she rubbed it away. There were three young boys, one about the same age as Owen had been. A man was with them, a great big man with a fat belly and wearing a floppy black hat. They were pelting him with snowballs and as he caught hold of them they shrieked with laughter and fell in a sprawling heap bringing him down with them. Jennet smiled as the four bodies rolled over and over, their clothes covered in snow. The memory came back to her of Papa, in the days when he was big and strong and used to played with her and Owen like this. How well she remembered the thrill of the first fall of snow, before the newness and excitement of it palled. No longer able see through her tears, Jennet turned to look for her clothes.

Fumbling with the unfamiliar points and laces, she dressed and covered herself in her mother's old hooded robe. It was the only item of clothing she had taken from the farm and only then because it happened to be lying forgotten in a corner of the stable. Knowing she had needed it, she had overcome her revulsion and later, when she had curled up in that dark mine like a creature in its burrow, the smell of it had brought her traitorous comfort even while it had filled her with horror. Now she wrapped it around her and drew from it only comfort, remembering her mother's love, yearning for the feel of her arms, and as she did so, a tiny bit of Jennet's anger fell away.

By the time she had found her way outside, the man and his children had gone. The moor was heavy with silence. She was at the back of a low sprawling house. All around were trees laden with snow; the ground beyond sloped away like a white blanket, drifted by eddies of wind into strange billowing shapes and blue shadows. The great sweep of the distant hills lay stark against the leaden sky. It had not been a heavy fall; the ground where the children and the man had been playing was mushy and stained with mud. Jennet walked away from the house, down through the trees and saw the spore of a rabbit. Her heart went out to it and to all the creatures that must somehow survive the cold and hunger that was to come. A black feather lying in the snow caught her attention; she picked it up and smoothed it holding it to the light to admire its dark blue sheen. She had a collection of such things at home, feathers, twigs crusted with lichen, beautifully shaped leaves and unusually coloured pebbles.

Home. Where was home, now? She tucked the feather in her belt with a pang of sadness. Heard a soft footfall behind her. Her heart leaping, face alight, she swung round, but it was not he. It was the big man who had been playing with the boys. He stood looking at her smiling kindly, his hands held behind his back, his coat still powdered with snow.

'Good morrow to you, Jennet; I am Cobb, Sarah's husband. She has sent me to find you – and I warn you she will scold you for coming out in the snow with nothing on your feet.'

Jennet looked down at her toes, which she could no longer feel, and bit her lip.

Cobb laughed. 'Don't worry; her bark is infinitely worse than her bite. I think these might fit you.' He brought from behind his back a pair of leather shoes and held them out to her. 'Try them for size.'

She took them gratefully and smiled up at him shyly. 'Thank you.' They fitted her cold feet perfectly, but felt strange and hard. She had become accustomed to going barefoot since her own shoes had disintegrated. The soles of her feet were like leather and her toes criss-crossed with scratches. She became aware that Cobb was studying her face. Embarrassed she looked away; his gaze made her feel uncomfortable. For the want of something to say she pointed to the lowering sky. 'I think there is going to be another fall.'

He nodded. 'For sure.' As he spoke, a gust of wind knocked a flurry of snow from the trees onto his head. He took off his hat to shake it and she saw the top of his head was bald and rimmed with hair like a monk's. It reminded her of a hen's egg lying in a nest of straw and she giggled. He looked at her in surprise then chuckled and she saw that his rubicund face was wreathed in laughter lines and his clear grey eyes were twinkling at her. She warmed to him and of a sudden lost her shyness. When he held out his hand, she took it without hesitation and he led her back to the house.

By mid-morning, Jennet had met too many people to remember their names; they looked at her with pity, but all were kind. The boy whose clothes she was wearing had stuck out his tongue and getting a clip round the ear from Cobb was forced to apologise. When Cobb turned away she smiled sympathetically at the boy and gave him her feather. He took it with delight, held it to the light as she had done and rewarded her with a grin. His name she remembered; it was Barnabas, but everyone called him Bas. Zach had greeted her with a hug, his dark, seamed face filled with concern, but seeing her looking around for Alexander, grinned. 'Yon Lapwing is nursing his head. He'll be out directly, but a word of warning, tiptoe around him quietly and whatever you do, don't shout.' Cobb had roared with laughter and Jennet, not really understanding why, had found she was laughing too.

The big man spent some time talking with her as if she were a woman grown. He explained that her father's livestock were being brought to the Warren for the winter and asked her advice about their care, particularly the big black sow. As she told him what Mochyn liked best to eat and how Seacoal, the cat, preferred his milk still warm straight from the cow, Cobb listened, nodding. He took her to see the sty where Mochyn would live and which he promised would be filled with clean straw and as many apples as the old sow could eat. Jennet, who had been worrying about Mochyn's fate, wept with relief, whereupon Cobb enveloped her in his big arms and hugged her to him, stroking her hair. 'There now, hush, my girl, you can come and see your Mochyn whenever you want to if your mama will allow.'

Comforted, with no shred of embarrassment, she hugged him back. She did not see the tears standing bright in his eyes. 'Come,' he said, his voice gruff, 'we must go and find Tawford. He wants to take you home to see your mama, who will be yearning for the sight of you, my pet.'

When they went back inside to the big, shared room of the longhouse, most of the men had gone out to shovel snow and everywhere was covered in feathers. Two women were sitting by the fire plucking a goose each and two small infants gurgling with laughter were plunging sticky fingers into the growing pile of down and throwing it into the air. Alexander, covered head to toe in feathers, a fiddle under his chin, was standing in the middle of the room playing a mournful air and making faces at the half dozen children who clustered round him, clinging to his legs and giggling.

As Jennet and Cobb came into the room, he stopped playing and directed his gaze at Cobb, eyebrow raised. The gypsy looked pink about the gills and decidedly sheepish, but Jennet's cheeks were glowing from the cold, her eyes sparkling and her lips curved in smile. With a small nod, Alexander grinned at Cobb, repositioned the fiddle and began to play again, this time a jig; slow at first then faster and faster, the children clapping their hands as they tried to keep time, shrieking with laughter as they failed. He ended on a high squeaking note, took the fiddle from his chin and bowed in a cloud of feathers to a chorus of noisy pleas for more. Sarah came bustling in from the kitchen wiping her hands on her apron, tutted as she saw the mess and shooed them all away.

'Outside. Give Master Tawford some peace. Off you go.' And because there was snow to play with, they all went running without further protest out into the cold.

While Alexander went out with Cobb to saddle up Biscuit, Jennet found herself once again smothered in Sarah's arms. Zach stood by and waited. As she turned to go he brought from behind his back a small package, which he gave to her with a smile. It was no bigger than her fist and wrapped in cloth tied round with a piece of red ribbon, beneath the ribbon was a single holly leaf, scarlet berry attached. Jennet looked at it wonderingly.

'It is naught but a small gift to wish you joy at Christmas, but you mustn't open it until tomorrow,' Zach said.

Reaching up she flung her arms around him and kissed his cheek. 'Oh, thank you.'

He flushed. 'It is just a little thing.'

They went outside and she saw Alexander standing with Biscuit and beside him, Cobb holding the reins of a small grey mare, its ears pricked forward watching her. Jennet looked first at Alexander and then at Cobb, who was grinning from ear to ear. He held out the reins to her and bowed.

'This is Peg and she is for you.' For a moment Jennet did not take in the implication of his words, was thrilled to be loaned a mount and permitted to ride on her own. She had ridden before, of course, but not since her father's old workhorse had died.

'It is short for Pegasus,' Alexander explained. 'But as you can see, she is a bit long in the tooth and much too fat for a winged horse, so you need have no fear she will take off with you.'

Jennet smiled. 'She is lovely.' She looked uncertainly at Alexander, who had mounted and was sitting on Biscuit's back, looking thoughtfully down at Cobb. She reached out to stroke the little mare's grey muzzle, laughing with delight as Peg blew into her hand. Pleadingly she looked up at Cobb.

'Thank you for letting me ride her. May I keep her for a little while? I will take good care of her until you want her back. May I? Please?'

Cobb smiled. 'I know you will, but you don't have to bring her back, my girl. She is not a loan. She is yours to keep – in exchange for Mochyn,' he added quickly, glaring at Alexander.

Jennet could hardly believe it; a horse of her own. She flung her arms as far as she could reach around Cobb's great girth and hugged him with a cry of pleasure. 'Oh thank you. Thank you.' And burst into tears.

Cobb gently eased her arms away, pulled from his sleeve a large grubby handkerchief into which he loudly trumpeted. Wiping his face, he lowered it and looked hungrily into Jennet's face, drinking in the promise of loveliness, the bright intelligence that shone from her tear-filled, beautiful eyes.

'Hush girl; no need for that – I think I have the best of the bargain. Old Mochyn will keep me company of a night when Sarah is too bad tempered to put up with me.'

Jennet laughed through her tears as he pulled the hood of her dreadful robe up and over her hair, tucking it close at her neck. 'There you are then, my lovely. God speed. Come and see us again some time if your mama will allow.' He bent and cupped his hands for her foot and lifted her into the saddle.

As they trotted up the track that had been cleared of snow, Jennet turned to look back at the Warren. Cobb and Zach were watching, standing side by side: Cobb tall and fat, Zach short and thin. It made her laugh; she waved at them and they raised their arms and waved back. Nudging Peg close to Biscuit's flank, she smiled happily at Alexander. 'I think your friends are lovely.'

He twisted his head to look down at her. 'Do you? I think they think you are lovely too. You look as though you are feeling a good deal better, Pixy. I told you Cobb would make you laugh. I am glad.'

The smile left Jennet's face. For just a brief space of time she had almost forgotten Papa. Realising it, she was stricken with guilt as the pain and misery came thudding back into her chest. She gasped. Aware of it – and the reason for it – Alexander slowed to a walk. 'I told you about Henry, did I not?'

Unable to speak, Jennet nodded.

'After he was killed there were times when I would forget he had gone and the manner of his dying. When it came back to me, it hurt even more because I felt I had betrayed his memory, for if I had really loved him how could I forget – even for a moment? How could I take pleasure in things that no longer included him? I used to punish myself with guilt, until one day I came to understand I could be happy about some things and sad about others all at the same time. There was no need to feel guilty for being happy. It did not mean I had forgotten Henry or that I loved him any less. He was still there in my heart. I did not have to feel sad all the time to prove to myself that I loved him.'

Alexander smiled down at Jennet's stricken face looking up at him from beneath her hood. 'Your father would not rest easy if he thought he had condemned you to a lifetime of misery for his sake, Pixy. You cannot think about him all the time. Being happy does not detract from his memory; quite the reverse. Just because he is not at the forefront of your mind does not mean you have forgotten what he meant to you; that will be within you always. So don't look like that. You will curdle the milk and put the hens off lay and poor Peg there will think it is her fault.' He puffed out his cheeks and blew at a lingering feather that had drifted down from his hat to the tip of his nose.

Jennet pushed the hood back from her head and considered

his words and though she did not smile he could tell from her expression she was comforted.

As they rode down from the moor the snow gradually thinned and soon they were able to nudge their mounts into a canter.

Ellen was strolling arm in arm with Adam on the foreshore. She was thinking at that moment about Robert. With the stoop gone from his shoulders and his face less gaunt, he no longer looked old before his time, was almost boyish in fact. What gladdened her heart more than anything was the sound of his ringing laughter; a sound she had not heard for more years than she cared to remember. Bella had been teaching him to speak French. He already spoke it quite well as Ellen knew, but Bella obviously did not and he teased her mercilessly when she lost patience with his deliberate mistakes. Their mischievous banter had brought Ellen to tears of laughter, but impatient to be alone with Adam, she had not been sorry when yesterday they had ridden away to Marley Court. On the morrow, she and Adam would ride over to St Peter's, the tiny church on the Marley estate, where they would attend the Christmas Day service, after which, at Ellen's insistence, they would all return for dinner at Tawford Barton. She was fairly certain Alexander had gone to look for Jennet and prayed he would find her, but even if he did not, that he would come home from wherever he had gone.

Yesterday, before Robert had left, Ellen had walked in on her brother deep in conversation with Adam. They had been in the parlour and as she came through the door, both men had stopped speaking and looked up at her, Adam slightly flushed, Robert with a half-smile hovering around his mouth. Feeling she was interrupting, she had muttered an apology and left them to it, but something about their secretive expressions had excited her. She was fairly sure she knew what they were discussing.

Her hopes were well founded. When the cavalcade had ridden away, Adam had put his arm about her waist, guided her to the parlour and indicated she should sit. When she had done so, he bowed low, took her hand and asked the question she had so longed to hear, assuring her Lord Westley had approved and given them his blessing; indeed, her brother had said he dared not do otherwise! Ellen, with a delighted laugh, had jumped up from the settle, wrapped her arms about Adam's neck and accepted without hesitation.

It was bitter cold walking by the sea, even the seaweed was crusted with ice; an east wind whipped up the waves of the incoming tide and flung sand stinging into their faces. The distant hills were white against the leaden sky and already the light was beginning to fade. Feeling Ellen shiver, Adam pulled her close, rubbing his hands up and down her back, his breath warm on her cheek. 'You are cold. Come, we will go back and sit by the fire.' He bent his head and kissed her.

Drawing away from him, Ellen looked anxiously into his eyes. There was something she yet had to tell him and she was finding it immensely difficult. She had been hugging the secret to her heart since her courses had stopped in October. Knew she must do it sooner rather than later, but was so afraid he would not share her joy.

Adam gave her a quizzical smile. 'What is it, sweetheart? You have changed your mind? I would not blame you. I know I have not much to offer you.'

She stopped his mouth with her icy fingers. 'No, of course not – never – you are everything I could ever want or need, but I have something to tell you and I am afraid it may not please you.'

He looked at her, anxiety furrowing his brow. So she drew a deep breath and told him, gazed into his eyes, watched his anxiety change to delight. It was all the reassurance she needed and her legs trembled with relief. He picked her up and whirled her round, laughing exultantly, then gently put her down, held her close and murmured happy nonsense in her ear. Walking slowly back to the house, they heard horses. Grabbing Adam by the hand Ellen started to run.

She had thought her happiness was complete, but when she saw Alexander come grinning down the track accompanied by Jennet, she knew she had been wrong. She was beside herself with joy and barely conscious of Adam's concerned voice in her ear. 'Steady sweetheart – your condition.' Laughing she ignored him and flung herself at Alexander the moment his feet touched the ground.

'Unhand me, woman. Adam, help! Get this hoyting girl off me, for goodness' sake. Whatever have you done to make her like this?' He took one look at Adam's face and his face split in a huge grin. 'You don't need to tell me. I can guess. You are going to make her into a respectable married woman. And about time too, though I must warn you, you will have your work cut out!' He ducked as Ellen swiped at him, knocking off his hat in a cloud of goose-down. Jennet giggled. He reached for her and lifted her out of the saddle.

'I found this strange child pretending to be a ghoul in a churchyard and thought I'd bring her home. I understand she's good with livestock and might be useful about the place if we fatten her up a bit. Oh – and by the way, she speaks and is nowhere near as green as she is cabbage-looking.'

Jennet gave him a haughty look, but her eyes were sparkling as she directed her gaze to Ellen and dropped a curtsey. 'I have so much to thank you for. I am sorry that I worried you so. Please forgive me. It was just that...' She faltered unable to say what she was thinking.

'Hush, child.' Ellen held out her arms and Jennet walked into them. 'There is nothing to forgive. It gladdens me more than I can say to see you safe. Your mother will be overjoyed.' She gestured over Jennet's head at Adam who came forward.

'This is my betrothed, Adam Hartley, and don't dare to curtsey or he will get ideas above his station.' Gently she released Jennet and turned her to face Adam.

He smiled. 'I am delighted to meet you at last. How like your mother you are.'

Jennet looked anxiously towards the house. 'She is here?'

Alexander shook his head. 'No, Pixy, but you go in with these two lovebirds and get warm and I will go and fetch her for you.' He looked at her, the smile fading from his face as he saw tears of despair starting to her eyes. He reached out a finger to her cheek. 'There is nothing to fear, sweetheart. Your mother will understand. I promise you. You must not be angry with her. She is no more to blame than you are. Remember her love, it will help you.'

Ellen, watching Jennet's face as she looked up trustingly at Alexander, felt a sudden qualm. The child clearly doted on him. She wondered if he was aware of it. Puppy love was an anguish of painful emotions, as she – little older than Jennet when she had first met Adam – remembered only too well. She would have to have a word with him later. She gave him a little push. 'Off you go then and don't be long.' She looked up; the gathering clouds were heavy with snow. 'It will be dark soon. Come with me, Jennet, we must get you out of those clothes and find you something more suitable to greet your Mama, and then we shall have a feast – we have so much to celebrate. And tomorrow it is Christmas Day and we will go to church and give thanks to the Lord for His bountiful goodness and mercy.' She seized Jennet's hand and marched her firmly down the track towards the house.

With a backward glance at Alexander, Jennet allowed herself to be led away. He mounted up and grinned down at Adam. 'The expression "dog with two tails" comes to mind as I look at you. Is there something you haven't told me, Adam?'

Adam flushed. 'I think Ellen would want to tell you herself.'

'Oh Lord – don't tell me! There is going to be the patter of tiny Hartleys. I can't bear it!' Laughing at Adam's indignant expression, Alexander cheerily waved his hand and set Biscuit up the track.

Shaking his head with a rueful smile, Adam led Peg to the stables, unaware of the change in Alexander's expression as he had turned away, nor, had Adam seen it, would he have understood.

30

As he rode away from the Barton, Alexander knew that something inside him was hurting – he refused to give it a name or even think about it. Instead, he buried it and allowed Ellen's face to fill his mind: the way she had looked at Adam, the light shining from her eyes, her delirious happiness seeming to glow around her like an aureole. Did it matter so very much that someone other than he had caused her to look that way? He thought he could probably live with it so long as she was happy, but by God, if Adam ever hurt her, quite simply, he would kill him. But Adam never would, not knowingly. He was a good man and a dear friend, as close as a brother. Ellen would be safe with Adam. Reaching deep, Alexander found it in himself to be immensely glad for them both. With a shadow of concern he prayed it would go right for them. Ellen was old to be having a babe – but at least she would have her own physician! The thought made him smile, the smile broadened and suddenly he was laughing out loud.

His thoughts moved to Jennet. He had hardly dared hope he would find her. That he had done so filled him with a sense of deep satisfaction. He had achieved something with that child. Helped her at least begin to come to terms with her father's death. He was glad he had been able to do that. In time she would heal. Only now, as he reflected on it, did it occur to him that in comforting Jennet he had found some sort of peace for himself. His words to her had been as much about his own grief as hers, for in a way he too had lost a father. He knew that now. He had never stopped to consider why he had felt such empty despair when those devastating words had chiselled into his brain. *'You are not my son.'* Instead he had filled the vacuum with bitterness and anger, too blinded by self-pity to recognise Robert had acted out of love. Too proud to acknowledge to himself his greatest fear: that he had lost that love. Well he was all done with self-pity!

He could not wait to tell Bethan that Jennet was alive and safe – except, of course, she would already know. He chuckled. He could well understand why folk thought Bethan a witch. There was something about her intuitiveness that was otherworldly. Even he, who did not believe it, sometimes could not suppress a superstitious shiver when she seemed to look deep into him with those faraway eyes of hers. Thinking of her led his thoughts to Cobb. That had been a shock! Alexander prided himself on being able to read people, could usually predict how they would react in certain situations and anticipate events that might result, but never in a thousand years would he have guessed about Cobb and Bethan. A more unlikely pairing he could not imagine! And yet there was a depth to Cobb even he had not fully plumbed, though Bethan undoubtedly would have done so. It did not trouble him that Jennet was Cobb's daughter; if anything it made the child even dearer to him, for with Cobb he shared an affinity. One he had never tried to explain – it just was.

His mind strayed to the war and to Cornwall. There had been no news since they had ridden from Torrington. They would move against Plymouth in January. He had half expected Sir Ralph to recall him and was not sure whether to be glad or sorry that he had not. Not that he particularly enjoyed fighting – who in his right mind did? But he enjoyed the challenge of war; the mental stimulation of strategic planning and the satisfaction of seeing his plans come to fruition. And though he preferred to operate alone, at one level he was forced to admit that the camaraderie of his men was important to him.

Even so, he hoped the King would succeed in negotiating terms with Parliament and bring this war to an end. He was not alone in finding it stuck in his craw to kill his fellow countrymen. There was plenty of fighting to be had elsewhere if one wanted it. Did he want it? He was not sure. But he could not stay and be a farmer for the rest of his life. There was nothing to hold him here, not now. He might go to sea again when the war was over. The thought brought a stir of excitement as it always did. But first, what he wanted more than anything else was to find out who he was. Clearly the answers he sought were in Ireland. He was drawn to it like a moth to a candle flame. All his instincts told him this was where he needed to be. He had once thought his mother was a princess – a childish notion – he was now convinced she was a whore. It no longer mattered; he could cope with being a whore's bastard. He smiled to himself – being knighted had undoubtedly helped! He knew she must be dead: why else was she always reaching out for him in his dreams – for who else could she be, the fair-headed, green-eyed woman of his dreams, but his mother? As soon as he could, he would find out about her; he would go to Ireland. His mind made up, he nudged Biscuit into a canter.

As he approached Marley Court the light had almost gone. It felt warmer – a sure sign of more snow. A lantern was lit outside the lodge and the gates were open. He rode through them and up the sweeping carriageway, Biscuit's hooves slipping and crunching on frozen snow. He could see the ground floor of the house glowing dimly with light and realised for the first time since Robert's tearful confession that he was not filled with dread to be riding towards it. He reined in for a moment and sat looking at it and as he did so, he caught sight of his guardian with Bella on his arm, strolling in front of the house. Alexander chuckled. Another surprise! Bella may not be right for Robert, but it was clear she had given him back his pride and *joie de vivre* and maybe that was enough for now. That too, made him feel glad for as he had finally acknowledged in the porch of Challacombe church, he loved the man, dammit; wanted him to be happy. Like Jennet, he must learn to forgive. And it was Christmas Eve. There was no better time than this to make his peace. Grinning with pleasure at the thought, he gathered the reins and nudged Biscuit forward, leaning over her neck to give her a playful hug, laughing at her whickered response as she tossed her mane in his face.

A shot rang out.

Startled he looked up, saw Robert thrown backwards, crumple and lie still. Heard Bella scream. Saw a dark shape shambling across the snow.

With a cry he dug his heels into Biscuit's flanks and leaving the carriageway galloped forward over the lawns, shouting, dimly aware of the frenzied, muffled barking of the hounds. The man turned, tossed away his pistol. Alexander, unarmed but for his dagger and still some distance away, saw him level a carbine to his shoulder. As he closed the gap he recognised Dewett. Barely able to comprehend what he was seeing, he bent low over Biscuit's neck and rode full at Dewett, knocking him to the ground. The carbine's shot went harmlessly over Alexander's head. Pulling his dagger from his boot he leapt from Biscuit's back and dived. Dewett grinned up at him. Alexander hesitated, his blade at Dewett's throat. The man did not try to defend himself. He could not. His grin was a rictus – he was already dead.

Dropping the blade Alexander ran to where Bella bent over Robert's body. She looked up at him, her face a white mask of terror. He put his hand to Robert's neck and felt for the pulse, it fluttered weakly beneath his fingers. 'He lives. Bella, help me. Bella!' Between them they picked him up, carried him into the house, and because it was near and the door was open, into his library where they laid him gently on the floor. Alexander spoke between gritted teeth. 'Where is everyone?'

'He sent them home for Christmas.'

'Godamme his generosity of spirit! Get Bethan.'

Her face streaming with tears, Bella jumped to his

command.

'Alexander?' Robert whispered. 'Is it you?'

'Yes. Do not try to speak. The ball has lodged in your chest.'

He knelt beside his guardian and cradled his head.

'I fear I am done for.'

Alexander shook his head, tears starting to his eyes. 'No!'

'Don't weep for me. It is a long time since I was so happy. I had not expected it. It is good to die happy.'

'You are not going to die. Don't try to talk.'

'I must talk.' Robert tried to smile. 'For once in your life you will just have to listen! In the drawer over there is a document assigning to you the lands in Munster. It wants only your signature. Bella will witness it. I know you refused it before, but will you do this for me now? Please. I beg you.'

'Yes, of course, if you want it, but why? Why have you done so much for me when I am not your son? Dear God, am I even your kin? Distant, you said once. How distant? You must know that I love you. I have always loved you. I am sorry, so sorry. I thought I had killed him. Please don't die. I will be content, I promise, but don't die. Please don't die,' Alexander repeated, babbling helplessly in the grip of despair.

Robert held up his hand, splaying out his fingers and Alexander moved to intertwine them with his own, gripping them tightly. 'Is the pain very bad?' A harsh sob tore from his throat. 'Dear God, it is my fault. I might as well have put a pistol to your head and pulled the trigger.'

Robert smiled gently. 'I am glad you did not. Do not blame yourself. Things sometimes happen that are meant to be and we are powerless to prevent them. It is God's will. I think at last I can accept that.' A spasm of pain crossed his features. 'I could not have loved you more had you been my son, Alexander. We are indeed kin, but not distant,' Robert gasped, the blood draining from his face. 'It is right that you should know who you are – I should not have kept it from you. Your father and mine was Sir Cleve Dynam. He sired us both. We are half-brothers. Henry was your nephew.'

Unable to fully comprehend what Robert was saying, Alexander gazed at him in shock, speechless, tears catching on his lashes, spilling down his cheeks.

Drawing an agonising breath, Robert spoke again. 'After my mother died and our father returned to Cork, he met the daughter of an Irish chieftain, he was a rebel leader; one of a secret army of outlaws who hide in the bogs and mountains and have sworn to rid their land of the planters who ousted them – men like our father.'

Alexander nodded, weeping. 'You mean the woodkerne? I know of them. It doesn't matter – none of it matters – please, just stop talking.'

'I must tell you what I know while I still can. Our father loved your mother passionately and she him. Fool that he was, he risked both their lives persuading her to run away with him. They were wed in secret, but some weeks later she disappeared and though he searched the length and breadth of Munster, he could find no trace of her. Then he received word that she was dead and thinking she was lost to him he came home to Devon. He was a broken, lonely old man when Anne Fisk insinuated her way into his life. The woman besotted him and trapped him into marrying her, but she was the death of him. Not long afterwards he learned what had happened to your mother, but by then it was too late.'

Robert's voice faltered, his breath rasping with effort as he clung to Alexander's hand. 'The woodkerne had taken her back to her father and discovering she was with child, he forced her to wed one of her own kind. She was terrified they would find out she was already wed to our father and would stop at nothing to kill him – and her. So she went through with a bigamous marriage, but sent her woman to tell our father she was dead, knowing he would then leave Ireland and be safe. She was convinced they would not allow her child to live, if a boy, and pleaded with her woman to give out that the babe was stillborn. As it happened there was no need; your mother gave birth to twins, you and a girl, but nobody knew except your nurse and she stole you away.'

'Shoonah…' Alexander breathed.

'Yes. She was loyal to your mother; it was not a coincidence that she married our agent, Art O'Neill. Our father paid them handsomely for their silence. I have continued to do so. I knew nothing of it until father was dying. He was so afraid, both for you and your mother: your very existence makes bastards of her Irish sons. If the woodkerne found out about you they would not hesitate to hunt you down. He begged me to keep you safe; fetch you back from Ireland and raise you as my own.'

Robert coughed, his voice sinking to a thread. 'Our father's marriage to Anne Fisk was illegal – albeit unknowingly – it is our half-brother George who is illegitimate, not you, but there is no proof. I was forced to destroy it. Dear God, Alexander, I wish I had not, but father begged me. On his deathbed he made me promise to destroy evidence of his marriage to your mother in order to protect her. He made me swear by everything I hold most holy to conceal your identity. Forgive me if I have wronged you. You will never come into the inheritance that is yours by right, but I did what I must for your safety.'

The breath rattled in Robert's throat, a trickle of blood escaping from the corner of his mouth. With the last of his strength he gripped Alexander's hand and attempted to pull himself up. 'I do not know if your mother still lives, but you must swear to me you will not try to find her; if you do and are discovered, your mother's sacrifice will have been for nothing. I beg you. Please, Alexander, swear it. Swear it…'

Alexander bent his head to Robert's lips. 'Who are my mother's people? Tell me her name and I will so swear.'

'Eithne…' the word escaped as a whispered sigh and Robert slumped unconscious.

Gazing at his brother's waxen face in despair, Alexander started, suddenly aware that Bethan was standing behind him. Bella rushed into the room, her face taut and wet with tears, her arms full of bandaging.

'Alexander, move!' Bethan knelt at Robert's side and put

her hand to his neck. 'Go fetch Ellen. Now. Quickly. Bella, fetch me warm water and a sharp knife – the sharpest you can find. If you can find any brandy bring that too, but any spirit will do. Alexander! Do as I say. Fetch Ellen. Tell her what has happened. She will know what to bring. Go. Now.'

Through the numbness of shock, Alexander responded to her urgency. Brushing his lips to Robert's brow, he gently unclasped his fingers and got to his feet. 'Can you save him?'

'I do not know. It is bad. The ball is in his lung. I will try. Now go. Hurry!'

His breath sobbing in his throat, he ran to where Biscuit was nosing Dewett's body in the snow. Averting his gaze, Alexander scrambled into the saddle and careless of the ice, set the mare into a gallop. Valiantly she responded to his need.

He heard again and again the tortured whisper of his mother's name and saw behind his eyes the fair-haired woman of his dreams: his mother or his twin? But his mind was clamouring with grief. He could not take in the enormity of what Robert had told him and because it no longer seemed important, he rejected it. All that mattered was that Robert should not die.

'Please God, let him live. Please God. Please God.' Alexander prayed in a way he had never done in his life before, his words echoed by the thrumming of Biscuit's hooves.

As he came within sight of Tawford Barton, the snow came drifting silent from the sky. 'Just a little bit further,' he pleaded as his gallant horse began to stumble.

On her last reserves of strength Biscuit carried him to the Barton and came to a shuddering standstill. Shouting for Ned, Alexander flung himself sobbing from her back and ran stumbling to the front door.

It opened and she stood before him, a lantern clutched in her hand, her red hair loose and wild about her face, her eyes widening in alarm. 'Alexander?'

For an instant he stared at her before it hit him; a gut wrenching blow that knocked all the breath from his body and bent him double with the force of it.

Ellen, his love, was his half-sister.

Author's Note

I have taken liberties with my characterisation of Captain James Dewett, about whom I can find nothing recorded beyond his involvement in leading a Parliamentarian troop to arrest the Earl of Bath at his home in Tawstock in September 1642 – according to Lady Bath's diary, at 11 o'clock at night – and deliver him to the Tower of London, where he was held until the following April. Lady Bath also mentions that Dewett and his troop plundered the house and stole Lord Bath's best horses. Should James Dewett have any living descendants, I apologise most wholeheartedly for any misrepresentation of his character, which is completely imaginary and totally unfounded.

Sir Ralph Hopton's flight from Sherborne to Minehead and across Exmoor, his meeting with Peter Bold in Chittlehampton and escape to Sir Bevill Grenville's house in Stow, are all matters of recorded fact. His subsequent campaign in the South West is described in his own memoirs, *'Bellum Civile'*. (For those who may be interested, I have appended a list of people whose names appear in my book and who are recorded in history, but since this is a work of fiction, I have not included a bibliography.)

My book's title is taken from the words of Prince Charles (later Charles II) in his reply to the overture of General Sir Thomas Fairfax in 1645: *Rogues; rebels; are not they content to be rebels, themselves, but would have me in their number.*

(Historical Manuscripts Commission, *Portland*, Vol. 1).
A writer's life is full of curious coincidences: some time after
I had invented the robbery of William Strode's stocks of ale
at Barrington Court (incidentally the first house to be owned
and opened to the public by the National Trust – and well
worth a visit!) I discovered that such a robbery did in fact take
place and was thought at the time to have been perpetrated
by Hopton's soldiers. Parliamentarian soldiers subsequently
plundered Hopton's own home in Witham.

Opinion differs as to the date of Hopton's failed first attempt
to take Exeter. It is possible that two such attempts were made,
one in November 1642 and the other in early January 1643
(at this time in the 17th Century, the New Year commenced
in March, so the date is recorded as January 1642). I have
combined the various descriptions of what happened on both
those dates, including the loss of Captain Nutt's ship off
Topsham (which is recorded as having been 'due to neglect'!)
and moved them to December to better fit my story.

Another coincidence: although I was unaware of it when I
was writing about Burrow Mump, it seems my use of it as a
Royalist hideaway has some basis in fact: defeated Royalist
soldiers hid in St Michael's Church after the battle of Langport
in 1645.

Alexander's story will continue in Book 2 of the Tawford
Chronicles: *Secrets & Ciphers*.

Jo Field
West Yelland, May 2008

Names occurring in Rogues and Rebels that are recorded in history

Bourchier, Henry, 5ᵗʰ Earl of Bath: a leading member of the ruling class in North Devon; member of the King's Privy Council and holder of the Privy Seal. Branded a delinquent by Parliament and imprisoned in September, 1642. Released in April 1643, but took little part in the Civil Wars thereafter.

Cary, Sergeant: one of the Clovelly Carys, a Parliamentarian soldier sent by the Earl of Bedford to Ilfracombe in search of Sir Ralph Hopton after the Royalists had escaped from Sherborne.

Charles I: King of England, 1600-1649, beheaded by Parliament for crimes against the State.

Chichester, Edward, Viscount Carrickfergus: served with the Marquis of Ormonde in Ireland. Beyond his presence in South Molton with the Earl of Bath in September, 1642 when he went to publish the Commission of Array and was met by a howling mob, he took no further part in the Civil Wars.

Devereux, Robert, Earl of Essex: Commander-in-Chief of Parliament's armies at the Battle of Edgehill, nicknamed 'Old Robin' by his troops.

Dewett, Captain James: a Roundhead captain who arrested the Earl of Bath on the orders of the Earl of Bedford.

Fane, Lady Rachel, Countess of Bath: during the Civil Wars, Lady Bath rescued members of the clergy and their families from persecution and was famed for her charitable works in and around North Devon.

Fiennes, Captain Nathaniel: second son of Lord Say and Sele, who fought for Parliament and led the charge against Prince Rupert at Powick Bridge.

Fisk, Sir John: notorious squire from Tavistock, father of Sir Richard Grenville's estranged wife, Mary.

Goring, Lord George: infamous for his drunken lechery but popular with his men and considered a brave commander; he betrayed the Army Plot to John Pym, surrendered Portsmouth to William Waller and fled to Holland. Thereafter he was leading Royalist protagonist in the Western Campaign.

Green, Lieutenant Arthur: a Parliamentarian officer in Exeter's Trained Band.

Grenville, Sir Bevill: grandson of the Elizabethan hero Sir Richard Grenville, he raised an army of Cornishmen which, under his leadership, became one of the most effective Royalist forces in the early Western campaigns. His death at the Battle of Lansdown Hill in 1643 caused an outpouring of grief.

Henrietta Maria, Queen: wife to Charles I and daughter of Louis XIII of France.

Herbert, Philip, 4th Earl of Pembroke: Lord Chamberlain to Charles I; sided with Parliament in 1640.

Hopton, Sir Ralph: Leader of the House of Commons and Member of Parliament for Wells. Sided with the King and was later commissioned Lieutenant General of Horse in the West. Following his escape across Exmoor in September 1642, he united the South West and eventually defeated Parliament at Roundaway Down in 1643.

Luke, Sir Samuel: Governor of Newport Pagnell, became Scoutmaster-General to the Earl of Essex.

Lunsford, Sir Thomas: a Royalist artillery captain who escaped to Wales with the Marquis of Hertford in September 1642. He was captured at Edgehill and imprisoned until 1644.

Luttrell, Sir Thomas: Parliamentarian governor of Dunster Castle who rebuffed Hertford and his army after their escape from Sherborne, having disabled most of the boats in an attempt to prevent their escape to Wales.

Lynn, William: Steward to the Earl of Bath in Lincoln's Inn Fields, London.

Nicholas, Sir Edward: Secretary of State to Charles I and thereafter to Charles II.

O'Néill, Domnhall: an Irish folk hero recorded in the Annals of Ireland.

Peard, George: Member of Parliament for Barnstaple and a patron of its Parliamentarian garrison.

Pollard, Richard: Steward to the Earl of Bath at Tawstock Court.

Poulett, Lord John: leading member of Royalist gentry from Somerset who escaped with Hertford to Wales.

Pym, John: leader of the opposition in Parliament who sided vociferously against the King.

Rupert, Prince of the Rhine: King Charles's nephew and Commander-in-Chief of the Royalist cavalry, becoming Captain-General of the Royalist army in 1644.

Russell, William, 5th Earl of Bedford: Lord Lieutenant of Exeter and Devon and Commander of Parliament's Western campaign in the autumn of 1642, but later changed sides and fought for the King.

Ruthin, Colonel William: Scottish mercenary who fought for Parliament in the South West.

Saunders, Major Richard: Commanding Officer of Exeter's Trained Band.

Seymour, William Marquis of Hertford: former tutor to the Prince of Wales, he commanded the King's Western Army until his escape from Minehead.

Slanning, Sir Nicholas: a naval officer and Royalist Governor of Pendennis Castle.

Southcott, Lady Margaret: wife to the Royalist officer, Sir Popham Southcott of Luppit.

Strode, Colonel William: Member of Parliament for Ilchester (not to be confused with the other William Strode, one of the five men whom the King famously attempted to arrest in the House of Commons).

Waller, William: Parliament's Major General of the West, nicknamed 'William the Conqueror' by his troops.

Wentworth Thomas, Earl of Strafford: Lord Deputy of Ireland, executed by Parliament in 1641 for crimes against the State.

Voysin, Sara: Daughter of Monsieur Voysin, a Syndique of Geneva, granddaughter of Henricus Stephanus, and niece of Isaac Causabonn. Sara was both a friend and lady-in-waiting to Lady Bath.

ROGUES & REBELS

Enjoyed this book?

Find out more about the author,
and a whole range of exciting titles at
www.discoveredauthors.co.uk

Discover our other imprints:

DA Diamonds traditional mainstream publishing

DA Revivals republishing out-of-print titles

Four O'Clock Press assisted publishing

Horizon Press business and corporate materials